OXFORD WORLD'S CLASSICS

MARCEL PROUST

In the Shadow of Girls in Blossom

Translated by
CHARLOTTE MANDELL

with an Introduction by
EDWARD J. HUGHES
and Notes by
ADAM WATT

OXFORD
UNIVERSITY PRESS

OXFORD
UNIVERSITY PRESS

Great Clarendon Street, Oxford, OX2 6DP,
United Kingdom

Oxford University Press is a department of the University of Oxford.
It furthers the University's objective of excellence in research, scholarship,
and education by publishing worldwide. Oxford is a registered trade mark of
Oxford University Press in the UK and in certain other countries

Translation © Charlotte Mandell 2025
Introduction © Edward J. Hughes 2025
Explanatory notes © Adam Watt 2025

The moral rights of the authors have been asserted

Published in the United States of America by Oxford University Press
198 Madison Avenue, New York, NY 10016, United States of America

British Library Cataloguing in Publication Data

Data available

Library of Congress Control Number: 2024939414

ISBN 978-0-19-284567-2

Printed and bound in the UK by
Clays Ltd, Elcograf S.p.A.

Links to third party websites are provided by Oxford in good faith and
for information only. Oxford disclaims any responsibility for the materials
contained in any third party website referenced in this work.

The manufacturer's authorised representative in the EU for product safety is
Oxford University Press España S.A. of el Parque Empresarial San Fernando de
Henares, Avenida de Castilla, 2 – 28830 Madrid (www.oup.es/en).

IN THE SHADOW OF GIRLS IN BLOSSOM

MARCEL PROUST (1871–1922) is best known as the author of the seven-volume masterpiece *A la recherche du temps perdu* (*In Search of Lost Time*, 1913–27). He was born in Auteuil, to the west of Paris, to well-to-do parents; at the age of 10 he suffered a near-fatal asthma attack and his life from that point onwards was marked by ill health. He began writing reviews, short stories, and society journalism whilst studying at the Lycée Condorcet and published a collection of these pieces, *Les Plaisirs et les jours* (*Pleasures and Days*) in 1896. Family connections and schoolfriends gave him access to the highest Parisian social circles, on which he would later draw for his portrayal of the society life in *In Search of Lost Time*. His first attempt at an extended narrative (posthumously published as *Jean Santeuil*, 1952) was abandoned; subsequent stages in his apprenticeship as a writer include translating works by the English art historian and social critic John Ruskin and producing dazzling pastiches of major French writers. Finally, during 1908–9, whilst working on a critical essay taking to task the great nineteenth-century critic Sainte-Beuve, Proust began to draft fragments of a first-person narrative that coalesced into what would become *In Search of Lost Time*. The first volume appeared in 1913. Unfit for military service, Proust spent the wartime years expanding his novel, the subsequent volumes of which appeared between 1919 and 1927. Proust's devotion to his work, sleeping by day then writing and making additions and revisions through the night, was ruinous for his already fragile health and he died in 1922, while still engaged in the corrections to his final volumes.

CHARLOTTE MANDELL has translated over fifty books, including works by Maurice Blanchot, Jonathan Littell, Gustave Flaubert, and Jean-Luc Nancy. She recently received the Thornton Wilder Translation Prize from the American Academy of Arts and Letters and the honor of Chevalier dans l'Ordre des Arts et des Lettres from the French government.

EDWARD J. HUGHES is Emeritus Professor of French at Queen Mary University of London, and a Fellow of the British Academy. His research interests lie in the field of modern and contemporary French and francophone literature, specializing in the socio-critical reading of a range of authors. He has a long-standing interest in the work of Marcel Proust on whom he has published numerous studies.

ADAM WATT is Professor of French & Comparative Literature at the University of Exeter, where he is Deputy Pro-Vice-Chancellor of the Faculty of Humanities, Arts and Social Sciences. His books include *Reading in Proust's* A la recherche*: Le Délire de la lecture* (2009); *The Cambridge Introduction to Marcel Proust* (2011); a critical biography of Proust (2013); and, as editor, *Marcel Proust in Context* (2013) and *The Cambridge History of the Novel in French* (2021). He has published comparative work on Proust and a range of writers from Valéry, Rivière, Beckett, and Barthes to Eve Kosofsky-Sedgwick and Anne Carson.

THE OXFORD PROUST

GENERAL EDITORS: BRIAN NELSON AND ADAM WATT

CONTENTS

ACKNOWLEDGEMENTS

I AM grateful to Brian Nelson, co-editor of this new edition of Proust, and translator of the first and last volumes, for his valuable editorial suggestions; Rowena Anketell, for her helpful copy-editing; Éric Trudel, Marina van Zuylen, and Odile Chilton of Bard College, for all their help and support over the years; Pierre Joris and Nicole Peyrafitte, for their friendship and advice; and, above all, to my husband, Robert Kelly, for his careful reading and insightful comments, especially in matters of poetry.

CHARLOTTE MANDELL

GENERAL EDITORS' PREFACE

IN SEARCH OF LOST TIME, published between 1913 and 1927, is recognized as the undisputed masterpiece of twentieth-century fiction. Endlessly rich in its themes and idioms, it is a philosophical novel about time, memory, imagination, and art; a psychological novel about human behaviour, love, and jealousy; a social novel about France, especially high society, as it evolved from the end of the nineteenth century to the aftermath of the 1914–18 War; and a comic novel of manners, character, and language. It is also an experimental novel, quite unlike what contemporary readers normally understood to be a work of fiction. Part of Proust's importance historically is that he redefined the boundaries of fiction. Instead of a conventional linear story with a clearly identifiable plot, the *Search* uses a kaleidoscope of memories to create a startlingly new form of narrative. For those who come to the *Search* for the first time, it reads very much like an autobiography. There is an 'I', a first-person narrator who is telling the story of his childhood experiences and the life that follows, adding analytical comments as he goes. But although there are strong autobiographical elements in the novel—the places and characters can be matched with Proust's own experience, and the narrator's name is eventually revealed to be Marcel—these elements have been transformed, and a world created out of them which, though based on real experiences, is an imaginary one, a fictional creation. Moreover, the narrative 'I' is a double 'I', moving fluidly between the present of the narrator and the past of his younger self, building multiple perspectives into a symphonic structure and promoting a dramatic narration as the narrator comes slowly to understand the significance of his past experiences. The novel invites the reader to enter the narrator's mind, to accompany him on his journey of discovery as he explores the workings of his own consciousness and seeks to understand not only the meaning of his own life but also the nature of the human condition.

There is no ideal, ultimate translation of a given original. There cannot be, given that nothing is exactly the same in one language as in another. Moreover, as Kevin Hart has noted, following Jacques Derrida, while any text is always open to translation, 'no version, faithful or free, will ever exhaust its meaning. There will always be a supplement of signification which remains outside even the most successful translation, and that supplement will always entice another translator to begin work.'[1] Classic texts in particular, from Homer onwards, are susceptible of multiple readings and retranslations over time. Gustave Flaubert's *Madame Bovary* has been retranslated into English over twenty times since its publication in 1857. Retranslation of classic works, and the ability to compare different versions of a given text, afford an opportunity to celebrate not only the expressive capacities of the English language, the role of the translator, and the creativity involved in the translator's art, but also 'the rich multiple presence of the translated text'.[2] Our aim with this series of new translations, accompanied by detailed notes and readable introductions by leading scholars, is to contribute to that richness—to widen still further the appeal of a work that offers inexhaustible rewards.

Publication will be in seven volumes. There will be a different translator for each volume (except the first and last). We have chosen to standardize certain terms, recurrent phrases and expressions, modes of address, personal titles, use of elision and so forth across the translations, and, more generally, have attempted to facilitate unity of voice, a stylistic consonance, across the various volumes (while bearing in mind shifts in Proust's voice and tone as his work progressed). The views on translation expressed in the Translator's Note in the first volume (*The Swann Way*) are, broadly speaking, those of the team. Ultimately, however, the best guarantee that Proust's voice will come through in each volume is the artistry of the translators themselves.

Proust's themes and preoccupations, the threads with which the seven individual volumes of the *Search* are stitched together into a coherent whole, are as relevant and speak as directly to us now as they ever have in the course of the last century. Desire, attraction, betrayal; ageing, memory, and identity; death, loss, and the solace of art: all of these human concerns speak to us from the pages of Proust's novel. But in their interweaving—and this cuts to the core of the

[1] Quoted by Paolo Bartoloni, 'The Virtuality of Translation', in Christopher Palmer and Ian Topliss (eds.), *Globalising Australia* (Melbourne: La Trobe University, 2000), 77–83, at 78.

[2] Dominique Jullien, 'The Way by Lydia's: A New Translation of Proust', in Suzanne Jill Levine and Katie Lateef-Jan (eds.), *Untranslatability Goes Global* (New York: Routledge, 2017), 64–76, at 72.

Search's remarkable hybrid status—we encounter a quite extraordinary array of cultural and historical references. From cave paintings to music hall, Renaissance sculpture to advertising hoardings, high culture to lowbrow ephemera, Proust's novel throngs with allusions to centuries' worth of history and cultural production. Though contemporary readers, unlike those of Proust's own time, have the facility of consulting a search engine to learn in a matter of seconds, for example, who painted the Virtues and Vices of Padua, or who Planté and Rubinstein were, we felt nevertheless that incorporating a set of explanatory endnotes in each volume was at once desirable and valuable. Those who choose to ignore them can of course forge ahead in their reading uninterrupted; but those who are curious will find socio-cultural, historical, geographical, and artistic allusions illuminated and contextualized. The notes seek not to offer any sort of critical commentary on Proust's novel, but rather to clarify dates and details that will enrich readers' appreciation of its unique breadth of reference.

The introductory essay to each volume outlines the key concerns and preoccupations of the volume in question, providing a broad frame of reference for readers tackling the novel for the first time and reflecting on the role of that volume in the wider structure of the novel as a whole. These essays will prime readers for the journey that lies ahead but should be read with the awareness that they—inevitably—contain 'spoilers' or anticipations of what is to come.

BRIAN NELSON
ADAM WATT

TRANSLATOR'S NOTE

To read Proust is to enter a person's mind, to watch a thought as it unfolds, slowly or quickly, intricately or straightforwardly, but always lucidly, insightfully. To translate Proust is to take up residence in that mind for a while, to see things as it sees them, to learn to think and write in a completely different way, a way that is foreign to one's 'usual' way of thinking and writing. My goal in translating Proust was to stay as faithful as possible to the syntax, rhythm, and register of the original text, while making it sound as convincing as possible in English; there is beauty in the way a Proustian sentence unfurls and develops a thought from seed to fruit, slowly, over time, the way a thought unfolds. I tried to preserve the integrity of the sentences by not breaking them up (interrupting the thought), by adhering to the rhythm of the phrases, and by trying as much as possible to stay true to the order of the syntagms, so that the reader can see the images and concepts in the same order the writer saw them, one after the other, culminating in the final, crowning word or phrase. Describing his admiration for both the writings of Madame de Sévigné and the paintings of Elstir, the narrator of *In the Shadow of Girls in Blossom* writes: 'I realized in Balbec that she presents things to us in the same way as he does, in the order in which we perceive them, instead of starting out by explaining what brought them about' (p. 203). This is one of the extraordinary qualities of Proust's sentences: they present things to us as the narrator sees them, as he tries to understand them and tease out their meaning, not as we ourselves might see them, all at once or objectively, and not as most of the writers of Proust's time did, in an explanatory, linear way. We learn to see everything in a different light, as if for the first time, the way Elstir sees things: the shadow cast on the water by a boat may look like a dolphin clinging to its hull; a church's reflection might make it look like a mirage seen from afar. The true skill of an artist—whether painter or writer, Elstir or Proust—is to transform reality, to make the mundane seem extraordinary. My goal as translator was not to smooth out the strangeness of some of these sentences, or to explain what I thought they meant in my own words, or to edit them by adding or removing words, but simply to say what they said, as faithfully and carefully as

I could, so that the remarkable way the narrator has of seeing 'reality' can be conveyed and appreciated in its complexity.

Translating a canonical and groundbreaking text that has been translated before—translated well, and beautifully—like *A l'ombre des jeunes filles en fleurs* demands a conscious effort to bring that text into English afresh. For half a century, C. K. Scott Moncrieff's translation was the only version available in English; this was followed by James Grieve's translation for the Penguin series. I am grateful for all the light their translations have cast upon Proust's work. Moncrieff's version is poetic, wonderfully evocative, and, overall, faithful to the original; Grieve's is idiomatic, straightforward, easier to understand. Moncrieff pays more attention to the shape of the sentences; Grieve stresses meaning over syntax, the story told over the voice of the storyteller. Moncrieff's English tends to be more flowery and ornate than Proust's French; Grieve's version tends to go in the opposite direction, opting for an idiom that sounds more like spoken English, with difficult expressions glossed over or rephrased to make their meaning easier to grasp. My goal is to render Proust's language in an English as mellifluous and poetic as Moncrieff's, and as understandable and unaffected as Grieve's. Moncrieff remained largely faithful to the structure of the sentences, while Grieve took a more liberal approach to the French, changing the order of the phrases in a sentence so that it would sound smoother in English, sometimes adding his own glosses of a cryptic term or poetic metaphor, and sometimes even breaking up sentences, or merging two shorter sentences into one. I tried to remain faithful to the length and poetry of Proust's sentences while also conveying their meaning and register; a successful translation captures the 'voice' of the original, so that what we read is not an approximate rendering of the translator's idea of the original, but a convincing re-creation of the voice of the writer/ narrator—his style, as it were.

One common misconception about Proust's sentences is that they are needlessly verbose; on the contrary, Proust is surprisingly concise and exact in his wording, and there are hardly any extraneous words or phrases. The tendency of both Moncrieff and Grieve to add words, either as explanatory glosses or for rhetorical effect, and, in Grieve's case, to restructure some sentences so that they read more smoothly in English, sometimes detracts from Proust's elegant simplicity and intricate, purposeful rhythm. Proust is such a distinctive writer that

I have tried as much as possible to let his prose speak for itself. In Grieve's Introduction to *In the Shadow of Young Girls in Flower*, he writes: 'The translator wishing to make a seamless text for his reader is often thwarted by Proust's seams, which tend to be rough . . . In translating, it is sometimes necessary to edit.'[1] I think these 'seams' are a necessary part of the text, and one of the qualities that make Proust's novel so different from any other; the abruptness with which a scene, or a thought, can shift is, I would argue, purposeful; our thoughts are not often seamless, and one of the most striking qualities of *A la recherche* is to show us a person thinking. There is also a poetic power in the 'seams': they require us to think on our feet, to fill in the gaps ourselves, the way a poem of Mallarmé might. Making a text smoother can make it lose some of its poetry, some of its intentional artifice (in its original sense of 'making art'). Syntax, rhythm, alliteration, poetic metaphor, all go into forming the narrator's voice; I have tried my best to preserve all these things so that this voice can come across (be 'translated') as Proust's own.

Moncrieff's translation, while unsurpassed in the richness of its language, sometimes tends towards preciosity—especially when it avoids alluding to obviously sexual themes—and has come to sound somewhat archaic in its old-fashioned turns of phrase. Grieve, on the other hand, gives the narrator a more modern, breezy style of speech which to my mind sounds foreign to the original. Proust's language in *A la recherche* is not colloquial or idiomatic; as Brian Nelson says in his Translator's Note to *The Swann Way*, 'Proust sounded strange in French, to his French audience, because of the particularity of his voice, a strikingly original new voice given shape in his native language.'[2] There is an inherent strangeness in Proust's voice and syntax, an otherness that transcends nationality or era. To make the narrator sound like a modern British or American person, or like an old-fashioned character from the Ancien Régime, would be to stray from that distinctive 'otherness'.

Finally, as to the title: this volume's title, *A l'ombre des jeunes filles en fleurs*, is arguably the most difficult title to translate out of the

---

[1] Marcel Proust, *In the Shadow of Young Girls in Flower*, trans. and introd. James Grieve (Allen Lane, The Penguin Press, 2002), p. xii.

[2] Marcel Proust, *The Swann Way*, trans. Brian Nelson, ed. Adam Watt (Oxford: Oxford University Press, 2023), p. xiv.

seven volumes of *A la recherche*, largely because of all that it leaves unspoken, and because almost every word in the title has several meanings, including (not so subtle) sexual innuendos. *A l'ombre* can mean either 'in the shade' or 'in the shadow'; *jeunes filles* can refer to either girls or young women (while *filles* by itself can mean 'prostitutes'); *en fleurs* literally means 'in flower' or 'in blossom', but it has an antiquated connotation of girls entering puberty, 'blossoming' into adulthood. There is no precise English equivalent for *en fleurs*. I wavered back and forth between *In the Shade of Young Women in Blossom* to the present title, *In the Shadow of Girls in Blossom*, for several reasons: I chose 'shadow' instead of 'shade' because, throughout the book, the narrator is very much in the girls' shadow, first in Gilberte's shadow and then in the shadow of all the girls in the 'little band'. He is never their equal; his love for them borders on a kind of idolatry, so that the girls take on a kind of superhuman power to bestow or withdraw an elusive (and never truly attained) happiness. And shadows themselves play an important part in the narrative, especially in the paintings of Elstir as the narrator describes them; shadows take on human qualities and almost become personified, undergoing the same sort of poetic transformation that the girls undergo as they gradually morph from goddesses to humans. I opted for 'girls' instead of 'young women' because the girls in the 'little band' are still very much girls, playing childish games like hide-and-seek and King of the Mountain and ring-on-a-string; they are not, as Grieve has them, 'young girls', however, since their ages range from about 14 to 16 or 17 (though their exact ages are never entirely clear, since they can shift from rough pranksters to sophisticated literary critics in the space of a few paragraphs). I chose 'in blossom' instead of 'in flower' because I thought it had a little more of a sexual, first-bloom-of-youth connotation. (And I chose 'blossom' instead of 'bloom' mainly for the rhythm of the phrase.) Moncrieff's *Within a Budding Grove*, while it does hint at a budding sexuality, loses all the nuances and hidden meanings of the original title, and leaves out the main subjects of the novel, the girls themselves. The plethora of choices suggested by the title alone gives one some idea of the complexities involved in any attempt to translate an entire novel by Proust—I can only hope I've managed in some way to make Proust 'sound like Proust'.

C.M.

INTRODUCTION

*Readers new to the novel should note that this Introduction
makes details of the plot explicit.*

ONE of Marcel Proust's concerns as a novelist was that his readers
might be failing to see the underlying structure in what would eventually
become his seven-volume *A la recherche du temps perdu* (*In Search of Lost
Time*). Not that his work ran to that length in November 1913 when *Du
côté de chez Swann* (*The Swann Way*) appeared. The size of that first
volume still had to be restricted nevertheless when the publisher,
Bernard Grasset, explained to Proust the need for individual volume
lengths that would be attractive to readers and also manageable from
a printer's point of view. The outbreak of the First World War in the
following year then saw the suspension of publication of the novel. The
substantial material which had to be held back from the first volume for
the pragmatic reasons Grasset had given was already at galley-proof
stage with the publisher in 1914. Proust then worked extensively on
these unpublished proofs, incorporating much of the revamped,
expanded material into what became the 500-page section that is the
present volume, under the fresh title *A l'ombre des jeunes filles en fleurs* (*In
the Shadow of Girls in Blossom*). This was part of his wider expansion of
the novel during the war years. For the new volume, Proust was now with
a different publisher, Gaston Gallimard. With a print run of 3,300 copies
completed by late November 1918, it finally appeared in June 1919.

We can see signs of Proust's rejigging of material caused by the
pressure to subdivide his work into a series of volumes. Thus, the title
for the 1919 instalment refers essentially to the last third of the text
where the central character meets the 'girls in blossom' at Balbec on
the Normandy coastline. This seaside setting forms what critics have
seen as the second panel of *In the Shadow of Girls in Blossom*, the
first being the Parisian backdrop against which the account of the
young protagonist's family life and his obsession with members of
the Swann family is set. That first panel, 'Madame Swann's Circle'
('Autour de Madame Swann'), itself builds on the relationship
between Odette and Swann which is recounted in the first volume, in
the section entitled 'Swann in Love'.

Proust was nevertheless inventive in turning to his advantage publishers' requirements to cut. In fact, in some respects, he succeeds in giving *In the Shadow of Girls in Blossom* an almost free-standing appearance. Adept at orchestrating textual sequences, he has the volume open with news of a change of direction involving some key characters. A mid-volume partition is worked around Madame Swann's majestic presence on Paris's Avenue du Bois de Boulogne (there are echoes here of the close of *The Swann Way*). And Proust closes the volume again on a note of ceremony and spectacle, as we will see at the end of this Introduction. Convincing his readers that the novel overall was structurally coherent remained one of his most pressing concerns.

A l'ombre des jeunes filles en fleurs was awarded France's Prix Goncourt, ahead of *Les Croix de bois* (*Wooden Crosses*) by Roland Dorgelès. It was a controversial choice given the year, 1919. Many felt that Dorgelès, a war veteran, should have received the honour for a novel that delivered a searing evocation of life in the trenches in the conflict that had just ended. But by a majority of six to four, the Goncourt jury opted for what in the eyes of many was an unpatriotic choice. The communist newspaper *L'Humanité* argued that the verdict disregarded Edmond de Goncourt's stated wish, which had been that the prize be given to a young writer. The paper claimed that the decision of the ten-man jury to honour an older author (Proust was 48 by then, Dorgelès 33) was part of a wider disdain directed against a heroic younger generation. By contrast, the conservative *Le Figaro* expressed satisfaction that one of its contributors had won the prize.

Unlike Dorgelès's novel, *In the Shadow of Girls in Blossom* is centred on a pre-First World War culture of leisure and social parade. It describes dinners in bourgeois homes and in the Grand-Hôtel in Balbec; children playing in the Champs-Élysées Park; crowds on holiday; trips by horse-drawn carriage to visit the coastal region around Balbec; idle looking; the jockeying for social position; new patterns of consumption. Nevertheless, *In the Shadow of Girls in Blossom* often confronts the reader with a world which, though familiar in many respects, is narrated from unfamiliar angles. Details of the plot are frequently straightforward. For example, the younger 'I' (the adolescent protagonist the first-person narrator once was) obsesses about Gilberte Swann and her mother; he travels by train from Paris to Balbec on the Normandy coast; he drinks too much port in a restaurant in Rivebelle, near Balbec. Yet the narrator's accounts of adolescent infatuation, of the train journey, and of the effects of a hangover trigger a string of analogies. In a similar way, the flurry of activity around the circular tables in the busy Rivebelle restaurant is imagined as planetary movement. Another analogy sees Françoise, the family cook, carefully choosing ingredients for a stew, just as Michelangelo went to a quarry in Carrara to select blocks of marble for his sculpture. Proust's appetite for copious and inventive comparison-making is one of the hallmarks of his compositional style and this has a bearing on our encounter with textuality in this volume where we find these detours, parallels, and asides.

New Volume, New Angles

This second book of Proust's novel opens with a dramatic character reshuffle that sees two figures from the first volume now recast. The twin reversal shows unexpected sides to Charles Swann and Dr Cottard. The mother of the main character had suggested to her husband that Swann and Cottard would make ideal dinner guests to be invited along with the senior diplomat Monsieur de Norpois, whom the parents are keen to impress. In *The Swann Way*, Swann is the discreet, urbane socialite who so impresses the family in provincial Combray, but is also a member of Paris's prestigious Jockey Club. Now, to the disgust of the protagonist's father, Swann has become besotted with everything to do with Odette, embracing the tastes, social contacts, and ambition of his new wife. Meanwhile, Cottard, who at Madame Verdurin's salon in 'Swann in Love' is socially hesitant, emerges as an international authority whose medical diagnoses are greatly valued. The narrator conveys with verve the drama signalled by these changes and the father's outburst about Swann. Later, the novelist Jean Genet was to read the opening sentence of *A l'ombre* and quickly close the book, knowing that a delight lay in store for him.

The explanation of the Cottard and Swann reversals and the question of appropriate dinner guests feed quickly into the plot, forming a number of strands: the incandescent rage of the boy's father; his mother's diplomatic planning of the meal for Norpois; the latter's social eminence which contrasts, we soon see, with the lower-level civil servants in France's Third Republic who are now regulars at the

Swanns'; and the high professional standing of Cottard whose aesthetic tastes remain nevertheless lowbrow.

The reversals also bolster the narrator's reflection on the place of discontinuity in the human personality. He sees change as intrinsic to an individual's psychology. Swann's second life, in his role as Odette's husband, will not be the last, the narrator notes. He also observes how Cottard, now much in demand as a doctor, has dropped his shyness and hesitancy and assumed a 'glacial demeanour' (p. 7) in order to give himself gravity. But spotting these changes takes time, the narrator cautions, given the frequent lag in our perception of people. Habit blocks our eyes and ears, to use his image. The mind is therefore often slow to grasp how people and their situations may have changed. The assertion provides an early example of the regular moves made by the 'I' of the narrative to formulate what are presented as laws of human behaviour.

Proust was also an astute observer of political power, as the portrayal of Norpois early in the present volume demonstrates. The aristocrat is an influential figure at the heart of government, having succeeded over several decades in maintaining his position as a state functionary. He has moved nimbly from serving a reactionary regime to working for the new Republic, which positions itself as being more progressive. The diplomat's language captures, in the narrator's summing-up, a career, a social class, and an era. Indeed, when he expresses regret at not having a fuller recall of Norpois' vocabulary, the narrator signals a key dimension in Proust's social observation, namely characters' use of language. We have copious illustrations of this. The narrator records Odette's Anglicisms, the howlers made by the manager of the Grand-Hôtel, and the larking about with high-flown language indulged in by Bloch and his sisters. Within the band of girls in Balbec, a school examination question awakens lively discussion about the register in which Sophocles might have addressed Racine. And on the question of vocabulary use, an artist like Elstir, the narrator comments, shares with others not only the same baker but also the same popular speech.

Proust's ear for language use includes the interaction between human voices in conversation. Thus, when the boy's father and Norpois are in discussion, their interventions are likened to that of a cello (in the case of the father) to which a piano replies, as in a Mozart concerto. The narrator also notes styles of intonation passing from parents to their children and sees them as revealing a whole outlook on the world: 'our intonations contain our philosophy of life' (p. 426). Knowledge of human psychology thus comes via attentiveness to language. For the young hero and his grandmother, their system of three knocks on the partition wall separating their hotel rooms in Balbec is as intimate a voice and language as any in the entire novel. The absence of those knocks, from the grandmother's side of the wall, strikes the painful closing note of the first half of 'Place Names: The Place'.

Returning to Norpois, we see alongside his exercise of political power the clout he wields as an invited guest. The protagonist's parents show him great deference, while he in turn influences their family dynamic. Contrary to what Marcel's father would have imagined, the diplomat endorses literature as a possible career for their son and encourages the boy to go to see La Berma in the lead role in Racine's play *Phèdre* (Proust modelled La Berma on the famous actress of the day, Sarah Bernhardt).[1] Norpois also unsettles other assumptions made by the boy's parents. He is a guest in the home of Odette and Charles Swann and whereas the protagonist's parents avoid the Swanns, Norpois sings Odette's praises. Indeed, he comments that the Swanns' guests are mostly men, his sly suggestion being that the allure of the former courtesan might explain this. With the boy's respectable bourgeois parents believing that an aristocrat would necessarily look down on a social climber like Madame Swann, the reversal of that expectation adds to the intrigue.

Through Norpois' social diary, then, the culture of leisure that is widespread in this volume begins to be mapped out. His contacts take the narrative beyond the adolescent protagonist's home to the world outside: to the theatre; to the home of the Swanns; and to the encounter with Bergotte, the writer whom the young 'I' of the narrative idolizes. This last link, however, sees Norpois launch a scathing attack on Bergotte, whom he dismisses as 'what I call a flute player' (p. 42). Seeing Bergotte's style as lacking virility, Norpois taps into a culture war of Proust's day around the role of the writer by suggesting that the nation needs a would-be vigorous, patriotic art and an end to aestheticism. With Norpois' career stretching back to before the

---

[1] See editorial note in Marcel Proust, *A l'ombre des jeunes filles en fleurs*, ed. Pierre-Louis Rey (Paris: Gallimard, 1988), 520.

Franco-Prussian War of 1870–1, his jibe against art comes in an age when the threat posed by Germany aroused great tensions. Even the career diplomat's more usual, measured tones mask a steely will to dominate. Later, his psychology is carefully gauged by the narrator, who sees that this skilled manipulator of situations invariably protects his own position while appearing to foster the interests of others. Norpois' social manoeuvres thus illustrate what Proust terms 'the principle of multiple uses' (p. 452).

Exploring the Human Mind

These scenes of rivalry, influence, and insecurity feed into the social comedy and show the narrator to be a busy student of the human mind. Questions concerning behaviour and motivation intrigue him, with sections of often intense psychological analysis forming a seam that runs through much of the novel. One of his central convictions is that the mind has the capacity to be both distracted and accurately focused. He marvels at how both memory and forgetting are part of everyday living. He also gives an acerbic, comic account of situations involving human misguidedness. Aspiring writers delude themselves about the merit of their work, he muses. Likewise, a person in love may blindly believe in the commitment of the one who, they know, betrays them. Probing what he presents as the concurrent strands that make up our mental life, the narrator identifies 'the shared life led by the ideas within our minds' (p. 49).

The young protagonist's own actions amply demonstrate how fallible the mind is. When he goes to see La Berma onstage, he yearns to grasp fully the nature of her performance. Yet his overly analytical approach to working out the artist's achievement means that he fails. Only when the other spectators break into rapturous applause does he begin to feel enthusiasm for La Berma's acting. Later, a glowing press review of her interpretation of the Phèdre role confirms how the verdict of others allows the adolescent to grasp mentally her exceptional talent. With anxious anticipation, then, comes the risk of disillusionment. The pattern repeats itself later in the volume when, with the protagonist sure that, thanks to Elstir, his long-awaited introduction to the band of girls is about to take place, the meeting fails to materialize. The run of sentences carrying the complex narrative of expectation ends with a pithy 'All was lost' (p. 381).

Individual paragraphs in Proust's novel, then, can deliver dramas in miniature. Indeed, they sometimes appear to stand as self-contained units of linguistic performance, with a punchy line often delivering a local denouement to the situation or issue being explored. A case in point is the scene where the protagonist, travelling through Paris with a friend of his father's, unceremoniously jumps out of the carriage to run after an unknown young woman, only to discover, on catching up with her, that the person in question is a now ageing Madame Verdurin whom he has been trying to avoid. The comic snapshot helps illustrate the narrator's broader view of his younger self as having 'a neurotic nature' (p. 218). Or again, when the adolescent receives a letter from Gilberte inviting him to tea in her parents' home, the narrator tracks the complex dissection that allows his mind to assimilate the written message. The paragraph ends with the briefest of sentences recording his cognitive breakthrough: 'Finally, I was able to experience my happiness' (p. 66). Similarly, when the young hero first enters the Swanns' home, he is described as being in a state of mental impotence, so overwhelmed is he at being admitted. After a lengthy attempt to gauge his incoherent response to Charles Swann, who is showing him round his library, the narrator settles for the ready-made explanation provided by the 'fine popular expression [. . .] "I didn't know whether I was coming or going"' (p. 74). In its inventiveness, everyday idiom here brings direct knowledge and interrupts the flow of micro-observation.

At times, Proust opts for compact formulations of what are offered as punchy psychological truths. A human being never forms a straight path, runs one of the narrator's aphorisms. Love's viewpoint is one of selfishness, is another. A future without those we love would bring 'a real death of our selves' (p. 218), which would then lead to the birth of a new but different self. The aristocrat Charlus, speaking with his aunt about the seventeenth-century writer Madame de Sévigné's feelings for her daughter, insists that 'the important thing in life is not *whom* you love [. . .] it's the fact of loving' (p. 299).

Other attempts at psychological understanding translate into lengthier reflections. Thus, the narrator's nuanced portrait of Andrée, one of the band of fun-loving girls in Balbec, draws out her intellectual side. Moreover, her conspicuous tact is a subject carefully dissected, the narrator wondering what that quality might tell us about the moral standpoint of the person showing it. Alongside this, a searching mental portrait of Andrée's mother reveals the ramifications of her social insecurity and her capacity for personal loyalty. The play-acting of Monsieur Nissim Bernard allows the narrator to probe the behaviour of the compulsive liar, a mindset that Robert de Saint-Loup is no less curious to understand.

The narrator applies a comparable technique of dissection to self-knowledge, with intense impressions providing privileged moments of access to this. For example, the sighting of three trees at Hudimesnil from a passing train triggers sudden, deep affect in the young protagonist, who wonders if their beauty might be connected with his earliest childhood. The moment of appearance is presented as holding a mysterious, elusive truth, the narrator likening the movement of the trees to a person suffering from aphasia and desperately unable to communicate their message. He explains how the sighting of the steeples at Martinville back in 'Combray' had released a similar intensity (we can see parallels here too with the madeleine episode in the same section of the first volume). These are among his deepest experiences and yet their revelatory potential remains tantalizingly unavailable to a principal character who longs to access such revelation and thus 'finally start a true life [*une vraie vie*]' (p. 259).

Seeing Across Time

Alongside this drilling down, Proust's novel also works to create a telescopic perspective on life, this connecting with the enduring theme of time's passing.[2] The conception of experience as something lived in time is regularly featured in the pages of *In the Shadow of Girls in Blossom*. The protagonist's appreciation of Vinteuil's music, for instance, develops across a series of hearings. Also set necessarily in time are the different stages in his getting to know St Mark's, Venice, the actual sight of the church being a step beyond the knowledge gathered from seeing a photograph earlier. Some characters appear to embody the past. Princesse Mathilde, a niece of Napoleon I, exudes charm by dressing in an old style, as if to satisfy people's expectations of the exotic era they see her as still inhabiting. Similarly, Odette Swann's outfits as she moves into middle age have younger

---

[2] In *Le Temps retrouvé* (*Time Regained*), the final volume of Proust's novel, the narrator will stress the importance of the telescopic viewpoint.

people admiring these 'remnants . . . of former years' (p. 172). The sight of Françoise in old-fashioned clothes, dressed for the train journey to Balbec, calls to the narrator's mind the historic figure of Anne de Bretagne. Charlus is likewise drawn to a small number of women whose noble lineage feeds his nostalgia for 'all the glory and elegance of the Ancien Régime' (p. 294). Later in this volume, Elstir waxes lyrical about the new dress designer Fortuny, who is resurrecting the old styles of the Venetian painter Carpaccio.

In parallel with this harking back, the novel also explores scenarios of projection forward. How much time needs to elapse for a work of artistic genius to be understood, the narrator wonders (in the same reflection, he considers the dislocation caused were we to be confronted in our youth with the traits of the person we would become in middle age). Modernity is another performer in the field of time passing. The prospectus for the Grand-Hôtel preaches the need to keep up with the latest styles. The technological change evident in urban life sees Madame Verdurin in a new home with electricity, a friend of hers having a telephone line installed, and electric lighting coming to the streets of Paris. The Gare Saint-Lazare is hailed as 'one of those vast, glass-roofed garages' (p. 195). In the arts, innovation with lighting effects is a feature of Leon Bakst's work on the set for the Ballets Russes. The narrator hears talk of a future invention, 'the phototelephone' (p. 445), which would provide both voice and face in the act of communication over distance. Odette's Anglicisms, already mentioned, reflect a new fashion which the young protagonist enjoys and his father dislikes. His grandmother appears keen to embrace modernity when she agrees to be photographed by her grandson's friend Robert de Saint-Loup, who has a Kodak camera. The protagonist thinks she is being vain and his insensitivity causes her to abandon the idea.

Linked to these signs of time passing, the theme of life's brevity colours numerous situations in the volume. Memory is fallible, the narrator observes, citing the phenomenon of senility. But long before old age, the signs of change and impermanence in life encroach. Saying goodbye to his mother at the Saint-Lazare station while he and his grandmother board the train for Balbec, the adolescent son sees for the first time that she might have a life separate from his. Or when he reminds Elstir of the remarkable artistic legacy the painter will leave, Elstir cannot separate the compliment from the sense of his mortality. A similar paradox occurs when the protagonist's father concedes that his son, no longer a child, should be allowed to pursue his wish to be a writer. The permission leaves the son feeling that he has already embarked on his existence, as he puts it. As the narrator stresses, we are subject to Time's laws, a process as inevitable as planet Earth turning. Capturing Time (with a capital T (*le Temps*), as Proust insists) is central, then, to his conception of the novelist's endeavour.

Other attributes, the narrator notes, are also required of the writer. Bergotte, whose works he had avidly read as a boy in the garden of the family home back in Combray, now appears as a guest in the Swann household. While the adolescent is star-struck at finding himself in the novelist's company, the mature 'I' offers a different angle. Successful writers, he cautions, are not those who move in high circles. Rather, their achievement is the ability to 'reflect their personalities like a mirror' (p. 115). They attend to what the narrator presents as a duty to imagine the lives of others. That act of imagination extends to the representation of social posturing. To cite just one example, we have the dialogue scene in which Madame Swann casts herself as a prejudice-ridden petite bourgeoise, her aim being to provoke protests to the contrary from her adoring guests. This tuning into the speech and posing of Madame Swann illustrates the narrator's view that novelists have a gift for grasping ways of living diametrically opposed to their own. While he recreates, often with great elan, scenes that centre on characters parading their importance, this does not equate to an endorsement of that social parade. Thus, while guests who have met Bergotte's family travel home in their Rolls-Royces, sure in the conviction that their hosts are socially unimportant, the narrator thinks differently. In his analogy, the achievements of Bergotte the writer see him climb skywards, as though in a modest aircraft.

Yet however accomplished he is, Bergotte is not averse to backbiting. The adolescent protagonist is amazed when someone who is so endearing when with the Swanns makes scathing comments to him about Madame Swann and pities her husband for the marriage in which he finds himself. For the teenager, the remarks herald an abrupt initiation into the ways of fashionable society (or *le monde*, to use the term in the French original). Bergotte's words highlight the gap that exists between *le monde* and the lifestyle and values of Combray, the narrator reflecting that his great-aunt Léonie may have been grumpy but would never have engaged in malicious gossip. The protagonist himself comes nevertheless to betray those values by choosing to give to a brothel the furniture he has inherited from her. He is wracked with guilt at what amounts to a desecration of the virtues of Combray. Similarly, his later selling of his great-aunt's silverware to pay for expensive gifts of flowers for Madame Swann leads to further self-recrimination and an awareness of the vanity of such ostentatious giving. The subject of his misspent inheritance returns towards the end of 'Madame Swann's Circle' where a fresh attempt by the protagonist to impress, this time involving Gilberte, has unexpected consequences. His moral fall can only sharpen the narrator's conviction that his mother and grandmother are 'creatures absolutely unspoiled' who belong to 'the race of Combray [which] seems to be almost extinct' (p. 284).

Proust's narrator is scathing about the scramble for social position, pointing comically to how those recently decorated want to see an immediate end to the conferral of any new honours. Likewise, he dismisses as vacuous Madame Verdurin's energetic calculations about her guest list. Her picking and choosing amount to what he derides as 'the Arts of Nothing' (p. 155), the use of capitals intensifying his scorn. Importantly, the moralizing tone does not mean the excision of the 'nothingness' of frivolity from the novel. Rather, the scenes of vanity and the blasts of trenchant dismissal directed against it run in tandem.

Commenting sharply on the jockeying for position is not restricted to the narrator. In an age of conspicuous male domination both in the domestic and public spheres, his mother may play a subservient role in relation to her husband yet she is altogether more perceptive than he is in her observation of the dynamic at work in Madame Swann's ambition. Observing the Swanns' desire to extend and, crucially, to parade their contacts, she depicts Madame Swann as a conquering warrior locked in colonial battle. To her mocking account of that particular merry-go-round, the narrator adds the broader, more damning verdict that our quest for fame is only hampered by the poverty of our imagination.

Proust's way of describing society thus shows multiple perspectives: austere detachment, mischievous playfulness, and moments of self-recrimination too, as we have seen. Self-mockery is part of this, as when the adolescent, finally gaining admission to the Swanns' home, is presented as reaching 'their Inner Sanctum' (p. 74). Other examples of hyperbole reinforce the sense of comedy. These visits by the young hero are compared to guests being presented to the King at the Palace of Versailles, the mock grandeur of the comparison seeing him mistake a male servant for Madame Swann in a dimly lit ante-room. Infatuated with Gilberte, the protagonist would prefer to have a photo of her rather than of artwork by Leonardo da Vinci. For all that, his exaggerated view of the Swanns' standing is deflated when his father comments matter-of-factly that houses of the kind the Swanns live in are fairly standard, the son inwardly dismissing the comment, just as a devout Christian might refuse to read Ernest Renan's account of the life of Christ.[3] These gaps in perspective between the experience of the younger 'I' and the viewpoint of the mature narrator are a pivotal aspect of *In the Shadow of Girls in Blossom*. They relativize the adolescent's travails and repeatedly generate comic dislocation. The gaps also highlight how an older self can reconstruct without partisanship the intense desires of a younger self. To cite a much earlier writer's reflection on how memory experiences the past differently: 'when I remember that I once wanted something, I can do so without wishing to have it now'.[4]

The narrator works the account of the protagonist's love for Gilberte (who is about 14 or 15 at the time, Norpois estimates) on to a wider canvas. Reflecting often sombrely on what love involves in the course of a lifetime, he contends that it brings a 'permanent suffering' (p. 138) that is merely kept at bay in periods of joy. A clear gender asymmetry marks these aphorisms, with the troubled lover being invariably male and the person loved, female. The narrator's pithy definitions sometimes strike a lofty, idiosyncratic note, as when he argues that, when in love, we are incapable of being 'worthy predecessors' (p. 142) to the person we will become when love ends.[5] Thinking laterally, he suggests that, in their dealings with the person loved, the lover is like 'someone who barely understands the principle of causality'

---

[3] The nineteenth-century writer Renan's depiction of Christ's life drew a hostile reception from the Catholic Church.

[4] See St Augustine, *Confessions*, Book 10, section 14, trans. and introd. R. S. Pine-Coffin (1961; Harmondsworth: Penguin, 1976), 220.

[5] David Ellison writes of the 'coherent, if sometimes strange and idiosyncratic theory of love' to be found in Proust's novel. See Ellison, *A Reader's Guide to Proust's 'In Search of Lost Time'* (Cambridge: Cambridge University Press, 2010), 66.

(p. 142). While the narrator gives free rein to his urge to speculate and make analogies, the inexperienced hero obsesses about Gilberte. The immediate arrangements surrounding their day-to-day contact feed the adolescent's obsession. Desperate for a letter from her, he overanalyses in a state of perpetual apprehension. In the dense paragraphs that chart the lover's state of mind, we see a return to the link forged in 'Swann in Love' between love and sickness.

As the relationship with Gilberte evolves, the protagonist is torn between the desire to end it and the hope that it will revive. Either way, his mental investment remains unrelenting. In the narrator's hard-hitting assessment, he is 'the creator—conscious, wilful, pitiless, and patient—of this anguish' (p. 164). The indecision and volatility of the younger 'I' allow the narrator to draw, again on the wider canvas of life's experience, one of the laws of the human soul, as he frames it, namely the intermittency that marks our emotional life. Proust set great store by this notion, as shown by the title he had originally envisaged for the novel overall: *Les Intermittences du Cœur* (*Intermittences of the Heart*). With this discontinuity come the many anachronisms, to use his term, that disrupt the present moment. The transition from love to detachment is fraught as a consequence, with the experience of forgetting Gilberte being disturbed at times by memories of her. These memories counteract the otherwise inevitable movement towards forgetting. The self that loved is thus stored away. In Proust's analogy, it's like a book one might deposit in the Bibliothèque nationale to ensure its preservation.

In Part Two of *In the Shadow of Girls in Blossom*, the protagonist, now two years older, meets Albertine. There too, the fate of the relationship is inextricably bound up with his individual psychology. Indeed, the narrator more than hints at a force of psychological determinism when he asserts that it is 'our character or nature [. . .] which itself creates the loves we experience' (p. 141).

Social Chronicling

While tracking the troubled inner life of the hero in love, Proust is also keen to establish historical perspective. Emphasizing in particular the concept of periodic societal and political change, he coins a particular metaphor for this, that of the social kaleidoscope. When its 'little coloured lozenges' (p. 133) are disturbed, a new configuration

comes into focus. In this second of seven volumes, Odette is at a relatively early stage in the social ascent she will make in the course of the
novel overall. Here, she frequents families where the husbands are part
of the machinery of government in the Third Republic, founded in
1871. The narrator provides a rough gauge, without precise dates, for
the first decades of that new regime, calibrating points in the first part
of his life with changes in French society. At the time of his earliest
years, fashionable society was dominated by conservatives hostile to
the new Republic and its supporters. Before the time of his First
Communion, social mobility sees Jews gaining visibility in smart
salons. The adolescent protagonist, the text also explains, starts visiting the Swanns in the years just before the outbreak of the Dreyfus
Affair (which began with the sentencing of Captain Alfred Dreyfus in
1894 before escalating dramatically in late 1897). The pattern of Jewish
assimilation is then abruptly halted, the Affair triggering intense anti-
Semitism. The kaleidoscope would turn again, the narrator surmises,
were there to be war with Germany, such a conflict unleashing a wave
of Germanophobia.[6] These periodic expressions of collective hatred
thrive on blind social adherence, he insists, citing how those in fashionable salons detest 'what they think they should detest' (p. 84).
Nevertheless, his overarching contention is that people fundamentally
assume that nothing can ever change. Evolutions in material culture
disprove this. We move, Proust says, from oil lamps and horse-drawn
omnibuses to telephones and then aeroplanes and yet conformity
spawns a conservatism of outlook. The view that the present is best is
encapsulated in the stance of those dubbed 'newspaper philosophers'
(p. 81), who dismiss everything associated with a previous age.

How society functions is never reduced to a subject for exclusively
serious treatment, however, in Proust. The narrator paints a social
comedy in frequently lively and irreverent ways. Swann adds to this
to the extent that, in the guest lists he proposes to Odette, he takes
perverse pleasure in bringing together people from contrasting backgrounds. This 'amusing [. . .] sociology', as Swann sees it, and the
'social "bouquets"' (p. 85) it assembles feed into the situations of
rivalry that mark many of the encounters in the novel.[7]

---

[6] As noted above, the world depicted in this volume predates the First World War.

[7] For an analysis of the particular nature of social representation in Proust, see Jacques
Dubois, *Le Roman de Gilberte Swann: Proust sociologue paradoxal* (Paris: Seuil, 2018).

How might *In the Shadow of Girls in Blossom* compare with other literary works of the period? Its general tone contrasts strikingly with Virginia Woolf's *Night and Day*, for example, also published in 1919. Both texts are set in the period before 1914. But in Woolf, a rigid demarcation of social structures in early twentieth-century England ensures that cross-class encounters involve often tense meetings between characters from different worlds. An atmosphere of social gloom pervades much of the novel, Leonard Woolf, the writer's husband, referring to its 'melancholy'. In reply, the novelist observed that 'if one is to deal with people on a large scale & say what one thinks, how can one avoid melancholy?'[8] Woolf's often sombre account of London life partitions off the domestic milieu of the privileged from public spaces that are regularly cast as unsettling. The segregation mirrors the 'kind of boundary to her vision of life' affecting one of the main characters, Katherine Hilbery.[9] With its consciously traditional novelistic form, Woolf's text also endorses many of the structures of social conservatism. *In the Shadow of Girls in Blossom*, on the other hand, offers an ebullient account of contact across classes, nowhere with more dash than when the protagonist's first visit to Balbec is recounted.

Kafka's 'In the Penal Colony', also published in 1919, again differs radically from the narrative of Balbec as pleasure colony, though for reasons altogether dissimilar to those applying in the case of *Night and Day*. In Kafka's short story, a European explorer visits a penal colony and witnesses a judicial system in which guilt is never in doubt and bloody execution is lauded for its machine-like efficacy. To honour one's superiors is the punitive message literally to be etched on the body of the prisoner whom the explorer sees facing execution on that particular day. Still, with the European visitor's opposition to the practice of capital punishment and in particular to the gruesome mechanical means of execution used, the practice of killing comes to be dismantled and the machinery of death spectacularly malfunctions. The nightmarish world depicted in Kafka's 'In the Penal Colony' and the often playful eagerness with which Proust explores *fin-de-siècle* leisure in Balbec are poles apart, then. Anchored to the

---

[8] Quoted by Suzanne Raitt in her Introduction to Virginia Woolf, *Night and Day*, ed. S. Raitt (Oxford: Oxford University Press, 2009), p. xvi.

[9] Woolf, *Night and Day*, 35.

image of a killing machine, Kafka's short story might, if anything, bear limited comparison with the war novel *Les Croix de bois* of the same year, where Dorgelès's narrator observes 'how the pain of others seems slight to the one not experiencing pain'.[10]

Balbec

'Place Names: The Place', the title of Part Two of *In the Shadow of Girls in Blossom*, echoes the earlier 'Place Names: The Name' used for the closing section of *The Swann Way*. The switch from name to place sees the protagonist move from Paris to the Normandy coast, with the imagined Balbec now juxtaposed with the hero's actual experience of the town. The jolt to his keen anticipation of the new location is most striking in the case of the Balbec church. Previously, Swann had praised its architectural beauty. The protagonist must now make the mental move from the romantic location he himself had expected to find (he imagined the church perched on a cliff face overlooking the sea) to its actual setting, quite far inland and in a drab square. Sharing a space with, among other buildings, a café and a branch of a savings bank, the church is subjected to what the narrator calls 'the tyranny of the Particular' (p. 208), with the stone statue of the Virgin Mary covered in the same soot that stains the surrounding houses.

Yet whereas Balbec Town is the hero's train stop for viewing the church and for the unexpected confrontation with urban grime, Balbec-Plage is where he, his grandmother, and Françoise are staying. The Grand-Hôtel is part of an international chain of luxury hotels, Le Palace, the development reflecting a new culture of early twentieth-century leisure. Guests from different classes and from both Paris and the provinces and a considerable number of hotel staff converge there. Thus, while promoting itself as a venue for fashionable leisure, the hotel is paradoxically a place of unpredictable encounter for those staying there, the narrator imagining it as a 'Pandora's box' (p. 213).

Now two years on from his relationship with Gilberte, the protagonist busily takes in the seaside location, with the large bay window of

---

[10] Dorgelès, *Les Croix de bois* (Paris: Albin Michel, 2014), 88; my translation.

the hotel dining room providing an ideal viewing platform for this new, mobile world. He marvels at how 'social standings' (p. 221) are so changed in the seaside location and he relishes being exposed to the unknown and the unfamiliar. Others are wary of such exposure. For a group of provincial bourgeois notables (three prominent legal figures and their spouses) who are regular summer guests there, snobbery shields them from what comes both from 'above' and 'below'. The narrator points out that, like most of the residents at the hotel, they prefer not to experience what he alluringly refers to as 'the delightful thrill of getting involved in an unfamiliar life' (p. 224). The elderly aristocrat Madame de Villeparisis practises shielding of a different sort, bringing with her some of her servants and many of the furnishings from her Paris home, the combination creating a bubble of protection against the surrounding social mix. Similarly, for much of the season, a group of four (a woman and three men) pointedly avoid interacting with other hotel residents. The most striking image of separation is the glass frontage of the Grand-Hôtel dining room, which serves as a class border. As though standing outside a giant aquarium, ordinary local folk peer in at the wealthy guests being served on the inside. The physical segregation prompts the narrator to wonder if revolution might one day see it all swept away.

Class affiliation is thus an important strand in the Balbec narrative. In the case of the hotel manager, we read that social position is the only thing to which he pays attention. With his obsession come multiple errors in his assessment of hotel guests' status, as the narrator gleefully reports. While the local manager greatly fears the hotel chain's general manager, who comes periodically to inspect, he confidently assumes that the minor aristocrat Monsieur de Cambremer is from a very ordinary background. A similar miscalculation sees him surprised when the protagonist's grandmother is greeted by her long-standing friend Madame de Villeparisis, who is a marquise. His gaffes are the stuff of slapstick humour but no less comical is the reaction of the provincial regulars to the spectacle of the man reputed to own an island in Oceania as he returns from the beach at lunchtime with his woman companion. The president of the Bar in Caen cannot suppress his visceral hatred for these new rich: '"It's enough to make you want to leave France!"' (p. 245), he protests in an expression of outrage that is both chauvinistic and staunchly bourgeois. Far from being covert, then, class tensions in Balbec are conspicuous and comically relayed. Proust was 'a phenomenal observer' of society and the social landscape of Balbec illustrates this well.[11]

The fixation with the who's who of the hotel is anathema to the young hero's grandmother. For her, a seaside holiday means bracing contact with the sea air and escaping the Parisian round of social politeness. Her rigid resolve adds to the mirth in the narrator's commentary. His gaze, by contrast, is often drawn towards social rank and in this, he both minds his own class interests and stands aloof from them. In each class, he asserts, deep-seated codes are at work. With no one social stratum enjoying dominance, the text spells out how the 'most stringent protocol' (p. 236) regulates the new relations which Françoise forms in the Grand-Hôtel. Her wish to protect the rights and interests of those who, like her, work in the service of others, comes to have material consequences for the hero and his grandmother.[12] As the narrator wryly comments, Françoise now puts the schedule and needs of the hotel staff she has befriended before those of her employer. Aimé's approach is different. The maître d'hôtel takes vicarious pleasure in the social standing of his guests and seems to want to enhance his own status through the pride he takes in the personal connections between the different tables he serves.

The narrator is not alone in savouring tales about servants' styles of engagement with their would-be superiors. Madame de Villeparisis tells of how her father's concierge had once instructed the Duc de Nemours who was visiting to take the post and papers upstairs since he was going that way. She clearly relishes the story of momentary insubordination. As an exception to the rule, it taps into the social concern with rank, a subject eagerly explored by Proust.

Social spaces are also often playfully theatrical in this volume. The recognition scene when the grandmother and her old friend Madame de Villeparisis run into each other in a doorway in the hotel is likened to a scene from a Molière play. The comparison with theatre is entirely apt since, for many, the hotel is a form of stage. Self-importance is part of this, the general manager of the Palace hotel chain regarding himself 'not as a lowly stage manager or orchestra conductor, but as a veritable generalissimo' (p. 236). Vaudeville is another comic form

---

[11] Jean-Yves Tadié, *Proust et la société* (Paris: Gallimard, 2021), 14.

[12] Of the 40 million who made up France's population in 1900, 1 million were in domestic service. See Tadié, *Proust et la société*, 38.

evoked specifically in relation to the Princesse de Luxembourg, who is a niece of the King of England. In her dealings with the hero and his grandmother, she treats them with the condescension she might show to animals in a zoo. Her farcical disdain is in turn matched by that shown her by the provincial bourgeois guests, for they remain unconvinced that she is a royal. In Proust's Balbec, hierarchy frequently rhymes with hilarity. But the narrator also deploys a wider optic when he speculates, more seriously, that the bourgeoisie and the aristocracy each hold an imaginary view of the other, just as people on one side of the Bay of Balbec do of those who inhabit the other. Beyond the slapstick, therefore, Proust is here making a more searching point about the place of illusion and imagination in class ideology.

The forms of insecurity Proust depicts are not restricted to groups such as the provincial notables at the hotel. Jewishness attracts social hostility in this and other volumes of the novel. Himself the son of a Jewish mother, Proust was alert to the virulent anti-Semitic prejudice of his day while also observing the process whereby Jews had come to be culturally assimilated in France, as mentioned above. In *The Swann Way*, Charles Swann epitomizes this social integration. Here in Balbec, Charlus makes anti-Jewish comments, complaining that a residence that once belonged to his family is now owned by wealthy Jewish financiers. The aristocrat's sectarianism is unsurprising in an age of openly anti-Jewish sentiment. In a similar way, Albertine declares without the slightest inhibition that she is not allowed to play with 'Israelites' (p. 421). There is a suggestion of scandalous behaviour surrounding the sisters and adolescent cousin of the protagonist's Jewish friend Bloch. The protagonist is nevertheless taken aback to overhear Bloch himself launching into an anti-Semitic tirade on the beach (the Jewish anti-Semitism here is directed against immigrants recently arrived in the country).[13] Bloch's father speaks Yiddish at home but declares it to be vulgar when in the presence of outsiders. Desperate for recognition, he tries bluffing his way in society by showing the card of Sir Rufus Israels. He pretends to be on

---

[13] I consider the question of Jewishness in Proust in a short essay, 'The Dreyfus Affair', in Adam Watt (ed.), *Marcel Proust in Context* (Cambridge: Cambridge University Press, 2013), 167–73. For a full account of the Dreyfus Affair, see Ruth Harris, *The Man on Devil's Island: Alfred Dreyfus and the Affair that Divided France* (London: Allen Lane, 2010).

close terms with the writer Bergotte and also hires a coach on certain days in order to be seen being driven through the Bois de Boulogne. Describing Bloch senior's striving to give the impression of having arrived socially, the narrator also inserts a brief, essay-style commentary on envy, pride, and the fear of exclusion.

Social hierarchy brings other surprises. Robert de Saint-Loup disowns the values of his aristocratic background and immerses himself in the works of radical figures from the nineteenth century such as Nietzsche and Pierre-Joseph Proudhon. His social contacts too run counter to the fixed codes that guide the parents of the narrator, who groups those codes under the rubric of 'the sociology of Combray' (p. 277). As for the protagonist's own response, a lingering conservatism ensures that he remains fascinated by Saint-Loup's noble lineage. Françoise is a royalist and so cannot take seriously the suggestion that a young aristocrat like Saint-Loup could have republican views. He in turn wants to treat his coachman as his equal and occasionally shouts at him, his argument being that to be overly polite would be to patronize him.

Saint-Loup's family also intrigues the protagonist. Announcing the imminent arrival in Balbec of his uncle, Palamède, the Baron de Charlus, who is visiting an aunt, Saint-Loup talks of the visitor's elegance as well as his notorious arrogance and disdain. Charlus' body language and violent mood swings leave the protagonist baffled. He manages, however, to piece together, thanks in part to Saint-Loup's explanation, that Charlus is a member of the Guermantes family, as is his aunt, Madame de Villeparisis. The adolescent now also realizes that Charlus is the man who had stared at him when, as a boy in Combray, he had walked past the Swanns' house in Tansonville and heard Madame Swann calling the name Gilberte. Memory of that episode and the emergence of the Guermantes trio in Balbec (aunt, nephew, great-nephew) provide important throwbacks to 'Combray'. The details again show Proust carefully attending to the broader weave of his novel.

Life Through Literature and Art

While a social earnestness marks Saint-Loup's reading, the encounter with books in this volume often has a comfortable, almost domestic feel to it. With various characters drawn to literature, the narrator thrives on the forms of textual play and resonance that can result. The letters between Madame de Sévigné and her daughter frame many of the conversations involving the young protagonist, his mother, and grandmother. Indeed, the de Sévigné exchanges form an enduring point of loving connection between his mother and grandmother. Literature also gets entangled with gossip about writers' lives. The hero reveres giants of nineteenth-century French literature such as Chateaubriand, Balzac, and Victor Hugo, but Madame de Villeparisis doesn't share his enthusiasm. She sees herself as best placed to comment on their merits since, she tells him matter-of-factly, they all came to her father's house. She sides with the nineteenth-century literary critic Sainte-Beuve, for whom knowing a writer in person was the key to understanding their work.[14]

Literary borrowing in the Balbec pages of the novel can also work in unruly, irreverent ways. We see this in the ludic account of how the president of the Bar, the *bâtonnier*, manages briefly to get above his position by having lunch with Monsieur and Madame de Cambremer. He then panics at the prospect of his fellow provincial guests at the hotel joining in. With the lawyer's temporary advantage threatened, the narrator throws in a line from Racine's tragedy *Esther*, the solemn moment in the play when the Persian king Ahasuerus asks his Jewish queen, Esther: ' "Of my Estate, must I give you half?" ' (p. 232).[15] By having two registers collide (the comedy around provincial snobbery being momentarily paired with the prospect of a grave obligation to share across an ethnic divide), Proust gleefully repurposes high literary reference to disruptive, comic effect.

Literature is also appealed to for its therapeutic value, as when the hero's mother tries to make him more resilient by reminding him of his aptitude for reading. Seeing him nervous about leaving her as he boards the train for Balbec, she discourages any emotional weakness by reminding him of how pleased Ruskin had been to travel. Long before becoming a published novelist, Proust studied Ruskin extensively. In collaboration with others, he undertook the translation of

---

[14] Proust was very familiar with Sainte-Beuve's highly influential work and he distanced himself from the critic's approach in a series of essays which were published posthumously under the title *Contre Sainte-Beuve* (*Against Sainte-Beuve*).

[15] Racine's *Esther* (1689) tells the story of a heroine who accedes to the throne of Persia and uses her influence to protect her fellow Jews from genocide. Ahasuerus' line in the French original is 'Faut-il de mes États vous donner la moitié?' (Act II, scene vii).

two of Ruskin's works, *The Bible of Amiens* and *Sesame and Lilies*. This deep engagement allowed him to appreciate the Victorian art historian's conviction that nature's creations were no less attractive than those of art. Bloch may tease the protagonist in Balbec about merely wanting to pose in Venice with a copy of Ruskin's *The Stones of Venice*. Yet the influence of that work is present in this volume, as evidenced by the hero imagining the joy of arriving by gondola to view paintings by Carpaccio at the Scuola di San Giorgio degli Schiavoni and also a Titian at the church of Santa Maria Gloriosa dei Frari.[16]

For Ruskin, the art of Venice was inseparable from its natural setting and he confessed to being 'as much in awe in gazing on' the Ducal Palace as on the backdrop formed by the Alps.[17] Similarly in the Balbec pages, art and nature converge. Elstir sees the Balbec church as a cliff and likens the cliffs at Les Creuniers on the Normandy coast to rock that has been chiselled as in the construction of a cathedral. The sea also creates, as though pictorially. With its constantly changing appearance, it seizes the hero's attention so that he anticipates in his mind the seascape he hopes to find when he contemplates the ocean. With nature creating its own canvases, his hotel room with its glass-fronted bookcases allows nature's works of art to be mirrored in an interior setting. More technically, he imagines these reflective bookcase fronts to be volets or panels that are linked to the panel produced outside his window by light, sky, and sea.

To nature's work as artist is added the work and striving of Elstir. The adolescent's initial motivation in going to the fictional painter's studio is merely to satisfy his grandmother, who sees doing so as having educational benefits. Still, the reluctant young visitor quickly marvels at the world he finds in the painter's canvases. In the seascapes, any demarcation between sky and sea is often unavailable, so strong is the sense of a reciprocal carrying over between the one and the other. The work of transferring is again present in the interpenetration of sea and land forms. This, the text explains, is another of the artist's favourite metaphors. With boats appearing to stand in the middle of the town and the town's inhabitants seeming to be

---

[16] See editorial note in Proust, *A l'ombre des jeunes filles en fleurs*, ed. Rey, 520–1.

[17] See John Ruskin, *The Stones of Venice*, ed. E. T. Cook and Alexander Wedderburn, 3 vols. (1903–4; Cambridge: Cambridge University Press, 2010), ii. 439.

'amphibious' (p. 364), the narrator explores how the painter's endeavour involves capturing the optical illusions that are part of our initial visual apprehension of the world. To translate that evanescent impression, the artist in Elstir must set aside his considerable intelligence and make himself 'ignorant', as Proust puts it (p. 366). This does not detract from the painter's considerable erudition, however, and indeed he provides his young visitor with a detailed commentary on the iconography of the medieval church in Balbec. It is, he enthuses, 'a whole vast theological and symbolic poem' (p. 367).[18]

Yet just as Bergotte has his failings as a social being, so the visit to the artist's studio draws out another side to Elstir. Intrigued by the androgynous portrait of 'Miss Sacripant', the protagonist comes to realize that the watercolour, dated October 1872, depicts the young Odette in the days when she frequented the Verdurin salon. This takes the reader back to *The Swann Way*. A second throwback to those days comes with the no less sudden realization that Elstir is none other than the pretentious and vulgar Monsieur Biche, as he was then known. When the protagonist asks if this is the case, the painter does not deny the suggestion. Instead, he seeks to provide instruction to his interlocutor in a poised, methodical fashion. Authentic wisdom, he argues, is not something that is handed down; rather, the individual must find it. Accepting the unlikeable things of one's past, the evil and the banality of the age one was a part of, is pivotal in that struggle. At the core of Elstir's philosophy of life, then, lies the conviction that past actions are not to be disowned but rather to be seen as signs of having lived. The lessons the protagonist takes away from his meeting with the painter are therefore not exclusively aesthetic. Elstir formulates a complex moral account of a struggle or combat around what is discreditable and what is good in a life. The message is received by an adolescent who, we see elsewhere in the volume, puts off the work which a fuller encounter with self would entail.

The question of how self-knowledge might be achieved is part of the wider trajectory of Proust's novel. The narrator describes the youth he once was as having been of a nervous disposition, as we have seen. In conversation with his grandmother, the adolescent confesses

---

[18] For Elstir's commentary on the porch of the Balbec church, Proust borrowed heavily from Émile Mâle's *L'Art religieux du XIIIe siècle en France*. See editorial note in Proust, *A l'ombre des jeunes filles en fleurs*, ed. Rey, 555.

his need for the reassurance of her presence. In a forthright assessment of those earlier years, the older 'I' sees his youth as belonging to a 'ridiculous phase' (p. 270). It is an age marked by upheaval, intense spontaneity, and insecurity. However, it's also a time of learning, the older self insists. Indeed, he applies this to the human experience of youth more generally. Rejecting the common view that it is an awkward age, he insists on its richness.

The Young Women of Balbec

Frequently in this volume, an insecure young hero looks on, longing to be noticed. Whether it be in relation to the Swanns, his brief contact with the peasant woman on the rural station platform and the feverish expectation this awakens in him, or the band of girls commemorated in the volume title itself, the protagonist displays the same nervous searching. The 'girls in blossom' make their appearance in the last third of the volume. Just as, in 'Madame Swann's Circle', Gilberte is the intermediary who facilitates access to the writer Bergotte, now, in a form of reverse symmetry, Elstir introduces the protagonist to the *petite bande*. Mesmerized on first spotting them, he likens their sudden appearance to that of a flock of seagulls landing on the Balbec beach. Drawn initially to what he sees as their 'fluid, collective, shifting beauty' (p. 324), the adolescent quickly projects on to them all the attributes he lacks. Whereas he is diffident, self-conscious, and sickly, he sees them as being physically vigorous and more interested in pleasure than in morality or intellectual life. He confesses to a long-held fascination with the sight of young women as they pass swiftly by, hence the motif of the phantom-like *passante* whom he is destined never to meet. The mobile band of girls now intensifies the male adolescent's sense of an ephemeral, inaccessible beauty. The narrator puts this more extravagantly, likening the uncertain movements of love to a patient search for the laws of a 'passionate astronomy' (p. 359). Now in love with all the members of the small band, the protagonist finds that they have 'eclipsed' his grandmother (p. 360). But as their individual selves gradually emerge, he corrects some of his sweeping projections. Most notably, Andrée has had to overcome sickness, he discovers, and, as already noted, is intellectual in her outlook.

The young protagonist also finds that his former attachment to Gilberte now translates into a new love, this time for Albertine.

He contends that the choice of successive loves in an individual's life derives from 'an inverted image or projection, a "negative" of our own sensibility' (p. 413). He views the process almost mathematically, using the language of repetition and detecting within the repetition a principle of variation. As he fixates about 'the little Simonet girl' whose name he overhears on the beach ('Simonet' will turn out to be Albertine's surname), he argues that it is as if the person we love can become more us than we are ourselves. In the immediate term, the introduction to Albertine brings with it a sense of 'gravity' (p. 394). With the relationship set to have a momentous sequel some years later, Proust begins preparing what is to come by threading into *In the Shadow of Girls in Blossom* occasional pointers to its subsequent impact. Receiving a note in which Albertine declares her affection for him, the hero decides that 'it was with her that my great romance would be written' (p. 431). Balbec marks the beginning, then, of a fateful liaison. Two later volumes of the novel, *The Captive* (*La Prisonnière*) and *The Fugitive* (*Albertine disparue*), form the core of what critics have called the Albertine cycle, which tells the story of their intense cohabitation and eventual separation. The cycle was central to the overall enlargement of Proust's novel, which eventually grew to 3,000 pages, thus doubling the length it stood at in 1914.

In the Shadow of Girls in Blossom feeds into the volume immediately following, *The Guermantes Way* (*Le Côté de Guermantes*), in numerous ways. That next instalment sees the narrative switch back from Balbec to Paris; we move from social classes in close proximity in the seaside setting to the rigid compartmentalization in the capital, where Marcel once again imagines the aristocratic Guermantes as inhabiting a mysterious world; the return to Paris also sees the deteriorating health of the protagonist's grandmother, who refers glancingly to her mortality in Balbec; and the enigma surrounding Charlus and the liaison with Albertine will continue.

While working to secure these strands of thematic continuity across the wider novel, Proust also displays a talent for fashioning endings for its various instalments. Just as *The Swann Way* closes with the narrator's recollection of Odette's walks in the Bois de Boulogne in an earlier decade, so 'Madame Swann's Circle' ends with his vivid recall of her midday appearances on the Avenue du Bois in the month of May. In this second, intensely theatrical scene, the protagonist and other male onlookers, aristocrats among them, gaze admiringly at Odette. Looking back, the narrator celebrates as something poetic his enduring memory of the minutes after a quarter past midday, in late spring, when he would watch the performance unfold. A further 'happy ending', with a comparable note of ceremonial performance, is worked into the closing pages of this second volume of the novel. This time, it is an intensely private moment, one that unfolds away from the public gaze. The background is that, on doctor's orders, the excitable young hero has to rest in the mornings while the bustle of seaside life in high season carries on outside beneath his hotel room window. Now, with midday striking, Françoise enters to open the curtains. She is seen as ushering in the intense light of the summer's day as though she were unveiling a millennial mummy. The zenith moment generates an impression of fixity and seems to suspend the narrative, bringing to a serene close the busy world of *In the Shadow of Girls in Blossom*, 'one of the most beautiful sections' of Proust's work.[19]

---

[19] See Ellison, *A Reader's Guide to Proust's 'In Search of Lost Time'*, 57. Pierre-Louis Rey uses the term 'serenity' in relation to the second part of *A l'ombre*, arguing that such an atmosphere is especially present on the last page of the volume. He attributes this mood to the maturity of perspective of Proust the novelist rather than to the daily experience of the young protagonist; see editorial preface to Proust, *A l'ombre des jeunes filles en fleurs*, ed. Rey, p. xxvii.

NOTE ON THE TEXT

THE translation is based on the 'new Pléiade' edition of Proust's novel in French: *A la recherche du temps perdu*, ed. Jean-Yves Tadié et al., 4 vols., 'Bibliothèque de la Pléiade' (Paris: Gallimard, 1987–9). This edition provides the text for the single-volume French publication of the novel, *A la recherche du temps perdu*, 'Quarto' (Paris: Gallimard, 1999), which is an economical means of obtaining a hard-copy version of all seven volumes of the novel. The Pléiade text is also reproduced in individual volumes in the readily available paperback series 'Collection Folio' (published 1988–90, Gallimard) and 'Collection Blanche' (published 1992, Gallimard).

SELECT BIBLIOGRAPHY

WE have indicated the standard editions of key works by Proust in French. For practical reasons, we have included only secondary sources written in English or those readily available in English translation.

Works by Proust

A la recherche du temps perdu, ed. Jean-Yves Tadié et al., Bibliothèque de la Pléiade, 4 vols. (Paris: Gallimard, 1987–9).

Contre Sainte-Beuve précédé de Pastiches et mélanges et suivi de Essais et articles, ed. Pierre Clarac and Yves Sandre, Bibliothèque de la Pléiade (Paris: Gallimard, 1971).

Against Sainte-Beuve and Other Essays, trans. John Sturrock (Harmondsworth: Penguin, 1988).

Essais, ed. Antoine Compagnon, Christophe Pradeau, and Matthieu Vernet, Bibliothèque de la Pléiade (Paris: Gallimard, 2022).

Jean Santeuil précédé de Les Plaisirs et les jours, ed. Pierre Clarac and Yves Sandre, Bibliothèque de la Pléiade (Paris: Gallimard, 1971).

Jean Santeuil, trans. Gerard Hopkins (1955; Harmondsworth: Penguin, 1985).

Pleasures and Days, trans. Andrew Brown (London: Hesperus, 2004).

Correspondence

'Corr-Proust' Digitization Project: http://proust.elan-numerique.fr/

Correspondance de Marcel Proust, ed. Philip Kolb, 21 vols. (Paris: Plon, 1970–93).

Marcel Proust: Selected Letters, 4 vols., ed. Philip Kolb et al., trans. Ralph Manheim (vol. i), Terence Kilmartin (vols. ii and iii), and Joanna Kilmartin (vol. iv) (New York: Doubleday; London: Doubleday/Collins/HarperCollins, 1983–2000).

Marcel Proust: Lettres 1879–1922, ed. Françoise Leriche (Paris: Plon, 2004).

Biography

Carter, William, *Marcel Proust: A Life* (2000; New Haven: Yale University Press, 2013).

Picon, Jérôme, *Marcel Proust: Une vie à s'écrire* (Paris: Flammarion, 2015).

Tadié, Jean-Yves, *Marcel Proust* (1996), trans. Euan Cameron (New York: Viking, 2000).

Watt, Adam, *Marcel Proust*, Critical Lives (London: Reaktion Books, 2013).

White, Edmund, *Proust* (London: Weidenfeld & Nicolson, 1999).

Critical Studies

Bales, Richard (ed.), *The Cambridge Companion to Proust* (Cambridge: Cambridge University Press, 2001).

Beckett, Samuel, *Proust* (1931), in *Proust and Three Dialogues with Georges Duthuit* (London: John Calder, 1987).

Benjamin, Walter, 'The Image of Proust' (1929), in *Illuminations*, trans. Harry Zohn, ed. Hannah Arendt (London: Jonathan Cape, 1970; Pimlico, 1999), 197–210.

Bowie, Malcolm, *Proust Among the Stars* (London: HarperCollins, 1998).

Compagnon, Antoine, *Proust Between Two Centuries*, trans. Richard Goodkin (New York: Columbia University Press, 1992).

Deleuze, Gilles, *Proust and Signs*, trans. Richard Howard (London: The Athlone Press, 2000).

Ellison, David, *A Reader's Guide to Proust's 'In Search of Lost Time'* (Cambridge: Cambridge University Press, 2010).

Elsner, Anna, and Stern, Thomas (eds.), *The Proustian Mind* (London: Routledge, 2022).

Hughes, Edward J., 'The Renewal of Narrative in the Wake of Proust', in John D. Lyons (ed.), *The Cambridge Companion to French Literature* (Cambridge: Cambridge University Press, 2016), 187–203.

Karpeles, Eric, *Paintings in Proust: A Visual Companion to 'In Search of Lost Time'* (London: Thames & Hudson, 2008).

Landy, Joshua, 'Proust, His Narrator, and the Importance of the Distinction', *Poetics Today* 25/1 (2004), 91–135.

Landy, Joshua, *The World According to Proust* (Oxford: Oxford University Press, 2022).

Lucey, Michael, 'Becoming Proust in Time', in Christopher Prendergast (ed.), *A History of Modern French Literature: From the Sixteenth Century to the Twentieth Century* (Princeton: Princeton University Press, 2017), 514–33.

Lucey, Michael, *What Proust Heard: Novels and the Ethnography of Talk* (Chicago: Chicago University Press, 2022).

McDonald, Christie, and Proulx, François (eds.), *Proust and the Arts* (Cambridge: Cambridge University Press, 2015).

Prendergast, Christopher, *Mirages and Mad Beliefs: Proust the Skeptic* (Princeton: Princeton University Press, 2013).

Schmid, Marion, 'Marcel Proust (1871–1922): A Modernist Novel of Time', in Michael Bell (ed.), *The Cambridge Companion to European Novelists* (Cambridge: Cambridge University Press, 2012), 327–42.

Watt, Adam, *The Cambridge Introduction to Marcel Proust* (Cambridge: Cambridge University Press, 2011).

Watt, Adam, 'État présent: Marcel Proust', *French Studies* 72/3 (2018), 412–24.

Watt, Adam, 'Marcel Proust's *A la recherche du temps perdu*', in Adam Watt (ed.), *The Cambridge History of the Novel in French* (Cambridge: Cambridge University Press, 2021), 456–72.

Watt, Adam (ed.), *Marcel Proust in Context* (Cambridge: Cambridge University Press, 2013).

Wood, Michael, *Marcel Proust: My Reading* (Oxford: Oxford University Press, 2023).

Further Reading in Oxford World's Classics

Flaubert, G., *Sentimental Education*, trans. Helen Constantine, ed. Patrick Coleman.

Joyce, J., *Ulysses*, ed. Jeri Johnson.

Kafka, F., *The Metamorphosis and Other Stories*, trans. Joyce Crick, ed. Ritchie Robertson.

Proust, M., *Swann in Love*, trans. Brian Nelson, ed. Adam Watt.

Proust, M., *The Swann Way*, trans. Brian Nelson, ed. Adam Watt.

Woolf, V., *Jacob's Room*, ed. Urmila Seshagiri.

Woolf, V., *Night and Day*, ed. S. Raitt.

A CHRONOLOGY OF MARCEL PROUST

1871 (10 July) Marcel Proust is born to Jeanne Proust née Weil and Dr Adrien Proust in the village of Auteuil, to the west of Paris. He is very weak in infancy.

1872 The Proust family moves to an apartment on the Boulevard Malesherbes in the 8th *arrondissement* of Paris.

1873 (24 May) Robert Proust, Marcel's brother, is born.

1878–86 Family holidays at Illiers (renamed Illiers-Combray in 1971) in the Eure-et-Loir.

1881 Proust's first, and near fatal, asthma attack. Respiratory and other health problems will henceforth be a permanent part of his life.

1882–9 Proust attends the Lycée Condorcet (named Lycée Fontanes until 1883); attendance poor due to ill health, but various friendships formed.

1889 Proust turns 18. *Classe de philosophie*; (Nov.) signs up for one year's voluntary military service.
Inauguration of the Eiffel Tower as the entrance arch to the World's Fair.

1890 (3 Jan.) Death of Proust's maternal grandmother, Adèle Weil. Enrols at the Faculty of Law and the School of Political Science.

1891 Journalism appears in *Le Mensuel*.
Thomas Hardy, *Tess of the D'Urbervilles*.

1892 Proust and friends from Condorcet found a review, *Le Banquet*. Increased socializing.

1893 Publications in the important journal *La Revue blanche*. Completes *Licence en droit*.

1894 (June) President Carnot assassinated in Lyons by an anarchist. (December) Court martial judges Captain Albert Dreyfus guilty.

1895 Completes *License ès lettres*. Unpaid position at the Bibliothèque Mazarine; scarcely attends due to 'ill health'. Stay in Brittany with Reynaldo Hahn. Begins notes towards *Jean Santeuil*.
Trial of Oscar Wilde.

1896 (Mar.) Publication of *Les Plaisirs et les jours*.

1897 Duels with journalist Jean Lorrain over Lorrain's public insinuations of Proust's homosexual relation with Lucien Daudet.
Henry James, *What Maisie Knew*.

1898 (13 Jan.) Zola's 'J'accuse' in *L'Aurore*. Later in the year Proust attends Zola's trial.

1899 *Jean Santeuil* abandoned; Proust starts work on a translation of Ruskin's *The Bible of Amiens*.
Freud, *Die Traudeutung* (*The Interpretation of Dreams*); Conrad, *Heart of Darkness*.

1900 Proust publishes a series of articles on Ruskin. (Apr.) Travels to Venice with his mother and friends; (Oct.) returns to Venice alone.
Deaths of Ruskin and Nietzsche.

1901 Thomas Mann, four years Proust's junior, publishes *Buddenbrooks*.

1902 Travels to Belgium and Holland with Hahn, visits Bruges and Amsterdam amongst other places. Sees Vermeer's *View of Delft* and numerous old Dutch masters.

1903 (Feb.) Marriage of Robert Proust. Society journalism published in *Le Figaro*. (Nov.) sudden death of Proust's father.
Gertrude Stein moves to Paris from the United States.

1904 *La Bible d'Amiens* published; translation of Ruskin's *Sesame and Lilies* begun; society journalism continues.

1905 (June) Proust's important essay on reading, the preface to *Sésame et les lys*, is published. (July) Madame Proust is taken ill in Évian and rushed back to Paris by Robert; (26 Sept.) Death of Madame Proust. (Dec.) Proust checks in to the clinic of Dr Sollier, fulfilling a promise to his mother.
French government passes a law separating Church and State.

1906 (Aug.–Dec.) Sollier's treatment having made little difference to his health, he stays in the Hôtel des Réservoirs in Versailles, unwilling to be alone in the family home. *Sésame et les lys* is published. He resolves to move into what was his great-uncle Georges Weil's Paris residence, 102 Boulevard Haussmann.
Dreyfus reinstated in the Army.

1907 Various articles and stories published. Summer in Cabourg on the Normandy coast. Meets Alfred Agostinelli, a young taxi-driver. Proust will return to Cabourg every year between 1907 and 1914. Picasso's *Demoiselles d'Avignon* completed in Paris.

1908 Plans a project 'Against Sainte-Beuve', part critical essay, part dialogue. Features of what will become *A la recherche du temps perdu* take shape. Succession of brilliant pastiches, around the Lemoine Affair, appear in *Le Figaro*.

1909 *Contre Sainte-Beuve* amounts to around 400 pages; publishers show no interest.
Marinetti's first *Manifesto of Futurism* in Paris; Gustav Mahler's Symphony No. 9.

1910–11 Develops the core sequences of his novel that will become *Du côté de chez Swann*, *Le Temps retrouvé*, part of *Le Côté de Guermantes* and, latterly, parts of *A l'ombre des jeunes filles en fleurs*.

1912–13 Successive rejections from publishers.

1913 (Spring) Agostinelli moves into Proust's apartment as secretary. *Du côté de chez Swann* is accepted for publication at the author's expense by Grasset and (14 Nov.) is published.
Stravinsky's *Rite of Spring*; Lawrence's *Sons and Lovers*; Duchamp's *Bicycle Wheel*.

1914 (May) Agostinelli dies, drowned in the Mediterranean as a result of a flying accident. Céleste Albaret officially enters Proust's service.
(Aug.) French forces mobilized; printing presses cease activity during the war. James Joyce, *Dubliners*.

1915 Proust develops *Sodome et Gomorrhe* and the 'Albertine cycle', *La Prisonnière* and *Albertine disparue*.

1916 Negotiations with the *Nouvelle revue française* (*NRF*) who wish to take over publication of *A la recherche* from Grasset. (May) Proust reports suffering a seventy-hour period of insomnia.
(July) First Dada manifesto proclaimed in Zurich.

1917 (18 May) In Paris, Proust attends the premiere of *Parade*, performed by the Ballets Russes, with a scenario by Cocteau, score by Satie, set and costumes by Picasso, and programme notes by Apollinaire.
(Feb. and Oct.) Revolution in Russia.

1918 Proust's health, always fragile, becomes a near-constant preoccupation as he devotes more and more time to correcting his novel.

1919 (June) NRF reissues *Du côté de chez Swann*, publishes *Pastiches et mélanges* and *A l'ombre des jeunes filles en fleurs*. The relative who owned 102 Boulevard Haussmann decides to sell and Proust has to move twice; eventually settling (Oct.) at 44 Rue Hamelin. (Dec.) *A l'ombre* awarded the Prix Goncourt.

1920 André Breton employed by Gallimard as proofreader for *Le Côté de Guermantes*. (Oct.) *Le Côté de Guermantes I* published.
(May) Breton and Soupault's *Les Champs magnétiques*, the first work of surrealist (or proto-surrealist) 'automatic writing'.

1921   (May) Proust sees Vermeer's *View of Delft* once more, at an exhibition
        at the Musée du Jeu de Paume. *Le Côté de Guermantes II / Sodome et
        Gomorrhe I* published together.

1922   Increasing doses of self-medication. (Apr.) *Sodome et Gomorrhe II*
        published. (18 Nov.) Proust dies after developing pneumonia.
        Gaston Gallimard and Robert Proust undertake to publish the
        remaining volumes of *A la recherche*.
        Joyce's *Ulysses* published in Paris; T. S. Eliot's *The Wasteland* appears
        in *The Criterion*.

1923   Publication of *La Prisonnière*.

1925   Publication of *Albertine disparue*.
        Virginia Woolf, *Mrs Dalloway*.

1927   Publication of *Le Temps retrouvé*.

IN THE SHADOW
OF GIRLS IN BLOSSOM

PART ONE
MADAME SWANN'S CIRCLE

WHEN the subject of having Monsieur de Norpois to dinner for the first time was raised and my mother expressed regret that Professor Cottard was travelling and that she herself had entirely stopped seeing Swann, since both men would no doubt have interested the former ambassador, my father replied that an eminent guest, an illustrious scholar like Cottard, could never behave poorly at a dinner, but that Swann, with his ostentation, his way of shouting his slightest connections from the rooftops, was a common loudmouth whom the Marquis de Norpois would no doubt have found, as he would say, 'revolting'. Now this reply of my father's requires a few words of explanation, since some people might possibly remember a very mediocre Cottard and a Swann carrying discretion in social matters to the most extreme degree of delicacy and refinement. But regarding Swann, it had happened that to 'Swann the younger' and also to the Swann of the Jockey Club,* my parents' former friend had added a new personality (and one that would not be the last), that of the husband of Odette. Adapting to the humble ambitions of this woman the instinct, desire, and industry he'd always had, he'd endeavoured to build, well below his former status, a new position that was appropriate to the companion who would occupy it with him. And so he appeared a different man. Since (while still continuing to see his personal friends, on whom he didn't want to impose Odette when they didn't spontaneously ask to meet her) it was a second life he was beginning, in common with his wife, in the midst of new people, it would still have been understandable if, in order to measure their rank, and consequently the pleasure and pride he might feel when entertaining them, he'd used, as a point of comparison, not the brilliant people among whom he moved before his marriage, but Odette's previous connections. But even when one knew that it was with coarse civil servants, with dull-witted women, the ornaments of government balls, that he desired to associate, it was surprising to hear him (who in the past, and even today, would so graciously hide an invitation to Twickenham or Buckingham Palace*) proclaim quite loudly that the wife of a cabinet minister's clerk had come to call on Madame Swann. One might say it stemmed from the fact that the simplicity of the fashionable Swann had only been a more refined form of vanity and that, like certain Jews, my parents' old friend had been able to present by turns all the successive states through which those of his race had passed, from the most naïve snobbery and the rudest boorishness to the most delicate politeness. But the main reason—and the one applicable to humanity in general—was that our virtues themselves are not something free-floating, whose permanent availability we keep within us; they are in fact so closely associated in our minds with the events in connection with which we made it our duty to exercise them, that if an activity of another order presents itself to us, it catches us unawares and without our having the least idea that it could bear with it the practice of these same virtues. Swann, fawning over these new connections and citing them with pride, was like those great artists, modest or generous who, if at the end of their lives they apply themselves to activities like cooking or gardening, display a naïve satisfaction with the praises given to their dishes or their flower beds, for which they will not brook the criticism they readily accept if it concerns their great achievements; or who, though they might give away one of their canvases for nothing, can't help but feel annoyed if they lose forty sous* at dominos.

As for Professor Cottard, we will see him again, at great length, much later, at the Patronne's home,* the Château de la Raspelière. Concerning Cottard, let it suffice for the moment to note this first of all: in Swann's case, the change might seem surprising, since it was already complete and unsuspected by me when I used to see Gilberte's father at the Champs-Élysées,* where, as he never spoke to me, he couldn't try to dazzle me by talking about his political connections (it's true that if he *had* done so, I might not have noticed his vanity right away, since the conception one has already long formed of a person blocks one's eyes and ears; for three years, my mother could no more make out the rouge one of her nieces applied to her lips than if it had been invisibly dissolved in liquid, until the day when an extra layer, or else some other cause, brought about the phenomenon called supersaturation; then all the unperceived colour crystallized and, faced with this sudden riot of colour, my mother declared, as she would have done in Combray,* that it was shameful, and nearly broke off all relations with her niece). For Cottard, on the contrary, the period when we saw him attending Swann's first visits to the Verdurins' was already quite distant; and honours and official titles come with the years. Secondly, one can be uncultivated and make silly puns and yet possess a particular talent—one that no general culture can replace—like the gift of a great strategist or a great clinical practitioner. It was not solely, in fact, as an obscure physician who over the years had obtained European fame that his colleagues regarded Cottard. The most intelligent of the young doctors declared—for a few years, that is, since fashions change, being themselves born out of the need for change—that if ever they fell ill, Cottard was the only one of the leading medical men to whom they would entrust their persons. No doubt they preferred the company of certain more literate, more artistic chief physicians, with whom they could talk about Nietzsche or Wagner.* When music was played at Madame Cottard's, on the evenings when, in the hope he might one day become a dean of Faculty, she received her husband's colleagues and students, instead of listening, Professor Cottard would prefer to play cards in a neighbouring room. But the swiftness, the profundity, the soundness of his examinations and diagnoses were praised. Thirdly, concerning all the ways Professor Cottard appeared to a man like my father, we should note that the nature we cause to make manifest in the second part of our lives is not always (though it often is) our first nature which has been developed or diminished, coarsened or refined; it is sometimes an inversion of that nature, like clothes that have been turned inside out. Except at the home of the Verdurins, who had become infatuated with him, Cottard's hesitant air, his excessive shyness and kindness, had in his youth been a source of constant taunts. Was there a charitable friend who advised him to adopt a glacial demeanour? The importance of his position made it all the easier for him to assume it. Everywhere, except at the Verdurins', where he'd instinctively become himself again, he made himself cold, deliberately silent, peremptory when he had to speak, purposefully saying disagreeable things. He could try on this attitude in front of patients who, not having seen him previously, weren't able to make comparisons and would have been quite surprised to learn that he was not a man to whom such rudeness came naturally. He made a special effort to display impassivity, and even in his hospital ward, when he reeled off some of the puns that made everyone laugh, from the head clinician to the newest intern, he would always do it without moving a muscle in his face—which was already hard to recognize now that he'd shaved off his beard and moustache.

Finally, we'll turn to Monsieur de Norpois. He'd been a minister plenipotentiary before the war and ambassador on the Sixteenth of May,* and, despite that, to the great surprise of many, had been entrusted several times since then with representing France in extraordinary missions—even as Comptroller of Public Finances, in Egypt, where his great financial abilities had enabled him to render important services—by Radical cabinets that a simple reactionary bourgeois would have refused to serve, and in whose eyes Monsieur de Norpois' past, his connections, his opinions should have made him suspect. But these progressive ministers seemed to realize that by such an appointment they were showing how broad-minded they were when it came to the higher interests of France; were placing themselves above the normal rank of politicians by earning the distinction of being described by the *Journal des débats** itself as statesmen; and finally, were benefiting from the prestige linked to an aristocratic name and from the interest awakened by an unexpected choice, like a *coup de théâtre*. And they also knew that by relying on Monsieur de Norpois, they could glean these advantages without having to fear from him any lack of political loyalty, of which the marquis's birth, far from giving them cause for concern, should have given them every assurance. And in this, the government of the Republic was not mistaken. First of all because a true aristocracy, raised since infancy to regard its name as an innate asset that nothing can take away (and the precise value of which its peers, or those who are even higher by birth, are well aware), knows it can spare itself the effort (since it would gain virtually nothing thereby) which so many bourgeois men make to profess only conventional opinions and frequent only right-thinking people. On the other hand, concerned to grow in the eyes of princely or ducal families beneath which it is immediately situated, this aristocracy knows it can do so only by adding to its name something it didn't already contain, something that makes it prevail over an equal name: political influence, a literary or artistic reputation, great wealth. And the money they don't waste on the useless country squire so sought out by the bourgeois or the sterile friendship for which a prince would not be in the least grateful, they lavish on politicians—even if they're Freemasons—who can gain them entry into embassies or sponsor them in elections, on artists or scholars whose support helps them 'pierce' the branch where they take precedence—on all those, finally, who are able to confer a new distinction or make them secure a wealthy marriage.

But concerning Monsieur de Norpois, it was above all true that, in a long practice of diplomacy, he'd been imbued with that negative, rule-bound, conservative spirit, called the 'governmental mind', which is, in fact, that of all governments and, in particular, under all governments, the spirit of foreign ministries. He had acquired, in the course of his career, a dislike, a fear, and a contempt for those more or less revolutionary, at the very least incorrect, procedures which are the practice of an opposition. Except in a few uncultivated individuals among the common people or among society, for whom differences are unimportant, what brings people together is not a community of opinions but a consanguinity of minds. An academician like Legouvé, a promoter of the classics, would have more readily applauded the praise of Victor Hugo by Maxime Du Camp or Mézières than that of Boileau by Claudel.* The same nationalism suffices to bring Barrès closer to his electors, who will probably see little difference between him and Monsieur Georges Berry, but not closer to those of his fellow academicians who, though sharing his political opinions but having a different way of thinking, will even prefer adversaries like Ribot and Deschanel, to whom faithful monarchists feel much closer than to Maurras or Léon Daudet, even though they too desire the return of the King.* Sparing of his words not just out of professional habit, caution, and reserve, but because they have more value and offer more nuance to men whose decade-long efforts to bring two countries closer together are summarized and conveyed—in a speech or a protocol—by a simple adjective that seems ordinary but conveys a whole world to them, Monsieur de Norpois was considered very cold at the Commission,* where he sat next to my father, whom everyone congratulated for the friendship the former ambassador showed him. This friendship surprised my father most of all. For, being generally not very sociable, my father was used to not being sought out outside the circle of his close friends, and admitted this candidly. He was aware that the diplomat's friendly advances were the result of that entirely individual point of view everyone takes in choosing friends, and where all a person's intellectual qualities and refined sensibility will not be as good a recommendation to someone who is bored or annoyed by him as the candour and cheerfulness of another who would seem empty, frivolous, and dull in the eyes of many. 'De Norpois invited me to dinner again; it's extraordinary; everyone on the Commission is amazed, since he has no private relations with anyone. I'm sure he's going to tell me thrilling things again about the war of '70.'* My father knew it was possibly Monsieur de Norpois alone who had warned Napoleon III of the growing power and bellicose intentions of Prussia, and that Bismarck had particular respect for his intelligence. Even recently, at the Opéra, during the state visit of King Theodosius, the newspapers had noted the long conversation the sovereign had had with Monsieur de Norpois.* 'I must find out if this visit of the King really amounts to anything,' said my father, who took a great interest in foreign policy. 'I know old Norpois doesn't give much away, but with me he opens up in a very pleasant way.'

As for my mother, perhaps the ambassador did not himself have the kind of intelligence towards which she felt most attracted. And I should say that Monsieur de Norpois' conversation was such a complete compendium of antiquated forms of speech typical of a career, a class, and a time—a time which, for that career and that class, might be said not to have entirely ended—that I sometimes regret not having simply written down the expressions I heard him utter. I would thus have achieved an old-fashioned effect, as cheaply and in the same way as that actor from the Palais-Royal* who was asked where he managed to find his remarkable hats, and replied: 'I don't find my hats, I keep them.' In a word, I think my mother thought Monsieur de Norpois a little 'old-fashioned', which was far from making him seem unpleasant where manners were concerned, but charmed her less in the realm, not so much of ideas—for Monsieur de Norpois' ideas were quite modern—as of expressions. Yet she felt she'd be gently flattering her husband if she spoke to him admiringly of the diplomat who showed him such a rare predilection. By strengthening in my father's mind the good opinion he had of Monsieur de Norpois, and thereby leading him to have an equally good opinion of himself, she was aware of fulfilling one of her duties, which consisted in making life pleasant for her husband, just as she did when she made sure his meals were carefully prepared and served in silence. And since she herself was incapable of lying to my father, she trained herself to admire the ambassador so she could praise him with sincerity. What's more, she naturally enjoyed his kindness, his slightly old-fashioned politeness (of such a ceremonious sort that when, as he was walking along the street, his tall figure stiffly upright, upon seeing my mother going by in a carriage, before tipping his hat to her, he'd fling away a newly lit cigar); his measured conversation, in which he spoke of himself as little as possible and always kept track of what might be pleasant to his interlocutor; his punctuality in answering a letter, which was so surprising that when returning from posting him one, my father's first instinct upon recognizing Monsieur de Norpois' writing on an envelope was to think that by bad luck their letters had crossed: it was as if there existed for Monsieur de Norpois additional deliveries and special treatment at the post office. My mother marvelled that he could be so punctual while being so busy, so friendly although with so many commitments, not realizing that 'althoughs' are always unrecognized 'becauses', and that (just as old men can be remarkable, kings full of simplicity, and country folk so well informed about everything) these were the very habits that allowed Monsieur de Norpois to fulfil so many occupations and to be so regular in his replies, to be well liked in society and to be so friendly towards us. What's more, my mother's error, like that of all overly modest people, stemmed from the fact that she placed the things that concerned her beneath, and consequently apart from, the concerns of others. The reply she thought my father's friend was so considerate to write so quickly, since he wrote so many letters every day, she felt was distinct from the large number of letters of which this was just one; similarly, she didn't think that a dinner at our house was for Monsieur de Norpois just one of the countless deeds of his social life: she didn't realize that long ago the ambassador had been accustomed in his life as a diplomat to regard dinners in town as being part of his duties, and to deploy an inveterate charm which it would have been asking too much to make a special effort to abandon when he came to our house.

The first dinner Monsieur de Norpois attended at our house, one year when I was still playing at the Champs-Élysées, has remained in my memory, because the afternoon of that same day was the one when I finally went to see La Berma, in a matinee performance of *Phèdre*,* and also because, as I was chatting with Monsieur de Norpois, I realized all of a sudden, and in a new way, how much the emotions awakened in me by everything regarding Gilberte Swann and her parents differed from those that same family aroused in any other person.

It was probably when she noticed the dejection into which I was plunged by the approaching New Year's holiday when, as she herself had told me, I wouldn't see Gilberte, that one day, to distract me, my mother said: 'If you still want so much to see La Berma, I think your father might let you go: your grandmother could take you.'

But it was because Monsieur de Norpois had told him that he should let me see La Berma, that it was, for a young man, a memory to treasure, that my father, who until then had been so hostile to the idea of my wasting my time and risking getting sick again for what he called, to my grandmother's great indignation, pointless things, now almost thought of this evening recommended by the ambassador as somehow forming part of a set of prescribed activities for anyone hoping to have a brilliant career. My grandmother, who, by giving up for my sake the advantage I'd have derived (according to her) from seeing La Berma, had made a huge sacrifice in the interest of my health, was surprised to see such a sacrifice come to nothing at a single word from Monsieur de Norpois. Placing her invincible rationalist hopes in the regime of fresh air and early bedtimes that had been prescribed for me, she deplored as a disaster this transgression I was about to make against it, and, in an annoyed tone, said: 'How careless you are' to my father, who replied furiously: 'What, now it's *you* who don't want him to go! That's a bit much, you were the one who kept going on about how useful it could be.'

But Monsieur de Norpois had changed my father's plans for me in another way, which mattered much more to me. My father had always wanted me to become a diplomat, and I couldn't bear the thought that even if I did remain attached to the ministry for a while, I'd risk being sent one day as ambassador to capitals in which Gilberte didn't live. I'd have preferred to return to the literary projects I'd once formed and abandoned during my walks by the Guermantes way.* But my father had been adamantly opposed to my devoting myself to a literary career, which he deemed far beneath diplomacy, even denying it the name of 'career', until the day when Monsieur de Norpois, who didn't much like the new social strata of diplomatic officials, had assured him that, as a writer, one could attract as much esteem and exercise as much influence as in the diplomatic world, while at the same time keeping more independence.

'Well, well! I never would've thought it, old Norpois is not at all opposed to the idea of your doing literature,' my father had said. And since he himself was not without influence, he believed there was nothing that couldn't be settled, nothing that couldn't find a favourable solution, in conversation with important people: 'I'll bring him to dinner one of these evenings when we leave the Commission. You can chat with him a little, so he can get to know you. Write something good you can show him; he's very close to the editor of *La Revue des Deux Mondes*,* he can get you in there, he'll manage it, he's a clever old chap; and, upon my word, he seems to think diplomacy, today . . .!'

My happiness at the prospect of not being separated from Gilberte made me eager, but incapable, of writing something fine that could be shown to Monsieur de Norpois. After a few preliminary pages, boredom would make the pen fall from my hands, and I'd cry with rage at the thought that I'd never have any talent, that I was not gifted and couldn't even take advantage of the opportunity that Monsieur de Norpois' imminent visit offered me to remain forever in Paris. Only the idea that I was going to be allowed to see La Berma distracted me from my sorrow. But just as I only wanted to see storms on the coasts wherever they were most violent, so all I wanted was to see the great actress in one of the classic roles in which Swann had told me she touched the sublime. For when it's in the hope of a precious discovery that we desire to receive certain impressions from nature or art, we have qualms about letting our minds welcome lesser impressions in their place that might deceive us about the precise value of Beauty. La Berma in *Andromaque*, in *Les Caprices de Marianne*,* in *Phèdre*, was one of those famous things my imagination had so desired. I would have the same delight as on the day when a gondola would bring me to the foot of the Titian of the Frari or the Carpaccios at San Giorgio dei Schiavoni,* if ever I heard La Berma recite the lines:

> They say that an imminent departure is taking you from us,
> My Lord . . .*

I knew them from simple black-and-white reproductions in printed editions; but my heart pounded when I thought that I'd finally see them (as if I were completing a voyage) actually bathed in the atmosphere and sunshine of the golden voice.* A Carpaccio in Venice, La Berma in *Phèdre*: masterpieces of pictorial or dramatic art that the glamour attached to them made so alive for me, so indivisible, that if I'd been to see the Carpaccios in a gallery at the Louvre or La Berma in some play I'd never heard of, I wouldn't have felt the same delicious astonishment at finally having my eyes open in front of the inconceivable and unique object of so many thousands of my dreams. And, expecting from La Berma's performance revelations about certain aspects of nobility and suffering, it seemed to me that whatever there was that was great and real in this performance would be even more so if the actress superimposed it on a work of real value instead of embroidering truth and beauty on a mediocre, common fabric.

Finally, if I went to see La Berma in a new play, it wouldn't be easy for me to judge her art or her diction, since I wouldn't be able to distinguish between a text I didn't know beforehand and what might be added to it by intonations and gestures that were seemingly organic parts of it; whereas old works I knew by heart seemed to me like vast, ready-made expanses, reserved for me, where I could freely appreciate the inventions with which La Berma would cover them, like a fresco, from the perpetual discoveries of her inspiration. Unfortunately, since the time she'd left the classic stage and was making the fortune of a boulevard theatre where she was the star, she no longer played the classics, and despite my consulting the posters, they never announced anything but quite recent plays, made expressly for her by fashionable authors; when one morning, searching through the posters on the theatre columns for the matinees being given during the first week of January, I saw for the first time—at the end of a performance, after a probably insignificant curtain-raiser whose title seemed opaque since it contained all the particulars of actions unknown to me—two acts from *Phèdre* with Madame Berma, and for the following matinees *Le Demi-Monde** and *Les Caprices de Marianne*,* titles which, like *Phèdre*, were transparent, filled only with brightness, so well known were the works, illuminated through and through with the smile of art. They seemed to add nobility to Madame Berma herself when I read in the papers, after the programmes for these performances, that it was she who had decided to show herself again to the public in a few of her former creations. So, the artist knew that certain roles have an interest that survives the novelty of their appearance or the success of their repeated performances; she regarded them, interpreted by her, as museum pieces it could be instructive to place again before the eyes of the generation that had admired her in them, or the one that had not seen her in them. By advertising in this way, amidst plays that were intended only to let one while away an evening, *Phèdre*, whose title was no longer than theirs and was not printed in different typeface, she added to it something that was like the innuendo of a hostess who, introducing you to her guests when everyone was proceeding to dinner, mentions among the names that are only names, and in the same tone in which she has announced all the others: 'Monsieur Anatole France.'*

The doctor who was looking after me—the one who had forbidden any travel—advised my parents not to let me go to the theatre; I'd come home ill, and remain so for a long time perhaps, and in the end I'd derive more suffering than pleasure from my outing. This fear might have stopped me, if what I'd expected from such a performance had been merely a pleasure that subsequent suffering could cancel out, as recompense. But—like the trip to Balbec,* or the journey to Venice I'd so desired—what I expected from this matinee was something entirely different from pleasure: it was access to truths belonging to a world more real than the one in which I was living, truths that, once acquired, could not be taken away from me by insignificant incidents in my idle existence, even if they were painful to my body. At best, the pleasure I'd experience during the performance seemed to me perhaps the form needed to perceive these truths; and that was enough for me to wish that the predicted illnesses would begin only once the performance was over, so that it wouldn't be compromised or distorted by them. I implored my parents, who, ever since the doctor's visit, were no longer willing to let me go to see *Phèdre*. I recited to myself over and over the monologue beginning:

> They say that an imminent departure is taking you from us . . .*

seeking out all the subtleties of intonation one could wrest from it, the better to appreciate the unexpected quality of the one La Berma would find. Hidden like the Holy of Holies* behind the curtain that screened her from me and behind which I pictured her differently with each passing moment, according to whichever words by Bergotte—in the booklet Gilberte had found for me—came to my mind: 'plastic nobility', 'Christian self-torment', 'Jansenist pallor', 'Princess of Troezen and of Cleves', 'Mycenean tragedy', 'Delphic symbol', 'solar myth',* the divine Beauty that La Berma's acting would reveal to me, night and day, on an altar that was perpetually illumined, sat enthroned in the depths of my mind; and now it was up to my stern but fickle parents to decide whether or not it would enclose, forever, the perfections of the unveiled Goddess in the very place where her invisible form now stood. And with my eyes fixed on the unimaginable image, I struggled from morning to night against the obstacles my family placed in my way. But when they had fallen away, when my mother—even though the matinee was to take place on the very same day as the meeting of the Commission, after which my father was to bring Monsieur de Norpois to dine with us—had said: 'Well, we don't want to you to be upset, if you think you'd enjoy it so much, you must go,' when the outing to the theatre, until then forbidden, was entirely for me to decide, then, for the first time, no longer having to trouble myself with the thought that it might stop being impossible, I wondered if it was desirable, if other reasons besides the prohibition of my parents should perhaps make me stay at home. At first, after hating their cruelty, their consent made them so dear to me that the idea of causing them grief made me feel grief too; the goal of life now appeared not as truth, but as tenderness, and now seemed good or bad depending only on whether my parents would be happy or unhappy. 'I'd rather not go, if it would upset you,' I said to my mother, who, on the contrary, tried to dispel my lurking suspicion that she might be saddened by my going, since this thought, she said, would spoil my enjoyment of *Phèdre*, and it was for this reason that they had both changed their minds about letting me go. But now that I seemed under some sort of obligation to enjoy myself, I found it rather a burden. If I came home feeling unwell, would I recover quickly enough to be able to go to the Champs-Élysées, after the holiday, as soon as Gilberte went back there? To all these reasonings, in order to decide which would win out, I compared the idea, invisible behind her veil, of La Berma's perfection. In one of the scale pans I placed 'Making Maman unhappy; the risk of not being able to go to the Champs-Élysées'; in the other, 'Jansenist pallor' and 'solar myth'; but those very words ended up turning opaque in my mind, no longer meant anything to me, lost all their weight; little by little my hesitations became so painful that if I'd now opted to go to the theatre, it would only be to put an end to them and to be freed of them once and for all. It would have been to shorten my suffering, not in the hope of intellectual enrichment, yielding to the attraction of perfection, that I would have let myself be led not towards the Wise Goddess, but towards the implacable Divinity without face or name that had been stealthily substituted for her beneath her veil. But suddenly everything was changed, my desire to go and see La Berma received another stimulus that allowed me to look forward to the matinee with joy and impatience: I'd gone to take up my daily posture as a stylite, lately so painful, in front of the theatre columns,* and I'd seen the detailed poster for *Phèdre*, still damp, which they'd just pasted up for the first time (and on which, frankly, the rest of the cast offered no new attraction that might help me make up my mind). But it gave to one of the poles between which my indecision wavered a form that was more concrete, and—since the poster was dated not the day I was reading it, but the day when the performance would take place, and even the precise time when the curtain would rise—almost imminent, already on the point of realization, so much so that I jumped for joy in front of the column as I thought that on that day, at that precise hour, I'd be sitting in my seat ready to see La Berma; and fearing that my parents would not now have time to find two good seats for my grandmother and me, I rushed back home, excited as I was by the magical words that had replaced 'Jansenist pallor' and 'solar myth' in my thinking: 'Ladies wearing hats may not sit in the stalls; doors will close at two o'clock.'

Alas! That first matinee was a great disappointment. My father offered to drop off my grandmother and me at the theatre, on his way to the Commission. Before leaving the house, he said to my mother: 'Try to have a good dinner ready; remember I have to bring Norpois back.' My mother hadn't forgotten. And since the day before, Françoise, happy to devote herself to the art of cooking for which she certainly had a gift, stimulated moreover by the announcement of a new guest, and knowing she would have to produce, following methods known only to herself, a dish of *bœuf à la gelée*,* had been living in an effervescent state of creativity; since she attached extreme importance to the intrinsic quality of the ingredients that would go into the making of her masterpiece, she herself went to Les Halles* to find the finest cuts of rump steak, beef shank, and calves' foot, just as Michelangelo spent eight months in the Carrara mountains choosing the most perfect blocks of marble for Julius II's monument.* Françoise put so much ardour into these comings and goings that Maman, seeing her flushed cheeks, feared our old servant might fall ill from overexertion, like the creator of the Medici tombs in the Pietrasanta quarries.* The day before, Françoise had sent what she called a 'Nev'York ham' to be cooked in the village baker's oven, like breadcrumb-encrusted pink marble. Thinking the language less rich than it is, and since her own ears were not very sharp, no doubt the first time she'd heard of York ham she'd thought—finding it an unlikely extravagance of vocabulary that both York and New York could exist at the same time—she'd misheard, and that they'd meant to say the name she knew already. And so, ever since, the word 'York' was preceded in her ears (or to her eyes if she was reading an advertisement) with *New* which she

pronounced 'Nev'. And it was in the sincerest way possible that she
said to the kitchen maid: 'Go and get me some ham at Olida's.
Madame recommended the Nev'York.'* That day, while Françoise
had the ardent confidence of great creators, my lot was the cruel anxiety of the seeker after truth. To be sure, so long as I hadn't yet seen
La Berma, I enjoyed myself. I felt happy in the little square in front
of the theatre where, two hours later, the bare chestnut trees would
gleam with metallic reflections as soon as the gas lamps were lit, illu-
minating the detail of their branches; and I was happy when faced
with the theatre staff, whose selection, promotion, and fate depended
on the great artist—for she alone held sway in that theatre, in which
there was an obscure succession of temporary and purely nominal
managers—and who took our tickets without looking at us, concerned as they were to find out if all Madame Berma's orders had
indeed been conveyed to the new personnel, if it was clearly understood that the claque* should never applaud her, that the windows
should be open only when she wasn't onstage, and every single door
shut tight thereafter, that a bowl of hot water should be concealed
near her to make the stage dust settle: and, in fact, any moment now,
her carriage, drawn by two long-maned horses, would stop in front of
the theatre, she'd get out wrapped in furs, and, responding to greetings with a moody wave of the hand, she'd send a member of her
entourage to check that the right loge had been reserved for her
friends, to see that the temperature of the auditorium was right, to
find out who would be in which boxes, and monitor the behaviour of
the attendants, since the theatre and audience were for her no more
than a second, outer garment she'd put on, and the medium, of
greater or lesser conductivity, through which her talent would have to
pass. I was also happy in the auditorium itself; from the moment
I knew that—unlike what my childish imaginings had so long pictured to me—there was only one stage for everyone, I thought we'd
be prevented from seeing clearly by other spectators, as one is when
standing in the middle of a crowd; but now I realized that, on the
contrary, thanks to an arrangement that is symbolic of our way of
perceiving, everyone feels as if he's in the centre of the theatre; which
explained to me why, when we'd once treated Françoise to a seat in the
gods at a melodrama, she'd assured us when she came home that
she'd had the best seat in the house, and instead of finding herself too
far away, had felt intimidated by the mysterious, living proximity of

the curtain. I felt even happier when I began to distinguish confused sounds behind the lowered curtain, the kind one hears inside an eggshell when the chick is about to emerge; they soon grew louder, and all of a sudden, from that world impenetrable to our gaze but which could see us, it became clear that these sounds were addressed to us in the imperious form of three knocks, as exciting as a message from Mars.* And—once the curtain was raised—my enjoyment continued when, on the stage, a writing table and a fireplace, ordinary as they were, signified that the characters who were about to enter would be, not actors come to recite as I had seen once in an evening performance, but men in the process of living a day of their lives in their home, into which I would penetrate by breaking and entering without their being able to see me. It was interrupted by a moment's anxiety: just as I was pricking up my ears before the play began, two men walked on to the stage, very angry, since they were speaking loud enough, in this auditorium where there were over a thousand people, for everyone to be able to make out every word they said, whereas in a little café one has to ask the waiter what two individuals who are fighting are saying; but in the same instant, surprised to see that the audience was listening to them without protesting, submerged as it was in a universal silence broken now and then by a ripple of laughter, I understood that these insolent men were the actors and that the little play, called the curtain-raiser, had just begun. It was followed by such a long interval that the spectators who had returned to their seats were growing impatient, tapping their feet. I was frightened by this; for, just as in a report of a trial, when I read that a noble-hearted man was going to give evidence for an innocent man, with no regard for his own interests, I was always afraid lest he not be shown enough gratitude, or wasn't generously recompensed, and that, disheartened, he would go over to the side of injustice; similarly, likening genius to virtue, I was afraid that La Berma, vexed by the bad manners of a rather ill-bred audience—among whom, on the contrary, I would have wished that she could have the satisfaction of recognizing a few celebrities to whose judgement she would have been able to attach some importance—might express her discontent and disdain by performing badly. So I watched in a beseeching way those stomping brutes who in their fury were about to shatter the fragile, precious impression I'd come to seek. Finally, my last moments of enjoyment were during the opening scenes of *Phèdre*. The character of Phèdre doesn't appear in those early scenes of the second act; and yet, as soon as the curtain went up, and a second curtain, this one made of red velvet, had parted, thus doubling the depth of the stage, as in all the plays in which the star performed, there entered from the back an actress who had the face and voice I'd been told were those of La Berma. They must have changed the cast; all the care I'd put into studying the role of Theseus' wife became pointless. But then another actress entered into a dialogue with the first one who had entered. I must have been mistaken when I took her for La Berma, for the second one resembled her even more and, more than the other, had her diction. What's more, both added noble gestures to their role— which I could clearly make out and whose relationship with the text I understood, as they raised the beautiful folds of their robes—as well as ingenious intonations, now passionate, now ironic, which made me understand the meaning of a line I'd read at home without paying enough attention to what it meant. But all of a sudden, in the opening of the red curtain of the inner sanctum, as in a frame, a woman appeared and immediately—from the fear I felt (much more acute than La Berma's must be) at the thought that she might be annoyed by someone opening a window, that the sound of one of her words might be altered by the rustling of a programme, that she might be upset if her comrades were applauded, or she wasn't applauded enough; and from my way, even more absolute than La Berma's, of regarding, from that moment onwards, the auditorium, the audience, the actors, the play, and my own body as nothing but an acoustic medium having no importance except insofar as it enhanced the inflections of that voice—I realized that the two actresses I'd been admiring for several minutes looked nothing at all like the one I'd come to hear. But at the same time all the pleasure I felt had completely dissipated; despite straining my ears, eyes, and mind towards La Berma, so as not to let a single crumb escape of the reasons she would give me to admire her, I couldn't manage to find any. I couldn't even make out in her diction or her movements, as I had with the other actresses, any intelligent intonations or beautiful gestures. I listened to her as I would have read *Phèdre*, or as if Phèdre herself had said in that moment the things I was hearing, without La Berma's talent seeming to have added anything to them. I wanted to arrest, to immobilize before me, each of the artist's intonations, each of her facial expressions, in order to study them in depth and discover in them what was beautiful; at least I tried, by dint of mental agility, by making sure that all my attention was focused and at the ready before a line, not to waste on preparations a single particle of the length of each word, each gesture, and, through the intensity of my attention, to penetrate them as deeply as I would have done if I'd had many hours to spend on them by myself. But how short their duration was! As soon as one sound was registered by my ear it was replaced by another. In one scene, where La Berma remains motionless for a moment, with one arm raised to the level of her face, bathed thanks to an effect of lighting in a greenish glow, in front of a backdrop representing the sea, the audience burst into applause, but already the actress had changed her position and the tableau I'd have liked to study no longer existed. I told my grandmother I couldn't see properly, and she passed me her opera glasses. But, when one believes in the reality of things, using an artificial means to see them better isn't quite the same as feeling close to them. I thought it was no longer La Berma I was seeing, but her image in the magnifying glass. I put the glasses down; but perhaps the image my eye was receiving, diminished by distance, was no longer exact—which of the two La Bermas was the real one? As for Phèdre's declaration to Hippolyte,* I'd been specially looking forward to the part where, judging by the unsuspected subtleties of meaning her fellow actors kept revealing to me in less beautiful passages, she'd certainly have more striking intonations than the ones I'd tried to imagine when I'd read the play at home; but she didn't even attain those that Œnone or Aricie would have managed, she reduced the entire monologue to a toneless uniformity, blurring contrasts which were so clear-cut that not even a novice tragedian, not even lycée students, could have failed to bring them out; what's more, she began it so quickly that it was only when she'd arrived at the last line that my mind became aware of the deliberate monotone she'd imposed on the first lines.

Finally my first feeling of admiration blazed forth: it was provoked by the frenzied applause of the spectators. I added my own, trying to prolong it, so that, out of gratitude, La Berma would outdo herself; I was sure I'd heard her on one of her best days. The curious thing, though, is that the moment when this enthusiasm of the audience is unleashed was, as I learned later, the one when La Berma is at her most inspired. It seems that certain transcendent realities emit a kind of radiation to which the crowd responds. This is how, for example, when a major event occurs (as when an army at the border is in danger, or defeated, or victorious) and we receive unclear reports about it, an educated person may find it difficult to glean much from it, but it excites in the crowd an emotion that surprises him and, once the experts have informed him about the actual military situation, he recognizes the perception by the people of the 'aura' that surrounds great events and is visible hundreds of kilometres away. We learn of victory either afterwards, when the war is over, or right away from the joy of the concierge. We discover a brilliant feature of La Berma's performance either eight days after seeing her, from the critics, or right away from the cheers in the back stalls. But since this immediate awareness of the crowd was mingled with a hundred other ones, all erroneous, the applause usually occurred at the wrong times; what's more, it was mechanically increased by the force of previous applause, just as in a storm, once the sea has been churned up enough, the waves keep getting higher, even if the wind is no stronger. Nevertheless, the longer I applauded, the better La Berma seemed to me to have acted. 'At least,' a rather common-looking woman next to me said, 'she really gives her all, she hits herself until she hurts, she runs; now that, *that's* what I call acting.' And, happy to accept these reasons for La Berma's superiority, while still wondering if they explained it any better than a peasant's exclamation on seeing the *Mona Lisa* or Benvenuto's *Perseus*:* 'Nice work, that! It's all gold, and so beautiful! Really well done!', I let the cheap wine of this popular enthusiasm go to my head. Once the curtain had fallen, though, I still felt disappointed that the pleasure I'd so longed for hadn't been greater, but at the same time I felt the need to prolong it, not to quit forever, when I left the auditorium, the theatre life that for a few hours had been mine, and from which I'd drag myself away as if I were departing into exile, going straight home, had I not hoped to learn a great deal there about La Berma from the admirer to whom I was indebted for allowing me to go to *Phèdre*, Monsieur de Norpois. I was introduced to him after dinner by my father, who called me into his study. As I entered, the ambassador got up, held out his hand, bowed his tall frame, and fixed his blue eyes attentively on me. Since, when he represented France, visiting foreigners who had been introduced to him were all more or less (even well-known singers) persons of distinction about whom he knew that he could say later, when their names were mentioned in Paris or St Petersburg, that he remembered very well the evening he'd spent with them in Munich or Sofia, he'd formed the habit of showing them, by his affability, how pleased he'd been to meet them; but what's more, being convinced that in the life of foreign capitals, in contact both with interesting individuals passing through them and the customs of the people inhabiting them, one acquires a deeper knowledge than books can give of the history, geography, and customs of different nations, and of the intellectual trends of Europe, he would exercise upon each newcomer his keen faculties of observation in order to find out what manner of man he was dealing with. It had been a long time since the government had given him a foreign posting, but as soon as he was introduced to someone, his eyes, as if they hadn't received notification that he was no longer on active duty, began to pursue their work of profitable observation, while by his attitude he sought to show that the stranger's name was not unknown to him. Thus, as he spoke to me with the kindliness and air of importance of a man who is aware of his vast experience, he never stopped examining me with great curiosity, for his own benefit, as if I were some exotic custom, an instructive monument, or a star on tour. And in this way he showed towards me both the majestic amiability of the wise Mentor and the studious curiosity of the young Anacharsis.*

He offered me absolutely no entrance to the *Revue des Deux Mondes*, but asked me a number of questions about what my life and studies were like, and about my tastes, which I heard discussed for the first time as if it might be reasonable to follow them, whereas I'd thought until then that it was a duty to resist them. Since they inclined me towards literature, he didn't turn me away from it; on the contrary, he spoke of it with respect as if it were a venerable, charming person whose select circle one remembers fondly from having been admitted to it in Rome or Dresden, and whom one would gladly see more often, if it weren't for life's multifarious demands. Smiling almost roguishly, he seemed to envy me—for I was happier and freer than he was—the good times such a mistress would afford me. But the very terms he used showed me Literature to be too different from the image I'd had of it in Combray, and I understood how right I'd been to renounce it. Until then I'd realized only that I didn't have a gift for writing; now Monsieur de Norpois took from me even the desire to write. I wanted to explain to him what I'd dreamed; trembling with emotion, I had qualms that all my words were not the sincerest possible equivalent of what I'd felt and had never tried to formulate to myself; which is to say, my words had no clarity. Perhaps out of professional habit, perhaps by virtue of the calm any important man acquires whose advice is solicited and who, knowing that control of the conversation remains in his hands, lets his interlocutor become agitated, overexerted, distressed while he himself sits at ease, perhaps also to show off the character of his countenance (Hellenic according to him, despite his long side whiskers), Monsieur de Norpois, as something was being explained to him, preserved an immobility of face as absolute as if you were addressing some ancient—and deaf—bust in a museum. Suddenly, falling like an auctioneer's gavel, or like the Delphic oracle,* the ambassador's voice, as he replied to you, was all the more impressive because nothing in his face had led you to suspect the kind of impression you'd made on him, or the advice he was about to give.

'Exactly,' he said suddenly, as if the case were decided, and after letting me stammer before his unwavering gaze, his motionless eyes not having left mine for a second, went on: 'A friend of mine has a son who, mutatis mutandis, is like you' (and, to speak of our shared predispositions, he used the same reassuring tone as if they had been predispositions not for literature, but for rheumatism, and as if he wanted me to know it would not be fatal). 'And so he decided to leave the Quai d'Orsay,* even though his path was all laid out for him there by his father, and without worrying about what people would say, he set himself to writing. He has indeed had no reason to repent of his decision. Two years ago—he's quite a bit older than you, of course—he published a book having to do with the sense of the Infinite over the western shore of Lake Victoria Nyanza, and this year he published a treatise that was less substantial but written with a keen, even at times biting, pen, about the repeating rifle in the Bulgarian army; these books have put him in a class entirely his own. He has already gone pretty far, he's not one to stop halfway, and I know that, while a candidacy for him hasn't been mentioned, his name has been dropped two or three times in conversation, not at all unfavourably, at the Academy of Moral Sciences.* In short, while I can't yet say he has climbed as high as he can go, he has fought hard to achieve a fine position, and success—which doesn't always come only to the muddlers and meddlers of this world, to the troublemakers, who are nearly always show-offs—success has rewarded his efforts.'

My father, envisaging me already as an academician in a few years, exuded a satisfaction that Monsieur de Norpois brought to an even higher pitch when, after a moment's hesitation during which he seemed to be calculating the consequences of his action, he handed me his card and said: 'You should go and see him; mention my name. I'm sure he'll be able to give you some useful advice,' inducing in me a feeling of anxiety that was as distressing as if I'd been told I was about to be shipped off the next day as a cabin boy on board a schooner.

My aunt Léonie had bequeathed to me, along with more objects and pieces of furniture than I knew what to do with, almost the whole of her liquid assets—thereby revealing after her death an affection for me that I'd scarcely suspected while she was alive. My father, who had to manage this fortune until I came of age, consulted Monsieur de Norpois about a certain number of investments. He recommended some low-yield stocks he deemed particularly safe, especially English consols and Russian four-per-cents.* 'With first-rate stock like those,' Monsieur de Norpois said, 'if the return isn't very high, at least you can be sure the capital will be safe.' My father mentioned the other stocks he'd bought. Monsieur de Norpois gave him a barely perceptible congratulatory smile: like all capitalists, he deemed wealth an enviable thing, but considered it tactful to compliment others on the wealth they possessed with no more than a discreet, knowing look; what's more, since he himself was colossally rich, he thought it in good taste to appear impressed by the lesser incomes of others, while enjoying a quiet reminder of the superiority of his own. On the other hand, he didn't hesitate to congratulate my father on the 'composition' of his portfolio as being 'very sound, very discerning, very fine'. It was as if he attributed something like aesthetic merit to the way investments related to each other, and even to the intrinsic values of stocks. About one stock, quite new and unknown, which my father mentioned to him, Monsieur de Norpois, like those people who have read books you thought you alone were familiar with, said: 'Yes of course, I amused myself for a while watching how it performed, it was interesting'; and he smiled with the retrospectively captivated smile of a subscriber who has read the latest serialized novel in a magazine. 'I wouldn't advise against signing up for the issue that will soon be floated. It's attractive, the shares are being offered at tempting prices.' For some older investments, on the other hand, my father, who had forgotten their precise names, since they were easy to confuse with those of similar stocks, opened a drawer and showed the certificates themselves to the ambassador. They enchanted me; they were embellished with cathedral spires and allegorical figures, like some old romantic publications I'd leafed through long ago. All things that exist at a certain time resemble one another; the artists who illustrate the poems of one era are the same as those employed by financial companies. And nothing reminds me more of certain instalments of *Notre-Dame de Paris*,* or of the works of Gérard de Nerval* as displayed in the window of the grocery store in Combray, than, in its rectangular, flowery frame supported by river gods, a registered stock from the Water Company.

As far as my kind of intelligence was concerned, my father's attitude was one of scorn sufficiently tempered by affection that, on the whole, his feeling about anything I was doing was a kind of blind indulgence. Thus he didn't think twice about sending me off to look for a little prose poem I'd once written in Combray when I returned from a walk. I'd written it in a state of exhilaration which I thought would be communicated to anyone who read it. But it must not have won over Monsieur de Norpois, since he handed it back to me without saying a word.

My mother, who was full of respect for my father's activities, came to ask, timidly, if she could serve dinner. She was afraid of interrupting a conversation in which she wasn't expected to participate. And indeed, my father kept reminding the marquis of some useful measure they'd decided to propose at the next meeting of the Commission, and he did so in the special tone used in a different setting by two colleagues (similar in this to two schoolchildren) whose professional habits create shared memories to which others have no access, so they apologize for alluding to them in their presence.

But the absolute control over his facial muscles that Monsieur de Norpois had attained allowed him to listen without seeming to hear anything. Finally my father became unsettled: 'I had thought to ask the opinion of the Commission . . .', he said to Monsieur de Norpois, after lengthy preambles. Then, from the face of the aristocratic virtuoso, who had maintained the passivity of an instrumentalist whose cue to play had not yet come, there emerged with an even delivery, in a sharp tone seeming only to finish the phrase my father had begun in a different timbre, the words: '. . . which of course you will not hesitate to call to a meeting, especially since the members are all known to you and can easily make themselves available'. This was obviously not in itself a very extraordinary conclusion. But the immobility that had preceded it made it stand out with the crystalline sharpness, the almost mischievous unpredictability of the phrases by which the piano, silent until then, replies, at the right moment, to the cello one has just heard, in a concerto by Mozart.*

'Well, were you happy with your matinee?' my father asked me as we were going in to dinner, to give me a chance to shine, and in the hope that my enthusiasm would win Monsieur de Norpois' esteem. 'He's just been to see La Berma; remember, we talked about it earlier,' he said, turning to the diplomat with the same tone of retrospective, specialized, mysterious allusion as if they were in a Commission meeting.

'You must have been delighted, especially if it was the first time you saw her. Your father was alarmed at the after-effect that little outing might have on your health, since you're a little delicate, a little frail, I think. But I reassured him. Theatres today are not what they were even twenty years ago. You have more or less comfortable seats, and the air is a little fresher, although we have a long way to go before we reach the level of Germany and England, which in that respect as well as in many others are far ahead of us. I haven't seen Madame La Berma in *Phèdre*, but I heard she was admirable. You must have found it thrilling.'

Monsieur de Norpois, a thousand times more intelligent than I, must have possessed the truth I hadn't been able to extract from La Berma's performance, and he'd be able to reveal it to me; answering his question, I'd beg him to tell me what this truth consisted of; and in this way he'd justify the desire I'd felt to see the actress. I just had a moment—I had to take advantage of this and make my questions address the essential points. But what were they? Focusing my entire attention on my confused impressions, and not thinking in the least of making Monsieur de Norpois admire me, but rather of obtaining from him the desired truth, I didn't try to substitute ready-made expressions for the words that failed me; I stammered and, in the end, to try to provoke him to declare what was admirable about La Berma, I confessed that I'd been disappointed.

'What's all this?' my father cried, appalled at the poor impression my confession of incomprehension might make on Monsieur de Norpois. 'How can you say you didn't enjoy it? Your grandmother told us you didn't miss a word of what La Berma said, that your eyes were starting out of your head, that you were the only one in the auditorium like that.'

'Yes, I listened as hard as I could to find out what was so remarkable about her. No doubt she *is* very good . . .'

'If she is very good, what more do you want?'

'One of the things that definitely contributes to Madame La Berma's success,' said Monsieur de Norpois as he turned courteously towards my mother so as not to leave her out of the conversation, and in order to fulfil conscientiously his polite duty to a hostess, 'is the perfect taste she evinces in her choice of roles; this always earns her complete, well-deserved success. She rarely plays mediocre roles. So, you see, she's taken on the role of Phèdre. What's more, she carries this good taste over into her appearance, her acting. Even though she has toured frequently in England and America, the vulgarity—I won't say of John Bull, which would be unfair, at least to Victorian England—but of Uncle Sam* has not rubbed off on her. Her colours are never garish, her exclamations never exaggerated. And then there's that admirable voice, which serves her so well, on which she plays so delightfully, I'd almost be tempted to say like a musician on an instrument!'

My interest in La Berma's acting had continued to grow after the play was over, because it was no longer subject to the compression or constraints of reality; but I felt the need to find explanations for this interest, which had been focused with equal intensity, as La Berma was performing, on everything she offered, in the indivisible experience of life, to my eyes, to my ears; there was nothing separate or distinct; and so I was glad to discover a reasonable cause for my interest in these praises of her simplicity and fine artistic taste; it attracted them to itself by its power of absorption, latched on to them the way a drunken man's optimism seizes hold of a passer-by's actions to justify his own emotion. 'He's right!' I thought. 'What a beautiful voice, what an absence of histrionics, what simple costumes, what intelligence she showed in choosing *Phèdre*! No, I was not disappointed.'

The cold beef with carrots made its appearance, nestled by the Michelangelo of our kitchen on enormous crystals of aspic resembling blocks of transparent quartz.

'You have a first-rate cook, Madame,' said Monsieur de Norpois. 'And that's no small thing. Since I had to maintain quite a number of servants abroad, I know how difficult it often is to find a perfect chef. This is a veritable feast you've invited us to!'

Indeed, Françoise, overexcited by the ambition of bringing off for a distinguished guest a dinner full of difficulties worthy of her expertise, had gone to lengths she didn't take when we were alone, and had rediscovered the incomparable style she had in Combray.

'This is something you can't find in any hostelry, even the best ones: braised beef with aspic that doesn't taste like glue, in which the meat has taken on the aroma of the carrots, what an admirable thing! I hope you'll let me come back,' he added, motioning for more aspic. 'I'd be curious to see how your Vatel does on an entirely different dish—to see him tackle a beef Stroganoff, for instance.'*

To add his own contribution to the meal's charm, Monsieur de Norpois served us various stories with which he often regaled his professional colleagues, citing now a ridiculous sentence uttered by a politician known for his long-winded phrases full of mixed metaphors, now some pithy saying from a diplomat who was a master of Attic wit.* But the criterion he used to distinguish these two kinds of sentences was not at all like the one I applied to literature. Many nuances escaped me; the words he recited mockingly didn't seem very different to me from those he found remarkable. He was the sort of man who would have said of the books I liked: 'You understand them, then? As for me, I must confess I don't have a clue, I'm not an initiate,' but I could have said much the same to him, since I couldn't grasp the wit or stupidity, the eloquence or bombast he found in a retort or a speech, and the absence of any obvious reason for which this was bad or this good made these sorts of literary standards seem more mysterious to me, more obscure, than any other. The only thing I could make out was that repeating what everyone else thought was not, in politics, a mark of inferiority but of superiority. When Monsieur de Norpois used certain clichéd expressions that could be found in any newspaper and uttered them with conviction, one felt they were becoming an official proclamation simply by virtue of the fact that he'd used them, and a proclamation that would give rise to much commentary.

My mother had high hopes for the pineapple and truffle salad. But the ambassador, after briefly training his penetrating observer's gaze on the dish, ate it with an air of diplomatic discretion, and didn't convey his opinion to us. When my mother insisted he have a second helping, Monsieur de Norpois complied, but instead of offering the hoped-for compliment, merely said: 'I obey, Madame, since I see it's a veritable ukase* you've issued.'

'We read in the papers you had a long talk with King Theodosius,' my father said.

'That's right; the King, who has a rare memory for faces, had the kindness to recall, when he saw me in the stalls, that I'd had the honour of seeing him over the course of several days at the Bavarian court, at a time when he wasn't contemplating his Eastern throne (as you know, it fell to him as the result of a European Congress; he even entertained some grave doubts about accepting it, deeming that sovereignty rather unworthy of his race, the noblest—heraldically speaking—in all of Europe). An aide-de-camp came down to bid me greet His Majesty, an order I naturally hastened to follow.'

'And were you satisfied with the results of his visit?'

'Delighted! One might well have been justified in being a little apprehensive about how a monarch, still so young, would manage this difficult situation, especially in such delicate conditions. For my part I had complete faith in the sovereign's political acumen. But I must confess that my expectations were exceeded. The toast he gave at the Élysée,* which, according to information I have from an entirely sound source, had been composed by him from the first word to the last, was in every way worthy of the universal interest it aroused. It was simply a masterstroke; a little bold, I'll admit, but of an audacity fully justified by the event. There are indeed some good things about diplomatic traditions, but in this case they ended up making his country and our own live in an isolated atmosphere that was no longer breathable. Well! One of the ways of bringing in new air, obviously not one to be recommended but one that King Theodosius might allow himself to adopt, is to break the windows! And he did so with a fine humour that delighted everyone, as well as an accuracy in his choice of words in which one could immediately recognize the race of cultivated princes from which he is descended through his mother. It's plain to see that when he spoke of the "affinities" that unite his country with France, the expression, little-used though it may be in the diplomatic lexicon, was singularly apt. As you can see,' he added, addressing me, 'there's nothing wrong with literature, even in diplomacy, even on a throne. It's true that shared interests had long been apparent, and relations between the two powers had become excellent.

But still, it needed to be said. The word was what we were all hoping for; it was wonderfully chosen, you've seen what an effect it's had. I for one applaud it wholeheartedly.'

'Your friend Monsieur de Vaugoubert, who had been paving the way for this rapprochement for years, must have been happy.'

'All the more so since His Majesty, up to his old tricks, was keen to surprise him with it. In fact it was a complete surprise for everyone, beginning with the Minister of Foreign Affairs, who, I've been told, was none too pleased with it. They say that when someone mentioned it to him, he apparently replied very sharply, loud enough to be heard by people nearby: "I was neither consulted nor forewarned," clearly indicating he took no share of responsibility for the event. It should be said that the occurrence caused quite a fuss, and far be it from me to confirm', he added with a mischievous smile, 'that certain of my colleagues, who seem to live by the law of expending as little effort as possible, may have had their peace of mind disturbed. As for Vaugoubert, you know he'd been harshly attacked for his policy of urging rapprochement with France, and he must have suffered all the more from that since he's a sensitive, warm-hearted soul. I can testify that even though he's my junior (and by quite a bit), I've worked with him closely, we're old friends, and I know him well. Who wouldn't want to know him, for that matter? He has a heart of crystal. That may even be the sole defect with which he could be reproached; a diplomat's heart doesn't need to be as transparent as his. Despite this, there's talk of sending him to Rome, which would be a fine promotion, but a big pill for him to swallow. Between ourselves, I think that Vaugoubert, though he's utterly devoid of ambition, would be quite happy with it, and wouldn't ask for *that* cup to pass from him. He might work wonders there; he's the candidate favoured by the Consulta, and I for one can easily see him, artistic as he is, in the setting of the Farnese Palace and the Carracci Gallery.* You might think no one would be able to hate him; but there is around King Theodosius a whole camarilla more or less subservient to the Wilhelmstrasse,* whose wishes its members docilely follow, and this clique has tried its best to throw a spanner in his works. Vaugoubert has had to face not only these backstairs intrigues but also the insults of paid hacks who later on, cowardly as any corrupt journalists are, were the first to raise the white flag, but who in the meantime were quick to hurl the baseless accusations of dishonourable lackeys against our representative.

For over a month Vaugoubert's enemies danced around him, ready to scalp him,' said Monsieur de Norpois, stressing the word 'scalp'. 'But forewarned is forearmed; he shoved those insults aside,' he added even more energetically, with such a fierce glare that for a moment we stopped eating. 'As a fine Arab proverb goes: "The dogs may bark, but the caravan moves on."' After offering up this quotation, Monsieur de Norpois paused to look at us and to gauge the effect it had produced. It was great; the proverb was well known to us: that year among the cultivated it had replaced this other maxim: 'Who sows the wind reaps the whirlwind', which needed some rest, since it was not as tireless or steadfast as 'To work for the King of Prussia'. For the culture of these men of distinction was an alternating one, changing usually every three years. Not that the articles Monsieur de Norpois wrote for the *Revue des Deux Mondes* would have seemed less solid or well informed if they weren't expertly sprinkled with quotations of this sort. Even stripped of the embellishment they brought to his prose, Monsieur de Norpois had only to write at the appropriate point (which he unfailingly did): 'The Court of Saint James's was not the last to perceive the danger', or else 'Emotions were running high at the Choristers' Bridge, where an anxious eye was kept on the selfish but clever policy of the Double-Headed Eagle', or 'A cry of alarm rose up from the Montecitorio', or else 'The eternal double-dealing which is so characteristic of the Ballplatz'.* From these expressions, the lay reader immediately recognized and hailed the career diplomat. But what led some to say that he was not just a diplomat but a man of superior culture was his studied use of quotations, of which the highest form at that time was: 'Give me sound policies and I'll give you sound finances, as Baron Louis used to say.'* (They hadn't yet imported from the East: 'Victory goes to the side that can hold out a quarter of an hour longer than the other, say the Japanese.') This reputation as a well-read man, together with a real genius for intrigue hidden beneath a mask of indifference, had led to Monsieur de Norpois' election to the Academy of Moral Sciences. And there were some who even thought he wouldn't be out of place at the Académie française, when, wanting to show that it was by strengthening the Russian alliance that we could arrive at an agreement with England, he didn't hesitate to write: 'Let it be well known at the Quai d'Orsay, let it be taught henceforth in all the geography textbooks, which appear to be incomplete in this respect, let any undergraduate be pitilessly refused a degree, if he cannot say: All roads may lead to Rome, but the road that goes from Paris to London must necessarily pass through Saint Petersburg.'*

'In short,' Monsieur de Norpois went on, addressing my father, 'Vaugoubert has made a great success of this affair, even greater than the one he'd anticipated. He was in fact expecting a polite toast (which, after the dark clouds of the last few years, would already have been good enough), but no more than that. Several people among those present assured me that if one merely read the speech, one couldn't gauge the effect it produced when it was so beautifully spoken and delivered by the King, who, being the master in the art of public speaking that he is, brought out every intent, every nuance. On this subject, I was told a rather striking anecdote, which once again emphasizes the King's charming youthful bonhomie which wins him so many hearts. I was assured that the instant he uttered the word "affinities", which was the surprising innovation of the speech, and which—as you'll see—will be the talk of the chancelleries for a long time to come, His Majesty, foreseeing the joy it would cause our ambassador, who would find in that word the well-deserved crowning of all his efforts, of all his dreams, one might well say, his marshal's baton, half turned towards Vaugoubert and, fixing the intense gaze of the Oettingens* on him, clearly spoke the word "affinities", so apposite, so inspired, in a tone of voice that let everyone know it was being used intentionally, with full knowledge of the facts. Apparently Vaugoubert had difficulty mastering his emotions, and, to an extent, I sympathize. A reliable source even confided to me that the King went over to Vaugoubert after dinner, when His Majesty was holding court to a select few, and whispered to him, "Well then, are you satisfied with your student, my dear Marquis?" It's indisputable', Monsieur de Norpois concluded, 'that such a speech has done more than twenty years of negotiations ever could to strengthen the "affinities", to use Theodosius II's picturesque expression, between the two countries. True, it's just a word, but look at the good fortune it has created, how all the European press has taken it up, what interest it awakens, what a new chord it has struck! What's more, it's quite in keeping with the sovereign's style. I won't go so far as to say that he comes up with pure gems like that every day. But it's quite rare in his prepared speeches—indeed, even in his off-the-cuff conversations—for him not to leave some characteristic stamp (I was going to say not to attach his signature) with some incisive phrase. I'm all the less to be suspected of bias in this, since I'm an enemy of innovation in such matters. Nine times out of ten it's dangerous.'

'Yes, it occurred to me that the Kaiser's recent telegram might not be to your liking,' my father said.

Monsieur de Norpois raised his eyes to the sky as if to say 'Ah, that man!' and went on: 'First of all, it's an act of ingratitude. It's worse than a crime, it's an offence, of a stupidity I'd describe as monumental! For another thing, unless someone puts a stop to it, the man who got rid of Bismarck is quite capable of repudiating all of Bismarck's politics, one by one; and what a leap into the unknown that would be!'

'My husband tells me, Monsieur, that you might take him to Spain one of these summers; I'm so glad to hear it.'

'Yes indeed, it's an enticing prospect, which I'm looking forward to very much. It would be a pleasure to go on such a trip with you, my dear fellow. What about you, Madame, have you given any thought to how you will spend your holidays?'

'I might go to Balbec with my son, but I'm not sure yet.'

'Ah! Balbec is lovely, I stopped by a few years ago. They're starting to build some charming little villas: I'm sure you'll find the place delightful. But may I ask what made you choose Balbec?'

'My son has a great desire to see some of the region's churches, especially the one in Balbec. I was a little afraid that the journey, and especially the stay there, might tire him and be bad for his health. But I've heard they've just built an excellent hotel there, where he can live in all the comfort he requires.'

'Ah! I'll have to pass that information on to a certain person. She's not one to turn her nose up at something like that.'

'The church at Balbec is admirable, isn't it, Monsieur?' I asked, overcoming my sadness at learning that one of Balbec's attractions lay in its charming villas.

'Well, yes, but it can't bear comparison with such true gems wrought of stone as the cathedrals of Rheims and Chartres, or with what I regard as the crown jewel of them all, the Sainte-Chapelle here in Paris.'*

'But the Balbec church is partly Romanesque,* isn't it?'

'Quite right, it *is* in the Romanesque style, which is cold in itself, and doesn't at all foreshadow the elegance or fantasy of the Gothic architects, who could carve stone like lace.* The Balbec church is worth a visit if you're in the area, it's something to see; if you don't know what else to do on a rainy day, you should go inside and look at the tomb of Admiral de Tourville.'*

'Did you happen to attend the Foreign Affairs banquet last night?' my father asked. 'I couldn't go.'

'No,' Monsieur de Norpois replied with a smile, 'I must confess I passed up that pleasure for an evening that was of rather a different nature. I dined at the home of a woman you may have heard of, the beautiful Madame Swann.'

My mother suppressed a shiver; being more keenly sensitive than my father, she often grew alarmed on his behalf over what might not upset him until a moment later. Any unpleasantness that came his way was perceived by her first, just as bad news for France is heard earlier abroad than it is at home. But, curious to find out what sort of people the Swanns might be entertaining, she asked Monsieur de Norpois about whom he'd met there.

'Well, now . . . it's a house that seems to be frequented mostly by . . . gentlemen. There were a few married men there, but all their wives were indisposed that evening, and didn't come,' the ambassador replied with a crafty look sheathed in geniality, his glances full of a gracious discretion that pretended to temper their impishness while making it more obvious.

'I must say,' he added, 'to be entirely fair, women do go there, but . . . only ones who belong . . . how should I put it? . . . to the republican world rather than to Swann's' (he pronounced it 'Svann'). 'Who knows? Perhaps someday it will be a political or literary salon. In any case, they seem happy as they are. I think Swann even shows it a little overmuch. He was naming the people who had invited him and his wife over for the next week, claiming an intimacy of which there's no reason to be proud, with a lack of reserve and taste, even of tact, which surprised me in such a refined man. He kept repeating: "We don't have a single evening free!" as if that were something to boast about, like a real parvenu, which he is not in the least. For Swann had many friends, both men and women, and without meaning to overstep the mark, or to be indiscreet, I think I may safely say that not all of those ladies, not even the majority, but one at least, who is of quite noble lineage, may not have appeared entirely opposed to the idea of befriending Madame Swann, in which case it's quite likely that more than one of Panurge's sheep would have followed her lead.* But apparently there has been no move on Swann's part in that direction. What's this? A Nesselrode pudding as well! I'll need to take the cure at Karlsbad to restore me after such a Lucullan feast!*—Perhaps Swann felt there would be too much resistance to overcome. One thing is certain, the marriage was not well received. People spoke of the wife's wealth, which is the basest lie. In any case, the whole affair was frowned upon. Swann too has an extremely rich and highly regarded aunt, whose husband is, financially speaking, quite a one to be reckoned with. And not only did she refuse to meet Madame Swann, but she waged a full-scale campaign for her friends and acquaintances to do the same. I don't mean to say that anyone in reputable Parisian society has shown a lack of respect for Madame Swann . . . No! A hundred times no! Especially since her husband isn't the least bit reluctant to send round his seconds! Anyway, the curious thing is how Swann, with all his acquaintances, of such high calibre as well, is so eager to please members of a circle about which the best one can say is that it is extremely mixed. I used to know him in the old days, and I confess I was both surprised and amused to see a man so well bred, so at ease in the most fashionable and exclusive circles, effusively thanking the chief under-secretary of the Postmaster General for coming to their home, and asking him if Madame Swann might *have leave* to call on his wife! He must be feeling out of his element; obviously it's not a society to which he's accustomed. But I don't think Swann is unhappy. It's true that in the years before their marriage, she made some rather sordid attempts at blackmail; whenever he refused her anything, she'd deprive Swann of his daughter. Poor Swann, as naïve as he is sophisticated, believed each time that whenever his daughter was taken away it was a mere coincidence, and refused to face the facts. She made so many scenes that everyone thought if the day ever came when she got what she wanted and was married, nothing would hold her back, and their lives would be a living hell. Well, it's been just the opposite! People laugh quite a bit about the way Swann talks about his wife; it's become something of a joke. Of course no one expected that, more or less aware of being . . . (you know Molière's word),* he'd go and proclaim it *urbi et orbi*;* still, people think it a bit much when he keeps telling you how wonderful his wife is. But it's not as far-fetched as they might think. In her own way (which is not one all husbands might prefer, but still, between us, it seems hard to believe that Swann, who has known her for a long time and is far from being a complete dunce, didn't know what he was getting himself into), it can't be denied that she seems to be fond of him. I'm not saying she isn't fickle, and Swann himself is certainly no saint, if we listen to all the nice tongues that (as you may well believe) have been set wagging. But she *is* grateful to him for what he's done for her, and, contrary to everyone's fears, she seems to have become as sweet as an angel.' This change in Odette was perhaps not as extraordinary as Monsieur de Norpois thought. Odette had never believed that Swann would end up marrying her; whenever she announced to him in a meaningful tone that some respectable man had just married his mistress, she'd been met with an icy silence, and, at the very most, if she questioned him directly by asking him: 'Well then, don't you think it's it's a fine, noble thing he's done, for a woman who sacrificed her youth to him?', he'd reply drily: 'I'm not saying it's a bad thing; everyone does as he sees fit.' She even came close to believing that he'd carry out the threats he sometimes made in moments of anger and would abandon her completely, since she'd recently heard a woman sculptor say 'You shouldn't be surprised at anything men do, they're such brutes,' and, struck by the profundity of this pessimistic maxim, she had adopted it as her own, and would repeat it over and over in a discouraged way that seemed to say: 'After all, anything could happen, it would be just my luck.' As a result, all the strength had been drained from the optimistic maxim that had hitherto guided Odette through life: 'You can do anything you like to the men who are in love with you, they're such idiots,' which she conveyed with the same twinkle in her eye that might have accompanied a statement like 'Don't be afraid, he's quite tame!' In the meantime, Odette was tormented by how Swann's behaviour might appear to one of her friends, who had recently married a man she'd been with for less time than Odette with Swann, didn't have a child, and was now relatively high up on the social scale, receiving invitations to balls at the Élysée Palace. A wiser clinician than Monsieur de Norpois could no doubt have diagnosed that it was this feeling of humiliation and shame that had made Odette bitter, that the devilish temper she showed was not her true nature, or an incurable illness, and he could easily have predicted what had in fact happened: namely that a new regimen, the matrimonial one, would bring to a stop with an almost magical swiftness these painful attacks which, though daily, were in no way organic. Almost everyone was surprised by this marriage, and that in itself is surprising. Doubtless few people understand the purely subjective phenomenon that is love, or how it creates a kind of supplementary person, distinct from the one who bears our beloved's name in the outside world, and is mostly formed from elements drawn from our own selves. And so there are few who can find anything natural in the enormous proportions a person comes to assume in our eyes who is not the same as the one they see. In Odette's case, however, it should have been possible for people to realize that even though she'd never entirely understood Swann's mind, at least she knew the titles and details of his written works, so that the name of Vermeer* was as familiar to her as that of her dressmaker; about Swann himself, she was thoroughly acquainted with those character traits that were unknown or ridiculed by everyone else, the true, beloved image of which only a mistress or a sister possesses; and we are so attached to these features in ourselves, even to the ones we'd like most to correct, that when a woman comes to have an indulgent, amicably mocking familiarity with them, similar to the one we ourselves have, and to the one our relatives have, a lengthy affair can come to have something of the sweetness and strength of family affections. The bonds that unite us to another being are sanctified when that person adopts the same stance that we do in judging one of our flaws. And among these particular traits, there were others that belonged as much to Swann's intellect as to his character, but which, because they had roots in the latter, Odette had been able to discern more easily. She complained that when Swann turned his hand to writing and published his essays, these features couldn't be recognized as well as they could in his letters or conversation, where they abounded. She suggested he make them more prominent. Her reason for this was that it was these features she liked best in him, but since she preferred them because they were most his own, she may not have been wrong in wishing them to be more visible in his writings. Perhaps she also thought that if these writings were livelier, they might finally make him more successful, which might in turn enable her to form what at the Verdurins' she'd learned to prize above all else: a salon of her own.

Among the people who found this sort of marriage ridiculous, people who would have wondered in their own case: 'What will Monsieur de Guermantes think, what will Bréauté have to say, when I marry Mademoiselle de Montmorency?', among people who had that sort of social ideal, there would have figured, twenty years earlier,

Swann himself, the same Swann who had gone to such trouble to be elected to the Jockey Club, and who at that time had fully expected to make a brilliant marriage that, by consolidating his position, would have finally made him one of the most prominent men in Paris. However, for the images presented by such a marriage not to fade away and vanish completely, they must be nourished from without. Your most ardent dream may be to humiliate the man who has offended you. But if you hear nothing more of him, having moved to a different country, your enemy will end up having no importance whatsoever for you. If you've lost touch for twenty years with all the people for whose sake you would have liked to enter the Jockey Club or the Institut de France, the prospect of being a member of either of those associations will not be tempting in the least. In the same way, a long-standing love affair can do as much as retirement, illness, or a religious conversion to substitute new images for old. There was on Swann's part, when he married Odette, no renunciation of worldly ambitions, for Odette had long since detached him, in the spiritual sense of the word, from them. Besides, if it had not been so, it would have been all the more to his credit. It's because they entail the sacrifice of a more or less flattering position to a purely private pleasure that scandalous marriages are usually the worthiest of all (a marriage for money can't be deemed a 'scandalous marriage', since there's no instance of a couple in which one partner sold himself or herself to the other that wasn't eventually accepted by society, if only on the strength of tradition, or precedent, or in order to avoid a double standard). Perhaps, on the other hand, the artistic, if not the perverse, side of Swann would in any case have derived a certain pleasure from coupling, in one of those cross-breeding of species as practised by the Mendelians* or as narrated in mythology, with a being of a different race, an archduchess or a *cocotte*,* from contracting a royal alliance or marrying beneath himself. There had been only one person in the world whose opinion concerned him whenever he thought about his possible marriage with Odette: it was—and not out of snobbishness—the Duchesse de Guermantes. Odette, on the other hand, wasn't overly worried about her, since she thought only of the people immediately above her, rather than of those who inhabited such a vague empyrean. But when Swann in his daydreams envisaged Odette as his wife, he invariably pictured the moment he would bring her—and especially their daughter—to the home of the Princesse des Laumes,

or the Duchesse de Guermantes as she'd become upon the death of
her father-in-law. He had no desire to introduce them anywhere else,
but he'd feel deeply moved when, murmuring the words to himself,
he imagined everything the duchess would say about him to Odette,
and everything Odette would say to Madame de Guermantes, as well
as the tenderness the latter would shower upon Gilberte, spoiling her,
making him proud of his daughter. He'd act out this scene of introduction in his imagination in precise detail, just like people who picture to themselves how they'd spend a lottery prize whose amount
they've arbitrarily decided. Just as a mental image that accompanies
one of our resolutions motivates it, it could be said that the purpose
of Swann's marrying Odette was to introduce her and Gilberte,
without anyone else being present—if necessary without anyone ever
finding out—to the Duchesse de Guermantes. We'll see in time how
this social ambition, the only one he'd desired for his wife and daughter, was precisely the one whose fulfilment turned out to be denied
him, and by a veto so absolute that Swann died assuming the duchess
would never meet them. We'll see, too, how the Duchesse de Guermantes
did become friends with Odette and Gilberte after Swann's death.
And perhaps he would have been wise—since he attached so much
importance to such a trifling thing—not to form too dark an idea of
the future in this respect, and to entertain the possibility that the
desired meeting could well take place when he was no longer there to
enjoy it. The work of causality, which ends up producing pretty much
all possible results, and consequently even those that had been
thought to be the least possible, is sometimes slow, made even a little
slower by our own desire, which, by trying to accelerate it, impedes it,
or even by our very existence, and may come to fruition only after
we've stopped desiring, sometimes even living. Wasn't Swann aware
of this from his own experience, and wasn't there, in his life—like
a foreshadowing of what would happen after his death—a posthumous happiness in this marriage with Odette, whom he'd loved passionately (even though he hadn't been attracted to her at first sight),
and whom he'd married when he no longer loved her, when the being
who, in Swann, had so desired and so despaired of living his whole
life with Odette, was dead?

I began to talk about the Comte de Paris,* asking if he was a friend
of Swann's, since I was afraid the conversation might veer away from
the Swanns. 'Yes, he is,' Monsieur de Norpois replied, turning

towards me and fixing on my modest person his blue eyes in which his powers of assimilation and his great capacity for intellectual exertion floated, as if in their vital element. 'And, upon my word,' he added, addressing my father again, 'I don't think I'm overstepping the bounds of the respect I profess for the Prince (though I do not entertain personal relations with him, which would compromise my situation, unofficial though it may be) if I mention to you the rather intriguing fact that, no more than four years ago, in a little railway station in one of the Central European countries, the Prince happened to catch a glimpse of Madame Swann. Of course, no one in his entourage dared ask His Royal Highness what he thought of her. That would not have been seemly. But when by chance her name came up in conversation, then from certain signs—barely perceptible, but unmistakable—the Prince seemed quite ready to let it be understood that his impression was, in short, far from unfavourable.'

'There couldn't have been any possibility, though, that she was actually introduced to the Comte de Paris?' asked my father.

'Well! No one knows; with princes you never can tell,' Monsieur de Norpois replied. 'The most illustrious, the ones who know best how to obtain what must be rendered them, are also sometimes those who are least embarrassed about the dictates of public opinion, even the most justified sort, if it's a matter of rewarding certain connections. And it's quite certain that the Comte de Paris has always looked very kindly upon the devotion of Swann, who is a man of wit if ever there was one.'

'And what was your own impression, Your Excellency?' my mother asked, as much from politeness as from curiosity.

With all the force of an old connoisseur, which contrasted sharply with the usual moderation of his statements, Monsieur de Norpois replied: 'Quite excellent!'

And, aware that the acknowledgement of being strongly impressed by a woman (provided it's playfully done) fits into a certain widely appreciated category of conversational banter, the old diplomat chuckled to himself for a moment, until his eyes began to water and his nostrils, with their network of thin red veins, quivered.

'She is quite charming, I must say!'

'Was a writer by the name of Bergotte* at that dinner, Monsieur?' I asked shyly, to try to keep the conversation about the Swanns going.

'Yes, Bergotte was there,' Monsieur de Norpois replied, courteously inclining his head towards me, as if in his desire to be friendly with my father he attached real importance to anything connected to him, even to the questions of a boy of my age who was not used to being shown so much politeness by people like him. 'Do you know him?' he added, fixing on me that brilliant gaze whose penetration Bismarck admired.

'My son doesn't know him, but admires him very much,' my mother said.

'I must say,' said Monsieur de Norpois (who filled me with graver doubts about my own intelligence than those that usually tormented me, when I saw that what I valued a thousand times more than myself, what I considered the most exalted thing in the world, was for him on the very lowest rung of the ladder of his admirations), 'I do not share your view. Bergotte is what I call a flute player; one must, however, acknowledge that he plays pleasantly, although with many mannerisms and affectations. But it's not just that; that in itself wouldn't amount to much. His books lack musculature; you can never find what you might call a structure in his books. There's no action—or hardly any—and especially no range. His books fail at the foundation, or rather there's no foundation whatsoever. In a time like our own, when life's increasing complexity scarcely leaves us time to read, when the map of Europe has undergone profound alterations and may be on the verge of undergoing even greater ones, when so many new and threatening problems are springing up everywhere, you will surely admit that we have a right to ask a writer to be something more than a man of intellect who makes us forget, in irrelevant and Byzantine discussions on the merits of pure form, that we can be invaded at any time by a twofold influx of barbarians—from within and from without. I know that's blaspheming against the Sacrosanct School of what those gentlemen call Art for Art's Sake,* but in our time there are more urgent tasks than stringing words together in a harmonious fashion. Bergotte's style can sometimes be rather appealing, I won't deny that, but on the whole it's all quite insipid, quite flimsy, and not virile in the least. Now that I'm aware of your overblown admiration for Bergotte, I have a clearer understanding of the few lines you showed me earlier, which would be ungracious of me to overlook, since you yourself said quite straightforwardly that they were just a child's scribblings' (I had indeed said as much, but I didn't mean a word of it). 'All sins may be forgiven, especially the sins of youth. After all, quite a few others besides you have such things on their conscience, and you're not the only one who has fancied himself a poet at some point. But it's easy to see Bergotte's pernicious influence in what you showed me. Obviously, you won't be the least bit surprised when I tell you it has none of his qualities, since he's a past master in the art of a certain style (an entirely superficial art, for that matter), the bare rudiments of which you cannot begin to possess at your age. But already the defect is the same: the nonsense of putting mellifluous words together and only bothering about the meaning after the fact. That's like putting the cart before the horse. Even in Bergotte's books, all those chinoiseries of form, all those subtleties of a doddering mandarin, seem quite pointless to me. A writer has only to set off a few verbal fireworks in a pleasing manner and suddenly everyone hails a masterpiece. Masterpieces are not as commonplace as that! Bergotte does not have to his credit—in his arsenal, if I can put it that way—a novel with its sights set high, one of those books you put in the choicest section of your library. I can't see a single one like that in all his work. Still, with him, the work is infinitely better than its author. You know, he's the perfect example of what that clever fellow said, the one who claimed we should know writers only through their books. It's impossible to imagine a writer less like his books, or anyone more pretentious, more pompous, more difficult to get along with. At times he's vulgar, at other times he talks like a book—and not even like one of his own books, but like a boring book, which at least his are not—that's your Bergotte in a nutshell. He's one of the most muddle-headed, convoluted people there is—he's what an earlier generation called a sibylline, someone who makes the things he says even more unpleasant by his way of uttering them. I forget if it's Loménie or Sainte-Beuve who said the same of Alfred de Vigny.* But, unlike Vigny, Bergotte has never written anything like *Cinq-Mars* or *Le Cachet rouge*,* entire pages of which are real anthology gems.'

Stunned by what Monsieur de Norpois had just said about the piece I'd given him, thinking too of the difficulties I experienced whenever I wanted to write an essay or just give myself over to serious thought, once again I felt a keen sense of my intellectual poverty, and that I was not born for a literary life. It was true that long ago in Combray, certain humble impressions, or my reading of a few pages of Bergotte, had led me to a state of reverie that had seemed to me of great worth. But my prose poem was a reflection of that state; without a doubt Monsieur de Norpois had grasped and immediately seen through what I found beautiful in it as merely a completely deceptive mirage, since the ambassador wasn't fooled by it. On the contrary, he'd just taught me how little my work counted when I was judged from outside, objectively, by an expert who was not only extremely intelligent but also well disposed towards me. I felt dismayed, diminished; and just as my mind, like a fluid that has no dimension except that of the vase it's given, had once expanded to fill the immense capacities of genius, it now contracted, and was enclosed wholly within the narrow confines of mediocrity to which Monsieur de Norpois had suddenly enclosed it.

'Our introduction—Bergotte's and mine—' he added, turning to my father, 'couldn't help but be somewhat prickly (though even thorns, you could say, have their points). Some years ago now, Bergotte paid a visit to Vienna while I was ambassador there; he was introduced to me by the Princesse de Metternich,* came to sign the register, and intimated he would like to be invited to dinner. Now, being the representative abroad of France, to which he does after all pay honour in his work to some extent (a very limited extent, to be quite accurate), I would have overlooked the poor opinion I have of his private life. But he was not travelling alone, and what's more, he let it be known that he should not be invited without his companion. I don't think I'm any more prudish than the next man, and being a bachelor, I may perhaps have been in a position to open the Embassy's doors a little wider than if I'd been married and father of a family. Still, I confess that there is a degree of ignominy to which I could not stoop, made even more disheartening by the high moral—nay, moralizing—tone Bergotte takes in his books, where we find nothing but constant and, between ourselves, rather dull analyses, obsessive remorse, and, for minor indiscretions, veritable sermonizing (we know what that's worth) while he shows so much cynicism and lack of conscience in his private life. In short, I avoided answering; the princess took up the charge, but with no more success. As a result I doubt I'm in that individual's good books, and I'm not sure how much he appreciated Swann's thoughtfulness in inviting him at the same time as me. Unless Bergotte was the one who requested it. You never can tell, since when it comes down to it he's not all there. In fact that's his sole excuse.'

'Was Madame Swann's daughter at the dinner?' I asked Monsieur de Norpois, taking advantage, to ask my question, of the moment when we were passing into the drawing room, which enabled me to hide my emotion more easily than I could have done while sitting still at the brightly lit table.

Monsieur de Norpois, looking for a moment as if he were trying to remember, replied:

'Yes, a young lady of fourteen or fifteen? Indeed, I remember she was introduced to me before dinner as the daughter of our host. I can only say I didn't see much of her, and she went to bed quite early. Or perhaps she went out to see a friend; I'm afraid I can't quite recall. But I see you're very well informed about the Swann household.'

'I play with Mademoiselle Swann at the Champs-Élysées; she's lovely.'

'Aha, I see, I see! Indeed, she seemed charming to me as well. But I should confess to you that I doubt she'll ever come close to her mother, if I may venture to say such a thing without any intention of wounding your feelings.'

'I prefer Mademoiselle Swann's face, but I also admire her mother immensely; I go for walks in the Bois just in the hope of seeing her go by.'

'Really? But I must tell them that, they'll be flattered!'

As he was saying these words, and for a few seconds after he spoke them, Monsieur de Norpois was in the position of anyone who, hearing me talk about Swann as an intelligent man, of his family as respectable stockbrokers, of his house as a fine house, thought I would as readily speak of another man just as intelligent, of other stockbrokers just as respectable, of another house just as fine; it's the moment when a sane man chatting with a madman has not yet realized he's mad. Monsieur de Norpois knew it was only natural to take pleasure in looking at pretty women, that it's only polite, when someone speaks warmly about one of them, to pretend to believe he's in love with her, to joke about it with him and promise to aid in his designs. But by saying he would mention me to Gilberte and her mother (which would allow me, like a deity from Olympus who has taken on the fluidity of a breeze or the old man whose appearance Minerva assumes,* to penetrate, unseen, into Madame Swann's salon, to attract her attention, to occupy her thoughts, to arouse her gratitude for my admiration, to appear to her as the friend of an important man, to seem like

someone worthy of being invited to her home in the future and of
being welcomed into her family circle), this important man who was
going to exercise on my behalf the great prestige he must have in the
eyes of Madame Swann, suddenly inspired in me such a feeling of
tenderness that I could scarcely keep from kissing his soft white wrin-
kled hands, which looked as if they had stayed too long in water.
I almost acted on the impulse, though I thought no one else noticed this.
It is in fact difficult for each of us to calculate exactly the impact our
words or movements make on others; from fear of exaggerating our
own importance, and by overestimating the range of memory others
must have in order to cover a lifetime, we imagine that all the minor
details of our speech and our behaviour scarcely enter the consciousness, even less remain in the memory, of our interlocutors. That's the
sort of assumption, incidentally, criminals make when they subsequently 'rephrase' a statement they made earlier, thinking the new
version can't be compared with the one before it. But it's quite possible that, even when it comes to the immemorial existence of
humanity, the newspaper journalists' philosophy that everything is
doomed to oblivion is less true than a contrary philosophy predict-
ing that all things will last. In the same paper in which the author of
the leading article, a moralist commenting on an event, or a masterpiece, or, even more likely, a singer who has had her 'hour of fame',
writes: 'Who will remember any of this in ten years' time?', page 3
will report on a session at the Academy of Antiquities regarding
something that is in itself far less important, some minor poem, say,
dating from the time of the Pharaohs, yet which is still known in its
entirety. Perhaps it's not quite the same for a brief human lifespan.
But a few years later, when I was a guest in a house along with
Monsieur de Norpois, who seemed the surest ally I might find there
because he was a friend of my father's, indulgent, favourably inclined
towards us, and moreover accustomed by his profession and his
background to be discreet, I was told after the ambassador had left
that he'd referred to an evening long ago when he'd 'seen me about
to kiss his hand', I not only blushed to the tips of my ears, but I was
astonished to learn how different from what I would have expected
was the way in which Monsieur de Norpois spoke about me and the
very composition of his memory. This piece of gossip enlightened
me on the unexpected proportions of absent-mindedness and presence of mind, of remembrance and forgetfulness, of which the human

mind is made; and I was as marvellously surprised as on the day when I read for the first time, in a book by Maspero, that there was an exact list of hunters Ashurbanipal used to invite to his outings, ten centuries before Christ.*

'Oh! Monsieur,' I exclaimed to Monsieur de Norpois when he told me he'd let Gilberte and her mother know about the admiration I felt for them, 'if you did that, if you spoke about me to Madame Swann, my whole life would not be long enough to show you my gratitude, and that life would be forever in your debt! But I should make it clear that I don't know Madame Swann, and we've never been introduced.'

I added those last words out of a sense of scruple, so as not to seem as if I were boasting of a connection I didn't have. But even as I was uttering them, I sensed they were already to no avail, for as soon as I'd begun my little speech of thanks, its ardour provoked a glacial response: I'd seen the ambassador's face cloud over with an expression of hesitation and displeasure, and his eyes took on that vertical, narrow, oblique look (like the receding line, in the drawing of an object in perspective, of one of its sides), a look meant for that invisible listener we have inside ourselves the moment we're told something that the other listener, the person with whom we'd been conversing until then—myself, in this instance—is not supposed to hear. I realized at once that those words I'd uttered which, weak though they were when compared to the grateful effusiveness sweeping over me, I'd thought would move Monsieur de Norpois and convince him to perform a service that would have given him so little trouble, and me so much joy, were perhaps the very ones (among all those that could have been chosen, with evil intent, by people who wished me harm) that could cause him to change his mind. And, just as when a stranger with whom we've just been pleasantly exchanging seemingly mutual impressions about passers-by we agreed were vulgar suddenly reveals the pathological abyss separating us by carelessly adding, tapping his pocket: 'It's too bad I don't have my revolver with me, I'd have picked them off one by one,' Monsieur de Norpois, who knew there was nothing easier or less costly than to be recommended to Madame Swann and introduced into her circle, and who saw that for me, on the contrary, it was so valuable that it must entail great difficulty, thought that the desire I'd expressed, though seemingly normal, must be hiding an ulterior motive, some dubious intention, some previous misdeed which must explain why no one had ever

wanted to risk offending Madame Swann by putting in a good word
for me. And I understood that he'd never perform this service, that
even if he saw Madame Swann every day for years to come he wouldn't
mention me once to her. A few days later, however, he did ask her for
some information I wanted, and had my father pass it on to me. But
he hadn't thought it necessary to mention the person who was
requesting it. So she would never learn that I knew Monsieur de
Norpois, or that I so yearned to visit her house; yet this may have been
less grave a misfortune than I thought. For the second of these revelations would probably not have added much to the effectiveness,
uncertain as it was, of the first. Since the notion of her own life and
home awakened no mysterious turmoil in Odette's heart, she didn't
regard a person who knew her, who went to her home, as the fabulous
creature he appeared to one who, like me, would readily have thrown
a stone through the Swanns' window if I could have written on it that
I knew Monsieur de Norpois: I was convinced that such a message,
even if delivered in such a shocking way, would have done more to
increase my prestige in the eyes of the mistress of the house than it
would to turn her against me. But even if I *had* been able to foresee
that the mission Monsieur de Norpois didn't carry out would have
been pointless, or that it might actually have biased the Swanns
against me, I'd never have had the courage, even if Monsieur de
Norpois had been willing to carry out my request, to relieve the
ambassador of it and give up the pleasure—however disastrous its
consequences might be for me—of knowing that my name and my
person might, just for a moment, be in the same space as Gilberte,
inside her unknown house and life.

After Monsieur de Norpois had left, my father leafed through the
evening paper, while I returned to my meditations about La Berma.
The pleasure I'd felt in seeing her demanded to be brought to com-
pletion, all the more so since it fell far short of the pleasure I'd been
anticipating; and so it immediately absorbed everything able to nourish it—the merits Monsieur de Norpois had recognized in La Berma,
for instance, which my mind had swallowed in a single draught, like
a parched meadow when water is poured on it. But my father handed
me the paper, pointing to a paragraph that ran as follows: 'The performance of *Phèdre* that was given today before an enthusiastic audience, where the leading figures in the world of the arts, as well as in
the circle of critics, were noted by all, was for Madame La Berma,

who played the leading role, the occasion for a resounding triumph such as she has rarely known over the course of her prestigious career. At a later time we will dwell more fully on this production, which is a veritable landmark in the history of the theatre; let us confine ourselves here to stating that the best-qualified judges are united in declaring that such an interpretation has shed fresh new light on the role of Phèdre, which is one of the finest and most studied roles in Racine, and constitutes the purest and highest manifestation of art our era has ever been privileged to witness.' No sooner had my mind grasped this new idea of 'the purest and highest manifestation of art' than the concept joined the imperfect enjoyment I'd experienced at the theatre, adding to it a little of what it had been lacking, and their union formed something so exalting that I cried out: 'What a great artist she is!' Doubtless one might think I didn't sound entirely sincere; but one should consider, rather, all those writers who, dissatisfied with the piece they've just written, may happen to read some eulogy of Chateaubriand's genius,* or may call to mind some great artist they've dreamed of equalling, humming to themselves for example some phrase of Beethoven* the sadness of which they compare to what they wanted to portray in their prose, and are then so filled with this perception of genius that they allow it to affect how they look back on their own work, so that they see it in quite a different light than they had at first, and, hazarding an act of faith in the value of their labours, say to themselves: 'It's not so bad after all!' without realizing that the sum total which determines their final satisfaction includes the memory of Chateaubriand's brilliant pages, which they've incorporated into their own, but which they themselves did not in fact write; we should remember, too, all those men who continue to believe in the love of a mistress even though they know of nothing but her betrayals; think, too, of all those who, on the one hand, hope for some vague life-after-death (such as the inconsolable widower remembering a beloved wife, or the artist imagining the posthumous fame he might enjoy in the future) or who, on the other hand, long for a reassuring oblivion, when their conscience thinks back on the sins they might otherwise have to expiate after death; or think about the tourists delighted by the overall beauty of a journey they've just completed, although during it, day by day, they felt nothing but boredom; and then let us say whether, in the shared life led by the ideas within our minds, there's a single one of those that make us happiest that didn't first seek out, like a veritable parasite, a foreign, neighbouring idea to glean from it the greater part of the strength it lacked.

My mother didn't seem entirely pleased that my father was no longer contemplating a career in the diplomatic service for me. I think she hoped above all that a well-regulated life might discipline my nervous instability, and so her main regret was not so much that I was giving up diplomacy as that I was devoting myself to literature. 'Let it be,' my father remonstrated. 'The main thing is to take pleasure in what one does. And he's no longer a child. He knows very well now what he likes, it's not very likely he'll change, and he's capable of realizing what will make him happy in life.' My father's words, despite the freedom they granted me to attain happiness, or not to do so, at some future time, caused me a great deal of unease. His unforeseen acts of kindness, when they occurred, had long given me such a desire to kiss the flushed cheeks above his beard that it was only out of fear of displeasing him that I didn't give in to that urge. Now, just as an author might be taken aback when he sees his own dreams, which seem valueless to him because he can't separate them from himself, oblige a publisher to choose a certain kind of paper or use a typeface that might be finer than they deserve, I wondered if my desire to write was something that was important enough for my father to lavish so much kindness on its account. But especially when he spoke of my tastes that would not change, and of what was destined to make my life happy, he caused two terrible suspicions to arise in my mind. The first was that, though every day I thought of myself as being on the threshold of a life that was still pristine and would only begin the next morning, my life had already begun, and even worse, that what was about to come next wouldn't be very different from what had come before. The second suspicion, which was really nothing but another form of the first, was that I did not live outside Time, but was instead subject to its laws, just like those characters in a novel whose lives, for that very reason, used to plunge me into such sadness when I read about them in Combray, deep in my wicker basket chair. Theoretically, we know the earth turns, but in fact we do not perceive it; the ground on which we walk seems not to move, and we calmly go on with our lives. The same is true for Time in life. And to make its flight percept-ible, novelists, by wildly accelerating the speed of the hour hand, are forced to cause the reader to advance ten, twenty, or thirty years in two minutes. At the top of one page, we've left a lover full of hope; at the bottom of the next, we find him an octogenarian, painfully taking his daily walk in the courtyard of a nursing home, barely answering the words addressed to him, having forgotten the past. By saying about me: 'He isn't a child anymore, his tastes won't change,' and so on, my father had suddenly showed me myself living inside Time, and caused me to feel the same kind of sadness as if I were, though not yet the doddering inmate, one of those heroes whose life is summed up by the author, in a tone of indifference that's particularly cruel, at the end of a book: 'He seldom leaves the countryside now. He has finally settled there once and for all.'

My father, however, to forestall any criticism we might make about our guest, said to my mother: 'I must say that old Norpois was a little "stilted", as you say. When he said it wouldn't have been "seemly" to ask the Comte de Paris a question, I was afraid you'd burst out laughing.'

'Not at all,' my mother replied; 'I like it when a man of that stature and age has kept that sort of simplicity, which only goes to prove his basic honesty and good breeding.'

'I should think so! And it doesn't keep him from being sharp and intelligent either, as I know from seeing him at the Commission, where he's quite different from the way he seems here,' my father exclaimed, happy to see that Maman appreciated Monsieur de Norpois, and wanting to convince her that he was even better than she thought, since a good-hearted person magnifies a friend's qualities with as much pleasure as a small-minded one takes in minimizing them. 'What was that he said: "With princes you never know"?'

'Yes, that was it. I noticed that, it was very clever. It's so obvious he has a vast experience of life.'

'It's extraordinary he dined at the Swanns' and found respectable people there, government officials. Where on earth could Madame Swann have dug all those people up?'

'Did you notice the mischievous way he said: "It's a house to which mostly men go"?'

And they both tried to reproduce the way Monsieur de Norpois had said this phrase, as they would have done for some intonation of Bressant's or Thiron's voice in *L'Aventurière* or in *Le Gendre de Monsieur Poirier*.* But the person most delighted by one of Monsieur de Norpois' sayings was Françoise, who, even years later, couldn't 'keep a straight face' if she was reminded that she'd been described by the ambassador as a 'first-rate chef', a compliment my mother had conveyed to her in the kitchen like a minister of war passing on the congratulations of a visiting sovereign after reviewing the troops. I, incidentally, had preceded my mother into the kitchen. For I'd made Françoise, a cruel pacifist, promise that she wouldn't make the rabbit she had to kill suffer too much, and I hadn't yet received news of its death; Françoise assured me it had passed away as peacefully and swiftly as possible: 'I never saw an animal like that; it died without saying a single word, you'd have thought it was dumb.' Not very well informed about the language of beasts, I inferred that perhaps the rabbit didn't squawk, the way chickens do. 'Just you wait and see', Françoise said to me, indignant at my ignorance, 'if rabbits don't squawk just as much as chickens. Their voices are even louder!' Françoise accepted the compliments of Monsieur de Norpois with the proud simplicity, the joyful and—even if it was momentary—intelligent look of an artist hearing his art discussed. My mother had once sent her to certain great restaurants to see how the cooking was done there. That evening I heard her call the most famous ones 'chop shops' with the same pleasure I felt once when I learned, about actors, that their degree of merit did not at all equal that of their reputation. 'The ambassador', my mother told her, 'is adamant that cold beef or soufflés as good as yours can't be found anywhere else!' Françoise, with the modest air of one accepting a simple statement of fact, agreed, without being at all impressed by the title of ambassador; she said about Monsieur de Norpois, with the benignity due to one who had taken her for a chef: 'He's a good old soul, just like me.' She'd tried to catch a glimpse of him when he arrived, but, knowing that Maman hated it when people hid behind doors or windows, and thinking that Maman would find out from the other servants or gossips that she was on the lookout for him (for Françoise saw everywhere nothing but 'rumour-mongers' and 'telltales', who played the same unchanging sinister role in her imagination as, for some others, the intrigues of the Jesuits or the Jews), she'd confined herself to peering through the kitchen hatch 'so as not to have words with Madame' and, from a brief glimpse of Monsieur de Norpois, she'd thought he was 'the spitting image of Monsieur Legrandin' because of his 'agility', even though there was not a single thing in common between them.

'But really,' my mother asked her, 'how do you explain why no one can make aspic as well as you (when you set your mind to it)?' 'I don't know how that becomes about,' replied Françoise (who made no clear distinction between the verbs 'to come', in some of its usages, and 'to become'). She was telling the truth, moreover, at least in part, and was no more capable—or desirous—of unveiling the mystery behind the superiority of her aspics or custards than a smartly dressed woman of her toilette, or a great singer of her voice. Their explanations don't tell us much; the same was true for the recipes of our cook. 'They cook in too much of a hurry,' she said, speaking of the grand restaurants, 'and they don't make everything together. The beef has to become like a sponge, so it can drink up all the juice to the last drop. Still, there *was* one of those cafés where they seemed to know a little about cooking. I'm not saying it was the same as my aspic, but it was done slowly, and the soufflés had lots of cream.'

'Do you mean at the Henry?' asked my father, who had joined us, and who had a high opinion of the restaurant on the Place Gaillon, where he went regularly for official dinners with his colleagues. 'Oh no!' said Françoise, concealing her profound contempt in a mild tone. 'I meant a little restaurant. At that Henry's, they're very good of course, but it's not a restaurant, it's more of a . . . soup kitchen!' 'Weber's, then?' 'Oh, no, Monsieur, I meant a *good* restaurant. Weber's is on the Rue Royale, and it's not a restaurant but a brasserie. I don't even know if what they give you is properly served—I think they don't even use tablecloths! They just plop things down willy-nilly on the table, without even a by-your-leave.' 'Cirro's, then?' Françoise replied with a smile: 'Oh! there I think the dishes are mostly ladies of the world.' (For Françoise, *monde* meant *demi-monde*.*) 'Of course, you need them to draw the young folk.' We could see that with her seeming simplicity, Françoise was for famous chefs a more daunting 'colleague' than the most demanding and self-satisfied actress. But we felt that she had a proper feeling for her art and a respect for tradition, for she added: 'No, I mean a restaurant where it looked like they had good old plain home cooking. It's still a grand sort of place. It did a lot of business—you should see how they were raking in the sous!' (The economical Françoise counted in sous, leaving the golden louis* to reckless gamblers.) 'Madame knows it well, on the right, along the big boulevards, set back a little bit . . .' The restaurant she spoke of with such fair-mindedness mingled with pride and kindly indulgence was . . . the Café Anglais.*

When New Year's Day arrived, I first paid a round of family visits with Maman, who, so as not to tire me, had (with the help of an

itinerary drawn up by my father) sorted them in advance by neighbourhood rather than by precise degree of kinship. But scarcely had
we entered the drawing room of a rather distant cousin (visited first
because her home was not far from ours) than my mother was horrified to see there, with his candied or chocolate-covered chestnuts in
hand, the best friend of the most sensitive of my uncles, who would
then be informed that we hadn't begun our round with him. This
uncle would surely be offended; he would have thought it only natural for us to go all the way from the Madeleine to his house, near the
Jardin des Plantes, then come all the way back to Saint-Augustin
before setting off for the Rue de l'École de Médecine across the river.

Once the visits were over (my grandmother excused us from calling
on her, since we'd be dining with her later that day), I ran to the
Champs-Élysées to carry to our favourite stall-holder, so that she'd
deliver it to the person who came by several times a week from the
Swanns' to buy gingerbread, the letter which, on the day my dear
friend had made me so unhappy, I'd decided to send her at the New
Year, and in which I told her our former friendship had died with the
old year, that I'd forget my grievances and disappointments, and that
starting from this New Year, we'd build a new friendship, so solid that
nothing would be able to destroy it, so marvellous that I hoped
Gilberte would go out of her way to preserve it in all its beauty, and
would warn me in good time (as I promised to do myself) of any danger, however slight, that might jeopardize it. On my way back,
Françoise made me stop at an open-air stall on the corner of the Rue
Royale, where she picked out, for her own New Year's gifts, some
photographs of Pope Pius IX and Raspail,* and where I bought one
of La Berma. She inspired such a myriad of admiring expressions
that the single face she had to respond to them seemed slightly impoverished, unchanging, and fragile, like an outfit worn by someone who
has no other clothes to change into; and all she could reveal in this
face was the little groove above her upper lip, her arched eyebrows,
and a few other physical peculiarities, always the same ones, which,
when it came down to it, were at the mercy of a burn or a wound. It
was a face that wouldn't have seemed beautiful to me on its own, but
it gave me the idea—and consequently the desire—to kiss it because
of all the kisses it must have received before and because, from the
'album photo', it seemed to be beckoning still with that coquettishly
tender gaze and that artificially ingenuous smile. For La Berma must

in fact have felt for many young men the desires she confessed in the guise of Phèdre; and everything, even the prestige of her name, which added to her beauty and extended her youth, must make it easy for her to satisfy those desires. Night was falling; I paused in front of a Morris column* where the performance that La Berma was giving on New Year's Day was posted. A humid, gentle breeze was blowing. It was weather I knew well; I had the sudden feeling and presentiment that New Year's Day was not a day any different from the others, that it was not the first day of a new world in which, with my fate still undecided, I could remake my acquaintance with Gilberte as though on the very first day of Creation, as if the past didn't yet exist, as if the disappointments she'd sometimes caused me had been wiped away, along with the conclusions I could have drawn from them for the future: a new world where nothing survived of the old . . . except one thing: my desire that Gilberte would love me. I understood that if my heart yearned for this renewal, around it, of a universe that had not satisfied it, it was because my heart hadn't changed; and I told myself that there was no reason for Gilberte's to have changed either; I sensed that this new friendship was exactly the same, just as each new year is not separated from the one before by a chasm; they lie beyond our reach, oblivious to our attempts to change them by giving them a different name. Though I might dedicate this New Year to Gilberte, and try to imprint on New Year's Day the particular idea I'd formed of it, just as we superimpose a religion on the blind laws of nature, it was in vain; I felt it did not know we called it New Year's Day, that it was coming to an end in dusk in a way that was not new to me: in the gentle breeze wafting around the poster kiosk, I'd recognized, I'd sensed, the reappearance of all the old days, with their shared, eternal substance, their familiar humidity, their oblivious fluidity.

I went back home. I had just experienced the New Year's Day of old men, who are unlike the young on that day, not because no one gives them New Year's gifts anymore, but because they no longer believe in the New Year. Gifts I'd received, but not the only one that could have given me any pleasure: a note from Gilberte. But I was still young all the same, because I'd been able to write one to her which, by telling her the solitary dreams arising from my affection, I hoped would awaken similar ones in her. The sadness of men who have grown old lies in not even thinking of writing such letters, since they've learned how pointless they are.

After I'd gone to bed, the noises of the street, which continued late into that celebratory evening, kept me awake. I thought of all the people who would be ending their night in pleasure, the lover, or the band of debauchees perhaps, who must have gone looking for La Berma after the performance I'd seen advertised for this evening. To calm the agitation this idea aroused in me on that night of insomnia, I couldn't even tell myself that La Berma might not have been thinking of love, since the lines she'd recited, which she'd studied for so long, reminded her every moment how delightful love is, which of course she already knew so well that she projected its familiar heartaches—though fraught with fresh violence and unsuspected sweetness—to spectators who were amazed, even though each had felt them for himself. I lighted my extinguished candle again to look once more at her face. At the thought that it was probably at that moment being caressed by those men whom I couldn't help but imagine with La Berma and receiving from her superhuman, vague joys, I experienced an emotion more cruel than voluptuous, a yearning that was soon made more painful by the sound of the hunting horn, the kind you hear on the night of mid-Lent and often on other celebrations, which, because it's devoid of poetry, is sadder, coming from a tavern, than it is 'at evening, from deep within the woods'.* At that moment a note from Gilberte may not have been what I needed. Our desires interfere with each other, and in the confusion of existence, it's rare for happiness to pair with the same desire that had longed for it.

I continued going to the Champs-Élysées on days when the weather was fine, along streets whose elegant, rose-coloured houses seemed bathed (since it was a time when watercolour exhibitions were so in fashion) in a shifting, pastel sky. I'd be lying if I said that in those days Gabriel's palaces* struck me as seeming more beautiful, or even as belonging to another era, than the neighbouring houses. I found more style, and would have supposed more antiquity, if not in the Palais de l'Industrie, then at least in the Trocadéro.* Plunged in a restless sleep, my adolescence encompassed the whole neighbourhood through which it walked in a single dream, and I'd never have thought there could be an eighteenth-century building on the Rue Royale, just as I'd have been shocked to learn that the Porte Saint-Martin and the Porte Saint-Denis, masterpieces from the time of Louis XIV, were not contemporary with the most recent apartment houses in these sordid *arrondissements*.* Only once did one of Gabriel's palaces make me pause at length: night had fallen, and its columns, dematerialized by the moonlight, looked as if they were cut out of cardboard, and, reminding me of a set from the operetta *Orphée aux Enfers*,* struck me for the first time as beautiful.

Gilberte, however, still hadn't returned to the Champs-Élysées. And yet I needed to see her, for I couldn't even remember her face. The searching, anxious, demanding way we have of looking at the person we love, our expectation of the word that will give or take from us the hope for a meeting the next day, and, until that word is said, our alternating, or even simultaneous, imaginings of joy and despair— all this conspires, when we're in the presence of our beloved, to make our attention too tremulous to be able to obtain a clear image of her. Perhaps, too, this activity of all the senses at once, trying to discover with the eyes alone what lies beyond them, may be too taken in by all the myriad forms, tastes, movements of the living person whom usually, when we are not in love, we immobilize in our minds. The beloved subject, on the other hand, is forever in motion, and so we retain only blurred images of her. I no longer really knew what Gilberte's features were like, except in those exquisite moments when she revealed them to me; I could remember nothing but her smile. And, unable to see again that beloved face, however much I strove to remember it, I was irritated to find, drawn in my memory with minute precision, the meaningless, striking faces of the merry-go-round attendant and the lady who sold barley sugar, just as people who have lost a beloved, whom they can never manage to see again in their sleep, are exasperated to find their dreams incessantly filled with so many of those who were hard enough to bear in the waking state. In their inability to envisage the object of their grief, they almost accuse themselves of having no grief. As for myself, I was not far from believing that, unable to remember Gilberte's features, I'd forgotten her very being, and I no longer loved her. At last she came back to play almost every day, setting before me new things to desire, to ask of her, for the next day, in this sense indeed transforming my affection for her into a new one every day. But then, abruptly, something happened that would change once more the way in which, around two o'clock in the afternoon, I was confronted with the problem of my love. Had Monsieur Swann discovered the letter I'd written to his daughter, or was Gilberte only admitting to me long afterwards, so that I'd be more prudent, a state

of affairs that was already quite old? As I was telling her how much
I admired her father and mother, she began to have that vague look,
full of reticence and secrecy, which she always wore whenever we
spoke about her obligations, her errands and visits, and she suddenly
blurted out: 'They can't stand you, you know!' and she burst out
laughing, as she slipped away like the water-spirit she so resembled.
Often her laughter was at odds with her words and seemed, like music,
to be outlining an invisible surface on another plane. Monsieur and
Madame Swann were not demanding that Gilberte stop playing with
me, but she thought they'd rather our relationship had never begun.
They took a dim view of our friendship, didn't think my intentions
were honourable, and were convinced I could only be a bad influence
on their daughter. I pictured the sort of unscrupulous young person
Swann thought I resembled as hating the parents of the young woman
he loves, flattering them when they're present, but mocking them
when he's with her, urging her to disobey them, and, once he's won
their daughter over, going so far as to prevent them from seeing her.
With these characteristics (which are never those with which the
worst scoundrel views himself), how violently my heart contrasted
the feelings it actually had for Swann, which were so passionate that
I had no doubt that, if he'd suspected them, he would have repented
of his condemnation of me as an egregious error of judgement! All
I felt for him I dared to write in a long letter that I entrusted to
Gilberte, asking her to deliver it to him. She agreed. Alas! he must
have seen me as an even greater impostor than I thought; the feelings
I'd thought fit to describe, in sixteen pages, with so much candour,
made him suspicious; the letter I wrote to him, as ardent and sincere
as the words I'd said to Monsieur de Norpois, met with no more success. Gilberte told me the next day, after pulling me aside behind
a thicket of laurels, in a little lane where we each sat down on a chair,
that as her father had read the letter, which she had brought to give
back to me, he'd shrugged and said: 'None of this means anything, it
just proves how right I was.' I, who knew the purity of my intentions
and the goodness of my soul, was indignant that my words hadn't had
any effect whatsoever on Swann's absurd error. For it was an error;
I had no doubt about that. I felt I'd described so precisely certain
undeniable characteristics of my generous sentiments that the only
reason Swann hadn't immediately recognized them, or come to ask
my forgiveness and acknowledge his mistake, must be because he'd

never felt such noble sentiments himself, and was therefore incapable of understanding them in others.

But perhaps it was simply because Swann knew that magnanimity is often only the outward aspect our selfish motivations assume when we haven't yet named or recognized them. Perhaps he'd recognized my declarations of affection for him as merely the effect—and enthusiastic confirmation—of my love for Gilberte; and perhaps he foresaw that my subsequent actions would inevitably be governed by this love, and not by my secondary veneration for himself. I couldn't share his surmises, for I hadn't managed to abstract my love from myself, to make it fit into the same general category as any other love, and to make an experimental calculation of its consequences; I was in despair. I had to leave Gilberte for a moment since Françoise had called me. She wanted me to go with her to a little green-trellised pavilion, somewhat like the disused tollbooths of old Paris,* in which there had recently been installed what the English call a *lavabo* and the French, in their misguided Anglomania, *water-closets*.* In the entrance, where I stood waiting for Françoise, the damp old walls gave off a cool musty smell which, immediately relieving me of the anxiety provoked by Swann's words as conveyed by Gilberte, filled me with a pleasure not of the same kind as other pleasures, which leave us more unstable, incapable of holding on to them or possessing them, but rather with a substantial pleasure on which I could depend: delightful, peaceful, rich with lasting truth, inexplicable and sure. I'd have liked to try, as I did in my walks along the Guermantes way long ago, to fathom the charm of this impression that had come over me and, without moving, to examine this bygone redolence which invited me not to enjoy the pleasure it gave me simply as something added, but to delve down into the reality it hadn't yet revealed to me. But the matron of the establishment, an old lady with thickly powdered cheeks and a red wig, began talking to me. Françoise thought she came from 'her own localities'. Her daughter had married what Françoise called 'a well-off young man', which meant that he differed more from a common labourer in her eyes than, in Saint-Simon's, a duke did from a man 'belonging to the dregs of the people'.* Doubtless the matron had suffered some setbacks before she became what she was. But Françoise swore she'd been a 'marquise' and belonged to the Saint-Ferréol family. This 'marquise' advised me not to stay out in the cold and even opened a stall for me, saying: 'Don't you want to go in? Here's a nice clean one, no charge for you.' Perhaps she was doing this only the way the young ladies at Gouache's,* when we'd just placed an order, would offer me one of the sweets they kept under glass domes on the counter, which Maman, alas, forbade me from accepting; or perhaps it was done less innocently, like the old florist who used to help Maman fill her flower-stands, who would make eyes at me while offering me a rose. In any case, if the 'marquise' had a weakness for little boys when she opened for them the hypogeal door of these stone cubicles, where men crouch like sphinxes, the aim of her generosity must have been less a hope to corrupt them than the pleasure we all feel in selflessly indulging those we love, for I never saw her with any visitor other than an old park warden.

A moment later I took my leave of the 'marquise' along with Françoise, then left her to return to Gilberte. I saw her right away on a chair behind the thicket of laurels; she was hiding from her friends, with whom she was playing hide-and-seek. I went over to sit beside her. She was wearing a flat toque that came down low over her eyes, giving them the same furtive, dreamy, sly look I remembered from the first time I'd seen her in Combray. I asked her if there was some way I could talk things over with her father. Gilberte said she'd suggested that to him, but he thought it pointless. 'Here,' she went on, 'take your letter back. We should get back to the others, since they haven't found me.'

If Swann had arrived then before I'd taken back that letter, the sincerity of which I thought he'd been so unreasonable to doubt, he might have seen that he was the one who was right. For, as I came close to Gilberte, who, leaning back in her chair, told me to take the letter but didn't hold it out to me, I felt so attracted by her body that I said: 'Come on then, try to stop me from getting it, we'll see who's stronger.'

She put it behind her back; I slid my hand behind her neck, lifting the braids she wore over her shoulders, either because she was still the age for it, or because her mother wanted to keep her looking like a child so that she herself would appear younger, and we wrestled, interlocked. I tried to pull her towards me, and she resisted; her cheeks, flushed by the effort, were red and round as cherries; she laughed as if I'd tickled her; I held her tight between my legs like a sapling I wanted to climb; and, in the middle of all my exertions, not much more breathless than I already was by the muscular exercise and the fervour of the game, like a few drops of sweat wrung from me by the effort, I spilled my pleasure, before I even had time to analyse it; immediately I snatched the letter from her. Then Gilberte said in a friendly tone: 'You know, if you like, we could wrestle a bit more.'

Perhaps she'd obscurely sensed my sport had a different purpose from the one I claimed, yet hadn't realized that I'd already attained it. And since I was afraid she'd noticed (and a slight movement of recoil and restraint, as of offended modesty, which she made a moment later made me think I wasn't far wrong), I agreed to carry on wrestling, lest she think I had no other goal than the one that left me wishing only to sit calmly beside her.

On my way home I perceived—I suddenly remembered—the image, hidden till then, of which the cold, almost sooty smell of the trellised pavilion reminded me, without letting me see or recognize it. This image was that of my uncle Adolphe's little room in Combray, which in fact gave off the same musty smell. But I was unable to understand, and I put off till later my investigation into why remembering such an insignificant image had given me such happiness. In the meantime, it seemed to me that I truly deserved Monsieur de Norpois' contempt: from the whole panoply of writers, I'd chosen the one he called a simple 'flute player', and a real exaltation had been conveyed to me, not by some important idea, but by a smell of mildew.

For some time, in certain families, the name of the Champs-Élysées, if a visitor uttered it, would be greeted by mothers with the hostile air they reserve for a renowned doctor they claim has made too many wrong diagnoses for them to place any trust in him; they'd insist that its gardens weren't good for children, and that they could list more than one sore throat, more than one case of measles, and a number of fevers for which the gardens were responsible. While not openly calling into question the affection of Maman, who continued to let me go there, some of her friends deplored her lack of foresight.

Neurotics are perhaps, despite the expression used for them, the least 'hypersensitive' of all: they diagnose themselves as having so many disorders which they subsequently realize they were wrong to be worried about, that they end up paying no attention whatsoever to any of them. Their nervous system has so often cried 'wolf', as if it were faced with some grave illness, when it was simply a matter of impending snow or a move to a new apartment, that they acquire the habit of taking no more account of these warnings than a soldier who, in the heat of battle, pays so little attention to them that, even though he's dying, he's able to go on leading the life of a healthy man for a few more days. One morning, bearing within me my usual ailments, keeping my mind as averted from their constant internal circulation as I did from the circulation of my blood, I was running cheerfully into the dining room, where my parents were already seated, and—having told myself as usual that feeling cold can mean not that you should try to get warm, but, for instance, that you've been scolded, and that not feeling hungry meant it was going to rain, rather than that you should refrain from eating—I sat down, and, the instant I swallowed the first mouthful of an appetizing cutlet, nausea and dizziness made me stop: this was the feverish response of an illness that had just begun, the symptoms of which my cold indifference had masked and delayed, but which stubbornly refused the food I was not able to absorb. Then, in the same instant, like a wounded man's instinct of self-preservation, the thought that I'd be prevented from going out if my parents noticed I was ill gave me the strength to drag myself to my bedroom, where I saw I had a fever of forty degrees, and then to get ready to go to the Champs-Élysées. Through the sickly, weak body that enclosed them, my cheerful thoughts were already there, demanding to share the sweet pleasure of a game of prisoner's base with Gilberte, and an hour later, barely able to stand upright, but happy to be beside her, I still had enough strength to enjoy it.

When we returned home, Françoise declared I'd 'taken a turn', that I must have caught 'hot and cold', and the doctor, summoned immediately, declared he 'would rather have' the 'severity', the 'virulence' of the high fever that accompanied my lung congestion, and that it would be 'only a flash in the pan' compared to more 'insidious' and 'latent' forms. For some time now I'd been subject to fits of shortness of breath; and our doctor, despite the disapproval of my grandmother, who pictured me dying an early death as an alcoholic, had recommended that, in addition to the caffeine that was prescribed to help me breathe, I should have some beer, champagne, or cognac when I felt a crisis coming on. Such crises, he said, would be cut short by the alcohol-induced 'euphoria'. In order for my grandmother to allow me to have such a drink, I was often obliged, not to hide my shortness of breath, but rather to exaggerate it. What's more, as soon as I felt it coming on, never sure of how bad it might be, I was made even more anxious because of my grandmother's sadness, which

I feared much more than my own suffering. But at the same time, my body, either because it was too weak to keep this secret to itself, or because it feared that someone unaware of the imminent illness might ask me to make an effort that was impossible or dangerous for it, made me need to warn my grandmother of my discomfort with an exactitude which I came to invest with a sort of physiological compunction. If I perceived in myself an annoying symptom I hadn't yet fathomed, my body would remain distressed until I communicated it to my grandmother. If she pretended not to pay any attention to it, it would make me insist. Sometimes I'd go too far; and the beloved face, no longer as capable of mastering its emotions as it used to be, winced with pain and let an expression of pity appear. Then my heart would be wrung by the sight of her suffering, and, as if my kisses could chase away her grief, as if my love could give my grandmother as much joy as my recovery, I'd throw myself into her arms. And since its scruples were appeased by the certainty that she was aware of the illness I felt, my body wouldn't stop me from comforting her. I'd assure her that there was nothing really painful about this ailment, that I was not to be pitied at all, that she could be certain I was happy; my body had wanted to obtain precisely the amount of pity it deserved, and as long as someone knew it had a pain in its right side, it had nothing against my declaring that this pain was neither serious nor an obstacle to my happiness, since my body didn't pride itself on philosophy; that was outside its jurisdiction. I had these fits of breathlessness almost every day during my convalescence. One evening, when my grandmother had left me in a relatively good state, she returned to my room very late in the evening, and seeing that I was struggling to breathe, she exclaimed, her features contorted with grief: 'Oh, my dear, how you're suffering!' She left me at once; I heard the door to the street open, and she returned a little later with some brandy, which she'd rushed out to buy since there was none in the house. Soon I began to feel better. My grandmother, a little flushed, looked embarrassed, and there was a look of weariness and despondency in her eyes.

'I think I should leave you alone now, and let you enjoy this improvement a little,' she said, turning quickly to go. I kissed her, however, and felt something wet on her cool cheeks, but I couldn't tell if it was from the damp night air she'd just walked through. The next day, she didn't come to my room till evening because, I was told, she had to go out. I thought this showed a rather indifferent attitude towards me, and it was all I could do not to reproach her for it.

Since my attacks of breathlessness inexplicably persisted, long after my congestion had gone away, my parents called in Professor Cottard for consultation. It's not enough for a doctor called in for cases like this to be knowledgeable. Faced with symptoms that can be those of three or four different illnesses, ultimately it's his intuition, his cursory glance, which decide which illness, despite appearances that are all more or less alike, is the probable cause. This mysterious gift does not imply superiority in other areas of intelligence, and a person of great vulgarity, who admires the worst paintings, the worst music, and has no intellectual curiosity, could certainly possess it. In my case, what was externally observable might have been caused by nervous spasms, an early stage of tuberculosis, asthma, toxic-alimentary dyspnoea* brought on by poorly functioning kidneys, chronic bronchitis, or even a complex condition in which several of these factors were at play. While nervous spasms should be treated with scorn, tuberculosis should be treated with great care and with a kind of overfeeding which would be bad for an arthritic condition like asthma and could be dangerous in a case of toxic-alimentary dyspnoea, which requires a diet quite harmful for a tubercular patient. But Cottard hesitated only briefly, and his orders were imperious: 'Strong, drastic purgatives. Milk for several days, nothing but milk. No meat, no alcohol.' My mother murmured that I still needed to have my strength built up, that I was already quite nervous, that this drastic purge and diet would weaken me. I saw in Cottard's eyes, which looked anxious, as if he were afraid of missing a train, that he was wondering whether he'd allowed his naturally mild manner to show through. He was trying to recall if he'd remembered to assume his cold mask, the way you look for a mirror to see if you've forgotten to knot your tie. In his doubt, and so as to compensate just in case, he replied rudely: 'I am not in the habit of repeating my prescriptions. Give me a pen. Milk above all. Later on, when we've curbed the fits of breathlessness and the agrypnia, I want you to take some soup, then some broth, but always with milk, milk! You'll like that, since Spain is all the rage these days—*olé! au lait!*'* (His students were very familiar with this pun, which he'd make at the hospital whenever he placed a patient with a heart or liver disorder on a milk diet.) 'Then you'll slowly get back to normal. But whenever the cough and breathlessness return, purgatives, enemas, bed, and milk!' Without replying, he listened coldly to my mother's final objections, and as he left us without deigning to explain the reasons for this regime, my parents decided it had no relation to my case, was needlessly debilitating, and did not make me try it. Naturally they sought to hide their disobedience from the professor, and in order to make sure of this, they avoided all the houses where they might have met. Then, since my state was worsening, they decided to have me follow Cottard's orders to the letter; after three days I had no more rattles in my chest, no more coughs, and I could breathe easily. Then we understood that Cottard, while finding me as he later said quite asthmatic and, above all, prone to 'make things up', had discerned that what predominated in me at that moment was a toxic reaction, and that by clearing out my liver and cleaning my kidneys, my lungs would be decongested and my breath would return, along with sleep and strength. And we realized that this seeming idiot was a great clinical practitioner. At last I was able to get up. But I heard my parents say I might not be allowed to go to the Champs-Élysées anymore. They said it was because of the bad air, but I thought they were using that excuse to stop me from seeing Mademoiselle Swann; and I made myself say Gilberte's name over and over, like the native language the conquered try to keep using so as not to forget the homeland they'll never see again. Sometimes my mother would stroke my forehead and say:

'So, then, little boys don't tell their mothers their sorrows anymore?'

Every day Françoise would come over to me and say: 'Monsieur looks something terrible! You should see yourself, you look like death warmed up!' Of course, if I'd had a simple cold, Françoise would have assumed the same funereal air. These laments stemmed more from her 'class' than from my state of health. I couldn't figure out if this pessimism of Françoise's was sorrowful or gleeful. I concluded provisionally that it was social and professional.

One day, after the post had arrived, my mother put a letter on my bed. I opened it absent-mindedly since it couldn't possibly bear the only signature that could have made me happy—Gilberte's, with whom I hadn't had any contact away from the Champs-Élysées. At the foot of the page, stamped with a silver seal showing a helmeted knight surmounting the scrolled motto *Per viam rectam*,* at the end of a letter written in sprawling handwriting, in which almost all the sentences seemed to be underlined simply because the crosses of the *t*s were written not through them but above them, thereby placing a line beneath the corresponding word in the line above, it was indeed Gilberte's signature that I saw. But because I knew this was impossible in a letter addressed to me, this sight, unaccompanied by belief, brought me no joy. For an instant it only gave everything around me an air of unreality. With dizzying speed, this unlikely signature sent everything in my room—the bed, the fireplace, the wall—reeling. Whatever I looked at seemed to be swaying, as if I'd just fallen from a horse; and I wondered whether there might not be an existence entirely different from the one I knew, in contradiction to it but more real than it, which, suddenly revealed to me, filled me with the hesitation that sculptors portraying the Last Judgement show on the faces of the awakened dead, who find themselves on the threshold of the other world. 'My dear friend,' the letter said, 'I heard you've been very ill and aren't going to the Champs-Élysées anymore. I myself hardly ever go there because there are so many sick people. But my friends come to my house for tea every Monday and Friday. Maman asks me to tell you that we would be very happy if you came too, as soon as you're better, and we could go on having at home the nice chats we had at the Champs-Élysées. Goodbye, my dear friend, I hope your parents will allow you to come very often to tea, and I send you all my best wishes. Gilberte.'

While I was reading these words, my nervous system, with admirable diligence, was receiving the news that great joy had befallen me. But my mind—that is, I myself, the main interested party—was still unaware of that. Happiness—happiness from Gilberte—was a thing I'd constantly dreamed of, existing only in thought; it was, as Leonardo da Vinci said about painting, a *cosa mentale*.* A leaf of paper covered with characters is not something which thought can assimilate right away. But as soon as I'd finished reading it, I reflected on it, and it became an object of daydream; it too became a *cosa mentale*, and I felt such love for it that every five minutes I had to read it over again and kiss it. Finally, I was able to experience my happiness.

Life is strewn with these miracles, for which people who love can always hope. It's possible that this particular miracle might have been artificially brought about by my mother, who, seeing that for quite some time I'd lost all pleasure in living, may have had someone ask Gilberte to write to me, just as, when I was learning to swim in the sea, in order to make me enjoy swimming underwater, which I hated

beeause it cut off my breath, she'd secretly give my swimming instructor wonderful boxes made of shells and branches of coral, which
I thought I myself had discovered on the sea floor. In any case, it's
best not to try to understand how life, with all its contrasting situations, influences love, since, in both their inexorable and unhoped-
for qualities, they seem to be ruled by laws more magical than rational.
When a multimillionaire—a charming man despite his money—is
abandoned by a poor, unattractive woman with whom he's been living, and in his despair summons up all the powers of his wealth and
sets in motion all the influences of the world, without managing to get
her to come back to him, it's better, faced with his mistress's stubborn
resolve, to suppose that Fate wants to crush him and make him die of
a broken heart than to look for a logical explanation. The obstacles
against which such a lover has to struggle, which his imagination,
overstimulated by suffering, seeks in vain to fathom, may lie in some
singularity of character in the woman he can't bring back, in her stupidity, in the influence exercised on her by people the lover doesn't
know, in fears they may have put in her mind, or in the kind of pleasures she wants out of life at that moment, pleasures that neither her
lover nor her lover's wealth can offer her. Whatever the case, the lover
who seeks to know the nature of these obstacles, which the woman
cleverly hides from him, is hindered by his own judgement, which is
distorted by love, preventing him from assessing it accurately. They're
like tumours the doctor succeeds in reducing without ever learning
their cause: though temporary, they keep all their mystery. Only, such
obstacles usually last longer than the love itself. And since love is not
a disinterested passion, the lover who has stopped loving doesn't try
to find out why the penniless, flighty woman he once loved kept
obstinately refusing to stay with him.

In love, the same mystery that can hide from our eyes the causes of
catastrophe just as often shrouds sudden outcomes that are happier
(like the one Gilberte's letter brought me). Or rather, they seem happier, since none can be truly happy where a feeling is concerned:
whatever satisfaction we can bring to it usually only shifts the pain it
entails. Sometimes, though, a truce is granted, and for a time we may
have the illusion of being cured.

Concerning this letter (at the foot of which Françoise refused to
recognize Gilberte's name because the storiated *G*, leaning on an
undotted *i*, looked like an *A*, while the last syllable was extended

indefinitely with the help of a curling flourish), if one were to try to find a rational explanation for the change of heart it expressed, and which filled me with such joy, one might find that I was to some extent indebted to an incident that I'd actually thought was the kind that might make me lose favour with the Swanns forever. Not long before, Bloch had come to see me, at a time when Professor Cottard, who'd been visiting regularly since I started following his regimen, was in my room. After the consultation was over, and Cottard was lingering simply as a visitor because my parents had asked him to stay for dinner, Bloch was allowed in. As we were all chatting, Bloch having said that he'd heard that Madame Swann liked me very much—this from a person with whom he'd dined the previous evening, and who was very close to Madame Swann—I'd have liked to reply that he must be wrong, and to make it clear, by the same scruple that made me declare it to Monsieur de Norpois, and from fear that Madame Swann might take me for a liar, that I did not know her and had never spoken with her. But I didn't have the courage to correct Bloch's mistake, because I understood it was intentional, and because if he was inventing something that Madame Swann had not in fact said, it was in order to convey something he thought flattering but was not true, namely that he'd dined with one of Madame Swann's friends. Now it happened that whereas Monsieur de Norpois, learning that I did not know Madame Swann but would very much like to, had been careful to avoid mentioning me to her, Cottard, who was her doctor, having deduced from what he'd heard from Bloch that she knew me well and liked me, thought to himself that, when next he saw her, if he told her I was a charming boy whom he knew well, it would be of no advantage to me but would make him appear in a good light—two reasons which made him decide to put in a good word for me to Odette as soon as the opportunity arose.

And so I was introduced to the apartment from which Madame Swann's perfume wafted out even into the staircase, a scent made even more fragrant by the distinctive, melancholy charm emanating from the life of Gilberte. When I asked the erstwhile implacable concierge, now transformed into a kindly Eumenid,* if I could go up, he took to raising his cap with an auspicious hand, to show he was granting my prayer. Sometimes, when the weather was warm and I'd spent a whole afternoon with Gilberte in her room, it fell to me to open the very windows which, from the outside, had once interposed between me and the treasures not meant for me a bright, distant, superficial gaze that seemed to me the very gaze of the Swanns; now I was the one to let a little fresh air in and even lean out of them beside her, if it was her mother's at-home day, to see the arrival of the visitors who would often look up as they stepped out of their carriages and wave hello to me, taking me for a nephew of their hostess. At such moments, Gilberte's braids would brush against my cheek. They seemed, in the fineness of their weave, at once natural and supernatural, and the power of their foliated art looked like a unique work made of grasses grown in Paradise. To an infinitesimal section of them, what heavenly herbarium would I not have given as a setting! But with no hope of obtaining an actual piece of these braids, if at least I could have owned a photograph of them, how much more precious that would have been than one of the florets drawn by Leonardo!* To acquire one, I made obsequious overtures to friends of the Swanns and even to photographers, which didn't get me what I wanted, but tied me forever to some very tiresome people.

Whenever I entered the dark antechamber, in which constantly hovered the possibility of coming face to face with Gilberte's parents, who for so long had prevented me from seeing her (an encounter more formidable yet more ardently desired than a glimpse of the King would have been long ago at Versailles), after I'd stumbled against a massive seven-branched coat rack like the Candlestick in Scripture* and effusively greeted a footman who was seated, in the skirts of his long grey frock coat, on the firewood chest, and whom in the darkness I'd mistaken for Madame Swann, if one of them happened to be passing by at that moment, I'd be greeted with no sign of irritation whatsoever, and would be asked, in a friendly tone:

'How do you do?' (They both pronounced this 'how d'you do', running all the words together, a mannerism that, as soon as I was back home, I constantly indulged myself in imitating.) 'Does Gilberte know you're here? She does? Good, good, I'll leave you to her, then.'

Even more importantly, the tea parties Gilberte gave for her friends, which had for so long seemed the most insuperable of the many barriers separating her from me, now became an opportunity for us to be together; she'd tell me about them in a note, written (since I was still quite a recent acquaintance) on notepaper that was never the same. Once it was embossed with a blue poodle over a humorous caption written in English and ending in an exclamation mark;

another time it was stamped with an anchor, or with the initials G.S.,
exaggeratedly elongated and enclosed within a rectangle that took up
the entire length of the page, or else with the name 'Gilberte' either
written across one corner in gilt letters imitating my friend's signature and ending with a flourish, beneath an open umbrella printed in
black, or else enclosed in a monogram in the shape of a Chinese hat
with the name written entirely in capitals but in such a way that it was
impossible to make out a single one. Finally, since Gilberte's collection of notepaper, extensive as it was, was not limitless, after a number
of weeks, I'd see again the one that bore, like the first one she'd written to me, the motto *Per viam rectam* under the helmeted knight, on
his seal of burnished silver. At the time, I thought that each of them
was chosen on one particular day rather than another by virtue of
certain rituals, but now I think it was just because she was trying to
remember the ones she'd used before, so as never to send the same
one twice to any of her correspondents (at least those for whom she
took a little trouble), save at intervals as far apart as possible. Because
their lessons took place at different times, some of the friends Gilberte
invited to these teas were obliged to leave as others were just arriving;
as I was walking upstairs I could hear, drifting down from the ante-
room, a murmur of voices which, in the emotional turmoil aroused
by the momentous ceremony in which I was about to take part,
abruptly—long before I reached the landing—broke the ties that still
attached me to my previous life and even prevented me from remembering to take off my scarf once I was in the warmth of the apartment
or to keep an eye on the time so as not to get home late. This staircase,
all of wood, as was customary at the time in certain rental properties
in that faux Renaissance style which had so long been Odette's ideal
but which she'd soon abandon, bore a sign unlike any of those in our
building, which read: 'It is forbidden to use the lift to go down', which
seemed to connote such prestige that I said to my parents it was an
antique staircase brought from very far away by Monsieur Swann.
My respect for the truth was so great that even if I'd known this to be
untrue, I'd still have said the same thing, for this was the only way to
induce them to have the same esteem as I had for the dignity of the
Swanns' staircase. It's in just this sort of way that, when we're talking
with some ignorant person who doesn't recognize the genius of
a great doctor, we decide it's best to say nothing about the fact that he
doesn't know how to cure the common cold. But since I had no power

of observation, just as in general I knew neither the name nor the nature of things that were right in front of my eyes, and understood only that if they had anything to do with the Swanns, they must be extraordinary, it didn't strike me as a certainty that, by alerting my parents to the aesthetic value and distant provenance of this staircase, I was telling a lie. It didn't strike me as a certainty, but it must have seemed probable, for I felt myself blushing quite red when my father interrupted me with the words: 'I know those houses well; I've seen one, and they're all alike. Swann just occupies a few floors, it's Berlier who built them all.'* He added that he'd wanted to rent an apartment in one of them, but that he'd decided against it, finding them inconvenient and the main entrance badly lit; so said my father; but I sensed instinctively that my mind must make whatever sacrifices might be necessary to preserve the Swanns' prestige and my own happiness, and so, bringing an inner authority to bear, despite what I'd just heard, I banished once and for all, just as a devout Catholic might shun Renan's *Life of Jesus*,* the insidious notion that the Swanns' apartment was a quite ordinary apartment we could have been living in ourselves.

So, on those afternoon-tea days, walking up the staircase step by step, already stripped of reason and memory, being nothing more than the plaything of the basest reflexes, I'd reach the zone where Madame Swann's perfume could be smelled. I felt I could already glimpse the majesty of the chocolate cake set in a circle of dainty dishes laden with petits fours and intricate little grey damask napkins, required by etiquette and unique to the Swanns. But this unchanging, well-ordered arrangement seemed, like Kant's necessary universe,* to be dependent on a supreme act of free will. For when we were all gathered in Gilberte's little salon, all of a sudden, looking at the clock, she'd say:

'Listen, it feels as if lunch was hours ago, dinner's not till eight, and I'm feeling a bit peckish. How would you like a little something?'

And she'd usher us into the dining room, dark as the inside of an Asian temple as painted by Rembrandt,* where an architectural cake, as friendly and familiar as it was imposing, seemed to be sitting in state just by chance, as it might on any day, in case Gilberte was taken with the whim to uncrown it of its chocolate crenellations and knock down its steep brown slopes, baked in the oven like the bastions of Darius' palace.* The best thing was that, in proceeding to the destruction of that Ninevite pastry,* Gilberte didn't just consult her own hunger; she also enquired about mine, as she extracted for me from the fallen monument a whole glazed section studded with scarlet fruits, in the Oriental style. She'd even ask what time my parents dined, as if I still knew, as if the confusion that was overwhelming me allowed the sensation of satiety or hunger, the notion of dinner or the image of family, to persist in my vacant memory and paralysed stomach. Unfortunately, this paralysis was only temporary. There would come a time when the cakes I consumed without noticing them would have to be digested. But that time was still far away. In the meantime, Gilberte would make me 'my tea'. I'd go on drinking it indefinitely, whereas a single cup would prevent me from sleeping for twenty-four hours. And so my mother used to say: 'It's such a pity this child can't go to the Swanns' without making himself sick.' But did I even know when I was at the Swanns' that it was tea I was drinking? Had I known, I would have drunk it all the same, for even if I had recovered for a moment an awareness of the present, that would not have restored my ability to remember the past or predict the future. My imagination was incapable of reaching that distant time when I might think of going to bed or feel the need for sleep.

Gilberte's friends were not all plunged into that state of intoxication when any decision is impossible. Some refused tea! Then Gilberte would say, using a well-known phrase of the time: 'My tea isn't much of a success, is it?' And, to drive any idea of ceremony even further away, she'd rearrange the chairs set in order around the table, adding: 'It looks like a wedding breakfast; how stupid the servants are!'

She nibbled her cake, sitting sideways on an x-shaped chair placed askew. And if Madame Swann—whose 'at-homes' usually coincided with Gilberte's tea parties—looked in quickly after showing out a visitor, sometimes wearing blue velvet, often in a black satin dress trimmed with lace, she'd exclaim in a tone of surprise, as if Gilberte could have had all those petits fours to eat without her mother's permission: 'Oh my, how scrumptious that looks! It makes my mouth water to see you all sitting there eating cake.'

'Well, you're welcome to join us, Maman!' Gilberte would reply.

'No, no, my darling, what would my visitors say? I still have Madame Trombert, Madame Cottard, and Madame Bontemps—you know how dear Madame Bontemps never pays short visits, and she's only just arrived. What would all those nice people say if I left them to their own devices? If no one else comes, I'll come back and chat with you (which I'll enjoy much more) after they've all left. I think I deserve a little peace and quiet, I've had forty-five visitors today, and forty-two of them have talked about Gérôme's new painting!* But you should come on your own one of these days,' she said to me as she was about to rejoin her ladies, 'and have your tea with Gilberte—she'll make it for you just the way you like it, as you take it in your little "studio",' she added, as if all I was looking for in this mysterious world was something as familiar to me as my own habits (such as the one I supposedly had of taking tea; and as for a 'studio', I was not at all sure whether I had one or not). 'When could you come? Tomorrow? We'll make you *toast* as good as at Colombin's.* You can't? How mean you are!', she'd say, for ever since she too began to form a salon, she'd assumed the mannerisms of Madame Verdurin, especially her tone of simpering tyranny. Since *toast** was as unknown to me as Colombin's, that promise did nothing to tempt me further. When Madame Swann went on to praise our old 'nurse', it might seem strange, since everyone talks that way now (possibly even in Combray), that I didn't under-stand at first to whom she was referring. Despite my ignorance of English, I soon realized that this word referred to Françoise. Having been so afraid of the bad impression Françoise must have made at the Champs-Elysées, I learned from Madame Swann that it was all the things Gilberte had told her about my 'nurse' that had made her and her husband view me in a favourable light. 'She seems so devoted to you, so kind!' (Immediately I completely changed my opinion of Françoise. Now, having a governess equipped with a raincoat and a feather in her hat no longer seemed so necessary to me.) Finally I understood, from a few words Madame Swann let slip about Madame Blatin (whose kindness she appreciated but whose visits she dreaded), that being on friendly terms with that lady would have been of less value to me than I'd thought, and would in no way have improved my standing with the Swanns.

Though I'd begun, trembling with this respect and joy, to explore the enchanted realm which against all expectations had flung open to me its hitherto closed avenues, it was still only in my capacity as a friend of Gilberte. The domain into which I was welcomed was itself encompassed by an even more mysterious one, in which Swann and his wife led their supernatural lives, and towards which they were heading in the opposite direction to mine, when they shook my hand as our paths crossed in the anteroom. But soon I too was able to penetrate into their Inner Sanctum. For example, if Gilberte was out when I called, Monsieur or Madame Swann might be in. They'd ask who had rung, and learning it was me, would ask me to stay with them for a while, wanting me to influence their daughter towards a certain course of action in some matter or other. I remembered that letter—so exhaustive, so persuasive—that I'd once written to Swann and to which he hadn't even deigned to reply. I marvelled at the powerlessness of the mind, of reason, and of the heart to bring about the slightest change in people, or to resolve a single one of those difficulties, which life, without our even knowing how it goes about it, subsequently untangles so smoothly and easily. My new position as a friend of Gilberte, endowed with the capacity to influence her for the better, put me in the favourable position of someone who was a friend of a king's son at a school where I was also head of the class, and, because of these fortuitous facts, now receives invitations to the Palace and is granted private audiences in the Throne room; with infinite kindness, and as if he were not preoccupied with lofty considerations, Swann would show me into his study and for an hour would allow me to respond with stammerings and shy silences interspersed with brief, incoherent surges of courage to statements of which my emotion prevented me from understanding a single word; he showed me books and works of art which he thought might interest me, and which, even before I'd seen them, I was convinced infinitely surpassed in beauty all those owned by the Louvre and the Bibliothèque nationale, which it was impossible for me to view. At such moments, if his butler had asked me to give him my watch, my tiepin, my boots, or to sign a document recognizing him as my heir, I'd have been only too delighted: in the words of the fine popular expression of which the author, like the author of the greatest epic poems, is unknown, but which, like them, and contrary to Wolf's theory,* must have had one (one of those inventive, modest wits we come across every year, who think up phrases like 'putting a name to a face', without putting a name to their own face), 'I didn't know whether I was coming or going'. All I could summon up from these visits, however long they were, was a sense of astonishment at the utter lack of understanding, the complete absence of a satisfying outcome, to which these hours spent in the enchanted realm led me. But my disappointment stemmed neither from any deficiency in the masterpieces displayed, nor from the impossibility of fixing on them my distracted gaze. For it wasn't the intrinsic beauty of these things that made it seem miraculous for me to be in Swann's study, but rather the way these things—which could have been the ugliest in the world—were linked to the special, melancholy, voluptuous emotion I'd invested in this place for so many years, with which it was still impregnated; likewise, Madame Swann's multitude of mirrors, silver brushes, and shrines to Saint Anthony of Padua,* painted or sculpted by the greatest artists, who were her friends, were as nothing to me, so overwhelmed was I by the feeling of my unworthiness and her own regal benevolence which were aroused in me whenever Madame Swann received me for a moment in her bedroom, where three beautiful and imposing creatures, her first, second, and third maids, were smiling and laying out wonderful outfits, and to which, at the command given by the footman in breeches and hose that Madame wished to speak to me, I made my way along a winding corridor fragrant from afar with precious oils from her dressing room, constantly wafting their scented exhalations.

When Madame Swann had returned to her visitors, we could still hear her laughing and talking, for even with only a few people, she'd raise her voice and enunciate her words loudly as if she had to hold forth in front of all her 'confidantes', as she'd heard the 'Patronne' do so often in the 'little clan'* when she was 'leading the conversation'. Since the expressions we've borrowed recently from others are those we most like to use, at least for a while, Madame Swann would sometimes choose those she'd learned from the distinguished people whom her husband had been unable to avoid introducing to her (it was from them she'd acquired the mannerism of omitting the article or demonstrative pronoun before an adjective describing a person), and sometimes more plebeian ones (for example, 'It's just a little whatnot!', a favourite phrase of one her friends), and tried to include them in all the stories she liked to tell, in keeping with a habit picked up from the 'little clan'. She'd then continue with: 'I'm *so* fond of that story', or 'Come now, admit it, it's a *lovely* story'; which came to her, through her husband, from the Guermantes, whom she did not know.

Madame Swann had left the dining room, but her husband, who had just come home, would look in on us.

'Do you know if your mother is alone, Gilberte?'

'No, she still has visitors, Papa.'

'What, still? At seven o'clock! How awful. The poor woman must be exhausted. It's odious.' (At home I'd always heard the first syllable of this word pronounced with a long *o*, as in 'ode', but Monsieur and Madame Swann made it short, as in 'odd'.) 'Just think of it, she's been at it since two o'clock!' he continued, turning to me. 'And Camille told me that between four and five o'clock, at least twelve people came. Did I say twelve? I think he said fourteen. No, twelve; I can't remember. When I came home I'd quite forgotten it was her at-home day, and when I saw all those carriages outside, I thought there must be a wedding in the house! Even in the last few minutes, while I've been in my study, the doorbell hasn't stopped ringing; upon my word, it's given me a quite a headache. And there are still a lot of visitors with her?'

'No, just two.'

'Do you know who?'

'Madame Cottard and Madame Bontemps.'

'Ah! the wife of the private secretary to the Minister of Works.'

'I know her husband works in some ministry or other, but I don't have a clue which one,' Gilberte replied, in a childish voice.

'What's this? Silly girl, you sound like a two-year-old. What do you mean, "works in some ministry or other"? He's actually the *main* private secretary to the minister, head of the whole thing! and what's more—wait, what was I thinking? Good grief, I'm as foolish as you are, he's not just the private secretary, he's the *chief* private secretary.'

'So what? Is that a big thing, to be a chief private secretary?' replied Gilberte, who never lost an opportunity to show indifference towards anything her parents took pride in (or perhaps she thought she was only increasing the brilliance of their acquaintance with such a personage by seeming not to attach too much importance to it).

'What do you mean, is it a big thing!' exclaimed Swann, who preferred exaggeration over modesty, which might have left me in doubt. 'He's simply the head of everything, after the minister! He's even *more* important than the minister, since he's the one who does everything. I hear he's very capable, too, first-rate, as distinguished as they come. He's an Officer of the Legion of Honour.* A delightful man—very handsome, too.'

His wife, in fact, had married him against everyone's advice because he was 'a charmer'. He had all the attributes necessary to form a rare and delicate whole: a silky blond beard, handsome features, a nasal voice, bad breath, and a glass eye.

'I can tell you', Swann added, turning to me, 'that it amuses me no end to see people like that in the present government, because they're the Bontemps of the Bontemps-Chenuts, typical of the narrow-minded bourgeoisie, priest-ridden reactionaries. Your poor grandfather was very familiar, at least by reputation and sight, with old Chenut, who never tipped a cabman more than a sou, even though he was rich for those days, and he also knew the Baron Bréau-Chenut. They lost everything in the Union Générale crash*—you're too young to remember that, and since then they've had to salvage whatever they could.'

'He's the uncle of a girl who used to go to my school, but she was in a class much lower than mine—the famous "Albertine". She'll definitely be very "*fast*"* someday, but for now she's a funny-looking thing.'

'What a surprising daughter I have, she knows everyone!'

'No, I don't know her. I'd just see her going by, and hear everyone shouting "Albertine" here, "Albertine" there. But I *do* know Madame Bontemps, and I don't like her either.'

'You couldn't be more wrong, she's charming, pretty, and intelligent. Witty too. I'll just go in and say hello to her, and ask her if her husband thinks we're going to war, and if we can count on King Theodosius. He must know all about it, since he's such an insider, don't you think?'

This was not how Swann used to talk; but who hasn't seen an unaffected, plain-spoken princess of royal blood who, after eloping with a footman, tries ten years later to re-enter society, but, sensing no one wants to call on her, spontaneously adopts the language of boring old gossips, and when the name of some fashionable duchess is dropped, instantly say: 'She visited me only yesterday', and 'I live quite shut away'? Which shows how pointless it is to study mannerisms, since they can be deduced from the laws of psychology.

The Swanns shared a shortcoming common to people with few friends: a visit, an invitation, a simple friendly word from anyone even slightly prominent was for them an event to be publicly announced. If bad luck had it that the Verdurins were in London when Odette happened to give even a slightly noteworthy dinner-party, arrangements were made for the news to be cabled to them across the Channel by a mutual friend. It wasn't just that the Swanns couldn't keep to themselves the flattering letters and telegrams

Odette received; they spoke of them to friends, passed them around. And so the Swanns' salon was like one of those seaside hotels where telegrams are tacked to the wall.

Also, the people who had known the former Swann not just apart from society, as I did, but also in the Guermantes circle, where stringent demands were made of its members (except princesses and duchesses) when it came to wit and charm, and from which even eminent men who were found boring or vulgar were barred—such people may have been surprised to note not only that the former Swann had become someone who was indiscreet when he talked about his connections, but that his selection of them was hard to fathom. How was it that Madame Bontemps—so common, so spiteful—didn't exasperate him? How could he maintain that she was pleasant? The memory of the Guermantes circle should have prevented him from doing so, one would have thought; but in fact, it spurred him on. The Guermantes, unlike the great majority of social circles, certainly had taste, even of quite a refined sort, but also a snobbishness which allowed for the possibility of momentary interruptions in the exercise of that taste. When it came to someone not indispensable to their set—a Minister of Foreign Affairs, say, who was a slightly pompous republican, or an academician who talked too much—their taste would turn heavily against him; Swann would express sympathy for Madame de Guermantes for having to sit next to such guests at an embassy dinner; and the whole Guermantes set would infinitely prefer a fashionable man (that is, a man of their own circle), with nothing remarkable about him, but of the same cast of mind as the Guermantes, someone who belonged to the same clique. However, if a grand duchess or a princess of the blood were to dine frequently at the home of Madame de Guermantes, she'd soon find that she too was part of their set, without having any right to be there, without having its cast of mind. But with the naïvety of society people, from the moment she was welcomed in, they'd go out of their way to find her pleasant, though they couldn't say that it was because they'd found her pleasant that they welcomed her in. Swann, coming to the rescue of Madame de Guermantes, would say to her after Her Highness had left: 'She's really quite nice, she even has a certain sense of humour. Of course, I doubt she's an expert on the *Critique of Pure Reason*,* but she's not a bad sort.'

'I share your opinion entirely,' the Duchess de Guermantes would reply. 'Mind you, she was a little intimidated today, but you'll see that she can be quite charming.' 'She's much less boring than Madame X' (the long-winded academician's wife, who was actually a remarkable woman) 'who keeps quoting books at you!' 'There's really no comparison!' Swann had acquired the ease with which he said such things, and said them sincerely, at the Duchesse de Guermantes', and had kept it. He used it now with regard to the people who came to his house. He'd endeavour to discern, and to love, the qualities that every human being reveals if examined with a favourable predisposition and not with the distaste of the overly fastidious; he praised the merits of Madame Bontemps as he'd once praised those of the Princesse de Parme, who should have been excluded from the Guermantes set if special exceptions weren't made for certain highnesses, even when they were accepted mainly because they possessed some wit and a little charm. We've seen already how Swann had an inclination (which he was now applying, except in a more permanent way) to exchange his position in society for another which, in certain circumstances, suited him better. It is only people unable to see the composite nature of what at first sight seems indivisible who think one's position is an integral part of one's person. The same person, taken at successive times in his life, dwells, on different rungs of the social ladder, in worlds that are not necessarily increasingly more exalted; and whenever, at any time in our lives, we form or re-form ties with a certain social circle, and feel at home in it, we naturally put down roots and start to feel attached to it.

As for Madame Bontemps, I think too that Swann, in speaking of her with such enthusiasm, was also quite pleased to think that my parents would hear that she'd come to see his wife. In fact, however, in our house the names of people that Madame Swann was getting to know aroused more curiosity than admiration. At the name of Madame Trombert, my mother exclaimed: 'Aha! A new recruit! And she'll bring in others as well.'

And as if she were comparing the rather summary, swift, and violent way in which Madame Swann conquered her new connections to a colonial war, Maman added: 'Now that the Tromberts are subdued, the neighbouring tribes will soon surrender.'

When she met Madame Swann in the street, she'd say upon her return: 'I saw Madame Swann all ready for battle—she must have been just about to set off for some successful offensive against the Massachutoes,* the Sinhalese, or the Tromberts.'

And when I told her about all the new people I'd seen at the Swanns', in that rather mixed, artificial milieu to which they'd been brought, often rather unwillingly, from quite disparate worlds, she'd immediately guess where they'd come from, and would speak of them as if they were dearly bought trophies:

'Brought back from an expedition to the So-and-Sos!'

As for Madame Cottard, my father was surprised that Madame Swann could see any advantage in inviting this unfashionable bourgeois lady to her house, and would say: 'Despite the professor's situation, I must say I can't understand it.' My mother, on the other hand, understood very well; she knew that a large part of the pleasures a woman finds when entering a class of society different from the one she used to live in would be lost if she couldn't inform her old connections of the relatively more brilliant ones with which she has replaced them. For this, a witness is required who will be allowed to penetrate this delicious new world, like a capricious insect buzzing into a flower, and then (this at least is the hope), as her visits increase, will spread the news, the secret seed of envy and admiration. Madame Cottard, who seemed ready-made to fulfil this role, belonged to that special category of guests whom Maman (who had some of her father's style of wit) called 'Stranger, go tell the Spartans!'* guests. Besides—along with another reason which we'd learn only many years later—since Madame Swann would invite this kind, reserved, modest friend only to her at-homes, she had no need to fear that she might be introducing into her home a traitor or a rival. She was well aware of the huge number of bourgeois calyxes this active worker-bee, armed with her feathered hat and her card case, could visit in a single afternoon. She knew the power of dissemination and, trusting in the laws of probability, she was justified in thinking that, almost certainly, some acquaintance of the Verdurins would learn within a few days that the commanding officer of the Paris region had left his card with her, or that Monsieur Verdurin himself would hear that Monsieur Le Hault de Pressagny, President of the Horse Show,* had taken her and Swann to the King Theodosius gala; she imagined the Verdurins would hear only of these two events, both of them flattering to herself, since the particular manifestations of fame which we imagine and pursue are quite few, given our limited minds, incapable as they are of imagining simultaneously all the forms this fame might take, though we still nurture a vague hope that it might actually assume these forms.

In any case, Madame Swann had met with success only in what was called 'the world of officialdom'. Fashionable ladies didn't visit her. It wasn't the presence of republican notables that had frightened them away. During my early childhood, anything that pertained to conservative society was fashionable, and in an established salon a republican would not have been welcomed. The people who lived in such a milieu thought that the impossibility of ever inviting an 'Opportunist', or even worse a frightful 'Radical', was a thing that would endure forever, like oil lamps or horse-drawn omnibuses. But like kaleidoscopes, which are turned from time to time, society is constantly rearranging elements believed to be immutable, forming ever-different patterns. I hadn't yet taken my First Communion when conventional ladies were stupefied to meet an elegant Jewish woman while paying a social call. These new arrangements of the kaleidoscope are produced by what a philosopher would call a paradigm shift. The Dreyfus Affair* led to a new shift, slightly after I started to visit Madame Swann, and the kaleidoscope once more reversed its little coloured lozenges. Anything Jewish—even the elegant lady—went down, and obscure nationalists climbed up to take its place. The most brilliant salon in Paris belonged to an ultra-Catholic Austrian prince. If instead of the Dreyfus Affair a war with Germany had occurred, the kaleidoscope would have turned in the opposite direction. The Jews, having shown (to general astonishment) that they were patriotic, would have kept their positions, and no one would have wanted to go—or even confess to ever having gone—to the Austrian prince's salon. The fact remains that every time society is temporarily stationary, those who live in it imagine that no further change will ever take place, just as, having witnessed the birth of the telephone, they don't want to believe in the aeroplane. In the meantime, newspaper philosophers denounce the previous age: not just the kinds of pleasures that were popular then, which seem to them the last word in corruption, but even the works of artists and philosophers, which in their eyes no longer have any value, as if they were indissolubly linked to the successive forms of fashionable frivolity. The only thing that does not change is the constant assertion that 'things aren't the way they used to be in France'. During the period I was visiting Madame Swann, the Dreyfus Affair hadn't yet erupted, and some notable Jews were very powerful. None more so than Sir Rufus Israels, whose wife, Lady Israels, was Swann's aunt. She personally didn't have intimate acquaintances as elegant as those of her nephew, who, since he didn't like her, had never much cultivated her society, even though he was presumably her heir. But she was the only one of Swann's relatives who was aware of Swann's position in society, the others always having remained, in that respect, in the same state of ignorance that had long been our own. When one member of a family migrates to high society—which seems to him a unique achievement, but which ten years later he realizes had been accomplished in other ways and for different reasons by more than one young man with whom he'd grown up—he draws around himself a zone of shadow, a *terra incognita,** quite visible in its slightest nuances to anyone inhabiting it, but only dark night and pure nothingness to all those who don't penetrate it, but brush against it without the slightest inkling of its existence so close to them. Since there was no news agency to inform Swann's cousins about the people he frequented, it was (before his horrible marriage, of course) with smiles of condescension that they'd tell each other at family dinners how they'd 'virtuously' employed their Sunday in going to see 'cousin Charles', whom, believing him to be a poor relation envious of their standing, they'd wittily call, playing on the title of Balzac's novel, 'Le Cousin Bête'.* Lady Rufus Israels, however, knew perfectly well the identity of the people lavishing on Swann a friendship of which she was jealous. Her husband's family, which was roughly the equivalent of the Rothschilds,* had for several generations overseen the business affairs of the princes of Orléans. Lady Israels, extremely wealthy, had great influence, and she'd used it to ensure that no one she knew would receive Odette. Only one woman had disobeyed, and that secretly. This was the Comtesse de Marsantes. As bad luck would have it, one day, when Odette went to visit Madame de Marsantes, Lady Israels arrived almost at the same time. Madame de Marsantes was on tenterhooks. With the baseness of those who know they can behave exactly as they please, she spoke not a word to Odette, who was thus not encouraged to pursue any further an incursion into a circle of society which in any case was not at all the one to which she'd like to belong. Now wholly ignored by the Faubourg Saint-Germain,* Odette went on being the ill-educated *cocotte*, quite different from those bourgeois who are experts on the minutest points of genealogy and who, by reading old memoirs, quench their thirst for aristocratic connections with which real life has failed to provide them. As for Swann, he probably went on being the lover who finds all these quirks of a former mistress charming or inoffensive, for I often heard his wife utter real social heresies without his trying to correct them (whether out of a lingering fondness for her, the lack of esteem in which he now held her, or laziness about improving her). Perhaps it was also another form of the simplicity that had so often deceived us in Combray, and that now, though he himself continued to know very grand people, prevented him from giving the impression, at least in his wife's drawing-room conversations, that those people were in any way important to him. Besides, they were less important than ever for Swann, since his life's centre of gravity had shifted. In any case, Odette's ignorance in society matters was such that if the name of the Princesse de Guermantes arose in conversation after that of her cousin the Duchesse de Guermantes, she'd say: 'Oh, they're *princes* now! So they've gone up in the world.' If someone said 'the Prince' in speaking of the Duc de Chartres, she'd correct them: 'You mean the *duke*, he's the Duc de Chartres, not a prince.'* As for the Duc d'Orléans, son of the Comte de Paris, she'd say: 'That's funny, the son is higher than the father,' adding, since she was an Anglophile: 'All these "royals", they're so confusing!'; and to someone who asked her which of the old provinces the Guermantes came from, she replied with the name of a *département*:* 'From the Aisne.'

Swann, however, was blind to all of Odette's deficiencies, not just to the gaps in her education, but also to the mediocrity of her intelligence. What's more, whenever Odette told a silly story, Swann would listen to his wife with an amused indulgence bordering on admiration, which must have been fuelled, at least in part, by a lingering desire; while, in the same conversation, whatever Swann himself said that was subtle or even profound was listened to by Odette usually without any interest, in an impatient, perfunctory way, and was sometimes sharply contradicted. The conclusion to be drawn from this is that this subservience of brilliance to vulgarity is the rule in many marriages, when we think, conversely, of all the highly intelligent women who fall for some boor who mercilessly censures their most delicate utterances, while they go into raptures, with the infinite indulgence of love, over his dullest jokes. To return to the reasons that prevented Odette at that time from being admitted to the Faubourg Saint-Germain, it should be said that the most recent turn of the social kaleidoscope had been caused by a series of scandals. Women to whose houses people were going in all confidence had been revealed to be common prostitutes and English spies. And so for some time thereafter people would be expected (or so it was believed) to have a certain solidity and respectability. Odette represented precisely all the things that had recently been condemned, but which (since humans, who cannot change overnight, seek to continue the old state of affairs in the new) would soon be welcomed back, but in a slightly different form, thereby allowing society to fool itself into believing it's no longer the same as it was before the scandal. Odette, however, was too like the 'branded' ladies of that society. Fashionable people are quite short-sighted; no sooner do they sever all relations with the Jewish ladies they know, and are wondering how to fill this void, than they perceive, delivered to them as if by the fortune of a stormy night, a new lady, also Jewish; but thanks to her newness, she is not associated in their minds, as the previous ones were, with what they think they should detest. She does not ask them to respect her God. They adopt her. There was no question of anti-Semitism during the time I began visiting Odette. But she was too like what people wanted, for a time, to avoid.

As for Swann, he'd often visit some of his old acquaintances, who, of course, all belonged to the highest society. When he spoke to us about the people he'd just gone to see, though, I noted that his choice among those he'd known previously was guided by the same kind of sensibility—half-artistic, half-historical—that shaped his taste as a collector. And remarking that it was often some great lady who had come down in the world who interested him because she'd been a mistress of Liszt* or because one of Balzac's novels had been dedicated to her grandmother (just as he'd buy a drawing if Chateaubriand had written about it), I had the suspicion that in Combray we'd replaced one mistake, of thinking Swann was a bourgeois who didn't go out into society, with another, that of thinking he was one of the most elegant men in Paris. Being the friend of the Comte de Paris meant nothing. How many of those 'friends of princes' are there who wouldn't be received in even a slightly exclusive salon? Princes know they are princes, are not snobs, and what's more see themselves as so far above anyone not of their blood that noblemen and bourgeois alike seem to them, although beneath them, almost on the same level.

Swann, however, wasn't content to seek the simple pleasure a cultivated, artistic man finds in society as it exists, by familiarizing himself with the names inscribed on it by the past and still legible now; he also enjoyed the rather vulgar entertainment of creating social 'bouquets' by forming groups of heterogeneous elements, bringing together people found here and there. These experiments in amusing (or so Swann thought) sociology didn't always elicit the same reaction from all his wife's friends. 'I think I'll invite the Cottards along with the Duchesse de Vendôme,' he'd say, laughing, to Madame Bontemps, in the epicurean tone of a gourmet contemplating using cayenne pepper instead of cloves in a sauce. But this plan, which the Cottards would certainly have found entertaining, had the knack of infuriating Madame Bontemps. She'd recently been introduced by the Swanns to the Duchesse de Vendôme, and had found it both pleasant and natural. The thought of winning the Cottards' admiration after telling them about this added just a little more spice to her pleasure. But like those newly decorated individuals who, as soon as they've received their award, would like the fountain of medals to be turned off at the tap immediately thereafter, Madame Bontemps would have preferred that after herself no one from her own circle should be introduced to the Duchesse de Vendôme. She inwardly cursed Swann's depraved taste that, in order to gratify a wretched aesthetic whim, had made him destroy at one fell swoop the dazzling impression she'd made on the Cottards when she told them about the Duchesse de Vendôme. How could she dare tell her own husband that the professor and his wife would in turn share in a delight she'd assured him was unique to themselves? If only the Cottards had known that they were not being invited seriously but merely for Swann's amusement! It is true that the Bontemps had been invited for the same reason, but Swann, having adopted the aristocracy's eternal 'Don Juan' attitude* that, given two ordinary women, each would believe she's the only one he truly loves, had assured Madame Bontemps that she was the perfect person to dine with the Duchesse de Vendôme. 'Yes, we're planning on having the Duchesse de Vendôme over with the Cottards,' Madame Swann said a few weeks later. 'My husband thinks something amusing will come of this conjunction'—for, while she'd kept from the 'little clan' certain habits dear to Madame Verdurin, such as shouting very loudly in order to be heard by all the faithful, she'd also picked up certain expressions (like 'conjunction') dear to the Guermantes set, whose attraction she was experiencing, at a distance and without their realizing it, as the sea is pulled by the moon, though she didn't seem to be coming any closer to them. 'Yes, the Cottards and the Duchesse de

Vendôme—don't you think that will be amusing?' asked Swann. 'I think it will go very badly, and it will cause nothing but problems for you; you shouldn't play with fire,' replied Madame Bontemps, furious. Both she and her husband, as it happened, as well as the Prince d'Agrigente, were invited to this dinner, which Madame Bontemps and Cottard had two ways of describing, according to the individuals they were addressing. To some, Madame Bontemps for her part, Cottard for his, would say offhandedly when asked who else had been invited to the dinner: 'Only the Prince d'Agrigente; it was very intimate.' But others ran the risk of being better informed (someone had even said once to Cottard: 'But weren't the Bontemps there too?' 'Oh, I forgot them,' Cottard had replied, blushing, to his tactless interlocutor, whom he classified ever after as a malicious gossip). For these the Bontemps and the Cottards each adopted, without consulting one another, a version with identical wording, but with only their respective names interchanged. Cottard would say: 'Well, there were only our host and hostess, the Duc and Duchesse de Vendôme' (smiling smugly), 'Professor and Madame Cottard, and also—heaven knows why, since they were like fish out of water—Monsieur and Madame Bontemps!' Madame Bontemps would recite exactly the same set piece, only it was Monsieur and Madame Bontemps who were named with a self-satisfied emphasis, in between the Duchesse de Vendôme and the Prince d'Agrigente, while the 'nobodies', whom in the end she accused of having invited themselves and who stood out like a sore thumb, were the Cottards.

Swann would often come home from his social calls not long before dinner. At that hour of six o'clock, when he'd felt so unhappy before, he no longer wondered what Odette might be doing, and wasn't very worried whether she was entertaining guests or had gone out. He sometimes recalled that, many years before, he'd tried to read a letter from Odette to Forcheville through the envelope. But this memory was not a pleasant one, and to avoid dwelling on his shame, he'd merely twitch the corners of his mouth, or give a little shake of his head, as though to say: 'What does that matter to me?' Indeed, he now thought that the hypothesis upon which he'd so often dwelled, namely that it was his jealous imagination alone that blackened what was actually the innocent life of Odette (which was after all a beneficial supposition, since it had diminished the sufferings of his lovesickness by making them seem imaginary) was not the correct one, but that it was his jealousy that had seen things clearly, and that although Odette might have loved him more than he thought, she'd also deceived him more. In those days, when he was suffering so much, he'd vowed that as soon as he'd stopped loving Odette and no longer feared annoying her or making her think he loved her too much, he'd give himself the satisfaction of sitting down with her and finding out, simply from love of the truth and as a point of historical interest, whether or not Forcheville was in bed with her the day he'd rung the bell and tapped on her window with no answer, and she'd written to Forcheville that it was an uncle of hers who had called. But this absorbing problem, which he'd been looking forward to clearing up as soon as his jealousy had subsided, had lost all interest for Swann precisely when he'd stopped being jealous. Not right away, however. Long after he'd ceased feeling any jealousy with regard to Odette, that afternoon when he'd knocked in vain on the door of the little house on the Rue La Pérouse had continued to arouse jealousy in him.* It was as if jealousy, somewhat akin in this respect to those maladies that seem to have their basis, their source of contagion, less in certain individuals than in certain places, in certain houses, hadn't had Odette herself as its object so much as that day, that hour in the long-lost past when Swann had knocked at all the entrances to Odette's house. It was as if that day, that hour alone, had captured the few remaining shreds of the amorous personality that had once been Swann's, and as if it was there alone that he could find it again. For a long time now, he'd stopped caring that Odette had been unfaithful to him and was so still. And yet for some years he'd continued to search for former servants of Odette's, so strongly had the painful curiosity persisted in him to know whether on that day, so long ago, at six o'clock, Odette had been in bed with Forcheville.* Then this curiosity itself had disappeared, yet without Swann ceasing his investigations. He went on trying to find out what no longer interested him, because his old self, though it had degenerated to extreme decrepitude, was still acting mechanically, in accordance with preoccupations so diminished that Swann couldn't even manage to picture to himself that anguish, even though it had once been so strong that he couldn't imagine at the time he'd ever be rid of it, and that only the death of the woman he loved (though death, as will be shown later in this book by a cruel corroboration, in no way diminishes the sufferings of jealousy) seemed capable of smoothing the obstacle-strewn path of his life.

To shed light on the things in Odette's life that had caused him such suffering hadn't been Swann's only wish; he'd also harboured the desire to avenge his sufferings when, having ceased to love Odette, he no longer feared her; and the opportunity to grant this desire was now at hand, for Swann loved another woman, a woman who gave him no grounds for jealousy but made him jealous all the same, because he was no longer capable of changing his old habits, and so he loved the other woman in the same way he'd loved Odette. For Swann's jealousy to revive, it wasn't necessary for this woman to be unfaithful; it sufficed that she was apart from him for some reason or other, at a soirée for instance, and seemed to be enjoying herself. That was enough to awaken his old anguish, the lamentable and counter-productive excrescence of his love, which distanced Swann from the actual woman and made him yearn for the unknowable (the real feel-ings she had for him, the hidden desires that filled her days, the secrets of her heart), for between Swann and the woman he loved this anguish interposed an impervious mass of previous suspicions ori-ginating in Odette, or in some other perhaps who had preceded Odette, so that the ageing lover could relate to his present mistress only through the old, collective phantasm of 'the woman who made him jealous' in which he arbitrarily embodied his new love. Often, however, Swann would accuse this jealousy of making him believe in imaginary betrayals; but then he'd remind himself that he'd allowed Odette to benefit from the same reasoning, and wrongly. And so everything the young woman he loved did in the hours when he was not with her ceased to appear innocent to him. But whereas before, he'd vowed that if he ever stopped loving the woman who, unbe-knownst to him, would one day become his wife, he'd mercilessly flaunt his indifference (which was at least sincere) in order to avenge his pride which had been humiliated for so long, now that he could safely carry out these reprisals (for what harm could come if Odette took him at his word and deprived him of her company, which had once been so necessary to him?), he no longer felt any need to do so; the disappearance of his love had taken with it his desire to show he no longer felt any love. And the Swann who, when he was suffering because of Odette, had so desired to let her see one day that he'd taken up with someone else, now that he was able to do so, took infinite precautions to keep his wife from suspecting this new love.

It was not only in those tea parties, which had once caused me such grief when I saw Gilberte leave me and go home early to prepare for them, that I was now allowed to take part, but also the excursions she went on with her mother, either to go for a stroll or to some matinee performance, and which, by preventing her from coming to the Champs-Élysées, had deprived me of her on the days when I lingered alone on the grass or in front of the merry-go-round; now Monsieur and Madame Swann included me in these expeditions— I had a seat in their landau,* and I was even the one they asked if I'd rather go to the theatre, a dance lesson at the home of one of Gilberte's friends, a social gathering at a friend of Madame Swann's (which the latter called 'a little *meeting*'*), or to visit the tombs at Saint-Denis.*

On those days when I was to go out with the Swanns, I would go to their house for lunch, which Madame Swann called 'le *lunch*'; as the invitation was for half past twelve, whereas my parents lunched at a quarter past eleven, it was after they'd left the table that I'd head towards that wealthy district, quite empty at any time, but especially at that hour, when everyone had gone home. Even on frosty winter days if the weather was fine, adjusting every now and then the knot of a magnificent tie from Charvet's* and making sure my polished boots weren't getting dirty, I'd pace up and down the avenues, waiting until it was twenty-seven minutes past noon. From afar, I could see the bare trees in the Swanns' little garden sparkling in the sun as though covered in frost. There were only two trees in the garden, but the unusual hour made the sight seem ever new. These pleasures of nature (made keener by the departure from habit, and also by hunger) were mingled with the exciting prospect of lunch with Madame Swann; far from diminishing them, it dominated them, overcame them, made them fashionable accessories; so that if, at that time of day when I usually didn't notice them, I seemed now to be discovering the fine weather, the cold, the winter light, it was like a sort of preface to the eggs coddled in cream, like a patina, an icy pink glaze added to the façade of that mysterious chapel which was Madame Swann's home, in the heart of which there was so much warmth, so many perfumes and flowers.

At half past twelve, I'd finally make up my mind to enter the house which, like an immense Christmas stocking, seemed destined to bring me supernatural delights. (The French word *Noël*, by the way, was unknown to both Madame Swann and Gilberte, who had replaced it with the English *Christmas*, and would speak of nothing but *le pudding de Christmas* and what they'd been given *pour leur Christmas*, or of going away—the mere idea filled me with grief—*pour Christmas*. Even at home, I thought it was beneath me to speak of *Noël*, so I always said *le Christmas*, which my father found extremely silly.)

At first I'd encounter no one but a footman who, after leading me through several large drawing rooms, brought me to a very small, empty one, already beginning to dream in the blue afternoon light from its windows; I'd be left alone there in the company of orchids, roses, and violets, which, like people waiting next to you but who don't know you, maintained a silence that their individuality as living things made all the more impressive, while they luxuriated in the warmth of a glowing coal fire, carefully laid behind a pane of crystal, in a deep white marble bowl over which from time to time it spilled its dangerous rubies.

I had sat down, but rose hurriedly when I heard the door open; it was only a second footman, then a third, and the paltry result of their pointlessly alarming comings and goings was the addition of a little coal to the fire or water to the vases. They would leave, and I'd find myself alone again once the door was shut, the very one that Madame Swann was bound to open. Indeed, I'd have been less flustered in a magician's cave than in this little waiting room where the fire seemed to be performing transmutations, as in Klingsor's laboratory.* Footsteps sounded again; I did not get up, assuming it was another footman—it was Monsieur Swann. 'What's this? You're alone? What can I say, my poor wife has never had any idea of time. Ten to one already. She gets later by the day. You'll see, she won't be in the least bit of a hurry when she does appear, she'll think she's early.' And since he was still subject to neuro-arthritis and had become rather ridiculous, having such an unpunctual wife who returned so late from the Bois de Boulogne, whiled away the hours at her dressmaker's, and was never on time for lunch, was upsetting for Swann's digestion, but flattering for his self-esteem.

He'd show me the new acquisitions he'd made and explain their significance, but my emotions, along with the novelty of not having already eaten at this hour, agitated my mind but left it empty, so that although I was capable of speech, I was incapable of listening. In any case, insofar as the works of art Swann owned were concerned, it was enough for me that they were in his house and formed part of the delicious hour preceding lunch. Even if the *Mona Lisa* had been there, it wouldn't have given me any more delight than one of Madame Swann's dressing gowns or her phials of smelling salts.

I'd continue to wait, alone or with Swann and often Gilberte, who came to keep us company. Madame Swann's arrival, for which so many majestic entrances had paved the way, seemed bound to be a stupendous event. I started at every sound. But we never find a cathedral, a wave in a storm, or a dancer's leap as high as we'd hoped; after the footmen in livery, just as the procession of extras on the stage both prepares for and diminishes the final appearance of the queen, Madame Swann, entering surreptitiously in a little otter-skin jacket, her veil lowered over a nose reddened by the cold, did not fulfil the promises my imagination had conjured up while I was waiting.

If, however, she'd stayed at home all morning, she'd come into the drawing room wearing a brightly coloured crêpe-de-Chine dressing gown, which struck me as more elegant than any evening gown.

Sometimes the Swanns would decide to stay at home all afternoon. And then, as we'd lunched so late, quite soon I'd see the sun setting over the garden wall on that day which had seemed as if it would be different from all other days, and despite the servants bringing lamps of all shapes and sizes, each burning on the consecrated altar of a console, an occasional table, a corner pedestal, or a stand, as if for the celebration of some unknown rite, nothing extraordinary would emerge from the conversation, and I'd leave disappointed, with the same crestfallen feeling we often have as children after Midnight Mass.

But this disappointment was merely in the mind. I was radiant with happiness in this house where Gilberte, when she wasn't already with us, was about to join us, and would bestow on me in a moment, for hours, her speech, her attentive, smiling gaze, just as I'd seen it for the first time in Combray. At worst, I might experience a little envy whenever I saw her disappear, as she often did, into some large rooms reached by an inner staircase. Obliged to remain in the drawing room, like an actress's lover who must remain in his seat in the stalls and anxiously envisages what might be happening backstage in the green room, I asked Swann some skilfully veiled questions about that other part of the house, but in a tone which I couldn't keep from sounding a little uneasy. He explained that the room Gilberte was going to was the linen room, offered to show it to me, and promised that whenever Gilberte had to go there, he'd tell her to take me with her. With those last words and the relief they brought me, Swann suddenly erased one of those terrifying inner perspectives which make the woman we love seem so far away. At that instant, I felt an affection for him which I believed to be more profound even than my affection for Gilberte. For, as his daughter's master, he was giving her to me, whereas she sometimes withheld herself; I didn't have the same direct hold over her as I did indirectly through Swann. What's more, I loved her, and could therefore not see her without that turmoil, that desire for something more, which deprives us, when we are with the one we love, of the sensation of loving.

Usually, though, we wouldn't stay indoors, but would go out for a drive. Sometimes, before going up to dress, Madame Swann would sit down at the piano. Her beautiful hands, emerging from the pink, or white, or often brightly coloured sleeves of her crêpe-de-Chine dressing gown, would stretch their fingers over the piano with the same melancholy that was in her eyes but not in her heart. It was on one of those days that she happened to play for me the passage from Vinteuil's sonata that contained the little phrase* Swann had loved so much. Often we hear nothing if the music is slightly complicated and we're hearing it for the first time. And yet later on, when this sonata was played two or three times for me, I found I knew it perfectly well. And so we're not wrong when we say we've heard something 'for the first time'. If we haven't really made much of our first hearing (though we thought we had), then the second and third could each be the first; and there would be no reason why we'd understand it any more upon hearing it for the tenth time. Probably what is lacking the first time is not comprehension, but memory. For our memory, compared to the complexity of impressions it must encounter as we listen, is minuscule, as brief as the memory of a man who as he sleeps thinks of a thousand things he instantly forgets, or as that of a man in his second childhood who can't recall a minute later what has just been said to him. Our memory is incapable of providing us with an immediate recollection of these multiple impressions. But that recollection itself takes shape slowly, and with regard to pieces of music heard two or three times, one is like a schoolboy who has read over and over again before falling asleep a lesson he thought he didn't know and yet recites it by heart the next morning. But I'd heard nothing of that sonata until that day, and the phrase that Swann and his wife could make out distinctly was as far from my clear perception as a name you try to recall but only draw a blank, a blank whence, without your realizing it, the syllables that had been vainly sought spring forth of their own accord, in a single bound. And not only do we not instantly remember truly rare pieces, but even within each of these works—as happened for me with Vinteuil's sonata—it's the least remarkable parts we notice first. So much so that not only was I wrong in thinking that the piece had nothing more in store for me (so that for a long time I didn't try to hear it again), since Madame Swann had played for me its most famous phrase (I was just as obtuse in this respect as those who expect to feel no surprise in front of Saint Mark's in Venice because they've seen the shape of its domes in photographs*); but much more important-antly, even when I'd listened to the sonata from beginning to end, it remained almost wholly invisible to me, like a monument that can only be partly glimpsed through mist or distance. Hence the melan-choly linked to knowledge of such works, or of anything that's only fully realized over time. When the most hidden part of Vinteuil's sonata was finally revealed to me, everything I'd at first noticed and preferred was already beginning to elude me, carried away by habit out of the reach of sensibility. Since I'd been able to appreciate everything this sonata brought to me only in successive periods of time, I never possessed it wholly: it was like life. But, less disap-pointing than life, great works of art do not start out by giving us the best they have. In Vinteuil's sonata, the beautiful things you discover soonest are also those of which you tire most quickly, no doubt for the same reason, which is that they differ the least from those you knew already. But when they've taken on some distance, we're left to admire a certain phrase that its structure, too new to offer anything but con-fusion to our minds, had kept impenetrable and made indiscernible to us; and so this phrase, which we'd passed over unthinkingly every day and which had held itself in reserve, and which, solely by the power of its beauty, had become invisible and remained unknown, comes to us last of all. But it will also be the last one we leave. And we will love it longer than the others, because we've taken longer to love it. This time that a person needs—as I needed for Vinteuil's sonata—to penetrate a work of some depth is nothing but the synopsis, the symbol, so to speak, of the years, or centuries sometimes, that go by before the public can love a truly new work of art. Thus the man of genius, to spare himself the ignorance of the crowd, might say to himself that since his contemporaries lack the necessary distance, works written for posterity should only be read by posterity, like certain paintings that look poorly executed when viewed from up close. However, any cowardly precaution taken to avoid misjudgements is pointless; they are unavoidable. The reason a work of genius isn't easily admired right away is that its creator is extraordinary; there aren't many like him. It is his work itself that, by fertilizing the rare minds capable of understanding it, will make them increase and multiply. It was Beethoven's quartets (numbers 12, 13, 14, and 15)* that, over the course of fifty years, created and expanded the audience for Beethoven's quartets, thus effecting, like all great works of art, progress if not in the quality of artists, then at least in the community of minds, largely composed today of what was nowhere to be found when the work of art first appeared—that is, of persons able to admire it. What we call 'posterity' is the posterity of the work of art. The work itself (leaving out, for the sake of simplicity, the geniuses who at the same period might be preparing for the future a better audience from which geniuses other than they will benefit) must create its own posterity. For if the work were held back in reserve so that it would be known only by posterity, that audience, for that work, would not be posterity, but rather a group of contemporaries who happened merely to be living fifty years later. And so if the artist wants his work to be able to find its own way, he must do what Vinteuil had done, and launch it where there's sufficient depth, straight into the distant future. And yet, if not taking into account this time to come—the true perspective of works of art—is the mistake made by bad judges, taking it into account is sometimes a dangerous scruple of good ones. No doubt it's easy to imagine, by an illusion like the one that makes everything on the distant horizon look the same, that all the revolutions that have taken place up until now in painting or music still respected certain rules, and that what is right in front of us—Impressionism, the pursuit of dissonance, the exclusive use of the Chinese scale, Cubism, Futurism*—differs outrageously from what came before. This is because we consider what came before without taking into account the long period of assimilation that has turned it all into a substance that is no doubt varied, but, when taken as a whole, is completely homogeneous, where Hugo figures alongside Molière. Just imagine the shocking disparities that would be presented to us if we didn't take into account the time to come and the changes it brings; it would be like reading a horoscope describing our middle-age cast for us when we were still young. Except not all horoscopes are accurate, and the obligation, in judging a work of art, to add the factor of time to its overall beauty entails something as dubious, and therefore as devoid of any real interest, as any prophecy that is never fulfilled, which in no way implies the mediocrity of the prophet, for the power to summon possibilities into existence or to exclude them from it is not necessarily due to genius; it's possible to have genius but not to have believed in the future of railways or planes, just as one can be a keen psychologist but disbelieve in the infidelity of a mistress or the treachery of a friend, both of which could be foreseen by someone of entirely average intelligence.

Although I didn't understand the sonata, I was delighted to hear Madame Swann play. Her touch, like her dressing gown, like the perfume in her staircase, like her coats, like her chrysanthemums, seemed to form part of a unique and mysterious whole, in a world infinitely superior to the one in which reason is capable of analysing talent. 'Isn't this Vinteuil sonata beautiful?' Swann asked me. 'The moment under the trees when night's falling, when the violin's arpeggios call a fresh coolness down to earth. You must admit it's lovely; it captures the whole static aspect of moonlight, which is its essential aspect. It's not surprising that a sunlight treatment like the one my wife's taking acts on the muscles, since moonlight keeps the leaves from stirring. That's what's portrayed so well in that little phrase—it's the Bois de Boulogne plunged into a state of catalepsy. By the seashore it's even more striking, since there are the soft responses of the waves, which of course you can hear quite clearly, since nothing else can move. In Paris it's just the opposite; at most, you might notice unusual shimmers on the old buildings, the sky illumined as if by a colourless and harmless fire, like some momentous event the nature of which you can only guess. But in Vinteuil's little phrase, and in the whole sonata for that matter, it's not like that; it all takes place in the Bois de Boulogne—in the *gruppetto** you can distinctly hear someone's voice saying: "I could almost see to read the paper!"' These words of Swann's might have distorted my understanding of the sonata later on, music being too inclusive to discount absolutely what someone suggests we might find in it. But I realized from other remarks he made that these nocturnal leaves were simply those under whose dense shelter, in many restaurants on the outskirts of Paris, on certain evenings, he'd heard the little phrase. Instead of the profound meaning

he'd so often sought in it, what it recalled for Swann were those leafy
canopies arranged, entwined, painted around it (so that he yearned to
see those leaves again, since the little phrase seemed to be their innermost being, like a soul); it brought back the whole springtime which
he hadn't been able to enjoy, lacking—feverish and sorrowful as he
was at the time—enough strength for it, and which it had kept for
him, just as one saves for an invalid all the nice things he'd been
unable to eat. The charm he'd felt on certain nights in the Bois de
Boulogne, a charm that could be communicated to him by Vinteuil's
sonata, he could not ask Odette about, even though she'd been just as
much with him on those evenings as the little phrase. But Odette had
been merely by his side (not inside him, like Vinteuil's motif), and so
had seen nothing—nor would she have, even if she'd been a thousand
times more understanding—of that which cannot be externalized for
any of us (at least I believed for a long time that this was a rule to
which there were no exceptions). 'It's quite lovely, don't you think,'
Swann said, 'that sound can reflect things, like water, or a mirror.
Mind you, the only things Vinteuil's phrase shows me now are all the
things I wasn't paying attention to then. It reminds me of none of my
worries or love affairs of that time; it has exchanged one set of things
for another.' 'Charles, I don't think that's very flattering to me, what
you're saying.' 'Not flattering! How extraordinary women are! I simply meant to point out to this young man that what music shows—to
me at least—is not at all "The Will-in-Itself" or "The Synthesis of
the Infinite"* but, for example, old Verdurin in his frock coat in the
Palm Court at the Jardin d'Acclimatation.* A thousand times, without my ever leaving this room, that little phrase has taken me along
with it to dine at Armenonville.* God knows it's much less boring
than going there with Madame de Cambremer!' Madame Swann
laughed. 'That's a lady they say was madly in love with Charles,' she
explained, in the same tone she'd used a little earlier when speaking
about Vermeer of Delft, with whose work I was surprised to learn she
was familiar, when she'd said: 'I should tell you that Monsieur Swann
was very taken with that painter when he was courting me. Isn't
that so, Charles my dear?' 'Don't talk nonsense about Madame de
Cambremer,' Swann said, at heart quite flattered. 'But I'm only
repeating what I've been told,' Madame Swann replied. 'Besides,
I hear she's very intelligent, though I don't know her myself. I believe
she's very *pushing*,* which surprises me in an intelligent woman. But

everyone says she was mad about you; there's nothing bad about that.' Swann maintained a marked silence, which seemed at once a kind of confirmation of what she said and a proof of his complacency. 'Since what I'm playing reminds you of the Jardin d'Acclimatation,' Madame Swann continued, playfully pretending to be offended, 'we could drive there this afternoon, if that's something the young might enjoy? It's lovely out, and you, my dear, could relive your fond memories. Speaking of the Jardin d'Acclimatation, this young man thought we were very fond of a person I actually "cut" as often as I can: Madame Blatin! I think it's rather humiliating for us that she's taken for a friend of ours. Just think, dear Doctor Cottard himself, who never speaks badly about anyone, declares she's revolting!' 'A repulsive woman! The one thing that can be said for her is that she looks so like Savonarola. She's the spitting image of the portrait of Savonarola by Fra Bartolomeo.'* This mania of Swann's for finding resemblances for people in paintings was understandable, for even what we call individual expression is something general (as we realize with such sadness whenever we love someone, and want to believe in the unique reality of that individual), something that could have been encountered at different eras. But if you listened to Swann, *The Procession of the Magi*, already so anachronistic when Benozzo Gozzoli inserted the Medicis into their midst, was even more ahead of its time, since it contained, according to him, the portraits of a host of men, contemporaries not of Gozzoli but of Swann—dating, that is, not only from fifteen centuries after the Nativity, but from four centuries after the time of the painter himself.* According to Swann, there wasn't a single Parisian of note missing from the retinue of the Magi, any more than there was from that scene in the Sardou play in which, out of friendship for the author and the leading lady, and because it was fashionable as well, all the noteworthy men of Paris—famous doctors, politicians, lawyers—amused themselves, each on a different evening, by appearing onstage.*

'But what does Madame Blatin have to do with the Jardin d'Acclimatation?' Swann asked.

'Everything.'

'Come again? You think she has a sky-blue behind, like monkeys?'

'How rude you are, Charles! No, I was thinking of what the Sinhalese chap said to her. Tell him, it's too funny for words.'

'It's just a silly thing. You know how Madame Blatin likes to accost everyone in a tone she thinks is friendly, but is actually quite condescending.'

'What our good neighbours across the Channel call *patronizing*,' Odette interrupted.

'Well, she went recently to the Jardin d'Acclimatation where there was an exhibition being given by some black people—from Ceylon, I think, or so says my wife, who's much more "in the know" about ethnography than I am.'*

'Come, come, Charles, don't make fun of me.'

'But I'm not making fun in the least. Anyway, she went up to one of these black fellows and said: "Hello, Black Man!" '

'Isn't it absurd?' interrupted Madame Swann.

'Anyway the black man took offence to this term and shot back: "If you call me 'Black Man', I'll call you 'Old Cow'!" '

'I think that's so funny! I just love that story. Isn't it a gem? Can't you picture old Blatin there: "If you call me 'Black Man', I'll call you 'Old Cow!' " '

I expressed a strong desire to go see these Sinhalese, one of whom had called Madame Blatin an old cow. They did not interest me in the least. But I thought that, in order to go to and from the Jardin d'Acclimatation, we'd cross the Allée des Acacias where I'd so admired Madame Swann; and I hoped that Coquelin's mulatto friend,* to whom I'd always wanted to show off by greeting Madame Swann, might see me sitting next to her in the back of a victoria.

During those minutes in which Gilberte, who had gone to get ready, wasn't in the room with us, Monsieur and Madame Swann would enjoy extolling all their daughter's rare virtues to me. And everything I observed seemed to prove them right. I remarked that, as her mother had told me, she was, not just to her friends, but to the servants and the poor, extremely attentive and thoughtful, and that she showed a desire to please and a fear of giving offence, all of which were conveyed by little things she did, which often put her to a great deal of trouble. She'd made a little piece of embroidery for our stall-keeping friend on the Champs-Élysées, and she went out into the snow to give it to her herself, so as not to lose a day. 'You have no idea how kind-hearted she is, she hides it so well,' her father said. Even at such a young age, she seemed much more sensible than her parents. When Swann spoke of his wife's high connections, Gilberte would look away and say nothing, but without any sign of reproach, for it seemed impossible to her that her father could be the object of the slightest criticism. One day, when I'd mentioned Mademoiselle Vinteuil to her, she said:

'I never want to know her, for one reason: she wasn't nice to her father, from what I hear—she made him very unhappy. You can't understand that any more than I can, isn't that so? I'm sure you couldn't live without your father any more than I could, which is quite natural after all. How could you ever forget someone you've always loved?'

And once, when she was being particularly affectionate towards Swann, and I pointed this out to her when he was out of the room, she said:

'Yes, poor Papa, it's the anniversary of his father's death round about now. You can understand what he must be feeling—we feel the same about these things, don't we? So I'm trying to be less mean than usual.' 'But he doesn't think you're mean, he thinks you're perfect.' 'Poor Papa, that's because he's too good himself.'

Her parents were not content with praising only Gilberte's virtues— that same Gilberte who, even before I'd ever set eyes on her, would appear to me standing in front of a church, in a landscape of the Île-de-France, and later, after my dreams had turned to memories, was always in front of a hedge of pink hawthorn, on the steep little lane I took to go to the Méséglise way.* Since I'd asked Madame Swann (attempting to assume the indifferent tone of a friend of the family, curious about a child's likes and dislikes) which among Gilberte's playmates she liked best, Madame Swann replied: 'But you must be more in her confidence than I am! Aren't you her great confidant, the *crack*, as the English say?'*

In such perfect coincidences, when reality folds back and fits perfectly over what we've dreamed of for so long, it hides it from us completely and merges with it, like two symmetrical figures superimposed one over the other so that they become one; whereas, in order to give our joy all its significance, we'd prefer every detail of our desires, at the very instant we attain them, to retain the prestige of being intangible, in order to be quite certain they're actually what we desired. Our mind can't even reconstruct the old state in order to compare it with the new, for it no longer has free rein: the acquaintance we've made, the memory of those first, unhoped-for moments, the words we've heard, are now blocking the entrance to our consciousness, and as they control the exits from memory far more than those from imagination, they have more of a retroactive effect on our past (which we can no longer see without taking them into account) than on the still shapeless form of our future. For years I'd believed that going to Madame Swann's was a vague fantasy that I'd never attain; now, after spending a quarter of an hour in her home, it was the time when I didn't yet know her that had become fantastical and vague, like a possibility which the realization of another possibility has destroyed. How could I ever again dream of her dining room as an inconceivable place when I couldn't make the least movement in my mind without encountering the infrangible rays emanating back into my most distant past from the lobster *à l'américaine** that I'd just eaten? Swann must have observed something similar occurring in his own case: this apartment where he was entertaining me could be seen as the place where two dwellings had merged and become one, not just the ideal apartment my imagination had created, but another still, the one that Swann's jealous love, as inventive as my dreams, had so often depicted to him—the home which he and Odette might one day share, but which had seemed so inaccessible to him when Odette had brought him and Forcheville to her house to drink orangeade; and what had come to be absorbed, for him, into the very structure of the dining room where we were lunching, was this unhoped-for paradise in which, years ago, he could not without a pang of distress imagine that he'd be saying to *their* butler the very words: 'Is Madame ready yet?' which I now heard him utter with a touch of impatience mingled with a certain self-satisfaction. No more, probably, than Swann himself could I truly grasp my own happiness, and when Gilberte herself once exclaimed: 'Who could ever have predicted that the little girl you used to watch playing prisoner's base, without speaking to her, would one day be your closest friend whose home you could go to whenever you liked?', she spoke of a change which I was forced to see from without, but which I did not possess within myself, for it was composed of two states, which I couldn't manage to think of at the same time without their merging into each other.

And yet because Swann had so intensely desired the apartment, it must still have retained for him some of its appeal, just as it hadn't lost all its mystery for me. By entering their house, I hadn't entirely banished from it the singular charm by which I had for such a long time imagined the life of the Swanns to be enveloped; I'd made it retreat a little, tamed as it was by the stranger I'd been, the pariah whom Madame Swann was now graciously motioning over to sit in a magnificent, hostile, scandalized armchair; but in my memory, I can still perceive this charm all around me. Is this because, while I sat waiting on those days when Monsieur and Madame Swann invited me to have lunch and then go out with them and Gilberte, I imprinted with my gaze, on the carpet, on the wingback armchairs, on the tables, the folding screens, and the paintings, the idea engraved in my mind that Madame Swann, or her husband, or Gilberte was about to enter? Is it because these things have lived on since then in my memory alongside the Swanns, until they absorbed something of them? Is it because, knowing they spent their lives in the midst of these objects, I made them all, as it were, emblems of their special existence, their habits, from which I'd been too long excluded for them not to continue to seem strange to me, even when I was permitted to share in them? Whatever the case, whenever I think of that drawing room which Swann found so ill-assorted (not that his criticism implied any intention on his part to contradict his wife's taste)—because, while it was still based on the half-conservatory, half-studio style which had been that of the apartment where he'd first known Odette, she had nevertheless begun to remove from this jumble a number of Chinese objects she now found a little 'tacky', a bit 'out-of-date', and to replace them with a host of little pieces upholstered in Louis XVI silks* (not to mention the works of art brought by Swann from his house on the Quai d'Orléans)—I see that composite room in my memory as possessing a cohesion, a unity, an individual charm lacking in even the most intact collections the past has bequeathed to us, or in those most vividly stamped with a person's unique imprint; for, by believing they have their own existence, we alone can give certain things we see a soul which lives in them, and which they go on to develop in us. All the ideas (at once thrilling and indefinable) I'd formed of the hours—different from those that exist for other people—that the Swanns spent in that apartment, which was for their everyday life what the body was for the soul, and which was bound to express the singular quality of their existence, were divided amongst and amalgamated with the placement of the furniture, the thickness of the carpets, the orientation of the windows, the ministrations of the servants. When, after lunch, we'd go into the sunshine to have coffee by the great bay window of the drawing room, and Madame Swann would ask how many lumps of sugar I'd like in my coffee, it wasn't just the silk-covered footstool she pushed towards me that emanated the melancholy charm I used to sense in the name of Gilberte—under the pink hawthorn, and then beside the thicket of laurels—along with the hostility that her parents had shown me, and which this piece of furniture seemed to have known and shared so well that I didn't feel worthy, and felt a little shy about setting my feet on its defenceless padding; an individual soul secretly connected it to the light at two in the afternoon, a light different from light anywhere else, as it made its golden waves play in the gulf around our feet, and as the bluish settees and hazy tapestries emerged from those waves like enchanted islands; and there was nothing, not even the painting by Rubens* hanging above the mantelpiece, that was not also endowed with the same quality and almost the same power of charm as Monsieur Swann's laced boots and voluminous cape, the like of which I so longed to wear, yet which Odette was now asking her husband to replace with another so as to be more elegant, when I did them the honour of driving out with them. She too would go to get dressed, even though I protested that no walking dress could even come close to the wonderful dressing gown of crêpe de Chine or silk, in old rose or cherry, Tiepolo pink,* white, mauve, green, red or yellow, plain or patterned, in which Madame Swann had taken lunch and out of which she was about to change. When I told her she should go out like that, she'd laugh, either out of mockery of my ignorance or delight in my compliment. She apologized for having so many tea gowns, claiming they were the only things she felt comfortable in, and then left us to don one of those regal outfits admired by all, after having summoned me at times to choose the one I'd like her to wear.

How proud I was at the Jardin d'Acclimatation, after we'd stepped down from the carriage, to be walking at Madame Swann's side! As she strolled along in her nonchalant way, letting her cloak float behind her, I kept glancing at her with a gaze of admiration to which she coquettishly responded with a lingering smile. Now, if we met any of Gilberte's schoolmates, girls or boys, who greeted us from a distance, I would be regarded by them as one of those beings I'd envied so, one of those friends of Gilberte who knew her family and were included in that other part of her life, the part not spent at the Champs-Élysées.

Often in the paths of the Bois de Boulogne or the Jardin d'Acclimatation we'd be greeted by some distinguished lady or other who was a friend of Swann's, whom he sometimes didn't notice and would be pointed out by his wife: 'Charles, don't you see Madame de Montmorency?' And Swann, with that genial smile stemming from a long friendship, would take off his hat, but with a flourish and an elegance uniquely his own. Sometimes the lady would stop, happy to show Madame Swann a courtesy that would have no repercussions, since she knew Madame Swann wouldn't use it to her advantage later, so well had Swann instructed her to show reserve. Madame Swann had nonetheless acquired all the manners of polite society, and however elegant and stately the lady was, Madame Swann would always match her; pausing for a moment by the friend her husband had just greeted, she'd introduce Gilberte and me with such ease, and would remain so relaxed and calm in her affability, that it would have been difficult to say which of the two—Swann's wife or the passing lady—was the aristocrat. The day we went to see the Sinhalese, on our way home we saw, coming towards us and followed by two others who seemed to be escorting her, an old but still beautiful lady wrapped in a dark cloak and wearing a little bonnet tied under her chin with ribbon. 'Ah! Here's someone who will interest you!' Swann said to me. The old lady, now quite close, smiled at us with an affectionate sweetness. Swann doffed his hat while Madame Swann curtsied and made as if to kiss the hand of the lady, who looked like a portrait by Winterhalter,* but she drew her up and kissed her cheek. 'Come now, do please put your hat on, you!' she said to Swann, in a rough, almost rasping voice, like an old friend. 'I'm going to introduce you to Her Imperial Highness', Madame Swann whispered to me. Swann drew me aside for a moment while Madame Swann chatted with Her Highness about the fine weather and the animals newly arrived at the Jardin d'Acclimatation. 'That's the Princesse Mathilde', he told me, 'you know, the friend of Flaubert, Sainte-Beuve, Dumas . . . Just think, she's the niece of Napoleon I!* Both Napoleon III and the Emperor of Russia have asked for her hand in marriage. Isn't that remarkable? Talk to her a little. But I hope she won't keep us standing here for an hour!— I met Taine* recently,' Swann went on, addressing the princess, 'who told me Your Highness had fallen out with him.' 'He has behaved like a pig!' she said gruffly, pronouncing the word *cochon* as if it were the name of Joan of Arc's contemporary, Bishop Cauchon.* 'After his article on the Emperor, I left him my card with *p.p.c.* written on it.'* I felt the sort of surprise one feels on first reading the letters of the

Duchesse d'Orléans, née Princesse Palatine.* And indeed Princesse Mathilde, animated by sentiments so thoroughly French, expressed them with a bluntness that recalled the Germany of an older generation, a trait which she had no doubt inherited from her mother, who was from Württemberg. Her slightly uncouth and almost masculine frankness was softened, when she smiled, with Italian languor. On top of this, she wore outfits that were so Second Empire in style* that, even though the princess no doubt wore them only out of attachment to the fashions she'd loved before, she seemed to have planned them so as not to commit the slightest mistake in historic colour, and to comply with the whims of those who expected her to evoke another era. I whispered to Swann to ask her if she'd known Alfred de Musset. 'Hardly, Monsieur,' she replied, in a tone that seemed to feign annoyance, whereas it was by way of a joke that she said 'Monsieur' to Swann, since they were close friends. 'I had him over for dinner once. I'd invited him for seven o'clock. At half past seven, as he hadn't appeared, we sat down to dinner. He arrived at eight, bowed to me, sat down, never once opened his mouth, and left after dinner without my hearing the sound of his voice. He was dead drunk. That hardly encouraged me to repeat the invitation.' Swann and I were standing a little way off. 'I hope this little meeting won't last much longer,' he said to me; 'the soles of my feet are hurting. And I don't know why my wife keeps on making conversation. After this, she'll complain about being tired, while I'm the one who can't bear standing so long.' Madame Swann, in fact, who had the news from Madame Bontemps, was saying to the princess that the government, having finally realized its faux pas, had decided to send her an invitation to be present on the dais during the visit that Tsar Nicholas was to make two days later at the Invalides.* But the princess, who despite all appearances and despite the character of her circle, which was comprised mainly of artists and writers, had remained at heart, whenever she had to take action, Napoleon's niece, replied: 'Yes, Madame, I received it this morning, and I sent it back to the Minister, who must have received it by now. I told him I did not need an invitation to go to the Invalides. If the government wishes me to go, it will not be on the dais, but in our vault, where the Emperor's tomb is. I don't need a card for that. I have my own keys. I go in whenever I like. The government has only to let me know if it wishes me to be present or not. But if I do go to the Invalides, it will be in the vault or not at all.' At that moment

Madame Swann and I were greeted by a young man who said hello to her in passing, and whom I didn't know she knew: it was Bloch. When I asked Madame Swann about him, she told me he'd been introduced to her by Madame Bontemps, and that he was on the minister's staff, which I hadn't known. At any rate, she must not have seen him often, or else she hadn't wanted to mention the name of 'Bloch', which she may not have thought very 'chic', for she said his name was Monsieur Moreul. I assured her she was mistaken and that his name was Bloch. The princess was straightening out the train unfurling behind her, which Madame Swann was admiring.

'It's actually made from a fur the Tsar sent me,' the princess said, 'and as I've just been to see him, I wore it to show him it could be made into a coat.'

'I hear Prince Louis has joined the Russian army;* Your Highness must be so sad not to have him nearby anymore,' said Madame Swann, not seeing her husband's signs of impatience.

'That's all he needed! As I said to him, "Just because you had a soldier in the family, that's no reason to join," ' replied the princess, thereby, with this abrupt simplicity, alluding to Napoleon I.

Swann could no longer keep still. 'Madame, I'm afraid I'm the one who must play the royal highness and ask your permission to take our leave; my wife hasn't been at all well, and I don't want her to remain standing much longer.'

Madame Swann curtsied again and the princess bestowed on us a divine smile, which she seemed to have summoned out of the past, from the gracious days of her youth, from evenings at Compiègne,* a sweet, unbroken smile that smoothed away the briefly annoyed expression from her face; then she walked away, followed by her ladies-in-waiting, who, like interpreters, nannies, or nurses, had done nothing but punctuate our conversation with insignificant remarks and pointless explanations. 'You should go and sign the book at her house one day this week,' Madame Swann said. 'One doesn't leave visiting cards with all these *royalties*, as the English say, but you'll get an invitation if you write your name down.'

Sometimes in those late winter days, before going for our ride, we'd go and see one of the little exhibitions opening at the time; Swann, as a noted collector, was greeted with special deference by the dealers in whose galleries they were held. And in that cold weather, all my old desires to leave for the South of France and Venice were reawakened by those rooms, in which spring was already advanced, and a fiery sun cast violet glints on the rosy Alpilles and gave the Grand Canal the dark transparency of emerald. If the weather was poor, we'd go to a concert or to the theatre, and afterwards refresh ourselves at a tearoom. Whenever Madame Swann wanted to say something to me that she didn't want the people at the neighbouring tables, or even the waiters, to hear, she'd say it in English, as if it were a language known only to ourselves. Whereas everyone knew English; I alone had not yet learned it, and I was obliged to say so to Madame Swann so that she'd stop making remarks I guessed were unkind about the people drinking tea, or about those serving it, none of whom—except, of course, myself—missed a word of what was said.

Once, in connection with a matinee, Gilberte took me completely by surprise. It was the very day she'd mentioned before, the anniversary of her grandfather's death. We were both supposed to be going, along with her governess, to hear selections from an opera, and Gilberte had changed into an outfit suitable for such a musical performance, preserving the air of indifference she customarily displayed towards whatever we were about to do, saying it didn't matter what it was so long as I liked it and her parents agreed to it. Before lunch, her mother took us aside to tell her it annoyed her father that we were going to a concert on that particular day. This seemed entirely natural to me. Gilberte remained impassive but turned pale with anger she was unable to hide, and said not a word. When Monsieur Swann came home, his wife took him to the other side of the drawing room and whispered in his ear. He called Gilberte and took her into the next room. We could hear their raised voices. Yet I could not believe that Gilberte, so obedient, so loving, so well behaved, would resist her father's request, on such a day and for such an insignificant reason. Finally Swann left the room, saying: 'You heard what I said. Now do as you like.'

Gilberte's face remained tense all during lunch, after which we went to her room. Then all of a sudden, without the slightest hesitation, and as if nothing were wrong, she exclaimed: 'Two o'clock! You know the concert starts at half past.' And she told her governess to hurry.

'But won't your father be annoyed?' I asked her.

'Not in the least.'

'But he was afraid it might seem strange because of the anniversary.'

'What do I care what people think? I think it's ridiculous to worry about other people when feelings are involved. You feel for yourself, not for an audience. Mademoiselle, who hardly ever goes out, was looking forward to this concert, so I won't deprive her of it just to please the gallery.'

And she picked up her hat.

'But Gilberte,' I said, taking her arm, 'it's to please your father, not the gallery.'

'You're not going to start criticizing me too, I hope,' she said angrily, snatching her arm away.

A favour the Swanns granted me even more precious than taking me with them to the Jardin d'Acclimatation or to a concert was to be included even in their friendship with Bergotte, which had been at the source of the charm I found in them when, long before meeting Gilberte, I thought that her closeness to that godlike old man made her the most fascinating friend of all, if it weren't for the fact that the disdain I thought I must inspire in her had forbidden me to hope that she'd ever take me with her to visit the towns Bergotte loved. Then, one day, Madame Swann invited me to a grand luncheon. I didn't know who the guests would be. When I arrived in the entrance hall I was disconcerted by an alarming incident. Madame Swann rarely missed an opportunity to adopt any of the customs that are thought 'smart' for a season but, failing to catch on, are soon abandoned (as, for example, many years before, she had her *hansom cab*,* or had it printed on a luncheon invitation that it was being held *to meet*,* a person of some importance). Often there was nothing mysterious about these customs, and they required no initiation. One of these was a little fad imported from England, which led Odette to have visiting cards made for her husband on which the title of 'Mr' appeared before his name. After my first visit to their house, Madame Swann had called on me and left me one of those 'pasteboards', as she called them. No one had ever left me a card before; I was overwhelmed with such pride, excitement, and gratitude that, scraping together all the money I possessed, I ordered a superb basket of camellias and sent it to Madame Swann. I begged my father to leave a card at her home, but first to have some made on which the title of 'Mr' appeared before his name. He granted neither of my prayers; for several days I was in despair, but then wondered if he might after all be in the right. Still, even though the use of 'Mr' was pointless, it was at least intelligible. This was not the case with another custom revealed to me, though without its meaning, on that day of Madame Swann's luncheon party. As I was about to proceed from the entrance hall into the dining room, the butler handed me a long, thin envelope on which my name was written. Taken aback, I thanked him, and stared blankly at the envelope. I knew no more what to do with it than a foreigner does with one of those little utensils given to guests at Chinese dinners. I saw it was sealed; I was afraid opening it right away might seem indiscreet, so I slipped it into my pocket with a knowing air. Madame Swann had invited me a few days before to come to a luncheon for 'a select few'. But there were sixteen of us, among whom I had no idea Bergotte was included. Madame Swann, who had just 'named' me, as she put it, to several of her guests, suddenly uttered after my name, in the exact same way she'd just said it (as if we were merely two luncheon guests who must each feel equally flattered to meet the other), the name of the gentle white-haired Bard. The name Bergotte gave me a start, like the sound of a revolver being fired straight at me, but instinctively, to put up a bold front, I bowed; before me, like one of those magicians in tails you see emerging unscathed from the smoke of a pistol shot out of which a dove flies up, I saw a young, uncouth, stocky, myopic little man with a red nose shaped like a snail-shell and a black goatee beard. I was heartbroken, for what had just been reduced to dust was not only the gentle old man of whom nothing remained, but also the beauty of an immense body of work that I'd contrived to house in the frail and sacred organism I'd constructed, like a temple, expressly for it, but for which no room was to be found in the thickset body, full of blood vessels, bones, and glands, of the little snail-nosed, black-goateed man standing before me. The whole Bergotte I had slowly and delicately built up, drop by drop, like a stalactite, from the transparent beauty of his books, had suddenly been rendered useless the instant the bulbous nose and the black goatee came into the picture, just as the solution found for a mathematical problem turns out to be useless because we haven't thoroughly read all its terms and have therefore failed to observe that the total must amount to a specific number. The nose and goatee were so prominent and impossible to ignore that they not only forced me to reconstruct completely the character of Bergotte, but also seemed to imply, to produce, to exude constantly a certain kind of overactive, self-satisfied mind, and this was not fair, for that mentality had nothing to do with the sort of intelligence that permeated all his books, which I knew so well, and which were infused with a gentle, godlike wisdom. Starting from them, I would never have arrived at that snail nose; but starting from that nose, which did not seem the least bit self-conscious, but stood out proudly and fantastically on its own, I went in an entirely different direction from Bergotte's work, one that must, it seemed, end up at the mentality of some sort of overworked engineer, the kind that, when greeted, think the correct response is 'Fine, thanks, and you?' even before being asked, and if you say you're delighted to make his acquaintance, replies with an abbreviation he thinks is fashionable, intelligent, and modern since it wastes no precious time in empty phrases: 'Likewise.' Names, no doubt, are whimsical painters, giving us such unlikely sketches of people and places that we often feel a kind of astonishment when we have in front of us, instead of the imagined world, the visible one (which, for that matter, is not the 'real' world, since our senses no more possess the gift of portraiture than our imagination does, so that the ultimately approximate sketches we obtain from reality are at least as different from the visible world as the visible world was from the imagined one). But in Bergotte's case, the difficulty I had with my preconception of his name was nothing compared to the one caused by the work that I knew, to which I was forced to attach, as if to a balloon, the goateed man, without knowing if that body of work would still have the strength to rise up. But apparently this *was* the man who had written the books I loved so much, for when Madame Swann made a point of telling him about my admiration for one of them, he showed no surprise that she'd told him rather than some other guest, and didn't seem to see it as the result of some misunderstanding; but, while his body, eager for the coming meal, swelled out the frock coat he'd worn in honour of all these guests, and his attention was focused on other, more important matters, it was only as at some far-off episode of his former life, as if some allusion were being made to a costume he'd worn as the Duc de Guise one year at a masked ball, that he smiled as he cast his mind back to the idea of his books, which immediately fell in my estimation (dragging down with them in their fall the whole value of Beauty, the universe, and life itself) until they seemed to have been no more than a trivial form of recreation for a man with a goatee beard. I told myself that he must have put some effort into them, but that if he'd lived on an island surrounded by oyster beds, he would instead have devoted himself equally success-fully to the pearl trade. His work no longer seemed so inevitable to me. And then I wondered if originality truly proves that great writers are gods, each reigning over a kingdom that is his alone, or if it was all something of a sham, and that the differences between one individu-al's books and another's might be the result of hard work rather than the expression of a radical, essential difference between distinct per-sonalities.

Meanwhile we'd taken our seats at table. Next to my plate I found a carnation with its stem wrapped in silver paper. It embarrassed me less than the envelope I'd been given in the entrance hall and had completely forgotten. Its purpose, though quite new to me, seemed to make more sense when I saw all the male guests pick up similar car-nations lying by their plates and slip them into the buttonholes of their frock coats. I did the same with the feigned naturalness of an atheist in church who isn't familiar with the Mass, but stands up and kneels down just a moment after everyone else. Another unknown, less ephemeral custom made me even more uneasy. On the other side of my plate was a little dish piled high with a blackish substance that I didn't know was caviar. I had no idea what to do with it, but was determined not to eat it.

Bergotte was seated quite close to me; I could hear perfectly everything he said. I understood then the impression Monsieur de Norpois had formed of him. He really did have a bizarre vocal organ; nothing alters the material qualities of the voice more than the quality of thought it contains: the resonance of the diphthongs, the energy of the labials are all influenced by it. So is diction itself. His own seemed entirely different from his way of writing, and even the things he said differed from the words that filled his books. But a voice emerges from a mask; it's not powerful enough at first to make us recognize the face we've seen laid bare in the speaker's style of writing. At certain points in the conversation, when Bergotte was in the habit of speaking in a way that Monsieur de Norpois was not alone in finding affected and displeasing, it took me a long time to discover an exact corres-pondence with the parts of his books where his style became so poetic and musical. At such times, Bergotte saw a plastic beauty in what he was saying that was independent of the meaning of his sentences, and since human speech is in communication with the soul but can't express it in the same way that written style does, Bergotte seemed almost to be talking nonsense, drawing certain words out and, if he was following a single image behind the words, running them together like a single sound, with a fatiguing monotony. But his pretentious, bombastic, and toneless delivery was actually the sign of the aesthetic quality of his words, and the manifestation in his conversation of the power that gave his books their harmonious flow of imagery. It was all the more difficult for me to perceive this at first since what he was saying at such moments, precisely because it was issuing from the real Bergotte, did not seem to be by Bergotte. It was a profusion of exact ideas that did not appear in the 'Bergotte style' appropriated by so many essayists; and this dissimilarity was probably—seen dimly through the conversation, like an image behind smoked glass—another aspect of the fact that when you read a page by Bergotte, it was never what would have been written by any of those shallow imitators who embellished their prose in newspapers and books alike with so many images and ideas 'à la Bergotte'. This difference in style stemmed from the fact that 'the Bergotte' was above all a kind of precious and real element hidden in the heart of every thing and then extracted from it by that great writer thanks to his genius, and that this extraction, rather than writing 'à la Bergotte', was the goal of the gentle Bard. Actually he did this despite himself precisely because he *was* Bergotte, and because in this sense every new-found element of beauty in his work was the small amount of Bergotte hidden in a thing, which he drew out of it. But even though each of these beauties was thereby connected to the others and was thus recognizable, it remained unique, like the discovery that had brought it to light; and also new, hence different from what is called the Bergotte style, which was a vague synthesis of all the Bergottes already found and written by the man himself, none of which enabled men without genius to predict what he might go on to discover in other things. This is true of all great writers; the beauty of their sentences is as unforeseeable as that of a woman we have not yet met; it is creative because it's centred on some external object they're thinking of—not on themselves—and which they have not yet expressed in words. A memoir writer of our time who wanted to write in the style of Saint-Simon without being obvious about it might at a pinch write the first line of his portrait of Villars: 'He was rather a tall, dark man . . . with a lively, open, expressive physiognomy', but what law of determinism could lead him to write Saint-Simon's next line, which begins: 'and in truth a trifle mad'?* True variety lies in this abundance of real, unexpected elements, in the branch laden with blue flowers soaring impossibly upwards from the spring hedgerow that seemed already overfull, whereas the purely formal imitation of variety (and the same could be argued for all other qualities of style) is nothing but empty uniformity, that is, the very antithesis of variety, and can only give the illusion or memory of it to a reader who has not grasped it from the masters themselves.

Hence, just as Bergotte's manner of speaking would no doubt have been charming if he had just been some amateur reciting imitation Bergotte, whereas it was bound up with Bergotte's thought, at work and in action, by vital connections that couldn't immediately be discerned by the ear, so the reason why there was something too matter of fact and overindulgent in his speech was that he applied his mind with precision to any aspect of reality he found pleasing, thereby disappointing those expecting to hear him speak only of 'the eternal torrent of appearances' or the 'mysterious thrill of beauty'. Finally, the quality, always rare and new, of what he wrote was conveyed in his conversation by such a subtle way of approaching a question, ignoring every aspect that was already familiar, that he seemed to be considering it from some petty angle, to be simply wrong, or to be speaking in paradox; and so, more often than not, his ideas seemed confused, since each of us sees clarity only in those ideas that have the same degree of confusion as our own. Besides, since every novelty requires that we first eliminate the cliché we were so used to that we'd come to view it as reality itself, any new style of conversation, like any originality in painting or music, will always seem convoluted and tiresome. It is based on figures of speech to which we're not accustomed; the speaker seems to be talking only in metaphors, which tires us and gives the impression of a lack of truth. (Of course, the old figures of speech were also once difficult images to follow when the listener wasn't yet familiar with the world they portrayed. But they've long since become the real world, the world of reference.) And so when Bergotte said Cottard was 'a Cartesian diver trying to find his balance'* or that Brichot 'was even more concerned than Madame Swann about the grooming of his hair, because, doubly anxious as he was about both his profile and his reputation, he always had to make sure that his hair was so arranged as to make him look like both a lion and a philosopher', people soon tired of it, saying they preferred to find their footing on something more concrete, by which they meant something they were more used to. The unrecognizable words issuing from the mask before me must indeed be connected to the writer I admired; they could not have been inserted into his books like pieces in a jigsaw puzzle, but were on a different level and required a transposition by means of which, one day when I was repeating phrases I'd heard Bergotte say, I discovered the whole foundation of his written style, which in spoken form had seemed so different that I'd been unable to recognize and name its different elements.

Less importantly, the special, somewhat too pedantic, overly emphatic, way he had of pronouncing certain words, certain adjectives, which often recurred in his conversation and which he always slightly over-emphasized, stressing all their syllables and intoning the last one (as for instance the word 'visage', which he always used instead of 'face', filling it with a number of extra *v*s, *s*s, and *g*s, which all seemed to explode from his open hand at such moments), corresponded precisely to the beautiful passages in his prose where he highlighted these favourite words, which were always preceded by a sort of margin, and arranged in the overall pattern of the sentence in such a way that, to avoid making a metrical mistake, you were obliged to include in your count their full 'quantity'. Yet you couldn't find in Bergotte's speech that sort of illumination which in his books, as well as in the books of a few other writers, often changes the appearance of words in the written sentence. No doubt this is because such illumination comes from deep within us, and its rays cannot reach our spoken words at those times when, open to others through conversation, we are to a certain extent closed to ourselves. In this respect there were more intonations, more emphases, in his books than in his spoken words: it was an emphasis independent of beauty of style, and which the author himself probably didn't notice, since it wasn't separable from his inmost personality. It was this stress that, at those times when, in his books, Bergotte was entirely natural, gave rhythm to the often quite insignificant words he was writing. This emphasis is not noted down in the text; there is nothing to indicate it, and yet it insistently imposes itself on the sentences; they cannot be uttered in any other way; it is what is most ephemeral yet most profound about that writer, what will bear witness to his true nature, what will show that, despite all the severe things he expressed, he was gentle, or that, despite all his sensualities, he was sentimental.

Certain peculiarities of elocution that existed as faint traces in Bergotte's conversation were not his alone, for when I came to know his brothers and sisters later on, I found those peculiarities much more pronounced. There was a sort of abruptness, a hoarse tone, in the final words of a cheerful sentence, or a fading, indistinct voice at the end of a sad one. Swann, who had known the Master as a child, told me he could hear these family inflections in him back then as well as in his brothers and sisters, shouts of fierce joy or whispers of lingering melancholy, and that in the room where they were all playing together, Bergotte could be heard over everyone in their concerts, alternately deafening and subdued. Unique as they may be, all the sounds we humans emit are fugitive, and do not survive us. But this was not the case for the Bergotte family's pronunciation. Though it may be difficult ever to understand, even in the *Meistersinger*, how an artist can invent music by listening to birdsong,* Bergotte had transposed and fixed in his prose the ways of drawing out words that are repeated in shouts of joy, or that fall, drop by drop, in sorrowful sighs. In his books, there are sentence endings in which the accumulated sounds are prolonged, as in the last chords of an opera's overture which can't bring itself to come to an end and repeats its final phrase several times before the conductor at last lays down his baton; I came to see this later as a musical equivalent of those phonetic 'brasses' of the Bergotte family. In Bergotte's case, however, the instant he transposed them into his books, he unconsciously stopped using them in his speech. From the day he began to write—and, all the more so, later on, when I knew him—his voice had forever lost its power to orchestrate them.

These young Bergottes—the future writer and his siblings—were doubtless not superior (quite the contrary) to more refined, spiritual young people, who found the Bergottes to be quite rowdy, even a little vulgar and annoying in their jokes, which characterized the partly pretentious, partly puerile style of the house. But genius, or even great talent, stems less from intellectual elements and social refinement superior to those of other people than from the ability to transform and transpose them. To heat a liquid with an electric lamp, you don't need the strongest lamp possible, but one whose current can be diverted from illumination in order to produce heat rather than light. To soar up into the sky, it's not necessary to have the most powerful vehicle, but one that can shift from moving along the ground to ascending vertically, one that's capable of converting its horizontal speed into upward thrust. Similarly, those who produce brilliant works are not the ones who live in the most refined environment, who are the most cultured and whose conversation is the most intellectual, but the ones who, suddenly ceasing to live for themselves alone, have the ability to reflect their personalities like a mirror, so that their lives, mediocre as they may be socially and even, to a certain degree, intellectually, are reflected by their work, since genius consists in the ability to reflect and not in the intrinsic quality of the scene reflected. The day the young Bergotte was able to show to the world of his readers the tasteless household where he'd spent his youth and the not very amusing chatter he shared with his brothers, he rose higher than his family's friends, even though they were more intellectual and more distinguished: they could go home in their fine Rolls-Royces, expressing a slight contempt for the vulgarity of the Bergottes; but he, in his modest machine that had finally 'taken off', was soaring above them.

He now shared other traits of his elocution not with family members but with certain writers of his day. Younger men who were beginning to renounce him, and who claimed to have no intellectual affinity with him, nevertheless unconsciously revealed that affinity by using the same adverbs, the same prepositions he constantly repeated, by constructing their sentences in the same way, or by speaking in the same muted, languid tone, which had been his reaction against the facile grandiloquence of an earlier generation. Perhaps these young men—and we will see who they were—had never known Bergotte. But, having been inoculated with his way of thinking, they'd developed those changes in syntax and accent which are necessarily linked to intellectual originality. This connection requires interpretation. Although Bergotte wasn't indebted to anyone for his writing style, he owed his way of speaking to one of his old colleagues, a wonderful conversationalist who had worked his spell on him, whom he imitated without meaning to in conversation, but who, being less gifted, had never written any truly superior books. So that if one went no further than originality of speech, Bergotte would have been labelled a disciple, a second-rate writer; whereas, despite his friend's influence in conversational style, he was original and truly creative as a writer. Probably again in order to separate himself from the previous generation, which was overfond of abstractions and tiresome commonplaces, whenever Bergotte wanted to praise a book, the part he'd single out and quote was always a scene that created an image, a picture that had no rational significance. 'Ah yes!' he'd say, 'what a nice touch that is, the little girl with an orange shawl!', or else: 'The part where there's a regiment marching through a town, that's excellent, excellent!' As to style, he wasn't entirely of his time (though he remained firmly within his country; he detested Tolstoy, George Eliot, Ibsen, and Dostoevsky*) since the word that always came to him when he wanted to praise a particular style was 'smooth'. 'Yes, all the same I like the Chateaubriand of *Atala* better than the Chateaubriand of *Rancé*; he seems smoother.'* He said this word like a doctor who, when a patient assures him that milk gives him an upset stomach, replies: 'But it's very smooth.' And it's true that there was in Bergotte's style a kind of harmony similar to the one the ancients praised in some of their orators, the nature of which is difficult for us to fathom, accustomed as we are to our modern languages, in which we don't seek out such effects.

If anyone praised a piece of his, he'd say shyly: 'I think it's more or less true, more or less accurate; it may be worth something', but simply out of modesty, like a woman who, when told her dress, or daughter, is lovely, replies, about the former: 'It's comfortable', and about the latter: 'She's a good girl'. But the artisan's instinct was too deeply rooted in Bergotte for him not to be aware that the sole proof that what he'd constructed was useful and true lay in the joy his work had given him—him first of all, and others later on. Only, many years later, after he'd lost his talent, whenever he wrote something with which he wasn't happy, so as not to erase it as he should have done, but publish it, he'd repeat, to himself this time: 'Despite everything, it's not too bad, it may be of some use to my country.' Thus the phrases murmured long ago to his admirers out of feigned modesty came to be uttered, in the secrecy of his heart, out of a kind of proud anxiety. And so the very words that had served Bergotte as a superfluous apology for the value of his early work became, as it were, an ineffective consolation for the mediocrity of his latest.

A kind of austerity of taste that he possessed, a constant desire to write only things about which he could say: 'That's smooth', and that had made people regard him for so many years as a sterile, overly precious artist, a scribbler of trifles, was on the contrary the secret of his strength, for habit forms a writer's style as well as a man's character, and the author who has become satisfied with achieving a kind of pleasantness in the expression of his thoughts thereby sets the boundaries of his talent forever, just as, by yielding often to pleasure, or laziness, or fear of suffering, we ourselves trace the lineaments of our vices and the limits of our virtue on a character that, after a time, can no longer be touched up.

If, however, despite so many correspondences that I perceived later on between the writer and the man, I didn't at first believe at Madame Swann's that it was actually Bergotte, the author of so many divine books, who stood before me, perhaps I wasn't entirely in the wrong, for he himself did not, in the strict sense of the word, 'believe' it either. He didn't believe it because he showed a special eagerness to please fashionable people (though he himself wasn't a snob), literary men, and journalists, who were all quite inferior to him. True, he had now learned, from the approval of others, that he had genius, compared to which social position and official rank are nothing. He'd learned he had genius, but he didn't believe it, because he continued to feign deference towards mediocre writers in order to become an academician as quickly as possible, whereas neither the Académie nor the Faubourg Saint-Germain has any more to do with that part of the eternal Spirit which writes the books of a Bergotte than with the principle of causality or the idea of God. He knew this too, just as a kleptomaniac knows, but without benefiting from his knowledge, that it's wrong to steal. And so the goateed, snail-nosed man, like a gentleman guest who steals your spoons, knew all the tricks to get closer to the coveted chair at the Académie, or to some duchess who commanded several votes at each election, but to do so in a way that no one who would have thought it a vice to pursue such a goal could see through his little game. He was only partly successful; the real Bergotte's speech could be heard alternating with that of the selfish, ambitious Bergotte, who thought only of talking about certain powerful, noble, or wealthy men in order to increase his importance—the same man who in his books, where he was truly himself, had so clearly shown the charm, pure as a mountain spring, of the poor.

As for those other vices to which Monsieur de Norpois had alluded—that almost incestuous love affair, along with, rumour had it, a lack of discretion when it came to money—even though they stood in glaring contradiction to the tenor of his latest novels, full as they were of such a scrupulous, painful concern for all that's good that their heroes' slightest joys were poisoned by it, and the reader himself felt an anguish that made even the quietest life seem hard to bear, these vices (supposing they were justly imputed to Bergotte) did not prove that everything he wrote was a lie, or all his sensitivity a mere sham. Just as in pathology, certain conditions that seem similar may be due to different causes, some to high blood pressure and some to low, some to an excess of glandular secretions, some to an insufficient amount, so vice can arise from both hypersensitivity and insensitivity. Perhaps it's only in truly depraved lives that the problem of morality can arise in the full force of its anxiety. And to this problem the artist gives a solution pertaining not to his own personal life, but to what is for him his real life: a general, literary solution. Just as the great Fathers of the Church, virtuous though they were, often started out by experiencing the sins of all men, out of which they drew their own sanctity, great artists, however unvirtuous they may be, use their vices to develop a concept of the moral law that applies to us all. It's the vices (or merely the foibles and follies) of the environment in which they live, the trivial conversations, the frivolous or shocking lives of their daughters, the infidelity of their wives, or their own misdeeds, that writers have most often denounced in their diatribes, without, however, doing anything to rectify the problems or failings of their own family life. This contrast was less striking in Bergotte's time, partly because, as society became more corrupt, notions of morality became increasingly refined, and partly because the public had become more knowledgeable than it had ever been before about writers' private lives; and on certain evenings at the theatre, people would point out the author I'd so admired in Combray ensconced in the recesses of a fashionable box in a setting that seemed a singularly derisive or poignant commentary, a brazen denial of the theory he'd just been expounding in his latest book. Nothing of what anyone told me could teach me much about Bergotte's goodness or wickedness. Some intimate friend of his might provide proofs of his coldness, while some stranger might mention an example (touching because it obviously was supposed to be kept secret) of Bergotte's profound sensitivity. He had behaved cruelly towards his wife. But in a village inn where he'd spent the night, he had sat up to watch over a poor woman who had tried to drown herself, and when he was obliged to leave, he'd left a lot of money with the innkeeper so that he wouldn't turn the poor creature out but would see that she received the care she needed. Perhaps the more the great writer developed in Bergotte at the expense of the man with the goatee beard, the more his individual life drowned in the flow of all the lives he imagined, until he no longer felt obliged to perform practical duties, which were replaced for him by the duty to imagine those other lives. But at the same time, because he imagined the feelings of others as well as if they were his own, when circumstances brought him into at least temporary contact with an unfortunate person, rather than adopt his own point of view, he always put himself in the position of the person suffering; and from this standpoint, he would have been horrified to hear the language of those who go on thinking about their own petty concerns faced with another's grief. And so he gave rise around him to both justified anger and undying gratitude.

Above all, he was a man who took his deepest pleasure only in certain images, in composing and portraying them with words, like a miniature on the bottom of a little box. For a trifle you'd sent him, if the trifle provided him with the opportunity to embellish it with a few of those images, he'd be lavish in his expression of gratitude, whereas he'd evince none for an expensive present. If he'd ever had to defend himself in a court of law, despite his best interests, he'd have chosen his words not for the effect they might produce on the judge, but for the sake of imagery, which the judge would certainly not have noticed.

On that day when I first saw him at the home of Gilberte's parents, I mentioned I'd recently seen La Berma in *Phèdre*; he told me that in the scene where she stands still with one arm raised to shoulder height—precisely one of the scenes that had been so warmly applauded—she'd managed, with artistic nobility, to evoke masterpieces which she may perhaps never have seen: a Hesperid making the same gesture on a metope at Olympia, or the beautiful virgins on the ancient Erechtheion.*

'Perhaps she conjures them up on her own, but I imagine she goes to museums. It would be an interesting thing to "detect".' ('Detect' was one of Bergotte's favourite expressions, one that had been taken up by various young men who, though they'd never met him, spoke like him, as though they were under some sort of telepathic suggestion.)

'Do you mean the Caryatids?'* Swann asked.

'No, no,' Bergotte replied, 'except in the scene where she confesses her passion to Œnone, when she holds her hand just like Hegeso on the stele in the Kerameikos;* the art she brings back to life is much older. I mentioned the Korai from the old Erechtheion, and I admit there's probably nothing more remote from Racine's art than that, but there are already so many things in *Phèdre* . . . that one more . . . Oh, it's true, her Phèdre straight out of the sixth century* is very pretty indeed, the verticality of the arm, the coil of hair "like marble", yes, it's impressive that she discovered all that. There's much more antiquity there than in quite a few books on so-called "antiquity" this year.'

Since Bergotte had written a famous invocation to these archaic statues in one of his books, the words he was now saying were quite clear to me, and gave me another reason for taking an interest in La Berma's acting. I tried to remember what she'd looked like in that scene where she raised her arm to shoulder height. And I said to myself: 'There's the Hesperid at Olympia; there's the sister of one of those admirable praying figures on the Acropolis; *that's* the definition of noble art!' But in order for these thoughts to enhance La Berma's gesture for me, Bergotte needed first to provide me with a description of them. If this had occurred while the actress's posture was actually appearing in front of me, at that instant when the thing happening has all the fullness of reality, I could have tried to extract the idea of ancient sculpture from it. But all I'd retained of La Berma in that scene was a memory that could no longer be changed, as faint as an image that lacks the depth of the present into which we can delve and from which we can draw something truly new, an image on which we cannot retroactively impose an interpretation that can be verified by comparing it to its objective counterpart. To join the conversation, Madame Swann asked me if Gilberte had remembered to give me what Bergotte had written on *Phèdre*. 'My daughter is such a scatter-brain,' she added. Bergotte smiled modestly and protested it was just a little thing of no importance. 'That's not true, that little booklet—that *tract*—is delightful!' Madame Swann said, to show she was a good hostess, to make it seem as if she'd read the pamphlet, and also because she didn't want merely to compliment Bergotte, but to show that she made selections from among the things he wrote, and wished to exercise a degree of influence over him. And it's true that she did inspire him, but in an entirely different way from what she thought. But when all is said and done, there are connections between the elegance of Madame Swann's salon and a whole aspect of Bergotte's work such that each can be a commentary on the other, for the old men of today.

I became caught up in relating to Bergotte my impressions of La Berma. Often he didn't agree with them, but he let me continue. I told him how much I'd liked the green lighting when Phèdre raises her arm. 'Ah! The set designer would be very happy to hear that—he's a great artist, I'll tell him because he's quite proud of that particular lighting effect. I must say I don't like it very much, it bathes everything in a kind of glaucous glow, it makes little Phèdre look too much like a branch of coral at the bottom of an aquarium. You'll say it brings out the cosmic aspect of the tragedy. True. Still, it would be more fitting for a play set in Neptune's realm. I'm quite aware of Neptune's revenge in the play. Of course, I'm not saying that people should think solely of Port-Royal,* but really, Racine isn't talking about the love affairs of sea urchins. But it's what my friend wanted, and it *is* quite striking all the same; when it comes down to it, it's rather nice. Yes, you liked it, you understood it; we do agree in the end, it's a little crazy what he did, isn't it, but it's actually very clever.' When Bergotte's opinion differed in this way from my own, he never silenced me or made it impossible for me to reply, as Monsieur de Norpois would have done. That does not prove that Bergotte's opinions were less valid than the ambassador's; quite the contrary. A powerful idea communicates some of its power to the person who contradicts it. As part of the universal community of minds, it inserts itself into the mind of the one refuting it and takes root amongst other adjacent ideas, with the help of which, regaining some ground, he completes and amends it; so that the final verdict is in a way the work of both individuals discussing it. It's to ideas that are not, strictly speaking, ideas, to ideas that, being groundless, can find no support, no friendly branch on which to alight in the mind of the opponent, that the latter, grappling with thin air, can find no reply. Monsieur de Norpois' arguments (on the subject of art) left no room for discussion because there was no reality to be found in them.

Since Bergotte hadn't swept aside my objections, I confessed to him that they'd been treated with contempt by Monsieur de Norpois. 'But he's just an old canary!' he replied. 'He pecked at you because he always thinks whatever's in front of him is some birdseed or cuttle-fish.' 'What's this? You know Norpois?' Swann asked me. 'Oh! He's as dull as dishwater,' interrupted his wife, who put great stock in Bergotte's opinions and doubtless was afraid that Monsieur de Norpois had spoken ill of her. 'I wanted to chat with him after dinner—I don't know if it's age or digestion, but he seemed quite woozy. It was as if he'd been drugged!' 'That's very true,' said Bergotte, 'he's quite often obliged to stop talking before the evening's over so as not to use up the stock of inanities that keep his shirt front starched and his waistcoat white.'

'I think Bergotte and my wife are being rather hard on him', said Swann, who had taken on the role of the voice of reason in his house. 'I realize Norpois can't be very interesting to you, but from another point of view' (for Swann was also a collector of life's more interesting titbits), 'he's rather a curious man, rather curious as a "lover", I mean. When he was an attaché at the embassy in Rome,' he went on, after making sure that Gilberte couldn't hear him, 'he had a mistress in Paris with whom he was madly in love, and he'd find a way to hurry back twice a week to see her for two hours. Mind you, she was an extremely intelligent, beautiful woman back then; she's a dowager now. And he's had many other affairs in the meantime. I would have gone quite mad if the woman I loved had to live in Paris while I had to stay in Rome. Highly strung people must always love, as the lower classes say, "beneath them", so as to make sure that the women they love know it's in their best interest to be always at their disposal.' As he spoke, Swann realized that I might be applying this maxim to himself and Odette. This made him annoyed with me, since even high-minded people, when they seem to be soaring with you over life, are still weighed down by petty pride. But this irritation showed only in an uneasy look in his eyes. He said nothing to me at the time. Not that this should surprise us overmuch. When Racine (according to a story that's actually apocryphal, though it happens every day in Parisian life) made an allusion to Scarron in the presence of Louis XIV,* the most powerful king in the world said nothing to the poet that night. It wasn't until the next day that he fell from grace.

But since a theory likes to be expressed fully, after this moment of irritation, and after wiping the lens of his monocle, Swann completed his thought with these words, which would later assume in my memory all the weight of a prophetic warning, but which I didn't have the sense to heed: 'The danger of such liaisons, however, is that even though subjecting the woman in this way may calm the man's jealousy for a time, it also makes her more demanding. Eventually he makes his mistress live like one of those prisoners who have a light trained on them night and day to keep them closely guarded. And that usually ends in tragedy.'

I returned to the subject of Monsieur de Norpois. 'You shouldn't trust him; he has a wicked tongue!' Madame Swann said in a tone that seemed so obviously to imply that Monsieur de Norpois had spoken ill of her that Swann looked at his wife reprovingly, as if to stop her from saying anything more.

In the meantime, Gilberte, who had already been asked twice to get ready to go out, stayed there listening to us, between her mother and father, on whose shoulder she was leaning affectionately. At first sight, there was no greater contrast to Madame Swann, who was a brunette, than this red-haired, golden-skinned girl. But after a while, several features of her mother could be recognized in Gilberte, such as the nose abruptly and decisively shortened by the invisible sculptor plying his chisel for many generations, as well as her mother's expressions and gestures; to borrow a comparison from another art, she looked like a slightly inaccurate portrait of Madame Swann whom the painter, from some colourist's whim, had posed in partial disguise, ready to go to a costume ball in Venetian dress. It wasn't just the blonde wig she was wearing, but the fact that every dark atom had been expelled from her skin, which, stripped of its brown veils, seemed more naked, covered only in the rays emanating from an inner sun, as though the make-up wasn't merely superficial, but incarnate; Gilberte looked as if she were representing some fabulous animal, or wearing a mythological disguise. Her fair complexion was so much her father's that, when Gilberte had been created, Nature seemed to have had to solve the problem of making Madame Swann over again little by little, having nothing but Monsieur Swann's skin at its disposal. And nature had used this perfectly, like a master cabinetmaker who purposely leaves the knots and grain of the wood visible. In Gilberte's face, at the corner of a perfect reproduction of Odette's nose, the skin rose to preserve intact both of Monsieur Swann's moles. It was a new variety of Madame Swann that was produced there, next to her, like a white lilac next to a purple one. The line of demarcation between the two likenesses was not, however, clear-cut. At times, when Gilberte laughed, you could make out the oval of her father's cheek in her mother's face, as if the two had been juxtaposed to see what effect the mixture would produce; this oval took shape the way an embryo forms, lengthening diagonally, swelling, and then disappearing in a flash. Gilberte's eyes contained her father's kind, sincere gaze; it's the look she had when she gave me the agate marble, saying: 'Keep it in memory of our friendship.' But, if you asked Gilberte about what she'd done, you'd see in her eyes the same embarrassment, uncertainty, dissimulation, and sadness that Odette used to evince when Swann asked her where she'd been, and she'd give one of those lying replies which, back then, filled the lover with despair, but, now that he was an incurious, prudent husband, made him abruptly change the subject. Often at the Champs-Élysées, I'd been worried when I saw this look in Gilberte's eyes. But most of the time I was mistaken. For in her, a purely physical survival of her mother, this look—this particular one at least—did not signify anything. It was when she'd been to her class, or when she had to go home for some lesson or other, that the look in Gilberte's eyes underwent the same change that used to occur long ago in Odette's eyes, when she was afraid of revealing that she'd invited one of her lovers over that day, or that she was in a hurry to go to an assignation. Thus you could see the two natures of Monsieur and Madame Swann undulating, flowing, overlapping each other, in the body of this Mélusine.*

We are well aware, of course, that a child takes after its father and mother. Nevertheless, the distribution of qualities and defects the child inherits is effected so strangely that only one of two good qualities that seemed inseparable in one parent may be found in the child, and it may be blended with the very defect in the other parent that seemed irreconcilable with it. Similarly, the embodiment of some moral quality in an incompatible physical defect is often one of the laws of filial resemblance. Of two sisters, one will have, along with her father's proud bearing, her mother's petty mind; the other will have her father's intelligence but the mother's appearance, and so the mother's large nose, bulging waist, and even her voice, turn into the outer garments of gifts which were more familiar in a finer form. So that one can say about either sister that she's the one who takes after one parent or the other the most. It's true that Gilberte was an only child, but there were at least two Gilbertes. The two natures—her father's and her mother's—did more than mingle in her; they fought over her, and even that wouldn't be an accurate thing to say, since it would imply that there might be a third Gilberte who suffered at those times from the struggles of the other two. Whereas Gilberte was by turns one and then the other, and only one of the two at any given moment, which is to say that when she was the less good of the two, she was incapable of regretting it, since the better Gilberte, being absent at the time, couldn't be aware of the lapse. And so the less good of the two was free to enjoy base pleasures. When the better one spoke to you with her father's heart, her broad views inspired you to undertake grand projects with her; you told her as much, but just as you were putting the final touches to your preparations, her mother's heart had already taken over and was speaking through her; and then you'd be disappointed and annoyed—yet almost fascinated, as when one is confronted with an impostor—by a petty remark, or a deceitful snigger, in which Gilberte took pleasure, for they were emanating from the person she was at that moment. The discrepancy between the two Gilbertes was sometimes so great that you wondered (to no avail, of course) what you could have done to her for her to be so different. Not only had she not come to the meeting she'd arranged with you and not apologized for it later, but, whatever the reason for her change of heart, she'd seem so different afterwards that you could almost have believed it was a case of mistaken identity, like the one that forms the plot of the *Menaechmi*,* and that you weren't dealing with the person who had so sweetly asked to meet you, were it not that her ill humour revealed she felt at fault and wished to avoid explanations.

'Come along now, go and get ready; don't keep us waiting', her mother said.

'It's so nice here next to my little Papa; I want to stay a little while longer,' Gilberte replied, nestling her head under her father's arm as he affectionately ran his fingers through her hair.

Swann was one of those men who, having lived for a long time in illusions of love, have lavished their generosity on many women, thereby increasing their happiness, without being repaid with any gratitude or tenderness towards themselves; but they believe they can sense in their children an affection that, embodied in their own name, will make them live on after their death. When Charles Swann should cease to exist, there would still be a Mademoiselle Swann, or a Madame X *née* Swann, who would go on loving the dead father. Perhaps even loving him too much, Swann probably thought, for he replied to Gilberte: 'You're such a good girl!' in that tone softened by anxiety about the future of someone whose love for us is excessively passionate, and who is destined to outlive us. To hide his emotion, he joined our conversation about La Berma. He pointed out to me—though in a detached, bored tone, as if he wished to remain, as it were, outside what he was saying—with what intelligence, with what unexpected accuracy, the actress had said to Œnone: 'You knew it!'* He was right: for her intonation at least had a truly intelligible quality, and should therefore have satisfied my desire to find irrefutable reasons to admire La Berma. But it was because of its very clarity that it did not satisfy me in the least. The intonation was so ingenious, its intention and meaning so well defined, that it seemed to exist on its own, so that any intelligent actress might have adopted it. The idea was sound; but anyone else who could grasp it in all its fullness would also have been able to convey it. It's true that La Berma had discovered it, but can she be said to have 'discovered' it, when it was something that would be no different if she'd been given it, something that was not essentially hers alone, since it could be reproduced by someone else?

'Goodness,' Swann said to me, 'how your presence among us raises *the tone of the conversation!*', as if to excuse himself to Bergotte; for he'd acquired the habit from the Guermantes circle of entertaining great artists as if they were simply good friends whom one could please merely be serving them their favourite dishes, playing parlour games, or, in the country, indulging them in the sport of their choice. 'We do seem to be talking about *Art*,' he added. 'But that's very good, I do so enjoy it!' said Madame Swann, casting a grateful glance at me, out of kindness, and also because she still retained her old yearnings for more intellectual conversation. Bergotte went on to speak to other members of the party, Gilberte especially. I'd told him everything I felt with a freedom that surprised me, and which stemmed from the fact that I'd acquired from him (over so many hours of solitary reading, when he was nothing but the better part of myself) the habit of sincerity, openness, and trust, and so he intimidated me less than someone I'd been talking to for the first time. And yet for the same reason I was full of qualms about the impression I must have made on him, since the contempt I imagined he'd have for my ideas dated not from today, but from the already remote time when I'd first started reading his books, in our garden in Combray. Perhaps I ought to have told myself that, since both my love for Bergotte's works and the inexplicable disappointment I'd felt at the theatre were sincere and wholehearted, these two instinctive responses could not be so different from each other, but must obey the same laws; and that that mind of Bergotte's, which I had so admired in his books, was not likely to be something wholly alien and hostile to my disappointment and my inability to express it. For I must have only one mind; and perhaps there exists only one single mind shared by everyone, one mind to which everyone, from within his own particular body, directs his gaze, as at the theatre, where, even though everyone has his own separate seat, there is only a single stage. No doubt the ideas I was trying to disentangle were not the same ones Bergotte usually explored in his books. But if it was the same mind available to us both, he must, when he heard me express those ideas, remember them, cherish them, smile upon them, while probably keeping his inner eye fixed (despite what I supposed) on an entirely different part of his mind than the one that had left a remnant of itself in his books, on which I'd based all I'd imagined about his whole mental universe. Just as those priests who have the broadest knowledge of the human heart are best able to forgive sins they themselves do not commit, so can the genius with the broadest understanding of the mind best understand the ideas most opposed to those that form the foundation of his own works. I should have reminded myself of all this (which is not, for that matter, a very pleasant thought, for the benevolence of great minds has as its counterpart the obtuseness and hostility of mediocre ones; and the happiness one can find in the friendliness of a great writer, which can when needed be found in his books, is much less than the suffering caused by the hostility of a woman whom one has not chosen for her intelligence, but whom one can't help loving). I should have told myself all this, but I did not; I was convinced I'd appeared stupid to Bergotte, when Gilberte whispered in my ear:

'You can't imagine how happy I am—you've won over my dear friend Bergotte! He told Maman he thought you're very intelligent.'

'Where are we going?' I asked her.

'Oh, you know me, wherever you like . . .'

But ever since the incident that occurred on the anniversary of her grandfather's death, I'd been wondering if Gilberte's character was different from what I'd thought—whether her indifference to what we'd do, her submissiveness, her calm, her constant, gentle docility, might on the contrary hide passionate desires which her pride kept her from disclosing, and which were revealed only by her sudden resistance when, by chance, they were thwarted.

Since Bergotte lived in the same neighbourhood as my parents, we left together; in the carriage, he spoke to me about my health: 'Our friends told me you've been ill. I was very sorry to hear that. But not too sorry, because I can see you must be enjoying the pleasures of the intellectual life, and that's probably what counts most for you, as it does for anyone familiar with such pleasures.'

Alas, how deeply I felt that what he was saying wasn't true for me, how any discussion, however exalted, left me cold, how it was only in those moments of simple reverie that I felt truly happy and content; I felt how purely material whatever I desired in life was, and how easily I could do without the intellect. Since I was unable to distinguish between the pleasures—of varying depth and permanence—that came to me from different sources, I thought, as I replied to him, that I'd have liked an existence in which I was on friendly terms with the Duchesse de Guermantes, one that would allow me often to feel damp, cool air, as in that disused tollbooth by the Champs-Élysées, which would remind me of Combray. And in this ideal vision of life that I didn't dare confide to him, the pleasures of the intellect had no place.

'No, Monsieur, the pleasures of the intellect don't matter much to me; they're not what I'm looking for—I don't even know if I've ever experienced them.'

'Is that what you really think?' he replied. 'Come now, they *must* be what you like best—at least, that's what I believe.'

He didn't convince me, of course, but I did feel happier, less constrained. Because of what Monsieur de Norpois had said to me, I'd regarded my moments of daydreaming, of enthusiasm, of self-confidence, as purely subjective and devoid of reality. But according to Bergotte, who seemed to know what I was like, apparently it was my self-doubts, my disgust with myself, that should be ignored. Above all, what he'd said about Monsieur de Norpois took much of the force away from a judgement I'd thought was categorical.

'Are you being properly looked after?' Bergotte asked. 'Who's in charge of your treatment?' I told him I'd seen Cottard, and would probably go on seeing him. 'But he's not the one for you!' he replied. 'I don't know him as a doctor. But I've seen him with Madame Swann. He's an idiot. Even if that doesn't prevent you from being a good doctor, which is hard for me to believe, it prevents you from being a good doctor for artists, for intelligent people. People like you need the right doctors, even special diets and medications. Cottard will bore you, and boredom alone will prevent his treatment from being effective. Also, the treatment can't be the same for you as for any average person. With intelligent people, three-quarters of their illness comes from their intelligence. They at least need a doctor who's familiar with that kind of illness. How can Cottard possibly treat you?

He can diagnose a difficulty in digesting rich sauces, gastric trouble, but he can't diagnose the effects of reading Shakespeare! And so his calculations don't apply to you, the little Cartesian devil is thrown off balance, and so up it bobs again.* He'll declare you have a distended stomach; he won't need to examine you because it's already there in his eye. You can see it there, reflected in his pince-nez!' I was bewildered by this way of speaking; I said to myself, with the stupidity of common sense: 'A distended stomach can no more be reflected in Doctor Cottard's pince-nez than inanities hidden in Monsieur de Norpois' white waistcoat.' 'If I were you,' Bergotte went on, 'I'd see Doctor du Boulbon, who's extremely intelligent.' 'He's a great admirer of your work,' I replied. I saw that Bergotte knew this, and concluded that like minds soon seek each other out, and that one has few friends who come 'out of the blue'. What Bergotte told me about Cottard impressed me, but also contradicted everything I'd thought. I wasn't at all worried that my doctor might be a bore; I merely expected him, thanks to an art whose laws escaped me, to pronounce an infallible oracle about my health by consulting my entrails. I didn't require him, with his lesser intelligence, to understand my own, which I thought of only as a means, of no significance in itself, to the attainment of external truths. I very much doubted whether intelligent people needed another kind of hygiene than idiots, and I was quite willing to submit myself to the care of the latter. 'Our friend Swann is someone who needs a good doctor,' said Bergotte. And when I asked if he was ill, he replied: 'Well, he's a man who married a slut, and has to swallow a dozen insults a day from women who refuse to invite her to their homes, or from men who've slept with her. You can see it from that twisted smile of his. Look how his eyebrows go up when he comes home, to see who's there.' The harshness with which Bergotte spoke to a stranger about friends who had invited him so many times to their home was as new to me as the almost tender tone he always adopted with them in person. A person like my great-aunt, for example, would have been incapable of lavishing on us any of the compliments I'd heard Bergotte showering on Swann. Even to people she liked, she enjoyed saying disagreeable things. But behind their backs she'd never have uttered a word about them which she wouldn't have said to their faces. Our little coterie in Combray couldn't have been less like fashionable society, but the Swanns' circle was already on its way towards its ever-changing waves. It hadn't yet reached the open sea, but it was certainly in the inner harbour. 'This is all just between you and me,' Bergotte murmured as he dropped me off me outside my door. A few years later I would have answered: 'I never repeat anything I hear.' That's the ritual saying of people in society, whereby the scandalmonger is invariably filled with a false sense of security. It's the phrase I would have said to Bergotte that day, for we don't invent everything we say, especially when we're acting a social role. But I didn't know it yet. On the other hand, my great-aunt's saying on such an occasion would have been: 'If you don't want me to repeat it, why are you saying it?' That's the reply of people who don't care about being accepted in society, of those who 'go against the grain'. I was not such a one: I bowed my head in silence.

Literary people whom I regarded as being of considerable importance had to scheme for years before managing to establish a relationship with Bergotte; even then, their connection remained limited to vaguely literary matters that never went beyond his study, whereas I had just taken my place, suddenly and unobtrusively, among the great writer's friends, like a spectator who, instead of queuing up with everyone else for a bad seat, is ushered to one of the best, having been shown in through a door closed to the others. If Swann had opened such a door for me, it was doubtless because, just as a king finds it natural to invite his children's friends into the royal box or on to the royal yacht, so did Gilberte's parents welcome their daughter's friends among the precious things they owned, including them even in their more exclusive friendships. But at that time I thought, perhaps rightly, that this amiability of Swann's was aimed indirectly at my parents. I thought I'd heard once in Combray that Swann, seeing how I admired Bergotte, had offered to take me to dine with him, and that my parents had refused, saying I was too young and highly strung to go out. No doubt my parents made quite a different impression on some people—precisely those I found most exalted—from the one they made on me, so that, as on the occasion when the lady in pink had lavished such praise on my father, who had shown himself so unworthy of it, I'd have liked my parents to understand how priceless the gift I'd just received was, and to show their gratitude to that generous and courteous Swann who had given it to me, or to them, while seeming no more aware of its value than the charming Magi king with the hooked nose and blond hair in Luini's fresco,* to whom Swann had at one time been thought to bear a striking resemblance.

Unfortunately, this favour Swann had granted me, which I announced to my parents as soon as I came in, even before removing my overcoat, in the hope it would move them as much as it did me and would sway them to make some sort of grand, decisive gesture of courtesy towards Swann, did not seem to please them in the least. 'Swann introduced you to Bergotte, did he? Well, well, what an excellent acquaintance *that* is, what a wonderful connection to have!' my father exclaimed sarcastically. 'That just takes the cake!' And when I added that Bergotte didn't like Monsieur de Norpois at all, he replied: 'Naturally! That just goes to show what a false, evil mind he has. My poor boy, you didn't have much common sense to begin with; I'm very sorry to see you falling into company that will lead you even further astray.'

My parents were already far from delighted with the mere fact of my frequent visits to the Swanns'. My introduction to Bergotte seemed to them a pernicious but natural consequence of an initial fault: their own weakness, which my grandfather would have called a 'lack of perspicacity'. I sensed that all that was needed to complete their ill humour was for me to say that this immoral man who had such a low opinion of Monsieur de Norpois thought I was highly intelligent. In fact, whenever my father thought that someone, one of my schoolfellows for instance, was headed in the wrong direction—as I was at that time—if that person enjoyed the esteem of someone my father didn't respect, he viewed that approval as confirmation of his own severe verdict. The evil he saw seemed all the greater. I could already hear him exclaiming: 'Of course, it's all of a piece!', an expression that terrified me with the vagueness and vastness of the imminent reforms it suggested were about to be introduced into my quiet life. But since not telling them what Bergotte had said about me couldn't erase the impression my parents had already formed, it didn't much matter if I made it a little worse. Besides, they seemed to me so unfair, so mistaken, that not only did I no longer have any hope of bringing them around to a fairer point of view, but I'd almost lost all desire to do so. However, sensing as the words left my mouth how taken aback they'd be to think I was liked by someone who thought intelligent men stupid, was held in contempt by all decent people, and whose praise, since it was something I desired, would only spur me on into further wrongdoing, it was in a hesitant and slightly ashamed voice that I added the final damning touch to my account:

'He told the Swanns he thought I was extremely intelligent.' Like a poisoned dog in a field who rushes, without knowing why, straight to the one herb that's the antidote to the toxin it has swallowed, I'd just unwittingly said the one thing in the world that could overcome my parents' prejudice against Bergotte, a prejudice that would have firmly withstood all the well-reasoned arguments I could have made in his favour and all the praise I could have showered on him. At that instant the situation changed.

'Oh! He said you were intelligent, did he?' my mother said. 'I'm so glad to hear it, since he's such a talented man.'

'Really? He said that?' my father joined in. 'I've got nothing to say against his literary acumen, which everyone acknowledges; it's just a pity he leads that dishonourable life old Norpois alluded to,' he added, not realizing that against the supreme virtue of the magic words I'd just uttered, Bergotte's moral depravity couldn't hold out much longer than the falsity of his judgement.

'But darling,' my mother interrupted, 'there's no proof that's true. People say so many things. Anyway, Monsieur de Norpois is the nicest of men, but he's not always very kind, especially towards people who aren't his sort.'

'That's true, I've noticed that myself,' my father replied.

'In any case, we shouldn't judge Bergotte too harshly if he thinks so highly of my little boy,' Maman went on, gazing at me thoughtfully while running her fingers through my hair.

My mother had not in fact been waiting for this pronouncement by Bergotte to tell me I could invite Gilberte to tea whenever I had friends over. But I didn't dare to do so, for two reasons. The first was that at Gilberte's, only tea was ever served. At home, however, Maman insisted that hot chocolate be served as well. I was afraid Gilberte might think this was common of us, and scorn us for it. The other reason was a problem of etiquette which I was never able to solve. Whenever I arrived at Madame Swann's, she'd ask:

'And how is your dear mother?'

I'd made a few attempts to broach the subject with Maman to find out if she'd do the same when Gilberte came over, a point which seemed more serious to me than the use of 'Monseigneur' at the court of Louis XIV.* But Maman wouldn't hear of it.

'Of course not, because I don't know Madame Swann.'

'But she doesn't know you either.'

'I'm not saying she does, but we don't have to do everything the same way. I'll find other ways to be nice to Gilberte, different from Madame Swann's.'

But I was not convinced, and preferred not to invite Gilberte.

Leaving my parents, I went upstairs to change my clothes, and as I emptied my pockets I suddenly found the envelope the Swanns' butler had given me before ushering me into the drawing room. I was alone now. I opened it to find a card indicating the lady I was supposed to have taken in to lunch.

It was about this time that Bloch completely overturned my conception of the world and opened before me new possibilities for happiness (which, as it happens, would later change into possibilities for suffering) by assuring me that, unlike what I'd believed when I went for walks along the Méséglise way, women desired nothing more than to make love. He complemented this favour with another one, which I would only enjoy much later on: it was he who took me for the first time to a brothel. He had of course told me that there were many pretty women to be had. But I could only form a vague picture of their faces, which brothels would allow me to replace with particular ones. So it was that, on the one hand, because of Bloch's 'good news'— that happiness and the possession of beauty are not inaccessible things, and that we were wrong to despair of ever enjoying them— I owed him a debt of gratitude similar to the one we owe the optimistic doctor or philosopher who allows us to hope for a long life in this world, or not to be completely separated from it once we've passed into the other; and on the other hand, the houses of assignation I frequented some years later (by providing me samples of happiness, by allowing me to add to the beauty of women that element which we cannot invent, which is something more than the mere synthesis of former beauties, but the truly divine gift, the only one we cannot bestow on ourselves, before which all the logical constructs of our mind pale, and which we can only acquire from reality: an individual charm) deserve to be ranked alongside those other benefactors, more recent in origin but similar in usefulness (before the discovery of which we could only form vague notions of the seductive charms of Mantegna,* Wagner, and Siena, based on other painters, other composers, other cities): illustrated editions of the history of painting, symphonic concerts, and studies on the 'Cities of Art'.* But the house Bloch took me to, which he himself had long stopped frequenting, was too inferior, the personnel too mediocre and too unvarying, for me to be able to satisfy old curiosities or to acquire new ones. The madam of this house knew none of the women you asked for, and always offered ones you didn't desire. She sang the praises of one woman in particular, about whom she said, with a promising smile, as if she were offering a rarity or a special treat: 'She's a Jewess! Doesn't that tempt you?' (That's probably why she called her 'Rachel'.) And with inane, artificial rapture, which she hoped would be infectious and which concluded with an almost orgasmic moan, she'd add: 'Just think of it, my boy, a *Jewess*! How thrilling is that? Mmmm!' I was able to look at this Rachel without her seeing me: she was a brunette, not pretty, but intelligent-looking, and would invariably run the tip of her tongue over her lips as she smiled impertinently at the customers who were introduced to her, and whom I could hear striking up a conversation with her. Her thin, narrow face was framed with dark, curly hair that looked uneven, as if cross-hatched in an Indian ink drawing. At every visit I'd promise the madam, who offered her to me with a special insistence, boasting of her great intelligence and learning, that I wouldn't fail to come someday expressly to meet this Rachel, whom I nicknamed 'Rachel, when of the Lord'.* But on that first evening, I'd heard the girl say to the madam as she was going out:

'So that's settled, then? I'm free tomorrow, so if you have someone don't forget to send for me.'

These words had prevented me from seeing her as a person, because they'd immediately made me put her in the category of women whose general practice was to turn up there in the evenings to see if they could earn a louis or two. Her phrase was always the same, varied only by 'if you need anyone' or 'if you need anybody'.

The madam, who wasn't familiar with Halévy's opera, didn't know why I kept calling the girl 'Rachel when of the Lord'. But failure to understand a joke has never prevented anyone from being amused by it, and she'd invariably say, with a loud guffaw: 'So, tonight's not the night for you and "Rachel when of the Lord"? Is that how you say it, "Rachel when of the Lord"? That's a good one, that is! Just you wait, I'll get you two hitched. You'll see, you won't regret it!'

Once I nearly gave in, but she'd already been 'called away'; another time she was in the hands of the 'hairdresser', an old gentleman who never did anything with the girls except pour oil over their loose hair and comb it. I grew impatient with waiting, even though a few of the humbler denizens of the place (supposedly working women but always out of work) would come and make a tisane for me, and would engage me in long conversations to which—despite the seriousness of the subject matter—the partial or complete nudity of my inter-locutors gave a delectable simplicity. However, I stopped going to this house because, anxious to prove my goodwill to the madam who was in need of furniture, I gave her a few pieces, notably a large sofa, which I'd inherited from my aunt Léonie. I'd never seen them, because there was no room in our home for my parents to install them, and so they were put into storage. But as soon as I saw them being used by the women in the brothel, all the virtues that perfumed the air of my aunt's bedroom in Combray appeared before me, tor-tured by the cruel contact to which I'd delivered the poor, defenceless things. I couldn't have suffered more if it had been the dead woman herself being violated. I stopped going to the procuress's house, for the furniture seemed to be living and crying out to me, like those seemingly inanimate objects in a Persian fairy tale in which souls are imprisoned, undergo torture, and cry out for deliverance. Furthermore, since our memory doesn't usually present our recollections to us in chronological order, but as a reflection that reverses the order of things, it was only much later that I remembered it was on that very same sofa on which, many years before, I'd experienced the delights of love for the first time with one of my little cousins who drove me to distraction, a girl who had urged me to take perilous advantage of an hour when my aunt Léonie was out of the room.

Another entire lot of Aunt Léonie's furniture—especially a mag-nificent set of antique silverware—I sold, against my parents' advice, so as to have more money with which to send flowers to Madame Swann, who said, upon receiving some immense baskets of orchids: 'If I were your father, I'd give you a good talking-to!' How could I imagine that there would come a day when I missed that silver ser-vice especially, and that paying court to Gilberte's parents would not only pale in comparison to certain other pleasures, but would come to mean absolutely nothing to me? Similarly, it was because of Gilberte, so as not to leave her, that I'd decided not to embark on a career as a diplomat. It's always when we're in a state of mind destined to be short-lived that we make our most irrevocable resolutions. I could scarcely imagine that this strange substance contained within Gilberte and radiating from her parents and her house, making me indifferent to everything else, could be liberated from her and could migrate into another person. It was truly the same substance, yet one that would have an entirely different effect on me. For the same illness changes over time; and a delicious poison can't be tolerated in the same way as before when, with the passing of the years, the heart's resistance has weakened.

My parents, meanwhile, would have liked to see the intelligence Bergotte had noticed in me manifest itself in some sort of remarkable piece of work. When I didn't yet know the Swanns, I thought I was unable to work because of agitation caused by my not being able to see Gilberte at will. But now that their door stood open to me, no sooner had I sat down at my desk than I'd jump up and rush to their house. And as soon as I'd left them and returned home, it was only in appearance that I was alone; my thoughts could no longer withstand the stream of words which had carried me automatically along for hours. All I could do was compose remarks the Swanns might like, and in order to make the game more interesting, I'd take the place of these absent partners; I'd ask myself made-up questions chosen only so that my brilliant answers would show off my skill at repartee. Even though conducted silently, this exercise was a conversation and not a meditation, my solitude a mental salon in which it was not I, but imaginary interlocutors, who controlled my words, and in which I could feel the formation not of thoughts I believed to be true but ones that came to me easily, without any influence of the outer world on the inner—the sort of entirely passive pleasure that someone burdened with poor digestion finds in staying still.

If I'd been less determined to settle down to work in earnest, I might perhaps have made an effort to start right away. But since I'd made a solemn resolution, and since within twenty-four hours, in the empty frame of the following day where everything fitted so easily because I hadn't yet entered it, my good intentions would easily be carried out, it was better not to choose an evening when I didn't feel quite ready—and of course the following days would prove just as unsuitable for a good starting point. But I was reasonable. For someone who had waited years, it would have been childish to be unable to bear a delay of a few days. Confident that by the day after tomorrow I'd already have written several pages, I didn't utter another word about my decision to my family; I preferred to wait patiently for a few hours and then bring the work in progress to my relieved and convinced grandmother. Unfortunately, the next day turned out not to be that vast, outward-looking day I'd so feverishly awaited. When it was over, my laziness and my painful struggle against my inner obstacles had simply lasted twenty-four hours more. When my plans still hadn't been carried out after a few days, my hope that they'd soon be realized faded, along with my courage to subordinate everything else to this goal: I began once more to stay up late, since, having lost my innermost conviction that the work would begin the next day, I no longer felt obliged to go to bed early in the evening. To regain my resolution, I needed a few days' relaxation, and the only time my grandmother dared, in a gentle, neutral tone of voice, to utter this reproach: 'Well then, what about that work of yours?' I was angry with her, convinced that, unable to see that my commitment to the work was irrevocable, she'd just postponed it even further, perhaps for a long time, by the anguish her unfairness caused me, which would make me lose all heart to begin. She sensed that her scepticism had unintentionally offended a firm resolve. She apologized and kissed me, saying: 'I'm sorry, I won't say another word.' And to keep me from feeling discouraged, she assured me that as soon as I felt better, the work would come of its own accord.

Besides, I said to myself, by spending all my time with the Swanns, am I not behaving just like Bergotte? My parents almost seemed to think that, despite my laziness, I was leading the life most favourable to the development of talent, since it was being spent in the same salon as a great writer. And yet the notion that someone could be excused from creating this talent himself, from within, and could receive it from another, is as far-fetched as the belief that one could become healthy, despite ignoring all the rules of hygiene and indulging in the worst excesses, merely by dining regularly with a doctor. The person, incidentally, who was most completely taken in by this illusion, shared by my parents and myself alike, was Madame Swann. Whenever I told her I couldn't come over, and that I had to stay at home and work, she'd act as if I was making a lot of fuss about nothing, that I was being silly and pretentious, and would say:

'But Bergotte keeps coming, doesn't he? Do you think what he writes is no good? He'll soon be even better', she added, 'because he's sharper, more focused, in newspaper articles than in books, where he tends to water things down a bit. I've even managed to get him into *Le Figaro*, where he's going to write the *leader article*. He'll certainly be

the right man in the right place.'* And she concluded: 'Do come, he can
tell you better than anyone what you should do.'

And so she'd tell me to be sure to come to dinner with Bergotte at
her house the next evening, as if I was a soldier being invited along
with his colonel in order to further his career, and as if works of art
were made by having 'the right connections'.

So it was that there was no more opposition from either the Swanns
or my parents—that is, from those who at various times had seemed
to be against it—to this sweet life in which I could see Gilberte whenever I liked, with delight if not with peace of mind. There can be no
peace of mind in love, since each gratification won is only a new point
of departure to desire even more. As long as I'd been unable to go to
her house, my sights had been trained on that inaccessible happiness,
and I couldn't even imagine the new sources of emotional turmoil
awaiting me there. Once her parents' resistance was overcome and the
problem finally solved, it kept rearising, each time in different terms.
In this sense it was indeed a new friendship that began afresh each
day. Every evening when I came home, I'd realize that there were
important things I had to say to Gilberte on which our friendship
depended, and these things were never the same. At least I was happy,
and there were no more threats to my happiness. One would arise,
alas, from a place I would never have guessed: from Gilberte and
myself. And yet I should have been tormented by the very thing that
reassured me, by what I took for happiness. Our state of mind when
in love is abnormal; it is capable of immediately attributing to the
simplest-seeming accident, which can happen at any time, a gravity it
would not possess just by itself. What makes us so happy is the presence in our hearts of something unstable, which we try constantly to
maintain, and which we almost don't notice so long as it isn't disturbed.
Whereas actually there is in love a permanent suffering, which joy
neutralizes, virtualizes, postpones, but which at any instant can
become what it would have been long since if we had not obtained
what we desired: excruciating.

Several times I sensed that Gilberte wanted to see less of me. Of
course, whenever my desire to see her got the better of me, I had only
to get myself invited over by her parents, who were more and more
convinced of my excellent influence on her. Thanks to them, I thought,
my love is in no danger; so long as I have them on my side, I can rest
easy, since they have complete authority over Gilberte. Unfortunately,

from certain signs of impatience Gilberte betrayed when her father invited me over, as it were, against her wishes, I wondered whether what I'd regarded as a protection for my happiness might not be the secret reason why it couldn't last.

The last time I went to see Gilberte, it was raining; she'd been invited to a dance lesson at the home of some people she didn't know well enough to take me along. Because of the humidity, I'd taken more caffeine than usual. Perhaps because of the bad weather, or perhaps because she had some sort of prejudice against the house where this lesson was to take place, just as Gilberte was about to leave, Madame Swann called out 'Gilberte!' in a sharp voice and pointed to me, implying that I'd come to see her and that she should stay with me. This 'Gilberte' was uttered—shouted, rather—with the best of intentions towards me, but from the way Gilberte shrugged her shoulders as she took off her outdoor things, I understood that her mother had unwittingly speeded up the change—which until then might possibly have been arrested—that was gradually pulling my dear friend away from me. 'You don't have to go dancing every day,' said Odette to her daughter, in a sensible tone she'd no doubt acquired long ago from Swann. And then, becoming Odette again, she began speaking English to her daughter. Immediately it was as if a wall was hiding part of Gilberte's life from me, as if an evil genie had taken my friend far away from me. In a language we know, we have replaced the opacity of sounds with the transparency of ideas. But a language we don't know is a closed palace in which our beloved can betray us, while, kept outside, frantic in our impotence, we can see nothing, prevent nothing. So this conversation in English, which would only have made me smile a month earlier, now interspersed with a few proper nouns in French which only increased and focused my anxieties, conducted as it was right next to me by two motionless people, had the same cruelty, and made me feel just as forsaken and alone, as a kidnapping. Finally, Madame Swann left us. That day, perhaps out of resentment for my being the involuntary cause preventing her from going out and having fun, perhaps also because, realizing her anger, I reacted defensively and became colder than usual, Gilberte's face, stripped of all joy, bare, ravaged, seemed all afternoon to be harbouring a melancholy regret for the *pas-de-quatre** my presence prevented her from dancing, and to challenge all living creatures, beginning with myself, to understand the subtle reasons that had swayed her to a sentimental

attachment to the Boston waltz.* Confined to brief remarks about the
weather, the rain that was coming down harder, or the clock that was
running fast, her conversation was punctuated by silences and monosyllables in which I too, with a sort of desperate rage, stubbornly
persisted in destroying those instants we could have devoted to
friendship and happiness. And all our remarks took on a kind of
supreme harshness by the glaring paradox of their pettiness, which
nonetheless consoled me, for it prevented Gilberte from being deceived
by the banality of my observations and the indifference of my tone.
I had only to say 'I think the clock was actually a little slow the other
day' for her to translate it as 'How mean you are!' Throughout that
rainy day, even though I persisted in reiterating these sunless words,
I knew that my coldness was not as intransigent as I pretended, and
that Gilberte must sense that if, after telling her three times already,
I hazarded a fourth time to say that the days were getting shorter, it
was only because I could barely prevent myself from bursting into
tears. When she was like this, when a smile didn't light up her eyes or
open up her face, I cannot describe the wretched monotony stamped
on her sad eyes and sullen features. Her face, grown almost ugly,
reminded me then of those boring beaches where the sea, having
ebbed far out, wearies you with a shimmer that's always the same,
bounded by a motionless, limited horizon. Finally, when after many
hours the happy change I was expecting to see in Gilberte failed to
appear, I told her she wasn't being nice. '*You're* the one who's not
being nice,' she snapped. 'Yes I am!' I replied. I wondered what I'd
done, and, unable to find the cause, asked her what it was. 'Of course
you think you're nice!', she replied, and went on laughing. It was at
that moment that I felt how painful it was for me to be unable to
fathom that other, more elusive realm of her mind hinted at by her
laughter. Her laugh seemed to mean: 'No, no, I'm not taken in by
anything you say; I know you're crazy about me, but I couldn't care
less about you.' But I told myself that laughter isn't such a well-defined
language that I could confidently say I understood it. And Gilberte's
words were affectionate. 'But in what way am I not nice?' I asked her.
'Tell me, I'll do anything you want.' 'No, that would be pointless,
I can't explain why.' For a moment I was afraid she thought I didn't
love her, and this was another kind of suffering for me, no less keen,
but requiring a different sort of reasoning. 'If you knew how unhappy
you're making me feel, you'd tell me,' I said. But this unhappiness,

which should have delighted Gilberte if she'd doubted my love, irritated her instead. And so, realizing my mistake, determined not to pay heed to her words, even when she said 'I really did love you, you'll see that someday' (that same 'someday' on which the guilty assert their innocence will be proven, and which, for mysterious reasons, is never the day when they're asked about it), I mustered the courage to make the sudden resolution that I wouldn't see her anymore, but didn't tell her yet, because she wouldn't have believed me.

Sorrow caused by a person you love can be bitter, even when it occurs amidst other preoccupations, occupations, and joys, which are not centred on that person and which, most of the time, divert our mind from it. But when such sorrow arises—as it did now—at a time when the happiness of seeing this person fills us completely, the sudden depression that takes hold of our spirits, which just before had been sunny, resolute, and calm, creates in us such a raging storm that we don't know if we can weather it. The storm howling in my heart was so violent that I headed home battered and bruised, feeling as if I could only get my breath back by retracing my steps and making some excuse or other to return to Gilberte. But she would have said: 'Him again! Obviously I can do whatever I like, he'll come back every time, and the more miserable he is when he leaves me, the more docile he'll be when he comes back.' And then my thoughts drew me irresistibly back to her, and these alternating inclinations, this wild spinning of my inner compass, persisted after I reached home, and were conveyed by the drafts of contradictory letters I wrote to her.

I was about to go through one of those difficult conjunctures that challenge most of us several times in a lifetime, and which, even though we haven't changed our character or nature—which itself creates the loves we experience, and almost the women we love, down to their very faults—we confront differently each time, depending on our age. At moments like these our life is divided, as if distributed in its entirety over a pair of scales, on two opposite pans. In one is our desire not to offend the woman we love (whom we don't truly understand) by seeming too subservient, but we think it wise to conceal this wish so that she won't think she's indispensable to us, which would soon make her tire of us; in the other scale pan there is a feeling of pain—though not a localized or mild one—which can only be appeased if, giving up our resolve not to annoy this woman or make her believe we can do without her, we seek her out. If we take from the scale pan

containing our pride a little of the willpower we've allowed to weaken
with age, and if we add to the pan containing our emotional pain a physical pain we have acquired and have allowed to get worse, instead of
the courageous solution that would have won the day at twenty, it's
the other one, which without a counterbalance has become too heavy,
that drags us down at fifty. This is all the more true since situations,
even though they repeat themselves, change; and there is a possibility
that in middle age or late in life, one may have had the disastrous self-
indulgence of mingling love with an element of habit, which adolescence, wrapped up in too many other duties and less free to do as it
likes, has not yet acquired.

I had just written a letter to Gilberte in which I unleashed the
thunder of my fury, not without throwing her a lifebuoy of a few
words placed here and there as if by chance, to which my dear friend
could cling if she wished for a reconciliation; a moment later, the
wind having shifted, I wrote her nothing but tender phrases chosen
for the sweetness of certain sorrowful expressions, such as 'never
again', so poignant to the one writing them, yet so tiresome to the
woman who reads them, either because she suspects them of being
false and translates 'never again' as 'this very night, if you want me',
or because she believes them to be true and sees in them the announcement of the sort of final separation to which we're completely indifferent when we're not in love with the person in question. But since,
while we're in love, we're incapable of acting as worthy predecessors
to the next person we'll become, the one who will no longer be in love,
how could we accurately imagine the state of mind of a woman who,
even though we knew we meant nothing to her, has always appeared
to us in our reveries as whispering, in order to lull us into a happy
dream or console us for a great sorrow, the same sweet nothings that
she'd have used if she loved us? Faced with the thoughts or actions of
a woman we love, we're as completely bewildered as the first physi-
cists were when faced with natural phenomena (before science had
progressed and shed a little light on the unknown), or, worse still, like
someone who barely understands the principle of causality, who is
therefore incapable of forming a link between one phenomenon and
another, and for whom the spectacle of the world is as uncertain as
a dream. Of course, I tried my best to make sense of this incoherence
and to identify its causes. I even tried to be 'objective' by noting the
disparity that existed not just between Gilberte's importance to me

and mine to her, but also hers to everyone else, since overlooking this disparity might have made me mistake mere amiability on her part for a passionate avowal, and a ridiculous, demeaning gesture on mine for the simple, friendly impulse that attracts a man to a pretty face. But I was also afraid of going to the opposite extreme and seeing Gilberte's lateness when she was in a bad mood as an act of irremediable hostility. Between these two equally distorted viewpoints, I attempted to find the one that would allow me to see things clearly; the calculations this required distracted me for a while from my distress; and either in obedience to the answer supplied by these reckonings, or because I made them say what I wanted to hear, I resolved to go to the Swanns' the next day, happy, but only as happy as those who, having long been tormented by the thought of a journey they didn't want to make, go no further than the train station, and return home to unpack their luggage. And since, as one is hesitating, the mere idea of a possible resolution (provided one hasn't made this idea void by deciding one won't make such a resolution) develops, like a hardy seed, all the delineations and details of the emotions that will arise from performing such an action, I told myself that, by planning never to see Gilberte again, it had been silly of me to cause myself as much suffering as if I'd actually put this plan into effect, and that, since I'd end up going back to her house, I could have saved myself the vexation of so many conflicting impulses and painful moments of resignation. But this resumption of friendly relations lasted only as long as it took me to go to the Swanns': not because their butler, who was very fond of me, told me that Gilberte had gone out (which I learned that very evening was true, from people who had seen her), but because of the way he said it: 'Monsieur, Mademoiselle has gone out; I can assure Monsieur I'm not lying. If Monsieur would like to make sure, I can call for the maid. Monsieur should rest assured that I would do anything in my power to please him and that if Mademoiselle were here, I would immediately take Monsieur to her.' These words, as important as only spontaneous words can be, giving us at least a basic X-ray of the unimaginable reality that a memorized speech would conceal, proved that in Gilberte's household I was deemed a nuisance; and so, scarcely were the words out of the butler's mouth than they engendered in me a hatred which I preferred to direct at him rather than at Gilberte; all the feelings of rage I had for my friend were focused on him; freed from my anger thanks to these words, only my love remained; but at the same time, his words had shown me that I should let a little time elapse before I tried to see Gilberte again. Surely she would write to me to apologize. Even so, I wouldn't go back right away to see her, to prove I could live without her. Besides, once I'd received her letter, visiting Gilberte would be something I could easily do without for a time, since I'd be sure of seeing her again whenever I liked. All I needed to bear this voluntary absence more cheerfully was to feel my heart freed from the terrible uncertainty about whether we'd fallen out with each other forever, whether she'd become engaged, had left Paris, or had been abducted. The days that followed resembled the first week of that previous New Year I'd had to spend without seeing Gilberte. But once that week was over, I was certain not only that my friend would return to the Champs-Élysées and I'd see her as before, but also that it wasn't worth going to the Champs-Élysées so long as the New Year's holiday lasted. So, during that miserable week, which already seemed so remote, I'd borne my misery calmly, because it wasn't mingled with fear or hope. But this time my suffering was intolerable, because I was tormented by a hope that was almost as strong as my fear. When I didn't receive a letter from Gilberte that evening, I made allowance for her forgetfulness, her other concerns; I was sure I'd find one from her in the next morning's post. Every day I awaited the post with a beating heart, only to fall into a state of utter dejection when I found only letters from people other than Gilberte, or no letters at all, which wasn't as hard to bear as those letters, since the tokens of another girl's friendship made Gilberte's indifference all the more cruel. Then I'd start hoping for the afternoon delivery. Even between deliveries I didn't dare go out, since she might be sending the letter by hand. Finally the moment would arrive when neither the postman nor the Swanns' footman could come, and I'd have to postpone my hope of reassurance until the next day, and so, since I believed my suffering wouldn't last, I was forced, so to speak, to renew it constantly. The sorrow may have been the same, but rather than uniformly prolonging an initial emotion, as before, it started up again several times a day with such a frequently renewed emotion that this entirely physical, temporary state ended up becoming stabilized, so that the vexations caused by the wait scarcely had time to subside before a new reason for waiting arose, and there wasn't a single minute in the day when I wasn't consumed by that anxiety which is so difficult to bear even for an hour. And so

my suffering was infinitely more cruel than on that previous New
Year's Day, because this time I was full not of a pure and simple
acceptance of it but of the hope, at every instant, that it would end.
I did, however, finally arrive at this acceptance; I realized it must be
permanent, and so I renounced Gilberte forever, for the sake of my
very love, but also because above all I wanted her not to remember me
with contempt. And so, whenever she sent me invitations later on, I'd
often accept them, so that she wouldn't think I was suffering from
heartache, and then, at the last minute, I'd write that I couldn't come,
with the same effusive apologies I'd have made to someone I had no
desire to see. It seemed to me that these expressions of regret, which
we usually reserve for those to whom we are indifferent, would serve
better to convince Gilberte of my own indifference than would the tone
of feigned indifference we affect only towards the woman we love.
Once I'd proved to her not just with words but, even better, with constantly repeated actions that I had no wish to see her, perhaps she'd
rediscover her own desire to see me. Alas! All my attempts were fruitless: by trying to revive her interest in seeing me by not seeing her,
I lost her forever; first of all because, if her interest began to come
back to life, if I wanted it to last, it was vital for me not to give in right
away; besides, the most painful hours would be over by then; it was in
that instant that I needed her most, and I wished I could warn her
that soon, by seeing me again, she'd only be soothing a grief so diminished that it would cease to be (as it still was at this moment) a motive
for capitulating, reconciling, and seeing each other again. And later
on, when Gilberte's liking for me had become so strong that I could
at last safely confess mine for her, my own desire wouldn't have been
able to survive such a long absence, and would no longer exist; Gilberte
would have become indifferent to me. I knew this, but couldn't tell her;
she'd have thought that if I claimed I'd stop loving her by not seeing
her for too long, it could only mean I was trying to get her to tell me
to hurry back to her. In the meantime, one thing that eased my mind
about condemning myself to this separation was that (in order for her
well and truly to realize that despite my contradictory assertions, it
was my own free will, not an obstacle or my state of health, that prevented me from seeing her) whenever I knew ahead of time that
Gilberte would not be at home, but was going out with a friend and
not returning for dinner, I'd go to see Madame Swann (who had once
again become for me what she'd been when I had such difficulty

seeing her daughter, when on the days that Gilberte didn't come to the Champs-Élysées I'd go for a walk along the Avenue des Acacias*). In this way I'd hear about Gilberte, and I was sure she'd hear about me later, in a way that would show her I was no longer attached to her. Also, like all those who endure suffering, I reasoned that my sad situation could have been worse. For, having full access to the house in which Gilberte lived, I kept telling myself (although I was determined not to take advantage of the possibility) that if ever my suffering grew too keen, I could make it stop. I was only unhappy from day to day. And even that was an overstatement. How many times an hour (but now no longer in the grip of that anxious waiting during the first few weeks after our quarrel, before I'd gone back to the Swanns') did I recite to myself the letter Gilberte would surely send me someday, perhaps even bring to me by her own hand! The constant vision of this imagined happiness helped me to bear the destruction of my actual happiness. With women who don't love us, as with those who have died, knowing we have nothing left to hope for doesn't prevent us from continuing to wait. One lives with one's eyes and ears always on the alert; a mother whose son has sailed out to sea on a dangerous expedition imagines at every instant, even after she has long known for certain he has died, that he'll come through the door, miraculously safe and sound. And this expectancy, depending on the power of her memory and her bodily strength, either allows her to get through the years, after which she'll be able to bear the fact that her son is no longer alive, to forget little by little and to survive—or else it makes her die. Also, my sorrow drew a little comfort from the idea that it benefited my love. Every visit I paid to Madame Swann without seeing Gilberte was painful to me, but I felt it made Gilberte's opinion of me that much higher.

If I always made sure, before going to Madame Swann's, that her daughter would be away, it may have had as much to do with my resolution to break with her as with the hope for a reconciliation superimposed upon it (very few of these resolutions are absolute, at least in a permanent way, since one of the laws of human nature, strengthened by unexpected surges of various memories, is intermittency), a hope that masked its unbearably cruel aspect. I was quite aware of how illusory this hope was. I was like a poor man who sheds fewer tears over his stale bread if he tells himself that at any moment a stranger might leave him his entire fortune. To make reality bearable, we must all entertain a few little fantasies. And so my hope remained more intact—while at the same time the separation was more effectively maintained—if I did not see Gilberte. If I'd found myself face to face with her in her mother's drawing room, we might have exchanged a few irrevocable words that would have made our quarrel permanent, killed my hope, and, by causing yet more anguish, reawakened my love and made my resignation even harder to bear.

For quite some time, long before my break with her daughter, Madame Swann had been saying to me: 'It's all very well, your coming to see Gilberte, but I'd also like it if you came to see *me* sometimes—I don't mean my *Choufleury*,* where you'd be bored because of all the people, but on the other days, when you'll always find me at home a little later in the day.' And so, by going to see her, I might have appeared merely to be belatedly obeying a wish she'd expressed long ago. Very late in the afternoon, when it was already dark and my parents were just about to sit down to dinner, I'd set out to pay Madame Swann a visit during which I knew I wouldn't see Gilberte and yet would think only of her. In this neighbourhood, regarded at the time as remote, in a Paris that was darker than today, and which, even in the city centre, had no electricity on public streets and very little in private houses, the lamps of a drawing room on the ground floor or a low mezzanine (which was where Madame Swann's reception rooms were) were enough to light up the street and draw the gaze of a passer-by, who recognized their glow as the obvious, though veiled, reason for the presence outside the door of a number of impressive carriages. This passer-by may have thought, not without some alarm, that there might be some other mysterious reason for this event when he or she saw one of the carriages start moving; but it was just a coachman who, to keep his horses warm, trotted them back and forth now and then, and the silent rubber tyres made the clatter of the horses' hooves sound even clearer and more distinct.

The 'winter garden', which the passer-by would also usually glimpse in those days, whatever street he was on, if the apartment was not too high above the pavement, can only be seen now in the photogravure illustrations of P.-J. Stahl's New Year's giftbooks;* such a winter garden, in contrast to the sparse floral arrangements (a rose or a Japanese iris in a long-necked crystal vase, which couldn't contain a single flower more) of today's Louis XVI drawing rooms, because of the profusion of indoor plants in fashion at the time, and the complete lack of style in their arrangement, seemed to be the fruit of some spirited and delightful passion for botany among the mistresses of the house rather than any cold concern for lifeless decoration. It brought to mind, though on a larger scale, in the *hôtels* of those days,* those miniature, portable greenhouses placed under a bright lamp (since children didn't have the patience to wait until daylight) on New Year's morning among the other New Year's gifts, but the loveliest gift of them all, consoling them for the bareness of winter with real plants they could grow; and even more than the miniature terraria, the winter gardens looked more like the greenhouse you could see portrayed right beside the one in a handsome book, another New Year's gift and one which, although it was given not to the children but to Mademoiselle Lili, the book's heroine, so delighted them that, even now when they were almost old, they wondered whether in those happy years winter wasn't the loveliest of the seasons. And finally, in the depths of this winter garden, through the varied foliage which from the street made the glowing window look like the glass of those children's terraria, fictional or actual, the passer-by, standing on tiptoe, could usually see a gentleman in a frock coat with a gardenia or carnation in his lapel, standing in front of a lady who was sitting, both of them hazy, like two intaglios in topaz, deep within the drawing room's atmosphere, turned amber by the steam from the samovar—a recent import at the time, but so common today that it's become invisible. Madame Swann was very attached to this 'tea'; she thought she was displaying her originality and charm when she said to a man: 'You can always find me at home in the late afternoon; do come and take tea with me,' and she'd smile sweetly and delicately while with a fleeting English accent she uttered these words, which her interlocutor duly noted with a solemn bow, as if they were something singular and important that commanded deference and required attention. There was another reason, apart from those noted already, why flowers played more than an ornamental role in Madame Swann's drawing room, a reason that had nothing to do with the era but to some degree with the life Odette had once led. A high-class courtesan, as she had been, lives mainly for her lovers, that is to say at home; in time, this might lead her to live for herself. The things that can be seen at a 'respectable' woman's home, which she might indeed regard as somewhat important, are even more so for the courtesan. The high point of her day is not when she gets dressed to go out in society, but when she undresses for a man. She must be just as elegant in a kimono or nightgown as in full outdoor attire. Other women might show off their jewellery; she lives in the privacy of her pearls. This kind of existence requires, and eventually gives one a taste for, secret luxury, that is to say, it comes close to appearing disinterested. Madame Swann extended this to her flowers. Next to her armchair there was always an immense crystal bowl full to the brim with Parma violets or daisy petals in water, which seemed to a newcomer to indicate some favourite pastime that was interrupted, like the cup of tea Madame Swann may have been drinking alone, for her own pleasure; but a pastime so private and mysterious that the guest might be prompted to apologize for his intrusion when he sees the flowers spread out there, as one might apologize for seeing the title of a book left open that might reveal Odette's recent reading, and hence her present thoughts. But the flowers were even more alive than a book; if you came to visit Madame Swann, you'd be embarrassed to note that she wasn't alone, or, if you were accompanying her home, to find the drawing room wasn't empty, so enigmatic a place did they occupy, recalling as they did the hours in the life of the mistress of the house that were unknown to you; these flowers, which had not been arranged for Odette's visitors but looked as if they'd been forgotten there by her, as if they'd been having, and would continue to have, special conversations with her that you were afraid of disturbing, whose secret you tried in vain to fathom by studying the faded, fluid, mauve, dissolute colour of the Parma violets. By the end of October, Odette would come home as regularly as possible for tea, which was still in those days called the *five o'clock tea*,* since she'd heard (and liked to repeat) that if Madame Verdurin had been able to form a salon, it was because people could be sure of finding her at home at the same time each day. She imagined she had a salon of her own similar to it, but freer, *senza rigore** as she liked to say. She saw herself as a kind of Julie de Lespinasse, founding a rival salon by stealing away from the Madame du Deffand of the little set its most attractive men,* especially Swann who had followed her in her secession and retreat, according to a version she understandably urged upon newcomers who knew nothing of the past, without believing it herself. But we play certain favourite roles so often before the public, and we rehearse them so assiduously in private, that we find it easier to subscribe to their fictitious testimony than to that of an almost completely forgotten reality. On the days when Madame Swann had not gone out at all, she could be found in a crêpe-de-Chine dressing gown, white as new-fallen snow, or sometimes in one of those long, pleated chiffon robes that look like nothing more than a cascade of pink or white petals, and which people nowadays would regard, wrongly, as inappropriate for winter. For in the stifling heat of the drawing rooms of those days, with their heavily curtained doors, about which the most elegant thing the fashionable novelists of the time could find to say was that they were 'cosily padded', these light fabrics and soft colours made a woman look as if they must feel as cold as the roses standing beside her, despite the winter, in their incarnadine nudity, as if it were spring. Since the carpets muffled all sounds, the mistress of the house, sitting secluded in an alcove, was not alerted to your entrance as she would be today, and would keep reading even when you were standing almost in front of her, which added even more to the impression of the romantic, the charm of uncovering a secret, which we can recapture today when we think back to those already out-of-fashion robes, which Madame Swann alone, perhaps, still wore, and which give us the feeling that their wearer must be the heroine of a novel, because most of us have only come across them in the romances of Henry Gréville.* Now, at the beginning of winter, Odette had in her drawing room enormous chrysanthemums in a variety of colours such as Swann would never have seen in her old apartment. My admiration for them—when I'd go to pay Madame Swann one of those melancholy visits during which, in my sorrow, I'd rediscover all the mysterious poetry in her role as the mother of Gilberte to whom she'd say the next day: 'Your friend paid me a visit'—came no doubt from my impression that, pale pink like the Louis XV silk on her armchairs, snow-white like her crêpe-de-Chine dressing gown, or metallic red like her samovar, they gave to the drawing room an additional decorative array that was just as rich in colour and just as refined, but alive, though it would last only a few days. But I was moved not by the ephemeral nature of these chrysanthemums but by their relatively enduring nature compared to the equally pink or copper-coloured tones that the setting sun kindled so magnificently in the mist of those late November afternoons, and that, after seeing them fade away in the sky before I entered Madame Swann's house, I'd rediscover transposed into the fiery palette of the flowers. As if a master colourist had snatched their flaming lights from the sun and the

changeable atmosphere to adorn a human dwelling, these chrysanthemums invited me, despite all my sadness, to drink deeply during this
teatime hour of November's fleeting pleasures, whose intimate, mysterious splendour they set ablaze so close to me. Such splendour,
however, was not to be found in the conversations I heard; far from it.
Even with Madame Cottard, and despite the late hour, Madame
Swann would say in a cajoling way: 'But it's not the least bit late!
Don't look at the clock, that's not the right time, it's stopped. You
can't be in *that* much of a hurry!' and she'd offer one more tartlet to
the professor's wife as she clutched her calling cards.

'It's so difficult to tear oneself away from this house,' Madame
Bontemps would say to Madame Swann, while Madame Cottard,
surprised at hearing her own thoughts spoken out loud, would blurt
out: 'That's just what I'm always saying in my own simple way, in my
heart of hearts!' And this would win the approval of the gentlemen of
the Jockey Club, who had outdone one another in exaggerated greetings earlier, as if they were overwhelmed by such a great honour,
when Madame Swann had introduced them to this plain little bourgeois woman who, when surrounded by Odette's brilliant friends,
would stay on her guard, or on what she called 'the defensive', since
she always used flowery language for the simplest things.

'That's hard to believe,' Madame Swann said to Madame Cottard,
'since it's three Wednesdays in a row now that you've let me down.'
'It's true, Odette, it's been *ages*, simply *an eternity* since I saw you last.
I plead guilty, but I must tell you', she added in a vague and prudish
way (for, despite the fact that she was a doctor's wife, she could only
speak in a roundabout way about rheumatism or renal colic), 'that
I've had so many little *aches and pains*. As we all do, I'm sure. And I've
also had a crisis in my male domestic staff. While I don't abuse my
authority any more than the next person, I had to set an example and
fire my Vatel* who, I think, was looking for a more lucrative position
in any case. But his departure almost led to the resignation of the
whole Cabinet! My own maid didn't want to stay either; there were
some Homeric scenes. Despite everything, though, I steered a steady
course, and it's a real object lesson I won't forget in a hurry. I'm boring you with all these servant tales, but you know as well as I do what
a bother it is when you're forced to reshuffle your staff.' And she
added, finally: 'We won't be seeing your delightful daughter, then?'
'No, my delightful daughter is dining with a friend,' Madame Swann

replied, and then remarked, turning to me: 'I think she wrote to you, asking you to come and see her tomorrow. And how are your *babys?*'* she asked the professor's wife.

I breathed a sigh of relief. These words of Madame Swann's, which proved to me that I could see Gilberte whenever I liked, gave me precisely the solace I'd come to seek; it was the reason why my visits to Madame Swann during this period were so necessary. 'No, I'll write her a note tonight. Besides, Gilberte and I can't see each other anymore,' I added, as if to ascribe our separation to some mysterious cause; and this in turn gave me an illusory feeling of love, which was sustained by the affectionate way in which Gilberte and I continued to refer to each other.

'You know how much she cares for you,' Madame Swann said. 'Do you *really* not want to come tomorrow?'

All of a sudden I felt a thrill of joy, and I said to myself: 'Well, why not, since it's her own mother who's asking me?' But as soon as the thought occurred to me I relapsed into my dejected state. I was afraid that if she saw me, Gilberte would think my recent indifference had been feigned, and so I thought it best that the separation should continue. During these asides, Madame Bontemps had been complaining of how bored she was by politicians' wives, for she made a show of finding everyone tedious and ridiculous, and of deploring her husband's position in the ministry.

'So you can entertain fifty doctors' wives in a row, just like that?' she asked Madame Cottard, who, on the contrary, was full of goodwill towards everyone and respect for her obligations. 'How virtuous you are! I have my own duties because of the Ministry, of course. But all those wives of *civil servants* are more than I can stand—I can't help sticking my tongue out at them! My niece Albertine is just the same. You have no idea how cheeky she is. Just last week the wife of the under-secretary of state at the Treasury was at my at-home, and she said she had no idea how to cook. "But, Madame," my niece replied with her most charming smile, "you *must* know how, since your father was a scullery boy!"'

'Oh! what a wonderful story!' exclaimed Madame Swann. 'I think it's delightful! But', she said to Madame Cottard, 'on your husband's consulting days you should have a little *home** of your own, with your flowers and books and all the things you like.'

'Just like that, bang, point-blank!' Madame Bontemps continued. 'She said it straight to her face. And she was so deadpan, she didn't give me the least little warning—she's as clever as a monkey. You're lucky you can restrain yourself; I so envy people who can hide their thoughts.' 'But I don't need to, Madame: I'm very easy-going,' Madame Cottard replied gently. 'For one thing, I don't have quite as many obligations as you do,' she added in the slightly louder voice she used for emphasis whenever she slipped into the conversation one of those delicate compliments or flattering phrases which her husband so admired, and which helped in the advancement of his career. 'And also I'm only too happy to do anything that might be useful to the professor.'

'Ah, but not everyone is as *capable* as you are! You're probably not very highly strung. But when I see the wife of the Minister of War contorting her face the way she does, I immediately start imitating her. It's terrible to have a temperament like mine.'

'Oh yes, I've heard she has tics,' Madame Cottard replied. 'My husband also knows someone quite high up, and of course, when these gentlemen get talking . . .'

'And it's the same with the head of Protocol who's a hunchback, it's automatic, he just has to be in my house for five minutes before I go over to touch his hump. My husband says I'll get him fired. Who cares! Let the Ministry be damned! Yes, let the Ministry be damned, I say! I'd like to have that printed on my notepaper. I'm sure I'm shocking you because you're so good, but I must confess that nothing amuses me as much as these little jibes. Life would be so *dull* without them.'

And she went on talking about the ministry as if it were Mount Olympus. To change the subject, Madame Swann turned to Madame Cottard, and said: 'My, but you're looking stunning today! *Redfern fecit?**

'No, you know how I devoted I am to Raudnitz.* But it's just a little old thing I've had altered.'

'Well, it does look chic!'

'Guess how much? . . . No, change the first number.'

'But that's a steal! I heard it was three times as much.'

'And *that's* how History gets written,' the doctor's wife said. And, pointing to a choker Madame Swann had given her, she asked her: 'Look, Odette, do you recognize it?'

Through the door curtains a face might appear with a look of cere-monious deference, playfully assuming a pretence of not wishing to disturb the gathering: it was Swann. 'Odette, the Prince d'Agrigente, who's with me in my study, is wondering if he could come and pay his respects. What should I tell him?' 'That I'd be delighted, of course,' Odette would reply contentedly, while not losing any of the composure which came to her all the more easily since she had always, even as a courtesan, entertained fashionable men. Swann would withdraw to deliver the message and return accompanied by the prince, unless Madame Verdurin had made her entrance in the meantime. When Swann had married Odette, he'd asked her to stop visiting the 'little clan' (he had many reasons for this, and would still have done so even if he had none, out of obedience to a law of ingratitude which, without exception, demonstrates the lack of foresight, or perhaps the disinterest, of all go-betweens). His sole concession was that Odette could pay two visits a year to Madame Verdurin, which still appeared excessive to some of the 'faithful' who were indignant at the insult to the 'Patronne' who had treated Odette and even Swann as beloved children of the house for so many years. Although the little group contained traitors who slipped away on certain evenings so that they might secretly accept an invitation from Odette, ready, in case of discovery, with the excuse that they were curious to meet Bergotte (even though the Patronne claimed he never went to the Swanns' and had no talent, she still tried, to quote one of her favourite expressions, to 'reel him in'), the little clan also had its 'fanatics'. Ignorant of the particular rules of behaviour that often dissuade people from an extreme attitude they're being urged to adopt in order to annoy someone else, they wished, to no avail, that Madame Verdurin would cease all relations with Odette, thus depriving her of the satisfaction of saying with a laugh: 'We hardly ever go to the Patronne's house, ever since the Schism. It was still possible when my husband was a bachelor, but now that we're married, it's not that easy . . . To tell the truth, Monsieur Swann can't stand old Mother Verdurin, and he wouldn't take kindly to my taking up with her again. And since I'm a loyal wife . . .' Swann would accompany his wife to a soirée at the Verdurins', but would make sure not to be present when Madame Verdurin returned the visit. So it was that if the Patronne was in the drawing room, the Prince d'Agrigente would come in alone. He was also the only person to whom Odette introduced Madame Verdurin, so that she wouldn't hear any of the more obscure names, and, when she saw more than one unknown face in the room, she might think she was among the cream of the aristocracy; this ruse was so successful that when Madame Verdurin came home that evening, she said to her husband in disgust: 'Charming people she has there! Nothing but Reactionary bigwigs!' As for Odette's illusion about Madame Verdurin, it was quite the opposite. It wasn't that Madame Verdurin's salon at that time had even begun to develop into what we will one day see it become. Madame Verdurin hadn't even reached that period of incubation when one postpones one's grander parties lest the few recently acquired celebrities should be lost in the crowd, and when one prefers to wait for the generative power of the ten just men one has managed to 'reel in' to multiply them a hundredfold. As Odette would soon do, Madame Verdurin did indeed adopt 'Society' as her objective; but her zones of attack were still so limited, and what's more so remote from those by which Odette had some chance of arriving at an identical result on her way up, that Odette lived in complete ignorance of the strategic plans the Patronne was developing. And it was with all the sincerity in the world that, when anyone spoke to her of Madame Verdurin as a snob, Odette would laugh and say: 'It's quite the opposite. For one thing, she doesn't have any of the requirements; she knows no one. And then, to do her justice, she seems quite content with things as they are. No, what she likes most of all are her Wednesdays and her pleasant, ordinary conversations.' And she secretly envied Madame Verdurin those arts (though she entertained the hope that she'd mastered them herself thanks to such a great teacher) to which the Patronne attached such importance, even though they did nothing but limn the non-existent and sculpt the void, being as they are, strictly speaking, the Arts of Nothing practised by hostesses: the ability to know how to 'bring people together', to 'match people', to 'draw people out', to be 'self-effacing', to act as a 'go-between'.

In any case, Madame Swann's friends were impressed to see in her house a woman they usually pictured only in her own drawing room surrounded by her close-knit clutch of habitués, her little group, which they were amazed to see thus evoked, summarized, condensed into a single armchair, in the form of the Patronne-turned-visitor ensconced in her feather-trimmed cloak, as downy as the white furs carpeting this very salon, in which Madame Verdurin herself was her own salon. The shyer women thought it best to withdraw discreetly, and, using the plural, as people do when they want to hint to others that they shouldn't tire an invalid on her first outing, said: 'We'll just be on our way now, Odette.' They envied Madame Cottard, whom the Patronne called by her first name.

'Shall I whisk you away, then?' said Madame Verdurin, who couldn't bear the thought that one of her 'faithful' might stay behind.

'I'd be only too pleased, but this dear lady has been kind enough to offer me a lift,' replied Madame Cottard, loath to appear as if she might be forgetting, when approached by a more famous personage, the offer Madame Bontemps had made earlier to drive her home in her carriage with its ministerial crest. 'I must say I'm especially grateful to friends who so kindly offer to take me with them in their carriages. It's such a godsend for little old me, with no charioteer of my own.'

'Especially', replied the Patronne (not daring to say too much, since she knew Madame Bontemps slightly and had just invited her to her Wednesdays), 'since you're so far from your home here at Madame de Crécy's.—Oh dear, I'll never get into the habit of saying "Madame Swann"!' It was a running joke in the little clan, for those of the 'faithful' who had little wit, to make out that they couldn't get used to saying 'Madame Swann': 'I've become so accustomed to saying "Madame de Crécy" that I nearly said it again by mistake.' Madame Verdurin was the only one, when she spoke to Odette, not to nearly make the mistake by accident, but to do so on purpose.

'Doesn't it make you afraid, Odette, living in the middle of nowhere like this? I'm sure I'd be scared witless coming home after dark. And also it's so damp. That can't be good for your husband's eczema. At least you don't have any rats, do you?' 'Of course not! How awful!' 'That's a relief; I heard you did. I'm so glad to know it's not true, because I have a terrible phobia of them, and I'd never be able to visit you again. Goodbye, my dear, we'll see each other soon; you know how happy I am to see you.—You don't know how to arrange chrysanthemums,' she added on her way out, as Madame Swann rose to accompany her. 'They're Japanese flowers, you have to arrange them the way the Japanese do.'

'I don't agree with Madame Verdurin,' declared Madame Cottard after the Patronne had shut the door behind her, 'even though everything she says and does is gospel to me. No one but you, Odette, can find such beautiful chrysanthemums—or should I say *chrysanthema*, since it seems that's what they're called nowadays.'

'Our dear Madame Verdurin is not always very kind about other people's flowers,' Madame Swann gently replied. 'Who's your florist, Odette?' asked Madame Cottard, to cut short any further criticism of the Patronne. 'Is it Lemaître?* I must say the other day in front of Lemaître's there was such a lovely pink shrub that I couldn't help myself!' Her sense of propriety, however, kept her from divulging the exact price of the shrub; she confined herself to saying that the professor, even though he was usually 'as meek as a lamb', had 'thrown a fit' and told her she 'spent money like water'.

'Oh no, the only florist I go to is Debac,' Madame Swann replied. 'Me too, but I must confess I desert him once in a while for Lachaume.'*
'Aha, so you cheat on him with Lachaume, do you? Just wait till I tell him!' Odette exclaimed, anxious as always to show her wit and lead the conversation in her own home, where she felt more at ease than among the little clan. 'Really, though, Lachaume is becoming much too expensive. His prices are exorbitant, don't you think? Positively indecent!' she added, laughing.

Meanwhile Madame Bontemps, who had declared a hundred times that she had no desire to go to the Verdurins', was overjoyed at being invited to their Wednesdays, and was calculating how she could arrange things so that she could attend as many times as possible. She wasn't aware that Madame Verdurin didn't want her guests to miss a single Wednesday; moreover, she was one of those people whose company isn't much sought after, and who, when a hostess invites them to a 'series' of at-homes, instead of going whenever they have the time and inclination, like people who know they'll always be welcome, resist the urge to attend, for example, the first and third soirées, imagining that their absence will be noted, and save themselves up for the second and fourth, unless they've heard from a reliable source that the third will be a particularly brilliant soirée, in which case they reverse the order, with the excuse that 'they were unfortunately tied up the last time'. So Madame Bontemps was estimating how many Wednesdays were left before Easter, and how she could fix it so that she could get herself invited to an extra one without seeming to impose. She was counting on Madame Cottard to give her a few hints on their drive home.

'Oh, Madame Bontemps, I see you're getting up—it's very wicked of you to give the signal for retreat like that!' Madame Swann exclaimed. 'You owe me for not coming last Thursday . . . Do sit down again, just for a minute. You can't have any other visits to make before dinner! Really, can't I tempt you with one of these?' she asked, holding out a plate of cakes. 'They're not bad at all, these frightful little things. They may not be much to look at, but if you taste one, you'll see what I mean.'

'Oh, they do look delicious,' Madame Cottard interrupted. 'In your house, Odette, one never goes hungry. I don't need to ask you who made them—I know you order everything from Rebattet's.* I have to say I'm more eclectic. For petits fours and other little sweets, I often use Bourbonneux.* But I admit they don't know much about ices. When it comes to ice cream, mousse, or sorbet, Rebattet are true artists. As my husband would say, they're the *nec plus ultra*.'*

'But these are home-made! I really can't tempt you?' 'I wouldn't have any room left for dinner,' Madame Bontemps replied, 'but I will sit down again just for a minute—you know how I love chatting with an intelligent woman like you. Odette, you might think I'm being very indiscreet, but I'd very much like to know what you think about the hat Madame Trombert was wearing. I know big hats are all the fashion these days, but can't one go a little too far? And compared to the hat she wore the other day at my house, the one she was wearing just now is microscopic!'

'Oh no, I'm not at all intelligent,' Odette said, thinking this was the right thing to say. 'I'm such a gullible person—I'll believe anything people say—and I get all worked up over the silliest things.' And she insinuated that she'd suffered terribly early on in her marriage with Swann, who had a life apart from hers and was unfaithful.

Meanwhile, the Prince d'Agrigente, who had heard the words 'I'm not intelligent', felt duty-bound to protest, but unfortunately didn't have the gift of repartee.

'Nonsense!' Madame Bontemps exclaimed, 'not intelligent, *you*?'

'In fact I was just saying to myself: "What's this I'm hearing?"' the prince said, rising to the bait. 'My ears must be playing tricks on me.'

'It's true, I assure you,' Odette said, 'I'm really just a little middle-class housewife, easily shocked, full of prejudices, living in her own little corner, and terribly ignorant.' And then, in case he had any news of the Baron de Charlus, she asked: 'Have you seen the dear baronet recently?'

'*You*, ignorant!' Madame Bontemps exclaimed. 'Well then, what would you call the world of officialdom, what about all those ministers' wives who can only talk about their dresses! . . . Let me tell you, Madame Swann: just last week I mentioned *Lohengrin* to the wife of the Minister of Education. She replied: "*Lohengrin?* Oh yes! The new revue at the Folies-Bergère, I heard it's a riot!"* Well, Madame, I mean to say, when you hear things like that it just makes your blood boil. I could have slapped her. Because I have a bit of a temper. What do you think, Monsieur,' she asked, turning to me, 'wasn't I right?'

'Still,' Madame Cottard broke in, 'it's understandable for someone to get it wrong when they're asked point-blank like that, without warning. I know what it's like, because Madame Verdurin has a habit of putting people on the spot.'

'Speaking of Madame Verdurin,' Madame Bontemps said to Madame Cottard, 'do you know who'll be there on Wednesday? . . . Oh! I've just remembered that my husband and I have accepted another invitation for this coming Wednesday. Would you like to dine with us the Wednesday after that? That way we could go to Madame Verdurin's together. I'm too intimidated to go alone—I don't know why, but I've always been frightened of that grande dame.'

'I know why!' Madame Cottard replied, 'It's her booming voice. But not everyone can have as lovely a voice as Madame Swann's. As soon as you find your tongue, as the Patronne says, you'll break the ice. Deep down she's very friendly. But I completely understand how you feel, it's never easy to venture into new territory.'

'You could dine with us as well,' Madame Bontemps said to Madame Swann. 'We could all go together after dinner to Verdurate—or rather to Verdurinize; and even if that means upsetting the Patronne so she doesn't invite me anymore, once we're there, we three can keep each other company; I'm sure that's what I'd like best.' But this assertion must not have been very truthful, since Madame Bontemps went on to ask: 'Who do you think will be there the Wednesday after this? What's planned? You don't think it will be too crowded, do you?'

'I definitely won't be going,' Odette said. 'We'll just put in a brief appearance on the last Wednesday of all. If you don't mind waiting till then . . .' Madame Bontemps, however, did not seem to take to this suggestion.

Although the intellectual merits of a salon are usually in inverse rather than direct proportion to how fashionable it is, we must assume, since Swann found Madame Bontemps pleasant, that accepting one's diminished status makes one more easy-going towards those with

whom one is resigned to get along, and less demanding of their qualities, intellectual and otherwise. If that is so, individuals, like nations,
must see their culture and even their language disappearing, along
with their independence. One of the effects of this indulgence is to
aggravate the tendency we have after a certain age to be gratified by
words that pay homage to our own opinions and inclinations, so that
we feel encouraged to give them free rein; this is also the age when
a great artist, instead of mingling with original geniuses like himself,
prefers to associate with his students, who have nothing in common
with him except the letter of his teachings, and who praise him to the
skies and hang upon his every word; it is the age when a prominent
man or woman who lives only for love will deem most intelligent the
person at a party who might be inferior, but who says something that
shows they can understand and approve of an existence devoted to
affairs of the heart, thereby pleasantly flattering the voluptuous lean-
ings of the amorous individual; it was the age, too, when Swann, in his
role as Odette's husband, liked hearing Madame Bontemps say how
ridiculous it is to invite only duchesses to one's house (concluding
from this, contrary to what he would have thought in the old days at
the Verdurins', that she was a sensible and witty woman, not snobbish
in the least) and enjoyed telling her stories that 'left her in stitches',
because she hadn't already heard them and also because she was quick
to 'get the point', being eager to please and easily amused.

'So the doctor isn't as mad about flowers as you are, then?' Madame
Swann asked Madame Cottard.

'Well, you know how sensible he is, how he practises moderation in
all things.—Oh, but he does have one passion.'

'And what might *that* be, Madame?' asked Madame Bontemps, her
eyes sparkling with gleeful malice and inquisitiveness.

'Reading,' Madame Cottard replied innocently.

'What a soothing passion for a husband to have!' exclaimed Madame
Bontemps, stifling a diabolical laugh.

'Yes, all he needs is a good book . . .'

'Well then, Madame, you have nothing to fear.'

'Oh, but I do!—for his eyesight!' replied Madame Cottard. 'I must
get back to him, Odette, but I'll come knocking on your door as soon
as I can. Speaking of eyesight, did you hear that the *hôtel* Madame
Verdurin has just bought will be lighted by electricity? I didn't find
that out from my own little secret service, but from the electrician

himself, Mildé!* See, I always quote my sources! Even the bedrooms will have their own electric lamps, with shades to soften the light. Such a charming luxury, don't you think? It seems everyone we know must have the very latest thing, even if it isn't available yet. Just imagine, the sister-in-law of one of my friends had a telephone installed! She can order something without ever going out! I must confess that I've been scheming shamelessly for an invitation to go and speak into the instrument one day. I'm sorely tempted, but I'd rather have it in a friend's house than at my place. I don't think I'd like having a telephone in my own home. Once the novelty wears off, it must be a real headache.—Well, Odette, I must be off; don't try to keep Madame Bontemps any longer, since I'm in her charge. I really must tear myself away, you'll get me into trouble if I don't get home before my husband!'

I too had to go home, even though I hadn't yet been able to enjoy the winter pleasures that seemed to be contained within the dazzling chrysanthemums. These pleasures had not materialized, and yet Madame Swann didn't seem to be expecting anything else. She let the servants carry away the tea things as if she'd cried 'Closing-time!' And finally she said: 'Really, must you go? Well then, *goodbye!*' I felt that even if I did stay on, I would never experience those secret pleasures, and that it wasn't just my sadness that was depriving me of them. Were they to be found not on the beaten path of hours that always leads so quickly to the moment of departure, but rather on some unknown, intersecting byway on to which I should have turned? At least the object of my visit had been attained; Gilberte would know I'd come to her house when she was away, and that I had, as Madame Cottard kept saying, 'won Madame Verdurin over right away, from the very first moment'. ('You must be soulmates,' added the doctor's wife, who had never seen her 'make such a fuss' over anyone.) Gilberte would know that I'd spoken about her affectionately, as I couldn't help but do, but that I did not in fact have that inability to live without her which I thought was at the root of the boredom she'd evinced at our recent meetings. I'd told Madame Swann that I couldn't see Gilberte again. I'd said it as if my decision were irrevocable. The letter I was going to send Gilberte would imply this as well. Except, to keep my courage up, I told myself I'd make a final, supreme effort that would last just a few days. I said to myself: 'This is the last invitation from her I'll refuse; I'll accept the next one.' To make the separation less difficult for me, I didn't think of it as definitive. But I knew it would be.

New Year's Day was especially painful that year. No doubt that's true for any day that marks a milestone or anniversary when one is unhappy. But if our unhappiness comes from having lost someone dear to us, for example, the suffering stems solely from the sharp contrast between present and past. Added to this in my case was the unspoken hope that Gilberte might have wanted me to take the first steps towards a reconciliation, but when she saw I hadn't, was only waiting for the pretext of New Year's Day to write to me, saying: 'What's wrong, then? I'm mad about you, please come over so we can talk things through, I can't live without seeing you.' In the last days of December, such a letter seemed possible. It may not have been the least bit likely, but in order for us to think it is, our desire, our hope, are enough. The soldier is convinced that a certain period of time, which can be extended indefinitely, will be granted him before he's killed; the thief, before he's caught; humans in general, before they have to die. This is the amulet that protects individuals—and sometimes nations—not from danger but from the fear of danger, which is actually the belief in danger; in some cases, it's what allows them to brave those dangers without having to be brave. It's this sort of unfounded confidence that sustains the lover who's counting on a reconciliation or a letter. For me to stop expecting either of these, I had only to stop hoping for them. However uninteresting we may know we are to the woman we still love, we endow her with a series of thoughts—even indifferent ones—along with an intention to express those thoughts and a complicated inner life in which we figure as the object not just of antipathy, but of constant attention. To imagine what was going on in Gilberte's mind, however, all I needed was the ability to feel the way I would on one of the following New Year's Days, when Gilberte's attention, silence, affection, or coldness would go almost unnoticed by me, and when I would not have thought, or even been able to think, of looking for the solution to problems that would have stopped arising for me. When we are in love, our love is too vast to be contained wholly within ourselves; it radiates out to the beloved, encounters in her a surface that stops it and forces it to return to its starting point, and it's this return shock of our own affection that we call the feelings of the other person and that casts a spell on us even more than it did on the way out, because we don't realize it comes from us. All the hours of New Year's Day chimed without the arrival of that letter from Gilberte. And since I received some New Year's cards late or delayed by the overload of mail at that time of year, I still held out some hope on the third and fourth of January, but it was fading fast. On the following days I cried a great deal. This was owing, of course, to the fact that I'd been less than sincere when I'd renounced Gilberte, and had clung to the hope for a New Year's letter from her. And seeing that hope extinguished before I had time to fortify myself with another, I suffered like an invalid who has emptied his vial of morphine without having a second one ready. But perhaps—and these two explanations are not mutually exclusive, since a single emotion may be made of opposites—the hope I had of finally receiving a letter had brought the image of Gilberte closer to me, and had recreated the emotions I'd felt when I was waiting to be with her, or when I saw her, or when I observed the way she was with me. The immediate possibility of a reconciliation had suppressed the one thing whose enormity we never realize: resignation. Neurasthenics* can't believe people who assure them that they will gradually grow calm if they just stay in bed without reading any letters or newspapers. They think such a regimen will only worsen their anxiety. Similarly, lovers are unable to believe in the beneficial power of renunciation, since they're looking at it from within an opposite state of mind, and haven't yet begun to experience it.

Because I was having violent palpitations, my caffeine intake was reduced, and the palpitations stopped. Then I wondered if the caffeine might have been at least partly responsible for the anguish I'd felt when I'd fallen out with Gilberte, and which I'd attributed, whenever it recurred, to the suffering of not seeing my friend anymore, or the risk of seeing her only when she was in the same bad mood. But if this drug had been at the root of the suffering which at that time my imagination had interpreted wrongly (which would not be at all extraordinary, since, for lovers, the worst mental suffering is often due to the physical habit of living with the women they love), then it was like the love potion that continues to link Tristan to Iseult long after they drink it.* For the physical improvement brought about almost immediately by the decrease of caffeine did not arrest the evolution of the grief which my absorption of the toxin had, if not created, at least made more acute.

Then, around the middle of January, after my hopes for a New Year's letter had been crushed, and after the additional suffering that had accompanied this disappointment had abated, my old sorrow from before the holidays started up again once more. Perhaps the cruellest thing about it was that I myself was the creator—conscious, wilful, pitiless, and patient—of this anguish. The only thing that mattered to me was my relationship with Gilberte, but I myself was rendering it impossible by gradually bringing about, through this prolonged separation from my friend, not her indifference, but something that would amount to the same thing in the end: my own. It was a long, cruel suicide of the self that loved Gilberte that I was constantly working away at, with a clear idea not only of what I was doing in the present, but of what the result would be in the future: I knew not just that within a certain period of time I would no longer love Gilberte, but also that she herself would regret the separation, and that the attempts she would make then to see me would be as fruitless as today's, not because I'd love her too much, as I did now, but because I'd certainly be in love with another woman whom I would continue to desire and for whom I would spend hours waiting, hours from which I wouldn't dare subtract a second for the sake of Gilberte, who would be nothing to me then. And no doubt at that very moment, when (since I'd made up my mind not to see her anymore, unless she herself frankly requested a reconciliation, or made a complete declaration of love, neither of which was the least bit likely) I'd already lost Gilberte, and loved her more than ever (I felt all that she meant to me even more acutely than the year before when, spending all my afternoons with her, or whenever I chose, I believed that nothing could threaten our friendship), no doubt at that moment the idea that someday I'd feel the same emotions for another woman was hateful to me, for this idea took me away from Gilberte, my love, and my suffering, the very love and suffering that caused me to try to grasp, through my tears, precisely what Gilberte was, but that forced me to acknowledge that they did not belong solely to her but would, sooner or later, be linked to some other woman. In this way—at least this was how I thought at the time—we are always detached from the other: when we love, we sense that this love does not bear her name, but could arise again in the future, and could even, in the past, have arisen for another woman and not for this one: and during the time when we are not in love, if we are able to consider the contradictory nature of love philosophically, it's because we don't feel the love about which we speak so easily, and so we don't know it, since knowledge in these matters is intermittent and does not survive the actual presence of the emotion. Of course, there would have been time for me to warn Gilberte that the future in which I would no longer love her, which my suffering helped me guess at but which my imagination couldn't yet picture clearly, would gradually take shape, and that its arrival was, if not imminent, then at least inevitable, if Gilberte herself didn't come to my aid and nip my future indifference in the bud. How often I came close to writing to Gilberte, or of going to say to her: 'I'm warning you; I've made my decision; the step I'm about to take is final. This is the last time I'll see you. Soon I won't love you anymore!' But what would be the use? By what right could I have reproached Gilberte for an indifference that, though I didn't consider myself guilty on that account, I displayed towards anything that was not Gilberte? The last time! To me, that seemed immense, because I loved Gilberte. To her it would doubtless have made the same impression as those letters in which friends ask to pay us a visit before they leave the country, requests that, like those of tiresome women who are in love with us, we deny, because we're looking forward to pleasures of our own. The time we have at our disposal every day is elastic; the passions we feel expand it, the ones we inspire contract it, and habit fills the rest.

Besides, even if I had spoken to Gilberte, she wouldn't have heard me. We always think, when we converse, that it's our ears and minds that are listening. But if my words had reached Gilberte, they would have been distorted, as if they had had to pass through the shifting curtain of a waterfall before reaching her, and would have been unrecognizable, ridiculous-sounding, devoid of meaning. The truth we put into words doesn't forge its own direct path; it is not endowed with undeniable self-evidence. A certain time must elapse before a truth of the same order can take shape within those words. Then the political opponent who, despite all arguments and proofs to the contrary, upheld that his adversary, who maintained an opposite view, was a traitor, himself shares the hated conviction in which the one who had so ineffectively tried to spread it no longer believes. The masterpiece which, to admirers who read it out loud, seemed to demonstrate clearly the proofs of its excellence, but to those who listened sounded merely nonsensical or mediocre, will after a time be proclaimed a masterpiece by the latter, but too late for the author to hear it. Likewise, in love, barriers cannot be broken down from without by the one whom they fill with despair, no matter how hard he tries; it's only when he no longer cares about them, thanks to efforts coming from the other side, from the beloved who did not love him, that these barriers, which he'd attacked before in vain, suddenly fall, but to no purpose. Even if I had gone to tell Gilberte of my future indifference and how to prevent it, she would have inferred from this that my love for her, the need I had for her, were even greater than she'd thought, and her annoyance at seeing me would have increased. And it is indeed true that it was this love which, because of the series of discordant states of mind it produced in me, helped me to foresee, even better than she could, the end of this love. And yet I might still have given Gilberte such a warning, by letter or in person, after enough time had elapsed, which would, it's true, have made her less indispensable to me, but might also have proved to her that she was not so indispensable. Unfortunately, some well-meaning or ill-intentioned people spoke to her about me in a way that must have led her to believe that they were doing so at my behest. And so, whenever I heard that Cottard, my own mother, and even Monsieur de Norpois, with a few thoughtless words, had rendered null and void all the sacrifices I'd made, spoiling the whole effect of my reserve by wrongly making it seem as if I'd abandoned it, I faced a twofold difficulty. In the first place, I now had to date from that day alone my laborious and productive abstention that these busybodies, unbeknownst to me, had interrupted and consequently annihilated. Worse still, I would have less pleasure in seeing Gilberte, who now believed me to be not resigned in a dignified manner, but scheming in the shadows for a meeting that she hadn't deigned to give me. I cursed all this idle chatter of people who often, without even intending to help or harm, for no reason at all, just for the sake of having something to say, sometimes because we ourselves couldn't help saying things within their hearing and because they're indiscreet (as we are), cause us, at the most crucial moment, so much harm. It's true that in the deadly task of destroying our love they are far from playing a role comparable to that played by two people who are in the habit, one from an excess of kindness and the other from an excess of malice, of making everything fall apart just when it was starting to come together. But we're not as angry with those two people as we are with the meddling Cottards of this world, since the latter of these two is the one we love, and the former, ourselves.

Meanwhile, since almost every time I went to see Madame Swann, she'd invite me to come to tea with her daughter, and would tell me to

reply directly to Gilberte, I would often write to her, and in this correspondence I did not choose the phrases I thought might win her
over, but sought only to prepare a smooth stream-bed for my flood of
tears. For regret, like desire, seeks self-satisfaction rather than self-
analysis; when we first fall in love, we spend our time not in trying to
find out what love is, but in making arrangements for tomorrow's
meetings. When we stop loving, we seek not to know the nature of our
sorrow, but to offer to the one causing it the expression of sorrow that
seems tenderest to us. We say things that we feel we need to say, not
what the other will understand; we speak for ourselves alone. I wrote:
'I'd thought it wouldn't be possible. Alas, I see it's not that difficult.'
And although I said: 'I'll probably never see you again', I took care
not to adopt a coldness she might have thought affected, and these
words, as I wrote them, made me weep, because I felt they expressed
not what I'd have liked to believe, but what was actually going to happen. For I knew that the next time she suggested a meeting I would
still be brave enough, as I was now, not to give in; and, refusal after
refusal, I would gradually arrive at a time when, after not seeing her
for so long, I would no longer want to see her. I wept, but I found the
courage, the sweetness, of sacrificing the happiness of being with her
to the possibility of one day seeming desirable to her, a day when—
alas!—seeming desirable to her would no longer matter to me. The
very hypothesis, unlikely as it was, that at this moment she still loved
me, as she'd claimed during my last visit to her, and that what I took
as the boredom one feels with someone one is tired of might merely
be due to a sense of insecurity, or to feigned indifference like my own,
served only to make my resolution less cruel. It seemed to me that in
a few years, after we'd forgotten each other, when I'd be able to look
back on this letter I was writing now and tell her it wasn't the least bit
sincere, she would reply: 'So you really loved me? If only you knew
how I'd been looking forward to that letter, how I longed for us to
meet, how much it made me cry!' As I was writing to her, having just
come home from her mother's house, the thought that I might now be
consummating that very misunderstanding, by its sadness alone, by
the pleasure of imagining I was loved by Gilberte, made me go on
with my letter.

Whereas, as I was leaving Madame Swann's 'tea party', I was
thinking of what I was about to write to her daughter, Madame
Cottard was thinking along entirely different lines. During her little

'tour of inspection', she hadn't failed to congratulate Madame Swann on the new pieces of furniture, the recent 'acquisitions' she'd noticed in the drawing room. She could even spot among them some (though very few in number) of the objects Odette used to have in her *hôtel* on the Rue La Pérouse, notably her gemstone animals, her fetishes.

But ever since Madame Swann had learned the word 'tacky' from a friend she admired—a word which had opened new horizons to her, since it designated precisely the things she'd found 'chic' a few years earlier—all those things had, one after the other, followed into retirement the gilded trellis that had supported her chrysanthemums, along with countless bonbonnières from Giroux's* and her coronet-embossed notepaper (not to mention the cardboard coins strewn over the mantelpieces which, even before she met Swann, a man of taste had advised her to give up). Moreover, in the artistic disorder, the bohemian clutter, of the rooms whose walls were still painted in dark colours, which made them as different as possible from the white drawing rooms Madame Swann would have a little later on, the Far East was retreating more and more before the advances of the eighteenth century; and the cushions that, to make me more 'comfortable', Madame Swann kneaded and heaped up behind my back, were embroidered with Louis XV posies rather than the Chinese dragons of old. In the room where she could usually be found, of which she'd say: 'Yes, I'm fond of this room; I use it quite often. I couldn't live among cold, pretentious things; *this* is where I work' (though what this 'work' entailed was never clear—it could have been a painting, or perhaps a book, since the fashion of writing books was beginning to be popular among women who liked to 'occupy themselves' so as not to feel useless), she was surrounded by Dresden china (she liked that sort of porcelain—which she'd pronounce with an English accent—so much that she'd say about anything at all: 'How pretty that is! It looks just like Dresden flowers!'); and she was so fearful of the servants' clumsy handling of the china—more so even than she'd been in the old days for her Chinese figurines and vases—that she'd make the servants pay for the anxiety they caused her with tantrums which Swann, although such a polite, gentle master, would witness without being shocked by them. Seeing certain defects in those we love takes nothing away from our affection; on the contrary, that affection just makes them seem more endearing. Nowadays Odette would receive her intimate guests less often in a Japanese kimono, favouring the pale, frothy silk of Watteau dressing gowns* whose flowery spume she'd caress over her breasts, gowns in which she would bask, lounge, frolic with such deep breaths and such an air of well-being, of feeling the cool air on her skin, that she seemed to think of them not as a decorative setting for herself, but as necessary as her 'tub' or her daily 'constitutional', satisfying the requirements of her body and the subtleties of her hygiene. She had a habit of declaring that she could more easily do without bread than art or cleanliness, and that she'd have been more distressed by the burning of the *Mona Lisa* than by the annihilation of 'throngs' of her acquaintances. These theories seemed paradoxical to her friends, but made them think of her as being high-minded, and earned her a weekly visit from the Belgian ambassador, so that in the little world that revolved around her sun, people would have been most surprised to learn that elsewhere, at the Verdurins' for example, she was deemed stupid. It was because of her quick wit that Madame Swann preferred the society of men to that of women. But when she criticized the latter, it was always from a courtesan's perspective, calling attention to those of their flaws that might lower the opinion men had of them: thick ankles, a bad complexion, poor education, hairy legs, a rank odour, pencilled eyebrows. But towards a woman who had been kind or indulgent towards her in the past, she was more forgiving, especially if it was someone who had fallen on hard times. She'd defend her adamantly and would insist: 'People are unfair to her. She's a very nice woman, I can assure you.'

It wasn't just the interior decoration of Odette's drawing room, but Odette herself, that Madame Cottard and everyone who had known Madame de Crécy would have found difficult to recognize if they hadn't seen her in a while. She seemed years younger than before. No doubt this was thanks partly to the fact that she'd filled out, was in better health, and seemed calmer, cooler, more relaxed; but also because the new fashion of smooth, straight hair opened up her face, which was enlivened by the application of pink blusher, and in which her eyes and profile, which had been too prominent before, seemed to have become toned down. But another reason for this change was that, having reached middle age, Odette had finally discovered, or invented, her own personal way of presenting her face, with an unchanging 'character' and a certain 'style of beauty'; and on her unruly features—which for so many years, at the mercy of the haphazard, undisciplined whims of the flesh, briefly ageing by years at the slightest fatigue, had somehow composed for her, depending on her mood and health, a vague, changeable, shapeless, charming face—she had now applied this fixed style, giving her a kind of eternal youth.

In Swann's own bedroom, instead of the handsome photographs that were now being taken of his wife in which, whatever dress or hat she wore, the same enigmatic, imperious expression proclaimed her triumphant face and features, he kept a small old daguerreotype of her, quite plain, which predated that model, and from which Odette's youth and beauty, which she hadn't yet discovered, seemed absent. Doubtless Swann, having remained faithful, or having reverted, to a different conception of her, appreciated a more Botticelli-like charm* in this frail young woman with her pensive eyes and weary features, her pose suspended between movement and stillness. For he still loved seeing his wife as a Botticelli. Odette, however, who sought not to emphasize but to compensate for and cover up whatever she didn't like about herself, which may have revealed her 'character' to an artist, but which as a woman she regarded as flaws, wanted nothing to do with Botticelli. Swann owned a magnificent Oriental shawl, in blue and pink, which he'd bought because it was exactly like the one worn by the Virgin in the *Magnificat*.* But Madame Swann didn't want to wear it. Once only, she allowed her husband to order a dress completely covered in daisies, cornflowers, forget-me-nots, and bluebells, like that of *La Primavera*.* Sometimes, in the evenings, when she was tired, Swann would quietly draw my attention to the way, without realizing it, she gave her pensive hands the nimble, slightly agitated movement of the Virgin dipping her pen into the inkpot the angel holds for her, before writing in the holy book in which the word *Magnificat* is already inscribed. But he added: 'Whatever you do, don't tell her! She'd stop doing it if she knew.'

Except at such unselfconsciously relaxed moments when Swann would try to recapture Botticelli's melancholy attitude, Odette's body now seemed as if it were cut out to form a single silhouette completely surrounded by an 'outline' which, to follow the contour of the woman, had abandoned the jagged lines, the zigzags, the convexities and concavities, the disparate nature of all the composite elements of the fashions of former times, but which also, where her own anatomy erred by making pointless departures inside or outside the ideal design, was able, with a single bold stroke, to rectify these flaws of nature and, throughout a whole section, to compensate for the

failings of both the flesh and the material. All the padding, the preposterous bustles, had disappeared, along with the long, corseted bodices
which, overlapping the skirt and rigid with whalebone, had for so
long overemphasized her belly and made her look as if she were made
up of disparate parts not connected by any individuality. The vertical
fringes and the curved ruches had given way to the inflexion of a body
that made silk undulate as a mermaid ripples water and gave percaline* a human expression, now that it had freed itself, like a living
organism, from the long chaos and nebulous opacity of fashions now
dethroned. But Madame Swann had been able to preserve a vestige of
some of these fashions, in the very midst of the ones that had replaced
them. On some evenings, when I was unable to work and knew for
certain that Gilberte was at the theatre with her friends, I'd make
a surprise visit to her parents' house, where I'd often find Madame
Swann in an elegant house-dress of which the skirt, in one of those
beautiful dark shades, burgundy or sienna, which seemed to have
a special significance because they were no longer in fashion, was
crossed diagonally by a broad openwork band of black lace reminiscent of old-fashioned flounces. When, on one chilly spring day before
my break with Gilberte, she took me to the Jardin d'Acclimatation,
under her jacket, which she unbuttoned a little as she grew warm
from the walk, the serrated edging of her blouse looked like the half-
glimpsed lapel of some absent vest similar to one she'd worn a few
years before, when she liked them to have those slightly jagged edges;
and her scarf—in that same 'tartan' to which she'd remained faithful,
although its tones were so softened (the red became pink and the blue,
lilac) that it almost resembled one of those dove-coloured taffetas that
were the latest fashion—was knotted under her chin in such a way
that its fastening was invisible, irresistibly bringing to mind those
bonnet ribbons now no longer worn. She had only to 'hold out' a little
longer like this for young men, trying to understand her outfits, to
say: 'Madame Swann is quite a period piece, isn't she?' As in a fine
literary style layered with different forms of expression and strengthened by a hidden tradition, so in Madame Swann's attire those vague
memories of bodices and bows, an occasional, instantly repressed tendency towards a short 'monkey jacket',* or even a vague allusion to
long 'follow-me-lads' hat ribbons, suffused her actual form with the
incomplete suggestion of other, older ones, which could not have
been effected by a seamstress or milliner, but about which one's

thoughts constantly revolved, and which enveloped Madame Swann in a sort of nobility—perhaps because the very uselessness of these accoutrements made them seem to serve a more than utilitarian purpose, perhaps because of the remnants they preserved of former years, perhaps too because of a kind of sartorial individuality peculiar to this woman that gave her outfits, however different they were, the same family resemblance. It was as if she didn't dress solely for the comfort or adornment of her body; she was encompassed by her outfits as by the delicate, spiritualized trappings of a civilization.

When Gilberte, who usually held her tea parties on the same days her mother was 'at home', had to be away and I was therefore able to attend Madame Swann's '*Choufleury*', I'd find her in one of her beautiful dresses, sometimes of taffeta, sometimes of faille, or else of velvet, or crêpe de Chine, or satin, or silk, and which, not loose like the dressing gowns she usually wore indoors, but cinched tight as if she were about to go out, gave those leisurely afternoons at home a quality of alertness and energy. The bold simplicity of their cut suited her waist and gestures, which seemed to give her sleeves a mood that varied according to the day: it was as if there was a sudden determination in the blue velvet, an easy-going nature in the white taffeta; and, in order to become visible, a sort of supreme, dignified reserve in her way of holding out her arm had taken on the valiant smile of self-sacrifice expressed by black crêpe de Chine. But at the same time, the complication of these 'embellishments', which served no practical purpose and had no reason to be visible, added to these vivid dresses something detached, pensive, secret, which harmonized with the melancholy Madame Swann still retained, at least around her eyes and in the curve of her fingers. Beneath the profusion of sapphire charms, enamelled four-leaf clovers, silver medals, gold medallions, turquoise amulets, ruby necklaces, and topazes big as chestnuts, there would be in the dress itself some colourful design on an extra panel of cloth continuing its own previous existence, or some row of little satin buttons which buttoned nothing and couldn't be unbuttoned, or a braid attempting to please the eye with its intricacy, the unobtrusiveness of a delicate reminder, and all of these, quite as much as the jewels, seemed—having otherwise no possible justification—to imply an intention, to be a token of affection, to keep a secret, to comply with a superstition, to commemorate a cure, a vow, a lover, or a tryst. And sometimes a hint of a slash in the sleeve of a blue velvet bodice, or the slightly puffed shoulders in a black satin dress recalling the 'leg of mutton' style of the 1830s, or else something under the skirt that called to mind Louis XV hoop bustles, made the dress look almost like a costume and, by inserting a sort of hazy reminiscence of the past into the life of the present, added to the person of Madame Swann the charm of certain historical or fictional heroines. And if I pointed this out to her, she'd say: 'Unlike some of my friends, I don't play golf. So I'd have no earthly excuse to go about wearing *sweaters*, as they do.'*

In the crowded drawing room, after showing out one visitor or offering a plate of cakes to another, Madame Swann would take me aside for a moment to say: 'Gilberte has asked me specially to invite you to lunch the day after tomorrow. I wasn't sure I'd see you, so I was going to write you a note if you didn't come today.' But I continued to resist. And this resistance was costing me less and less, because however much we may love the poison that's harming us, when something forces us to be deprived of it for any length of time, we can't help but realize the value of the peace of mind we'd lost, along with its freedom from emotion and suffering. If we aren't entirely sincere when we tell ourselves we never want to see the one we love again, we wouldn't be any more so in saying we do. Of course, we can only bear her absence by assuring ourselves it won't last very long, and by thinking of the day when we'll meet again; on the other hand, we feel how much easier to bear are these daily dreams of an imminent, constantly postponed meeting than an actual encounter, which could be followed by jealousy, and so the news that we'll see the one we love again could cause us unwelcome distress. What we keep putting off, day after day, is no longer an end to the unbearable anguish of separation, but the dreaded renewal of pointless emotions. How infinitely we prefer, to such an encounter, the compliant memory we embellish at will with dreams in which the girl who, in reality, doesn't love us, tells us she does when we're all alone; how preferable this memory is, which we can make as sweet as we like by gradually adding to it whatever we like, to the deferred encounter in which we'd have to deal with someone to whom we could no longer dictate at will the words we wish her to say, but whose cold indifference and unexpected hostility we'd have to endure yet again! When we're no longer in love, we all know that forgetting the loved one, or merely having vague memories of her, causes much less suffering than unhappy love. It was the sweet tranquillity of such anticipated forgetfulness that I longed for, though I didn't admit as much to myself.

Moreover, however painful such a treatment of mental detachment and physical isolation may be, it grows progressively less so for another reason: while we wait for a cure, it weakens the obsessive fixation that love is. My own love was still strong enough for me to want to regain Gilberte's esteem, which, by my self-imposed separation from her, I thought must be steadily increasing, so that every one of these calm, sad days when I didn't see her, following one after the other without interruption, without a suggested end-date either (barring the interference of some busybody or other), was a day not lost, but gained. Resignation, one of the modes of habit, allows some elements of our inner strength to grow indefinitely. Those that had been too negligible to bear my sorrow on the first evening of my break with Gilberte gained immeasurably in strength. Only, the tendency of everything that exists to go on existing is sometimes interrupted by sudden impulses to which we allow ourselves to give way all the more easily because we know for how many days, or even months, we have been able, and might still be able, to abstain. Often, it's when the purse in which we've been putting our savings is almost full that we suddenly empty it; it's when we don't wait for the result of our treatment, when we've grown used to it, that we stop it. So one day, when Madame Swann repeated her usual words about how happy Gilberte would be to see me, thus placing within my reach the happiness of which I'd been depriving myself for so long, I was astounded to realize that it was still possible for me to enjoy it; I could hardly wait for the next day; for I had just made up my mind to surprise Gilberte by turning up at her house before dinner.

What helped me to endure waiting for an entire day was a plan I'd made. Now that all was forgotten, and Gilberte and I were reconciled, I was determined to go and see her only as her lover. Every day she'd receive from me the most beautiful flowers. If Madame Swann forbade me from making daily deliveries of flowers (not that she had any right to be such a severe mother), I'd find more precious, less frequent gifts. My parents didn't give me enough money to buy expensive things. But I thought of a large vase in old Chinese porcelain that my aunt Léonie had left me; every day Maman would envisage Françoise coming to her and saying: 'Oh no, it's all shattered to smithereens!' and there would be nothing left of it. In that case, wasn't it wiser to sell it, so I could procure as much delight as I wished for Gilberte? I thought I could easily get a thousand francs for it. I had it wrapped up; I'd grown so used to it that I no longer noticed it—parting with it at least had the advantage of making me more aware of it. I picked it up as I left for the Swanns' and, giving their address to the coachman, told him to go via the Champs-Élysées, at the corner of which was a large shop dealing in Oriental objects owned by a man my father knew. To my great surprise, he offered me on the spot not one thousand, but ten thousand francs. I took these notes joyfully; for a whole year, I could shower Gilberte with a daily delivery of roses and lilacs! After we left the shop, since the Swanns lived near the Bois de Boulogne, the coachman naturally drove up the Avenue des Champs-Élysées instead of taking the usual route. We'd already passed the corner of the Rue de Berri when, in the gloaming, I thought I recognized, quite close to the Swanns' house but moving away from it in the opposite direction, Gilberte, who was walking slowly but purposefully next to a young man with whom she was talking, though I couldn't see his face. I leaned forward in the cab, intending to signal the driver to stop; but then I hesitated. The strolling couple were already quite far away, and the two faint, parallel silhouettes outlined by their slow strides were gradually fading into the Elysian shadows. Soon we arrived at Gilberte's house. I was greeted by Madame Swann, who said: 'Oh dear, how disappointed she'll be! I don't know why she's not here. She felt very hot after a lesson, so she told me she was going out for a breath of fresh air with one of her girlfriends.' 'I think I saw her on the Avenue des Champs-Élyées,' I replied. 'Oh no, I don't think so. Whatever you do, don't tell her father; he doesn't like her going out this late. *Good evening!*'* I left, telling the coachman to take the same route, but couldn't spot the pair. Where had they been? What were they saying to each other, in such an intimate way?

I went home, hopelessly clutching my windfall of ten thousand francs that was to have allowed me to give so many little pleasures to Gilberte, whom I was now determined never to see again. Of course, my visit to the dealer's had filled me with joy by giving me the hope that from now on, my friend would be nothing but happy and grateful. But if I hadn't made this stop, if the carriage hadn't taken the Avenue des Champs-Élysées, I wouldn't have seen Gilberte with that young man. Thus a single event can lead to two contradictory ramifications, with the unhappiness it engenders cancelling the happiness it had caused. What happened to me was the opposite of what so often occurs; usually we desire some pleasure or other but we lack the material means to attain it. As La Bruyère says: 'It is sad to be a lover without wealth.'* And so all that's left for us is to try gradually to dampen our desire for that pleasure. In my case, however, the material means had been obtained, but at the same time, if not as a logical result, then at least as a fortuitous consequence of this initial success, my joy had been snatched from me. It would seem that this must always be the case—though not, as a rule, on the same evening we've acquired the thing that makes it possible. Usually we go on struggling and hoping for a little while longer. But happiness can never be attained. If we manage to overcome circumstances, Nature shifts the struggle from the external world to our inner selves, and gradually brings about a change in our heart until it desires something other than what it's about to possess. If the reversal occurs so quickly that our heart hasn't had time to change, Nature still doesn't despair of conquering us—more slowly, it's true, and more subtly, but just as effectively. Thus our possession of happiness is wrested from us at the last second, or rather it's by means of this very possession that, by a diabolical ruse, Nature destroys our happiness. Having failed with anything having to do with everyday reality and life, Nature creates one final impossibility: the psychological impossibility of happiness. The phenomenon of happiness doesn't come to pass, or else it gives rise to extreme bitterness.

I locked away my ten thousand francs. But they were of no use to me now. I spent them, as it happened, even more quickly than if I'd sent flowers daily to Gilberte, for when night fell, I was so unhappy that I couldn't stay at home, but went instead to drown my sorrows in the arms of women I didn't love. As for trying to please Gilberte, I no longer wished to do so; returning to her house would only have made me suffer. Even the sight of Gilberte, which would have given me such delight the day before, would not have helped me; for my anxiety would only have increased so long as I couldn't be with her. This is how, with each additional torment she inflicts on us, often without realizing it, a woman increases her power over us, but also increases our own demands on her. With each injury she does us, she imprisons us more and more, adding to our chains; but she also multiplies those chains we thought were sufficient to bind her to us in order to keep our minds at peace. Only the day before, if I hadn't been afraid of annoying Gilberte, I'd have been content to ask for occasional meetings with her; but now these could no longer have satisfied me, and my requests would have been completely different. For in love, unlike in war, the more we're defeated, the greater and harsher our demands become, provided we're still in a position to impose them. Such was not my case with Gilberte. And so I preferred at first not to return to her mother's house. I did, it's true, go on telling myself that Gilberte didn't love me, that I'd known this for some time, that I could see her again if I wished and, if I didn't wish, forget her with time. But these notions, like a remedy that has no effect on certain diseases, were completely powerless against those two parallel, vanishing silhouettes that I kept seeing of Gilberte and the young man as they made their slow progress along the Champs-Élysées. This was a new pain, which would also eventually wear itself out; it was an image that would one day present itself to my mind completely purified of every noxious element it had contained, like those deadly poisons that can be handled without danger, like a tiny piece of dynamite with which you can light your cigarette without fear of an explosion. In the meantime, there was another force in me that was struggling with all its might against the unhealthy force that kept showing me Gilberte walking along in the twilight: to repel the ever-renewed onslaughts of my memory, there was, working effectively in the opposite direction, my imagination. The first of these two forces did continue to show me that couple walking along the Champs-Élysées, and presented me as well with other unpleasant images from the past, such as Gilberte shrugging her shoulders when her mother asked her to stay with me. But the second force, working on the canvas of my hopes, outlined a future much more obligingly detailed than the limited view of my unfortunate past. For each minute during which I saw Gilberte's sullen face, how many more were spent imagining the steps she might take towards our reconciliation, possibly even towards our engagement! It's true that this force directed towards the future by my imagination drew, after all, from the past. As my exasperation with Gilberte's shrug faded, so too would my memory of her charm, a memory that made me wish she'd return to me. But I was still far from that death of the past. I still loved Gilberte, even though I thought I hated her. Whenever I was complimented on what I was wearing or how well I looked, I wished she was there. I was annoyed by the inclination so many people showed at that time to invite me over, and I refused all their invitations. There was a scene at home because I didn't accompany my father to an official dinner which was to be attended by the Bontemps and their niece Albertine, a young girl still hardly more than a child. So it is that the different periods of our life overlap. Because you're still in love with someone who will one day not matter to you, you scornfully refuse to see someone who doesn't matter to you today, but whom you'll love tomorrow, whom you might have been able, if you'd agreed to see her, to love earlier on, and who would thereby have curtailed your present sufferings (though they would, of course, have been replaced with others). My own sufferings were undergoing a transformation. I was surprised to observe within me one emotion one day and another the next, usually aroused by some hope or fear having to do with Gilberte. With the Gilberte I carried within me. I should have told myself that the other Gilberte, the real one, might be entirely different from my own, felt none of the regrets I ascribed to her, and probably thought much less about me than I did about her, but also much less than I imagined her thinking about me when I was alone conversing with my fictional Gilberte, wondering what her real feelings were towards me, and thus imagining her attention constantly revolving around me.

During those periods when grief, though dwindling, still persists, we must distinguish between the sorrow caused by the constant thought of the loved one and the sorrow revived by certain memories, some nasty remark, some verb used in a letter she wrote. Since all the various forms of grief will be discussed in the context of a love affair still to come, let it be said here that of these two kinds of sorrow, the former is infinitely less cruel than the latter. This is because the idea of the person, forever living inside us, is adorned with the halo with which we soon endow her, and is tinged, if not with the frequent palliatives of hope, then at least with the tranquillity of permanent melancholy. (It should be noted as well that the image of a person who makes us suffer counts for little among the complications which exacerbate and prolong the unhappiness of love and keep it from healing, just as in certain maladies the cause is out of proportion with the ensuing fever and the delayed recovery.) But if the idea of the person we love reflects an intelligence that is on the whole optimistic, the same is not true of those particular memories, those nasty remarks, that hostile letter (I received only one of that sort from Gilberte); it's as if the person herself dwelt in those fragments, however paltry, raised to a power which she is far from possessing in the usual idea we form of her as a whole. This is because we haven't contemplated the letter as we do the image of our beloved, in the calm melancholy of regret; we have read it, devoured it, in the same dreadful anguish that grips us during some unexpected disaster. These kinds of sorrows take shape in a different way; they come to us from without, and they reach our heart by way of the cruellest suffering. The image of our friend, which we believe to be original and authentic, has actually been revised many times by us. The cruel memory, on the other hand, is not contemporaneous with that restored image; it is from another age, it is one of the rare witnesses of a monstrous past. But since this past continues to exist, except in us, where we've seen fit to replace it with a miraculous golden age, a paradise where everyone is reconciled, these memories and letters bring us back to reality and can't help but make us feel, by the sudden pain they cause us, how far we've strayed from reality in the mad hope born from our daily expectations. Not that this reality must always remain the same, even though that is sometimes the case. In our lives there are many women whom we've never sought to see again, women who have naturally responded to our unintentional silence with a silence of their own. Only, since we never loved these women, we haven't counted the years spent apart from them; and this example, which would invalidate our argument, is ignored by us when we consider the efficacy of isolation, just as people who believe in premonitions forget all the occasions when their own haven't come true.

After a time, though, absence can be effective. The desire, the appetite to see us can finally be reborn in the heart that currently disregards us. But this takes time. With regard to time, however, our demands are no less exorbitant than those required by the heart to change. First of all, time is the one thing we have the most difficulty granting, for our suffering is acute, and we're eager for it to end. Secondly, the time it takes for the other heart to change helps our own to change as well, so that when the goal we've set ourselves becomes attainable, we no longer want to achieve it. In any case, the very idea that it will be attainable—that there's no happiness that, once it has ceased being happiness for us, we can't finally achieve—contains an element, but only an element, of truth. This happiness comes to us when we've become indifferent to it. But it's precisely this indifference that has made us less critical, and leads us to believe in retrospect that such a happiness would have delighted us, when at the time we may have found it extremely inadequate. We are not very demanding, not very good judges, of things that no longer matter to us. The friendliness of a person we no longer love, which in our indifference seems excessive, might not even have been enough when we were in love. These affectionate words, this offer of a meeting make us think of the joy they would have given us and not of all the others we'd have wanted immediately afterwards, which, by our greed, we may have prevented from occurring. So that we can never be certain that the happiness that comes too late, when we can no longer enjoy it, when we are no longer in love, is quite the same happiness which made us feel so wretched before, when we didn't have it. There's only one person who could decide this: our previous self; and that self no longer exists; no doubt if it did reappear, our happiness—identical or not—would vanish.

Before these belated fulfilments of a dream that would no longer matter to me, and because I went on inventing, as in the days when I still hardly knew Gilberte, words she might say and letters she might write in which she begged for forgiveness, swore that she'd never loved anyone but me, and asked me to marry her, a series of delightful images, incessantly recreated, came to occupy a larger place in my mind than the vision of Gilberte and the young man, which now had nothing to sustain it. By this time, I would probably have resumed my visits to Madame Swann if not for a dream I had in which one of my friends, who was not, however, someone I recognized, behaved with the vilest kind of treachery towards me and plainly believed I'd behaved in the same way towards him. Abruptly awakened by the pain this dream had caused me, unable to shake myself free of it, I tried to remember who the friend was that I'd seen in my sleep, someone with a Spanish name that I could no longer make out. Playing both Joseph and the Pharaoh, I set out to interpret my dream.* I knew that in many dreams one shouldn't assign too much importance to the appearance of people, who may be disguised and may have exchanged faces with each other, like those mutilated saints in cathedrals which ignorant archaeologists have restored by placing the head of one on the body of another and mixing up their attributes and names. The appearances people assume in dreams can mislead us. The person we love should be recognized solely by the intensity of the pain we feel. From my own suffering I learned that, having turned into a young man while I slept, the person whose recent treachery was still causing me pain was Gilberte. I then remembered that the last time I saw her, on the day her mother had forbidden her to go to a dancing lesson, Gilberte had laughed in an odd way and had, either sincerely or deceitfully, refused to believe that my feelings for her were entirely proper. By association, this memory led to another. Long before that, it was Swann who had doubted my sincerity and my suitability as a friend for Gilberte. I'd written to him in vain; Gilberte had brought my letter back and returned it to me with the same incomprehensible laugh. She hadn't given it to me right away; I remembered the whole scene behind the laurel bushes. Unhappiness sharpens one's sense of morality. Gilberte's present aversion to me seemed like a punishment inflicted by life because of my behaviour that day. Since we think we can avoid danger by paying attention while crossing the street, we think we can evade punishment. But punishments can come from within. The accident comes from the place you never suspected, from inside, from your heart. Gilberte's words: 'if you like, we could wrestle a bit more', now filled me with horror. I pictured her behaving like that, at home perhaps, in the linen room upstairs, with the young man I'd seen with her on the Champs-Élysées. And so, just as I'd been mad to believe, some time ago, that I'd reached a state of tranquil happiness, I was equally foolish, now that I'd given up happiness, to take it for granted that I had at least become, and could remain, calm. For so long as our heart constantly enshrines the image of another person, it's not just our happiness that can be destroyed at any moment; when this happiness has vanished, when we've suffered and then managed to allay this suffering, the thing that's just as deceptive and fragile as happiness itself had been is our state of tranquillity. My own state of tranquillity did eventually come back, for whatever enters our minds under cover of a dream, changing our inclinations and desires, also gradually fades away, since nothing can be permanent or everlasting, not even suffering. Besides, those who suffer from love are, as they say of certain invalids, their own physicians. Since consolation can come to them only from the person causing their pain, and since this pain originates from that person, it's in the pain itself that they finally find a remedy. At a certain point the pain reveals the remedy, for as they turn it over in their minds, this pain keeps showing them another aspect of the person they long for: sometimes she's so hateful that they lose all desire to see her again, since they'd have to make her suffer before they could enjoy being with her; sometimes so sweet that the gentleness they attribute to her becomes an intrinsic virtue, which gives them new reason to hope. But even though the suffering that had sprung up in me again did eventually subside, I no longer wanted to visit Madame Swann, except on rare occasions. In the first place because, for those who love and have been abandoned, the state of expectation in which they live—even if it is secret—is transformed into another seemingly identical but exactly opposite state. The first was the consequence, the reflection of the painful incidents that had upset us. Expectation of what might happen is mingled with fear, especially since at that moment, if we hear nothing new from the one we love, we want to take action, and we're not really sure if we'll meet with success after taking a step which might preclude any others. But soon, without our realizing it, our ongoing expectation is determined, as we've seen, not by our memory of the past we've just been through, but by the hope we place in an imaginary future. From then on, it is almost pleasant. And since the first state lasted for some time, it has accustomed us to living in expectation. The suffering we felt during our last meetings is still there, but is already becoming dormant. We're not in too much of a hurry to rouse it, especially since we're not quite sure what we want now. To possess a little more of the woman we love would only increase our need for the part we don't possess, which, since our needs are born out of our satisfactions, would remain irreducible.

In addition to this, one final reason arose later on to make me cease my visits to Madame Swann altogether. This belated reason was not that I'd already forgotten Gilberte, but that I must try to forget her more quickly. It's true that after the worst of my suffering was over, my visits to Madame Swann had again become, for what was left of my sadness, the balm and distraction that had been so precious to me at the beginning. But the reason for the efficacy of the balm was also the reason why the distraction was a drawback: my memory of Gilberte was inextricably bound up with these visits. The diversion would only have been useful to me if it had set thoughts, interests, and passions in which Gilberte played no part against a feeling no longer nourished by Gilberte's presence. These states of consciousness from which the person we love remains absent then occupy a place that, though it might be small at first, leaves less room in the heart for the love that had once occupied it entirely. We must try to nourish these thoughts and make them grow while the feeling that's now nothing but a memory diminishes, so that the new elements introduced into the heart combat that feeling, wrest from it an ever-increasing portion, and finally steal it away completely. I realized that was the only way to kill a feeling of love, and I was still young and brave enough to undertake the task, to take on that most cruel grief born out of the certainty that, however long it may take, we will succeed. The reason I now gave in my letters to Gilberte for my refusal to see her was an allusion to some mysterious misunderstanding between us both, one which I'd completely made up, about which I'd initially hoped that Gilberte would demand an explanation. But in fact never, even in our most insignificant relationships, is clarification sought by a correspondent who knows very well that an obscure, deceptive, or incriminating sentence has been purposely inserted so that he will protest; from this, he's only too happy to deduce that he's the one who has—and will continue to have—control of the situation, the one who retains the initiative. This is all the truer for more affectionate relationships, in which love is so eloquent and indifference so incurious. Since Gilberte neither disputed nor sought to learn the nature of this misunderstanding, it became real for me, and I alluded to it in every letter. There is in these exercises in misapprehension, in this pretence of coldness, a spell that makes us persevere in them. By writing again and again: 'Now that we've broken up' so that Gilberte would reply: 'That's not true at all! We have to talk', I ended up convincing myself of our permanent separation. By constantly repeating: 'Life may have changed for us, but it will never erase the feelings we had for each other', out of a wish to hear her say: 'But nothing has changed, our feelings are stronger than ever!', I was living with the idea that life had indeed changed, and that we'd preserve the memory of the emotion that had vanished, just as certain neurotics, having feigned an illness, end up becoming chronic invalids. Now, whenever I had to write to Gilberte, I'd refer to this imagined change, which, having been tacitly acknowledged by Gilberte's silence on the subject in her replies, would continue between us. But then Gilberte stopped ignoring my statements and adopted my point of view herself; and, as in official toasts when the visiting head of state adopts virtually the same expressions just used by his host, whenever I wrote to Gilberte: 'Life may have parted us, but the memory of the days we spent together will endure', she'd invariably reply: 'Life may have parted us, but it will never make us forget the precious hours that will be forever dear to us' (though it would have been difficult for us to pinpoint why exactly 'life' had parted us, or what change had occurred). By now my suffering had abated. One day, though, when I was telling her in a letter that I'd learned of the death of our old barley-sugar woman from the Champs-Élysées, as I wrote these words: 'I thought this must have made you sad; for me it stirred up so many memories', I couldn't help but burst into tears when I realized I was speaking about our love in the past tense, as if it were a dead friend who was already almost forgotten, although despite myself I had never stopped thinking about it as something alive, or at least capable of reviving. There could be nothing more tender than this correspondence between friends who no longer wished to see each other. Gilberte's letters were as tactful as those I used to write to people who didn't matter to me, and evinced the same apparent marks of affection, which seemed so sweet coming from her.

Little by little, the more I refused to see her, the less pain I felt. And since she was becoming less dear to me, my painful, incessantly recurring memories were no longer strong enough to destroy the budding pleasure I felt when I thought about Florence or Venice. At such times, I was sorry I'd rejected a career as a diplomat and had confined myself to a sedentary existence so that I could remain close to a girl I'd never see again and had already almost forgotten. We construct our lives for one person, and when we can finally welcome her into it, she doesn't come; eventually she is dead to us, and we go on living as prisoners in what had been intended only for her. Though my parents thought Venice too far away and too hot for me, it was at least easy and not too fatiguing to go to Balbec for a while. But that would have entailed leaving Paris and giving up those visits, infrequent as they were, to Madame Swann's, where I could hear her talk to me about her daughter. I was even beginning to find other pleasures in them, which had nothing to do with Gilberte.

As spring arrived, and as the Ice Saints* and the hailstorms of Holy Week brought back the cold, since Madame Swann thought her house was freezing, I'd often see her wrapped in furs while she entertained her guests, her shivering hands and shoulders disappearing beneath the dazzling white expanse of an immense flat muff and cape, both of ermine, which she hadn't removed when she came home, and which looked like the last remaining patches of winter snow that neither the heat from the fireplace nor the advancing season had managed to melt. And the whole truth of those freezing but already blossoming weeks was suggested to me in this drawing room I would soon no longer visit, by other more intoxicating gleams of white, such as the 'snowballs' of the guelder roses gathering, at the top of their tall stems, like the upright trees of the Pre-Raphaelites,* their separate but unified globes, white as the herald angels and enveloped in the scent of lemon. For Odette, the châtelaine of Tansonville,* knew that even the frostiest April is not without its flowers, and that winter, spring, and summer are not as hermetically sealed off from one another as might be supposed by the city dweller who, until the first warm weather arrives, imagines that the world contains nothing but bare houses in the rain. That Madame Swann was content with the deliveries sent by her gardener in Combray, and that she did not have her 'regular' florist fill the gaps in an inadequate evocation of springtime with the help of imported flora from the precocious Mediterranean, far be it from me to say, nor was it any of my concern. To fill me with yearning for the countryside, it was enough that next to the white swathe of Madame Swann's muff, the snowballs of the guelder roses (which, in the mind of my hostess, may have had no other purpose than to play in concert with her furniture and her outfit to make the 'Symphony in White Major'* that Bergotte spoke of) should remind me that the Good Friday Spell in *Parsifal** symbolizes a natural miracle that we could witness every year if we were wiser, and, with the help of the sharp, heady scent of other varieties of flowers unfamiliar to me which had made me pause so many times during my walks in Combray, should make Madame Swann's drawing room seem as virginal, as naturally in blossom without any verdure, as overladen with genuine scents, as the steep little lane that led up to Tansonville.

But it was still too hard for me to be reminded of this little lane. There was a danger that this memory might keep alive the little that remained of my love for Gilberte. And so, even though I no longer suffered at all during these visits to Madame Swann, I spaced them out more and tried to see her as little as possible. At most, since I continued to remain in Paris, I allowed myself to walk with her once in a while. The bright, warm days had finally returned. Since I knew that Madame Swann went out before lunch for an hour's stroll in the Avenue du Bois de Boulogne, near the Étoile and the spot they used to call, because of the people who would come to gawk at the rich people they knew only by name, the 'Down-and-Out Club', I obtained permission from my parents that on Sundays (since I was busy at that hour on weekdays) I could take my lunch long after they did, at a quarter past one, so that I could go for a walk beforehand. I never missed a Sunday during that entire month of May, since Gilberte had gone to visit some friends in the countryside. I would arrive at the Arc de Triomphe around noon. I kept watch at the entrance to the avenue, making sure not to lose sight of the corner of the little street by which Madame Swann, who had just a few metres to walk, would come from her house. Since by this time many of the people who had been strolling there were going home to lunch, those who remained were few in number and, for the most part, fashionable. All of a sudden, on the finely gravelled path, slow, unhurried, and luxuriant as the most beautiful flower that blossomed only at noon, Madame Swann would appear, blooming in a raiment that was never the same but that I recall as being usually mauve; then she would raise and unfurl on its long stalk, at the moment when her radiance was at its zenith, the silken flag of a large parasol of the same shade as the cascading petals of her dress. A whole entourage would surround her: Swann, along with four or five clubmen who had come to call on her that morning or whom she had just come upon; and their obedient black or grey assemblage, moving almost like mechanical figurines in an inanimate frame around Odette, made this woman, the only one whose eyes showed any intensity, appear to be looking straight ahead, past all these men, as from a window at which she had stationed herself, and made her stand out, frail, fearless, in the nudity of her soft colours, like the apparition of a being from a different species, an unknown race with an almost warlike power, which made her seem by herself alone a match for her numerous escort. Smiling, happy with the fine weather and the sunlight that wasn't yet bothersome, having the air of confidence and tranquillity of the creator who has completed his work of art and doesn't care about anything else, certain that her outfit— though vulgar passers-by might not appreciate it—was the most elegant of all, she wore it for herself but also for her friends, naturally, without excessive self-consciousness, but also without complete indifference, permitting the little bows on her bodice and skirt to flutter lightly in front of her like pets whose presence she was not unaware of but whose capricious gambolling she indulgently permitted, giving them free rein, so long as they matched her pace; and even on her mauve parasol, which she often kept furled when she arrived, she'd rest her gaze now and then as though on a spray of Parma violets, a glance so happy and gentle that when it lingered not on her friends but on an inanimate object, it seemed to be still smiling. She thus reserved this interlude of elegance, keeping it open for her outfits, and the men with whom Madame Swann spoke so familiarly respected its space and necessity, not without the sort of deference shown by the uninitiated, an admission of their own ignorance; and in this they deferred to her competence and jurisdiction, in the same way that we defer to an invalid about the special precautions he must take, or to a mother about the education of her children. Both by the retinue surrounding her, which didn't seem to notice the passers-by, and by the lateness of her appearance in the avenue, Madame Swann evoked the apartment in which she'd just spent such a leisurely morning and to which she'd soon have to return for luncheon; she seemed to convey its proximity by the calmness and leisureliness of her stroll, like the saunter one takes in one's garden; it was as if she still carried around her the cool, indoor shade of her salon. But this vision of her only made me feel more intensely the warmth and fresh air. All the more so since (already convinced as I was that, by virtue of the liturgy and rites in which Madame Swann was profoundly versed, her clothing was joined to the season and hour by a necessary, unique link) the flowers on her inflexible straw hat, the little ribbons on her dress, seemed to me to spring from the month of May even more naturally than the flowers in gardens and forests; and to experience the stirring newness of the season, I had to raise my eyes no higher than her parasol, open and outstretched like another, nearer sky, round, clement, mobile, and blue. These rites, sovereign though they were, made their— and consequently Madame Swann's—glory yield condescendingly to the morning, the spring, the sun, which to me didn't seem sufficiently flattered that such an elegant woman should deign to pay them heed, and because of them had chosen a dress in a brighter, lighter fabric, bringing to mind, with its flared collar and sleeves, the moist warmth of her neck and wrists; she had, finally, taken all the pains of a great lady who, having cheerfully stooped to visiting common folk in the countryside, and who is known to everyone, even the lowliest, still insists on wearing country clothes to match the occasion. As soon as she appeared, I would greet Madame Swann, and she would stop me and say '*Good morning*',* with a smile. We would walk a little way together. And I understood that it was for herself alone that she obeyed these rituals that governed the way she dressed, as if she were yielding to a superior wisdom of which she was the high priestess: for if by chance, feeling too warm, she opened, or even removed completely and handed to me to carry, her jacket which she'd planned to keep closed, I'd discover in her blouse a thousand details of handiwork which would most likely have gone unnoticed, like those orchestral passages on which the composer has lavished great care even though they might never reach the audience's ears; or, in the sleeves of the jacket folded over my arm, I would see, and gaze at length upon out of pleasure or fondness, some exquisite detail, a delightfully coloured band, a mauve sateen usually hidden from the eyes of everyone, but just as delicately executed as the outer parts, like those Gothic sculptures in a cathedral hidden on the inner face of a balustrade eighty feet high, as perfect as the bas-reliefs over the main portal, but which no one had ever seen before until, chancing upon it during his travels, an artist obtains leave to climb up there and stroll about in the open air, so that he could survey the whole town, between the two steeples.

What enhanced this impression that Madame Swann strolled along the Avenue du Bois as if along a path in her own garden, was—for those who knew nothing of her 'constitutionals'—that she had come on foot, without a carriage following her, even though as soon as May arrived, she could usually be seen sitting, languid and majestic as a goddess, behind the smartest pair of horses and the best-dressed coachman in Paris, enjoying the warm air in an immense eight-spring victoria.* On foot, especially when her pace was slowed by the heat, Madame Swann looked as if she were yielding to a whim of curiosity, committing an elegant breach of protocol, like those monarchs who, without consulting anyone, leave their royal box during a gala performance while their admiring but slightly scandalized entourage follows them, not daring to object, to visit the lobby of the theatre and mingle with other members of the audience for a little while. The crowd felt the barriers of a certain sort of wealth between them and Madame Swann, and these barriers struck them as the most impassable of all. The Faubourg Saint-Germain has its own barriers as well, though less obvious to the eyes and imaginations of the 'down-and-out'. When these people see a society lady who is quite unaffected, easier to confuse with an ordinary middle-class woman, and less remote from the people, they won't feel the same sense of inequality, almost of unworthiness, as they do when faced with someone like Madame Swann. Ladies of Madame Swann's sort are doubtless not as impressed by the dazzling opulence in which they move; they've stopped paying attention to it, but only because they've grown used to it—that is, they've come to see it as all the more natural and necessary by judging others according to how familiar they are with these luxurious customs: so that (since the superiority they themselves evince and recognize in others is entirely material, easy to verify, slow to acquire, and difficult to correct), if a woman like this ranks a passer-by as of the lowest sort, she does so in the same way that he has ranked her among the highest, that is to say immediately, at first sight, irrevocably. Perhaps that particular social class, which included in those days women like Lady Israels, who mingled with women of the aristocracy, and Madame Swann, who would one day be on familiar terms with them, that intermediate class, inferior to the Faubourg Saint-Germain which it courted, but superior to whatever was not of the Faubourg Saint-Germain, having the peculiarity that, though it existed apart from the world of the rich, it was still wealthy, but with a wealth that had become flexible, obedient to artistic ideas and goals— its money was malleable, poetically crafted, able to smile—perhaps that class no longer exists, at least not with the same character and charm. In any case, the women who belonged to it then would now no longer have the chief necessity of their reign, since with age they've almost all lost their beauty. Whereas it was both from the acme of her aristocratic wealth and from the glorious height of her ripe and still-ambrosial summer that Madame Swann, majestic, smiling, and kind, strolling along the Avenue du Bois, watched, like Hypatia,* worlds revolving beneath the slow tread of her feet. Young men passing by would look at her anxiously, unsure if their vague acquaintance with her (especially since, having been introduced to Swann only once, if that, they were afraid he wouldn't recognize them) was enough to allow them to greet her. They trembled at the thought of the consequences when they finally made up their minds to do so, wondering if their audaciously provocative and sacrilegious gesture, encroaching on the inviolable supremacy of caste, might unleash catastrophic events or call down upon them the chastisement of some unknown god. But all it did was set off, like clockwork, the gesticulations of little bowing figures who were none other than Odette's retinue, beginning with Swann himself, who raised his top hat lined with green leather with a gracious smile which he'd learned in the Faubourg Saint-Germain, but which no longer had the indifference that would have accompanied it then. This indifference was now replaced (since to a certain extent he'd been imbued with Odette's prejudices) both by annoyance at having to acknowledge someone so poorly dressed, and by satisfaction that his wife knew so many people, a mixed emotion he conveyed by saying to the elegant young men accompanying him: 'Another one! I must say, I'd like to know where Odette digs them all up!' Meanwhile, having nodded to the alarmed young man who was already out of sight but whose heart was still pounding, Madame Swann turned to me to ask: 'Is it all over, then? You won't come and see Gilberte anymore? I'm glad you've made an exception for me and that you won't *drop** me completely. I like seeing you, but I also like the influence you have on my daughter. I'm sure she's sorry about it all too. But I mustn't bully you, or you'll decide to stop seeing me as well!' 'Look, Odette, there's Sagan* bidding you good morning,' Swann remarked to his wife. And there indeed was the prince, as in some grand finale at the theatre or the circus or in an old painting, wheeling his horse round and bowing to Odette with a dramatic, almost allegorical flourish which conveyed all the chivalrous courtesy of the nobleman paying homage to Woman, even though she was embodied in a woman with whom his mother or sister would never associate. And in fact, recognized amidst the fluid transparency and luminous sheen in which the shade from her parasol enveloped her, Madame Swann was receiving a constant stream of greetings from the last belated riders, who looked as though they were galloping figures in a motion picture with the sunny, white backdrop of the avenue, fashionable clubmen whose names—Antoine de Castellane, Adalbert de Montmorency,* and many more—were celebrities to the public, but were the familiar names of friends to Madame Swann. And, since the average lifespan, the relative longevity, of our memories of poetic sensations is much greater than that of our memories of the heart's sufferings, long after the sorrows I once suffered because of Gilberte have faded, what now survives is the pleasure I feel whenever I want to read, in a kind of sundial, the minutes between a quarter past noon and one o'clock, in the month of May, when I picture myself talking like this with Madame Swann, beneath her parasol, as though in the dappled light of an arbour of wisteria.

PART TWO
PLACE NAMES: THE PLACE

I HAD reached a state of almost complete indifference towards Gilberte when, two years later, I left for Balbec with my grandmother. When I yielded to the charm of a new face, or when I imagined experiencing the Gothic cathedrals, palaces, and gardens of Italy with some other girl, I'd say to myself sadly that our love, insofar as it is a love for one particular being, might not be a very real thing, since, although the association of pleasant or painful musings can attach it for a while to a woman until we come to believe that it could be inspired by her alone, if we detach ourselves, consciously or unconsciously, from these associations, this love, as though it was spontaneous and sprang from ourselves alone, can revive and give itself to another woman. At the time of my departure for Balbec,* however, and during the first part of my stay there, my indifference was still only intermittent. Often (our life being so oblivious to chronology, injecting so many anachronisms into the sequence of our days), I'd find myself living in a time—much earlier than a day or two before—when I loved Gilberte. Then not seeing her would suddenly become painful, as painful as it would have been back then. The self who had loved her, which was now almost completely replaced by another, would reappear, and this was triggered far more often by a trivial than by an important event. For instance (if I may look ahead for a moment to when I'd already arrived in Normandy), in Balbec I overheard a stranger walking by on the esplanade say: 'The family of the Postmaster General's chief under-secretary'. Now, since I wasn't yet aware of the influence this family would have on my life, this phrase should have struck me as irrelevant; but it cut me to the quick with the same feeling of suffering that my old self, which had mostly long since disappeared, had experienced at being separated from Gilberte. For I'd never given a second thought to a conversation Gilberte and her father had once had in my presence about the family of 'the Postmaster General's chief under-secretary'. Now the memories of love are no exception to the general laws of memory, which themselves are ruled by the still more general laws of habit. Since habit weakens all things, what most calls someone to our mind is precisely what we have forgotten (because it was insignificant, and so we've allowed it to keep all its power). This is why the better part of our memory lies outside us, in a damp gust of air, in the musty smell of a room, or in the fragrance of that first woodfire—wherever we happen upon what our reasoning mind, having no use for it, had overlooked: the last remnant of the past, the best, the one that, when all our tears seem to have run dry, can make us weep again. Outside us? Inside us rather, but concealed from our own gaze, in a forgetting that can continue for a long or a short period of time. It's solely thanks to this ability to forget that we can recover now and then the person we were, see things as that person did, suffer again, because we are no longer ourselves, but that person, and because that person loved what we now no longer care about. In the broad daylight of habitual memory, the images of the past gradually fade and vanish; nothing more is left of them, we can't find that time again. Or rather we wouldn't find it, if a few words (like 'the Postmaster General's chief under-secretary') hadn't been carefully locked away and forgotten, just as a copy of a book is deposited in the Bibliothèque nationale to preserve it from oblivion.

But this suffering, and also this revival of love for Gilberte, lasted no longer than they would in a dream, because in Balbec, old Habit was no longer there to make them last. If these effects of Habit seem contradictory, it's because it obeys multiple laws. In Paris I'd become increasingly indifferent to Gilberte, thanks to Habit. The change of habit—that is, the temporary cessation of Habit—put its finishing touches to Habit's work when I left for Balbec. Habit weakens but stabilizes, leads to disintegration but causes disintegration to last indefinitely. Every day for years, I'd based my state of mind on that of the day before. In Balbec, however, a new bed, with, next to it, a different breakfast from the one brought to me in Paris, would no longer be able to nourish the thoughts on which my love for Gilberte had fed: there are cases (though admittedly quite rare) in which, the days having been brought to a halt by a sedentary lifestyle, the best way to gain time is to change locations. My journey to Balbec was like the first outing of a convalescent who needed nothing more than that to realize he's cured.

No doubt people would make this journey in a motor car today, thinking it would be more pleasant. We shall see that when it's done in this way, it might even in a sense be more faithful to reality, since you'd be following more closely, more intimately, the various gradations changing the earth's surface. But when it comes down to it, the specific pleasure we derive from travelling is not the ability to stay somewhere along the way, or to stop when we're tired, but in the way it makes the difference between departure and arrival not as imperceptible but as profound as possible, so that we can experience this difference in its totality, as intact as it was in our mind when our imagination carried us from the place in which we were living to where we longed to be, in a leap that seemed miraculous less because it covered such a distance than because it linked together two distinct individualities of the land, taking us from one name to another; this leap is epitomized (more so than a ride in a motor car, which, since you can get out wherever you like, does away with any sense of arrival) by the mysterious process that used to be enacted in those special places, railway stations, which are just barely part of a city but contain the essence of its personality, just as they bear its name on a signboard.

But in all sorts of ways, our age is obsessed with showing things only in the context of what surrounds them in reality, thereby suppressing the essential thing: the act of mind that isolated them from that reality. A painting is 'shown' in the midst of furniture, curios, or wall-hangings from the same period, the insipid interior decoration which the hostess, who had been so ignorant before but who now spends her time in archives and libraries, excels at composing, and in the midst of which the masterpiece we gaze upon during dinner doesn't give us the same intoxicating joy we can only expect from it in an art gallery, which, by its bareness and lack of any personality of its own, symbolizes much more aptly the inner spaces into which the artist withdrew to create it.

Unfortunately, these wonderful places, railway stations, from which we set out for a remote destination, are also tragic places, for in order for the miracle to be accomplished that allows places that existed only in our thoughts to become places where we will live, we must, as we leave the waiting room, give up all thought of presently returning to the familiar bedroom we left just a moment ago. We must abandon all hope of going home to sleep in our own bed, once we've made up our mind to enter the reeking cavern that serves as gateway to the mystery, one of those vast, glass-roofed garages, like that of Saint-Lazare where I went to find the train to Balbec, a station which spread out above the city it rent asunder one of those vast, bleak skies, pregnant with accumulated tragic menace, like those skies painted with an almost Parisian modernity by Mantegna or Veronese, beneath which only some terrible, solemn act could be carried out, such as a departure by train or the Elevation of the Cross.*

As long as I'd been content to see that storm-buffeted Persian church of Balbec from the comfort of my own bed in Paris, my body had made no objection to this journey. The objections began only when it realized it was going to be included among those making the journey, and that on the evening of my arrival I'd be taken to 'my' bedroom, which would be entirely unknown to it. Its rebellion became even more vehement on the very eve of my departure, when I learned that my mother would not be accompanying us, since my father, who was held up at the ministry until the time came for him to set off for Spain with Monsieur de Norpois, had preferred to rent a house on the outskirts of Paris. Still, being able to see Balbec seemed no less desirable because it had to be bought at the cost of an illness which seemed to symbolize and guarantee the reality of the impression I was going there to seek, an impression that couldn't be replaced by any sort of allegedly equivalent sight, any 'panorama'* that I could go and see without being prevented from returning home to sleep in my own bed. This wasn't the first time I felt that those who act out of love and those who act for pleasure are not the same. I thought I longed for Balbec as deeply as the doctor treating me who, surprised by my unhappy expression on the morning of my departure, said: 'Believe me, if I could get even a week off to go down to the seaside and breathe the fresh air, I'd be there at the drop of a hat. Just think of all the wonderful races and regattas you'll be seeing!' Long before I'd gone to see La Berma, I'd already learned that no matter what I loved, it could only be attained after a long and painful pursuit; and this supreme goal could be achieved only on condition that I sacrifice to it the pleasure I'd hoped to find in it.

My grandmother, naturally, viewed our departure from a slightly different angle; and, since she was as eager as ever to endow the presents I was given with an artistic quality, in order to offer me this journey as a kind of old 'print', she'd wanted us to follow, partly by train and partly by carriage, the route taken by Madame de Sévigné when she'd gone from Paris to 'L'Orient'* via Chaulnes and 'the Pont-Audemer'. But my grandmother had been forced to abandon this project because of the objections of my father, who knew, whenever she organized any expedition with a view to gleaning from it all the intellectual benefit it could yield, how many missed trains, lost luggage, sore throats, and contraventions of doctor's orders it would entail. She at least took comfort from the thought that, when the time came for us to go down to the beach, we'd never run the risk of being kept from doing so by the arrival of what her beloved Sévigné calls 'a beastly coach-load of visitors', since we wouldn't know a soul in Balbec, Legrandin having offered us no letter of introduction to his sister. (His failure to do so was not so well received by my aunts Céline and Victoire,* who, since they'd known this sister as a girl and had always referred to her, to emphasize their previous intimacy, as 'Renée de Cambremer' (who had given them the sorts of gifts that ornament a room or a conversation but which have nothing to do with everyday reality), thought to avenge the insult, when they visited Madame Legrandin, by never uttering her daughter's name, and even to congratulate each other as they left with phrases like 'I made no reference to you-know-who' and 'I think the point was taken'.

So we were simply to leave Paris by that one-twenty-two train which had delighted me so often when I looked it up in the railway timetable—where every time it gave me the thrill, almost the blissful illusion, of departure—that it was difficult for me to believe I hadn't already taken it. As the features of any future happiness are determined in our imagination more by the nature of the desires it awakens in us than by the exactitude of the information we have about it, I was certain I knew this happiness in all its detail, and had no doubt that I'd feel a special delight in my compartment when the day began to grow cool, or when some interesting detail struck me as we drew into a station; so that this train, which always awakened in me the images of the same towns that I pictured bathed in the light of those afternoon hours through which it travelled, seemed different from all other trains; and, as we often do with a person we've never met but whose friendship we like to believe we've won, I'd come to endow it with the distinctive, unchanging appearance of a handsome, artistic traveller who took me with him on his journey, and to whom I'd bid farewell beneath the Cathedral of Saint-Lô,* before he moved off into the setting sun.

Since my grandmother couldn't resign herself to 'just' going to Balbec, she'd decided to stop along the way and spend the night at a friend's house; I was to continue on alone that same evening so as not to be in the way, and also so that I'd arrive in the daytime to see the Balbec church, which, we'd learned, was quite far from the beach, and which I might not be able to visit later on after I started my bathing cure. And perhaps it was less painful for me to know that the admirable goal of my journey would come before that cruel first night when I'd enter a new dwelling place and resign myself to living there.

But first I had to leave the old one; my mother had arranged to move that very day into the rented house in Saint-Cloud,* and she had made—or had pretended to make—all the necessary arrangements to go there directly after seeing us off at the station so that she wouldn't have to go back to our own house, in case I should decide to return home with her instead of going to Balbec. She'd even decided, on the pretext that she had too much to do in the house she'd just rented and was pressed for time, but actually to spare me from the cruelty of these kinds of farewells, not to stay with us until the train's departure—that moment when the looming separation, which had been lurking in the seemingly endless comings and goings and preparations, suddenly appears, impossible to endure when it can no longer be avoided, wholly concentrated into one vast instant of powerless, utter awareness.

For the first time I sensed it was possible for my mother to live a life without me, unrelated to me, completely different from my own. She was going to live on her own with my father, whose existence she may have thought was made somewhat complicated and sorrowful by my poor health and nervous excitability. This separation made me all the more disconsolate because I told myself that she probably viewed it as a welcome respite from the series of disappointments I'd caused her, which she never mentioned, but which had made her realize the difficulty of spending our holidays together; and perhaps this was also a preliminary attempt at a kind of life to which she was beginning to resign herself for the future, as the years advanced for my father and her, a life when I'd see less of her, in which (and this had never appeared to me even in my worst nightmares) she'd already have become something of a stranger to me, a lady who might be seen returning home alone to a house where I didn't live, asking the concierge if there were any letters from me.

I could barely muster a word in response to the porter who offered to take my suitcase. My mother was trying to comfort me as best she could. Since she thought it futile to pretend not to notice my despair, she gently teased me about it: 'Come now,' she said, 'what would the Balbec church say if it only knew how unhappy you looked just as you're getting ready to see it? Is this the joyful traveller Ruskin writes about?* Whatever happens, I'll know if you've been brave—even when we're miles away I'll still be with my little darling. Tomorrow you'll have a letter from your Maman.'

'My dear,' said my grandmother, 'I can see you'll be just like Madame de Sévigné, following our every move with your eyes glued to a map!'*

Then Maman tried to distract me by asking what I'd order for dinner; she admired Françoise and complimented her on a hat and coat she didn't recognize, despite the fact that she'd been repelled by them before when she first saw them, brand-new and worn by my great-aunt, the hat because it had an immense bird perched on it, the coat because it was covered in jet and hideous designs. But since the coat had been cast off, Françoise had turned it inside-out so that it revealed a solid-coloured lining in a lovely hue. As for the bird, it had long since met its maker and been thrown out. And, just as it's sometimes strange to come upon refinements which the most deliberate artists have to strive for, in a popular song or on a farmer's cottage where a white or yellow rose is blooming at just the right spot over the door, so did the velvet bow, the loop of ribbon (which would have looked delightful in a portrait by Chardin or Whistler*), placed on the hat by Françoise with her infallible but simple taste, turn it into a charming thing.

Or, thinking back to an earlier era, the modesty and honesty that often lent nobility to our old servant's face having extended also to the clothes that, as a humble but by no means servile woman who 'knows her place', she'd worn for the journey so as to be worthy of being seen with us while not appearing to be trying to attract attention, Françoise, in the faded cerise material of her coat and the smooth nap of her fur collar, called to mind one of those pictures of Anne de Bretagne painted by an old master in a book of hours,* in which everything is so perfectly in place, the sense of the whole so evenly distributed throughout its parts, that the rich, old-fashioned singularity of the costume expresses the same pious gravity as the eyes, lips, and hands.

It was difficult to speak of thought in connection with Françoise. She knew nothing, in the fullest meaning of the term, by which 'knowing nothing' means to understand nothing, save the rare truths that the heart can grasp directly. The vast world of ideas didn't exist for her. But to see the clarity of her gaze, the delicate lines of her nose and lips—all those indications lacking in so many cultivated people in whom they would have signified the supreme distinction, the noble detachment of a superior mind—was to be struck as by the kind, intelligent eyes of a dog, though we know all human conceptions are alien to it; and one might wonder whether there might be, among our humbler brethren the peasants, individuals who are as it were the elite of the simple-minded world, or rather who, condemned by an unjust fate to live among the unlettered, deprived of light, but more naturally and essentially akin to higher natures than most educated people, resemble the dispersed, wandering, reason-deprived members of the holy family, the still-childlike kinfolk of the loftiest intellects, lacking— as can be seen in the unmistakable gleam in their eyes, though focused on nothing—only one thing needed to have skill: knowledge.

Seeing that I could barely hold back my tears, my mother said: ' "Regulus was accustomed, upon momentous occasions . . ."* And it's not very nice for your Maman either! As your grandmother would say, quoting Madame de Sévigné: "I'll have to draw on all the courage you lack." '* And, remembering that feeling affection for others distracts us from grief for ourselves, she tried to cheer me up by saying she thought her trip to Saint-Cloud would go well, that she was happy with the hansom cab she'd rented, that the coachman was polite and the seats comfortable. I tried to smile at these details, and nodded with an air of agreement and satisfaction. But they only made me imagine Maman's departure more vividly, and it was with a heavy heart that I looked at her as if she were already apart from me, in the round straw hat she'd bought for the countryside and the light summer dress she'd put on in view of the long, hot drive, and this costume made her someone else, someone who already belonged to the Villa Montretout,* where I would never see her.

To prevent the fits of breathlessness the journey might bring on, the doctor had advised me to drink a little too much beer or brandy just before departure so as to achieve the state of what he called 'euphoria', in which the nervous system is for a time less fragile. I was still unsure if I'd comply, but I wanted my grandmother at least to acknowledge that if I did make up my mind to do so, I'd be acting on good authority and wise advice. And so I spoke about it as if I was only unsure about where I should go for a drink, the station buffet or the dining car. But my grandmother's face looked so disapproving, and she seemed so unwilling even to consider the idea, that I suddenly resolved to have a drink, an act that had now become necessary to prove my freedom, since my mere mention of it had aroused her displeasure, and I exclaimed: 'What's this? You know how ill I am, you know what the doctor told me, but this is how you react!'

When I explained to my grandmother how unwell I felt, she looked so disconsolate, and so kind, as she replied: 'Oh dear, run quickly and find some beer or a liqueur, if that will do you good!', that I flung myself on her and kissed her over and over. After that, the only reason I drank too much in the bar on the train was because I felt I'd have a severe attack if I didn't, and that would distress her even more. When I returned to our compartment at the first stop, I told my grandmother how happy I was to be going to Balbec, how I felt everything would turn out for the best, that after all I'd soon grow used to being away from Maman, that the train was comfortable, the bartender and other attendants so pleasant that I'd like to make the journey often so I could see them again. My grandmother, however, did not seem to feel quite as overjoyed as I was at all this good news. Avoiding my eyes, she replied: 'Perhaps you should take a little nap', and turned towards the window; the shade, though we'd lowered it, didn't cover it entirely, so that the sun was able to shed on the waxed oak of the door and the cloth of the banquette (like a far more persuasive advertisement for a life in nature than the ones posted by the railway company, too high up in the compartment for me to read the names of the landscapes they depicted) the same warm, languorous light that drowsed in the forest glades outside.

But when my grandmother thought my eyes were closed, I could see her steal glances at me now and then from beneath her polka-dot veil, then look away and back again, like someone striving to get used to a painful exercise.

Then I'd speak to her, but she didn't seem to enjoy this. And yet to me the sound of my voice was pleasant, as were the slightest, innermost movements of my body. And so I tried to prolong them; I lingered over every word, enjoyed each glance as it rested on a spot and remained there longer than usual. 'Come now, try to sit still,' my grandmother said. 'Read something if you can't sleep.' And she handed me a volume by Madame de Sévigné which I opened, while she settled down to the *Mémoires* of Madame de Beausergent.* She never travelled without a volume of each; these were her two favourite authors. Unwilling to move my head at this moment, and experiencing great pleasure from maintaining a position once I had taken it, I sat holding the volume of Madame de Sévigné without opening it or lowering my gaze to look at it, but instead staring straight ahead at the blue window-blind. Contemplating this shade seemed a worthy thing to do, and I wouldn't have gone to the trouble of replying to anyone who tried to distract me from this contemplation. The blue colour of the blind seemed, not perhaps by its beauty but by its intense vividness, so completely to erase all the other colours that had passed before my eyes from the day I was born up to the moment my drink had begun to take effect, that compared with this blue, they were as dreary, as null, as the darkness must be retrospectively for a man born blind who can finally see colours after an operation. An old conductor came by to ask for our tickets. The silvery glints reflected off the metal buttons on his tunic fascinated me. I wanted to ask him to sit down next to us. But he continued on to the next carriage, and I thought nostalgically about the lives of railwaymen who spend all their lives on the train and so must see this old ticket-collector almost daily. The pleasure I felt in gazing at the blue blind and sensing that my mouth was half open finally began to diminish. I became more mobile; I shifted about a little; I opened the book my grandmother had given me and was able to focus my attention on pages I chose at random. As I read, I could feel my admiration for Madame de Sévigné growing.

One shouldn't be taken in by the purely formal features of Madame de Sévigné's style which stem from her era or from salon life, and which lead some people to believe they've captured the Sévigné spirit when they say things like 'Instruct me, my good lady' or 'That count struck me as being quick of wit' or 'Haymaking is the merriest thing to do'. Even Madame de Simiane imagines she takes after her grandmother when she writes: 'Monsieur de la Boulie is in excellent health, sir; he's quite ready to hear news of his death' or 'Oh, my dear Marquis, how I enjoyed your letter! I can't help but answer it', or 'It strikes me, Monsieur, that you owe me a reply, and I owe you some snuffboxes of bergamot. I'm fulfilling my part of the deal with eight of them, and more to come . . . never has the soil been so generous—it's obviously being so for your pleasure.'* She continues this style in her letters on being bled, on lemons and so on, which she believes are in the manner of Madame de Sévigné. But my grandmother, who had come to Madame de Sévigné from within, from her love for family and nature, had taught me to appreciate the true beauty of her letters, which is to be found in quite different things. This beauty would soon strike me all the more forcibly since Madame de Sévigné is a great artist of the same tribe as a painter I was about to meet in Balbec, Elstir, who was to have such a profound influence on my way of seeing things.* I realized in Balbec that she presents things to us in the same way as he does, in the order in which we perceive them, instead of starting out by explaining what brought them about. But already that afternoon in the railway carriage, as I reread the letter in which moonlight appears, where she writes: 'I couldn't resist the temptation, I put on all my bonnets and cloaks, unnecessary though they were, and walked along the mall where the air is as sweet as in my chamber; I came upon a myriad of phantasmagorical images, *monks black and white, several nuns grey and white, garments thrown every which way, shrouded men upright against trees*';* I was captivated by what I would later have called the Dostoevsky side (for doesn't she portray landscapes in the same way as he portrays characters?) of Madame de Sévigné's *Letters.**

That evening, after accompanying my grandmother to her friend's house and spending a few hours there, when I once again took the train, by myself this time, at least I wasn't distressed by the night that followed; this was because I didn't have to spend it imprisoned in a bedroom whose somnolence would have kept me awake; I was surrounded by the calming activity of all those movements of a train which kept me company, offered to chat with me if I couldn't fall asleep, lulled me with their sounds which I linked together, as I used to do with the bells in Combray, sometimes according to one rhythm, sometimes to another (hearing, depending on my whim, first four equal semiquavers, then one semiquaver hurled furiously against a crotchet); they neutralized the centrifugal force of my insomnia by exercising over it counterbalances that kept me in equilibrium, and on which my immobility and soon my sleep felt supported with the same impression of refreshment I'd have felt from sleep guarded by the powerful forces of nature and life, if I could have been transformed briefly into a fish sleeping in the sea, carried along in its slumber by currents and waves, or into a soaring eagle borne aloft by the storm.

Sunrises go with long train journeys just as hard-boiled eggs, illustrated papers, card games, and rivers with boats straining forward without seeming to make any progress do. At a certain moment, as I was sifting through the thoughts that had just been filling my mind in order to determine whether or not I'd been asleep (and as the very uncertainty that made me ask the question was giving me a reply in the affirmative), in the windowpane, above a small, dark copse, I saw some ragged clouds whose soft down was tinged with a fixed, lifeless pink, as unchanging as the pink tinting the feathers on a wing or daubed by an artist's whim on a pastel drawing. But I felt that this colour was neither immutable nor fanciful, but necessary and alive. Soon reserves of light marshalled behind it. It caught fire, and the sky took on a incarnadine hue that I strove, as I stared out the window, to see more clearly, for I felt that it was connected to the innermost life of nature, but since the tracks had changed direction, the train curved away, and the dawn scene was replaced in the window frame by the blue, moonlit rooftops of a nocturnal village, its wash-house smeared with the nacreous opalescence of night, beneath a sky still strewn with all its stars, and just as I was grieving for the loss of my band of pink sky I glimpsed it again, but red this time, in the opposite window which it then abandoned at a second curve in the line; so that I spent all my time rushing from one window to the other to reassemble, to realign the intermittent, opposing fragments of my beautiful, scarlet, ever-changing morning, so as to form a complete view, a continuous panorama of it.

The landscape became hilly and steep, and the train stopped at a little station between two mountains. At the bottom of the ravine, beside the swift-flowing river, all that could be seen was a lone guard-house lashed by the waves up to its windowsills. If a person can be the product of a place and embody its particular charm, then, even more than by the peasant girl I'd so longed to see when I wandered by myself along the Méséglise way in the woods of Roussainville, such a possibility was demonstrated by the tall girl I now saw emerge from the house, climb the path lit by the slanting rays of the rising sun, and come towards the station carrying a jug of milk. In this valley, hidden from the rest of the world by the steep mountains, she must never see anyone except travellers in these trains which stopped only briefly. She walked beside the carriages, offering coffee with milk to the few passengers who were awake. Flushed with the morning's rays, her face was rosier than the sky. Looking at her, I felt that desire to live that's rekindled in us whenever we once again become aware of beauty and happiness. We always forget that beauty and happiness are personal qualities, and, substituting for them a conventional model that we form in our minds by making a sort of average of all the different faces we've admired, all the pleasures we've known, we're left with nothing but abstract images that are lifeless and vapid because they lack precisely this quality of something new, different from what we've been familiar with, the quality that's unique to beauty and happiness. So we view life with a jaundiced eye and think we're justified in doing so, for we believed we were taking happiness and beauty into account, whereas we've actually left them out and replaced them with synthetic replicas that contain nothing of them. So it is that a well-read man immediately starts yawning with boredom when someone talks to him about the latest 'great book', because he imagines a sort of composite of all the great books he's read, while a truly great book is unique, unforeseeable, and is not made of the sum of all previous masterpieces, but of something which the most thorough assimilation of every one of them would not enable him to discover, precisely because it lies beyond that sum. But as soon as he learns of this new book, the well-read man, who had previously been so jaded, becomes interested in the reality the book portrays. In the same way, unaware of the types of beauty my mind conjured up when I was alone, the beautiful girl immediately gave me the taste for a particular happiness (the only form, always unique, in which we can have the taste of happiness), the happiness I might feel if I lived with her. But here again the temporary cessation of Habit played a large part. I was giving the dairymaid the benefit of the fact that it was my whole being, ready to taste the keenest joys, that confronted her. We usually live with our whole being reduced to a bare minimum; most of our faculties lie dormant because they rely on habit, which knows what has to be done and has no need of them. But on this morning of travel, the interruption of the routine of my existence, the change in place and time, made the presence of my faculties indispensable. My habit, which was sedentary and not matutinal, had slipped away, and all my faculties came rushing in to replace it, each more zealous than the other, rising like waves to the same unaccustomed level, from the basest to the noblest, from breath, appetite, and the circulation of blood to sensitivity and imagination. I don't know whether, by leading me to believe this girl was unlike other women, the wild charm of this region added to her beauty, but her own certainly enriched it. Life would have seemed delightful to me if only I could have spent it, hour upon hour, with her, accompanying her to the river, to the cow, to the train, being always by her side, feeling I was known by her, that I had a place in her thoughts. She would have initiated me into the charms of rural life and the early morning hours. I gestured to her to bring me some of her coffee. I needed to be noticed by her. She didn't see me, so

I called out. Above her tall body, her face looked so rosy and golden that I felt as if I were seeing her through a stained-glass window. She turned and walked back towards me; I couldn't take my eyes off her face, which grew larger and larger, like a sun you could stare at which kept coming nearer until it was right next to you, letting itself be seen from up close, dazzling you with red and gold. She fixed her piercing eyes on me, but since the conductors were closing the doors, the train started to move away; I watched her as she left the station and went back to the footpath; it was broad daylight now, and I was travelling away from the dawn. Regardless of whether my exaltation was aroused by this girl or had on the contrary caused most of the pleasure I'd felt in her presence, it was so intermingled with her that my desire to see her again was above all a mental desire not to let this state of excitement die away completely, not to be separated forever from the person who had, even unwittingly, been a part of it. It wasn't just that this state was enjoyable. It was above all that (just as increased tension on a string or the more rapid vibration of a nerve produces a different note or colour) it gave another tonality to what I saw, and introduced me as an actor into an unknown, infinitely more interesting universe; that beautiful girl whom I could still see, as the train gathered speed, was like part of a life other than the one I knew, separated from it by a thin border, a life in which the sensations aroused by objects were no longer the same; to leave that state now would have been like a kind of inner death. To have the solace of feeling I was at least linked to this new life, I'd have needed to live near enough to the station to be able to come to it every morning and ask this country girl for coffee. But, unfortunately, she would always be absent from the other life towards which I was hurtling ever more quickly, a life I could bring myself to accept only by thinking up plans that would someday enable me to take this same train again and stop at this same station, a scheme that had the added advantage of nourishing the self-motivated, active, practical, reflexive, lazy, centrifugal predisposition which is that of our mind, for it is all too ready to shy away from the effort required to analyse in a general and disinterested way any pleasant impression we've experienced. And since we also want to go on thinking about this impression, the mind prefers to imagine it in the future, cleverly arranging the circumstances that could make it recur, which teaches us nothing about its essence, but saves us the trouble of recreating it within ourselves, and allows us to hope that we might receive it again from without.

Certain names of towns—Vézelay or Chartres, Bourges or Beauvais—
are often used to stand, by abbreviation, for those towns' principal
churches.* This use of the whole to signify a part often leads us—if
we're not yet acquainted with the places—to sculpt the name as
a whole, so that henceforth, whenever we want to introduce into that
name the idea of the town (which we've never seen), it will impose on
it, as on to a mould, the same carvings, in the same style, and will turn
it into a sort of great cathedral. It was, however, in a railway station,
above a refreshment room, in white letters on a blue panel, that I read
the name, almost Persian in style, of Balbec. I strode briskly through
the station and across the boulevard leading up to it, and asked for
directions to the beach, so as to see only the church and the sea; but
no one seemed to understand what I meant. Balbec-le-Vieux, Balbec-
en-Terre, where I'd arrived, had neither beach nor harbour. True, it
was in the sea that fishermen, according to legend, had found the
miraculous Christ statue,* as depicted in a stained-glass window in
the church that was just a few metres away from me; it was indeed
from the wave-battered cliffs that stone for its nave and steeples had
been quarried. But this sea, which for those reasons I'd imagined
sending its spray right up to the window, was almost twenty-five kilometres away, at Balbec-Plage, and, next to its dome, the steeple which,
because I'd read that it was itself a rugged Norman cliff assailed by
squalls, with sea-birds wheeling around it, I'd always pictured as being
drenched at its base by the last flecks of foam of the surging waves,
stood on a square where two tramlines crossed, opposite a café that
bore, in golden letters, the word *Billiards*, against a background of
houses whose rooftops were bare of masts. And the church—catching
my attention along with the café, the passer-by I'd asked for directions, and the station to which I would soon return—merged with
everything else, seemed an accident, a product of this late afternoon,
in which the mellow, bulbous dome against the sky was like a fruit
whose rosy, golden, succulent skin was ripened by the same light that
bathed the chimneys of the houses. But when I recognized the
Apostles, copies of which I'd seen in the Trocadéro Museum,* and
which, on either side of the Virgin at the entrance to the deep recess
of the porch, were waiting for me as if to pay me their respects, all
I wanted to contemplate now was the eternal significance of the carvings. With their kindly, worn, gentle faces and their slight stoop, they
seemed to be walking towards me in welcome, singing the Hallelujah

on this beautiful day. But then I noticed that their expressions were as frozen as those of the dead, and changed only if I moved round them. I said to myself: 'Here I am, this is the church at Balbec! This square, which looks as if it's aware of its fame, is the only place in the world that possesses the Balbec church. All I've ever seen of it until now have been photographs and replicas of the famous Apostles and of the Virgin of the porch. Now it's the church itself, the statue itself, the original ones: this is so much more.'

It was also, perhaps, much less. Just as a young man on the day of an examination or a duel feels that the fact about which he has been questioned or the bullet he has just fired are quite insignificant compared with the vast reserves of knowledge and courage he would have liked to display, so my mind—which had elevated the Virgin of the porch above the reproductions I'd seen, invulnerable as she was to the vicissitudes that could threaten them, intact even if they were destroyed, ideal, endowed with a universal value—was astonished to see the statue it had sculpted countless times reduced now to nothing but its own stone appearance, occupying in relation to my arm's reach a place where it competed with an election poster and the tip of my walking stick, shackled to the square, inseparable from the end of the main street, unable to flee the gazes of people in the café or the horse-tram depot, sustaining on her face half of the setting sun's rays—and soon, in a few hours, half of a street lamp's brightness—the other half of which shone down upon the branch of a savings bank, and enveloped at the same time by the aromas emanating from the pastry-cook's kitchens, subjected to the tyranny of the Particular to such a point that, if I'd wanted to write my name on this stone, it was she, the illustrious Virgin whom until then I'd endowed with an existence of her own and an intangible beauty, the unique (which meant, alas, the only) Virgin of Balbec, who, on her body encrusted with the same soot as the neighbouring houses, unable to rid herself of it, would have displayed, to all the admirers who came to contemplate her, the marks of my piece of chalk and the letters of my name, and it was she, finally, the immortal work of art so long desired, whom I found transformed, like the church itself, into a little old woman made of stone, whose height I could measure and whose wrinkles I could count. Time was passing, and I had to return to the station where I was to await my grandmother and Françoise, so that we could travel on together to Balbec-Plage. I recalled what I'd read about Balbec, and

Swann's words: 'It's delightful, it's as beautiful as Siena.'* And blaming my disappointment solely on contingencies, my ill humour, my fatigue, my inability to know how to look at things properly, I tried to console myself with the thought that there were other towns that still remained intact for me, that presently I might be able to venture, as into a shower of pearls, into the cool pleasant babble of the rain in Quimperlé, or walk through the green and rosy glow that bathed Pont-Aven;* but as for Balbec, as soon as I'd set foot there, it had seemed as if I'd split open a name that should have been kept hermetically sealed, and into it, taking advantage of the opening I'd foolishly offered them, and expelling all the images that were living in it until then, there came a horse-tram, a café, the people passing by on the square, the savings bank, all irresistibly propelled by an external pressure and a pneumatic force, rushing into those two syllables, which had now closed over them, letting them frame the porch of the Persian church, and would contain them evermore.

I found my grandmother on the train of the little local branch line that was to take us to Balbec-Plage, but she was alone; she'd sent Françoise ahead of her so that everything could be prepared in advance, but, misdirecting her, she'd sent her off on the wrong train, and so Françoise, quite oblivious, was now rushing at full speed towards Nantes, and might not wake up until she reached Bordeaux. No sooner had I sat down in the carriage, which was filled with the fleeting light of the setting sun and the persistent heat of the afternoon (the former, alas, allowing me to see clearly on my grandmother's face how much the latter had wearied her) than she asked me: 'Well, what do you think of Balbec?' with a smile so enthusiastically lit up by her hope for the great pleasure she thought I'd experienced that I didn't dare confess my disappointment. Besides, the impression my mind had been seeking in visiting Balbec was becoming less and less important as we approached the place to which my body would have to grow accustomed. Despite being over an hour away from our journey's end, I was trying to picture the manager of the hotel in Balbec, aware of the fact that, at that moment, I did not exist for him; and I'd have liked to appear before him in more prestigious company than that of my grandmother, who would without a doubt ask him for a reduced rate. I imagined him as being somewhat haughty, but I could form only a vague picture of him as a whole.

Every few minutes the train would stop at one of the stations which came before Balbec-Plage, and their very names (Incarville,

Marcouville, Doville, Pont-à-Couleuvre, Arambouville, Saint-Mars-le-Vieux, Hermonville, Maineville*) struck me as strange, whereas, if I'd read them in a book, I would have recognized their connection to the names of actual places in the vicinity of Combray. But to a musician's ear two themes, despite having several notes in common, can seem completely dissimilar if they differ in the colour of their harmony and orchestration. In the same way, in these dreary names made of sand, empty air, and salt, from which the word *ville* flew off like the 'gull' in 'seagull', there was nothing to remind me of those other names, Roussainville or Martinville, which, because I'd so often heard them uttered by my great-aunt at the dining-room table, had acquired a certain sombre charm that might have been intermingled with the taste of jam, the aroma of the wood fire, the smell of the paper in a book by Bergotte, or the colour of sandstone on the house across the way, and which, even today, when they rise like bubbles from the depths of my memory, preserve their own specific quality through the successive layers of all the contexts they must pass through before they reach the surface.

These places, overlooking the distant sea from the tops of their dunes or already settling down for the night at the foot of some garishly green and oddly shaped hill, as misshapen as the sofa in a hotel room seen for the first time, each town comprising a few villas, a tennis court, and sometimes a casino with its flag clanking in the freshening, hollow, fretful wind, these little stations gave me my first glimpse of their inhabitants, but only from their habitual exteriors—tennis players in white caps, the stationmaster living there next to his tamarisks and roses, a lady in a straw boater who, following the everyday routine of an existence I would never know, was calling to her dawdling greyhound on her way back to her cottage where the lamp was already lit—and, with these strangely ordinary and scornfully familiar images, cruelly wounded my stranger's eyes and my homesick heart. But my sufferings were increased tenfold when we made our way into the lobby of the Grand-Hôtel at Balbec with its monumental staircase of imitation marble, and my grandmother, unconcerned with the growing hostility and disdain of the strangers among whom we were about to live, discussed 'terms' with the manager, a portly little man whose face and voice alike were full of scars (left behind by the removal of countless pimples from the former, and, in the case of the latter, made by all the various accents stemming from distant origins and

a cosmopolitan upbringing); he wore the tails of a fashionable gentleman and had a psychologist's gaze, which enabled him, whenever the
'omnibus' arrived, invariably to mistake noblemen for hagglers and
hotel thieves for noblemen. No doubt forgetting that his own monthly
salary wasn't anywhere near five hundred francs, he had profound
contempt for anyone to whom five hundred francs (or, as he put it,
'twenty-five louis') was a substantial sum, and regarded them as
belonging to a race of pariahs who did not belong at the Grand-Hôtel.
It's true that, even in this luxury hotel, there were people who didn't
pay very much yet still kept the manager's esteem, provided he was
certain they were frugal not out of poverty but out of avarice. For
miserliness can in no way affect prestige, since it's a vice, and may
consequently be found in any social class. Social position was the only
thing to which the manager paid any attention—social position, or
rather the signs that seemed to imply high rank, such as not removing
one's hat when entering the lobby, wearing plus-fours with a short-
waisted jacket, or taking a purple-and-gold-banded cigar out of
a crushed morocco case (all advantages which I, alas, lamentably
lacked). He peppered his commercial banter with choice expressions,
which he misused.

As I sat on a banquette and heard my grandmother, unperturbed
that he was listening to her while whistling to himself with his hat on,
ask him in an artificial tone of voice: 'And what are your . . . charges?—Oh!
far too high for my little budget,' I took refuge in my innermost self,
strove to soar off into eternal thoughts, to leave nothing of myself,
nothing living, on the surface of my body—desensitized like the body
of an animal that plays dead when attacked—so as not to suffer too
much in this place, to which I felt so foreign that I was even more
stung by the familiarity with it evinced at the same moment by an
elegant lady to whom the manager showed his respect by taking liber-
ties with the little dog following her about or the young dandy with
a feather in his hat who came in asking if there were 'any letters' for
him—all these people for whom climbing those imitation marble
steps meant they were going home. At the same time the glare of
Minos, Aeacus, and Rhadamanthus* (into which I plunged my bare
soul as into an unknown element where there was nothing to protect
it) was cast upon me severely by three gentlemen who, little versed as
they may have been in the art of 'reception', still bore the title 'reception clerks'; further on, behind a glass partition, some people were

sitting in a reading room to describe which I'd have had to borrow turn by turn the colours Dante uses to depict Paradise and Hell,* depending on whether I was thinking of the bliss of the chosen who had the right to sit there quietly reading, or of the terror my grand-mother would have caused me if, in her complete obliviousness to outward appearances, she'd ordered me to enter it alone.

My sense of loneliness increased even more a moment later. After I confessed to my grandmother that I wasn't feeling well, that I thought we might have to go back to Paris, she made no protest, and said merely that she was going out for a few things which would be just as useful whether we stayed or left (and which I later discovered were all for me, since some items I might have needed were still with Françoise); while I waited for her, I paced up and down the streets, so packed with people that they felt as warm as a stuffy apartment, pass-ing by a barber's shop which was still open and a tearoom where cus-tomers were eating ices opposite the statue of Duguay-Trouin.* This statue gave me about as much pleasure as a picture of it might to a patient leafing through a magazine in a surgeon's waiting room. I was amazed that there could be people so different from myself that the manager would think I'd enjoy taking this stroll through the town as an amusing diversion, and also that the torture-chamber that is a new abode could appear to some as a 'dwelling-place of delight', as it was called by the hotel brochure, which, though it might have been exaggerating, was directed at a wide clientele to whose tastes it must have appealed. To attract such a clientele to the Grand-Hôtel of Balbec, it elaborated not only on the 'exquisite cuisine' and the 'enchanting view from the Casino gardens', but also on the 'decrees of Her Majesty Queen Fashion, which must be followed to the letter if one doesn't want to be taken for a philistine, a risk no well-bred man would willingly run'.

The need I felt for my grandmother was increased by my fear that I'd disappointed her. She must be feeling discouraged that if I couldn't bear this fatigue, there was no hope that any trip could do me good. I decided to return to the hotel to wait for her; the manager himself came over and pushed a button, and a personage hitherto unknown to me, whom they called the '*lift*'* (and who, like a photo-grapher under his hood or an organist in his loft, dwelt at the topmost level of the hotel, where the lantern would be in a Norman church*) began his descent towards me with the agility of a tamed, industrious, captive squirrel. Then, gliding again on his column, he drew me up towards the dome of this commercial nave. At each floor, on either side of a narrow communicating stairway, shadowy galleries fanned out, in one of which a maid carrying a bolster passed by. Over her face, blurred by the twilight, I applied the mask of my most passionate dreams, but what I read in her eyes as they turned towards me filled me with the horror of my own nonentity. Meanwhile, throughout the interminable ascension, to dissipate the mortal anguish I felt in silently crossing the mystery of this tedious chiaroscuro, lit by a single vertical row of windowpanes from the sole water-closet on each floor, I spoke to the young organist, the artisan of my journey and my companion in captivity, who kept pulling the stops and pushing the knobs of his instrument. I apologized for taking up so much space, for putting him to such trouble, and asked if I was getting in the way of the exercise of his art, for which, to flatter the virtuoso, instead of merely seeming curious about it, I confessed my extreme admiration. But he said nothing, either out of surprise at my words, preoccupation with his work, concern for etiquette, hardness of hearing, respect for place, fear of danger, slowness of mind, or his manager's orders.

There is perhaps nothing that makes us see the reality of the external world more clearly than a change of location, relative to ourselves, of a person, however insignificant, before we knew that person, and after. I was the same man who in the late afternoon had taken the little train from Balbec; I had the same mind. But in this consciousness, in the place where, at six o'clock, there had been, along with the impossibility of visualizing the manager, the hotel, and its employees, a vague, fearful anticipation of the moment when I'd arrive, there could now be found the pimples excised from the face of the cosmopolitan manager (who was actually a naturalized citizen of Monaco, despite being—as he put it, because he always used expressions he thought were distinguished, without realizing they were incorrect—'of Romanian originality'); his ringing for the lift; the lift-boy himself: the whole frieze of puppet-like characters emerging from this Pandora's box which was the Grand-Hôtel, undeniable, irremovable, and, like anything actual, banal. But at least this change, which I had not brought about, proved that something had happened that was external to myself—however devoid of interest that thing might be in itself—and I was like a traveller who, having had the sun in front of him when he set out on a journey, notes that time has passed when he sees it behind him. I was feverish and exhausted, and would gladly have gone to bed, but all my night things were missing. I'd have liked at least to lie down for a while, but I didn't see the point, since I wouldn't have been able to find any repose for that mass of sensations that our conscious, if not material, body is for each of us, and since the unknown objects that surrounded my body, forcing it to keep its perceptions in a constant state of defensive vigilance, would have held my eyes and ears—all my senses—in as cramped and uncomfortable a posture (even if I'd stretched out my legs) as that of Cardinal La Balue in the cage in which he could neither stand nor sit.* It is our attention to things that places them in a room, and our habit that takes them away and makes room for us in it. There was no room for me in my bedroom in Balbec ('mine' in name only); it was full of things that didn't know me, returned the mistrustful glance I gave them and, paying no heed whatsoever to my existence, demonstrated that I was disturbing the routine of theirs. The clock—which I heard at home only a few seconds a week, when I emerged from profound meditation—continued without a moment's interruption to utter, in an unknown language, remarks that must have been disparaging to me, for the long violet curtains listened to it without replying but with an attitude similar to the one adopted by people who shrug their shoulders to show they're annoyed by an outsider. They gave to this high-ceilinged bedroom an almost historical character that would have made it the perfect place for the assassination of the Duc de Guise,* and, later on, for tours of visitors led by a guide from Cook's*—but certainly not for me to sleep in. I was tormented by the presence of the little glassed-in bookcases that lined the walls, but especially by a tall cheval-glass* that stood athwart a corner of the room and which I knew would have to leave if I was going to get any rest there. I kept raising my eyes—which the objects in my room in Paris disturbed no more than did my own pupils, for they were nothing more than extensions of my senses, an amplification of myself—to the lofty ceiling of this belvedere at the hotel's summit which my grandmother had chosen for me; and deep down, in that region more private than the one where we see and hear, in that region where we experience the quality of smells, almost in the innermost part of myself, the aroma of vetiver* came to lead the assault on my last remaining defences, an aroma I wearily counter-attacked with the useless and continuous riposte of a frightened sniffling. Having no world of my own, no bedroom, no body even except the one being threatened by the enemies surrounding me, and invaded down to my bones with fever, I was alone, and wanted to die. It was then that my grandmother came in, and all at once my constricted heart opened up to an infinite expansiveness.

She was wearing a cotton cambric tea gown that she'd wear about the house whenever any of us was ill (because she felt more comfortable in it, she said, always attributing selfish motives to whatever she did), and which was her servant's smock, her nurse's uniform, her nun's habit, in which she would tend to us and watch over us. But, while the attentions of servants, nurses, and nuns, the kindness they show, the goodness we find in them and the gratitude we owe them, do even more to increase the impression we have of being, for them, a stranger, of feeling we're alone, keeping to ourselves the weight of our thoughts and our own desire to live, I knew, when I was with my grandmother, however great the sorrow that I expressed, it would be met with an even greater sympathy; that whatever was in me—my anxieties, my hopes—would be bolstered by my grandmother's desire, even stronger than my own, to preserve and enhance my own life; and my thoughts were continued in her without deviating because they passed from my mind into hers without any change of context or person. And—like a man who tries to knot his tie in front of a mirror without realizing that the end he sees reflected is not on the side to which his hand is moving, or like a dog chasing on the ground the dancing shadow of an insect—misled by her body's appearance as we are deceived in this world where souls can't be directly perceived, I threw myself into my grandmother's arms and pressed my lips to her face as if I were in this way gaining access to that immense heart she opened to me. When my mouth was pressed to her cheeks, her forehead, I drew something from them that was so beneficial, so nourishing, that I became as motionless, serious, and placidly gluttonous as an infant nursing.

I never wearied of gazing upon her large face, outlined like a beautiful, glowing, peaceful cloud, radiating tenderness. Anything that shared, however remotely, in her sensations, anything that could in this way be said to be still a part of her, was immediately so spiritualized, so sanctified, that I smoothed her beautiful hair, which still had only a touch of grey, with as much awe, care, and gentleness as if I were caressing her goodness itself. She took such pleasure in taking any trouble that spared me trouble, such joy in a moment of rest and peace for my weary limbs, that when I tried to prevent her from helping me take off my boots and get ready for bed, making as though to undress myself, her imploring gaze stopped my hands, which were fumbling with the top buttons of my jacket and boots.

'Please, let me!' she said. 'It's such a joy for your old grandmother. And don't forget to knock on the door if you need anything during the night, my bed is just next to yours, and the partition is very thin. As soon as you're in bed, try it, and we'll see how easy it is.'

And, that evening, I did give three knocks—a ritual which, a week later, when I was ill, I would repeat every day for a few days, because my grandmother wanted to give me some milk early in the morning. As soon as I thought I could hear her stirring—so that she wouldn't have to wait and could go back to sleep straight afterwards—I'd venture three little knocks, timidly, weakly, but distinctly, for if I was afraid of waking her up in case I was mistaken and she was still asleep, I also didn't want her to keep listening for a summons she might not have heard at first and which I wouldn't dare repeat. Scarcely had I given my taps than I heard three more, in a different tone, betokening calm authority, repeated twice for more clarity and as if to say: 'Never fear, I heard; in a few minutes I'll be there'; and soon afterwards, my grandmother arrived. I told her I was afraid she hadn't heard me or thought it was a neighbour knocking; laughing, she replied: 'Mistake my poor lamb's knocking for anyone else's? Your grandmama would know it a mile away. Do you really think there's anyone else in the world who's as silly and anxious and torn between the fear of waking me up and not being heard? All she needs is a tiny scratch to recognize her little mouse, especially such a special and sorry one as hers. I could hear it just now, trying to make up its mind, stirring in its bed, up to all its little tricks.'

She would open the shutters; the sun had already settled on the roofs of the protruding annex of the hotel like an early-rising slater working quietly so as not to rouse the still-sleeping town, whose motionlessness makes him seem all the more agile. She'd tell me what time it was and what the weather was like, that I shouldn't bother to come to the window, that there was mist over the sea, whether the bakery was open yet, what kind of carriage it was that we heard: the whole insignificant curtain-raiser, that trifling *introit* of the day* which no one attends, a little slice of life that was ours alone, which

I'd happily talk about later on with Françoise or with strangers, prattling on about the fog you could cut with a knife at six o'clock that morning, speaking with the ostentation not of knowledge that I'd acquired, but of a mark of affection that had been bestowed on me alone; it was a sweet morning moment that opened like a symphony with the rhythmic dialogue of my three taps to which the thin partition, imbued with love and joy, grown melodious and ethereal, singing like the angels, answered with three other taps, eagerly awaited, twice repeated, by which it skilfully transported my grandmother's soul in its entirety, along with the promise of her coming, with a musical fidelity and the swiftness of an annunciation. But on that first night after our arrival, after my grandmother left me, I once again began to suffer just as I had in Paris upon leaving home. Perhaps this fear I had—shared by so many people—of sleeping in a strange room is only the humblest, most obscure, most organic, almost unconscious form of that supreme, desperate resistance offered by things that make up the better part of our present life to our theoretical acceptance of a future that does not include them; this resistance was at the root of the horror I'd so often felt at the thought that my parents would die someday, that life's demands might force me to live far from Gilberte or simply to settle permanently in a place where I'd never see my friends again; this resistance was also at the root of the difficulty I had in thinking about my own death, or about an afterlife like the one Bergotte promised in his books, into which I would not be able to carry my memories, my faults, my very character, which did not resign themselves to the idea of ceasing to exist, and which desired for me neither nothingness, nor an eternity that excluded them.

When Swann had said to me in Paris, one day when I'd been feeling particularly unwell: 'You should go off to one of those delightful islands in the South Pacific; you'll see, you'll never come back!' I'd have liked to reply: 'But then I wouldn't see your daughter anymore, I'd live among people and things she's never seen.' Yet my rational mind murmured: 'What does that matter to you, since you won't be affected by it? When Monsieur Swann says you won't come back, he means you won't want to come back, and if you don't want to, it's because you'll be happy there.' For my rational mind knew that habit—the same habit that was now about to take on the responsibility of making me like this unfamiliar abode, change the position of the mirror, adjust the hue of the curtains, and silence the clock—also undertakes to make us care for people whom we disliked at first, alter the appear-ance of their faces, improve their tone of voice, change the heart's inclinations. It's true that this new-found liking for places and people is based upon our forgetting the old ones; but my rational mind thought I could fearlessly envisage the prospect of a life in which I'd be separated forever from people I'd cease to remember, and although it offered my heart a promise of forgetting as a sort of consolation, it only deepened its despair. Not that our heart won't also experience the analgesic effects of habit when the separation is complete; but until then, it will continue to suffer. The fear of a future in which we can no longer see or talk with those we love—the very ones from whom we now derive our deepest joy—this fear, far from dissipating, increases, if we imagine such a deprivation being compounded by something that now seems even more cruel: not to feel it as pain, but to view it with indifference; for then our very self would be changed: not only would we cease to be surrounded by the delight of our par-ents, our mistress, and our friends, but our affection for them would have been so completely torn from our hearts, in which it plays such a large role now, that we'd be able to enjoy this life apart from them, the very thought of which horrifies us today; and so it would be a real death of our selves—a death followed, it's true, by resurrection, but as a different self, which the parts of the old self condemned to die cannot bring themselves to love. It is these parts—even the most insignificant, like our obscure attachment to the dimensions or atmos-phere of a room—that take fright and refuse to comply, and rebel in ways that must be seen as the secret, partial, tangible, and true ways that we resist death, that daily, desperate resistance to the fragmen-tary, continuous death that insinuates itself into the whole course of our lives, tearing off pieces of us at every moment, which are replaced with new cells fed and multiplied by their mortification. And for a neurotic nature such as mine (one, that is, in which the functioning of those intermediaries, the nerves, is impaired, so that they fail to prevent the lament of the humblest elements of the doomed self from reaching consciousness, but rather allow it to arrive there, distinct, exhausting, innumerable, and painful), the anxious alarm I felt beneath that strange, lofty ceiling was merely the protest of an attachment that still survived in me to a ceiling that was familiar and low. Doubtless this predilection would disappear and another take its place (when death, and then another life, had, in the guise of Habit, completed their twofold task); but until that annihilation, every night it would suffer and, on that first night especially, confronted with a future that had already become real and in which there was no room for it, it rebelled, it tortured me with the sound of its lamentations whenever my eyes, unable to turn away from the source of their suffering, tried to come to rest on that inaccessible ceiling.

But the next morning!—after a servant had come to wake me and bring hot water, and while I was washing, trying in vain to find what I needed in my trunk, which yielded up only a jumble of things I had no use for, what a joy it was for me, thinking already of the pleasure of lunch and a stroll, to see in the window, and reflected in all the glass panes of the bookcases, as in the portholes of a ship's cabin, the open sea, casting no shade, yet with shadows over half of its expanse, its horizon thin and ever-shifting, and to follow with my eyes the waves crashing one after the other like divers leaping from their boards! Holding the stiff, starched towel bearing the name of the hotel, with which I was making futile attempts to dry myself, I kept going back to the window to gaze again upon this vast, dazzling, mountainous amphitheatre and upon the snowy summits of its emerald waves, here and there polished and translucent, which with placid violence and leonine frown caused their slopes, on which the sun added a faceless smile, to collapse and hurtle down. It was at this window that I would take my place every morning as at the window of a coach in which you've been sleeping to see whether during the night a longed-for chain of mountains had come closer or receded—for here these hills of the sea, before they come dancing back towards us, can retreat so far that often it was only beyond a long sandy plain that I could glimpse far away their first undulations, in a transparent, hazy, bluish remoteness, like the glaciers you see in the backgrounds of paintings by Tuscan primitives.* At other times the waves were quite close; and the sun would laugh on these swells of a green as soft as that pre-served in Alpine meadows (among mountains where the sun tumbles haphazardly down like a giant gleefully leaping downhill in uneven strides) less by the moisture of the soil than by the liquid mobility of the light. In this breach opened by the shore and the waves in the middle of the world to allow the light to pass through it and accumu-late, it is this light, depending on the direction from which it comes and which we follow with our eyes, that shifts and positions the sea's undulations. Changes in light can modify the orientation of a place, set before us new goals and make us want to reach them, just as effectively as could the route travelled on a long journey. When the sun appeared in the morning from behind the hotel, revealing before me the sands illuminated all the way to the first foothills of the sea, it seemed to be showing me another side of the sea and to be encouraging me to follow, on the winding path of its rays, a motionless but changeful journey through the most beautiful sites of the hours' shifting landscape. On this first morning, the sun pointed out, with a smiling finger, those faraway blue summits of the sea that have no name on any map, until, dizzy with its sublime excursion over the thundering and chaotic surface of their crests and avalanches, it came to take shelter from the wind in my room, lounging about on the unmade bed and scattering its riches on the wet washstand and open trunk, and adding, by its very splendour and incongruous luxury, even more to the room's disorderly appearance. As to the sea breeze, it seemed unfair to my grandmother—as we were lunching an hour later in the grand dining room and sprinkling a few golden drops from a lemon's leather gourd on to two soles which soon left on our plates the plumes of their skeletons, curled like feathers and resonant as zithers—that we couldn't enjoy its invigorating breath because of the glass partition, transparent but closed, which, like a shop window, separated us from the beach while at the same time letting us see its whole expanse, into which the sky fitted so perfectly that its azure seemed the colour of the windows, and its white clouds like flaws in the glass. Imagining I was 'sitting on the jetty' or in 'the boudoir' as in Baudelaire,* I wondered if his 'sun shining on the sea'—unlike the rays of evening, simple and insubstantial as a quivering golden shaft— might be just like this sun that was at this very moment burnishing the sea to a topaz yellow, fermenting it, turning it into a pale milky ale, frothy like milk, while every now and then great blue shadows played over parts of it, as though some god were shifting them about for his own amusement by moving a mirror in the sky. Compared to the 'parlour' in Combray which looked out at the houses opposite, unfortunately it was not only in its appearance that this Balbec dining room—uncluttered, full of sunlight that was green as the water in a pool—differed, while just a few metres away, as though guarding the celestial city, the high tide and broad daylight raised their indestructible, ever-shifting ramparts of emerald and gold. In Combray, where we were known by everyone, I wasn't concerned about anyone. At seaside resorts, however, one is surrounded by strangers. I was not yet old enough, and was still too sensitive, to have given up the wish to please others and to win them over. I hadn't yet acquired the nobler indifference a man of the world would have felt towards the people lunching in the dining room or the boys and girls strolling by on the esplanade: the thought that I couldn't accompany them on their outings pained me, though not as much as if my grandmother, heedless of conventions and concerned only with my health, had humiliated me by asking them to let me join them. Whether they were returning to some villa unknown to me, or leaving one to stroll, racquet in hand, to a tennis court, or riding horses whose hooves trampled my heart, I gazed at them with passionate curiosity, in that blinding light of the beach where social standings are altered; I followed all their movements from the transparency of that wide bay window that let so much light through. But it intercepted the sea wind, and that was a defect for my grandmother, who, unable to bear the thought that I might lose the benefit of an hour's worth of fresh air, surreptitiously opened one of the panes and thereby sent flying the menus, newspapers, veils, and hats of all the people who were eating lunch; while she herself, uplifted by the heavenly breeze, remained calm and smiling like Saint Blandina* amid the torrent of abuse which, increasing my sense of isolation and misery, united the contemptuous, dishevelled, furious tourists against us.

To a certain extent—and this, at Balbec, gave a rather marked regional character to the usually monotonously wealthy and international population of that sort of luxury hotel—the guests were composed of eminent personalities from the principal *départements* of that part of France: one of Caen's first presidents; a *bâtonnier* from Cherbourg; an eminent notary from Le Mans*—who at every holiday season, leaving from the various points over which they'd been scattered all year long like skirmishers or draughts on a chequerboard, converged on this hotel. They always reserved the same rooms, and with their wives, who had aristocratic pretensions, they formed a little group which also included a prominent lawyer and a famous doctor from Paris, who would say when it came time to leave:

'Oh yes, of course, you're not taking the same train as we are—how lucky you are, you'll be home in time for lunch!'

'Lucky, you say? You live in the capital, Paris, the big city, while I live in a puny little country town of a hundred thousand souls—or rather, a hundred and two thousand, at the last census—but what's that compared to your two and a half million and your asphalt pavements, and all the glamour of Paris?'

They'd say this with a provincial rolling of the *r*, without any bitterness, for they were the leading lights of their provinces, and could have gone to Paris if they'd liked—the first president from Caen had several times been offered a seat at the Cour de Cassation*—but they'd chosen to stay where they were, out of love for their towns, or a desire for obscurity, or for local fame, or because they were reactionary, or else enjoyed being on friendly terms with the neighbouring owners of châteaux. Besides, quite a few of them weren't going back to their county towns right away.

Since the Bay of Balbec was a little world apart within the greater one, a basketful of seasons composed of different sorts of days and a string of months all gathered together in a ring, so much so that not only on days when you could make out Rivebelle (indicating a coming storm, when you could see the sun shining on its houses while Balbec was covered in darkness), but also, when the cold weather had returned to Balbec, you could always be sure of finding two or three additional months of warmth on that opposite shore, those regulars of the Grand-Hôtel whose vacations began late or lasted longer gave orders, when the rain and fog arrived with the approaching autumn, for their trunks to be loaded on to a boat so they could cross the bay to rejoin summer in Rivebelle or Costedor.* This little clan at the Balbec hotel would look suspiciously at each new arrival and, feigning nonchalance, would all interrogate their friend the head waiter about him. For it was the same head waiter—Aimé—who returned every year for the season, and kept their tables for them; and their good ladies, knowing Aimé's wife was expecting, would each work after meals on one of the items for the infant's clothes, glaring through their lorgnettes at my grandmother and me because we were eating salad with hard-boiled eggs, which was deemed common and 'was not done' in the respectable society of Alençon. They affected an attitude of scornful irony towards a Frenchman who was called 'His Majesty' and who had, in fact, proclaimed himself king of a little island in the South Pacific inhabited only by a few 'savages'. He was staying at the hotel with his pretty mistress, who, as she made her way to the shore to bathe, was greeted by the children with shouts of 'Long live the Queen!' because she showered them with fifty-centime coins. The first president and the *bâtonnier* made as if not to see her, and if one of their friends looked at her, they thought it incumbent upon themselves to warn him that she was only a little shopgirl.

'But I was told they used the royal bathing machine at Ostend!'*

'Of course! Anyone can rent it for twenty francs—you can have it, if you like. And I know for a fact that he asked for an audience with the King, who let him know in no uncertain terms that he'd have nothing to do with that pantomime king!'

'Really, now? How interesting! It takes all kinds . . .'

No doubt this was true, but it was because they resented the fact that to most of their fellow guests they were nothing but ordinary bourgeois gentlemen who didn't know this prodigal king and queen that the notary, the first president, and the *bâtonnier* felt such rancour whenever what they called the 'carnival' went by, and gave vent so loudly to their indignation, which was well known to their friend the head waiter, who, obliged as he was to be civil to these more generous than genuine sovereigns, would nevertheless, as he took their order, give a meaningful wink from afar to his regular customers. Perhaps some of this same resentment at being mistakenly thought less fashionable while being unable to explain they were actually *more* so lay behind the epithet 'Pretty boy!' with which they referred to a young fop, the consumptive and profligate son of an industrial magnate, who appeared every day in a new jacket with an orchid in its buttonhole, took champagne with his lunch, and then went off smiling blithely, pale and impassive, to the baccarat tables at the Casino, where he spent enormous sums 'which he could ill afford to lose', as the notary said with a knowing air to the first president, whose wife had it 'on good authority' that this *fin-de-siècle* young man was making his parents die of sorrow.

The *bâtonnier* and his friends were similarly unstinting with sarcastic remarks on the subject of an old woman, wealthy and titled, because she never travelled anywhere without her entire household. Whenever the wives of the notary and the first president saw her in the dining room during meals, they'd inspect her insolently through their lorgnettes with the same meticulous and defiant scrutiny as if she were some pompously-named but suspicious-looking dish which, after methodical examination, is deemed unsuitable and waved haughtily away with a grimace of disgust.

No doubt by this behaviour they meant only to show that, if there were certain things they lacked—namely, certain prerogatives enjoyed by the old woman, and the distinction of being acquainted with her—it was not because they were unable to acquire them, but because they were unwilling to do so. But they had ended up convincing themselves of this; and it was this suppression of all desire for, or curiosity about, ways of life unknown to them, all hope of winning new friends—replaced in these women by feigned disdain and artificial cheerfulness—that had the drawback of making them label displeasure as contentment, and lie to themselves constantly, two reasons for their unhappiness. But everyone else in that hotel was doubtless acting in the same way, though in different forms, and sacrificing, if not to self-esteem, at least to certain acquired principles or intellectual habits, the delightful thrill of getting involved in an unfamiliar life. Of course, the microcosm in which the old woman isolated herself was not poisoned with virulent rancour like that of the group in which the wives of the notary and the first president sneered with rage. Despite being imbued with a delicate, old-world fragrance, however, the old woman's world was no less artificial than theirs. If she had tried to attract, to win over, the mysterious affection of new people (while being renewed in the process), she would probably have discovered a charm that is entirely absent from the pleasure of mixing only with the people of one's own world and reminding oneself that, since one's own society is the best there is, other people's ignorant disdain doesn't matter. But perhaps she felt that, by arriving incognito at the Grand-Hôtel of Balbec, with her black woollen dress and old-fashioned bonnet, she might have aroused an amused smile from some old reprobate who, looking up from his rocking chair, might have murmured 'Good grief, what a wreck!' or, even worse, some worthy who, like the first president with his salt-and-pepper sideburns, still had the fresh face and intelligent eyes she liked, and who would at once have drawn the attention of the conjugal lorgnette's probing lens to the apparition of this outlandish specimen; and it was perhaps due to this unconscious anxiety about that first minute, which, though we know is brief, we dread all the same—like that first dive into the water—that this lady sent a servant ahead of her to inform the hotel of her personality and habits, and, cutting short the manager's greetings, made her way swiftly, though more from shyness than from pride, to her room, where her own curtains, replacing the hotel's, her own screens and photographs, erected so effectively the bulwark of her own habits between herself and the outer world (to which she would otherwise have had to adapt) that it was her own home, in which she had remained, that travelled rather than herself.

From then on, having placed between herself on the one hand and the hotel employees and tradesmen on the other her own servants, who took it upon themselves to endure contact with this new-found race and who maintained her accustomed atmosphere around their mistress, having inserted her prejudices between herself and the holidaymakers, unconcerned about offending people her friends wouldn't have entertained, she continued to live in a world all her own, through corresponding with her friends, through her memories, through her innermost awareness of her own situation, through the quality of her manners and the adequacy of her politeness. And every day, when she walked downstairs to go for a drive in her carriage, her lady's maid carrying her things behind her and her footman in front of her seemed like those sentries who at the gate to an embassy flying its country's colours are the guarantors, on foreign soil, of its privilege of extraterritoriality. She didn't leave her room until mid-afternoon on the day we arrived, so we didn't see her in the dining room to which, since we were newcomers, the manager conducted us at lunchtime, taking us under his wing, as a non-commissioned officer leads recruits to the quartermaster to have them kitted out; but we did see, a moment later, a country squire and his daughter, of an obscure but very ancient Breton family, Monsieur and Mademoiselle Stermaria, whose table had been given to us in the belief that they wouldn't return until evening. Since they had come to Balbec solely to see some country squires they knew in the district, the time they spent in the hotel dining room, what with the invitations they accepted and the visits they paid, was as brief as possible. Their haughtiness guarded them against any sympathy for their fellow humans, from any curiosity about the strangers seated around them, among whom Monsieur de Stermaria preserved the frosty, hurried, distant, stiff, fastidious, and spiteful air one has in the buffet car on a train among passengers one has never seen, will never see again, and with whom one can't conceive of any connection other than defending from them one's chicken salad and window seat. Scarcely had we begun our lunch than we were asked to leave the table on the order of Monsieur de Stermaria, who had just arrived and, without the slightest gesture of apology towards us, loudly requested the head waiter to see to it that such a mistake would never occur again, for it was repellent to him that 'people he did not know' had taken his table.

Of course, in the sentiment that compelled a certain actress (better known, however, more for her elegance, wit, and fine collections of German porcelain than for the occasional parts she played at the Odéon*), her lover, a wealthy young man for whose sake she had acquired these cultural tastes, and a pair of prominent men of the aristocracy to form a little band apart, to travel always together, to take lunch (when at Balbec) very late, when everyone else had finished, to spend the day playing cards in their own drawing room, there was no malice, but merely the requirements of their predilection for certain types of witty conversation and for particularly refined food and wine, which made them find pleasure in living and taking their meals only with one another, and would have made a life shared with people uninitiated into their preferences unbearable. Even at a dinner table or card table, each of them needed to be certain that, in their fellow guest or partner at cards, there lay, latent and untapped, a certain knowledge that allows one to recognize as fake the rubbish that passes for genuine medieval or Renaissance with which so many Parisian homes are decorated and, in all things, that they share the requisite criteria to distinguish good from bad. No doubt at such moments it was only by some rare and amusing interjection uttered amid the silence of the meal or game, or by a charming new dress the young actress had worn for lunch or poker, that the special existence in which these friends wanted to remain immersed wherever they went was revealed. But cocooning themselves in this way with habits they knew by heart was enough to safeguard them against the mystery of the life around them. All throughout the long afternoons, the sea was suspended before their eyes like nothing but the pleasing colour of a painting on the wall of a wealthy bachelor's sitting room, and it was only between hands that one of the players, having nothing better to do, would raise his eyes to it to see what the weather was like or what the time might be, and to remind the others that tea was waiting. And in the evenings they never dined in the hotel, where electric fountains flooded the big dining room with light so that it became like an immense and wonderful aquarium, while against its glass wall the working population of Balbec, the fishermen, and also families from the lower middle class, invisible in the darkness, pressed their faces to see the luxurious life of these people, floating gently on the golden eddies, a sight as extraordinary to the poor as the life of strange fish or molluscs (and herein lies a great social question: whether the glass wall will forever protect the feasts of these wondrous creatures, or whether the obscure onlookers greedily watching them in the dark will break into their aquarium to catch and devour them). In the meantime, perhaps among the motionless, dazzled crowd in the dark, there may have been some writer, some fancier of human ichthyology, who, as he watched the jaws of old female monsters clamping down on a gulped morsel of food, was taking pleasure in classifying them by species, by innate characteristics, as well as by acquired characteristics, which may lead an old Serbian lady whose buccal cavity is like that of a great ocean fish to eat her salad—because since childhood she has swum in the fresh waters of the Faubourg Saint-Germain—like a La Rochefoucauld.*

At that hour, the three men in dinner jackets could be seen waiting for the woman, who was late; soon, though, wearing a different dress almost every night along with scarves chosen according to a particular whim of her lover's, after ringing for the lift from her floor, she'd emerge from it as if from a toy chest. Then all four of them, who thought the international phenomenon of the palatial hotel, having been planted in Balbec, had caused luxury to blossom there rather than fine cuisine, piled into a carriage and went to dine a mile or so away in a reputable little restaurant where they'd hold endless discussions with the chef about the composition of the menu and the preparation of the dishes. During their drive, the road from Balbec, lined with apple trees, was nothing to them but the distance—hardly distinguishable to them in the dark night from the space separating their Parisian homes from the Café Anglais or the Tour d'Argent*—that had to be covered to reach the elegant little restaurant where, while the rich young man's friends envied him for having such a well-dressed mistress, her scarves provided the little band with something like a perfumed, floating veil, but one that kept it separate from the rest of the world.

Unfortunately for my own peace of mind, I was far from resembling these people. I was concerned about the opinions of many of them; I'd have liked not to be ignored by a man with a low forehead and a gaze that flitted between the blinkers of his prejudices and his education, the local grandee, who was none other than the brother-in-law of Legrandin; he came to visit Balbec once in a while, and the weekly garden parties he and his wife gave on Sundays emptied the hotel of a large number of its residents, because one or two of them were invited to these parties and the others, so as not to appear to have been left out, chose that day to go on a lengthy excursion. He had, as it happened, been very poorly received at the hotel on the first day of the season, when the staff, freshly arrived from the Riviera, didn't yet know who he was. Not only was he not dressed in white flannels, but, following the old French rules of courtesy and unaware of the ways of establishments such as the Grand-Hôtel, when he entered the lobby in which women were present, he'd removed his hat at the door, causing the manager not even to touch his own in reply, since he thought this must be someone of the humblest birth, what he called a man 'extracted from the ordinary'. Only the notary's wife felt drawn to the newcomer, who emanated all the starched vulgarity of 'respectable' people, and she had declared, with all the infallible discernment and unerring authority of a person for whom the highest society of Le Mans holds no secrets, that in his presence one could sense a man of great distinction and perfect breeding, a man who was a cut above all the other people one usually met in Balbec, those she deemed unworthy of knowing, so long as she didn't know them herself. The favourable judgement she had pronounced on Legrandin's brother-in-law may perhaps have stemmed from the drab demeanour of a man who had nothing intimidating about him, or perhaps from her recognizing in this gentleman farmer with the look of a sexton the Masonic signs of her own brand of clericalism.

Despite learning that the young men who rode past the hotel every day on horseback were the sons of the devious owner of a fancy-goods shop whose acquaintance my father would never have sought, 'seaside resort life' had elevated them in my eyes to equestrian statues of demigods, and the best I could hope for was that they'd never let their eyes fall on the poor boy that I was, who left the hotel dining room only to go and sit on the sand. I'd even have been happy to be liked by the adventurer who had been king of a desert island in the South Seas, or the young consumptive whom I liked to think of as hiding beneath his insolent exterior a timid and loving heart, and lavishing on me alone the treasures of his affection. Besides (contrary to what is usually said about acquaintances made during travel), since being seen about with certain people at a spa to which you return from time to time can give you a certain status that has no equivalent in real society, there is nothing that, far from keeping resolutely at a distance, we cultivate more assiduously after our return to Paris, than friendships struck up at seaside resorts. I was anxious about what opinion all these temporary or local celebrities might have of me; my tendency to put myself in the place of others and recreate their state of mind made me place them not in their true rank, the one they would have had in Paris, for example, which was quite low, but in the rank which they must have thought was theirs, and which actually was so in Balbec, where the lack of a common denominator gave them a kind of relative superiority and singular interest. Alas, among all these personages, there was no contempt more painful to me than that of Monsieur de Stermaria.

For I'd noticed his daughter as soon as she came in—her pretty face, pale and almost bluish, the particular way she carried her tall frame, her distinctive gait—all of which (rightly) suggested to me her heredity and her aristocratic education, all the more clearly because I knew her name, like those expressive themes invented by talented composers which so splendidly paint the flicker of a flame, the rushing water of a river, and the peace of the countryside, for listeners who, glancing through the programme in advance, have set their imagination on the right track. 'Breeding', by adding to Mademoiselle de Stermaria's charms the idea of their origin, made them more intelligible, more complete. It also made them more desirable, proclaiming they were difficult to achieve, just as a high price adds to the value of an object we like. And the hereditary stock gave her complexion, made up of so many select elixirs, the savour of an exotic fruit or a celebrated vintage.

As it happened, for my grandmother and me, chance suddenly placed in our hands an opportunity to acquire instant prestige in the eyes of all the hotel's inhabitants. For on our very first day there, as the old woman was coming downstairs from her rooms, making a profound impression—thanks to the footman leading the way and the maidservant running behind with a forgotten book and blanket—on everyone present, and arousing in them curiosity and respect, which Monsieur de Stermaria evinced more visibly than anyone else, the manager leaned over to my grandmother and out of politeness (as one might point out the Shah of Persia or Queen Ranavalo* to an obscure onlooker who can obviously have no connection to the powerful sovereign, but who might be impressed by seeing one a few feet away) whispered in my grandmother's ear: 'The Marquise de Villeparisis!' while at the same time that lady, catching sight of my grandmother, couldn't conceal a look of joyful surprise.

One might easily think that the sudden appearance, in the guise of a little old lady, of the most powerful of fairy godmothers couldn't possibly have given me more pleasure, devoid as I was of any means of access to Mademoiselle de Stermaria, in a place where I knew no one. No one, that is, from a practical point of view. Aesthetically, the number of types of humans is so limited that we often have the joy, wherever we go, of seeing people we know (even without looking for them in the paintings of the old masters, as Swann did). This is how in the first few days of our visit to Balbec I'd happened to meet Legrandin, Swann's concierge, and Madame Swann herself, transformed into a café waiter, a passing stranger whom I never saw again, and a beach guard respectively. A kind of magnetism attracts, and keeps so inseparably together, certain features of physiognomy and mentality that when nature introduces a person into a different body in this way, it's done without too much mutilation. Legrandin, transformed into a café waiter, kept intact his stature, the contour of his nose, and part of his chin; Madame Swann, in her new embodiment as a beach guard, had retained not only her usual facial features, but also her mannerisms of speech. Only she could be of no more use to me, in her red belt and, at the slightest swell, hoisting the flag that bans swimming (for beach guards are nothing if not prudent, since they rarely know how to swim), than if she were in the fresco of *The Life of Moses* wherein Swann had recognized her long ago in the guise of Jethro's daughter.* Whereas this Madame de Villeparisis was the real thing; she hadn't been the victim of a spell robbing her of her power, but on the contrary was capable of casting a spell that could affect my own power and multiply it a hundredfold, thanks to which, as if I'd been carried aloft on the wings of some mythical bird, in a few seconds I was about to cross the infinite social distances—infinite in Balbec, at least—that separated me from Mademoiselle de Stermaria.

Unfortunately, it would have been difficult to find anyone who lived more enclosed in her own little world than my grandmother. It wasn't that she would have despised me, she wouldn't even have understood me if she'd known that I was so concerned about others and attached so much importance to the opinions of people of whose existence she wasn't even aware, and whose names she wouldn't even have bothered to learn by the time we left Balbec; I didn't dare confess to her that if these same people had seen her chatting with Madame de Villeparisis, I would have been profoundly happy, because I sensed

that her friendship with the marquise, who had such prestige in the
hotel, would have elevated us in the eyes of Monsieur de Stermaria.
Not that I viewed my grandmother's friend as a member of the aristocracy: I was too used to her name, which had become familiar to my
ears before my mind had taken note of it, when as a child I'd heard it
uttered at home; and her title added nothing but a curious detail, as
an unusual first name might do, or as sometimes happens with street
names when one can't imagine the Rue Lord-Byron, the vulgar and
working-class Rue Rochechouart, or the Rue de Gramont being any
nobler than streets named after commoners, like the Rue Léonce-
Reynaud or the Rue Hippolyte-Lebas.* The name of Madame de
Villeparisis no more made me think of a person from a special world
than did the name of her cousin Mac-Mahon,* whom I couldn't really
tell apart from Monsieur Carnot, also a president of the Republic,* or
from Raspail, whose photograph Françoise had brought along with that
of Pius IX.* It was a firm principle of my grandmother's that when you
travel, all social interaction should cease; that one doesn't go to the seaside to see people—you have all the time in the world for that in Paris;
that they would make you waste in polite remarks and banal conversations the precious time that should be spent entirely out of doors, in the
fresh air, by the waves; and, finding it more convenient to assume that
this opinion was shared by everyone else and that, between old friends
thrown together by chance in the same hotel, it authorized the fiction of
a reciprocal incognito, on hearing the name the manager whispered, my
grandmother merely averted her eyes and pretended not to have seen
Madame de Villeparisis, who, realizing my grandmother didn't want to
be recognized, likewise looked off into space. She continued on, and
I stayed there in my isolation like the survivor of a shipwreck watching
as a vessel approaches, but then disappears without stopping.

Madame de Villeparisis also took her meals in the dining room, but
at the other end. She knew none of the people staying at the hotel or
visiting it, not even Monsieur de Cambremer; I noticed that he didn't
greet her on the day when he and his wife came to lunch at the invitation of the *bâtonnier*, who, giddy with the honour of having the gentleman at his table, avoided his everyday friends and confined himself to
winking at them from afar to mark this historic event, but discreetly
enough for them not to take this as an invitation to come over.

'Well, well, I see you've come up in the world! Aren't you grand!'
the first president's wife said to him that evening.

'Grand, whatever do you mean?' rejoined the *bâtonnier*, concealing his joy with exaggerated surprise. 'Do you mean because of my guests?' he went on, sensing he wouldn't be able to keep up the pretence any longer. 'How is having some friends over for lunch "grand"? They have to eat somewhere!'

'Of course it's grand! They were the *de* Cambremers, weren't they?* I recognized them at once. She's a marquise. A *real* one, not from the distaff side.'*

'Oh, but she's just a simple woman, she's charming, there's nothing arrogant about her. I thought you'd join us, I was signalling to you . . . I could have introduced you!' he said, tempering with a slight irony the enormity of the proposition, like Ahasuerus when he says to Esther: 'Of my Estate, must I give you half?'*

'No, no, we hide ourselves away, like the shrinking violet!'

'But you're quite wrong, I assure you,' replied the *bâtonnier*, emboldened now that the danger was past. 'They wouldn't have eaten you. Shall we go and have our little game of bezique,* then?'

'But of course! We didn't dare suggest it, now that you're hobnobbing with marquises!'

'Come now, there's nothing so extraordinary about them. Look, I'm supposed to go over to their place tomorrow for dinner. Would you like to go in my place? I mean it, really. Honestly, I'd be just as happy staying here.'

'No, no! I'd be struck off the bench as a reactionary!' exclaimed the first president, laughing until tears came to his eyes at his own joke. 'But you often go to Féterne too, don't you?' he added, turning to the notary.

'Oh, I go there on Sundays—in one door and out the other. But they don't come and have lunch with me, unlike our *bâtonnier* here.'

Monsieur de Stermaria wasn't at Balbec that day, to the *bâtonnier*'s great regret. But he slyly said to the head waiter:

'Aimé, you can tell Monsieur de Stermaria that he's not the only nobleman who has graced this dining room. You saw the gentleman who had lunch with me today? Eh? Toothbrush moustache, military bearing? Well, *that* was the Marquis de Cambremer!'

'Is that so? I'm not at all surprised!'

'That'll show him he's not the only man with a title. That'll teach him! Does these noblemen good to be taken down a peg or two.—You know what, Aimé, don't say anything to him if you don't want to—those aren't my own opinions, you understand. Besides, he knows the man quite well.'

The next day, Monsieur de Stermaria, who knew the *bâtonnier* had represented one of his friends in court, went over to introduce himself.

'Our mutual friends, the Cambremers, have been wanting to bring us together, but it was never the right day, or something like that,' said the *bâtonnier*, who, like many liars, assumed that other people don't bother to verify an insignificant detail which, however, can be enough (if chance provides the humble fact that contradicts it) to reveal the liar's true character and give rise to permanent distrust.

As usual, though more easily now that her father had moved off to chat with the *bâtonnier*, I gazed at Mademoiselle de Stermaria. The forthright and ever-beautiful distinctiveness of each of her gestures (as when, with her elbows on the table, she would lift up her glass with both hands), the brevity of her easily bored glances, the fundamental, congenital hardness which could be sensed, ill-concealed by her own personal inflections, deep within her voice, and which had shocked my grandmother, a sort of atavistic dagger which she would sheathe as soon as she had conveyed her thoughts through a glance or an intonation—all that led an observer's thoughts back to the ancestral lineage that had bequeathed her this lack of human sympathy, these gaps in sensitivity, this failure of generosity in her make-up. But from certain glints in her eyes which burned brightly and then were quickly extinguished, and which hinted at that almost humble docility which a penchant for sensual pleasures gives to even the haughtiest woman, who soon comes to recognize only one kind of prestige, the one any man who can make her experience these pleasures takes on in her eyes, whether he be an actor or an acrobat for whom she might one day leave her husband; from a certain sensual, vivid flush of pink that spread over her pale cheeks, like the hue that turns incarnadine the hearts of the white water lilies on the Vivonne, I thought I could sense that she might readily have allowed me to taste on her person the poetic life she led in Brittany, a life to which, either out of a surfeit of habit, an innate superiority, or disgust at the penury or avarice of her family, she seemed not to value very highly, but which she neverthe-less held enclosed in her body. From the meagre reserve of willpower which had been handed down to her, and which gave a hint of timidity to her expression, she might not have found the strength to resist. And, crowned by a feather that was slightly old-fashioned and pretentious, the grey felt hat that she invariably wore at meals made her seem more endearing to me, not because it harmonized with her glowing, rosy complexion, but because, by making me think she was poor, it drew her closer to me. Obliged to assume a conventional attitude because of her father's presence, but already bringing principles quite different to his to the way she perceived and classified people around her, perhaps she saw in me not my lowly rank, but my sex and age. If Monsieur de Stermaria had left the room without her, or especially if Madame de Villeparisis, by coming to sit at our table, had given her an opinion of us that might have emboldened me to approach her, perhaps we could have exchanged a few words, arranged a meeting, become closer. And if her parents had left her alone for a month in her romantic château, we might have been able to wander together in the gloaming, where the pink flowers of the heather would glow more softly above the darkening water, beneath the oaks battered by the lapping waves. Together we might have roamed her island, which held so much charm for me because it had enclosed the everyday life of Mademoiselle de Stermaria, and because its memory remained in her eyes. For it seemed to me that I could truly possess her only there, when I'd traversed those landscapes that wrapped her in so many memories—a veil which my desire yearned to tear off, one of those veils that Nature interposes between a woman and certain men (with the same intention as when, for all humans, she interposes the act of reproduction between them and their keenest pleasure, and, for insects, sets between them and their nectar the pollen they must carry away) so that, under the misapprehension that they can possess her more completely in that way, they feel compelled to start out by taking possession of her landscapes, which, though more useful to their imagination than sensual pleasure, would not have attracted them otherwise.

But I had to avert my gaze from Mademoiselle de Stermaria, for already, doubtless thinking that making the acquaintance of an important person was one curious, brief act that was sufficient in itself and that, to elicit whatever interest it contained, all that was needed was a handshake and a penetrating glance without any immediate conversation or subsequent interaction, her father had taken his leave of the *bâtonnier* and was returning to sit opposite her, rubbing his hands like a man who has just made a valuable acquisition. As for the *bâtonnier*, once the initial emotion of this exchange had subsided, he could be heard, as on other days, addressing the head waiter every few minutes: 'You know, Aimé, I'm not a king! Go off and see to the king!—Look over there, Your Worship, those little trout look quite good, let's ask Aimé for some. Aimé, those little fish you have over there look just the thing: be a good fellow, Aimé, and bring us some, as much as you like!'

He kept repeating the name *Aimé*, so that whenever he had anyone to dinner, his guest would say: 'I see you're quite at home here,' and thought he too should say 'Aimé' over and over, by the propensity certain people have—part shyness, part vulgarity, and part stupidity— to believe it's witty and stylish to imitate to the letter the people they happen to be with. The *bâtonnier* kept repeating Aimé's name, but with a smile, for he wanted to display both his good relations with the head waiter and his own superiority. And the head waiter, whenever his name was mentioned, would smile and look both moved and proud, showing he appreciated the honour and shared the joke.

As intimidating as mealtimes always were for me in the Grand-Hôtel's vast restaurant, which was usually full, they became even more so when there arrived for a few days the owner (or possibly the general manager, appointed by a board of shareholders) not just of this luxury hotel, but of seven or eight others scattered over the four corners of France, in each of which, shuttling from one to the other, he would spend a week from time to time. Every evening, just as dinner began, there would appear, at the dining room's entrance, that little white-haired, red-nosed man, extraordinarily impassive and correct, who was known, apparently, from London to Monte Carlo as one of the leading hoteliers in Europe. Once, when I'd gone out for a moment at the beginning of dinner, I passed by him as I came in again, and he gave me a stiff bow, no doubt to show he was the host; but I couldn't tell whether his coldness stemmed from the reserve of someone who never forgets his position, or from disdain for a customer of no importance. With those, however, who were of great importance, the general manager bowed with equal formality but more deeply, and he lowered his eyelids with a sort of shy respect, as he would at a funeral when confronting the father of the deceased or the Blessed Sacrament. Except for these rare and frosty salutations, he didn't make a single movement, as if to show that his glittering eyes, which seemed to be protruding from his face, saw everything, controlled everything, and ensured that 'Dinner at the Grand-Hôtel' was perfect, from the smallest detail to the harmony of the whole. He obviously regarded himself not as a lowly stage manager or orchestra conductor, but as a veritable generalissimo. Deeming that extremely intense contemplation was enough to ensure everything was in order, that no mistake had been made that might lead to disaster, and, finally, that it was all he needed to take full responsibility of the proceedings, he carefully avoided not just making any gesture whatsoever but even moving his eyes, petrified as they were by the attention that embraced and directed the entire theatre of operations. I felt that the very movements of my spoon didn't escape him; and even if he slipped away after the soup, the inspection he'd just made spoiled my appetite for the rest of dinner. His own appetite was quite good, as could be seen at lunch, which he took like an ordinary person, at the same time as everyone else, in the dining room. There was only one unusual thing about his table: next to him as he ate, the other manager, the everyday one, remained standing the entire time, making conversation. For, as the general manager's subordinate, he sought to flatter him and stood in great fear of him. My own fear was not as great during these luncheons, since, lost among the clientele, he would exercise the discretion of a general who's sitting in a restaurant where there are soldiers present, but who pretends not to notice them. Still, when the desk clerk, surrounded by his bellboys, announced to me: 'He's leaving tomorrow morning for Dinard. Then he's going on to Biarritz, and after that to Cannes,' I could breathe more freely.

My life in the hotel was now not only glum, because I'd made no friends there, but also inconvenient, because Françoise had made many. One might think these friends should have made many things easier for us. But quite the opposite was true. Although members of the working class found it somewhat difficult to be treated as acquaintances by Françoise, and could achieve this only by behaving with extreme politeness towards her, once they'd won her over, they were the only people who mattered to her. Her time-honoured code taught her that she owed nothing to the friends of her employers; she could, if she was pressed for time, turn away a lady who had come to call on my grandmother. But towards her own acquaintances, that is, the select few of the lower classes allowed into her hard-won friendship, the subtlest and most stringent protocol ruled her actions. Thus Françoise, having made the acquaintance of the man who worked in the hotel café and of a little maid who sewed dresses for a Belgian lady, no longer went upstairs immediately after lunch to prepare my grandmother's things, but waited until an hour later, because the hotel worker wanted to make her a coffee or a tisane in the café, or the maid had asked her to come by and watch her sew, and to refuse them would have been not only out of the question but one of those things that are Not Done. What's more, particular consideration was due to the little maid, who was an orphan and had been brought up by strangers with whom she'd sometimes spend a few days. This situation aroused Françoise's pity as well as her benevolent disdain. Since Francoise had a family and a little farmhouse she'd inherited from her parents where her brother raised a few cows, she couldn't regard a person without roots as an equal. And since the girl hoped to go and stay with her benefactors during the August holiday, Françoise couldn't keep from repeating: 'How she made me laugh! She says, "I'm planning to go home for the holidays." Home, she says! Not only is it not her own place, but they're just people who took her in, and there she is saying "home" as if it really was her home. Poor little girl! How awful it must be not to know what it means to have a home.' Still, if Françoise had only struck up friendships with hotel visitors' maids, who ate with her in the servants' quarters and, seeing her fine lace cap and delicate profile, thought she might be some lady of noble birth forced to live in reduced circumstances or was perhaps motivated by personal attachment to serve as a lady's companion to my grandmother, if in a word Françoise had known only people who didn't belong to the hotel, the inconvenience for us wouldn't have been very great, because she couldn't have kept them from being of use to us, for the simple reason that, regardless of whether she knew them or not, there was no way they could possibly have been of any use to us in any case. But she had also befriended a sommelier, a man in the kitchen, and a floor housekeeper. And the result of this in our daily lives was that Françoise, who upon our arrival, when she didn't yet know anyone, would ring for the slightest thing at the drop of a hat during hours when my grandmother and I wouldn't have dared to do so, and if we made the slightest objection she'd reply: 'We're paying them enough for it, aren't we?' as if she was footing the bill herself, now that she was friends with a personage in the kitchen, which seemed to us to bode well for our comfort if my grandmother or I needed hot-water bottles, Françoise, even if it was an entirely normal time of day, didn't dare ring; she assured us it would be frowned upon because the ovens would have to be relit, or it would disturb the servants at dinner and they would be 'put out'. And she'd conclude with a locution which, despite the uncertain way she uttered it, was quite clear nonetheless and put us patently in the wrong: 'Well, the fact is . . .' We wouldn't insist, for fear of incurring one even worse: 'Why, the very idea!' The long and short of it was that we couldn't have hot water anymore because Françoise had become the friend of the person who was in charge of heating it.

Eventually we too made a friend, despite yet because of my grandmother, for she and Madame de Villeparisis encountered each other one morning in a doorway and were obliged to exchange words, not without first exhibiting signs of surprise and hesitation and performing gestures of withdrawal and uncertainty before finally giving way to polite exclamations and protestations of joy, as in those scenes in Molière where two actors who have been soliloquizing at length, each on his own but a few feet apart, are supposed not to have noticed each other yet, then all of a sudden catch sight of one another, can't believe their eyes, break off what they were saying, then finally start speaking at the same time, with the chorus following the exchange, and end up falling into each other's arms.* After the initial encounter, Madame de Villeparisis tactfully made as if to go on her way, but my grandmother wanted to continue the conversation until lunchtime, eager as she was to find out how Madame de Villeparisis arranged to have her mail delivered earlier than ours and to be served such lovely grilled dishes (for Madame de Villeparisis, who appreciated fine food, had a very poor opinion of the cuisine offered by the hotel, where we were served meals that my grandmother, forever citing Madame de Sévigné, described as being 'sumptuous enough to make you die of hunger'*). And the marquise formed the habit of coming every day, while waiting to be served, to sit with us for a little while in the dining room, insisting that we not rise for her or put ourselves out in any way. We would often linger to chat with her once lunch was over, at that squalid time when the knives are left lying on the tablecloth next to crumpled napkins. As for me, in order to maintain the illusion (which might help me come to like Balbec) that I was on the most far-flung headland in the world, I would try to look far out into the distance, to see nothing but the sea, to seek in it the effects described by Baudelaire,* and would let my gaze fall on our table only on those days when we were served some gigantic fish, some marine monster, which, unlike the knives and forks, was contemporary with the primitive epochs in which life began to surge in the Ocean, in the time of the mythical Cimmerians,* a fish whose body, with its countless vertebrae, its blue and pink veins, had indeed been constructed by Nature, but according to an architectural design, like a polychromatic cathedral of the sea.

Just as a barber, seeing an officer whom he treats with particular respect recognize a customer who has just come in and linger to chat with him, delights at the thought that the two men move in the same circles and can't help but smile as he goes to fetch the shaving mug, since he knows that his establishment doesn't merely perform the vulgar tasks of a simple barber's shop, but has the added advantage of social, even aristocratic pleasures, so Aimé, seeing that Madame de Villeparisis was treating us as old friends, went to fetch our *rince-bouches** with the proudly modest and knowingly discreet smile of a hostess who knows when to leave her guests to themselves. He also called to mind a happy, touched father quietly witnessing the joy of a young couple planning their future together at his table. It was enough for the name of a titled personage to be uttered for Aimé to look happy, unlike Françoise, in whose presence one couldn't say 'Count So-and-So' without her face darkening and her speech becoming dry and curt, which signified that she cherished the nobility not less than Aimé, but more. Françoise, however, had that quality which in others she thought was the worst possible defect: she was proud. She was not of that easy-going, good-natured race to which Aimé belonged. They feel and display true delight when you tell them about something that has occurred which may be of greater or lesser interest, but is new to them and hasn't found its way into the pages of any newspaper. But Françoise didn't want to appear surprised. If you announced in her presence that the Archduke Rudolf*—of whom she'd never heard— was not dead, as was universally assumed, but alive, she'd have replied 'Yes', as if she'd known it for a long time. Moreover, if Françoise couldn't hear the name of an aristocrat without having to repress an angry reaction, even if it was spoken by us (whom she humbly called her 'masters', and to whom she was, for the most part, subservient), this was because the family from which she came occupied in its village a comfortable, independent position, which could be disturbed in the respect it enjoyed only by those same noblemen in whose households an Aimé would have served ever since he was a boy, unless they'd taken him in out of charity. Therefore, in the eyes of Françoise, Madame de Villeparisis should ask forgiveness for being noble. Yet in

France, at any rate, that's precisely the talent, in fact the sole occupation, of lords and ladies. Françoise, after the manner of servants who perpetually gather from their masters' relations with other people fragmentary observations from which they sometimes make faulty deductions, as humans do about the lives of animals, was constantly inferring that we'd been 'slighted', a conclusion that was inspired as much by her excessive love for us as by the pleasure she took in being disagreeable to us. But having observed, without any possible error, the countless acts of consideration shown to us, and even to Françoise herself, by Madame de Villeparisis, Françoise forgave her for being a marquise, and, since she had never ceased to admire her for being one, she preferred her to all the people we knew. The fact was that no one else tried to be so continually nice to us. Whenever my grandmother remarked on a book Madame de Villeparisis was reading, or admired the fruit Madame de Villeparisis had received from a friend, an hour later a footman would come up and deliver the book or fruit to us. Then, the next time we saw her, in answer to our thanks, she'd merely say, as though trying to excuse her gift by some special usefulness it might have: 'It's not a masterpiece, but the papers arrive so late, one must have something to read', or 'It's always wiser at the seaside to have fruit one can be sure of'.

'I don't think I've ever seen you eating oysters,' Madame de Villeparisis said to us (increasing the sense of disgust I felt at the time, for the living flesh of oysters revolted me even more than the viscosity of the jellyfish sullying the Balbec beach); 'they're exquisite on this coast!—Oh, I must tell my maid to fetch your letters at the same time as mine. Did you say your daughter writes to you *every day*? What on earth can you find to say to each other?' My grandmother said nothing, probably out of disdain, for she used to quote the words of Madame de Sévigné to my mother: 'As soon as I've received one letter, I want another at once; I can't breathe until it comes. Few people are worthy of understanding what I feel.' And I was afraid she might apply to Madame de Villeparisis the conclusion: 'I seek out those few, and I avoid the others.'* My grandmother fell back on praising the fruit Madame de Villeparisis had sent us the day before. And they were in fact so fine that the manager, despite his wounded pride caused by our neglect of his fruit bowls, said to me: 'I'm like you, I'm more preferential to fruit than to any other dessert.' My grandmother told her friend that she'd appreciated it all the more because the fruit served at the hotel was usually horrid. 'I can't say,' she went on, 'like Madame de Sévigné, that if we had an urge for bad fruit, we'd have to order it from Paris.' 'Oh yes, you read Madame de Sévigné! I've seen you with her *Letters* ever since your first day here.' (She forgot that she'd never seen my grandmother in the hotel before encountering her in the doorway.) 'Don't you find it a bit much, her constant concern for her daughter? She mentions it too often to be really sincere. It seems forced.' My grandmother thought it pointless to argue, and to avoid having to speak about things she loved with someone incapable of understanding them, she hid, by placing her handbag over it, Madame de Beausergent's *Mémoires*.

If Madame de Villeparisis happened to come upon Françoise at the time (which Françoise called 'the midday') when, wearing a handsome bonnet and an aura of extreme respectability, she was coming downstairs 'to eat with the service', Madame de Villeparisis would stop to ask after us. When Françoise conveyed the marquise's message to us later, with: 'And she said, "Be sure to say hello to them from me"', she'd mimic the voice of Madame de Villeparisis, whose words she thought she was repeating verbatim, though she distorted them no less than Plato distorted the words of Socrates, or Saint John those of Jesus.* Françoise was naturally deeply moved by these attentions. But she didn't believe my grandmother, and thought she was lying in the interests of class (since the wealthy always support each other) when she assured us that Madame de Villeparisis had once been extraordinarily beautiful. It was true that only faint vestiges of this beauty survived, from which it would have been quite impossible, unless one was more of an artist than Françoise, to reconstruct her lost loveliness. For in order to understand how pretty an elderly woman may once have been, one must not only observe, but translate each feature.

'I must remember one day to ask her if I'm mistaken in thinking she's related somehow to the Guermantes,' my grandmother said to me, thereby arousing my indignation. How could I have believed there was a common origin between two names which had entered my consciousness, one through the lowly, shameful door of experience, the other through the golden door of the imagination?

For several days now, we had often seen, driving by in an elegant carriage, tall, beautiful, red-haired, with a slightly prominent nose, the Princesse de Luxembourg, who was spending her holiday for a few weeks in the vicinity. Her barouche* had stopped in front of the hotel; a footman had come in to speak with the manager, returned to the carriage, and reappeared holding some magnificent fruit (which, like the bay itself, combined several seasons in a single basket), with a card bearing the legend *The Princesse de Luxembourg* on which a few words were written in pencil.* For what princely traveller, residing here incognito, could they be intended, those plums that were as blue-green, luminous, and spherical as the encompassing sea was at that moment, those translucent grapes on their dried twig like a bright autumn day, those pears of a celestial ultramarine? It couldn't be my grandmother's friend the princess wanted to visit. The next evening, however, Madame de Villeparisis sent us the bunch of fresh, golden grapes, with some plums and pears that we recognized too, even though the plums, like the sea at dinner time, had turned to mauve, and in the ultramarine of the pears there floated the shapes of a few rosy clouds. A few days later, we met Madame de Villeparisis as we were leaving the symphony concert given every morning down at the beach. Convinced the pieces I'd just heard (the Prelude to *Lohengrin*, the Overture to *Tannhäuser*,* etc.) conveyed the highest truths, I was trying to raise myself up to their level; I plumbed my innermost depths to understand them, and offered up to them the best, most profound parts of my being.

As we were wending our way back to the hotel after the concert, pausing for a moment on the esplanade to exchange a few words with Madame de Villeparisis, who told us that she'd ordered some croque-monsieurs and coddled eggs in cream for us at the hotel, I saw in the distance, coming in our direction, the Princesse de Luxembourg, leaning just slightly on a parasol in such a way as to impart to her tall, wonderful body that slight inclination, to make it trace that arabesque, so prized by women who had been beautiful during the Second Empire and who knew how, with relaxed shoulders, arched backs, swaying hips, and svelte legs, to make their bodies float as languidly as a silken scarf around the armature of an invisible, inflexible rod transfixing it slantwise. She went out for her stroll on the beach every morning, almost at the time when everyone else had finished swimming and was coming back up for lunch, and since her lunch wasn't until half past one, she would return to her villa long after the bathers had abandoned the deserted, torrid esplanade. Madame de Villeparisis introduced my grandmother to her and wanted to introduce me, but had to ask my name, since she didn't remember it. She may never have known it, or else years ago had forgotten the name of the man to whom my grandmother had married her daughter. This name seemed to make a keen impression on Madame de Villeparisis. Meanwhile the Princesse de Luxembourg had shaken our hands and, from time to time, as she stood there chatting with the marquise, she would turn to glance tenderly at my grandmother and myself, with that hint of a kiss we add to our smile when it's intended for a baby with its nanny. Despite her desire not to seem to be enthroned in a sphere above our own, she had probably miscalculated the distance, for her eyes, not properly adjusted, were brimming over with such benevolence that I could imagine her reaching out and patting us like two friendly animals who had stuck their heads out for her through the bars of their cage at the Jardin d'Acclimatation. And immediately, as it happened, this idea of animals at the zoo was reinforced for me. It was that time of day when the esplanade was teeming with strolling vendors loudly hawking cakes, sweets, and pastries. Not knowing quite what to do to show us her goodwill, the princess stopped the first one to come past; all he had left was a single loaf of rye bread, the kind you throw to the ducks. The princess took it and said to me: 'This is for your grandmother.' But she handed it to me, saying with the mere wisp of a smile: 'You can give it to her yourself,' thinking that in this way, with no intermediary between me and the animals, my pleasure would be more complete. Other vendors came over, and she filled my pockets with whatever they had: little packages tied up with string, biscuits, sponge cakes, barley sugar on sticks. 'You should eat some yourself, but give some to your grandmother as well,' she said, and the vendors were paid by the little black servant boy dressed in red satin who followed her everywhere and was the talk of the whole resort. Then she took her leave of Madame de Villeparisis and held her hand out to us with the intention of treating us just as she treated her friend, to show she wasn't above us. But this time, she must have classified us as not quite so lowly in the scale of creatures, for the princess indicated her equality with us to my grandmother by means of that tender and maternal smile you give a little boy when you say goodbye to him as if he were a grown-up. By miraculous evolutionary progress, my grandmother was no longer a duck or an antelope, but was already what Madame Swann would have called a *baby*.* Finally, having said her farewells to us all, the princess resumed her stroll on the sunny esplanade, curving her magnificent form, which, like a snake coiled round a stick, twined round the blue-and-white parasol which she carried furled in her hand. She was my first royal—I say my first, since Princesse Mathilde didn't act like one. The second, as we shall see later on, would astonish me just as much by her graciousness. One aspect of the benevolence of the nobility, kindly intermediaries between kings and commoners, was revealed to me the next day, when Madame de Villeparisis said to us: 'She found you quite charming. She's a woman of sound judgement and she has a kind heart. She's not like so many royals and highnesses—she has a real warmth about her.' And, in a tone of conviction and joy at being able to say so, Madame de Villeparisis added: 'I think she'd be delighted to see you again.'

But on the morning when we left the Princesse de Luxembourg, Madame de Villeparisis had said something to me that impressed me even more, and didn't stem from mere politeness.

'Aren't you the son of the department head at the Ministry?' she asked. 'Well, I hear your father is a charming man. He's having a lovely holiday just now.'

A few days before, we had learned in a letter from Maman that my father and his travelling companion Monsieur de Norpois had lost their luggage.

'It's been found—or rather it was never really lost; let me tell you what happened,' said Madame de Villeparisis, who, without our knowing how, seemed much better informed than we about the details of the trip. 'I think your father is coming home earlier than planned, next week in fact, since he'll probably decide against travelling on to Algeciras.* But he's eager to spend one more day in Toledo, since he's an admirer of one of Titian's pupils*—I forget the name—and that's the best place to see his work.'

And I wondered by what strange chance the impartial telescope through which Madame de Villeparisis observed from afar the nebulous, rudimentary, insignificant movements of the host of people she knew happened to focus on my father through a tiny piece of glass of such powerful magnification that she could see, with such clarity and detail, everything that was pleasant about him, the circumstances that obliged him to return, his difficulties with the border customs, his liking for El Greco, and, by changing the scale of her vision, showed her this single man, looming so large over all the others, like the Jupiter to whom Gustave Moreau, portraying him next to a mere mortal, gave a superhuman stature.*

My grandmother took leave of Madame de Villeparisis so that we could linger for a moment to breathe in the fresh air outside the hotel as we waited for a signal to be given behind the glass partition that our lunch was ready. We heard a commotion. The young mistress of the king of that tropical island, having just finished her swim, was coming back up to the hotel for lunch.

'What an outrage! It's enough to make you want to leave France!' exclaimed the *bâtonnier* furiously as he passed by.

The notary's wife, however, was staring in amazement at the false queen.

'I can't tell you how annoyed I am when Madame Blandais looks at those people like that,' said the *bâtonnier* to the first president. 'It's enough to make me want to slap her. That's just the way to make that sort of riff-raff feel important, and of course all *they* want is for people to pay attention to them. Go and tell her husband to let her know how ridiculous it is. I for one will certainly not go out with them again if they keep gawking at those masqueraders!'

As for the arrival of the Princesse de Luxembourg, whose barouche, on the day she had brought the fruit, had stopped outside the hotel, it had not escaped the notice of the wives of the notary, the *bâtonnier*, and the first president, who had for some time been keen to know whether that Madame de Villeparisis, whom everyone treated with so much respect (of which all these ladies were dying to hear she was unworthy) was a real marquise and not an adventuress. Whenever Madame de Villeparisis crossed the lobby, the first president's wife, who could sniff out questionable women anywhere, would raise her nose from her embroidery and look at her in a such a way that her friends would burst out laughing.

'You know me,' she said proudly, 'I always start out thinking the worst. I won't admit a woman is really married until I've seen her birth certificate and marriage lines. Never you fear, I'll carry out my own little investigation.'

And every day all the ladies would run up to her, laughing and exclaiming: 'We've come for the latest!'

But on the evening of the Princesse de Luxembourg's visit, the first president's wife put a finger to her lips.

'I have news.'

'Oh! Isn't our Madame Poncin wonderful! I've never seen . . . but do tell, what is it?'

'Well, a woman with yellow hair and a ton of rouge and a carriage that reeked of loose morals a mile away—the kind of barouche only *that* sort of woman has—just came to call on the so-called marquise.'

'Ooh la la! Oh my, oh my! You don't say! But that's the same lady we saw, remember, *bâtonnier*? We didn't like the look of her at all but we didn't know she was coming to see the marquise. A woman with a black boy, yes?'

'That's the one.'

'You don't say! You don't know her name?'

'I do, I picked up her card as if by accident: she goes by the alias of the "Princesse de Luxembourg"! As if! That's just too much, having to rub shoulders with a Baronne d'Ange* like that!' The *bâtonnier* quoted Mathurin Régnier and *Macette** to the first president.

It shouldn't be assumed that this misunderstanding was temporary, like those that occur in the second act of a musical comedy only to be cleared up in the final scene. Whenever the Princesse de Luxembourg, a niece both of the King of England and the Emperor of Austria, came to call on Madame de Villeparisis for their carriage outings, they always looked like a pair of those ladies of easy virtue it's difficult to avoid in fashionable watering places. Three-quarters of the gentlemen of the Faubourg Saint-Germain are seen by a large part of the bourgeoisie as dissolute wastrels (which, taken one by one, they sometimes are) who are therefore not to be allowed into proper society. In this, the middle class is too moral, since the failings of those gentlemen would never prevent them from being received with the highest honour in houses where the bourgeoisie will never be welcome. And the gentlemen are so sure that the middle class knows this that they affect a simplicity in their own affairs, disparaging those of their friends who are especially 'on their beam-ends', that the misunderstanding is only made worse. If by chance a gentleman of high society has dealings with the lower middle classes because, being extremely rich, he happens to be director of the leading banking houses, the members of the bourgeoisie, thinking they've finally found a nobleman worthy of being one of their own, would swear he has no connection with the ruined, gambling marquis whom they think is all the more friendless because he's so approachable. And they can't believe it when the duke who is the managing director of the colossal enterprise marries his son to the daughter of said gambling marquis, who nevertheless bears the oldest name in France, just as a sovereign would prefer to have his son marry the daughter of a dethroned king rather than of a current president of the Republic. In other words, the two worlds have as fanciful a view of each other as the inhabitants of the shore at one end of the Bay of Balbec have of the shore at the other end: from Rivebelle you can just barely make out Marcouville l'Orgueilleuse; but even that is deceptive, because you might think the people in Marcouville can see you, whereas from there, the splendours of Rivebelle are almost entirely invisible.

The Balbec doctor, whom we'd summoned for a sudden fever I'd come down with, having decided that I shouldn't stay out all day on the beach in full sunlight during the hot weather, wrote out some prescriptions, which my grandmother received with an outward look of respect in which I immediately recognized her firm resolve not to have any of them filled; she did, however, heed his advice regarding matters of hygiene, and accepted Madame de Villeparisis' offer to take us out for drives in her carriage. I would spend the time before lunch going back and forth from my room to my grandmother's. Her room didn't have a direct view of the sea, as mine did, but it looked out on to three different views: a section of the esplanade, a courtyard, and the surrounding countryside; it was furnished differently from mine, with armchairs embroidered with metallic filigree and pink flowers from which there seemed to emanate the pleasant, fresh odour that met you when you came in. And at that hour when the sun's rays, coming as they did from different exposures and seemingly from different times of day, broke the angles of the wall, projected, alongside the sea's reflection on the chest of drawers, an altar of repose dappled like flowers along a path, suspended on the wainscotting the folded, trembling, warm wings of a brightness ready to resume its flight, and, by the window overlooking the courtyard, warmed like a bath a square of rustic carpet which the sun festooned like a vine, adding to the charm and decorative complexity of the furniture by seeming to pluck the armchairs' silken flowers and loosen their threads, this room where I lingered for a moment before getting dressed for our drive, suggested a prism in which the colours of the light from outside were dispersed, a beehive in which the nectars of the day I was about to taste were separated, scattered, intoxicating, and visible, a garden of hope which dissolved in a shimmer of silver rays and rose petals. But before all this I'd drawn back my curtains, impatient to find out which Sea was playing that morning by the shore like a Nereid.* For none of these

Seas ever stayed the same for more than a day. The next day there would be another, which sometimes resembled it. But I never saw the same one twice.

There were some that were of such rare beauty that, when I saw them, my pleasure was increased even more by surprise. By what privilege, on one morning rather than another, did the window, when opened, reveal to my astonished eyes the nymph Glauconome,* whose lazy beauty, breathing gently, had the misty transparency of an emerald through which I could see the ponderable elements that coloured it? She made the sunshine play, with a smile softened by an invisible mist that was nothing but an empty space hovering about her translucent surface, which was thus made more defined, more striking, like those goddesses a sculptor carves in relief into a block of marble while leaving the rest unpolished. In such a way, with her unique colour, she invited us to drive over those rough dirt roads, from which, seated in Madame de Villeparisis' carriage, we could glimpse, all day long but without ever reaching it, her cool, gentle breathing.

Madame de Villeparisis would have her horses harnessed early, so that we could have time to go all the way to Saint-Mars-le-Vêtu, or the rocks of Quetteholme, or to some other goal which, for such a slow vehicle, was distant enough to require the whole day. In my joy at the thought of the long drive we were about to take, I would hum some tune I'd recently heard as I paced back and forth waiting for Madame de Villeparisis to be ready. If it was Sunday, her carriage wouldn't be the only one outside the hotel; quite a few hired cabs would be waiting there, not only for the people Madame de Cambremer had invited to her château at Féterne, but for those who, rather than staying put like children being punished, declared that Sundays were exceedingly dull at Balbec, and immediately after lunch would rush off to hide in some nearby resort or visit one of the local sights. And so, whenever Madame de Blandais was asked if she'd been to the Cambremers', she'd reply brusquely: 'No, we went to the waterfalls at Le Bec', as if that was the sole reason she hadn't spent the day at Féterne. And the *bâtonnier* would reply charitably: 'I envy you—I wish we could have changed places. The falls are much more interesting.'

Beside the carriages, in front of the portico where I was waiting, planted there like a rare species of shrub, stood a young pageboy who was just as striking for the singular harmony of his hair colour as for his plant-like epidermis. Inside, in the lobby, which corresponded to the narthex or antechamber for catechumens in Romanesque churches,* and which could be entered by people who weren't staying at the hotel, the 'outside' page's counterparts didn't do much more work than he, but at least executed a few more movements. They probably helped with cleaning in the mornings. But in the afternoon, they would merely stand there like chorus members who, even when they're not singing, remain onstage to make up the numbers. The general manager, the one who filled me with such dread, was planning on increasing their number considerably the following year, for he was a man who could see 'the big picture'. And his decision greatly distressed the manager of the hotel, who regarded all these boys as 'obstructors', by which he meant that they got in everyone's way and served no purpose. At least, between lunch and dinner, between the entrances and exits of the guests, they filled the void in the action, like Madame de Maintenon's charges who, dressed as young Jews, provided an interlude whenever Esther or Joad left the stage.* But the 'outside' page, with his delicate hues and his tall, willowy figure, standing not far from where I was waiting for the marquise, maintained an immobility which included melancholy as well, for his older brothers had left the hotel for more brilliant careers, and he felt lonely on this foreign soil. Finally Madame de Villeparisis arrived. Tending to her carriage and helping her into it ought perhaps to have counted among the page's duties. But he knew that a person who brings her own servants with her expects them to wait on her and doesn't generally give many tips in a hotel, and that the nobles of the old Faubourg Saint-Germain behave in the same way. Madame de Villeparisis belonged to both these categories. The arborescent pageboy concluded that he could expect nothing from the marquise, and, leaving the head waiter and her own maid to settle her in with her things, he dreamed sadly of the enviable lot of his brothers and preserved his vegetal immobility.

We set off; a little while after turning past the train station, we would come to a country road which soon became as familiar to me as the roads in Combray, from the sharp bend where it wended its way between charming orchards to the turn where we left it, with its ploughed fields on either side. In the midst of these we could see here and there an apple tree, which, though denuded of its flowers and bearing no more than a sprig of pistils, was enough to delight me because I recognized those inimitable leaves whose wide expanse, like the ceremonial carpet just after a wedding, had been swept quite recently by the white satin train of their blushing flowers.

How often in Paris, in May of the following year, would I buy a branch of apple blossoms from the florist and then spend the night in the presence of its flowers, which spread the same creamy essence that still sprinkled its foam on the leaf buds; between their white blooms it looked as if the florist himself, out of generosity towards me, out of a taste for invention and ingenious contrast as well, had added on either side, as a bonus, a fetching pink bud; I would gaze at these blossoms, place them under my lamp—for so long that I was often still there when the dawn cast the same red glow on them that it must at the same time have been bestowing on Balbec—and I'd try to transport them in my imagination back to that road, to multiply them, to spread them out within the frame prepared for them, on the ready canvas, of those orchards whose contours I knew by heart, which I so longed to see, which one day I would see, again, at the moment when, with the magnificent enthusiasm of genius, spring covered their canvas with its colours.

Before getting into the carriage, I'd composed the seascape I was going to seek, which I hoped to see with Baudelaire's 'radiant sunbeams',* and which at Balbec I could glimpse only in discrete sections between so many vulgar eyesores that had no place in my dream—swimmers, bathing machines, pleasure yachts. But when, Madame de Villeparisis' carriage having reached the top of a hill, I could make out the sea between the leaves of trees, then, probably because it was so far away, those present-day details which had placed it as it were outside nature and history disappeared, and, as I watched the waves, I could try to think they were the same ones that Leconte de Lisle describes in his *Oresteia*, when 'like birds of prey taking flight at the break of day', the long-haired warriors of heroic Hellas 'with a hundred thousand oars pound the waves of the bay'.* But I wasn't close enough to the sea for it to look alive; it looked fixed in place, and I could no longer feel the power beneath its colours, spread like those of a painting among the leaves, where it looked as insubstantial as the sky, only of a darker hue.

Madame de Villeparisis, seeing how I loved churches, promised that we'd visit a few, especially the one in Carqueville 'quite hidden beneath its old ivy', she said with a movement of her hand which seemed tastefully to envelop the absent façade in an invisible, delicate tracery of leaves. With little descriptive gestures like this, Madame de Villeparisis would often find just the right way to define the charm and distinctive features of a historic building, always avoiding technical terms, but incapable of hiding her thorough knowledge of the subject. She seemed to be trying to excuse herself for this expertise by the fact that one of her father's châteaux, the one in which she'd been brought up, was located in a region where there were several churches in the same style as those around Balbec, so that it would have been unpardonable if she hadn't developed a taste for architecture, especially since this château was the finest example of Renaissance style. But as it was also an actual museum, and as, moreover, Chopin and Liszt had played there, Lamartine recited poetry,* and all the artists famous for an entire century had inscribed reflections, noted down melodies, drawn sketches in the family album, Madame de Villeparisis, whether from self-effacement, good breeding, actual modesty, or lack of a philosophical turn of mind, offered only this purely material origin for her knowledge of all these arts, and in the end seemed to regard painting, music, literature, and philosophy as the necessary accompaniment of a young lady brought up in the most aristocratic manner in an illustrious building listed as a national monument. It was almost as if no other paintings existed for her except those that were inherited. She was pleased that my grandmother admired a necklace she wore, which showed over her dress. It appeared in the portrait of one of her ancestors, by Titian, which had never left the family. And so one could be certain it was genuine. She didn't want to hear about paintings bought heaven knew where, by some Croesus;* she was already convinced they were forgeries and had no desire to see them. We knew that she herself painted watercolours of flowers, and my grandmother, who had heard them praised, mentioned them to her. Madame de Villeparisis modestly changed the subject, but without showing any more surprise or pleasure than a famous artist for whom compliments were a matter of course. She merely said it was a delightful pastime because, even if the flowers sprouting from the brush weren't remarkable, at least painting them allowed you to live in the company of real flowers, whose beauty, especially when you were obliged to look at them more closely in order to portray them, never grew wearisome. But in Balbec Madame de Villeparisis was taking a little break so that she could rest her eyes.

We were taken aback, my grandmother and I, to see how much more 'liberal' she was than even the majority of the middle class. Madame de Villeparisis was surprised that people were scandalized by the expulsions of the Jesuits,* saying that it had always been done, even under the monarchy, even in Spain. She defended the Republic, and criticized its anticlericalism only in this respect: 'I'd be just as upset if I was prevented from going to Mass if I wanted to as if I were forced to go if I didn't!' She even gave vent to sayings like: 'Oh, what does today's aristocracy really amount to?' or 'For me, a man who doesn't work doesn't count!', perhaps only because she sensed how scandalous, juicy, and memorable they became when uttered from her lips.

Upon hearing these progressive opinions—though they never went so far as to approach socialism, anathema to Madame de Villeparisis—so openly and frequently expressed precisely by one of those people whose intelligence we dare not, with our scrupulous and cautious impartiality, offend by condemning conservative ideas, we were not far, my grandmother and I, from believing that in our pleasant companion were to be found the measure and pattern of truth in all things. We took her at her word when she passed judgement on her Titians, the colonnade of her château, Louis-Philippe's wit and conversational skill.* But—like those scholars who dazzle us when they're holding forth on Egyptian painting or Etruscan inscriptions, yet say such banal things about modern literary works that we wonder whether we haven't overrated the interest of their specific area of expertise, since we can't see in it the same mediocrity of mind they must also have brought to their vapid essays on Baudelaire—Madame de Villeparisis, when I questioned her about Chateaubriand, Balzac, or Victor Hugo, all of whom had once been guests of her parents and had been glimpsed by her, chuckled at my admiration, told anecdotes about them that were as mordant as those she'd just been recounting about great aristocrats or statesmen, and took a severe view of these writers, precisely because they had been lacking in that modesty, that self-effacement, that sober art which confines itself to a single precise stroke without overdoing it, and which shuns above all else the absurdity of grandiloquence, because they had lacked the propriety, the qualities of measured judgement and simplicity, which she had been taught were the marks of genuine worth; and it was obvious that she felt no qualms about regarding those writers as inferior to the men who, by virtue of those very qualities, might well have upstaged a Balzac, a Hugo, a Vigny in a drawing room, an academy, or a cabinet, men like Molé, Fontanes, Vitrolles, Bersot, Pasquier, Lebrun, Salvandy, or Daru.*

'It's like those novels by Stendhal* which you seem so taken with. He'd have been quite surprised to hear you speaking so highly of him. My father, who used to see him at Monsieur Mérimée's*—now *there* was a man of talent—often told me that Beyle (that was his real name) was frightfully vulgar, but a good dinner companion, quite witty, and never bragged about his books. But I'm sure you've seen for yourself how he shrugged off the excessive praise Monsieur de Balzac heaped on him. At least in that respect he knew how to behave.'

She had the autographs of all these great men, and, based on the special relationships her family had with them, seemed to think that her judgement of them was more correct than that of young people like myself who had been unable to meet them. 'I think I'm well placed to talk about them, since they came to my father's house; and, as Monsieur Sainte-Beuve,* who was a highly intelligent man, used to say, you should take the word of people who saw them up close and were able to judge their worth accurately.'

Sometimes, as the carriage was climbing up a steep road with ploughed land on either side, a few hesitant cornflowers, just like the ones in Combray, would follow in our wake, making the fields more real, adding to them a stamp of authenticity like the precious tiny flower with which some of the old masters used to sign their paintings. Soon the horses would outdistance them, but after a few paces we would glimpse another, which as it waited for us had pricked up its azure star in front of us in the grass; some were so bold as to stand right next to the road, and a whole constellation would begin to take shape, formed from my distant memories and these tame flowers.

We would go down the hill; and we would encounter, climbing up on foot, or on a bicycle, or in a horse-drawn cart or carriage, one of those lovely creatures—flowers of the beautiful day, but not like the flowers of the field, for each of these beings harboured something none of the others had, which would prevent us from satisfying the desire she aroused in us with any of her counterparts—a farmgirl leading her cow or sprawled on a wagon, a shopkeeper's daughter out for a stroll, or some fashionable young lady sitting on the back seat of a landau, facing her parents. Bloch, of course, had opened a new era and changed the meaning of life for me the day he told me that the dreams I'd indulged in during my walks along the Méséglise way, when I wished some peasant girl would pass by whom I could take in my arms, were not fantasies with no connection to anything outside myself, but that all the girls one met, from villagers to young ladies, were only too willing to fulfil similar desires. And even if, now that I was ill and couldn't go out on my own, I'd never be able to make love to them, I was happy all the same, like a child born in a prison or a hospital who, having long believed that the human organism can digest nothing but dry bread or medication, has suddenly learned that peaches, apricots, and grapes are not simply countryside ornaments but delicious and digestible food. Even if his jailer or nurse doesn't allow him to pick these beautiful fruits, the world nevertheless seems a better place to him, and existence more merciful. For any desire seems more attractive, more reassuringly reliable, when we know that the reality outside us is compatible with it, even if for us it's not realizable. And we think more joyfully about a life in which—provided we set aside for a moment the thought of the little accidental, specific obstacle that prevents us personally from doing so—we can picture ourselves fulfilling that desire. As to the pretty girls who passed by, from the day I knew that their cheeks could be kissed, I'd become curious about their minds. And the universe had become more interesting.

Madame de Villeparisis' carriage moved quickly. I'd only glimpsed the girl who was heading in our direction; and yet—since the beauty of people isn't like the beauty of things, and we feel it belongs to a unique being, endowed with consciousness and free will—as soon as her individuality, with its unseeable mind, its desires unknown to me, resolved itself into a tiny, miniaturized, but complete image, in the depths of her absent-minded gaze, immediately, like the mysterious response of pistils ready for pollen, I could feel stirring within me the beginnings—just as indistinct and minuscule—of the desire not to let this girl go by without her consciousness becoming aware of my person, without my preventing her desires from turning to someone else, without my entering her daydreams and seizing hold of her heart. But our carriage was drawing away, the beautiful girl was already behind us, and since she had formed of me none of the notions that constitute an individual, her eyes, which had barely seen me, had already forgotten me. Was it because I had only glimpsed her that I found her so beautiful? Perhaps. For one thing, the impossibility of pulling up beside a woman, the risk of not finding her again some other day, suddenly give her the same charm a place acquires when illness or poverty prevents us from visiting it, or the struggle to which we will eventually succumb gives to the gloomy days that are left to us to live. So that, were it not for habit, life might seem delightful to those under constant threat of death—that is to say, everyone. For another thing, if our imagination is stirred by desire for what we cannot possess, its flight is not brought up short by a clearly perceived reality, in these encounters where the charms of the passing girl are generally in direct proportion to the swiftness of the passage. So long as night is falling and the carriage is moving swiftly, in the countryside, or in a town, there isn't a female torso—mutilated like an ancient sculpture by the speed carrying us off and the twilight drowning it—that doesn't aim at our heart, at every street corner, from within every shop, the arrows of Beauty, that Beauty of which we're sometimes tempted to wonder whether, in this world, it isn't anything more than the makeweight added to a fragmentary, fleeting passer-by by an imagination overwrought with regret.*

If I'd been able to get out and talk to the girl we were passing, perhaps I'd have been disillusioned by some defect in her complexion which hadn't been visible from the carriage. (In which case, any effort I made to delve into her life would have seemed suddenly impossible. For beauty is a series of hypotheses which ugliness contradicts by barring the way that we were just beginning to glimpse as it led into the unknown.) Perhaps a single word she said, or a smile, might have provided me with an unexpected key or clue, enabling me to read her expression and her movements, which might immediately have become banal. That's possible, for never in my life have I met girls who were as desirable as on those occasions when I was with some sententious person whom I couldn't shake off, despite repeated attempts: a few years after this first visit of mine to Balbec, as I was driving through Paris with a friend of my father's and glimpsed a woman walking quickly in the dark, I thought it was unreasonable, for the sake of propriety, to lose my share of happiness in what is probably the only life we have, and so, leaping to the ground without an apology, I set off in search of the unknown girl, lost her at a crossroads, found her again on another street, and finally fetched up, completely out of breath, beneath a street lamp, face to face with old Madame Verdurin, whom I'd been avoiding everywhere and who, overjoyed and surprised, exclaimed: 'Oh! how sweet of you to run all that way just to say hello!'

That year in Balbec, whenever we passed these girls, I'd assure my grandmother and Madame de Villeparisis that I had such a bad headache that it would be much better for me to go home alone on foot. But they would refuse to let me get out. And so I added the beautiful girl (much more difficult to find again than a historic building, for she was nameless and mobile) to the collection of all those whom I'd promised myself to see up close. I did happen to see one of them again, however, in such a way that I thought I'd be able to recognize her later. She was a milkmaid who came from a farm to bring cream to the hotel. I thought she recognized me too, and she did in fact look at me with an attentiveness that might perhaps have been caused only by my own surprise at seeing her. The next day, after I'd been resting all morning, when Françoise came in to open the curtains at noon, she handed me a letter that had been dropped off for me at the hotel. I knew no one in Balbec. There was no doubt in my mind that the letter was from the milkmaid. Alas, it was only from Bergotte; since he was passing through, he'd tried to see me, but on hearing I was asleep, he'd left me a charming note which the lift-boy slipped into an envelope and addressed in a hand which I'd thought was the milkmaid's. I was crestfallen, and the idea that it was much rarer and more flattering to receive a letter from Bergotte didn't console me in the least for the fact that it wasn't from the milkmaid. As for that particular girl, I never saw her again, or any of the others I'd glimpsed only from Madame de Villeparisis' carriage. Seeing and then losing all of these girls increased the agitated state in which I was living, and I found some wisdom in those philosophers who advise us to limit our desires (if, that is, they mean our desire for people, for that's the only kind that can lead to anxiety, linked as it is to an unknown sentient being. To assume they mean desire for wealth would be too absurd.) Yet I was inclined to think that there was something lacking in this wisdom, for I told myself that these encounters made me find even more beautiful a world which caused to grow along all the country roads flowers at once unique and common, fleeting treasures of the day, blessings of our outing, my enjoyment of which had been prevented only by contingent circumstances which might not always recur, and which created a new zest for life.

But perhaps, by hoping that one day, when I had more freedom, I might find similar girls on other roads, I was already beginning to distort the focused desire to live with a particular woman one has found pretty, and by the mere fact that I was admitting the possibility of deliberately arousing desire, I had implicitly recognized its illusory nature.

On the day that Madame de Villeparisis took us to Carqueville and the ivy-covered church she had spoken of which, built on a hillock, dominated the village and its river, still with its little bridge from the Middle Ages, my grandmother, thinking I'd rather be alone to observe the building, suggested to her friend that they take tea at the pastry-cook's in the village square, which we could see clearly and which, beneath its golden patina, seemed like another part of an ancient whole. We agreed I should meet them there later. In the mass of foliage I saw before me, in order to recognize a church I had to make a real effort to keep in mind the very concept of a church; in fact, as happens with students who are better able to grasp the meaning of a sentence when, by translating it or discussing it, they're obliged to divest it of the forms to which they're accustomed, the concept of a church, which as a rule I scarcely needed when faced with steeples that were recognizable in themselves, I was constantly forced to summon up so as not to forget that the arch in a clump of ivy was that of an ogival window, that a protrusion of leaves was due to the bulge of a capital.* But then a little breeze came up and sent a quiver through the mobile portico, which rippled and trembled like a stream of light; the leaves unfurled against each other; and, shivering, the caress of the arboreal façade made its columns shimmer and undulate.

As I was leaving the church, I saw by the old bridge some village girls who, probably because it was a Sunday, were standing there in their best clothes, hailing the boys passing by. Not as well dressed as the others, but seeming somehow superior to them—for she scarcely responded to what they said to her—and looking more serious and determined than they, was a tall girl who, dangling her legs from the parapet of the bridge, had in front of her a little bucket full of fish which she'd probably just caught. She had tanned skin and eyes that were gentle but looked scornfully around her, and a small, delicate, charming nose. My gaze rested on her skin, and my lips would readily have followed suit. But it wasn't only her body I'd have liked to possess; it was also the person who lived inside it, for whom there is only one kind of touch, which is to attract her attention, and only one kind of penetration, which is to awaken a thought in her.

But the inner self of the beautiful fisher-girl seemed still closed to me; I doubted that I'd entered it, even after I'd glimpsed my own image furtively reflected in the mirror of her gaze, following a refractive index which was as unknown to me as if I'd placed myself in the visual field of a deer. But just as I'd rather my lips gave pleasure to hers rather than take it from them, so I'd have liked the idea of myself entering this being and taking hold there to bring me not merely her attention, but her admiration and desire, and to force her to keep a memory of me until I could see her again. Meanwhile I could see not far away the square where Madame de Villeparisis' carriage would be waiting. I didn't have a second to lose; and already I could sense that the girls were beginning to laugh on seeing me hovering there. I had five francs in my pocket. I took them out, and before explaining to the beautiful girl the errand I was giving her, I held the coin up to her eyes for a moment, so that she'd pay more attention to me.

'Since you seem to be from here,' I said, 'would you be so kind as to deliver a message for me? I'd like you to go to a pastry-cook's which I hear is in a square, but I'm not sure where exactly—a carriage is waiting for me there. Oh, wait! Just to be quite sure, ask if it's the carriage of the Marquise de Villeparisis. But you can't mistake it, it has two horses.'

That was what I wanted her to know, so that she'd think highly of me. But no sooner had I uttered the words 'Marquise' and 'two horses' than I experienced a wave of relief. I felt the fisher-girl would remember me; and I felt a dissipation, not just of my fear that I wouldn't be able to find her again, but of part of my desire to do so. It seemed to me that I had just touched her person with invisible lips, and that I had pleased her. And this forcible capture of her mind, this disembodied possession of her, had stripped away her mystery just as much as physical possession does.

We drove down towards Hudimesnil; all of a sudden I was flooded with a profound happiness the like of which I hadn't often felt since Combray, a happiness similar to the one produced by, among other things, the steeples of Martinville.* But this time it remained incomplete. I'd just seen, set back from the cambered road we were following, three trees which must have served as an entrance to a shaded lane, and which made a pattern that I wasn't seeing for the first time; I couldn't manage to recall the place from which they had been, as it were, removed, but I sensed it had been familiar to me once; and as my mind lurched between some distant year and the present moment, Balbec and its surroundings wavered, and I wondered whether this entire outing wasn't fictional, Balbec a place I'd never visited except in my imagination, Madame de Villeparisis a character in a novel, and the three old trees the reality you rediscover when you lift your eyes from the book you were reading, a book describing an environment into which you'd come to believe you had in fact been transported.

I looked at the three trees; I could see them clearly, but my mind felt they were concealing something it couldn't grasp, like those things placed so far away that when we reach out our arm, our outstretched fingers merely brush against their surface but grasp only thin air. And so we take a deep breath for a moment before we fling our arm forward with renewed vigour and try to extend our reach. But in order for my mind to collect itself in this way and gather momentum, I needed to be alone. How I'd have liked to wander off as I used to on my walks by the Guermantes way when I broke away from my parents! It even seemed imperative I do so now. I recognized that kind of pleasure which, though it requires a certain amount of effort on the part of the mind, dissipates the allure of the laziness that would incline us to give it up. This pleasure, the object of which I could only sense, and which I myself had to create, I felt only on rare occasions, but on each occasion it seemed to me that the things that had occurred in the meantime were of scant importance, and that by clinging to the reality of that pleasure alone, I could finally start a true life. I placed my hand over my eyes for a moment so that I could close them without Madame de Villeparisis noticing. I remained like that, not thinking of anything, and then, when my thoughts were gathered and renewed, I leapt even further forward towards the trees, or rather further inward, towards the place where I could see them inside me. Again I sensed behind them the same object, known yet vague, which I couldn't bring nearer. And yet as the carriage advanced, I could see all three of them coming closer. Where had I seen them before? There was no place around Combray where a lane opened in this way. Nor was there any room for such a lane in the site they reminded me of, the German countryside I'd visited one year with my grandmother to take the waters. Must I suppose that they came from years that were already so far removed from my present life that the landscape surrounding them had been completely obliterated from my memory and that, like those passages we're suddenly moved to find again in a book we thought we'd never read before, they alone were surfacing from the forgotten book of my earliest childhood? Or did they belong only to those dream landscapes, always the same, at least to me for whom their strange appearance was only the objectification in my sleep of the effort I'd been making during the day, either to fathom the mystery of a place which I felt concealed something more behind its outward appearance, as I'd so often experienced along the Guermantes way, or to try to reintroduce this mystery into a place I'd longed to know, but which, as soon as I came to know it, had seemed merely superficial, like Balbec? Might they be nothing but an entirely fresh image from a dream of the night before, but already so hazy that it seemed to be coming from much further away? Or rather had I never in fact seen them before, and were they concealing behind them, like those trees or tufts of grass I'd seen by the Guermantes way, a meaning that was just as obscure, just as difficult to grasp, as a remote past, so that, while they seemed to be urging me to investigate an idea, I thought I had to recognize a memory? Or else were they not even hiding any thoughts, and was it merely my tired eyes that made me see double in time as we sometimes see double in space? I didn't know. And yet they kept coming towards me; perhaps they were a mythical apparition, a ring of witches or Norns offering to tell me their oracles.* I thought rather that they were ghosts from the past, beloved companions from my childhood, deceased friends who were invoking our shared memories. Like shades, they seemed to be asking me to take them with me, to bring them back to life. In their naïve, passionate gesticulations, I recognized the powerless regret of a beloved friend who has lost the use of speech and feels that he can't tell us what he wants, and that we won't be able to guess. Soon, at a crossroads, the carriage left them behind. It was taking me far from what I believed was the sole truth, from what would have made me truly happy; it was like my life.

I watched the trees move further away, waving their desperate arms, seeming to say: What you fail to learn from us today, you will never know. If you let us drop back into the depths of this path from which we were striving to reach you, a whole part of yourself which we were bringing to you will fall forever into nothingness. And in fact, though later on I did once again find the sort of pleasure and anxiety I had just felt, and though one evening—too late, but then for all time— I attained it, I never found out what those trees had wanted to convey to me, or where I'd seen them before. And when, the carriage having turned a corner, I could no longer see them behind me, as Madame de Villeparisis was asking me why I was looking so pensive, I was as sad as if I had just lost a friend, or felt something die in myself, or betrayed the dead, or denied a god.

It was time to think about making our way home. Madame de Villeparisis, who had a certain feeling for nature, not as sensitive as my grandmother's but able to recognize, even apart from museums and aristocratic homes, the simple and majestic beauty of certain ancient things, told the coachman to take the old road to Balbec, little used, but planted with old elm trees which we found very fine.

After we'd become familiar with this old road, for a change we'd return (unless we'd taken it on the way out) on another which went through the woods of Chantereine and Canteloup. The invisibility of countless birds calling to each other quite close to us in the trees produced the same restful feeling one has when one closes one's eyes. Chained to my back seat like Prometheus to his rock, I listened to my Oceanids.* And when I chanced to glimpse one of these birds flitting from one leaf to the shelter of another, there was so little apparent connection between it and these songs that I didn't think it possible that they could spring from this tiny fluttering body, startled and expressionless.

This road was similar to many others of its kind in France, climbing up a rather steep slope, then descending for some while. At that particular time, I didn't find it especially charming; I was simply happy to be going home. But afterwards it became a frequent source of joy for me, by remaining in my memory like a wellspring to which all similar roads I would take later on over the course of a walk or drive would immediately and seamlessly connect and, because of it, would communicate directly with my heart. For as soon as the carriage or motor car turned into one of these roads, which would seem to be the continuation of the road I'd travelled along with Madame de Villeparisis, what my awareness would focus on, as if it were in my most recent past, would be (all the intervening years having fallen away) the impressions I'd received from these late afternoons, on these outings near Balbec, when the leaves smelled fragrant, the mist was rising, and, beyond the next village, one could glimpse the setting sun through the trees, as if it were merely the next location on the road, wooded, distant, unable to be reached that evening. Linked to the impressions I was experiencing now in another place, on a similar road, wrapped up in all the attendant sensations—the ability to breathe freely, curiosity, indolence, appetite, lightness of heart—which went with them, excluding all others, these impressions would be reinforced, would take on the consistency of a particular type of pleasure, almost a framework for living, which I rarely had the luck to find again, but in which the awakening of memories blended the reality my senses could perceive with enough recalled, dreamt-of, elusive reality for these regions I was travelling through to give me, not just an aesthetic experience, but a desire, exalted yet fleeting, to live there forever. How many times since then has the mere whiff of fragrant leaves made me see the act of sitting in a folding seat opposite Madame de Villeparisis, passing the Princesse de Luxembourg as she waved from her carriage, going back to dine at the Grand-Hôtel, as one of those ineffable pleasures which neither present nor future can give back to us, and which we taste only once in life.

Often night would have fallen before we'd returned. Shyly, indicating the moon in the sky to Madame de Villeparisis, I would quote some fine phrase by Chateaubriand or Vigny or Victor Hugo: 'She spread the ancient secret of melancholy' or 'weeping like Diana beside her fountains' or 'The shadows were nuptial, august, and solemn'.*

'And you like that, do you?' she'd ask me. ' "Brilliant", you say? I must say, I'm always surprised to see how people these days take seriously things which these gentlemen's friends, though fully aware of their merits, were the first to laugh at. People weren't so liberal with the word "brilliant" as they are today, when if you tell a writer merely that he has talent, he takes that as an insult! You quote a fine phrase by Monsieur de Chateaubriand on moonlight. You'll see why I have my reasons to bristle at it. Monsieur de Chateaubriand would often visit my father. He was quite pleasant when you were alone with him, because then he was simple and amusing, but as soon as there were others present, he began showing off and became ridiculous; when my father was in the room, he claimed he'd flung his resignation in the King's face and led the voting in the Conclave of Cardinals, forgetting that he'd asked my father to beg the King to take him back, and that my father had heard him make the most absurd predictions about the papal election.* The one to listen to about that famous Conclave was Monsieur de Blacas,* who was quite a different sort of man from Monsieur de Chateaubriand. As to those lines about moonlight, they simply became a catchphrase at home. Whenever the moon was shining over the château, if there was some new guest, we'd suggest he take Monsieur de Chateaubriand out for a stroll after dinner. When they returned, my father never failed to take the guest aside, and would ask: "So, was Monsieur de Chateaubriand eloquent?"

"Yes, indeed!" "He talked about the moonlight?" "Yes, how did you know?" "And did he not say . . ." and he'd cite the phrase. "Yes, but how in the world . . .?" "And didn't he also talk about moonlight in the Roman countryside?" "But you're a magician!" My father wasn't a magician, but Monsieur de Chateaubriand was always happy to trot out the same well-rehearsed speech.'

At the mention of Vigny, she burst out laughing.

'He's the one who said: "I am the Comte Alfred de Vigny." Whether you are a count or you aren't is of no importance whatsoever!'

Yet perhaps she thought it might be of some importance, for she added:

'First of all, I'm not at all sure he *was* one, and even if he was, he was of very low stock, that gentleman with his "nobleman's coat of arms" in his verses. How tasteful and interesting that is to a reader! He's just like Musset, a simple bourgeois from Paris, who went on about "the golden hawk on my helmet's crest". A real aristocrat would never say such a thing. At least Musset had talent as a poet. But aside from *Cinq-Mars** I've never been able to read Monsieur de Vigny, it's so boring the book just slips from my fingers. Monsieur Molé, who had all the wit and tact that Monsieur de Vigny lacked, put him in his place in his welcome speech at the Académie française. What's that, you don't know his speech? It's a masterpiece of sly impertinence!'

She reproached Balzac, whom she was surprised to find her nephews admired, for having presumed to portray a society 'to which he was not even admitted', and so his descriptions were riddled with implausible details. As for Victor Hugo, she told us that her father, Monsieur de Bouillon, had been able to attend the premiere of *Hernani** thanks to some friends, but he couldn't bear to stay to the end, so ridiculous did he find the lines of that talented but overblown writer who acquired the title of 'Great Poet' only as the result of a bargain, as recompense for the self-interested partiality he professed for the dangerous deviations of the socialists.

We could now make out the hotel, with its lights that had looked so hostile on the evening of our arrival, but that now seemed gentle and protective, heralding the warmth of home. And when the carriage pulled up at the door, the concierge, bellboys, and lift-boy—all grouped together on the steps to receive us, eager, simple, vaguely anxious because of our lateness—had become familiar, joining the ranks of those beings who change so many times over the course of our lives, as we ourselves change, but in whom, when they are for a brief time the mirror of our habits, we are happy to feel ourselves faithfully and amicably reflected. We prefer them to friends we haven't seen for a long time, since they contain more of what we are now. Only the 'outside' pageboy, having been exposed to the sun all day, had been brought indoors to protect him from the evening chill, and swaddled in woollen garments which, combined with the reddish effulgence of his hair and the curiously pink bloom of his cheeks, called to mind, as he stood in the middle of the glassed-in lobby, a greenhouse plant being protected against the cold. We'd get out of the carriage, helped by many more servants than were necessary, but they sensed the importance of the scene and felt obliged to play a role in it. I was always famished. And so, often, so as not to delay dinner, I wouldn't go up to my room (which had ended up becoming so truly my own that to see again the long violet curtains and the low bookcases was to find myself alone with myself, that self of which things, like people, offered a reflected image), and so we'd all wait together in the lobby for the head waiter to announce that dinner was served. This was another opportunity for us to listen to Madame de Villeparisis.

'We're imposing on you,' my grandmother said.

'Not at all, I'm only too delighted, it's such a pleasure!' her friend would reply with an affectionate smile, intoning her words in a melodious drawl which contrasted with her usual simplicity.

The fact was that at those times she was not natural; she was remembering her upbringing, the aristocratic mannerisms a great lady must assume to show the middle class that she's happy to be with them, and that she doesn't look down on them. The only time she lacked real politeness was when she was excessively polite; for then one could recognize the occupational habit of a lady from the Faubourg Saint-Germain who, always seeing in certain bourgeois people the discontent she was bound to cause eventually, eagerly takes advantage of any opportunity which allows her, in the ledger of her friendship with them, to register a balance which will presently allow her to debit them the dinner or reception to which she will not invite them. And so, since the spirit of her caste had long ago had its indelible effect on her, and was unaware of the fact that circumstances had changed, people were different, and that in Paris she'd like to see us often at her house, she felt impelled, as if the time granted her to be friendly was brief, to multiply the occasions, while we were in Balbec, for her to send us roses or melons, lend us books, take us for rides in her carriage, and shower us with effusive words. In this way—as much as the dazzling brilliance of the beach, the multicoloured glints and undersea glimmers of the bedrooms, as much even as the riding lessons that transformed the shopkeepers' sons into godlike Alexanders of Macedonia*—the daily friendly overtures of Madame de Villeparisis, and the temporary, holiday ease with which my grandmother accepted them, have remained in my memory as typifying the life of seaside resorts.

'Give them your coats so they can be taken upstairs.'

My grandmother handed them to the manager, and, because of the kindnesses he had shown me, I was distressed by this lack of consideration, which seemed to wound him.

'I do believe the gentleman is hurt,' said the marquise. 'He probably thinks he's too high and mighty to take your wraps. I remember the Duc de Nemours,* when I was still quite little, coming into the apartment of my father, who was living on the top floor of the Bouillon château, with a thick bundle of letters and newspapers under his arm. I can still see the prince in his blue suit standing under the lintel of our door, which had lovely woodwork—I think it was by Bagard*—you know those delicate laths that are so soft the cabinetmaker sometimes shaped them into little bows and flowers, like ribbons tying up a bouquet. "Here, Cyrus," he said to my father, "your concierge gave me this for you. He said to me: 'Since you're going to visit Monsieur le Comte, it saves me the bother of climbing the stairs—just be careful not to break the string.'" Now that you've got rid of your things, come and sit down—here, take this armchair,' she said to my grandmother as she took her by the hand.

'Oh, not that one, if you don't mind! It's too small for two, but too big just for me, I'd feel uncomfortable in it.'

'That reminds me of another armchair, just like this one, that I had for a long time but finally had to get rid of because it had been given to my mother by the unfortunate Duchesse de Praslin.* My mother, even though she was the most unassuming person in the world, still had old-fashioned ideas which were already starting not to make sense to me; at first she didn't want to be introduced to Madame de Praslin, who at the time was only Mademoiselle Sebastiani,* while the latter, since she was a duchess, thought it wasn't her place to arrange an introduction. And really,' added Madame de Villeparisis, forgetting she wasn't supposed to care about such subtle distinctions, 'even if she *had* been Madame de Choiseul,* there was some basis for her claim. The Choiseuls are of the highest stock; they're descended from a sister of Louis "the Fat",* and were once true sovereigns in Bassigny. I'll admit that we trump them in marriages and distinctions, but in terms of lineage, our rank is almost the same. And so this question of precedence led to some amusing incidents, such as a luncheon that was served a whole hour late because neither lady could let herself be introduced. Despite that, they became great friends, and she gave my mother an armchair like this one in which everyone refused to sit, as you've just done. One day my mother heard a carriage in the courtyard of her *hôtel*. She asked a young servant who it was. "It's Madame la Duchesse de La Rochefoucauld, Madame la Comtesse."* "Oh, good, show her in." After a quarter of an hour, still no one. "Well then, where is Madame la Duchesse de La Rochefoucauld?" "She's on the stairs, catching her breath, Madame la Comtesse," replied the little servant, who had just arrived from the countryside, where it was my mother's sound practice to acquire her servants. Often she'd even been witness to their births. That's how to get decent people working for you. And they're the most important luxury of all. And in fact, the Duchesse de La Rochefoucauld was finding it difficult to mount the stairs, for she was an enormous woman—so enormous that when she came in, my mother wondered for a moment where she could seat her. At that point, the chair Madame de Praslin had given her caught her eye. "Won't you have a seat?" my mother asked as she nudged it towards her. And the Duchess filled it to overflowing. Despite her bulk, she'd remained quite a pleasant woman. "She still causes quite a stir when she enters a room," one of our friends said. "She certainly makes one when she goes out," retorted my mother, who had a slightly sharper tongue than is acceptable nowadays. Even at Madame de La Rochefoucauld's own home, no one felt any qualms about poking fun at her ample size—in fact she was the first to laugh. "Are you alone, then?" my mother asked Monsieur de La Rochefoucauld one day when she'd come to call on the Duchess, whose husband had met her at the door; she hadn't noticed his wife sitting in a bay window at the other end of the room. "Madame de La Rochefoucauld isn't here? I don't see her." "How kind you are!" replied the Duke, who had just about the worst judgement of anyone I've ever known, but who didn't lack a certain wit.'

After dinner, when my grandmother and I had gone upstairs, I said
to her that the qualities we found charming in Madame de Villeparisis—
tact, delicacy, discretion, self-effacement—were not, perhaps, of very
great value, since those who best exemplified them were only ordinary
men like Molé or Loménie,* and that even though the lack of such
qualities might make everyday relations unpleasant, their absence
hadn't hampered people like Chateaubriand, Vigny, Hugo, Balzac,
self-important men who had no judgement and were easy to mock,
just as Bloch did . . . But at the mention of Bloch my grandmother
protested, and went on to sing the praises of Madame de Villeparisis.
Just as it's said that concern for the preservation of the species is what
guides our individual preferences in love, spurring fat men to seek
out thin women and vice versa, so that the child will have the most
normal constitution possible, so it was somehow the requirements of
my happiness, which was threatened by nerves and my unhealthy tendency towards melancholy and isolation, which made her rank most
highly those qualities of level-headedness and good judgement which
were peculiar not just to Madame de Villeparisis but to a society that
might provide me with amusement and ease, a society similar to the
one which allowed a Doudan, a Monsieur de Rémusat, to flourish, to
say nothing of a Beausergent, a Joubert,* or a Madame de Sévigné—
qualities which bring more happiness and dignity to life than their
opposites do, which have led the Baudelaires, the Poes, the Verlaines,
the Rimbauds,* into suffering and disrepute, neither of which my
grandmother wanted for her grandson. I interrupted her to kiss her,
and asked if she'd noticed something Madame de Villeparisis had said
in which one could detect a woman who set more store in her birth
than she liked to admit. In this way, I'd submit my impressions to my
grandmother, for I never knew how much esteem someone was owed
until she pronounced judgement. Every evening, I'd submit to her
the mental sketches I'd formed during the day based on all those non-
existent people who were not her.

Once, I said to her: 'Without you I wouldn't be able to live.'

'You mustn't say that,' she replied in a troubled tone of voice.
'We must try to be a little tougher than that. Otherwise, what would
become of you if I went away on a trip? I hope you'd be sensible and
happy.'

'I could be sensible if you went away for a few days, but I'd count
the hours.'

'But if I went away for months . . .' (the very thought of it made my blood run cold) 'for years . . . for . . .'

We both fell silent. We didn't dare look at each other. Yet I suffered more from her anxiety than my own. And so I walked over to the window and said clearly, averting my eyes:

'You know how I'm a creature of habit. The first few days when I've just been separated from the people I love the most, I'm unhappy. But even though I still love them just as much, I get used to it, my life becomes calm and pleasant again; I could bear being away from them for months, years even.'

I had to stop talking, and to look straight out of the window. My grandmother left the room for a moment. But the next day I began talking about philosophy, in the most neutral tone possible, but in such a way that my grandmother would pay attention to my words: I said how curious it was that after the latest discoveries in science, materialism seemed to be on its way out, and that the most likely thing was still the eternal life of the soul, and reunion in a time still to come.

Madame de Villeparisis let us know that soon she wouldn't be able to see us so often. A young nephew who was preparing for Saumur, and who was then stationed in nearby Doncières,* was to spend a few weeks' furlough with her, and she'd have to devote most of her time to him. During our drives together, she had vaunted his great intelligence and especially his kindness; already I was imagining that he'd conceive a great liking for me, that I'd become his best friend, and when his aunt informed my grandmother, before his arrival, that he'd unfortunately fallen into the clutches of a dreadful woman with whom he was utterly infatuated and who wouldn't let go of him, since I was convinced that this sort of love always ended fatally in madness, crime, and suicide, thinking of the brief time allotted to our friendship, already so strong in my heart even before I'd set eyes on him, I wept over that friendship and over the misfortunes that were in store for it as if over a beloved person we've just heard is gravely ill and not expected to live long.

One very hot afternoon I was in the hotel dining room, which they'd left in semi-darkness to protect it from the sun by drawing the faded curtains, which let the blue of the sea flicker through the gaps between them, when, in the central walkway that led from the beach to the road, I saw, tall, slim, neck bare, head held erect and proud, a young man passing by with piercing eyes, his skin as fair and hair as golden as if they'd absorbed all the sun's rays. Dressed in a flowing, off-white material I'd never have thought a man would dare to wear, its thinness just as suggestive of the glorious, warm weather outdoors as the cool of the dining room, he was walking quickly. His eyes, from one of which a monocle kept falling, were the same colour as the sea. Everyone watched him curiously as he went by; they knew this young Marquis de Saint-Loup-en-Bray* was famous for his elegance. All the papers had described the suit he wore when he'd recently acted as second for the young Duc d'Uzès* in a duel. It seemed as if the special quality of his hair, his eyes, his skin, his figure, which would have made him stand out in a crowd like a precious vein of luminous, sky-blue opal embedded in the coarse earth, must signify a life different from that of other men. And so, when, before the affair Madame de Villeparisis so deplored, the prettiest women in society had vied for him, his presence, in a seaside resort for example, beside the renowned beauty to whom he was paying court, not only shone a spotlight on her, but also drew attention to him. Because of his 'stylishness', his insolent 'young lion' manner, and above all his extraordinary beauty, some even thought him effeminate, but didn't reproach him for it, since they knew how virile he was and how passionately he loved women. This was the nephew of Madame de Villeparisis of whom she'd spoken. I was delighted to think I'd enjoy his company for several weeks, and certain he'd lavish all his attention on me. He loped swiftly through the entire length of the hotel, seeming to be in pursuit of his monocle, which flitted before him like a butterfly. He was coming from the beach, and the sea, which filled the lower half of the lobby's windows, provided a background against which he stood out in full length, as in certain portraits in which the painter, without in any way departing from the most exact observation of real life, chooses to depict his model in an appropriate setting—a polo ground, a golf course, a racetrack, the deck of a yacht—producing a modern equivalent of those canvases in which the old masters used to portray the human figure in the foreground of a landscape. A carriage and pair awaited him at the door; and while his monocle resumed its frolicking on the sun-drenched road, with the elegance and mastery a great pianist manages to display in the simplest passage, one in which it didn't seem possible he could show his superiority over a second-rate performer, the nephew of Madame de Villeparisis, taking the reins the coachman handed him, sat next to him and, while opening a letter the hotel manager brought out to him, set the horses trotting.

What disappointment I felt in the days that followed when, every time I encountered him in or out of the hotel—high-collared, constantly adjusting the movements of his limbs to his fugitive, dancing monocle, which seemed to be their centre of gravity—I came to realize that he had no interest in making our acquaintance, and saw that he never greeted us, even though he must have known we were friends of his aunt. And, remembering the friendliness shown me by Madame de Villeparisis and Monsieur de Norpois before her, I thought perhaps they were only sham nobility, and that a secret article in the laws governing the aristocracy might allow women, perhaps, and certain diplomats, in their relations with commoners, for some reason unknown to me, to shed the arrogance which must on the contrary be mercilessly maintained by a young marquis. My intelligence should have told me otherwise. But the characteristic of the ridiculous phase I was going through—not an unrewarding phase, indeed a highly productive one—is that intelligence is not consulted, and the most trivial attributes of other people seem to form an integral part of their personality. Surrounded on all sides by monsters and gods, we hardly ever experience tranquillity. There's scarcely a single action we took then that we wouldn't like to take back later. What we should really regret, however, is the fact that we no longer possess the spontaneity that made us take those actions. Later, we see things from a more practical perspective, in complete accordance with the rest of society, but adolescence was the only time when we ever learned anything.

The insolence I attributed to Monsieur de Saint-Loup, and all the innate coldness it implied, was confirmed by his attitude whenever he passed by us, his body as inflexibly erect as before, his head always held just as high, his gaze just as impassive—that's an understatement, as implacable, as devoid of that vague respect one has for the rights of other beings, even if they don't know your aunt, which causes me to look somewhat differently at an old woman than I would a lamp post. These icy manners were as remote from the charming letters that, just a few days before, I'd imagined him writing to me to express his friendship, as the daydreams of an ordinary person who imagines the enthusiasm of the Chamber of Deputies roused to a standing ovation by his unforgettable speech are from the mediocre, obscure situation of that man after fantasizing this scenario by himself, for his ears only, out loud, who finds, once the imaginary cheers have died down, that he's still the same unremarkable person he was before. When Madame de Villeparisis, doubtless trying to remedy the bad impression made on us by Saint-Loup's outward appearance, suggestive as it was of a haughty, unfriendly nature, spoke to us again about the infinite kindness of her grand-nephew (he was the son of one of her nieces, and was a little older than I was), I marvelled at how, flying in the face of all truth, we attribute kindness of heart to those who are hard-hearted, so long as they're amiable towards the brilliant members of their own set. Madame de Villeparisis herself added, though indirectly, a confirmation of her nephew's essential traits, which were already quite apparent to me, one day when I met them both on a path so narrow that she had no choice but to introduce me to him. He seemed oblivious to the fact that a name was being announced to him; not a single muscle in his face moved; his eyes, in which not the slightest gleam of human sympathy shone, showed merely an exaggeration of the insensitivity and blankness of his gaze, which was the only thing that distinguished them from lifeless mirrors. Then, fixing on me those hard eyes, as if he wanted to make sure of me before returning my greeting, with a sudden release which seemed due more to a muscular reflex than to an act of will, placing between himself and me the greatest distance possible, he stretched out his arm to its full length and, from afar, offered me his hand. When he had his card sent to me the next day, I thought it must, at the very least, be a challenge to a duel. But he merely talked about literature, and, after a lengthy discussion, declared he'd like very much to see me for several hours a day. During this visit, not only did he show an extremely passionate taste for the things of the mind, but he displayed a liking for me which was hardly in keeping with his greeting of the day before. When I saw him repeat this gesture every time he was introduced to someone, I understood it was simply a social habit peculiar to a certain branch of his family, to which his mother, who was anxious for him to be well brought up, had made his body conform; he made these salutations with no more thought than he'd give to his fine clothes or his beautiful hair; it was devoid of the moral significance I'd seen in it, something he'd merely acquired, like the other habit he had of demanding to be introduced immediately to the parents of anyone he knew, which had become so instinctive to him that, upon seeing me the day after our conversation, he rushed up to me and, without even saying hello, asked me to introduce him to my grand-mother who was standing next to me, with the same feverish rapidity as if this request were due to some defensive instinct, like parrying a blow or closing one's eyes to a spurt of boiling water, without which self-protective actions it would have been dangerous to remain a second longer.

Once the first rites of exorcism were performed, just as a wicked fairy sheds its initial appearance and seems to be full of charm and grace, I saw this haughty being become the friendliest, most consid-erate young man I'd ever met. 'Fine,' I said to myself, 'I've already been mistaken about him once, I was the victim of a mirage, but I've triumphed over the first only to fall into a second, for he must be an aristocrat who has grown weary of his nobility and is trying to hide it.' In fact, all Saint-Loup's charming behaviour, all his friendliness, would before long allow me to see quite another person, but very dif-ferent from the one I suspected him of being.

This young man, who seemed from his appearance to be a disdain-ful aristocrat and sportsman, actually had respect and curiosity only for intellectual matters, especially for those modernist examples of literature and art which his aunt found so ridiculous; he was, more-over, imbued with what she called 'socialist ravings', had the deepest contempt for his caste, and spent hours poring over Nietzsche and Proudhon.* He was one of those 'intellectuals'* eager to shut himself away in a book, concerned only with exalted thoughts. Indeed, while I was moved by Saint-Loup's tendency towards the abstract, so far from my own usual preoccupations, it also annoyed me a little. For instance, after I realized who his father was, on days when I'd been reading memoirs chock-full of anecdotes about the famous Comte de Marsantes, who epitomized the extraordinary elegance of an already distant epoch, with my mind full of vague musings, wishing to know more about the life Monsieur de Marsantes had led, I'd be infuriated that Robert de Saint-Loup, instead of being proud to be his father's son, instead of being able to guide me through the old-fashioned romance his father's life had been, had elevated himself to things like love and Nietzsche and Proudhon. Not that his father would have shared my regret. He was an intelligent man whose interests extended beyond the limits of society life. He'd scarcely had time to get to know his son, but he'd wanted him to become a better man than he was. And I do think that, unlike the rest of the family, he would have admired his son, and would have been delighted that he'd abandoned the things that had made up his own trivial amusements in favour of austere meditations, and, without saying a word about it, like the witty but modest nobleman he was, he'd have secretly read his son's favourite authors in order to appreciate how superior Robert was to him.

There was, however, one rather sad thing: whereas Monsieur de Marsantes, open-minded as he was, might have appreciated a son so different from himself, Robert de Saint-Loup, because he was the kind of man who believes merit is linked to certain forms of art and life, had an affectionate but slightly scornful memory of a father who had devoted his entire life to hunting and racing, had yawned at Wagner and been passionate about Offenbach.* Saint-Loup was not intelligent enough to understand that intellectual worth has nothing to do with adhesion to any one aesthetic doctrine; and the disdain with which he viewed Monsieur de Marsantes' intellectual aptitude was akin to what might have been expected in a son of Boieldieu or of Labiche,* if either of them had had a son who was a lover of the most Symbolist literature or the most abstruse music. 'I hardly knew my father,' Robert would say. 'I gather that he was a charming man. His tragedy was the deplorable time in which he lived. To have been born in the Faubourg Saint-Germain and to have lived at the time of *La Belle Hélène** is enough to ruin anyone's life. Perhaps, if he'd been a middle-class fanatic of the *Ring*,* he'd have led quite a different existence. I've even heard he loved literature. But we'll never know, since what he meant by "literature" was made up of completely out-dated works.' As for me, while I found Saint-Loup a little serious, he couldn't understand why I wasn't more so. Judging all things solely by their intellectual content, and unaware of the delight my imagination took in what he deemed frivolous, he was surprised that I—whom he regarded as so much his superior—could be interested in them.

From the very beginning, Saint-Loup utterly captivated my grand-mother, not only by the constant acts of kindness he lavished on us, but by the naturalness with which he performed them, the same nat-uralness he brought to everything he did. Naturalness—doubtless because, beneath our artifice, it allows nature to be glimpsed—was the quality my grandmother preferred above all others; she disliked artificiality, whether in gardens, if, like our garden in Combray, its flower beds were too orderly; in cuisine, if it featured those 'elaborate concoctions' in which you can scarcely recognize the foodstuffs used to make them; or in piano performances, if they were too polished, too perfect (she had a special weakness for the missed or wrong notes of Rubinstein*). She even enjoyed the naturalness of Saint-Loup's clothing, which had a supple elegance with nothing 'foppish' or 'formal' about it, no stiffness, no starch. What she prized even more in this wealthy young man was the casual, carefree way he had of living in luxury without 'smelling of money', without giving himself airs; she even saw the charm of this naturalness in the inability Saint-Loup still had—which usually disappears with childhood along with certain physiological traits of that age—to prevent his face from reflecting every emotion. Something he desired, for instance, which he hadn't expected, even if it was merely a compliment, triggered in him such a sudden, ardent, volatile, effusive pleasure, that it was impossible for him to contain or hide it; a look of delight spread irresistibly over his face; the delicate skin of his cheeks let a deep red show through; his eyes gleamed with confusion and joy; and my grandmother was infinitely sensitive to this gracious appearance of candour and innocence which, in Saint-Loup, at least at the time I knew him, was never deceptive. I knew another person, though—and there are many—in whom the physiological sincerity of this fleeting blush didn't at all rule out moral duplicity; quite often, in people with a nature capable of the vilest treachery, it merely proves the intensity with which they feel pleasure. But above all, my grandmother admired Saint-Loup's naturalness in the straightforward way he had of confessing his affection for me, for which he used words that, she said, were truer and more genuinely affectionate than she herself could have found, words worthy of Mesdames de Sévigné and de Beausergent; he didn't shy away from poking fun at my defects—which he'd singled out with an acuteness that amused her—but just as she herself would have done, with tenderness, exalting my qualities with a warmth and enthusiasm that betokened none of the reserve or coldness which young men of his age usually evinced, thinking that it made them seem important. And, in forestalling my slightest discomforts, in covering my legs with blankets if the weather grew brisk without my noticing it, in discreetly rearranging his schedule so that he could stay with me later in the evenings if he thought I was sad or feeling a little unwell, he displayed a vigilance which, from the point of view of my health, for which a tougher approach might have been preferable, my grandmother found almost excessive, but which, as proof of his affection for me, touched her deeply.

It was quickly settled between us that we had become firm friends forever, and he'd say 'our friendship' as if he was speaking of something important and delightful that existed outside ourselves and which he presently called—setting aside his love for his mistress—the greatest joy in his life. These words saddened me in a way, and I was at a loss to respond to them, for, when I was with him, talking to him—and no doubt this would have been true for anyone else— I didn't feel any of the happiness I felt when I was alone. Alone, I would sometimes feel, welling up from deep within me, one of those impressions that gave me a sensation of delightful contentedness. But as soon as I was with someone else, as soon as I was talking to a friend, my mind did an about-turn, and it was towards that interlocutor and not myself that it directed its thoughts; and when they went in that contrary direction, they brought me no pleasure. Once I'd left Saint-Loup, with the help of words, I would put a kind of order into the confused minutes I'd spent with him; I'd tell myself that I had a good friend, that a good friend is a rare thing, and, feeling surrounded by good things that are hard to acquire, I experienced what was precisely the opposite of the pleasure that was natural to me, the opposite of the pleasure of having extracted from myself and brought out into the light something that had been hidden there in the darkness. If I'd spent two or three hours talking with Robert de Saint-Loup, and if he'd admired what I'd said to him, I'd feel a kind of remorse, a regret, a weariness at not having stayed by myself, ready finally to get to work. But I'd tell myself that one isn't intelligent just for oneself, that even the greatest people have wanted to be appreciated, that I couldn't regard as lost those hours when I'd built up a lofty idea of myself in my friend's mind; I had no difficulty in convincing myself that I should be happy about it, and I'd wish all the more keenly that this happiness, which I hadn't felt, would never be taken from me. The joys we most dread losing are those that have remained outside us, because our heart hasn't taken possession of them. Even though I felt I was better able than most to practise the virtues of friendship (because I'd always placed the well-being of my friends above the considerations of personal self-interest to which others are attached, and which for me counted for nothing), I realized I was unable to experience joy in a feeling which, instead of increasing the differences there were between my nature and other people's—differences that exist between all of us—would abolish them. At times, though, my thoughts would discern in Saint-Loup a being that was more generic than himself, the 'nobleman', which, like an inner spirit, moved his limbs and ruled his gestures and actions; then, at those moments, although I was near him, I was as alone as I would have been gazing at a landscape whose harmonious proportions I could understand. He was no more than an object my curious thoughts were trying to plumb. To find in him the earlier, age-old, aristocratic being which Robert aspired precisely not to be, I felt a keen joy, but one produced by the mind, not by friendship. In the moral and physical agility that gave so much grace to his friendliness, in the ease with which he offered his carriage to my grandmother and helped her into it, in his promptness to leap from the box when he was afraid I might be feeling cold, to throw his own coat over my shoulders, I sensed not only the hereditary deftness of generations of great hunters, the ancestors of this young man who aspired only to intellectuality, not only their disdain for wealth which, surviving in him along with his desire for it only to be able to entertain his friends more lavishly, made him shower his riches at their feet so carelessly; above all, I sensed in him the certainty (or illusion) those great noblemen had of being 'above other people', which had prevented them from bequeathing to Saint-Loup any desire to show he was 'the same as everyone else', any anxiety about seeming overeager to please, both feelings which were in fact truly unknown to him and which can spoil with so much stiffness and awkwardness even the sincerest expressions of civility on the part of 'commoners'. Sometimes I'd reproach myself for taking such pleasure in regarding my friend as a work of art, that is, in observing the play of all the parts of his being as being harmoniously regulated by a general idea on which they depended but of which he was unaware, and which, consequently, added nothing to his own qualities, to those personal values of intelligence and morality to which he attached so much importance.

Yet it was this atavism that was, to a certain extent, the source of these values. It was because he was a nobleman that this lively intelligence, these socialist aspirations, which made him seek out young, pretentious, unkempt students, indicated in him something truly pure and selfless, though the same could not be said of them. Believing himself to be the heir to an ignorant, selfish caste, he sincerely desired to be forgiven for his aristocratic origins which the students, on the contrary, found irresistibly appealing, and which was the reason they sought him out, while at the same time feigning coldness and even insolence towards him. This is what led him to make overtures to people whom my parents, faithful to the sociology of Combray, would have been astonished he didn't shun. One day when we were both sitting on the sand, we heard, from inside the canvas tent against which we were leaning, someone inveighing against the 'hordes' of Jews infesting Balbec. 'You can't take two steps without bumping into one of them,' said the voice. 'I'm not in principle completely hostile to those of the Jewish persuasion, but here, there are swarms of them. You hear nothing but "I thay, Apraham, I've chust theen Shakop". You'd think you were in the Rue d'Aboukir!'* The man who had been railing against Israel finally emerged from the tent; we raised our eyes to this anti-Semite. It was my friend Bloch. Saint-Loup immediately asked me to remind Bloch that they'd met before when they'd both sat for the *Concours général*, at which Bloch had won the top prize, and then again in an *université populaire*.*

Sometimes I couldn't help but smile when I recognized Robert's Jesuit training in the embarrassment he evinced whenever he feared hurting someone's feelings, as when one of his intellectual friends committed a social faux pas or did something silly, which didn't matter to Saint-Loup, but which he thought might make the other blush if he'd been aware of it. And so it was Robert who blushed as if he'd been the guilty party, for instance on the day when Bloch, promising to visit him at the hotel, added: 'Since I can't abide cooling my heels in the sham chic of these hotel caravanserais, and since those gypsy orchestras turn my stomach, tell the "lighft-boy" to shut them up, and to let you know forthwith that I'm waiting.'

Personally, I was not very pleased about Bloch coming to the hotel. He wasn't, unfortunately, alone in Balbec, but with his sisters, who had many relatives and friends there themselves. This Jewish colony was more picturesque than pleasant. Balbec was like certain countries— Russia, say, or Romania—where, as we're taught in geography lessons, the Jewish population doesn't enjoy the same favour, and hasn't achieved the same degree of assimilation, as in Paris, for example. Always together, never mingling with any outside element, when Bloch's female cousins or uncles, or any of their co-religionists of either sex, came to the Casino, some for the 'ballroom', others veering off towards the baccarat tables, they formed a homogeneous procession, completely unlike the people who watched them go by and saw them there every year without ever exchanging a greeting with them, whether they were the Cambremer set, the clan of the first president, or the upper middle class and petit bourgeois, or even simple grain merchants from Paris, none of whose daughters—beautiful, proud, irreverent, and as French as the statues in Rheims Cathedral—would have wanted to mingle with this horde of ill-bred trollops who cared so much about 'resort fashion' that they always looked as if they were just coming back from prawn-fishing or dancing the tango. As for the men, despite their shiny dinner jackets and polished shoes, their physical characteristics were so exaggerated that they brought to mind the so-called 'clever' ideas of painters who, having to illustrate the Evangelists or the *Arabian Nights*,* think of the country where the story takes place and give Saint Peter or Ali Baba exactly the same features as those of the most important 'bigwig' in Balbec. Bloch introduced me to his sisters, whom he would abruptly cut off in the midst of their chatter, and who burst out in peals of laughter at the slightest witticism of their brother, whom they idolized. No doubt this community, like any other—perhaps more than any other—contained many charms, qualities, and virtues. To discover them, however, one would have to enter this community. But no one liked its members; they felt this, and so they saw this as proof of anti-Semitism, against which they closed ranks in a compact, solid phalanx which no one would dream of penetrating.

As for Bloch's use of 'lighft', which he rhymed with 'knifed', it didn't really take me by surprise, since a few days earlier, when Bloch had asked why I'd come to Balbec (of course, it seemed to him entirely natural that he should be there) and if it was 'in the hope of making connections', and when I'd replied that this trip was the fulfilment of one of my oldest wishes, though not quite as profound as my desire to go to Venice, he'd answered: 'Yes, so you can sip iced drinks with pretty ladies, while you pretend to be reading *The Stones of Venaïce* by Lord John Ruskin,* who was a crashing bore, one of the dullest dotards ever.' Bloch obviously thought that in England, not only were all individuals of the male sex lords, but also that the letter *i* was always pronounced like the 'i' in 'ice'. Saint-Loup, however, viewed this mistake in pronunciation as all the more inconsequential since he saw it merely as a sign of a lack of those society mannerisms that my new friend despised as much as he was conversant with them. But the fear that Bloch might one day learn the correct pronunciation of 'Venice' and that Ruskin was not a lord, and that Bloch might retro- spectively suspect that Robert had thought him ridiculous, made Robert feel guilty, as if he'd been found wanting in the solicitousness with which he overflowed; and so the blush that would no doubt spread across Bloch's face when he discovered his error flushed Robert's face, out of his foresight and his ability to put himself in the other's place. For he was quite sure that Bloch would attach more importance to this mistake than he actually did. Which Bloch proved a little later, one day when he heard me pronounce 'lift', interrupting with 'Oh! it's "lift", is it?' And, in a dry, haughty tone, he added: 'It's of no importance in any case.' This phrase is like a reflex; it's the same with all self-important individuals, in the gravest as well as the most trivial circumstances, calling attention both there and in this instance to how important the subject in question seems to the person declaring it devoid of importance; it can also be a tragic phrase, when it's the first thing to emerge, so distressingly, from the lips of any man who takes a certain pride in himself, from whom the last shred of hope to which he'd been clinging has just been snatched away, when a favour has been refused him: 'Oh, that's fine, it's of no importance, I'll make some other arrangement'; the other arrangement on which he had to fall back, which was 'of no importance', being, sometimes, suicide.

Then Bloch said some very pleasant things to me. He was certainly anxious to be friendly. And yet he asked me: 'Are you friendly with Saint-Loup-en-Bray because you have your sights set on the nobility? It goes without saying that his branch of the nobility is nothing to write home about, but you always were naïve. You must be going through a nice little fit of snobbery. Come now, are you a snob? You are, aren't you?' It wasn't that his desire to be friendly had suddenly changed. But since he suffered from the defect that's commonly referred to as 'boorishness', it was this very defect that he didn't notice in himself, and so he didn't think anyone else could be shocked by it. In humankind, the frequency of the virtues shared by all is no more remarkable than the multiplicity of defects peculiar to each. Undoubtedly, it isn't common sense that is 'the commonest thing in the world',* but common kindness. In the remotest, most far-flung corners of the earth, we can be amazed to see it flourish of its own

accord, like a poppy in a distant valley which is just like other poppies
in all the rest of the world, even though it has never seen them, and
has known only the wind that sometimes ruffles its lonely red bonnet.
Even if this kindness, when paralysed by self-interest, isn't exercised,
it still exists, and whenever some selfish motive doesn't prevent it from
acting—when one is reading a book or a newspaper, for example—
it blossoms, even in the heart of someone who, though a murderer in
real life, has become tender-hearted thanks to his love of novels; and
it turns towards the weak, the righteous, and the persecuted. But the
variety of our defects is no less striking than the similarity of our
virtues. The most perfect person has a particular fault, which can
give rise to shock or fury. One man may have a fine mind, may see
everything from a lofty perspective, may never say a bad word about
anyone, but forgets that he still has in his pocket the most important
letters he himself offered to post for you, and then makes you miss an
important meeting, without a single apology, but with a smile, because
he takes pride in never knowing the time. Another is so sweet, mild-
mannered, and thoughtful that he only tells you things that might
make you happy, but you sense that he has entirely different thoughts
which he never voices and keeps buried in his heart, where they turn
sour, yet the pleasure he has in seeing you is so dear to him that he'll
make you die of fatigue rather than leave you alone. A third has greater
sincerity, but takes it so far that he insists on telling you, when you've
pleaded the state of your health as an excuse for not visiting him, that
you'd been seen going to the theatre and that you looked quite well, or
else that the action you'd performed on his behalf wasn't as helpful as
he'd hoped, that in any case three other people had already offered to
do it, and so he's only slightly indebted to you. In both of these circumstances, the second, less sincere friend would have claimed not to
know you'd gone to the theatre, or that others could have done him
the same good turn. As for the more sincere one, having felt the need
to repeat or disclose to someone else the very thing that can cause you
the most offence, he's extremely pleased with his frankness, and tells
you unapologetically: 'That's how I am!' While still others annoy you
by their exaggerated curiosity, or by their lack of curiosity, which is so
absolute that you can talk to them about the most sensational events
without their having any idea what you're talking about; and still others
let months go by without answering your letter if it has to do with
something important to you but not to them, or else, if they tell you

they're coming to see you to ask something and you don't dare go out for fear of missing them, they don't come and keep you waiting for weeks because, having received no reply from you even though their letter didn't require one, they thought you were angry with them. And some, responding to their own wishes but not yours, talk to you without letting you get a word in edgeways if they're in high spirits and want to see you, no matter how urgent your work might be, but if they feel tired due to the weather, or out of sorts, you can't get a word out of them; they meet all your efforts with languid inertia, and go to no more trouble to reply, even in monosyllables, to what you say than if they hadn't heard you at all. Each of our friends has so many faults that, in order to go on liking him, we must try to make allowances for them by thinking of his talent, or kindness, or affection; or else we must try to overlook their faults, by summoning all the willpower we have. Unfortunately, our complacent stubbornness in not seeing our friend's defect is surpassed by the obstinacy with which he persists in it, either because of his own blindness to it or because he attributes that blindness to others. Either he doesn't see it, or thinks others don't see it. Since the risk of giving offence stems mainly from the difficulty of discerning what will or won't pass unnoticed, we should at least, out of prudence, never talk about ourselves, since that's a subject about which we can be sure the views of others will never coincide with our own. Visiting a house that looks ordinary, if we find stolen treasure, burglars' jemmies, and corpses, we're just as surprised as we are by discovering others' real lives, the real world beneath the apparent one; we're just as taken aback if, instead of the image of ourselves we've built up as a result of what others say to us, we learn from the conversations they have about us in our absence how completely different is the image they were carrying in their own minds about us and our lives. So that every time we speak about ourselves, we can be sure that our inoffensive, prudent words, listened to with apparent politeness and hypocritical approbation, have given rise to the most unfavourable comments, full of exasperation or hilarity. If nothing else, we run the risk of irritating others by the disparity between our idea of ourselves and our words, a disparity that usually makes the things people say about themselves as laughable as the performances of those self-professed music-lovers who, when they feel the need to hum their favourite tunes, compensate for their flawed, inarticulate murmuring with an energetic pantomime and a look of admiration hardly justified by what reaches our ears. To the bad habit of talking about oneself and one's faults should be added, as forming part and parcel with it, the other habit of denouncing in other people the defects that are exactly the same in ourselves. Yet it's always those defects we talk about, as if it was a way of talking about ourselves, indirectly, so that we add to the pleasure of self-forgiveness the pleasure of confession. What's more, it seems that our attention, always drawn to whatever distinguishes us, notices that more than anything else in others. A near-sighted person says about someone else: 'He can barely see his hand in front of his face'; a consumptive has doubts about the pulmonary integrity of the most robust; a filthy man speaks of nothing but the baths others don't take; a foul-smelling man claims others smell bad; the deceived husband sees cuckolded husbands everywhere; a flighty woman sees other flighty women; the snob sees other snobs. Furthermore, every vice, like every profession, requires and develops a special knowledge which we're only too happy to display. It takes a homosexual to detect a homosexual; a dressmaker at a fashionable party, before he even opens his mouth to talk to you, has already been admiring the fabric of your clothing, the qualities of which his fingers are itching to discover, and if, after a few minutes' conversation, you were to ask a dentist's honest opinion about you, he'd tell you how many bad teeth you have. Nothing seems more important to him; and to you, who have noticed his own bad teeth, nothing more ridiculous. It's not only when we talk about ourselves that we think others are blind; we act as if they were as well. Each of us is watched over by a special god who hides our fault from us, or promises it shall be invisible, just as he closes the eyes and blocks the nostrils of people who don't bathe, so that they don't notice the streak of dirt around their ears or the smell of sweat emanating from their armpits, and convinces them that they can with impunity parade both of these things through the world without anyone noticing. People who wear fake pearls or give them as gifts imagine they'll be perceived as genuine. Bloch was ill-bred, neurotic, a snob, and, since he belonged to a family of no note, he suffered, as though he were at the bottom of the sea, the incalculable pressure brought to bear on him not just by the Christians on the surface, but by the superimposed layers of Jewish castes superior to his own, each one heaping its scorn on the one immediately beneath it. To break through to the fresh air by raising himself from Jewish family to Jewish family would have taken Bloch several thousand years. It made more sense to try to make his way out from some other direction.

When Bloch was talking about the fit of snobbery I was supposedly undergoing and asked me to confess I was a snob, I should have replied: 'If I were, I wouldn't be associating with you.' But I merely told him he wasn't being very pleasant. Then he wanted to apologize, but did so in a way that was precisely that of an ill-bred man who is only too happy to go over his words again and find an opportunity to make them even worse. 'Forgive me,' he'd say now whenever we met, 'I made you upset, I tortured you, I took pleasure in being mean to you. And yet, humans in general and your friend in particular being such a singular creature, even though I tease you so cruelly, you can't imagine the affection I have for you—so much affection that I'm genuinely moved to tears when I think of you.' And he'd weep a little as he said this.

There was one thing that surprised me about Bloch even more than his bad manners, and that was how uneven the quality of his conversation was. This contrary youth, who would say about the most fashionable writers: 'He's a complete idiot, an absolute fool', would tell, with great relish, anecdotes that weren't the least bit funny, and would label as 'a really interesting person' some complete mediocrity. This dual scale for weighing people's intelligence, worth, and interest never failed to surprise me, until the day I met Monsieur Bloch senior.

I hadn't thought Saint-Loup and I would ever be allowed to meet him, for Bloch junior had spoken ill of me to Saint-Loup and of Saint-Loup to me. In particular, he'd said to Robert that I was (still) a terrible snob. 'Yes, yes, he's overjoyed to know Monsieur LLLLegrandin,' he said. This habit Bloch had of drawing out a word was a sign of both irony and literature. Saint-Loup, who'd never heard of Legrandin, asked in surprise: 'You don't say? Who is he?' 'Oh, he's *someone*,' Bloch replied with a laugh, thrusting his hands into his jacket pockets as though for warmth, convinced he was at that instant contemplating the picturesque aspect of a provincial gentleman more preposterous than any in the pages of Barbey d'Aurevilly.* He consoled himself for his inability to describe Monsieur Legrandin by adding several *L*s to his name and savouring it like a fine old wine. But his subjective pleasures remained unknown to others. If he spoke ill of me to Saint-Loup, he spoke just as poorly about Saint-Loup to me. We would learn the details of his scandalmongering no later than the next day, not because we'd repeated them to each other, which would have seemed very wrong to us, but which seemed so natural and almost inevitable to Bloch that in his anxiety, and in his certainty that he wouldn't be telling us what each of us was bound to find out, he chose to take the initiative, and, taking Saint-Loup aside, confessed that he'd spoken ill of him on purpose, but only so that it would get back to him, and swore 'by the Kroniôn Zeus, keeper of oaths'* that he loved him, that he'd give his life for him, and wiped away a tear. That same day, he arranged to meet me alone, made his confession to me, and declared he'd acted in my own interests because he thought there were certain kinds of social relations that were harmful to me and that 'I deserved better'. Then, taking me by the hand with the maudlin sentimentality of a drunkard, even though his drunkenness was only nerves, he said: 'Believe me—and may the black Ker* seize me this instant and carry me through the gates of Hades, detestable to men, if yesterday, when I thought of you, and of Combray, and of my infinite affection for you, and of certain afternoons at school that you don't even remember, I didn't sob all night. Yes, all night, I swear! It's so sad, though, because I know human nature and I'm sure you won't believe me.' And indeed I didn't believe him, and his oath 'by Ker' added no great weight to the words which I sensed were invented that very instant and embellished as he went along, since Bloch's Hellenic cult was a purely literary one. What's more, as soon as he started to become emotional and wanted his interlocutor to be moved to tears over some falsehood, he'd say: 'I swear', more out of the hysterical, indulgent pleasure he felt in lying than out of a concern to make the other believe he was telling the truth. I didn't believe what he told me, but I wasn't angry with him, since I inherited from my mother and grandmother not only the quality of being incapable of holding a grudge, even against much guiltier parties, but also that of never condemning anyone.

It wasn't that Bloch was all bad; he was capable of great kindness. And now that the race of Combray, the race from which sprang creatures absolutely unspoiled like my grandmother and my mother, seems to be almost extinct, and since I hardly have a choice anymore except, on the one hand, simple brutes, straightforward and unfeeling, the mere sound of whose voice quickly shows they couldn't care less about your life, and, on the other, a race of men who, so long as they're with you, understand you, cherish you, are moved to tears by you, then take their revenge a few hours later by making a cruel joke about you, but come back to you, just as understanding, charming, and temporarily concerned about you, I think it's this latter race I prefer, if not for their moral value, then at least for their company.

'You can't imagine how sad I feel when I think of you,' Bloch went on. 'Actually, it's a little bit of my Jewish side,' he added ironically, narrowing his eyes as if he were measuring out under the microscope an infinitesimal amount of 'Jewish blood', as might (but never would) be said by a French aristocrat who, among his ancestors, all of them Christian, might still have included Samuel Bernard* or, even further back, the Virgin Mary herself, from whom, they say, the Lévys claim to descend. 'Yes, I do think it's my Jewish side showing through. I rather like', he added, 'to pick out from my emotions the share (which is really quite small) that might stem from my Jewish origins.' He uttered this phrase because it seemed to him both witty and brave to tell the truth about his race, a truth that, at the same time, he made sure to downplay quite a bit, like misers who make up their minds to pay their debts but can summon the courage to settle only half. The type of fraudulence that consists in having the boldness to proclaim the truth while diluting it with enough lies to falsify it is more widespread than we may think, and even in those who don't usually practise it, certain crises in life, especially those involving a love affair, give them an opportunity to indulge in it.

All these confidential diatribes of Bloch's to Saint-Loup against me, and to me against Saint-Loup, ended up in an invitation to dinner. It may well have been that he made a first attempt to invite Saint-Loup alone. Although such an attempt is entirely likely, it was not crowned with success, for it was to me and Saint-Loup that Bloch said one day: 'Gracious Lord, and you, knight cherished by Ares, de Saint-Loup-en-Bray, tamer of horses, since I've met you on the surf-resounding shores of Amphitrite, near the tents of Menier of the swift ships,* will you both come to dinner one evening during the week, at the home of my illustrious father with the blameless heart?' He was extending this invitation because he wished to become more intimate with Saint-Loup, who, he hoped, would give him access to aristocratic circles. If such a desire had been conceived by me, for my own purposes, Bloch would have seen it as the most hideous form of snobbery, quite in keeping with the opinion he had of a whole aspect of my nature (a side which, at least up until this point, he didn't regard as the main one); but the same desire on his part struck him as proof of the commendable curiosity of a mind eager to explore new social environments which he might find useful from a literary perspective. Monsieur Bloch senior, when his son had told him he'd be bringing to dinner one of his friends, whose name and title he'd announced with sarcastic satisfaction, 'the Marquis de Saint-Loup-en-Bray', had given a violent start. 'The Marquis de Saint-Loup-en-Bray! Gadzooks!' he exclaimed, using the oath which for him was the strongest sign of social deference. And he bestowed on his son, capable of having formed such an acquaintance, an admiring glance which meant: 'How amazing he is! Can this prodigy really be my son?' and which filled Bloch with as much gratification as if fifty francs had been added to his monthly allowance. For Bloch was ill at ease at home, and felt his father treated him like a reprobate because he admired Leconte de Lisle, Heredia,* and other 'bohemians'. But to be friends with Saint-Loup-en-Bray, whose father had been the president of the Suez Canal Company* (gadzooks!), was an 'indisputable' feather in his cap. It was all the more regrettable that they'd left the stereoscope in Paris,* for fear of its being damaged. Only Monsieur Bloch senior had the skill, or at least the right, to use it. He did so, moreover, only on rare occasions, judiciously, at his gala events when there were additional hired manservants. So that these stereoscopic exhibitions conferred upon those lucky enough to attend them a special privilege, and, for the master of the house who gave them, the same sort of prestige that talent confers on a man; this prestige couldn't have been greater if the images projected had been taken by Monsieur Bloch himself and the apparatus had been of his own invention. 'You weren't invited to Salomon's yesterday?' one family member would ask another. 'No, I wasn't among the chosen! What did I miss?' 'Oh, quite a show, with the stereoscope and the whole box of tricks!' 'Oh! If the stereoscope was there, I'm sorry I missed it—they say Salomon is really amazing when he demonstrates it.'

'You know, though,' Monsieur Bloch said to his son, 'we shouldn't give him everything at once; this way he'll still have something to look forward to.'

Out of fatherly tenderness, and a wish to gratify his son, he had actually thought of sending for the instrument. However, time was 'of the essence', or so they thought; but the dinner had to be postponed after all, because Saint-Loup was unable to leave the hotel, since he was waiting for an uncle who was coming to spend a few days with Madame de Villeparisis. This uncle was devoted to physical exercise, especially to long walks; and so, as he was travelling mostly by foot from the château where he was staying, and sleeping in farms along the way, the time of his arrival at Balbec was rather uncertain. Saint-Loup, not daring to stir out of doors, even tasked me with going to Incauville, where there was a telegraph office, to post the message he sent daily to his mistress. The first name of the awaited uncle was Palamède, a name he'd inherited from the princes of Sicily, his ancestors. Later on, whenever I read historical texts that mentioned this name, belonging to some *podestà* or prince of the Church*—a fine medallion of a name from the Renaissance, or, as some would say, a real antique, which had always stayed in the family, having passed from descendant to descendant, from the chancellery of the Vatican right down to my friend's uncle, I'd experience the pleasure reserved for those who, unable to afford a collection of medals or fine art, instead seek out old names (place names, as instructive and picturesque as an old map, an isometric projection, a signboard, or a custumal;* and baptismal names, in which we can hear, with their fine French final syllables, the resonance of the speech defects, or the intonation of some ethnic vulgarity, or mispronunciation, by which our ancestors made Latin and Saxon words undergo lasting mutilations which later became the revered standards of grammar books) and, in short, thanks to these collections of ancient sonorities, give themselves concerts, like those people who acquire a viola da gamba or a viola d'amore* to play early music on period instruments. Saint-Loup told me that even in the most exclusive aristocratic society, his uncle Palamède was famous for being extremely aloof, haughty, and infatuated with his own nobility, forming, with his brother's wife and a few other elect individuals, what was called the Circle of the Phoenixes. Even there, his insolent behaviour was so feared that once, when some fashionable people had asked his own brother for an introduction, they were met with a firm refusal. 'No, don't ask me to introduce you to my brother Palamède. My wife, or any of us, could try our best, but nothing would come of it. Or else you'd be running the risk of his being rude to you, and that I wouldn't want.' At the Jockey Club, the uncle and a few friends had drawn up a list of two hundred members to whom they'd never deign to be introduced. In the household of the Comte de Paris, he was called 'the Prince' because of his elegance and arrogance.

Saint-Loup told me about his uncle's youth, now long past. Every day he'd bring women to a bachelor's apartment he shared with two of his friends who were as handsome as he was, which earned them the sobriquet 'the Three Graces'.*

'Once, a man who's now one of the most prominent members of the Faubourg Saint-Germain, as Balzac would have said, but who was going through an unfortunate period in his younger days and was displaying odd tendencies, asked my uncle if he could come to this apartment. But almost as soon as he arrived, he began to make his intentions known not to the women, but to my uncle Palamède! My uncle pretended not to understand, and made some excuse to take his two friends aside; when they returned, they seized the guilty man, stripped him, beat him until he bled, and, on a night when it was ten below zero, threw him outside, where he was found half dead, so that the police started an investigation which the poor fellow had the greatest difficulty getting them to drop. These days, my uncle would never engage in such cruel behaviour, and you can't imagine how many ordinary people he, so haughty with those in his circle, has been kind to and protected, even if all he gets in return is ingratitude. It could be a servant who attended him in a hotel and whom he'll set up in Paris, or a peasant he'll sponsor to learn a trade. That's the rather nice side of his nature, as opposed to his society side.' Saint-Loup belonged to that type of young men of fashion who live at an altitude where certain expressions, like 'What's really rather nice about him', or 'his rather nice side', can take root and grow, like precious seeds; such expressions soon turn into a way of seeing things that makes one count oneself as nothing, but 'the people' as everything—quite the opposite, in fact, of plebeian pride. 'It would seem that we can't imagine how he set the tone, how he laid down the law for all of society when he was young. No matter the circumstance, he did whatever was most pleasing or useful to himself; but whatever it was, it was immediately taken up and imitated by all the snobs. If he was thirsty at the theatre and had a drink brought to him in his box, the next week all the little sitting rooms behind the boxes were full of refreshments. One very wet summer when he had a touch of rheumatism, he'd ordered an overcoat made of a soft but warm vicuña, which is used only for travelling rugs, and he'd kept its blue and orange stripes. Immediately all the best tailors were inundated with orders for shaggy blue and orange overcoats with a fringe. If for some reason he wanted to banish all solemnity from a dinner in a château where he was spending the day, and therefore hadn't brought evening clothes but sat down in his afternoon jacket, it became the fashion to dine in the country in a jacket. If, to eat a cake, he used a fork instead of a spoon, or some other implement of his own invention that he'd commissioned from a silversmith, or even his fingers, that was henceforth the only method allowed. When he wanted to hear certain Beethoven quartets again (for, even with all his preposterous ideas, he's far from stupid, quite talented in fact), he invited some musicians to play them every week, for himself and a few friends.* And so the height of fashion that year was to give small parties for a select few where chamber music was played. I don't think he's ever found life boring. Handsome as he was, think of all the women he's had! I couldn't tell you which ones precisely, because he's very discreet. But I do know he was very unfaithful to my poor aunt. But that didn't prevent him from being charming towards her; she adored him, and he mourned her for years. Whenever he's in Paris, he still visits the cemetery nearly every day.'

On the morning after Robert told me about his uncle while he was waiting (in vain, as it happened) for him, as I was walking by the Casino on my way back to the hotel, I had the sensation I was being watched by someone not far off. I turned my head and saw a man of about forty, very tall and rather stout, with a jet-black moustache, and who, while nervously tapping his trousers with a switch, was staring at me with eyes dilated by the strain of attention. At times, his eyes gleamed with an intense alertness, the kind that the sight of someone they don't know excites in some men and, for whatever reason, arouses thoughts that wouldn't come to anyone else—madmen, for example, or spies. On me, he fixed a supreme glare at once bold, cautious, swift, and profound, like the last shot you fire as you start to flee, and, after looking all round him, suddenly assuming an absent, haughty air, with an abrupt swivel of his entire person, he turned towards a playbill which absorbed all his attention, all the while humming a tune and arranging the moss rose in his lapel. He drew from his pocket a note-book into which he seemed to be inscribing the title of the upcoming performance, took out his watch two or three times, lowered over his brows a black straw boater whose brim he extended with his hand held like a visor, as if to try to see someone who wasn't coming, made that annoyed gesture you make when you want to look as though you've had your fill of waiting, but which you never make when you're actually waiting, then, pushing his hat back and exposing a brush-cut short on top but long and wavy on the sides, he let out a loud sigh, the way people do when they aren't too hot but want to seem as if they are. He looked to me like a hotel swindler who, having perhaps already in the past few days noticed my grandmother and me, and plotting some nefarious scheme, had just noticed I'd spotted him as he was spying on me; to put me off the track, perhaps he was merely trying to express absent-mindedness and detachment with this new attitude, but he did it with such overblown exaggeration that his goal seemed not just to dissipate the suspicions I must be having, but also to avenge some humiliation I'd unwittingly inflicted on him, and to give me the impression not that he hadn't seen me, but that I was of too little importance to attract attention. He threw back his shoulders with an air of bravado, pursed his lips, twirled his moustache, and adjusted his gaze so that it looked indifferent, hard, almost insulting. So much so that the singularity of his expression made me take him for either a thief or a lunatic. And yet his extremely studied attire was much more sober and uncomplicated than that of all the holidaymakers I'd seen at Balbec, and reassured me as to my jacket, so often humiliated by the glaring, banal whiteness of their seaside suits. My grandmother came to meet me, and we went for a stroll; an hour later, as I was waiting for her in front of the hotel, into which she'd gone for a minute, I saw Madame de Villeparisis emerge with Robert de Saint-Loup and the unknown man who had been staring at me so fixedly in front of the Casino. With lightning quickness his gaze skimmed over me, just as it had when I first saw him, and returned, as if he hadn't seen me, to settle a little lower down, just in front of his eyes, dimmed like the neutral gaze that pretends not to see anything outside the self and is incapable of reporting anything to the mind inside, the gaze that expresses merely the satisfaction of feeling its vacuous roundness parting the lashes encircling it, the sanctimonious, pious look of certain hypocrites, the smug look of certain idiots. I saw he'd changed his suit. The one he was wearing now was even darker; no doubt true elegance is closer to simplicity than is false elegance; but there was something else: at close range, one felt that if colour was almost entirely absent from these clothes, it wasn't because the person who had banished it from them was indifferent to colour, but rather because, for whatever reason, he denied himself the pleasure of it. And the sobriety they hinted at seemed the sort that comes from a self-imposed diet, rather than a lack of appetite. A dark green thread in the fabric of his trousers harmonized with the stripe in his socks with a refinement that revealed the vivacity of a taste curbed everywhere else and to which this sole concession had been made out of tolerance, while a spot of red on his cravat was as imperceptible as a liberty one dare not take.

'How are you? Allow me to introduce my nephew, the Baron de Guermantes,' said Madame de Villeparisis, while the stranger, without looking at me, muttering a vague 'Charmed, I'm sure', which he followed up with 'Hmm, hmm', to make his politeness seem forced, and, folding in his little finger, forefinger, and thumb, he held out his middle and ring fingers, bare of any ring, which I clasped through his suede glove; then, without raising his eyes to my face, he turned to Madame de Villeparisis.

'Good heavens, I must be losing my head!' she exclaimed. 'I called you the Baron de Guermantes. Allow me to introduce the Baron de Charlus. It's not such a big mistake after all,' she added, 'since you *are* a Guermantes.'

Meanwhile my grandmother had reappeared, and we all set out together. Saint-Loup's uncle didn't deign to honour me with a word, or even a glance. Though he glared at strangers (and during this brief walk he aimed his terrible and profound gaze like a sounding wand at insignificant passers-by of the humblest origins), he didn't at any time, judging by his behaviour towards me, look at people he knew, like a police officer on a secret mission who takes care that his friends are excluded from his task of professional surveillance. Letting him walk on with my grandmother and Madame de Villeparisis, I held Saint-Loup back and asked:

'Tell me, did I hear right? Madame de Villeparisis said your uncle was a Guermantes.'

'Yes, of course—he's Palamède de Guermantes.'

'The same Guermantes who have a château near Combray and claim descent from Geneviève de Brabant?'*

'Absolutely: my uncle, who knows everything there is to know about heraldry, would tell you that our "cry", our war cry, which later became "Passavant", started out as "Combraysis",* he said, laughing so as not to seem as if he was boasting about this privilege held only by houses of almost royal status, by the greatest feudal warlords. 'He's the brother of the present owner of the château.'

Madame de Villeparisis was therefore closely related to the Guermantes, though she had long remained for me the lady who would give me a box of chocolates held by a duck when I was little; this same Madame de Villeparisis seemed as remote from the Guermantes side as if she'd been shut away in the Méséglise way, less impressive, lower in my esteem than the Combray optician, and she was now suddenly undergoing one of those fantastic rises in value, parallel to the equally unexpected depreciations of other objects we possess, which— both rise and fall—introduce into our adolescence, and into those parts of our lives in which a little of our adolescence persists, transformations as numerous as Ovid's metamorphoses.*

'And doesn't the château contain the busts of all the former lords of Guermantes?'

'Yes, it's a fine spectacle!' Saint-Loup said ironically. 'Between us, I find all those sorts of things a little vapid. But there's something a little more interesting at Guermantes: a rather touching portrait of my aunt by Carrière.* It's just as beautiful as a Whistler or a Velázquez,'* added Saint-Loup, who in his neophyte zeal sometimes lost his sense of proportion when it came to degrees of greatness. 'There are also some moving paintings by Gustave Moreau.* My aunt is the niece of your friend Madame de Villeparisis, who brought her up, and she married her cousin, the present Duc de Guermantes, who was also the nephew of my aunt de Villeparisis.'

'What's your uncle's title, then?'

'It's the Baron de Charlus. Strictly speaking, when my great-uncle died, my uncle Palamède should have taken the title of Prince des Laumes, which was his brother's before he became the Duc de Guermantes; in my family, you see, people change their names as often as you'd change shirts. But my uncle has his own way of thinking about all that. So, since he thinks there are rather too many Italian duchies and Spanish grandees and all that sort of thing, even though he had his pick of four or five titles that would have made him "Prince So-and-So", he remained just plain Baron de Charlus, as a sort of protest, and with an apparent simplicity which concealed a great deal of pride. "These days," he says, "everyone's a prince, so you need something else to make you stand out; I'll keep my title of 'prince' when I want to travel incognito." According to him, there's no title older than that of Baron de Charlus; to prove to you that it came before the titles of the Montmorencys, who falsely claimed to be the first Barons of France, whereas they were merely Barons of Île-de-France,* where their fief was, my uncle will expound on the subject for hours, with great pleasure, because even though he's very clever and talented, he finds that topic of conversation fascinating,' Saint-Loup said with a smile. 'But since I am not he, you won't get me talking about genealogy—I can't imagine anything duller or more outdated; life is too short for that.'

I now recognized the fierce stare which had attracted my attention earlier near the Casino as the one I'd seen fixed on me in Tansonville, when Madame Swann had called to Gilberte.

'Might Madame Swann have been one of the many mistresses you said your uncle, Monsieur de Charlus, used to have?'

'Oh no, not at all! He's just a great friend of Swann's, and has always stood by him. But no one's ever said my uncle was his wife's lover. You'd cause quite a stir in Paris society if people thought you believed that.'

I didn't dare reply that I'd have caused much more of a stir in Combray if people had thought I didn't believe it.

My grandmother was delighted with Monsieur de Charlus. True, he attached extreme importance to matters of birth and social position, and my grandmother had noticed this, but she was free of the severity which as a rule is the result of secret envy and irritation at seeing someone else enjoying advantages one would like but can't have. Since my grandmother, happy with her lot and not in the least regretful that she didn't move in more brilliant circles, used only her intellect to observe Monsieur de Charlus' shortcomings, she spoke of Saint-Loup's uncle with the detached, smiling, almost sympathetic benevolence by which we reward the object of our disinterested observation for the pleasure it has given us, all the more so since in this instance the object was an individual whose pretensions, legitimate or not, were at least picturesque, and made him stand out rather starkly from the people with whom she usually mingled. But it was above all on account of his intelligence and sensibility, which one could sense were especially marked in Monsieur de Charlus, in contrast to so many of the fashionable people Saint-Loup made fun of, that my grandmother had so easily forgiven his aristocratic prejudice. Unlike the nephew, though, the uncle hadn't sacrificed this bias to higher values: he had reconciled it with them. As a descendant of the Ducs de Nemours and the Princes de Lamballe,* possessing archives, furniture, tapestries, portraits painted for his ancestors by Raphael, Velázquez, and Boucher,* and able to claim, quite rightly, that he could visit a museum or a major library merely by glancing at some family heirlooms, he respected all the heritage of the aristocracy as greatly as his nephew scorned it. Perhaps too, being less ideological than Saint-Loup, not quite so grandiloquent, and a more realistic observer of men, he didn't want to neglect what was to them an essential element of prestige, something which, while it provided his imagination with disinterested delights, could also be a powerfully effective aid to his practical activities. There can be no common ground between men of his sort and those who obey an inner ideal that motivates them to rid themselves of such advantages in order to devote themselves solely to realizing that ideal, similar in that respect to painters or writers who renounce their virtuosity, artistic people who embrace modernization, warlike people who choose global disarmament, dictatorial governments that turn democratic and repeal harsh laws, quite often without being rewarded for their noble effort; the men lose their talent, the nations lose their secular predominance; pacifism can sometimes multiply wars, and permissiveness can foster crime. However noble Saint-Loup's efforts towards sincerity and emancipation may have been, judging by their visible results, one could still be thankful they were not shared by Monsieur de Charlus, who had transferred most of the admirable wood panelling from the Guermantes *hôtel* to his house instead of opting, like his nephew, for a more 'modern' style of decoration, with paintings by Lebourg or Guillaumin.* The fact remained, though, that Monsieur de Charlus' ideal was extremely artificial, and, if the epithet can be applied to the word 'ideal', as much social as artistic. In some women of great beauty and extraordinary culture whose ancestors had two centuries earlier been part of all the glory and elegance of the Ancien Régime, he found a distinction that made them the only ones whose company he enjoyed; no doubt the admiration he had for them was genuine, but it was greatly influenced by countless reminiscences, historical and artistic, evoked by their names, just as memories of antiquity contribute to the pleasure a cultured man derives from reading an ode by Horace* which might be inferior to poems of our own day which would leave the same man indifferent. For Monsieur de Charlus, a pretty middle-class woman next to any of these women was like a contemporary painting of a road or a wedding party next to an old painting whose history we know—from the pope or king who commissioned it down to the various personages who have owned it, by either gift, purchase, inheritance, or theft—and which reminds us of some event or at the very least some alliance of historical interest, and consequently some knowledge we ourselves have acquired, gives it a renewed usefulness, and increases our sense of the richness of what we can possess through memory or learning. Monsieur de Charlus was pleased, too, that a prejudice like his own, by preventing these few great ladies from associating with women of lesser breeding, allowed him to worship them intact, in their unaltered nobility, like some eighteenth-century façade supported by flat columns of pink marble, unchanged by modern times.

Monsieur de Charlus extolled the virtues of the true *nobility* of mind and heart of these women, playing on the double meaning of the word, which misled him, and in which there lay not only the falsity of this ill-conceived notion, this medley of aristocracy, generosity, and art, but also its seductiveness, dangerous for people like my grandmother, for whom the coarsest but most innocent prejudice of a nobleman who cares only about heraldic quarterings* and nothing else would have seemed too ridiculous, but who was defenceless whenever something presented itself in the guise of spiritual superiority, to the point that she found princes the most enviable of men, because they were able to have a La Bruyère or a Fénelon as their tutor.*

The three Guermantes left us in front of the Grand-Hôtel; they were going to lunch with the Princesse de Luxembourg. As my grandmother was taking her leave of Madame de Villeparisis and Saint-Loup of my grandmother, Monsieur de Charlus, who up until then hadn't said a word to me, took a few steps back towards me and said: 'I'll be taking tea this evening after dinner in my aunt de Villeparisis' rooms. I hope you'll grant me the pleasure of attending, along with your grandmother.' And then he rejoined the marquise.

Even though it was Sunday, there were no more cabs outside the hotel than at the beginning of the season. The notary's wife especially found it quite expensive to rent a carriage every time just in order not to go to the Cambremers', so she settled on staying in her room.

'Is Madame Blandais not well?' her husband was asked. 'We haven't seen her today.'

'She has a slight headache—the heat, the bad weather. It takes the least little thing . . . But I think you'll see her tonight. I've told her she should come down. It can only do her good.'

I thought that by inviting us to take tea with his aunt, whom I was sure he'd informed of our visit, Monsieur de Charlus wanted to make up for the rudeness he'd shown me during that morning's stroll. But when we arrived in Madame de Villeparisis' drawing room and I went over to greet her nephew, despite my circling around him as, in a shrill voice, he was telling a rather malicious story about one of his relatives, I couldn't catch his eye; I made up my mind to say a loud hello to him, to apprise him of my presence, but I realized he had noticed me, for even before I'd uttered a word, as I was bowing to him, I saw his two fingers held out for me to clasp, though he never turned his eyes towards me or interrupted his conversation. He'd obviously seen me, without seeming to, and I noticed then that his eyes, which were never fixed on his interlocutor, were constantly roaming in every direction, like those of certain frightened animals, or of street hawkers who, while they're reeling off their sales pitch and exhibiting their illicit wares, without turning their heads, are scanning the different points on the horizon from which the police might come. At the same time, I was a little surprised to see that Madame de Villeparisis, though happy to see us, didn't seem to have been expecting us; I was even more surprised to hear Monsieur de Charlus say to my grandmother: 'Ah! What a good idea you had to drop in, it's lovely of them, isn't it, Auntie?' No doubt he'd noticed her surprise when we came in and thought, as a man accustomed to setting the tone, the 'right note', that all he had to do to change her surprise into delight was to indicate he was just as surprised, that it was perfectly natural for our entrance to cause such a reaction. And he was right in thinking this, for Madame de Villeparisis, who thought highly of her nephew and knew how difficult he was to please, seemed suddenly to have discovered new qualities in my grandmother, and kept making much of her. But I couldn't understand how, after just a few hours, Monsieur de Charlus could have forgotten the invitation—curtly delivered but seemingly so intentional, so premeditated—which he'd addressed to me that very morning, and which he called a 'good idea' of my grandmother's, while the idea was entirely his own. With a concern for exactitude that I retained until I was old enough to understand that we don't learn the truth about a man's intention by asking him about it, and that the danger of a misunderstanding that will probably go unnoticed is less than that of naïve insistence, I asked: 'But don't you remember, sir, that it was you who invited us to come this evening?' Not a sound, not a movement betrayed the fact that Monsieur de Charlus had heard my question. Seeing this, I repeated it, like a diplomat or a young man who, after a quarrel, endeavours with unflagging but futile goodwill, to reason with someone who is determined not to be reasoned with. Monsieur de Charlus still didn't answer. I thought I saw hovering over his lips the smile of those who from a great height pass judgement on the character and breeding of others.

Since he was refusing all explanation, I tried to find one myself, but I could only waver between several, none of which seemed the right one. Perhaps he didn't remember, or perhaps I was the one who hadn't understood what he'd said that morning . . . More probably, in his pride he didn't want to seem to have been seeking out people he disdained, and preferred to transfer to them the idea of dropping in. But in that case, if he was contemptuous of us, why had he insisted that we come—or rather, that my grandmother come, since he said not a single word to me but spoke to her alone all evening? Chatting with the greatest animation with her as well as with Madame de Villeparisis, while sitting almost hidden behind them, as though in a theatre box, he was content from time to time merely to divert the searching gaze of his penetrating eyes and rest it on my face, with the same seriousness, the same air of preoccupation, as if it were a manuscript difficult to decipher.

Probably, if it hadn't been for those eyes, Monsieur de Charlus' face would have been like that of many handsome men. And when Saint-Loup, telling me about other Guermantes, said to me later on: 'Believe me, they don't have that look of high breeding, of a nobleman down to their fingertips, that my uncle Palamède does!', confirming that there was nothing mysterious or new about a thoroughbred look or aristocratic bearing, but that they were comprised of elements I'd recognized without any difficulty and without feeling any particular impression, I felt another of my illusions vanishing into thin air. But although Monsieur de Charlus kept a hermetic seal on the expression of his face, to which a light dusting of powder gave a slightly theatrical look, his eyes were like two crevices or chinks in a wall which he had been unable to fill up and through which, depending on where you stood in relation to him, you suddenly felt yourself in the line of fire of some hidden weapon which seemed potentially dangerous, even for the person who, without being entirely in control of it, carried it about with him, unsafe and always on the point of exploding;

and the cautious, perpetually anxious expression of those eyes, with their low, dark circles, imparted a look of weariness to his face, however carefully he'd composed and arranged it, and made one think of an incognito, a disguise adopted by a powerful man in danger, or merely a dangerous but tragic individual. I'd have liked to guess what this secret was which other men didn't carry within them and which had already made Monsieur de Charlus' gaze so enigmatic to me when I'd seen him that morning outside the Casino. Now that I knew about his background, I could no longer believe his face was that of a thief, and, based on what I heard of his conversation, I could tell it wasn't that of a madman. If he was so cold towards me but so friendly to my grandmother, perhaps that stemmed not from any personal antipathy, for generally speaking he evinced as much benevolence towards women (about whose flaws he'd usually speak in only the most forgiving way) as he did hatred towards men—especially young men—which was redolent of the hatred certain misogynists have for women. When Saint-Loup happened to mention two or three 'gigolos' who were relatives or friends of his, Monsieur de Charlus said, with an almost ferocious expression which contrasted starkly with his usual coldness: 'They're absolute scum!' I realized that his main criticism of the young men of today was their effeminacy. 'They're women through and through!', he said scornfully. But what life wouldn't have seemed effeminate next to the one he wanted a man to lead, which he thought was never energetic or virile enough? (He himself, on his walking tours, after hours on his feet, would plunge his overheated body into freezing rivers.) He didn't even like a man to wear a single ring. But this defence of virility didn't prevent him from having qualities of the most delicate sensitivity. To Madame de Villeparisis, who asked him to describe for my grandmother a château where Madame de Sévigné had stayed, adding that she found Madame de Sévigné's despair at being separated from that 'tiresome' Madame de Grignanon rather contrived and 'literary', he replied:

'On the contrary, it seems only too genuine to me. It was a time when those feelings were well understood. The inhabitant of La Fontaine's Monomotapa, running to see his friend who appeared to him in a dream looking a little sad, or the pigeon thinking the greatest of all evils is the absence of the other pigeon,* might seem to you, my dear aunt, as exaggerated as Madame de Sévigné being unable to wait until she can be alone with her daughter. It's so beautiful, what she says when she leaves her: "This separation pains me in my soul, like an ache I can feel in my whole body. In absence, we make free with the hours; we move ahead to a time for which we yearn." '*

My grandmother was delighted to hear Madame de Sévigné's *Letters* spoken of exactly as she would have done. She was astonished that a man could understand them so well. She found a feminine delicacy and sensitivity in Monsieur de Charlus. Later, when my grandmother and I were discussing him together, we both said he must have been profoundly influenced by a woman—his mother, perhaps, or his daughter later on if he had children. To myself I thought: 'A mistress', remembering the influence Saint-Loup's mistress seemed to have on him, which led to my realizing how much the women with whom men live refine them.

'Once she was back with her daughter again, she probably had nothing to say to her,' Madame de Villeparisis replied.

'But of course she did; even if it was only what she called "things so slight that only you and I would notice them".* In any case, she was very fond of her. And La Bruyère tells us that means everything: "To be close to those one loves is enough: to speak with them or not to speak with them is all the same."* He's quite right; that's the only happiness there is,' Monsieur de Charlus added in a melancholy tone; 'and as to that happiness, alas, life is so poorly arranged that we rarely enjoy it; Madame de Sévigné was less to be pitied than many others. She spent most of her life with the person she loved.'

'You forget it wasn't "love"; it was her daughter she was with.'

'But the important thing in life is not *whom* you love,' he continued in an assured, authoritative, almost cutting tone, 'it's the fact of loving. What Madame de Sévigné felt for her daughter can more properly be said to resemble the passion Racine portrayed in *Andromaque* or *Phèdre* than the banal relationships the young Sévigné* had with his mistresses. It's like the love of some mystic for his God. The overly narrow demarcations we draw around love come solely from our great ignorance of life.'

'You're an admirer of *Andromaque* and *Phèdre*, are you?' Saint-Loup asked his uncle, in a slightly scornful tone.

'There's more truth in a tragedy by Racine than in all the plays of Victor Hugo,' replied Monsieur de Charlus.

'These society folk are the limit, aren't they?' Saint-Loup whispered in my ear. 'To prefer Racine to Victor Hugo—I ask you!' He was genuinely saddened by his uncle's words, but his relish at saying 'the limit' and especially 'I ask you!' consoled him.

In these reflections on the sadness of living far from the one you love (which would lead my grandmother to tell me that Madame de Villeparisis' nephew had a better understanding of certain books than his aunt did, and had a quality that made him far superior to most clubmen), Monsieur de Charlus not only revealed a delicacy of sentiment that men rarely show; his very voice, like certain untrained contralto voices whose singing sounds like a duet between a woman and a young man, lingered, at those times when he expressed such delicate thoughts, on the high notes, took on an unexpected sweetness, and seemed to contain lavishly tender choruses of brides and sisters. But the bevy of girls that Monsieur de Charlus, with his horror of effeminacy, would have been so taken aback at seeming to shelter thus in his voice, was not limited to the interpretation or modulation of scraps of sentiment. Often, as Monsieur de Charlus was talking, you could hear the high, fresh laughter of schoolgirls or coquettes gossiping mischievously and making sly remarks.

He spoke of an estate that had belonged to his family where Marie-Antoinette had slept, with a park designed by Le Nôtre;* it belonged now to the Israels, the wealthy financiers who had purchased it. 'Israels—at least that's the name these people go by, which strikes me as a generic, ethnic term rather than a proper name. Perhaps we're not aware that people of that sort don't have names but are merely designated by the collective tribe to which they belong. No matter! But really, to have been the home of the Guermantes and to belong now to the Israels!!!' he exclaimed. 'It reminds me of that room in the Château de Blois* where the guide giving the tour said to me: "This is where Mary Stuart used to say her prayers, and now it's where I store my brooms." Naturally I don't want to know any more about that Guermantes house, which has been dishonoured, than about my cousin Clara de Chimay,* who left her husband. But I do keep a photograph of the house when it was still pure,* just as I have one of the Princesse de Chimay when her large eyes looked at no one but my cousin. Photography acquires a little of the dignity it lacks when it stops being a reproduction of reality and shows us things that no longer exist. I could give you a copy,' he said to my grandmother, 'since you have an interest in that sort of architecture.' At that moment, noticing that the embroidered handkerchief in his pocket was letting its coloured edges show, he quickly pushed it back in with the alarmed look of a prudish but not in the least innocent woman hiding charms that, out of an excess of scruple, she deems indecent. 'Can you believe', he went on, 'that the first thing these people did was to destroy the park by Le Nôtre! That's as outrageous as slashing a painting by Poussin!* For that alone, those Israels should be thrown in prison. Though it's quite true', he added with a smile after a moment of silence, 'that there are undoubtedly quite a few other reasons they should be there! In any case, you can imagine the effect an English garden produces in front of the architecture of such a house.'

'Actually, the house is in the same style as the Petit Trianon,'* said Madame de Villeparisis, 'and Marie-Antoinette did have an English garden there.'

'Which completely spoils Gabriel's façade,' Monsieur de Charlus quipped. 'Obviously now it would be brutal to destroy the Hameau.* But whatever the fashions of the times may be, I very much doubt that a whim of Madame Israels has the same prestige as a memento of the Queen.'

Meanwhile my grandmother had been motioning to me that it was time for bed, despite the insistence of Saint-Loup who, to my great shame, had mentioned to Monsieur de Charlus the melancholy I often felt in the evening before going to sleep; I feared his uncle must not have found that very virile. I lingered a little while longer before leaving, and was quite surprised when, a little later, I heard someone knocking on my bedroom door; when I asked who it was, I heard the voice of Monsieur de Charlus, who said abruptly:

'It's Charlus. May I come in, Monsieur? Monsieur,' he went on in the same tone once he'd closed the door behind him, 'my nephew was saying just now that you tend to feel a little restless before you go to sleep, and also that you admire Bergotte's books. Since I have one in my trunk that you probably aren't familiar with, I'll bring it up to help you through those moments when you feel out of sorts.'

I thanked Monsieur de Charlus effusively and said I'd been afraid that what Saint-Loup had told him about my unease at nightfall made me seem more foolish than I was.

'Not at all,' he replied in a gentler tone. 'You may not, perhaps, have any personal merit; so few people have! But for a little while at least you have youth on your side, and that's always appealing. Besides, Monsieur, the greatest folly is to think that feelings one doesn't have oneself are ridiculous or blameworthy. I love the night, and you tell me you're afraid of it; I love smelling roses and I have a friend who becomes feverish from their smell. Do you think that makes him less worthy than I am? I try to understand everything, and I take care to condemn nothing. So don't fret, I won't say this melancholy isn't a difficult thing, I know how one can suffer from things that others wouldn't understand. But at least you've chosen well to direct your affection towards your grandmother. You can see her often. And it's a tenderness that's permitted; I mean a tenderness that's repaid. So many are not!'

He was pacing back and forth in the room, looking at one object, picking up another. I felt as if he had something he wanted to say to me but couldn't find the right words.

'I have another of Bergotte's books here, I'll have it sent up to you,' he added, and rang the bell. Presently a bellboy appeared. 'Go and fetch your head waiter. He's the only one here clever enough to run an errand,' Monsieur de Charlus said loftily.

'Do you mean Monsieur Aimé, Monsieur?' asked the bellboy.

'I don't know his name, but yes, now that I think about it I've heard him called Aimé. Go quickly, I'm in a hurry.'

'He'll be here right away, Monsieur, I just saw him downstairs,' replied the bellboy, who wanted to seem well informed. Some time passed. The bellboy returned.

'Monsieur, Monsieur Aimé has gone to bed. But I can run your errand.'

'No, you can just wake him up.'

'Monsieur, I can't do that, he doesn't sleep here.'

'In that case, leave us alone.'

'But Monsieur,' I said after the bellboy had left, 'you're too kind, a single volume by Bergotte is enough for me.'

'Yes, I think so too, after all.'

Monsieur de Charlus kept pacing up and down. A few minutes went by in this way, and then, after some hesitation, stopping several times to gather himself, he swivelled round and, in a voice that had resumed its biting tone, he said abruptly: 'Good evening, Monsieur,' and left. After all the lofty sentiments I'd heard him express that evening, the next morning, the day of his departure, on the beach, as I was about to go for my daily swim, when Monsieur de Charlus came over to let me know my grandmother would be waiting as soon as

I got out of the water, I was astonished to hear him say, as he pinched my neck, with a vulgar laugh and an air of familiarity:

'But he couldn't care less about his old granny, could he? Little rascal!'

'But I adore her, Monsieur!'

'Monsieur,' he said in an icy tone as he stepped back a pace, 'you're still young, you should take advantage of it to learn two things: the first is to abstain from expressing sentiments that are too natural not to be taken for granted; the second is not to take offence and reply out of hand to things people say to you without first trying to understand their meaning. If you'd taken that precaution just now, you wouldn't have seemed as if you were babbling nonsense like a deaf man, while to top it all off wearing a bathing costume embroidered with anchors! I lent you a book by Bergotte which I need. Have it sent to me in an hour by that head waiter with the ridiculous, inappropriate name, who I presume is not asleep at this time of day. I see now I was premature when I spoke to you last night about the charms of youth—I'd have done you more of a service if I'd pointed out its foolishness, its inconsistencies, its wrong-headedness! I hope, Monsieur, that this little shower of words will be no less salutary to you than your swim. But don't just stand there, you'll catch cold. I bid you good day, Monsieur.'

Monsieur de Charlus must have regretted these words, for a little while later, I received—in a morocco binding with a panel of tooled leather on the front cover showing a spray of forget-me-nots in half-relief—the book he'd lent me which I had sent back to him, not by Aimé, who was 'off duty', but by the lift-boy.

After Monsieur de Charlus had departed, Robert and I could finally go to dinner at Bloch's. During that little gathering, I learned that the stories our friend was only too ready to find amusing were those told by Monsieur Bloch senior, and that the 'truly remarkable' person featured in them was always one of Monsieur Bloch's friends, to whom he invariably applied this epithet. There are a certain number of people we admire as children, a father wittier than the rest of the family, a teacher who seems to us more philosophical because of the philosophy he teaches us, a classmate more advanced than ourselves (as Bloch had been for me) who despises the Musset of 'L'Espoir en Dieu'* when we still admire him, but who, by the time we've moved on to Leconte or Claudel,* will still be waxing lyrical over

> At Saint-Blaise, at Zuecca,
> You were so, so at ease . . .*

as well as

> Padua is a most beautiful place
> Where most grand legal scholars . . .
> But I prefer polenta . . .
> . . . La Toppatelle
> Goes past in her black domino*

and of all the 'Nuits' remembers only

> In Le Havre, before the Atlantic,
> In Venice, at the dreadful Lido,
> Where, on the grass round a grave,
> The pale Adriatic comes to die.*

So that, whenever we unreservedly admire someone, we note down and quote appreciatively things that are quite inferior to those that, left to the devices of our own intelligence, we'd sternly reject, just as a writer uses, on the pretext that they're true, phrases and characters in his novel which in real life are dead weights, mediocre elements. The portraits Saint-Simon wrote are admirable, though he probably didn't think they were; but what he describes as the charming traits of the witty men of his day has remained mediocre or become incomprehensible. He would never have stooped to invent what he reports as being so clever or colourful as said by Madame Cornuel* or Louis XIV; this characteristic is noticeable in many others, and can be interpreted in various ways, of which the only one that's relevant here is this: in the state of mind in which we 'observe', we are far below the level at which we create.

There was, then, embedded in my friend Bloch, Bloch senior, who lagged forty years behind his son and reeled off ludicrous anecdotes which were greeted with as much inner amusement by my friend as actual laughter by the external, visible Bloch senior, since whenever the father guffawed at his own jokes—making sure to repeat the punchline several times, so that his audience might fully appreciate the point—the son would add his own loud laughter, with which he never failed to acknowledge his father's stories at the dinner table. And so, after saying the most intelligent things, the younger Bloch, exhibiting the traits he'd inherited from his family, would tell us for the umpteenth time some of the gems his father would trot out (along with his frock coat) only on those ceremonial occasions when the younger Bloch had brought to the house someone worth impressing: one of his professors, a classmate who had won all the school prizes, or, as on that evening, Saint-Loup and myself. For instance: 'An expert military theorist, who had brilliantly proven without the shadow of a doubt why, in the Russo–Japanese war, the Japanese would be beaten and the Russians would be victorious',* or: 'He's an eminent gentleman who's viewed as a great financier in political circles and a great politician in financial circles'. These sayings were interchangeable with others about the Baron de Rothschild and Sir Rufus Israels, two individuals who were presented in an ambiguous way, so that one might have been led to believe that Monsieur Bloch had known them both personally.

I myself was taken in, and from the way Monsieur Bloch senior spoke of Bergotte, I thought he was an old friend. But Monsieur Bloch knew all these famous people only by 'knowing *of* them', having seen them from afar at the theatre or about town. He assumed, moreover, that his own face, his name, his personality, were known to them as well and that when they saw him, they were often obliged to stifle a furtive urge to bow to him. Although people in high society may know men of talent and have them to dinner, this doesn't mean they understand them any better. But after one has seen a little of society life, the vacuity of its denizens makes one overeager to associate with obscure people who know the famous only by 'knowing of them', and over-ready to assume they're intelligent. I would discover this when I spoke of Bergotte. Monsieur Bloch wasn't the only one to be a social success in his own house. My friend was even more so with his sisters, whom he kept hectoring while burying his face almost in his plate, which would make them laugh uproariously. They too had adopted their brother's peculiar language, which they spoke fluently, as if it were obligatory, and the only one that could be used by intelligent people. When we arrived, the eldest sister said to one of the younger ones: 'Go and tell our wise father and our venerable mother.' 'Fillies,' Bloch said to them, 'allow me to introduce the cavalier Saint-Loup of the swift javelins, who has come for a few days from Doncières to these dwellings of polished stone, abundant with horses.' Since he was just as vulgar as he was literary, his speech would usually end with some less-than-Homeric joke: 'Come, come, close your pepla with the lovely clasps,* what's all this I see? He is not my father!* And the Mesdemoiselles Bloch would double over in a tempest of laughter. I told their brother how much pleasure he'd given me by recommending I read Bergotte, whose books I loved.

Monsieur Bloch senior, who knew Bergotte only by sight, and Bergotte's life only from theatre gossip, had an equally indirect way of 'knowing' his books, with the help of judgements apparently literary in nature. He lived in a world of approximations, where one salutes the empty air and jumps to wrong conclusions. In this world, inexactitude and incompetence in no way diminish self-confidence; quite the contrary. Since so few of us can claim any intimacy with brilliant people or enjoy intellectual friendships, it's the beneficent miracle of self-esteem that allows those who lack them to continue in their belief that they are the most enviable, because the perspectives of the social strata make each rank seem best to the one who occupies it, and make him see as less fortunate, less well-off, more to be pitied, greater men whom he names and slanders without knowing them, judges and disdains without understanding them. Even in cases where self-esteem multiplies a person's modest personal advantages but can't manage to ensure him the dose of happiness, greater than that granted to others, that he requires, envy is there to make up the difference. Since envy must express itself in scornful terms, phrases like 'I don't want to know him' should be translated as 'I am unable to know him'. That's the intellectual translation. But the emotional meaning is indeed 'I don't want to know him'. We know that's untrue, but we don't say it out of simple dissembling; we say it because that's how we feel, and that's enough to bridge the gap between truth and untruth, which is all we need to be happy.

Egocentrism thus enabling every human being to see the world in descending tiers beneath himself as king, Monsieur Bloch allowed himself the luxury of absolute monarchy in the morning whenever, as he drank his chocolate, he saw Bergotte's name at the foot of an article in the newspaper: he would grant him a haughty and cursory audience, pronounce his sentence upon him and, between each scalding sip of his beverage, would give himself the comforting pleasure of repeating: 'That Bergotte fellow has become unreadable. It's enough to make you want to cancel your subscription. What convoluted, pleonastic nonsense!' And he would help himself to another slice of toast.

Monsieur Bloch's illusion of importance extended a little beyond the radius of his own self-perceptions. His children, for one thing, regarded him as a superior being. Children always tend either to belittle or to glorify their parents, and for a good son his father is always the best father there is, even aside from all the objective reasons there may be for admiring him. These reasons weren't entirely lacking in the case of Monsieur Bloch, who was well educated, shrewd, and affectionate towards his family. His closest relations were the ones who were happiest to be with him, because if, in 'society', people are judged by a standard (which is incidentally absurd) and according to rules that are false but fixed, based on comparison with the sum total of other fashionable people, in the subdivisions of middle-class life, on the other hand, dinner parties and family celebrations revolve around people who are declared easy-going and amusing, but who in society wouldn't be given a second chance. Moreover, in this bourgeois milieu where the artificial grandeurs of the aristocracy don't exist, they are replaced by distinctions that are even more ridiculous. And so in his family, and even among his remotest relations, an alleged similarity in the cut of his moustache and the bridge of his nose led to Monsieur Bloch's being called 'the spitting image of the Duc d'Aumale'.* (In the world of club bell-hops, isn't the one who wears his cap at a tilt and his tunic buttoned so as to make himself look, he imagines, like a foreign officer, the one who's viewed as something of a character by his fellows?)

This resemblance was extremely faint, but it was almost like a title. People would say 'Which Bloch do you mean? The Duc d'Aumale?' in the same way they might say 'Which Princesse Murat do you mean? The Queen of Naples?'* A few other minute features led his kinsfolk to proclaim him a man of distinction. Unwilling to go so far as to have a carriage of his own, on certain days Monsieur Bloch would hire an open victoria and pair, and have himself driven through the Bois de Boulogne, his body negligently sprawled, with two fingers on his temple and two under his chin, and though people who didn't know him may have thought he looked like 'a silly old man', his family members were convinced that when it came to matters of elegance, Uncle Salomon could show a thing or two to Gramont-Caderousse himself.* He was one of those people who, when they die, are described in the social column of *Le Radical*,* because they used to share a table in a restaurant in town with the editor of that paper, as 'a well-known

figure on the Paris scene'. Monsieur Bloch told Saint-Loup and me
that Bergotte knew very well why he, Monsieur Bloch, cut him in
public, so that whenever Bergotte saw him at the theatre or the club
he'd avert his eyes. Saint-Loup blushed, for he thought that club
couldn't be the Jockey Club, of which his father was president. Yet it
must have been a relatively exclusive club, since Monsieur Bloch had
said that Bergotte wouldn't be admitted to it now. And so, in some
trepidation that he might be 'underestimating the opponent', Saint-
Loup asked if the club was the Cercle de la Rue Royale,* which was
deemed 'beyond the pale' by his own family, and where he knew certain Jews were admitted. 'No,' Monsieur Bloch replied with an air at
once nonchalant, proud, and ashamed, 'it's just a little club, but much
nicer—the Old Codgers' Club.* We're very select, you know.' 'Isn't
Sir Rufus Israels the chairman?' the younger Bloch asked, to give his
father the opportunity to tell a lie that would show him in a good
light, not suspecting that the financier didn't have the same prestige
for Saint-Loup as he did for his family. Actually, the Old Codgers'
Club counted among its members not Sir Rufus Israels, but one of
his employees. This man, being on good terms with his employer, had
a supply of the great financier's calling cards, and gave one to Monsieur
Bloch whenever he was about to travel on a railway company of which
Sir Rufus was a director, so that Monsieur Bloch would say: 'I'll just
drop by the club and ask for a recommendation from Sir Rufus.' And
the card would enable him to dazzle the train conductors.

The Mesdemoiselles Bloch were more interested in Bergotte and,
returning to him so as to avoid prolonging the subject of the 'Old
Codgers', the youngest asked her brother in the most serious tone
possible (since she thought no other expressions existed in the world
to describe people of talent than the ones he employed):

'Is he such a cracking fellow, this Bergotte? Is he in the same category as the top lads, chaps like Villiers or Catulle?'*

'I've met him at a few opening nights,' said Monsieur Nissim
Bernard. 'He's rather uncouth, a sort of Schlemihl.'*

There was nothing very grievous about this allusion to the Count
von Chamisso's story in itself, but the epithet 'Schlemihl' was part of
the half-German, half-Jewish dialect, the use of which delighted
Monsieur Bloch in the privacy of his own family, but which he found
vulgar and out of place when spoken in the presence of strangers. And
so he shot a severe look at his uncle.

'He has talent,' said Bloch.

'Ah, I see,' his sister said in a serious tone, as if to say that in that case I could be forgiven.

'All writers have talent,' Monsieur Bloch senior said scornfully.

'I've even heard it said', said his son as he raised his fork and squinted with an air of devilish irony, 'that he's putting himself forward as a candidate for the Académie française!'

'Good grief! The man's a lightweight!' replied Monsieur Bloch senior, who didn't seem to have the same contempt for the Académie as his son and daughters. 'He's out of their league.'

'In any case, the Académie is a salon, and Bergotte has no influence,' declared Madame Bloch's wealthy uncle, a gentle, inoffensive individual whose surname, Bernard, might by itself have aroused my grandfather's diagnostic talents, but would have seemed too little in harmony with a face that appeared to have been brought back from Darius' palace* and recomposed by Madame Dieulafoy,* if it weren't for his first name, Nissim (chosen by some connoisseur wishing to crown this visage from Susa with an Oriental flair), which made the wings of some androcephalous bull from Khorsabad float above it.* But Monsieur Bloch never stopped insulting his uncle, either because he was irritated by his scapegoat's unguarded friendliness, or because, the villa being paid for by Monsieur Nissim Bernard, he wanted to show that, though his beneficiary, he still kept his independence, and above all that he wasn't trying to wheedle his way into the rich man's future bequest. Monsieur Bernard was particularly upset at being treated so rudely in front of the butler. He murmured an unintelligible phrase of which all that could be made out was: 'When the meschores are here.' In the Bible, *meschores* means 'servant of God'. Amongst themselves, the Blochs used this word to refer to the servants, and were always overjoyed to use it, since their certainty of being understood neither by Gentiles nor by the servants themselves increased the delight of Monsieur Nissim Bernard and Monsieur Bloch at having the distinction of being both 'masters' and 'Jews'. But this cause for satisfaction turned into a source of annoyance when company was present. When Monsieur Bloch heard his uncle say 'meschores', he felt he was allowing his Oriental side to show through too much, just as a courtesan entertaining some of her kind along with respectable people is irritated if they refer to their profession or use offensive words. So, instead of his uncle's admonition being heeded by Monsieur

Bloch, the latter, beside himself, could contain himself no longer. He made sure not to miss a single opportunity to berate the wretched uncle.

'Of course, whenever there's some stupid, sententious phrase to utter, we can be sure you won't miss a chance to say it. You'd be the first to lick Bergotte's boots if he was here!' Monsieur Bloch exclaimed, while Monsieur Nissim Bernard, aggrieved, lowered the ringleted beard of King Sargon towards his plate. My friend, who had also grown a beard just as frizzy and black, bore a strong resemblance to his great-uncle.

'What's that? You're the son of the Marquis de Marsantes? I knew him very well,' said Monsieur Nissim Bernard to Saint-Loup. I thought he meant 'knew' in the sense that Bloch senior said he 'knew' Bergotte, that is, by sight. But he added: 'Your father was one of my good friends.' Meanwhile Bloch had turned extremely red, his father looked deeply annoyed, and the Mesdemoiselles Bloch were stifling laughter. This is because in Monsieur Nissim Bernard the love of showing off, suppressed in Monsieur Bloch senior and his children, had created the habit of perpetually lying. For example, whenever he stayed at a hotel, Monsieur Nissim Bernard, as Monsieur Bloch senior would have done, had his valet bring him his newspapers in the dining room in the middle of lunch, when everyone was there, so they could see he always travelled with a valet. But if he became acquainted with any of the hotel guests, the uncle would say he was a senator, which his nephew would never have done. Despite the fact that he knew perfectly well it would eventually come out that he had no right to the title, at that moment he couldn't resist the urge to claim it. Monsieur Bloch suffered greatly from his uncle's lies and from all the difficulties they caused him. 'Pay no attention to him, he's always talking nonsense,' he murmured to Saint-Loup, whose interest was all the more piqued, for he was very curious about the psychology of liars. 'An even greater liar than Ithacan Odysseus, though Athena called him the greatest liar among mortals,'* our friend Bloch added. 'Just think!' Monsieur Nissim Bernard exclaimed. 'If I'd only known I'd be dining with my old friend's son! At home in Paris I have a photograph of your father, and any number of letters from him. He always called me "Uncle", though no one knew why. He was a brilliant, delightful man. I remember one dinner at my house in Nice, with Sardou, Labiche, Augier . . .' 'Molière, Racine, Corneille,' Monsieur

Bloch senior continued ironically, while his son completed the list with 'Plautus, Menander, Kalidasa'.* Wounded, Monsieur Nissim Bernard abruptly cut short his story, and, ascetically depriving himself of a great pleasure, remained silent for the rest of dinner.

'O bronze-helmeted Saint-Loup,' said Bloch, 'help yourself to a little more of this duck, its thighs thick with fat, whereon the illustrious high priest of poultry has poured copious libations of red wine.'

Usually, after fishing out from his store of anecdotes his choicest ones about Sir Rufus Israels and others for one of his son's important friends, Monsieur Bloch, feeling he'd won his son's approval, would withdraw so as not to 'overdo it' in front of 'the lad'. But if there was some extenuating circumstance, as, for example, when his son had passed the *agrégation*,* Monsieur Bloch would add to the usual series of anecdotes an ironic remark he usually saved for his personal friends, and which the younger Bloch was extremely proud to see trotted out for the benefit of his own friends: 'The government has committed an outrage. They didn't consult Monsieur Coquelin!* Monsieur Coquelin has let his displeasure be known.' (Monsieur Bloch prided himself on being reactionary and scornful of theatre people.)

Mesdemoiselles Bloch and their brother blushed to the roots of their hair, so impressed were they when Bloch senior, to prove how thoroughly princely he could be towards his son's 'old school chums', gave the order for champagne to be served, and casually announced that, 'as a special treat', he'd booked three seats for a performance a touring comic-opera company was giving that very night at the Casino. He was sorry he hadn't been able to get a box. They were all taken. In any case he'd tried all of them, and you were better off in the front stalls. If his son's failing (which he thought was invisible to others) was bad manners, the father's was miserliness. So what he called 'champagne' was actually a mediocre sparkling wine served from a carafe, and his so-called 'front stalls' were seats at the back, which cost half as much, miraculously convinced as he was by the divine intervention of his failing that no one would notice the difference at either dining table or theatre (where all the boxes were empty). After Monsieur Bloch had allowed us to wet our lips from shallow champagne glasses his son described floridly as 'hollow-flanked craters', we were invited to admire a painting he loved so much that he'd brought it with him to Balbec. He told us it was a Rubens.* Saint-Loup

naïvely asked him if it was signed. Blushing, Monsieur Bloch replied
that he'd had the signature cut off to fit the frame, which didn't matter, since he didn't want to sell it. Then he quickly took his leave in
order to bury himself in the *Journal officiel*,* copies of which were
strewn about the house; he was obliged to read them, he said, because
of his 'parliamentary situation', on the exact nature of which he
neglected to enlighten us.

'I'll just get a scarf,' Bloch said, 'for Zephyros and Boreas are bat-
tling over who shall control the fish-teeming sea, and if we tarry even
a little after the performance, we'll not return ere the first glimmers
of rose-fingered Eos.* By the way,' he asked Saint-Loup once we were
outside (and I quaked in my boots when I realized it was Monsieur de
Charlus to whom Bloch was referring so ironically), 'who was that
priceless clown in the dark suit I saw you parading about with the
other morning on the beach?'

'That was my uncle,' Saint-Loup replied, irked. But a faux pas like
that didn't trouble Bloch in the least. Shaking with laughter, he said:
'Heartfelt congratulations! I should have guessed; he has superb style,
and the mug of an old dodderer of the highest pedigree.'

'You can't be more mistaken,' Saint-Loup snapped, now furious.
'He's extremely intelligent.'

'I'm sorry to hear that, since it makes him less than perfect. Still, I'd
like to make his acquaintance, since I'm sure I could write some cracking pieces on old fellows like that. It's just priceless, seeing him go by!
But I'd leave out the caricatural aspect of his mug—because that would
hardly be worthy of an artist with any interest in the plastic beauty of
phrases—though (you'll have to forgive me) it had me in stitches for
quite a while, and I'd highlight the aristocratic side of your uncle, which
after all makes a smashing impression, and once you manage to stop
laughing it really does strike you with its grand style. But,' he added,
turning to me, 'on a completely different subject, there's something
I've been meaning to ask you, but whenever we're together, some god,
some blessed denizen of Olympus,* makes me completely forget to
request this piece of information which could already have been, and
which will surely be, extremely useful for me to know. Who was that
beautiful creature I saw you with at the Jardin d'Acclimatation? She
was with a gent I thought I knew by sight, and a girl with long hair?'

I'd noticed that Madame Swann hadn't remembered Bloch's name,
since she'd mentioned a different one to me, and had described my

friend as being attached to a ministry, though it had never occurred to me afterwards to ask him if this was true. But how was it that Bloch, who, according to what she'd said at the time, had got himself introduced to her, didn't know her name? I was so astonished that I was speechless for a moment.

'Whoever she was, you have my hearty congratulations,' he said. 'She must have given you a good time. I'd met her a few days before that on the belt line, and she was only too willing to undo her own belt for yours truly—I've never had such a good time, and we were just about to arrange to meet again when someone she knew had the poor taste to get on just before the terminus.'

Bloch didn't seem pleased by my silence. 'I was hoping', he said, 'to get her address from you so I could go there a few times a week to taste the pleasures of Eros, dear to the gods; but I won't insist, since you seem pledged to discretion with respect to a professional who gave herself to me three times running, in the most exquisite way, between Paris and the Point-du-Jour.* I'm sure I'll run into her again one of these nights.'

I went to see Bloch after this dinner; I was out when he returned my visit, but he was seen asking for me by Françoise, who, as it happened, had never seen him before, even though he'd visited us in Combray. She knew only that one of 'those Monsieurs'* I knew had come by to see me, but she didn't know 'to what effect', just that he was dressed 'any old way' and hadn't impressed her 'overmuch'. Though I knew that some of Françoise's notions about social matters would remain forever indecipherable to me, and that they probably stemmed, at least in part, from her tendency to mix up words and names (and these mistakes, once made, would never be corrected), I couldn't stop myself—despite long ago having given up wondering about such things—from trying (in vain, as it turned out) to discover what the immense significance the name of Bloch could have for her. For no sooner had I told her the young man she'd seen was Monsieur Bloch than she recoiled with a start, so great were her astonishment and disappointment. 'What! You mean *that's* Monsieur Bloch?' she exclaimed in amazement, as if such a prestigious personage should have an appearance that 'let you know' immediately that you were in the presence of a prodigy of nature; and, like someone realizing a historical figure doesn't live up to his reputation, she repeated in an awestruck tone in which one could already hear the beginnings of an all-embracing scepticism starting to take shape: 'What! So that's Monsieur Bloch! Ah! You'd never think it, to see him.' She seemed to be blaming me, as if I'd 'overrated' Bloch. And yet she was kind enough to add: 'Well, even if he *is* Monsieur Bloch, I'm sure Monsieur can say he's just as good as him.'

She would soon undergo a disillusionment of a different order, and of a lesser severity, with regard to Saint-Loup: she learned he was a republican. Despite the fact that when she spoke, for instance, about the Queen of Portugal, she'd say with the disrespect that among the lower classes is the supreme sign of respect: 'Amélie, that sister of Philippe's',* Françoise was a royalist. But that a marquis—not just any marquis, but one who had dazzled her—could be a supporter of the Republic didn't seem possible. She looked as upset by this as if I'd given her a box she thought was gold, for which she'd thanked me effusively, but which a jeweller later revealed to her was just gold-plated. She instantly withdrew her esteem for Saint-Loup, but soon gave it back to him, when she realized after some reflection that he couldn't, being the Marquis de Saint-Loup, *actually* be a republican, but that he was merely pretending, out of self-interest, for, the government being what it was, he could 'make a pretty penny' out of it. From then on, her coldness towards him, as well as her spite towards me, ceased altogether. And whenever she spoke of Saint-Loup, she'd say: 'He's such a hypocrite', with a broad, indulgent smile which showed only too clearly that she 'considered' him as highly now as she did before, and that she'd forgiven him.

Saint-Loup's sincerity and disinterestedness, however, were absolute; and it was this great moral purity that, unable to be wholly satisfied in a selfish emotion like love, and not conflicting in him—as it did in me—with the impossibility of finding its spiritual sustenance anywhere but within the self, made him as truly capable of friendship as I was incapable of it.

Françoise was equally mistaken about Saint-Loup when she said 'he just *looked* as if he didn't look down on people beneath him, but that wasn't true, since you only had to see him when he was angry with his coachman' to prove otherwise. In fact, Robert had upon occasion scolded his coachman with some severity, but in him this was less a proof of any feeling of class distinction than it was of class equality. 'But I say,' he said when I reproached him for speaking somewhat harshly to the coachman, 'why should I put on a show of speaking politely to him? Isn't he my equal? Isn't he as close to me as my uncles or cousins? You seem to think I should treat him with special consideration, like an inferior! You're talking like an aristocrat,' he added scornfully.

In fact, if there was a class against which he had a prejudice or bias, it was the aristocracy, to such an extent that he found it as difficult to believe in the superiority of a man of fashion as he found it easy to believe in that of a man of the people. When I mentioned the Princesse de Luxembourg, whom I'd met with his aunt, he said:

'She's just an old trout, like all her lot. She's a sort of cousin of mine, actually.'

With his prejudice against the people who composed it, Robert rarely went into society; and when he did, the scornful, hostile attitude he evinced towards it increased even more his close relatives' sorrow at his liaison with a woman 'of the stage', a liaison they believed would prove disastrous for him, especially since it had worsened his tendency towards disparagement and ridicule, and had 'led him astray' on a path that could only end with him losing his social position entirely. Hence the ruthlessness employed by many of the most frivolous men of the Faubourg Saint-Germain when they spoke about Robert's mistress. 'Harlots are just doing their job,' they'd say, 'one's no better than the next, but that one's crossed the line! There's no way we could forgive her—she's done too much harm to someone we care a great deal about.' Of course, Robert wasn't the first to be caught in such a snare. But the others took their pleasure as men of the world while they went on thinking about politics, and everything, as men of the world. Robert's family thought he'd become 'bitter'. They didn't realize that for many young men in fashionable society who might otherwise have remained uncultivated, unrefined in their friendships, and lacking in breeding and taste, it's often their mistress who is their true teacher, and affairs of this sort the only school of morals which initiates them into a higher culture and teaches them the value of selflessness in their relations with others. Even among the lower classes (who, when it comes to coarseness, so often resemble high society), it's the woman—more sensitive, more perceptive, more leisurely—who has a greater curiosity about certain refinements, and respects certain modes of beauty or art which, even though she may not understand them, she values more highly than things like money or social standing, which might have seemed more desirable to the man. Regardless of whether she's the mistress of a young clubman like Saint-Loup or a young workman (electricians, for example, can now be counted among the truest order of chivalry), her lover has too much admiration and respect for her not to extend them to what she herself respects and admires, so that his own scale of values is reversed. Because of her sex, she's weak and may have inexplicable nerve troubles, which, in a man—or even another woman, an aunt or cousin of his—would have made a sturdy youth smile. But he can't bear to see the woman he loves suffer. The young nobleman who, like Saint-Loup, has a mistress, gets into the habit, when he takes her out to dinner, of having in his pocket the valerian drops* she might need, or telling the waiter, sternly and without irony, to make sure he closes the doors quietly, and not to use damp moss in the table's centrepiece, so as to keep her from falling victim to one of those malaises he for his part has never experienced, but which to him is part of an occult world which she has taught him to see as real, and which now arouse his sympathy without his needing to experience them, and will continue to arouse it in the future even when others experience them. Saint-Loup's mistress—like the early monks in the Middle Ages teaching Christianity—had taught him to be merciful towards animals, for she was passionate about them and never went anywhere without her dog, her canaries, her parrots; Saint-Loup looked after them with motherly devotion, and called anyone who wasn't kind to them a brute. Moreover, an actress—or a so-called actress, like the one who was living with him—regardless of whether or not she was intelligent (and her intelligence was a subject I knew nothing about), by making him view the company of fashionable ladies as boring and the obligation to attend a soirée as a chore, had saved him from snobbery and cured him of frivolity. If, thanks to her, his society connections held a smaller place in the life of her young lover, his mistress had taught him to invest nobility and refinement in his friendships, which, if he'd been merely a frequenter of fashionable salons, would have been governed by vanity or self-interest and marked by coarseness. Her feminine instinct made her more capable of appreciating in men certain sensitive qualities, which, without her, her lover might have mocked or failed to recognize; this made her quick to distinguish which of Saint-Loup's friends had real affection for him, and to prefer that one over all the others. And soon Saint-Loup, without needing to be reminded by her anymore, began to care about all these things himself; in Balbec, where she wasn't present, for me, whom she'd never seen and whom he might not even have mentioned yet in his letters, on his own initiative he'd close the window of a carriage we were riding in, take away the flowers that might cause an attack, and, when he had to take his leave of several people at once, made sure to say goodbye to them a little sooner so as to be alone with me, marking a difference between them and me, treating me differently from the others. His mistress had opened his mind to the invisible; she had introduced seriousness into his life, delicacy into his heart—but his family were oblivious to all that, and only kept repeating, in tears: 'That strumpet will kill him, but not before she's dishonoured him first!' It's true that by this time Robert had derived all the benefit he could from her, and now she could cause him nothing but suffering, since she'd come to despise him and did nothing but torture him. One fine day, she began to find him silly and ridiculous, because the friends she had among the young writers and actors had assured her that this was the case; and she in turn had repeated what they'd said with all the passion and conviction you evince whenever you receive from others and adopt as your own opinions or customs of which you were entirely ignorant before. She was only too eager to proclaim, as her actor friends did, that the gulf between her and Saint-Loup was unbridgeable, because they came from different worlds, because she was an intellectual whereas he, whatever he might say to the contrary, was, by birth, an enemy of intellect. This point of view seemed profound to her, and she sought verification of it in the most insignificant words, the slightest actions, of her lover. But when these same friends had also convinced her that, by keeping such ill-suited company, she was destroying all the expectations she had raised, that her lover would end up being a bad influence on her, that by living with him, she was ruining her future as an artist, the scorn she felt for Saint-Loup was combined with the same hatred she'd have felt for him if he'd been trying to infect her with a fatal disease. She saw as little of him as she could while continually putting off a definitive break—an eventuality that seemed highly improbable to me. Saint-Loup made such great sacrifices for her that, even if she were incredibly beautiful (he'd never wanted to show me her photograph, saying: 'First of all, she's no great beauty, and also she doesn't photograph well—these are just some snapshots I took with my Kodak,* they'd give you a false idea of her'), it seemed unlikely that she'd find another man who would be prepared to do as much for her. It didn't occur to me that a passing fancy of making a name for yourself—even if you have no talent—or that the opinion, even if it's only the private opinion, of people who matter to you, can (though this may not perhaps have been the case for Saint-Loup's mistress), even for a little *cocotte*, be more powerful motives than the pleasure of acquiring money. Although Saint-Loup, without quite understanding what was going on in his mistress's head, didn't believe her to be completely sincere either in her unfair reproaches or in her promises of eternal love, he still had the feeling now and then that she'd break up with him when she could, and because of that, impelled no doubt by the instinct of his love to preserve itself, which may have been more clairvoyant than Saint-Loup himself, and, exercising a practical side of his nature which worked skilfully together in him with the loftiest—and blindest—impulses of the heart, had refused to advance her any large sums; though he borrowed a huge amount so she'd want for nothing, he had it doled out to her only as a daily allowance. No doubt, if she really was planning on leaving him, she was calmly waiting until she'd 'feathered her nest', which, in view of the money given to her by Saint-Loup, shouldn't take much time at all, although any time, however short, was a gift granted to prolong my new friend's happiness—or unhappiness.

This dramatic period of their relationship—which had now reached its cruellest, most acute phase, for she had forbidden him to remain in Paris, where his presence exasperated her, and had forced him to spend his leave in Balbec, near his garrison—had begun one evening at the house of one of Saint-Loup's aunts, after he'd prevailed on her to allow his mistress to recite, before the large gathering of guests, excerpts from a Symbolist play in which she'd once acted in an avant-garde theatre; her own enthusiasm for the piece was so great that it had infected him as well.

But when she appeared, with a large lily in her hand, in a costume copied from the *Ancilla Domini*,* which she'd convinced Robert was a true 'vision of art', her entrance had been greeted in this gathering of clubmen and duchesses by smiles which the monotonous intoning of her delivery, the outlandishness of certain words, and the frequent repetition of them, had changed into giggles, stifled at first, but then so uncontrollable that the poor monologist couldn't go on. The next day, Saint-Loup's aunt had been unanimously blamed for having allowed such a bizarre performer to appear in her home. A prominent duke made no secret of the fact that, if people were criticizing her, she had only herself to blame. 'Damn it all, what's the idea, serving up that sort of gibberish! It might be all right if the woman had talent, but that one has none whatsoever, not now, not ever! Good Lord, Paris isn't as dumb as people seem to think. Society isn't made up entirely of idiots. This little lady obviously thought she could surprise Paris. But Paris is harder to surprise than all that, and there are some things we just won't swallow.'

As to the artiste herself, she said to Saint-Loup as she was leaving: 'How *could* you land me with such empty-headed old cows, such asses, such brainless boors? What were you thinking? You can take it from me that there wasn't a single man there who didn't give me the eye or try to play footsie with me, and it's only because I rejected their advances that they wanted to get back at me!'

These words had changed Robert's antipathy towards society into a much deeper and more heartfelt loathing, which he felt especially keenly towards those who deserved it least: those devoted relatives who, at the family's behest, had tried to convince Saint-Loup's mistress to break up with him, a suggestion she told Robert was motivated by their own desire for her. Even though he had immediately broken off all relations with them, Robert thought, when he was away from his mistress as he was now, that either they or others would take advantage of his absence to renew their advances, and may even have won her favours. And when he spoke of the rakes who were disloyal to their friends and who tried to corrupt women and entice them into houses of assignation, his face contorted with pain and hatred.

'I'd kill them with less compunction than if they were dogs, who at least have the merit of being kind, loyal, faithful animals. Those kinds of people deserve the guillotine, much more than the poor wretches who've been reduced to crime by poverty and the cruelty of the rich.'

He spent most of his time in Balbec sending his mistress letters and telegrams. Whenever she found an excuse to quarrel with him from afar while at the same time forbidding him to return to Paris, I'd see it in his crestfallen look. Since his mistress never told him what she was blaming him for, Robert, suspecting that perhaps, if she wasn't telling him, it was because she didn't know why, and that she'd simply had enough of him, kept asking for an explanation, and would write: 'Tell me what I did wrong. I'm quite willing to acknowledge my faults.' The sorrow he felt had the effect of convincing him that he was the guilty party.

But she'd keep him waiting for her responses, and when they finally did arrive, they made no sense in any case. So it was almost always with a furrowed brow and quite often empty-handed that I'd see Saint-Loup returning from the post office; he was the only one in the hotel, apart from Françoise, who picked up and delivered his own letters, he out of a lover's impatience, she out of a servant's mistrust. (In order to send his telegrams, he had to venture further afield.)

When, a few days after the dinner party at the Blochs', my grandmother, looking overjoyed, told me that Saint-Loup had just asked her if she might like him to photograph her before he left Balbec, and when I saw that she'd worn her finest outfit for the purpose and couldn't make up her mind how best to style her hair, I felt a little irritated at this childishness, which surprised me in her. I even began to wonder if I'd been mistaken about my grandmother, if I hadn't placed her on too high a pedestal, if she was as indifferent as I'd always thought her to be about her appearance, and if she might after all have what I'd always thought so alien to her: coquetry.

Unfortunately, I allowed the displeasure that this plan for a photographic session caused me, and especially the satisfaction my grandmother seemed to derive from it, to be so apparent that Françoise noticed it and, unintentionally, lost no time in increasing it by making a sentimental, affectionate remark, which I met with a calculated look of disapproval.

'Oh, Monsieur, my poor mistress will be so happy to have her portrait taken, she's even going to wear the hat her old Françoise has done up for her—we should let her have her little treat, Monsieur.'

I persuaded myself that I wasn't being cruel to mock Françoise's sensibility by reminding myself that my mother and grandmother, my models in all things, often did so. But my grandmother, noticing how annoyed I looked, told me that if this photographic session bothered me, she wouldn't go through with it. I didn't want that; I assured her I saw nothing wrong with it and let her continue with her ministrations, but, thinking I should show how forceful and penetrating my mind was, I uttered a few sarcastic, hurtful words meant to neutralize the pleasure she seemed to be deriving from being photographed, so that although I was forced to see my grandmother's magnificent hat, at least I managed to wipe from her face the joyful expression that should have made me glad but which, as too often happens so long as those we love most are alive, seems to us to be the exasperating manifestation of some petty failing rather than the precious form of happiness we'd so like to procure for them. My ill humour stemmed especially from the fact that, during the last week, my grandmother had seemed to be avoiding me, so that I didn't have her to myself for a moment, either day or night. When I'd return in the afternoons to spend a little time alone with her, they'd tell me she wasn't in; or else she'd shut herself up with Françoise for long confabulations I wasn't allowed to interrupt. And when, having been out all evening with Saint-Loup, I'd be thinking during the return journey about the moment I'd see my grandmother again and kiss her, it was in vain that I waited for her to make on the wall the three little taps that would tell me to come and say goodnight to her; I heard nothing; at length I'd go to bed, a little upset with her for depriving me, with an indifference so unfamiliar in her, of a joy on which I'd set so much store; I'd stay awake a little longer, my heart throbbing as much as it did when I was a child, listening to the wall, which remained silent, and I'd cry myself to sleep.

That day, as on the preceding days, Saint-Loup had been obliged to go to Doncières where, until the time came for him to return permanently, his presence was required into the late afternoon. I was sorry he wasn't at Balbec. I'd seen alighting from carriages and going into either the Casino or the ice-cream parlour some young women who, from a distance, looked lovely. I was at one of those periods in youth—vacant, without any particular love object—when, like a lover seeing his beloved in all things, we desire, we seek, we see Beauty everywhere. All that's necessary is a single actual feature—the little we can glimpse of a woman at a distance, or from behind—for us to be able to project Beauty on to her; we imagine we've found it at last, our heart pounds, we quicken our pace, and, so long as the woman has disappeared, we'll always remain half convinced she was Beauty incarnate; it's only if we succeed in catching up with her that we realize our mistake.

What's more, as my health worsened, I was tempted to overrate the simplest pleasures because of how difficult it was for me to achieve them. I seemed to be seeing lovely women everywhere, because I was too tired if I was at the beach, too shy if I was at the Casino or a patisserie, to approach them anywhere. If I was to die soon, though, I'd have liked to know what the prettiest young women real life could offer looked like close up, even if it was someone else, or no one, who would enjoy this offer (I didn't realize that there was, in fact, a desire for possession at the root of my curiosity). I'd have been brave enough to go into the ballroom if Saint-Loup had been with me. Alone, I was idling in front of the Grand-Hôtel until it was time for me to join my grandmother, when, still almost at the far end of the esplanade where they formed a strange mobile patch of colour, I saw coming towards me five or six girls, as different in their appearance and manners from all the other people one was used to seeing in Balbec as could have been, appearing out of the blue, a flock of seagulls strutting in their leisurely way along the beach, the stragglers fluttering forward to catch up, in a procession that seems as obscure in its goal to the bathers, whom they seem not to see, as it is clearly determined in their own bird-minds.

One of these unknown girls was pushing her bicycle with one hand;* two others were carrying golf clubs; and their attire stood out from that of other girls in Balbec, who, even though some engaged in sports, didn't wear special outfits for the purpose.

It was the hour for ladies and gentlemen to take their daily stroll along the esplanade, exposed to the merciless line of fire from the lorgnette fixed on them by the first president's wife, who felt impelled to inspect each of them with minute scrutiny, as if they might be defiled with some physical defect, while she sat proudly in front of the bandstand, in the middle of the intimidating row of chairs in which they too, actors turned critics, would soon come to sit, to take their turn passing judgement on everyone else strolling past. All these people walking along the esplanade were pitching about as though they were on the deck of a boat (for they couldn't lift a leg without at the same time swinging an arm, glancing to the side, straightening their shoulders, counterbalancing the movement they'd just made on one side of their body with one on the other, and becoming flushed in the face), and though they pretended not to see anyone else so as to appear unconcerned, all the while darting furtive glances so as not to run into the people walking alongside them or towards them, they bumped into them nonetheless, or jostled them, because they themselves had been the object of the same secret attention, hidden beneath the same apparent disdain; love—hence fear—of the crowd being one of the most powerful motives in all individuals, whether they seek to please others, surprise them, or show them they despise them. In a recluse, his seclusion, even if it's absolute and lasts until the end of his life, is often based on an uncontrolled love of the crowd which takes such precedence over any other feeling that, unable when he goes out to win the admiration of the concierge, the passers-by, or the coachman who's come to a halt, he'd rather never be seen by them, and so renounces any activity that might require him to leave the house.

Among all these people, some of whom were following a train of thought while revealing its shifting nature by disjointed gestures or roving eyes, as uncoordinated as their neighbours' cautious lurching, the girls I'd seen, with that mastery of gesture which comes from perfect control of one's own body and a sincere contempt for the rest of humanity, were striding straight ahead, without any hesitation or stiffness, performing exactly the movements they wanted, each limb moving completely independently of the others, while most of their body kept that stillness so remarkable among expert waltzers. They weren't far away from me. Even though each girl was of a completely different type from the others, they were all beautiful; but, to tell the truth, I'd seen them so briefly and without daring to stare at them that I still hadn't individualized any of them. With the exception of one, whose aquiline nose and darker complexion made her stand out from the rest, as a king who looks Arabian would stand out in a Renaissance painting of the Magi, the other girls were recognizable only as a pair of hard, stubborn, mocking eyes in one of the faces, or as cheeks of that rosy pink tinged with coppery tones suggesting geraniums in another; but even these traits I hadn't yet indissolubly attached to one particular girl rather than another; and when (according to the order in which this marvellous ensemble unfurled before me, marvellous because utterly different aspects appeared next to each other, because all shades of colour were juxtaposed, but also as confused as a piece of music in which one can't isolate or recognize the phrases as they occur, which are no sooner heard than forgotten) I could see the emergence of a pale oval, or of black eyes, or green eyes, I didn't know if they were the same ones that had already charmed me a moment before, I couldn't connect them to any particular girl whom I might thereby have disentangled from the others and recognized. And this absence, in my vision, of the demarcations that I would soon establish between them, made their group shimmer with a kind of harmonious imprecision, the continuous transfer of a fluid, collective, shifting beauty.

It may not have been mere chance in life that, in bringing these friends together, had chosen such beautiful ones; perhaps these girls (whose attitudes alone revealed their bold, frivolous, or tough nature), extremely sensitive to every form of ridicule and ugliness, and incapable of experiencing any intellectual or moral attraction, had found each other naturally, from among other girls of their own age; they shared a feeling of revulsion at all those whose pensive or sensitive dispositions are revealed by shyness, embarrassment, or awkwardness; they called such girls 'loathsome' and were careful to avoid them; while they may have taken up with others to whom they were attracted by a certain mixture of gracefulness, suppleness, and physical elegance, the only form in which they could imagine the candour of an appealing character and the prospect of spending good times together. Perhaps, too, the class to which they belonged, which I couldn't label with any certainty, was at that stage in its evolution when, either thanks to an increase in wealth and leisure or because of new sporting habits (widespread even among certain working-class environments) and a new-found interest in physical training to which that of intellect hadn't yet been added, a social atmosphere, like those harmonious, fertile schools of sculpture which have not yet gone in for tortured expressions, produces naturally and in abundance beautiful bodies with lovely legs and shapely hips, with wholesome, calm faces and an air of agility and cleverness. And weren't these noble and tranquil models of human beauty I was seeing there, in front of the sea, like sunlit statues on a Grecian shore?

Just as if, from within their band moving forward along the esplanade like a shining comet, they'd decided that the crowd around them was made up of beings from another race who, even if they were suffering, couldn't possibly have awakened in them any feeling of solidarity, they didn't seem to see them, and forced people standing motionless to make way for them, as though for a machine that had been set loose which couldn't be expected to avoid pedestrians; and their only reaction, if some terrified or furious old gentleman, whose existence they didn't deign to acknowledge and whom they jostled aside, fled urgently or ludicrously out of their way, was to look at one another and laugh. For anyone who wasn't part of their group, they had no need to put on a show of scorn; their sincere scorn was enough.

They couldn't see an obstacle without taking pleasure in leaping over it, with a running start or from a standstill, because they were all brimming, overflowing, with the youthfulness which must have an outlet even if one is sad or ill, since one is more inclined to obey the needs of age than the mood of the day, and one never lets an opportunity to leap or slide go by without wholeheartedly indulging in it, interrupting, punctuating one's slow progress—as Chopin does with even his most melancholy phrase*—with graceful detours in which caprice and virtuosity are intermingled. The wife of an elderly banker, after hesitating between various places for her husband to sit, had finally settled him in a folding chair facing the esplanade, sheltered from wind and sun by the bandstand. Having seen him comfortably installed there, she had just gone off to buy a newspaper which she would read to him to divert him, one of her little absences during which she would leave him alone and would never prolong for more than five minutes, which seemed quite long to him, but which she repeated often enough so that her aged husband, the beneficiary of her close but unobtrusive care, might feel as if he was still capable of living like everyone else and didn't need any protection. The platform of the bandstand above him formed a natural, tempting springboard on which the oldest girl in the little band began straightaway to run: she leapt over the terrified old man, whose yachting cap was grazed by nimble feet, to the great amusement of the other girls, especially of a pair of green eyes in a round face which expressed, for this act, an admiration and amusement in which I thought I could detect a little shyness, or rather, a shyness that was at once ashamed and boastful, which wasn't present in the others' expressions. 'The poor old bloke, I almost feel sorry for him, he's got one foot in the grave!' said one of the girls in a husky voice, half ironically. They all walked on a few paces, then paused for a moment in the middle of the promenade without any concern about holding up the procession of strollers, in order to hold their confabulation, forming a compact, irregular, outlandish, high-pitched cluster, like birds gathering just before taking flight; then they resumed their slow stroll along the esplanade, above the sea.

By now their charming features were no longer indistinct and interchangeable. I could sort them out and assign them (for lack of names, of which I was still ignorant) to individual girls, such as the tall one who had leapt over the elderly banker; the short one who stood out against the sea's horizon with her plump, rosy cheeks and green eyes; the one with the darker complexion and straight nose, who contrasted so sharply with the others; another, with a face as white as an egg in which a small nose described the arc of a circle like a chick's beak, the sort of face some very young men have; yet another, tall, wearing a schoolgirl's cape (which made her look so poor, and was in such contrast with her otherwise elegant outfit that the only explanation that sprang to mind was that this girl's parents must be so highly placed, and have a sufficiently exalted opinion of themselves, that they had little concern for either the other Balbec visitors or their children's sartorial elegance, and couldn't care less if their daughter appeared on the esplanade in an outfit that people of the lower classes would have deemed too modest); a girl with bright, laughing eyes and plump, olive-coloured cheeks, with a little black toque pulled down low over her face, who was pushing a bicycle with such an exaggerated swing of her hips, and when I passed by was shouting such vulgar slang words (among which I could distinctly make out the rather tiresome phrase 'It's my life to live') that, abandoning the hypothesis I'd formed on the basis of her friend's cape, I decided that all these girls must belong to the crowds who frequent velodromes, and must be the very young girlfriends of racing cyclists. None of my conjectures, however, allowed for the possibility that they might be chaste. I knew this to be the case as soon as I'd set eyes on them—from the mocking way they looked at each other, or from the insistent stare of the one with the olive cheeks. Besides, my grandmother had always watched over me with such over-scrupulous care that I'd come to believe that the things one mustn't do form a single indivisible whole, and that girls who lack respect for the elderly are unencumbered by scruples when it comes to pleasures more tempting than that of leaping over an octogenarian.

Though the girls were now individualized, the way they kept exchanging glances full of smugness and complicity, with eyes that gleamed either with self-interest or insolent indifference, depending on whether they were looking at each other or at people passing by, the awareness, too, of knowing one another intimately enough to go about always together, a 'band of outsiders', as they made their slow progress, formed between their independent, separate bodies an invisible but harmonious bond, like a single warm shadow, like their own climate, making them into a whole as homogeneous in its parts as it was different from the crowd through which their procession wended its leisurely way.

For an instant, as I was passing by the brunette with the plump cheeks who was pushing the bicycle, I met her laughing, sidelong glance, aimed from the centre of that inhuman world that enclosed the lives of this little tribe, that inaccessible unknown where the idea of what I was could surely neither penetrate nor find a home. Engrossed as she was in what her companions were saying, did the girl with the toque pulled down low over her forehead see me the instant the dark beam from her eyes encountered me? From within what universe did she perceive me? It would have been as difficult for me to say as, when a telescope enables us to see certain features on a nearby planet, it's hard to tell if humans inhabit it, if they can see us, and, if so, what thoughts we might have aroused in them.

If we thought the eyes of such a girl were nothing but glittering little discs of mica, we wouldn't be too eager to know her or to link her life to ours. But we feel that the gleam emanating from those reflecting discs doesn't come solely from their material composition; that, unknown to us, they are the dark shadows of ideas this person is forming about the people and places she knows—the green turf of racecourses, the sandy paths on which, pedalling through fields and woods, she might have led me, this little *peri*,* more seductive than any of those in the Persian paradise—the shadows, too, of the house to which she'll soon return, the plans she's devising or that others have made for her; but most of all it is she herself who lies behind them, with her desires, her likes and dislikes, her unfathomable and unremitting will. I knew I could never possess this young cyclist unless I also possessed everything that lay behind her eyes. And so it was her entire life that awakened my desire; a desire full of pain, because I sensed it was unattainable, but also exhilarating, because what my life had been up until that point had suddenly ceased being my whole life, but was now only a small part of an immense expanse stretching out before me which I was longing to explore, and which was composed of the lives of these girls, offering me that expansion, that possible multiplication of the self, which is happiness. Doubtless the fact that there was no common ground between us—that we shared not one habit or idea—would make it more difficult for me to make friends with the girls and win their approval. But perhaps it was because of these very differences, because of my awareness that there wasn't a single element in the nature or actions of these girls that I knew or possessed, that my satiety had just been replaced by thirst—the burning thirst of parched earth—for a life that my soul, because it had never before received a single drop of it, would absorb all the more greedily, in long draughts, until I was soaked through with it.

I'd been looking so intently at this cyclist with the bright eyes that she seemed to notice it and said something to the tall one that I couldn't make out, but which made her laugh. To tell the truth, this brunette with the bicycle wasn't the one I liked best, precisely because she was a brunette, and because (ever since the day when, from the steep little lane by Tansonville, I'd seen Gilberte), a girl with auburn hair and golden skin had remained my unattainable ideal. But hadn't I fallen in love with Gilberte especially because she'd appeared to me wreathed in the halo of being a friend of Bergotte's, of visiting cathedrals with him? In the same way, couldn't I rejoice in the fact that I'd seen the brunette looking at me (which led me to hope it might be easier to make her acquaintance first), since she would introduce me to the others, to the ruthless one who had leapt over the old man, to the cruel one who had said: 'I almost feel sorry for him, the poor old bloke!'; and then to all of them, one after the other, those among whom she had the prestige of being their inseparable companion? And yet, in the assumption that I might one day be the friend of one or other of these girls, that these eyes that sometimes focused their unknown glances on me, unwittingly playing over me like sunlight on a wall, might ever, by some miraculous alchemy, allow their ineffable particles to be interpenetrated by the idea of my existence, or friendship for my person, that I myself might one day take my place among them in their gradual progression along the seafront—this assumption seemed to enclose a contradiction as insoluble as if, faced with some classical frieze or fresco depicting a procession, I'd thought it possible, as a spectator, to take my place, beloved by them, among the divine parading figures.

Was the happiness of knowing these girls really unattainable? It would certainly not have been the first happiness of its kind that I'd given up hope of achieving. I had only to cast my mind back to all those other unknown girls in Balbec I'd had to abandon forever as my carriage sped away. And the pleasure I felt at seeing this little band, as noble as if it were made up of Hellenic virgins, had something of the same quality as the longing I felt when I saw those elusive girls I passed on the road. The fleetingness of individuals who are not known to us, who force us to cast off from our habitual life in which the women we frequent inevitably end up revealing their flaws, impels us into that state of pursuit when nothing can stop the imagination. For to strip imagination away from our pleasures would be to reduce them to themselves—that is, to nothing. If they had been offered to me by a madam (whose services, as has been seen, I by no means scorned), stripped of the element that made them so nuanced and undefined, these girls would have enchanted me less. The imagination, aroused by the uncertainty of being able to attain its object, creates a goal that hides the other goal from us, and, by replacing sensual pleasure with the idea of penetrating someone's life, prevents us from recognizing that pleasure, experiencing its true flavour, and restricting it to its own domain. If the first time we saw a fish was when it was served on a dinner table, it wouldn't appear to be worth the countless ruses and devious ways required to catch it, unless there occurred between it and us afternoons spent fishing during which we saw, while being unsure what to do with them, beneath the water's rippling surface, the sheen of flesh, the imprecision of a shape, in the fluidity of a transparent, ever-shifting azure.

These girls also benefited from the change in social values characteristic of holiday life by the sea. All the advantages that, in our ordinary environment, extend and magnify our importance, become invisible there, indeed are abolished; while people to whom, without cause, we attribute similar advantages, appear to us amplified out of all proportion. It was this that made it easy for unknown women, like the group of girls on this day, to acquire enormous importance in my eyes, while at the same time making it impossible for them to know what importance I myself might possess.

But if this little band's stroll was only a brief excerpt from the endless flight of passing girls, which had always unsettled me, this particular flight was so slow that it approached immobility. And precisely because these faces, no longer disappearing in a whirlwind, but calm and distinct, still looked beautiful to me, I was prevented from believing, as I so often had when Madame de Villeparisis' carriage carried me off, that, closer up, if I were to pause for a moment, certain details—pockmarked skin, some defect in the nostrils, a vacant gaze, a twisted smile, an unshapely waist—would have replaced, in the woman's face and body, the features I'd imagined; for previously all I'd needed was a pretty figure or a glimpse of a fresh complexion for me to add, in all good faith, a lovely shoulder or charming eyes of which I always carried within me the memory or the preconceived idea, those rapid sight-readings of a being one glimpses in a fleeting moment, exposing us thereby to the same errors as those overly hasty readings of a text whereby, on the basis of a single syllable and without taking the time to identify the others, we substitute for the word that's written an entirely different one furnished by our memory. But this time it had to be different. I'd seen their faces clearly; I'd seen each of them, not from every angle, and rarely full-face, but still from two or three perspectives different enough to enable me either to rectify or to verify and 'prove' the different guesses at contour and colour hazarded at first sight, and to see, through their various expressions, the persistence of something inalterably material. And so I could say with certainty that, whether in Paris or Balbec, assuming the most favourable outcomes with any of the passing girls who had caught my eye, even if I'd been able to pause and chat with them, there had never been any whose appearance, and then disappearance, without my ever knowing them, would have left me with more regret than these girls would, or would have made me think their friendship could be so intoxicating. Not among actresses, or peasant girls, or young ladies at convent schools, had I seen anything so beautiful, impregnated with so much of the unknown, so inestimably precious, so seemingly unattainable. They were such a delightful and perfectly preserved example of the unknown, potential happiness of life, that it was almost for intellectual reasons that I'd despaired of being able to experience, in unique conditions leaving no room for any possible error, the profound mystery to be found in the beauty we desire, the beauty we console ourselves for never being able to possess by demanding pleasure—as Swann had always refused to do, before Odette—from women we haven't desired, so that we die without ever knowing what that other pleasure was. No doubt it was possible that it might not actually be an unknown pleasure, that on closer inspection its mystery might dissipate, that it was nothing but a projection, a mirage of desire. But in that case, I'd have only an inescapable law of nature to blame—which, if it was applicable to these girls, was applicable to all girls—and not any defect in the object of desire. For it was this object I'd have chosen from among all others, well aware, with a botanist's satisfaction, that it wasn't possible to find gathered together rarer specimens than these young blossoms who at this moment were interrupting before my eyes the line of sea with their slender hedge, like a thicket of wild roses adorning a clifftop garden, between the stems of which is contained the whole stretch of ocean crossed by some steamer, gliding so slowly on the blue horizontal line leading from one stalk to the next that if a lazy butterfly, lingering in a bloom that the ship's hull has long since passed, wants to time its flight so as to be sure of arriving before the vessel, it can wait until nothing but a single slice of blue separates the ship's prow from the first petal of the flower towards which it has set its course.

I went back to the hotel because I was going to dine with Robert at Rivebelle, and my grandmother insisted that on such evenings I should lie down for an hour, a siesta the Balbec doctor soon ordered me to extend to all other evenings as well.

To go indoors, there was now no need to leave the esplanade, walk around the back, and enter the hotel through the lobby. By virtue of a leap in time analogous to those Saturdays in Combray when we had lunch an hour early, now in midsummer the days had become so long that the sun was still high in the sky, as it would be during afternoon tea, when the tables were set for dinner at the Grand-Hôtel of Balbec. And so the tall sliding windows were kept open to the esplanade; I had only to step over a thin wooden frame to find myself in the dining room, which I crossed immediately to take the lift.

As I walked past the office, I gave the manager a smile and, without the least feeling of distaste, received one in return from a face which, ever since I'd been in Balbec, my studious attentiveness had been injecting and gradually transforming as if it were a natural history specimen. His features had become familiar, charged with a meaning that was commonplace but intelligible, like handwriting one can read; they no longer resembled those bizarre, unbearable characters that his face had presented to me on the first day, when I'd seen before me a personage now forgotten, or, if I managed to recall him, unrecogniz-able, difficult to equate with the insignificant, polite person of whom the former had been merely a caricature, a hideous and superficial sketch. Free from the shyness and sadness of the evening of my arrival, I rang for the 'lift', who now no longer kept silent as we ascended together, as though in a mobile ribcage gliding up the central column, but kept saying: 'There aren't as many people now as there were a month ago. They'll start leaving soon, the days are getting shorter.' He said this not because it was true, but because he had another job waiting for him on a warmer part of the coast, and he wished we'd all go away as soon as possible so the hotel could close and he might have a few days to himself, before 'restarting' his 'new' situation. 'Restarting' and 'new' weren't in the least incompatible terms for him, 'to restart' being for him the usual form of the verb 'to start'. The only thing that surprised me was that he condescended to say 'situation', for he belonged to the modern proletariat that wants to erase from language any trace of the system of domestic service. A moment later he also told me that in the 'situation' he was about to 'restart', he'd have a nicer 'tunic' and a better 'salary'; the words 'uniform' and 'wages' seeming outdated and unseemly to him. And since, by an absurd contradiction, despite everything, vocabulary has outlasted the concept of inequality in the minds of 'employers', I always had trouble understanding what the lift-boy said. For instance, if all I wanted to know was whether or not my grandmother was in the hotel, the lift-boy would anticipate my question and say: 'The lady has just left your rooms.' I was caught out every time, since I thought he meant my grandmother. 'No, the lady who I think is an employee of yours.' Since in old bourgeois language, which should really be abolished, a cook is not called an employee, I'd think for an instant: 'But he's wrong, we don't have a factory, or employees.' And suddenly I'd remember that the word 'employee' is as essential to the fulfilment of servants' self-esteem as wearing a moustache is to café waiters, and that the lady who had just left was Françoise (probably on her way to visit the person who makes the coffee, or to watch the young maid sewing for the Belgian lady), though even this wasn't enough to satisfy the lift-boy, who, as he bemoaned the lot of his own class, liked to say not 'workers' or 'commoners' but 'the worker' or 'the commoner', using the same singular form as Racine does when he says 'the poor man'.* Usually, though, since both my eagerness and my timidity of that first day were things of the past, I wouldn't speak to the lift-boy. Now it was he who received no reply during the brief journey as he piloted our craft at top speed through the hotel, hollow as a toy, and which extended around us, floor by floor, its branching corridors, in the depths of which the light grew velvety and soft, dematerializing the communicating doors and the steps of the service stairs, which it converted into that amber as golden, insubstantial, and mysterious as the half-light with which Rembrandt shapes a windowsill or the handle of a well.* And at every floor, a golden gleam reflected on the carpet signified that the sun was setting beyond the lavatory windows.

I wondered if the girls I'd just seen lived in Balbec, and who they might be. When desire is focused in this way on a little tribe of humanity which it singles out from the rest, anything that might be linked to it is the wellspring of some emotion, which in turn leads to reverie. I'd heard a lady on the esplanade say: 'She's a friend of the little Simonet girl' with that same superior air of someone in the know who says: 'He's the constant companion of La Rochefoucauld.' And immediately I could detect on the face of the person receiving this information a look of curiosity and a desire to get a better view of this person who was so special as to be the 'friend of the little Simonet girl'. Clearly this was a privilege not granted to everyone. For aristocracy is a relative thing: there are plenty of out-of-the-way little resorts where the son of a furniture salesman is an arbiter of fashion and holds court like a young Prince of Wales. I've often tried since then to remember how the name of 'Simonet' sounded to me on the esplanade, when I was still uncertain about its form, which I'd had trouble distinguishing, and about its significance as well, whether it designated one person or another; in short, it was imprinted with that vagueness and novelty so moving to us later on, when this name, the letters of which are every second more deeply engraved in our hearts by our constant attention, has become (as the name of 'the little Simonet girl' was to become for me, but several years later) the first word that comes to mind either upon waking in the morning or after a fainting spell, even before we have any idea of the time, or the place we're in, almost before the word 'I', as if the being it designates were more us than we ourselves are, and as if, after some moments of unconsciousness, the first interval to expire was the one in which we weren't thinking of the name. I don't know why I told myself on that very first day that the name of Simonet must have belonged to one of the girls; I couldn't stop wondering how I could go about getting introduced to the Simonet family, especially by people she regarded as superior to herself, which must not have been difficult if the girls were only working-class minxes, so that she wouldn't have a disdainful opinion of me. For one can't know someone thoroughly, one can't be completely absorbed in someone who looks down on you, so long as you haven't overcome her disdain. Whenever the image of women so different from us penetrates us, unless oblivion or other competing images wipes it out, we can have no rest until we've converted those alien women into something similar to ourselves, our soul being in this respect endowed with the same sort of reactivity and response as our physical organism, which can't tolerate the introduction of a foreign body into it without at once striving to digest and assimilate the intruder. The little Simonet girl must be the prettiest of them all—the one, too, who I thought could become my mistress, since she was the only one who, two or three times, half turning her head, had seemed to be aware of my intent stare. I asked the lift-boy if he knew of any Simonets in Balbec. Reluctant to admit he didn't know something, he replied that he seemed to have heard the name somewhere. When we reached the top floor, I asked him to have the latest list of guests sent up.

I stepped out of the lift, but instead of going to my room, I walked further down the corridor, since at that time of day the servant on duty, though fearful of drafts, had opened the window at the end, which looked out not on the sea but on the side of the hill and valley, though it never allowed them to be seen, since its panes, made of opaque glass, were usually closed. I paused in front of it for a moment, long enough to pay my devotions to the view which for once it revealed, beyond the hill that rose behind the hotel, a view encompassing nothing but a single house standing some distance away; but the perspective and the evening light, while preserving its mass, delicately embossed it and set it within a velvety case, so that it resembled one of those miniature structures, a tiny temple or chapel wrought in gold and enamel, which serve as reliquaries and are exposed only on rare occasions for the veneration of the faithful. But this moment of worship had already lasted too long, for the servant, holding a bunch of keys in one hand and touching the other to his sacristan's cap, though without raising it because of the cool, pure evening air, came and drew the two panes together, as if over a shrine, thus hiding the minute edifice and golden relic from my adoration. I went into my room. As the season advanced, the painting I perceived framed by the window changed. At first it was broad daylight, dark only if the weather was bad; and then, in the blue-green glass swelling with its rounded waves, the sea, set between the iron uprights of my casement window like stained glass, unfurled over all the deep, rocky border of the bay triangles plumed with motionless whitecaps delineated with the delicacy of a feather or a downy breast from Pisanello's pencil and fixed in place by that white, permanent, unctuous enamel used to depict fallen snow in glassware by Gallé.*

Soon the days grew shorter, and when I went into my room, the violet sky, which seemed to be branded by the rigid, geometrical, fleeting, flashing face of the sun (like the illustration of some miraculous sign or mystical apparition), leaned towards the sea over the junction of the horizon like a religious painting above the high altar, while the different aspects of the setting sun displayed in the glass panels of the low mahogany bookcases lining the walls, which I linked in my thoughts to the marvellous painting from which they'd been detached, seemed like those different scenes that some old master once depicted over a shrine of a religious order, the separate panels of which are now exhibited in a museum gallery so that only the visitor's imagination can restore them to their rightful place on the predella of the altar.* Some weeks later, when I went upstairs, the sun had already set. Like the one I used to see in Combray above the wayside cross when I was coming home from my walk and preparing to go down to the kitchen before dinner, a band of red sky over the sea, as dense and precisely defined as aspic, soon followed, over the sea already as cold and blue as grey mullet, by another sky, of the same pink as one of the salmon that would soon be served to us in Rivebelle, would rekindle the pleasure I was about to take in getting dressed for dinner. Over the sea, close to the shore, trying to rise above each other in ever-widening layers, were mists as black as soot, but also as smooth and dense as agate, and visibly heavy, so that the uppermost layers, pressing down over the misshapen base until they exceeded the centre of gravity of the layers that had been supporting them, seemed about to topple and drag down with them the scaffold already reaching halfway up the sky, pitching the whole edifice into the sea. The sight of a ship moving away, like a night traveller, gave me the same impression I once had in the train, of being liberated from the need to sleep and to be confined to a bedroom. Besides, I didn't feel imprisoned in this room, since within the hour I'd be leaving it and getting into a carriage. I threw myself on to my bed; and, as if I were in a bunk on one of the boats which I could see quite close to me and which catch us by surprise at night when they move slowly through the darkness, like shadowy, silent swans who never sleep, I was surrounded on all sides by images of the sea.

Quite often, though, they were nothing but images; I'd forget that beneath their colourful expanse lay the forlorn, empty shore scoured by the restless evening wind, which had made me feel so anxious when I arrived in Balbec; besides, even in my room, preoccupied as I was with the girls I'd seen, my mind was no longer calm or detached enough for it to apprehend truly profound impressions of beauty. My anticipation of dinner at Rivebelle made my mood even more frivolous, and my thoughts, dwelling at such moments on the surface of my body, which I was about to clothe in such a way as to appear as attractive as possible to the eyes of the women staring at me in the brightly lit restaurant, were incapable of adding any depth to the colours of things. If it wasn't for the indefatigable, soothing flight, beneath my window, of the swifts and swallows, rising up like a gushing fountain or living fireworks, alternating their dizzying rocketlike ascents with the motionless, white wake of their long, horizontal glide, if it wasn't for the lovely miracle of this natural, local phenomenon which linked the landscapes before my eyes to reality, I might have thought they were no more than a selection, made anew every day, of paintings displayed arbitrarily in the place where I happened to be, but without any necessary relation to it. One evening it would be an exhibition of Japanese prints: alongside the slim cut-out of the sun, red and round as the moon, a yellow cloud looked like a lake against which black swords were silhouetted like trees on its shore; a bar of soft pink, such as I hadn't seen since my first paintbox, swelled like a river, while boats beached on its shores seemed to be waiting to be launched and set afloat. And with the disdainful, bored, careless gaze of an expert, or of a fashionable lady hurrying through a gallery between social calls, I'd say to myself: 'It's an interesting sunset, it's different, but really I've already seen others just as delicate and surprising as this one.' I was more pleased on evenings when a ship, absorbed and dissolved by the horizon, looked so much as if it were of the same colour as it, as in an Impressionist painting, that it also seemed to be made of the same material, as though someone had merely outlined its hull and rigging until it dwindled into a filigree in the vaporous blue of the sky. Sometimes the ocean filled almost all of my window, lifted up as it was by a band of sky edged on top only by a line that was of the same blue as that of the sea, but because of that I thought it was still the sea, and owed its different colour only to a play of light. On another day, the sea was painted only in the lower part of the window, all the rest of which was filled with so many clouds thrust against one another by horizontal bands that the windowpanes seemed, by some premeditation or artist's trick, to present a 'Study of Clouds', while the different glass panes of the bookshelf, showing clouds that looked similar but appeared in another part of the horizon, and coloured differently by the light, seemed to offer a kind of repetition, dear to some contemporary masters, of a single effect, always observed at different hours, but able now, with the immobility of art, to be seen all at once in the same room, drawn in pastel, and mounted under glass. And sometimes, on a sky and sea uniformly grey, a little pink would be added with exquisite delicacy, while a tiny butterfly, which had fallen asleep on the windowsill, seemed with its wings to be adding, to the bottom of this *Harmony in Grey and Pink* after Whistler, the signature emblem of the Chelsea master.* Then the pink itself would disappear, and there would be nothing more to look at. I stood up for a moment, and before lying down again, closed the tall curtains. Above them, I could see from my bed the ray of light that was still there, growing steadily fainter and thinner, but it was without any feeling of sadness or regret that I let the last hour of daylight die at the top of the curtains at a time when I was usually seated at table, for I knew that this day was different from the others, longer, like those polar days interrupted by night for only a few minutes; I knew that from the chrysalis of twilight, by a radiant metamorphosis, the dazzling light of the Rivebelle restaurant was preparing to emerge. I thought: 'It's time'; I stretched out on the bed, then rose and finished my preparations; and I found a charm in these idle moments, relieved of all material burdens, when, while others were dining downstairs, I was employing the energy accumulated during the inactivity of this last hour of the day only in drying my body, slipping on a dinner jacket, tying my bow tie, and performing all those gestures already being guided by the anticipated pleasure of seeing again the woman I'd noticed the last time I was in Rivebelle, who had seemed to be looking at me, and had perhaps left her table for a moment only in the hope I'd follow her; and so I joyfully put on all my finery, so that I could devote myself wholly and willingly to a new life, free and without cares, when my hesitations could be soothed by Saint-Loup's calm certainty, and I could choose, from all those species of natural history and products from all countries, those that, composing the unusual dishes soon to be ordered by my friend, might tempt my appetite or my imagination.

And then at the very end came days when I could no longer pass straight from the esplanade into the dining room; its windows were no longer open, since night had already fallen, and the throng of the poor and the curious, chilled by the cold north wind and drawn by the blazing light which lay beyond their reach, huddled in dark clusters against the glowing sliding panels of our glass hive.

There was a knock on my door: it was Aimé, making a point of bringing me the latest guest list himself.

Aimé couldn't leave without telling me that Dreyfus was guilty a thousand times over.* 'It will all come out,' he said, 'not this year, but the next: a Monsieur who's very close to the General Staff told me so.' I asked him whether they might decide to divulge everything all at once, before the year's end. 'Look here, he put down his cigarette,' Aimé went on, acting out the scene and shaking his head and forefinger at me, as the guest he'd been serving had done, as if to say: We mustn't ask too much. ' "Not this year, Aimé," he said, touching my shoulder, "that's not possible. But just you wait until Easter comes, you'll see!" ' And Aimé tapped me lightly on my shoulder as he said: 'See, I'm telling you exactly the same way he told me,' either because he was flattered by this familiarity coming from a distinguished personage, or so that I could have full knowledge of the facts in order to appreciate the force of the argument and of our grounds for hope.

My heart almost skipped a beat when I saw, on the first page of the guest list, the words 'Simonet and family'. I harboured within me a reserve of old daydreams, dating from my childhood, in which all the tenderness that was in my heart, but that, when experienced, was indistinguishable from it, was brought flooding back to me by a person as different as possible from me. This person I once again invented by using the name 'Simonet' and the memory of the harmony that reigned among the young bodies I'd seen moving along the seafront in an athletic procession worthy of ancient Greece or Giotto.* I didn't know which, if any, of these girls was Mademoiselle Simonet, but I did know that I was loved by Mademoiselle Simonet, and that, thanks to Saint-Loup, I was going to try to make her acquaintance. Unfortunately, he had to return to Doncières every day, since that was the condition by which his leave was extended; to divert him from his military obligations, I'd thought I could depend, even more than on his friendship for me, on the same curiosity in human nature that had so often—even without seeing the person in question, only from hearing there was a pretty cashier working at the fruit market—made me want to learn more about a new variety of feminine beauty. But

I was wrong to hope I could arouse this curiosity in Saint-Loup by talking about my band of girls. For it had long been paralysed in him by the love he had for the actress whose lover he was. And even if he had felt a little of it welling up within him, he'd have repressed it, because of a kind of superstitious belief that his mistress's fidelity depended on his own to her. So he made no promise to take an active interest in my band of girls, and we set off to dine in Rivebelle.

The first few times we arrived there, the sun would just have set, but there would still be light; in the restaurant's garden, where the lamps hadn't yet been lit, the day's heat was subsiding and settling, as if at the bottom of a vase, around which the dark, transparent air was so gelatinous and dense that a tall rose bush attached to the shadowy wall that it streaked with pink looked like the veins inside an onyx. Before long it was already dark when we stepped out of the carriage, or even by the time we left Balbec, if there was a storm and we'd put off harnessing the horses in the hope of a break in the weather. But on those days, I wouldn't feel sad when I heard the wind howling; I knew it didn't mean I'd have to give up my plans or remain sequestered indoors, since I knew that, in the restaurant's spacious dining room which we'd enter to the music of the gypsy band, the countless lamps would easily triumph over the cold and dark by cauterizing them with their great golden light; and I'd cheerfully take my place by Saint-Loup's side in the brougham waiting for us in the rain. For some time, Bergotte's words declaring he was convinced that, despite my claims to the contrary, I was made to enjoy the pleasures of the mind above all else, would restore in me, with regard to what I might do with my life later on, a hope that was dashed every time I sat down at my desk to start a critical essay or a novel. 'After all,' I said to myself, 'perhaps the pleasure one derives from writing it isn't an infallible criterion of the worth of a fine page; perhaps it's only an accessory which is often added to it, but which one can't blame for being absent. Perhaps some masterpieces were written while the writer yawned all the way through.' My grandmother set my doubts to rest when she told me I'd work successfully and happily as soon as my health improved. Since our doctor deemed it wiser to warn me of the grave dangers to which my state of health could expose me, and had outlined all the hygienic precautions I must take to avoid having an attack, I subordinated all pleasures to the goal which I deemed infinitely more important: to become strong enough to be able to accomplish the work I might be carrying within me; and so, ever since arriving in Balbec, I'd been exercising constant and scrupulous self-control over myself. No one could have made me touch a cup of coffee, since it might have deprived me of the night's sleep I'd need so as not to be tired the next day. But as soon as we arrived in Rivebelle, because of the excitement any new pleasure aroused in me, and because I found myself in that new zone which an exceptional situation makes us enter after cutting the thread, patiently spun over so many days, that had been leading us towards careful control—as though there were no tomorrow, or any lofty achievements to be accomplished—the whole precise mechanism of prudent hygienic measures which had been set up to safeguard them would vanish. As a servant was offering to take my overcoat, Saint-Loup would ask: 'Won't you be cold? Perhaps you should keep it on, it's not very warm in here.' To which I'd reply 'No, no,' and perhaps I didn't feel the cold, but in any case I no longer knew the fear of falling ill, the necessity of not dying, or the importance of working. I'd hand over my coat; we'd enter the dining room to the strains of some warlike march played by the gypsies, and would stride between the rows of tables laid for dinner as though along a path of glory; and, though we felt the happy glow imparted to our bodies by the rhythms of the band which was bestowing these military honours and undeserved triumph, we'd hide it beneath a solemn, icy demeanour and a weary gait so as not to appear like those cabaret chanteuses who, about to sing a ribald verse they've set to a marching song, run on to the stage with the martial air of a victorious general.

From that moment on, I was a different person, no longer the grandson of my grandmother, whom I'd forget until we got up to leave, but rather the temporary brother of the waiters about to serve us.

The quantity of beer, not to mention champagne, that I wouldn't have wanted to drink in a week in Balbec, even though to my calm, lucid mind the taste of these beverages represented a pleasure that was clearly enjoyable but easily sacrificed, I now imbibed in an hour, interspersed with a little port, which I was too distracted to taste; and I gave the violinist who had just played for us the two louis I'd saved over the past month with a view to buying something I could no longer remember. Some of the waiters, who had been let loose in the rows between the tables, were rushing about at top speed, holding on their outstretched hands a dish that it was the apparent goal of this kind of race not to drop. And in fact the chocolate soufflés arrived at their destination without falling, the potatoes *à l'anglaise*, despite the gallop which must have shaken them about, were arranged around Pauillac lamb* just as they'd been at the start. I noticed one of these servers, quite tall, with a magnificent plume of black hair and some tinted make-up on his face which made him look like certain species of rare birds more than a human being; running without pause and seemingly without purpose from one end of the dining room to the other, he reminded me of one of those macaws that fill the large aviaries in zoos with their gorgeous colours and incomprehensible agitation. Soon the spectacle settled down, at least to my eyes, into a calmer, nobler order. All this dizzying activity resolved into a peaceful harmony. I could see the round tables, filling the restaurant in countless clusters, like so many planets, as depicted in allegorical paintings from long ago. An irresistible force of attraction was at work among these various heavenly bodies; at every table, the diners had eyes only for the tables where they were not, except for a wealthy host who, having managed to attract a famous writer, was doing his utmost to elicit from him, as if at a seance, inane remarks at which the ladies would marvel. The harmony of these astral tables didn't impede the incessant revolutions of the innumerable servers who, being on their feet instead of seated like the diners, moved in a higher sphere. Doubtless one was running over to bring hors d'oeuvres, another to change the wine or bring extra glasses. But despite these particular purposes, their constant race among the round tables eventually disclosed the law of its dizzying but well-regulated movements. Sitting behind a mountain range of flowers, two fearsome cashiers, engaged in endless calculations, resembled two witches bent on foretelling, by astrological computations, the upheavals that might occur from time to time in this heavenly vault fashioned according to the science of the Middle Ages.

And I felt a little sorry for the diners, because I sensed that for them the round tables were not planets, and that they weren't able to perform the sort of comparison of things that frees us from habitual appearances and enables us to perceive analogies. They thought they were dining with such-and-such a person, that the meal would cost a certain amount, and that they'd probably repeat the whole process the next day. And they seemed absolutely impervious to a procession of young assistant waiters who, probably having no urgent duties to attend to, were ceremoniously carrying baskets of bread. Some of them, too young, and harassed by the cuffs administered by the head waiters, had their melancholy eyes fixed on a distant dream, and were consoled only if some guest from the Balbec hotel, where they had formerly been employed, recognized them, spoke to them, and asked them personally to take away the champagne which was undrinkable, a request that filled them with pride.

I could hear the protestations of my nerves, though I still had a sense of well-being independent of any external objects which can supply it; but the slightest shift I made with my body or my attention was enough to renew that feeling, the way gentle pressure on one's closed eyes can create the impression of colour. I'd already drunk quite a bit of port, and if I was wondering whether I should have some more, it was less with a view to the euphoria more glasses of it might produce than an effect of the euphoria produced by the previous glasses. I let the music itself guide my pleasure to each note, on which it obediently came to rest. If, like the chemical industries that churn out huge quantities of substances that come together in nature only by chance and very rarely, this restaurant in Rivebelle gathered together at one and the same moment more women offering me prospects of happiness than I could have met by chance on walks or drives in a year, this music, on the other hand, which we were hearing—arrangements of waltzes, German operettas, cabaret songs, all of them new to me—was itself a sort of ethereal realm superimposed on the other, and more intoxicating than it. For every musical phrase, each as individual as a woman, did not hold in reserve, as she would have done for some privileged person, the sensual secret it contained: it offered it to me, ogled me, came to me with its whimsical or roguish ways, accosted me, caressed me, as if I'd suddenly become wealthier, more seductive, or more powerful; in these melodies, I could clearly sense a kind of cruelty, because any disinterested sense of beauty, any gleam of intelligence, was unknown to them; for them, physical pleasure alone existed. They are the most merciless form of hell, the one with no way out, for the jealous wretch to whom they offer that pleasure—the pleasure the woman he loves is enjoying with someone else—the only thing that exists in all the world for the woman who is all the world to him. But while I was softly humming the notes of this tune to myself, and returning its kiss, the unique voluptuous pleasure it made me feel became so dear to me that I would have left my parents to be able to follow the phrase through the singular, invisible world it created out of thin air, in musical lines by turns languid and lively. Even though such a pleasure is not the kind that increases the attractiveness of the person experiencing it, since that is perceived by him alone, and even though a woman who is not pleased by our appearance is ignorant of whether or not we possess this inner, subjective bliss, which consequently has no effect on the judgement she passes on us, I felt more powerful, almost irresistible. It seemed to me that my love was no longer something distasteful or amusing, but that it possessed precisely the touching beauty, the seductiveness of this music, which itself was like a friendly atmosphere in which my beloved and I might meet and quickly become very close.

The restaurant was frequented not just by women of the demi-monde, but also by people of the most fashionable society, who went there for five o'clock tea or else hosted lavish dinner parties. Afternoon tea was served in a long, glassed-in gallery, narrow as a corridor, leading from the entrance hall to the dining room and running alongside the garden, from which it was separated only by a few stone pillars and its tall glass windows, which could be opened here and there. The result of this, apart from frequent draughts, was that the room was filled with sudden, intermittent bursts of sunlight, a dazzling brightness that made it almost impossible to discern the ladies taking tea; and when they were there, with their tables ranged two by two all along the narrow channel, shimmering with every movement they made to drink their tea or greet one another, the room looked like a pool or a tank in which a fisherman has plunged the gleaming fish he's caught, which, half out of the water and bathed in the rays of the sun, dazzle everyone with their shimmering brilliance.

A few hours later, during dinner, which was served, naturally, in the dining room, the lamps would be lit, even though it was still light outside, so that we could see before us, in the garden, next to the pavilions still illumined by the twilight, and looking like pale ghosts of evening, arbours whose dusky foliage was shot through with the last rays of the sun; seen through the glass of the lamplit room in which we were dining, they resembled, unlike the wet, sparkling net enclosing the ladies taking late afternoon tea along the blue-gold corridor, the vegetation inside a huge, pale-green aquarium bathed in a supernatural light. People began to rise from their tables; and though the guests, having spent their time throughout the meal observing, recognizing, or asking the names of the guests at the next table, had been held in perfect cohesion around their own table, the force of attraction that had kept them gravitating around their host for the evening began to lose its power when they repaired for coffee to the same corridor where afternoon tea had been served; often, some migrating dinner party would in passing lose one or more of its corpuscles, which, having been too powerfully influenced by the attraction of the rival party, would detach themselves for a moment from their own, where they were replaced by the ladies or gentlemen who had come to greet their friends before returning to their own group, saying: 'I must get back to Monsieur So-and-So—he's my host tonight.' And for an instant the two groups looked like two separate bouquets that had exchanged some of their flowers. Then the corridor itself would begin to empty out. Often, since even after dinner there was still some lingering light, the long corridor was left unlit, and, skirted with trees leaning over it on the other side of the glass wall, it looked like a path in a wooded, shaded garden. Sometimes a woman, the last of her dinner party, lingered there in the half-light. As I was crossing the corridor on my way out one evening, I noticed, sitting among a group of people unknown to me, the beautiful Princesse de Luxembourg. I doffed my hat to her but didn't stop. She recognized me and nodded with a smile; from far above this greeting, emanating from the movement of her head, a few melodious words for me rose into the air, a somewhat drawn-out 'good evening' intended not to stop me, but merely to complete her nod, to make it a spoken greeting. But her words remained indistinct; all I could make out was the sound, which was so sweetly prolonged, and seemed so musical, that it was as if, in the shadowy branches of the trees, a nightingale had begun to sing. If by chance, to finish the evening with a group of his friends we'd run into, Saint-Loup decided to go with them to the Casino at a nearby resort, he'd put me into a carriage by myself; I'd tell the coachman to go as fast as possible, so as to shorten the time I'd have to spend without anyone's help in freeing me—by reversing course and shaking off the passivity in which I was caught as if in a trap—from the need to provide my own sensibility with distractions which, ever since I'd arrived in Rivebelle, I'd been receiving from others. Nothing—not a possible collision with an oncoming carriage on these pitch-dark lanes where there was room only for one; not the instability of the ground, sometimes crumbling at the cliff's edge; not the proximity to the sheer drop to the sea—none of that could rouse in me the little bit of effort required to bring the idea and fear of danger to the surface of my reasoning mind. For just as it's not the wish to become famous but the habit of hard work that enables us to produce a great work, it's not the light-heartedness of the present moment, but sober reflections on the past, that help us to safeguard the future. If, as soon as I'd arrived in Rivebelle, I'd cast far away from me the crutches that supported my rational thinking and self-control, both of which help our infirm selves to keep on a straight path, and had found myself prey to a kind of moral ataxia,* alcohol, by making my nerves even more highly-strung, had given to the present moment a quality, a charm, which were powerless to make me either more capable or even more determined to resist them; for, by making me see those present minutes as being vastly preferable to the rest of my life, my exalted state isolated them from it; I was trapped in the present, as heroes are, or drunkards; temporarily eclipsed, my past no longer projected before me that shadow of itself which we call our future; viewing the goal of my life now as no longer the realization of past dreams, but rather the enjoyment of the present moment, I couldn't see what lay beyond it. So that, by a contradiction that was so only in appearance, it was at the moment when I was experiencing an exceptional pleasure, when I felt my life could be happy, when it should have seemed more valuable to me—it was at that precise moment that, freed from the anxieties my life had until then inspired in me, I unhesitatingly surrendered it to the risk of some chance event. In fact, by doing this, I was only condensing into one evening the heedlessness that for everyone else is diluted throughout their entire lives, during which every day they needlessly face the dangers of a sea voyage, a ride in an aeroplane, a drive in a motor car, while the person whose heart would be broken if they died is waiting for them at home, or when, still stored in the fragile receptacle of their brain, is the book whose eventual publication is their sole reason for living. Similarly, in the restaurant in Rivebelle, on the evenings when we lingered there, if someone had come in with the intention of killing me, since I could no longer see, except in a future too remote to have any reality, my grandmother, my life to come, or my unwritten books, since I was totally absorbed by the fragrance of the woman at the next table, by the courtesies of the waiters, by the shape of the waltz being played, since I was glued to the sensation of the moment, having no existence beyond it or any wish except not to be separated from it, I would have died within that sensation, I would have let myself be torn limb from limb without lifting a finger to defend myself, without moving a muscle, like a bee stunned by tobacco smoke, who has lost all concern for preserving the store accumulated by his efforts, and all hope of reaching his hive.

I should add that the insignificance to which the gravest matters were reduced, in contrast with the intensity of my exaltation, eventually extended even to Mademoiselle Simonet and her friends. The whole enterprise of getting to know her now seemed easy but a matter of indifference, since nothing but my present situation, because of its extraordinary power, the joy provoked by its slightest variations, and even its mere continuity, had any importance; everything else— parents, work, pleasures, the girls in Balbec—weighed no more than a fleck of sea spray in a high wind that prevents it from coming to rest, and had no existence except in relation to the inner power I felt: for a few hours, drunkenness brings about subjective idealism, pure phenomenalism; all things are nothing more than appearances, and exist only as a function of our sublime selves. This doesn't mean that true love, if we feel such a thing, can't survive in such a state. But we feel so strongly, as if we've moved into a new sphere of being, that unknown pressures have altered the dimensions of this feeling, that we can no longer view it in the same way. We can still find this same love, but in a different place; it no longer weighs on us, it is satisfied by the sensation afforded it by the present, and this sensation is enough for us, since we have no concern for anything that is not in the present. Unfortunately, the coefficient that alters values in this way changes them only during this hour of drunkenness. The people who had lost all importance, whom we blew away like soap bubbles, will resume their substantiality the next day; and we'll have to try to resume the work that just yesterday had meant nothing. Even more seriously, these mathematics of the morrow are the same as yesterday's, with the same problems we must inevitably grapple with; they are the very same mathematics that, without our being aware of it, govern our lives even during our hours of drunkenness. If we happen to be with a chaste or unfriendly woman, the question that had seemed so difficult to us before—whether she might come to like us—now seems a million times easier without actually having become so in the least, for it's only in our own eyes, in our own inner view of ourselves, that we have changed. And she is as displeased at the instant when we became overfamiliar with her as we will be the next day at having tipped the porter a hundred francs, and for the same reason, which for us has simply taken longer to appear: an absence of drunkenness.

I knew none of the women who were in Rivebelle, and who, because they were a part of my drunkenness just as reflections are part of a mirror, seemed infinitely more desirable than the increasingly less existent Mademoiselle Simonet. A young blonde woman, on her own, with a melancholy air, wearing wildflowers in her straw hat, looked pensively at me for an instant and seemed attractive. Then my attention was caught by another, then a third; finally it was a brunette with a radiant complexion. Almost all of them were known, not by me, but by Saint-Loup.

Before meeting his current mistress, Saint-Loup had in fact lived so much in the limited world of licentiousness that, among all the women who dined on those evenings in Rivebelle, many of whom were there by chance, having come to the seaside either to meet their lover or try to find one, there were hardly any he didn't know, because either he or one of his friends had spent at least one night with them. He didn't greet them if they were with a man, and they, though they looked at him more than at some other man because the indifference he was known to feel towards any woman who wasn't his actress gave him, in their eyes, a singular prestige, pretended they didn't know him. One of them whispered: 'There's the young Saint-Loup. They say he still loves his tart—she's his one grand passion. What a charming boy! I think he's splendid; and look how stylish he is! Some girls have all the luck. He has it all, really. I knew him well when I was with d'Orléans. Those two were inseparable. He was living it up back then! But those days are over—he never cheats on her now. I hope she knows how lucky she is. I wonder what he sees in her. He must be easily fooled. She has feet like boats and a walrus moustache—and her undies are filthy! Even a little factory girl wouldn't want her knickers.—Just look at his eyes, you'd jump into the fire for a man like that. Oh, don't say a word, he has recognized me, he's laughing! How well he used to know me . . . Just mention me to him, you'll see.' I surprised a knowing look between him and them. I wished he'd introduce me to them, so that I could ask for an assignation, and so they could grant it, even though I might not be able to keep it. Otherwise their faces, as if hidden by a veil, would forever lack that element which varies with every woman, which we can't imagine in any woman when we haven't seen it there, and which appears only in the gaze that meets our eyes, and that acquiesces to our desire and promises us it will be satisfied. But even diminished in that way, the faces of these women were much more meaningful to me than those of women whom I suspected were chaste, whose faces were flat, with nothing behind them, made all of a piece, without any depth. No doubt these faces were not to me what they must have been to Saint-Loup, who could recall, and see, beneath the transparent indifference of motionless features that feigned not to know him, behind the banality of the same greeting that would have been offered to anyone else, the dishevelled hair, the parted lips, and the half-closed eyes, a whole wordless spectacle like those that painters, to deceive most visitors, cover with a decent canvas. For me, on the other hand, aware as I was that no part of my existence had penetrated any of these women, and that none of myself would be carried off on to the unknown paths they'd follow throughout their lives, these faces remained closed. But it was already enough to know that they could open for me to see them as being more valuable than if they'd been nothing but pretty medals, rather than lockets containing mementoes of love hidden inside. As for Robert, who could scarcely sit still when he was at table, and who hid beneath his courtier's smile a warrior's eagerness for action, when I looked at him closely, I realized how the emphatic bone structure of his triangular face must have been the same as that of his ancestors, better suited to an ardent archer than to a delicate scholar. Through his fine skin, the bold structure and feudal architecture showed. His head called to mind one of those ancient castle-keeps on which the disused battlements can still be seen, though inside they've been converted into libraries.

All the way back to Balbec, about one or other of those unknown women to whom he'd introduced me, I'd keep repeating, without a second's pause, and yet almost without realizing what I was doing: 'What a delightful woman!', as if singing a refrain. Of course, these words were dictated more by nervous excitement than by any definitive judgement. Nevertheless, if I'd had a thousand francs with me and if there were still any jewellers' shops open at that hour, I would have bought a ring for her. When the hours of our lives unfurl like sections utterly different from one another, we find we give too much of ourselves to all sorts of people who the next day may strike us as uninteresting. But we feel responsible for what we said to them the night before, and we want to honour it.

Since on those evenings I returned later than usual to the hotel, it was a pleasure to step into my bedroom, which was no longer unwelcoming, and to see the bed, on which I was sure I'd never be able to find rest, whereas now my weary limbs sought support from it; and one after the other, my thighs, hips, and shoulders tried to adhere at every point to the sheets enveloping the mattress, as if my fatigue were a sculptor trying to take a cast of the entire human body. But I was unable to fall asleep, since I could sense the approach of morning; peace of mind and well-being of body had deserted me. In my distress, I felt as if I would never find them again. I would have needed to sleep a long time to enjoy them again. But even if I had dozed off, I'd still have been awakened two hours later by the concert on the esplanade. All of a sudden I did fall asleep; I fell into that deep sleep that opens up for us a return to childhood, the rediscovery of years past and emotions once felt, disincarnation, the transmigration of souls, the recollection of the dead, the illusions of madness, regression to the most primitive forms of nature (for it's said we often see animals in our dreams, but we forget that, almost always when we dream, we ourselves are animals deprived of the rationality that projects the light of certainty on to things; on the contrary, all we can direct at the spectacle of life is an uncertain gaze constantly being obliterated by forgetfulness, each reality vanishing before the next takes its place like the ever-shifting projection of a magic lantern as the slides are changed), all these mysteries we think we don't know but into which we are actually initiated almost every night, just as we're introduced to the other great mystery of annihilation and resurrection. Since my difficulty in digesting the Rivebelle dinner caused me to be more restless, the fitful, wandering illumination of the various shadowy zones of my past made me a creature whose supreme happiness would have been to meet Legrandin, with whom I'd just been conversing in a dream.

Then even my own life would be completely hidden from me by a new setting, like the painted cloth lowered near the apron of the stage while actors provide a diversion as the scene is being changed behind it. The scene in which I was now playing a role was in the style of Oriental fairy tales; I knew nothing of my past or of myself, because of the extreme proximity of the interposed scene; I was nothing but a character getting a beating and being subjected to various punishments for a transgression I couldn't fathom, but which was actually that I had drunk too much port. Suddenly I awoke and saw that because of my deep sleep, I hadn't heard the concert. It was already afternoon; I verified this by my watch after several efforts to get up, efforts that were unsuccessful at first and interrupted by collapses on to my pillow, but the sort of brief tumbles that follow sleep as well as other kinds of drunkenness, whether they're produced by wine or convalescence; in any case, even before I'd looked at the time, I was sure it was past midday. The night before, I'd been nothing but an empty, weightless being, unable to stop moving or talking (and just as you have to be lying down before you can sit up, I had to go to sleep in order to stop talking); I was without density or a centre of gravity; I was set in motion, and I felt as if I could have kept going on my dreary course until I reached the moon. Though my eyes as I slept hadn't seen the time, my body had been able to calculate it; it had measured the time not from some superficial marks on a dial, but by the progressive weight of all my renewed energies, which, like a powerful clock, it had lowered, cog by cog, from my brain down into the rest of my body, where they now stored the unused abundance of their provisions all the way down to my knees. If it's true that the sea was once our life-giving environment into which we must reimmerse our blood so as to restore our vital forces, the same is true for forgetting, for mental oblivion; we seem absent from time for a few hours; but the unspent energy accumulated during that time measures it by itself, as precisely as the pendulum of a clock or the toppling sandhill in an hourglass. We emerge from such a sleep no more easily than we do from a prolonged spell of wakefulness, so strongly does everything tend to persist; and if it's true that some narcotics can bring on sleep, sleeping a long time is an even more powerful narcotic, after which it is quite difficult to wake up. Like a sailor who can clearly see the pier to which he must moor his boat still rocked by the waves, I had a firm intention of looking at the time and getting up, but my body was at every instant thrown back into sleep; landing was difficult, and before I could stand up and reach for my watch, to compare its time to the one indicated by the wealth of material stored in my tired legs, I fell back two or three more times on to my pillow.

Finally I could see it clearly, and exclaimed: 'Two o'clock in the afternoon!' I rang, but immediately fell into another sleep which this time must have been infinitely longer, judging by the depth of my repose, and by my vision on waking of having traversed an immense night. But since what woke me was Françoise coming in, in answer to my summons, this new sleep that had seemed so much longer than the one before it, and that had brought me such a feeling of well-being and so much forgetfulness, had lasted only half a minute.

My grandmother opened my bedroom door; I asked her a number of questions about the Legrandins.

It's not enough to say I'd regained peace of mind and good health, for it was more than merely distance that had separated them from me the night before; all night long I'd struggled against an opposing current, but now they were not only with me, but they were once again inside me. In precise and still slightly painful points of my empty head, which would one day be split open, letting my ideas escape forever, these ideas had once again taken their proper place, and resumed that existence by which, alas, they had until now failed to profit.

Once again I'd escaped the impossibility of sleeping as well as the floods and shipwrecks of my strained nerves. I no longer had any fear whatsoever of what had been threatening me the night before, when I was deprived of rest. A new life stretched before me; without moving a muscle (for I was still exhausted though already alert), I savoured my weariness with a light heart; it had isolated and broken the bones of my legs and arms, which I felt were all assembled before me, ready to be joined back together, and all I had to do to raise them up again was sing, like the builder in the fable.*

All of a sudden I remembered the wistful young blonde woman in Rivebelle who had looked at me for a moment. All evening long, many other women had seemed attractive; but now she alone rose up from the depths of my memory. It seemed to me that she had noticed me; I was expecting one of the Rivebelle waiters to come and deliver a note from her. Saint-Loup didn't know her, but thought she was respectable. It would be very difficult to get to see her, and to go on seeing her. But I was prepared to go to any lengths to make it possible, and could think of nothing but her. Philosophy often talks of free actions and necessary actions. Perhaps there is no act so completely involuntary as the one which, by virtue of a rising force which had been held down during activity, brings back, once our thoughts have come to rest, a memory that had been on the same level as all the others because of the oppressive force of distraction, and makes it spring to the surface, because, without our realizing it, it contained a charm the others lacked, and which we notice only twenty-four hours later. But perhaps this is the freest of all actions, since it is still unmotivated by habit, by the sort of obsessiveness which, in love, causes the exclusive image of a certain person to recur in one's mind.

That was the day after I'd seen the beautiful procession of girls going by, against the background of the sea. I asked several of the hotel guests who came almost every year to Balbec about them. They could tell me nothing. Later, a photograph showed me why. Who could have recognized now in these girls, who had just recently but definitively left behind the age at which we change so completely, the delightful, amorphous mass of little girls, still children, who, just a few years before, could be seen sitting in a circle on the sand, around a tent: a kind of vague, white constellation in which, even if one could make out a pair of eyes brighter than any other pair, a mischievous face, or blonde hair, one would soon lose sight of them and confuse them in the indistinct, milky nebula?

No doubt, at that time, just a few years before, it was not the vision of the group that lacked clarity, as it had been the day before, when they first appeared to me, but the group itself. In those days, the girls, still very young, were at that elementary stage in their formation when personality hasn't set its seal on each face. Like those primitive organisms in which the individual barely exists on its own, but functions as a colony of polyps rather than as any of the individual polyps that comprise it, the girls lived huddled all together. Sometimes one would push another over, and then a giggling fit, which seemed the only manifestation of their personal lives, would overcome them all at once, erasing and confusing these undefined, contorted faces as they congealed into a single sparkling, quivering cluster. In an old photograph they gave me later, which I've kept, their infantile troop already shows the same number of members as in their womanly procession later on; one can sense they must already have presented a singular spot of colour on the beach and must have drawn all eyes towards them, but one can't recognize any individual except by deduction, by taking into account all the possible transformations they could have undergone during their childhood, up to the point at which these reconstituted forms started to coincide with another individual set of features, which one must attempt to identify also in the beautiful face (accompanied now by a tall figure and hair that's been curled) that might once have been the wizened, scrunched-up face shown in the photo; and the distance travelled in such a short period of time by the physical characteristics of each of these girls was such an unreliable criterion, and the things they shared collectively were already so marked, that even their best friends sometimes mistook one for the other in this photograph, so that the uncertainty could be dispelled in the end only by some article of clothing that one of them, and she alone, was known to have worn. Different as those days were from the day I saw them on the esplanade—different, yet so close to it—the girls still succumbed to laughing fits, as I'd witnessed the day before, but this time their laughter wasn't the intermittent, almost automatic laughter of childhood, the spasmodic release that used to make all their heads bob down as one, just as a school of minnows in the Vivonne scatters and disappears before re-forming an instant later; now, however, their physiognomies were their own mistresses, their eyes were fixed on the goal they were pursuing; and it was only the indecision and vacillation of my initial perception on the day before that indistinctly confused the now separate and individualized beings, these spores of the pale madrepore.*

Many times, of course, when pretty girls passed by, I'd promise myself that I would see them again. Usually, such girls don't reappear; and memory, which soon forgets their existence, would have difficulty recalling their features; our eyes might not even recognize them—and in the meantime we will have seen other girls passing by, girls we won't see again either. At other times, though—and this is what would happen with the insolent little band—chance keeps bringing them back to us. Then chance strikes us as a beautiful thing, for we see in it the beginning of an effort to organize and compose our life; and this same chance makes it easy, inevitable, and sometimes—after interruptions that may have made us wish for a cessation of such memories—cruel for us to feel a fidelity to mental images that we may come to believe we were predestined to acquire, yet which, without that chance, we might so easily have forgotten at the very beginning, like so many others.

Saint-Loup's stay was about to draw to a close. I hadn't seen the girls on the beach again. He spent too few afternoons in Balbec to be able to pay attention to them or try to get to know them on my behalf. He had more time in the evenings, and he continued to take me regularly to Rivebelle. In such restaurants, as in public gardens or trains, people are encased in an ordinary appearance, but their names astonish us if, having casually asked for them, we discover that they're not the unremarkable nobodies we'd supposed, but nothing less than the government minister or duke we'd heard so much about. Two or three times already, in the Rivebelle restaurant, Saint-Loup and I had seen coming in and sitting down to dinner, just as everyone else was leaving, a tall man, very muscular, with regular features and a greying beard, whose pensive eyes stared steadily into space. One evening, when we asked the owner who this obscure, solitary, late diner was, he replied: 'You mean to say you don't know the famous painter Elstir?' Swann had once mentioned his name in my presence, though I'd completely forgotten in what connection; but the loss of a memory, like that of part of a sentence while reading, sometimes promotes not uncertainty, but the dawning of a premature certainty. 'He's a friend of Swann's, and a very well-known artist, extremely good,' I said to Saint-Loup. Immediately there passed through us both, like a shiver of excitement, the thought that Elstir was a great artist, a famous man; this was followed by the thought that, not distinguishing us from the other diners, he had no idea how thrilled we were by the idea of his talent. Doubtless the fact that he knew nothing of our admiration, and that we knew Swann, would not have irked us if we hadn't been at a seaside resort. But we were still at an age when enthusiasm can brook no silence, and, having been transported into a life in which our incognito seemed intolerable, we wrote a letter, which we both signed, in which we divulged to Elstir that the two diners seated a few feet away were ardent admirers of his talent, and were friends of his great friend Swann, and in which we asked his permission to present our compliments. A waiter delivered this missive to the famous man.

Elstir may not yet have been quite as famous at that time as the restaurant owner claimed, or as he would become not many years later. But he'd been one of the first to frequent this restaurant at a time when it was still nothing but a sort of farmhouse, and had brought to it a colony of artists (who had all, for that matter, migrated elsewhere as soon as the farmhouse, where they used to eat out of doors under a simple awning, had become an elegant meeting-place; Elstir himself had only come back to Rivebelle at that time because of a temporary absence of his wife, with whom he lived not far away). But a great talent, even when it's not yet recognized, necessarily gives rise to some manifestations of admiration, such as those the owner of the farmhouse had managed to discern in the questions of more than a few visiting Englishwomen, eager for information about the life Elstir led, or in the number of letters the artist received from abroad. The owner had also noticed that Elstir did not like to be disturbed when he was working, and that he got up at night, whenever there was a bright moon, to take a young model down to the sea's edge to pose nude; and he'd told himself that all the painter's hard work had not been in vain, nor the admiration of the tourists unjustified, when he recognized, in one of Elstir's paintings, a wooden cross that stood by the road leading to Rivebelle. 'It's the same one,' he would repeat in amazement. 'Those are all the four parts of it! How meticulous he is!'

And he wondered whether a little *Sunrise over the Sea** which Elstir had given him might not be worth a fortune.

We watched him read our letter, put it in his pocket, finish his dinner, ask for his things, get up to go; and we were so certain that what we'd done had offended him that our only wish now (just as it was our only fear before) was to slip away without being noticed by him. The one thing that should have seemed the most important of all didn't cross our minds for an instant: that our enthusiasm for Elstir, the sincerity of which we wouldn't have allowed anyone to doubt (offering as proof our bated breath and our eager willingness to do anything difficult or heroic for the great man), was not, as we imagined, real admiration, since we'd never seen anything by Elstir; it was possible that our emotion was inspired by the empty idea of 'a great artist', not by a work we'd never seen. At most it was theoretical admiration, the nervous framework and sentimental structure of an admiration without content—that is to say, something as inextricably linked to childhood as certain organs that no longer exist in the body of an adult: we were still children. Elstir had almost reached the door when suddenly he did an about-turn and headed towards us. I was overwhelmed by a thrill of delicious terror, the kind I'd have been incapable of experiencing a few years later, because, while age diminishes our ability to allow such extraordinary occasions to arise, habituation to the ways of the world takes away our inclination to feel these sorts of emotions.

In the brief conversation we had when Elstir came to sit at our table, even though I mentioned Swann several times, he never responded. I began to think he didn't know him. But he did ask me to visit him in his studio in Balbec, an invitation he didn't extend to Saint-Loup, and which I earned (as I might not have done, perhaps, by a recommendation from Swann, if Elstir was indeed a close friend of his, since a desire for impartiality plays a larger role in our lives than one might think) by a few words I said that made him think I appreciated the arts. The friendliness he lavished on me outdid Saint-Loup's as much as Saint-Loup's outdid that of a petit bourgeois. Compared to the kindness of a great artist, the amiability of a nobleman, charming as it may be, seems like play-acting, mere pretence. Saint-Loup sought to please; Elstir, on the other hand, loved to give, to give of himself. Whatever he possessed—ideas, works, and all the rest (which he valued much less), he would cheerfully have given to anyone who understood him. But, for lack of any company he could bear, he lived in isolation, with an unsociability that fashionable people regarded as affectation and poor breeding, the powers-that-be saw as rebelliousness, his neighbours as madness, and his family as selfishness and pride.

No doubt at first, even in his solitude, he must have taken pleasure in the thought that, through his work, he was addressing, from afar, those who had misunderstood or offended him, and was making them think more highly of him. Perhaps at that time he lived alone not out of indifference, but out of love of others, and, just as I'd given up Gilberte in the hope I'd eventually appear to her in a more favourable light, he painted with certain people in mind as a way of endearing himself to them, so that without actually seeing him, they would love him, admire him, speak about him; renunciation is not always definitive from the start, when we decide upon it in our original frame of mind, before we've felt its repercussions, whether it be the renunciation of an invalid, a monk, an artist, or a hero. But even if Elstir had wanted to work with certain people in mind, in working he had lived for himself, far from the society he shunned; the practice of solitude had given him a love for it, as happens with any great thing we at first fear, because we know it's incompatible with more trivial things to which we are attached, and from which it does not so much deprive us as release us. Before we experience it, our whole preoccupation is to know how we can reconcile it with certain pleasures—which stop being pleasures as soon as we've experienced it.

Elstir didn't sit talking with us for very long. I resolved to visit his studio in the next few days, but the day after that dinner, my grandmother and I having gone for a walk to the very end of the esplanade, near the cliffs of Canapville, as we were making our way back, at the corner of one of the little streets that ran at right angles down to the beach, we passed a girl: hanging her head like an animal being made to return to its stable against its will, and carrying golf clubs, she was walking in front of an authoritative-looking person, presumably her English governess, or a friend's governess, who looked like John

Jeffreys in the portrait by Hogarth,* with a complexion as red as if her favourite drink were gin and not tea, and with a black stain of chewing tobacco adding its curl to a grey moustache, which was quite pronounced. The girl walking in front of her looked like the girl in the little band with the black toque and a chubby, motionless face with laughing eyes. But the one walking home now, though she also had a black toque, looked even prettier than the first one; the line of her nose was straighter, and the wings of her nostrils were wider and fuller. The first one had struck me as a proud, pale young lady; this one looked more like an unwillingly submissive, rosy-cheeked child. However, as this one was pushing a similar bicycle, and wearing the same deerskin gloves, I concluded that the differences might be due to my present viewpoint and circumstances, for it was hardly likely that there was a second girl in Balbec whose face, in the final analysis, looked so much like hers, and who shared so many other similarities in clothing and accoutrements. She glanced quickly in my direction; over the following days, whenever I saw the little band on the beach, and even later when I knew all the girls who composed it, I never knew with absolute certainty whether any of them, including the first one with the bicycle, who looked most like her, was in fact the one I'd seen that evening at the far end of the beach, at the corner of the street, this one who was so similar to, but still slightly different from, the one I'd noticed in their procession.

From that afternoon on, even though my mind for the last few days had been occupied chiefly with the tall girl, it was the one with the golf clubs, whom I assumed to be Mademoiselle Simonet, on whom I began to dwell. While walking with the others, she would often stop, causing her friends, who seemed to respect her greatly, to pause as well. That is how I see her: bringing everyone to a standstill, her eyes shining under her toque, silhouetted against the backdrop of the sea, and separated from me by the transparent, sky-blue stretch of time elapsed since that first image, so slight in my memory, desired, pursued, then forgotten, then found again, of a face I've often since projected into the past, so as to say to myself, of a girl who was in my bedroom: 'That was her!'

Perhaps, though, it was the one with the geranium-coloured cheeks and green eyes I'd rather have come to know. But regardless of which one I preferred to see on any given day, the others, even without her, were enough to fill me with excitement; though my desire might shift from one to the other, it continued to merge them all together, as my indistinct vision did on the first day, into a single whole, a little world apart, animated by a life in common—which was probably, when it came down to it, how they imagined themselves; and if I could have befriended one of them, I would have penetrated, like a cultivated pagan or a scrupulous Christian among barbarians, a whole rejuvenating society based on health, recklessness, pleasure, cruelty, non-intellectuality, and joy.

My grandmother, whom I'd told about my conversation with Elstir, and who was pleased to think of all the intellectual advantage I could derive from his friendship, thought it absurd and impolite of me not to have paid him a visit yet. But I thought only of the little band, and, unsure of when these girls might pass by on the esplanade, I didn't dare go elsewhere. My grandmother was also surprised at how elegantly I was dressing, for I'd suddenly remembered some suits that until then had been left at the bottom of my trunk. Every day I wore a different one, and I'd even written to Paris to send for some new hats and neckties.

Life in a seaside resort like Balbec can acquire great charm if the face of a pretty girl, a vendor of seashells, pastries, or flowers, painted in vivid colours in our memory, becomes regularly, from the morning onwards, the goal of each of these leisurely, luminous days we spend on the beach. Because of this, our days, though idle, then become as busy as workdays, guided, magnetized, buoyed up by the thought of the approaching instant, the one when, merely by buying biscuits, roses, or ammonites, we can delight in seeing the colours on a feminine face displayed as purely as on a flower. But at least with these shop-girls one can talk with them first, thereby obviating the need to construct with our imagination other aspects than those provided by simple visual perception, to recreate their lives and exaggerate their charms, as we'd do if we were looking at a portrait; most importantly, by the mere fact that we're talking with them, we can find out where and at what time we can meet them again. But that was by no means the case for me when it came to the girls in the little band. I knew nothing of their habits; when I didn't see them on certain days, I was ignorant of the reason for their absence; I tried to find out if these absences were a regular thing, if they could be seen only every other day, or when the weather was just so, or if there were days when they were never to be seen. I pictured myself already a friend of theirs, asking them: 'Why weren't you there on such-and-such a day?' and being told: 'Oh, yes! That's because it was a Saturday, on Saturdays we never come because . . .' If only it were as simple as that, knowing that on sad Saturdays it was pointless to keep trying, that you could scour the beach in every direction, sit in the window of the patisserie, pretend to eat an eclair, go inside the gift shop, waiting until it was time to go for a swim, or to a concert, or for high tide, or sunset, or night, without ever seeing the longed-for little band. But perhaps that fatal day did not occur once a week. Perhaps it didn't always fall on a Saturday. Perhaps certain atmospheric conditions influenced it, or perhaps they had nothing whatsoever to do with it. How many patient but not at all serene observations we must record concerning the seemingly erratic movements of these unknown worlds before we can be sure we haven't been led astray by coincidences, that our expectations won't be disappointed, before we can finally deduce the definitive laws, acquired at the cost of cruel experience, of this passionate astronomy! Remembering that I hadn't seen them on a certain day the week before, I told myself they wouldn't come, that it was pointless to linger on the beach. And then I'd see them. On the other hand, on a day which, insofar as I'd assumed there were laws regulating the return of these constellations, I'd calculated would be an auspicious one, they didn't come. But this initial uncertainty about whether or not I'd see them on a particular day was followed by one even graver, namely, if I'd *ever* see them again, for I had no idea if they might be about to set sail for America, or go back to Paris. That was all that was needed to make me start to fall in love with them. One can have a liking for someone. But to unleash the sadness, the feeling of something irreparable having happened, the agonies that prepare the way for love, there must be the risk—and perhaps this, rather than any person, is the actual goal that passion seeks so anxiously to embrace—of an impossibility. These influences were already acting upon me, and they recur each time we fall in love (they can also be provoked, though mostly in city life, by working-class girls, when, because you don't know which day they have off, you become alarmed when you haven't seen them leaving the factory), or at least that's what has happened over the course of my own love affairs. Perhaps such influences are inseparable from love; perhaps the particularities of our first experience of love become incorporated into the following ones, thanks to memory, suggestion, habit, and, throughout the successive periods of our life, they give a common character to its varied phases.

I seized every possible pretext to go down to the beach at times when I hoped I might encounter them. Having seen them once while we were having lunch, I now invariably arrived late for it, having waited interminably on the esplanade for them to pass by; and throughout the short time I sat in the dining room, my gaze would question the azure of the glass doors, and I'd leave well before dessert so as not to miss them in case they went out for their walk at a different hour; and I became annoyed with my grandmother when, with unconscious cruelty, she made me stay with her beyond the time that seemed propitious. I'd try to extend the horizon by placing my chair at an angle to the table; if by chance I caught sight of any one of the girls, since they all shared the same special essence, it was as if I'd seen, projected before my eyes in a shifting, diabolical hallucination, a little of the daunting yet passionately desired dream that, just a moment ago, had existed only in my mind, where it lay perpetually dormant.

Loving them all, I didn't love any one of them; and yet the possibility of meeting them was the only thing that brightened my days, the only thing that made those hopes grow in me that lead one to believe all obstacles can be overcome, hopes that were often followed by fury if I hadn't seen them. At that time, these girls eclipsed my grandmother; I would happily have left for a long journey at once if it meant I could go to a place where they might be. It was on them that my thoughts contentedly dwelled when I thought I was thinking of something else, or of nothing. But when, even without realizing it, I thought of them, at an even deeper level of unconsciousness they were the hilly blue undulations of the sea, a procession silhouetted against the sea. It was the sea I was hoping to find again, if I went to some town where they might be. The most exclusive love for one person is always love for something else.

My grandmother, because I'd developed a sudden interest in golf and tennis and was wasting an opportunity to watch and listen to an artist whom she knew to be one of the greatest of all, evinced a disdain for me that seemed to stem from rather narrow-minded beliefs. At the Champs-Élysées I'd had an inkling, which later grew to a certainty, that when we're in love with a woman, we simply project on to her the state of our own soul; that, consequently, the important thing is not the merit of the woman, but the intensity of that state; and that the emotions that an ordinary girl arouses in us may enable us to bring to our consciousness aspects of ourselves that are more intimate and personal, more remote and essential, than we could acquire from the pleasure we feel when conversing with a great man, or even when we gaze admiringly at his work.

I eventually had to comply with my grandmother's wishes, with all the more annoyance because Elstir lived quite far from the esplanade, in one of the newest avenues of Balbec. The heat of the day made me take the train, which passed by the Rue de la Plage, and, so that I could think I was in the realm of the ancient Cimmerians, or possibly in the land of King Mark, or on the site of the Forest of Broceliande,* I made an effort not to look at the sham luxury of the buildings spreading out before me, among which Elstir's villa may have been the most sumptuously ugly of all; he'd rented it despite this because, of all those existing in Balbec, it was the only one that could offer him a vast studio.

I kept my eyes averted as I walked through the garden, which had a lawn (a small one, like that of any middle-class residence in the suburbs of Paris), a miniature statue of a courtly gardener, glass gazing globes, borders of begonias, and a little arbour sheltering rocking chairs arranged around a metal table. But after seeing all these peripheral accoutrements reeking of urban ugliness, I didn't mind the chocolate-coloured mouldings on the skirting boards once I was in the studio; I felt perfectly happy, for, with the help of all the studies around me, I sensed the possibility that I might rise to a poetic understanding, rich in delights, of many forms which until then I hadn't isolated from the general spectacle of reality. Elstir's studio looked to me like the laboratory for a sort of new creation of the world, in which, from the chaos of all the things we see, he had extracted particular things, by painting them on various rectangles of canvas which were strewn all around: an ocean wave crashing its lilac foam furiously on to the sand, or a young man in white twill leaning on a ship's taffrail. The young man's jacket and the foaming wave had acquired a new dignity from the fact that they continued to exist, even though they were deprived of their presumed characteristics, the wave now unable to make anything wet, and the jacket unable to be worn.

When I came in, the creator, paintbrush in hand, was just putting the finishing touches to the shape of the sun as it set.

The blinds were down on almost every side, so the studio was quite cool (save for one spot where the bright sun was decorating the wall with its dazzling, fleeting design) and dark; only a little rectangular window framed with honeysuckle was open, looking out beyond a strip of garden to an avenue; so that the atmosphere in most of the studio was dark, transparent, and compact in its mass, but liquid and glistening at the gaps where the light framed it, like a block of rock crystal one side of which, already cut and polished, gleams here and there like a mirror, and glows with iridescence. While Elstir continued to paint at my request, I wandered about in the chiaroscuro, pausing before one painting, then another.

Most of the paintings that surrounded me were not the kind I'd have preferred to see by him, namely those from his first and second periods, as described in an English art magazine lying on the table in the reading room of the Grand-Hôtel—that is, his mythological period, and the period in which he had undergone a Japanese influence, both admirably represented, the article noted, in the collection of Madame de Guermantes. The works in his studio were, of course, almost exclusively seascapes done here, in Balbec. But I could see that their charm lay in a sort of metamorphosis of the things they represented, like what in poetry is called metaphor, and if God the Father had created things by naming them, it was by removing their names, or by giving them different ones, that Elstir recreated them. The names that designate things always correspond to an intellectual idea, which is foreign to our actual impressions of them, and which forces us to eliminate from them anything that doesn't have to do with that idea.

Sometimes at my window, in the hotel in Balbec, on mornings when Françoise unfastened the covers keeping out the light, or on evenings when I was waiting until it was time to go out with Saint-Loup, thanks to an effect of sunlight, I might happen to mistake a darker section of the sea for a distant shore, or to look with joy at a wavering belt of blue not knowing if it belonged to sea or sky. Soon my mind would re-establish the separation between the elements that my first impression had abolished. Similarly, in my room in Paris, I sometimes heard an argument, almost a riot, until I'd linked the sounds to their cause—a carriage, for instance, rumbling towards me—a noise from which I eliminated those high-pitched, discordant vociferations which my ears had actually heard, but which my mind knew could not be produced by wheels. But those rare moments when we see nature as it is, poetically—it was those that formed Elstir's work. One of his most frequent metaphors in the seascapes he had with him at that time was precisely the one that, comparing earth to sea, blurred any distinction between them. It was this comparison, tacitly and tirelessly repeated in the same canvas, which gave it that powerful, multiform unity, the cause (though sometimes not clearly perceived by admirers of his work) of the enthusiasm that Elstir's painting aroused in them.

It was to a metaphor of this sort—in a painting depicting the harbour of Carquethuit,* a painting he'd finished just a few days before, and which I looked at for a long time—that Elstir had prepared the spectator's mind by using only marine vocabulary for the little town, and only urban vocabulary for the sea. Whether because the houses hid part of the harbour or a dry dock, or the sea itself was engulfing the land, as happened constantly in the region of Balbec, on the other side of the furthest promontory where the town was built, the roofs were surmounted (as if by chimneys or bell-towers) by masts, which seemed to make the ships to which they belonged town-like, as if they were built on land, an impression increased by other boats, moored along the pier, but in such serried ranks that you could see men conversing from one deck to the other without any separation or gap of water visible between them, and so this fishing fleet seemed to belong less to the water than, for instance, to the churches of Criquebec which, in the distance, surrounded by water on all sides because you saw them without seeing the town, in a sparkle of sun and wave, seemed to be emerging from the water, blown out of alabaster or foam, and, enclosed in the versicoloured sash of a rainbow, to form an unreal, mystical picture. On the beach in the foreground, the painter had cleverly accustomed the eye not to recognize any fixed border, any absolute line of demarcation, between the land and the ocean. Men pushing boats into the sea were running as much in the waves as on the sand, which, since it was wet, was already reflecting the hulls of the boats as if it too were water. The sea itself didn't come up in an even line but followed the irregularities of the shore, which the perspective of the painting made even more jagged, so that a ship out at sea, half hidden by the projecting structures of the arsenal, seemed to be sailing in the middle of the town; women gathering prawns among the rocks looked, because they were surrounded by water and because of the dip which, beyond the circular barrier of the rocks, lowered the beach (at the two points closest to land) to the level of the sea, as if they were in an undersea grotto, with waves and boats overhead, exposed yet protected in the midst of the miraculously parted waves. Though the whole painting gave the impression of ports where sea enters land, where land is already sea, and the population amphibious, the power of the marine element could be sensed everywhere; and near the rocks, at the entrance to the channel, where the sea was rough, you could feel from the efforts of the fishermen and from the steeply slanting angle of the boats lying in front of the calm verticality of the wharf, the church, and the houses of the town, which some people were entering while others were leaving to fish, that they were trotting roughly over the water as if it were a swift, spirited animal whose bucking and rearing might have thrown them if it weren't for their skill. A group of holidaymakers were setting gaily out to sea in a sailing boat that rocked like a horse-drawn cart; a cheerful but alert sailor controlled it as if with reins, trimming the luffing sail; each passenger stayed in place to avoid weighing down one side of the boat and making it capsize; and onwards they galloped through sun-spangled fields into shadowy places, racing down the slopes. It was a beautiful morning, despite a recent storm. You could even sense the powerful forces that had to be overcome in order to achieve the admirable equilibrium of the motionless boats, basking in the sun and the cool air, in the parts of the sea where it was so calm that their reflections were almost more solid and real than the hulls; these parts were made hazy by an effect of the light, and, because of the perspective, looked as if they overlapped each other. Or rather, they didn't look like other parts of the sea; for between any one of these areas, there was as much difference as between one of them and the church emerging from the water, or the boats beyond the town. Then the mind perceived as one single element what was black as if from a storm in one place, then, further on, the same colour as the sky and just as glossy, and, in another place, so white with sun, fog, and foam, so compact, so landlike, so surrounded by houses, that it brought to mind some stone causeway or field of snow, on which one was startled to see a ship rising up a steep, dry incline, like a carriage gushing water as it emerges from a ford, but which, on second thoughts, when you see other boats teetering on the high, uneven expanse of the solid plateau, you realize was identical in all these various aspects, and was still the sea.

Although it is said, and rightly so, that there can be no progress or new discoveries in art, but only in the sciences, and that each artist who sets out afresh on his own individual endeavour cannot be helped or hindered by the endeavours of any others, it must nevertheless be acknowledged that, insofar as art establishes certain laws, once technology has popularized them, the art that was first on the scene loses retrospectively a little of its originality. Ever since Elstir began to paint, we have seen so-called 'admirable' photographs of landscapes and cities. If we try to define what it is that art-lovers mean by that epithet, we will find that it is usually applied to some unusual picture of a well-known thing, an image different from those we're used to seeing, unique yet true, and which for that reason seems doubly striking, since it surprises us, jolts us out of our habits, but at the same time brings us back to ourselves by reminding us of an impression. For example, one of these 'magnificent' photographs will illustrate a law of perspective by showing us a cathedral we're used to seeing in the middle of the city, but taken from a point of view chosen to make it seem as if it were thirty times higher than the houses and jutting out over the river's edge, from which it is actually quite remote. Elstir's effort not to show things as he knew them to be but according to those optical illusions that comprise our first view of things had led him precisely to emphasize some of these laws of perspective, which were more striking at that time, because art was the first to reveal them. A river, because of a bend in its course, or a bay because of the seeming contiguity of the cliffs, seemed, in the middle of the plain or the mountains, to be hollowing out a lake completely landlocked on every side. In a painting done at Balbec on a sweltering summer's day, an inlet of the sea, enclosed in walls of pink granite, seemed not to be the sea, which began further off. The continuity of the ocean was suggested only by seagulls wheeling over what looked to the viewer like stone, whereas in fact they were inhaling cool air from the waves. Other laws were exemplified in this same canvas, such as, at the foot of immense cliffs, the Lilliputian grace of white sails* on the blue mirror where they looked like sleeping butterflies, and certain contrasts between the depth of the shadows and the pallor of the light. This play of shadows, which photography has also made commonplace, had fascinated Elstir so much that he used to take delight in painting actual mirages, in which a castle topped by a tower looked like a perfectly circular castle with a tower emerging organically from its highest point, with an inverted tower beneath it, either because the extraordinary purity of a fine day gave the shadow cast on the water the hardness and brilliance of stone, or because the morning mists made the stone as hazy as shadow. Similarly, beyond the sea, behind a line of woods, another sea began, pink from the sunset, but it was the sky. The sunlight, as though inventing new solids, struck the hull of a boat and thrust it behind a second hull in shadow, and, with the play of light and shadow on the morning sea, broke what was actually a flat surface into the tiered steps of a crystal staircase. A river flowing under the bridges of a town was painted from such a perspective that it looked entirely disjointed, spread out into a lake, narrowing to a rivulet, fragmented by the interposition of a hill crowned by woods, where the townsfolk go in the evenings to breathe in the cool night air; and the very rhythm of this topsy-turvy city was assured only by the inflexible verticality of the bell-towers, which didn't climb skywards, but rather, following gravity's plumb line as though marking the beat in a triumphal march, seemed to hold in suspense beneath them the whole confused mass of houses stacked on top of each other in the mist, all along the flattened, dismembered river. Even that half-human part of nature, a path along a clifftop or mountainside (since Elstir's early work dated from the period when landscapes were expected to include a human presence), was affected, like his ocean or river, by these eclipses of perspective. Either because a mountain ridge, or the mist of a waterfall, or the sea, prevented the viewer's gaze from following the continuity of the road, visible to the one walking on it but not to us, the little human figure in old-fashioned clothes lost in this wilderness often seemed to have stopped in front of an abyss, since the path he was following stopped there; and then, three hundred metres higher up in that evergreen forest, the viewer would be moved and reassured to see the reappearance at the traveller's feet of the thin white line of the footpath, which had been hidden by the mountain as it twisted and turned around the waterfall or gulf.

The effort Elstir made, when faced with reality, to rid himself of all the notions formed by his intelligence, was all the more admirable since this man, who before he set out to paint, purposely made himself ignorant, forgot everything out of a sense of integrity (for what we know does not belong to us), in fact had an exceptionally cultivated mind. When I confessed the disappointment I'd felt upon seeing the church in Balbec, he said: 'Really? You were disappointed by that porch? But it's the finest illustrated Bible the people have ever read!* That Virgin, and all those bas-reliefs telling the story of her life—they're the tenderest, most inspired expression of the long poem of adoration and praise that the Middle Ages ever made to the glory of the Madonna. If you only knew how scrupulously accurate the old sculptor was in rendering the sacred text, with what subtlety and delicacy his mind worked, how profound his thoughts were, how exquisite his poetry! The idea of the great veil in which the angels are bearing away the Virgin's body, too sacred for them to dare touch it directly' (I mentioned that the same subject was treated at Saint-André-des-Champs; he had seen photographs of the porch there, but pointed out that the bustling activity of the little peasants scurrying all at once around the Virgin was quite a different thing from the gravity of those two great angels, almost Italian, so willowy, so gentle); 'the angel bearing off the Virgin's soul to reunite it with her body; in the meeting between the Virgin and Elizabeth, the gesture of the latter as she touches Mary's breast, and her look of surprise when she feels it already swollen; or the bandaged arm of the midwife who had been unwilling to believe in the Immaculate Conception unless she touched it herself; or the sash the Virgin tosses to Saint Thomas as proof of her resurrection; the veil, too, that the Virgin tears from her own bosom to cover the nudity of her son, from whose pierced side the Church gathers His blood, the wine of the Eucharist, while on the other, the Synagogue, its reign finished, its eyes blindfolded, its crown falling from its head, holds a half-broken sceptre and lets the tablets of the old Law slip from its grasp; or the husband who, at the hour of the Last Judgement, helps his young wife step out of the tomb, and holds her hand against his own heart, to reassure her and prove it's really beating—isn't that a nice touch? And what about the angel taking away the sun and moon, useless now since it's written that the Light of the Cross will be seven times more powerful than that of the stars and planets; or the angel dipping his hand in Jesus' bathwater to see if it's warm enough; or the one emerging from the clouds to place his crown on the Virgin's brow; or all the angels leaning from the vault of heaven, between the banisters of the heavenly Jerusalem, raising their arms in horror or joy at the sight of the torments of the wicked and the bliss of the chosen! Don't you see, it's all the circles of heaven you have there, a whole vast theological and symbolic poem. It's mad, it's divine, it's a thousand times better than anything you'll see in Italy—where, as a matter of fact, this very tympanum was literally copied by sculptors with far less genius. For, don't you see, it's all a question of genius. There has never been a time when everyone had genius; that's all nonsense, it's even more non-existent than the golden age. The fellow who carved that porch, rest assured, was just as great, with ideas every bit as profound, as the people nowadays that you admire so much. I can show you all this, if we go there one day. There's a phrase from the liturgy for the Assumption that's illustrated with a subtlety unmatched by your Redon.'*

Though Elstir spoke of a vast heavenly vision, and made me realize that an epic theological poem had been written there, my eyes, full of desires, had seen nothing of any of that when I stood there looking at the façade. I mentioned the large statues of saints, standing there on stilts, which formed a sort of avenue.

'It's an avenue that begins at the dawn of time', Elstir said, 'and leads to Jesus Christ. On one side, you have his spiritual ancestors; on the other, the Kings of Judah, his ancestors in the flesh. All the centuries are there. And if you'd taken a better look at what looked to you like "stilts", you could have named the figures standing on them. Under Moses' feet, you'd have recognized the Golden Calf; under Abraham's, the ram; and under the feet of Joseph, the devil advising Potiphar's wife.'*

I also told him that I'd been expecting to find an almost Persian building, and that this was doubtless one of the reasons for my disappointment. 'Not at all,' he replied, 'there's a lot of truth in what you say. Some parts are entirely Oriental; one capital so exactly reproduces a Persian subject that the persistence of Oriental traditions isn't enough to explain it. The sculptor must have copied some casket brought back by navigators.' Indeed, he did show me, later on, a photograph of a capital on which I saw dragons that looked almost Chinese devouring each other, but in Balbec this small section of sculpture had gone unnoticed in the general effect of the building as a whole, which didn't look anything like what the words 'an almost Persian church' had conjured up in my mind.

The intellectual pleasures I experienced in this studio did not in the least prevent me from enjoying the soothing shimmer, the glowing penumbra in the room, although they surrounded us as if despite ourselves, and, beyond the little window framed with honeysuckle, in the rustic avenue, the hard dryness of the sun-scorched earth, veiled only by the haze of distance and the shade from the trees. Perhaps the unconscious feeling of well-being the summer day gave me helped to swell, like a tributary, the joy that had filled me upon seeing his *Harbour at Carquethuit.*

I had thought Elstir was modest, but I realized I was mistaken when I saw his face cloud with melancholy when, as I was thanking him, I uttered the word 'fame'. Those who believe their work is lasting—and this was the case for Elstir—become used to thinking of it as belonging to a time when they themselves will be nothing but dust. And so, by forcing them to think about their own annihilation, the idea of fame saddens them because it's inseparable from the idea of death. To dispel the cloud of proud melancholy I had unwittingly brought to Elstir's expression, I changed the subject. 'I was once advised', I said, thinking of my conversation with Legrandin in Combray, about which I was eager to consult his opinion, 'not to go to Brittany, because it was unhealthy for someone with a tendency to daydream.' 'That's not so at all,' he replied. 'When someone is inclined to dream, he must not be kept apart from this tendency; it shouldn't be rationed. So long as you turn your mind away from its dreams, it will not know them; you'll be the plaything of a thousand appearances, because you won't have understood their nature. If a little dreaming is dangerous, the cure for it is not less dreaming, but more dreaming, nothing but dreaming. It's important that we know our dreams thoroughly so as not to suffer from them; there's a certain separation between dream and life which it's so often useful to make that I wonder if we shouldn't, whatever the cost, practise it as a preventative measure, the way some surgeons maintain that the appendix should be removed from all children in order to prevent the possibility of appendicitis in the future.'

Elstir and I had walked to the far end of the studio, by the window that looked out over the garden to a narrow avenue branching off to the side, almost a little country lane. We'd gone there to breathe in the cool late-afternoon air. I thought I was far from the girls in the little band; it was only by sacrificing the hope of seeing them that I'd finally obeyed my grandmother's wish and gone to see Elstir. We never know where we'll find what we seek; and often, for a long time, we avoid the place to which others, for other reasons, have been inviting us. We don't suspect we'll see in that place the very person we've been thinking of. I was gazing absent-mindedly at the rustic path that passed quite close to the studio, but which didn't belong to Elstir. All of a sudden there appeared, striding quickly along it, the young cyclist from the little band, with her toque pulled down over her dark hair towards her plump cheeks, and with her cheerful, almost unwavering eyes; and on this blessed path miraculously filled with sweet promises, I saw her, under the trees, smile and give a friendly wave to the painter, a rainbow joining our terraqueous world to regions that until then I'd thought were inaccessible. She even came over to shake the painter's hand, without stopping, and I saw she had a little beauty spot on her chin. 'Do you know that young lady, Monsieur?' I asked Elstir, realizing he could introduce me to her, invite her to his house. And this peaceful studio, with its pastoral outlook, was suddenly filled with a delightful sense of something more, such as a child might feel in a house where he was already enjoying himself and learns that, in addition, by the generosity of lovely things and noble people that increases their gifts many times over, a splendid dessert is being prepared for him. Elstir told me her name was Albertine Simonet, and gave me the names of her friends as well, whom I described with enough accuracy for him to have no hesitation in identifying them. I had been mistaken about their social status, but not as I usually was in Balbec, where I'd readily take the son of a shopkeeper on horseback for a prince. This time, I had imputed a shady background to girls from extremely wealthy lower-middle-class families from the world of business and industry. That world was one which, initially, was the least interesting to me, having the mystery neither of the working class, nor of the society frequented by the Guermantes. Doubtless if the flamboyant vacuousness of life at a seaside resort hadn't made my dazzled eyes initially see the girls as possessing glamour, which they'd never lose, I might never have managed to overcome the idea that they were the daughters of wholesalers. All I could do now was admire how the French bourgeoisie was a wonderful studio full of the most plentiful and varied sculptures imaginable. How many unexpected types, what invention in the character of the faces, what decisiveness, what freshness, what simplicity in the features! The greedy old bourgeois families who had engendered these Dianas and nymphs* now seemed the greatest masters of statuary imaginable. Before I had time to register the social metamorphosis of these girls (for as soon as we discover our mistake, the notion we have of a person undergoes a change as swift as a chemical reaction), the idea had already appeared behind these faces—so roguish in appearance that I'd taken these girls for the girlfriends of racing cyclists or professional boxers—that they might very well be connected to the family of a notary we knew. I knew almost nothing about Albertine Simonet; and she of course had no inkling of what she would one day become for me. Even the name 'Simonet' which I'd already heard on the beach, if I'd been asked to write it I'd have spelled with two *n*s, not suspecting the importance this family attached to having only one. The further one descends the social scale, the more one's snobbery fastens on to utterly trivial things, which might not be more inconsequential than the distinctions valued by the aristocracy, but which, being more obscure, more peculiar to each individual, are even more surprising. Perhaps there had been some Simonnets who had failed in business, or worse. Whatever the case, the Simonets had always, apparently, taken offence, as if it were a matter of slander, whenever anyone doubled their *n*. They acted as if they were the only Simonets in the world with one *n* instead of two; they may even have taken as much pride in that as the Montmorency family did in being the premier barons of France. I asked Elstir if these girls lived in Balbec; he said most of them did. One girl's villa was actually situated at the far end of the seafront, near the cliffs of Canapville. Since that girl was a close friend of Albertine Simonet, this was one more reason to think it was indeed the latter I'd seen on that day when I was out walking with my grandmother. Of course, there were so many of those little streets running at right angles to the seafront, forming such similar corners, that I couldn't be sure of the precise corner where I saw her. We would like to have an accurate memory of something, but at the time, our vision is clouded. Albertine and the girl going to her friend's house were one and the same person—that much was almost certain. Despite that, although the countless images that the dark-haired golf-player would present to me later could be superimposed, however different they may have been (because I now know they all belonged to her), and even though, if I wind up the thread of my memories, I can, with this identity as a clue, and as if following an inner communicating passageway, go over all these images and still return to the same person, on the other hand, if I want to go as far back as the girl I saw on that day with my grandmother, I must re-emerge into the open air. I am convinced it is indeed Albertine I see again, the same one as the girl who kept coming to a standstill in the midst of her friends as they walked against the background of the sea; but all these images remain separate from that one, because I cannot in retrospect give it an identity it didn't have for me at the moment when it struck my eyes; however much the law of probabilities might assure me, this girl with the full cheeks who looked at me so boldly at the corner of the little side street and the seafront, who I thought might be able to love me, I have never, in the strict sense of the phrase, 'seen again'.

My hesitation between the various girls in the little band, each of whom retained some of the collective charm that had so thrilled me at first, along with those reasons, gave me, later on, even at the time of my greatest—and second—love for Albertine, a kind of intermittent, very brief, freedom not to love her. Having roamed over all her friends before coming to rest once and for all on her, my love sometimes kept a certain amount of 'leeway' between it and the image of Albertine that allowed it, like a poorly adjusted beam of light, to settle on others before returning to focus on her; the relation between the pain I felt in my heart and the memory of Albertine didn't seem an inevitable one; I could just as well have linked it to the image of someone else. And this enabled me, for a split second, to make reality disappear—not just external reality, as in my love for Gilberte (which I had recognized as an inner state, the source from which I drew from myself alone the particular quality, the special character of the person I loved, everything that made her indispensable to my happiness), but even inner, purely subjective reality.

'Not a day goes by when one or another of them doesn't call in at the studio and pay me a little visit,' Elstir said, thereby filling me with despair at the thought that if I'd only gone to see him as soon as my grandmother had asked me to, I'd probably long since have made Albertine's acquaintance.

She had walked on; we could no longer see her from the studio. I thought she'd gone to meet her friends on the esplanade. If I could only be there with Elstir, I might make their acquaintance. I invented a thousand excuses to make him agree to take a turn with me on the beach. I'd lost the calm I had before the girl appeared in the frame of the window, which had been so charming before with its honeysuckle, but which now was so empty. Elstir filled me with joy mingled with torment when he said that he'd walk a little way with me, but that first he had to finish the piece he'd been painting. It was of some flowers, but not those whose portrait I'd have liked to commission from him more than of any human, in order to learn, from what his genius revealed, what I'd so often looked for in vain when I stood before them—hawthorn, both white and pink, cornflowers, apple blossoms. As Elstir painted, he spoke to me of botany, but what he said fell on deaf ears; he was no longer enough on his own, he was now nothing but the necessary intermediary between those girls and me; the prestige which, just a few moments before, his talent had given him in my eyes, was now worth nothing except insofar as it gave me a little esteem in the eyes of the little band to whom he would introduce me.

I paced back and forth, impatient for him to finish; I picked up some studies to look at, many of which were turned to the wall, stacked against each other. In this way I unearthed a watercolour which must have belonged to a much earlier time in Elstir's life, and which stirred in me that particular kind of enchantment aroused by works of art that are not only delightfully executed but also represent a subject so unique and so appealing that we attribute part of their charm to it, as if the painter merely had to discover this charm and observe it, as if it were materially realized in nature and needed only to be reproduced. That objects like this can exist, beautiful even apart from the painter's interpretation, satisfies an innate materialism in us, against which our reason struggles and acts as counterbalance to the abstractions of aesthetics. It was—this watercolour—the portrait of a young woman who, though not pretty, was of an intriguing type: she wore a mob cap somewhat like a bowler hat, trimmed with a cherry-coloured silk ribbon; in one of her gloved hands she held a lit cigarette, and in the other, at knee-level, a sort of wide garden hat, a mere screen of straw against the sun. On the table next to her, a vase full of roses. Often (as was the case here) the singularity of these works stems especially from the fact that they were executed in particular conditions of which we aren't at first fully aware—if, for instance, the odd attire of a female model is her costume for a masked ball, or if, on the contrary, the red cloak of an elderly gentleman who looks as if he wore it to satisfy a whim of the painter is his professor's gown or cardinal's cape. The ambiguous nature of the person whose portrait I was studying stemmed, without my realizing it, from the fact that she was a young actress from an earlier period wearing predominantly male clothing. But her bowler hat, which covered hair that was full but short, and her velvet jacket, without lapels, which opened over a white dickey, made me hesitate about the date of the fashion and the sex of the model, so that I wasn't quite sure what I had before my eyes, except that it was a brilliant piece of painting. The pleasure it gave me was tempered only by the fear that, by continuing to delay, Elstir might make me miss the girls, for the sun was slanting low through the little window. There wasn't a single thing, in fact, in this watercolour that was simply observed as a fact and painted because of its usefulness for the composition, the costume there because the woman had to wear something, the vase to hold the flowers. The glass of the vase, adored for its own sake, seemed to be enclosing the water in which the carnation stems were floating in something as clear and almost as liquid as it; the woman's clothing encompassed her in a way that had an independent, fraternal charm about it, and, if man-made things can rival in charm the wonders of nature, it was as graceful, as sumptuous to the eye's touch, as ingeniously painted as the fur of a cat, the petals of a carnation, or the feathers of a dove. The shirt front, its whites as delicate as fine hail and its frivolous pleating smocked with little bells like lily of the valley, glittered with bright reflections from the room, themselves as vivid and finely shaded as if they were bouquets of flowers stitched on to the linen. The velvet of the jacket, pearly and gleaming, had here and there a rough nap, ruffled and creased, which was reminiscent of the frilly carnations in the vase. Above all, though, you felt that Elstir, unconcerned about whatever sort of immorality might be perceived in this young actress dressed like a man, for whom the talent with which she'd play her role doubtless had less importance than the arousing seductiveness she was about to offer the jaded or depraved senses of certain spectators, had on the contrary focused expressly on these ambiguous features as if on an aesthetic element which was worth being brought out, and which he'd done everything in his power to emphasize. Along the lines of the face, the sex of the person seemed about to reveal it was that of a slightly boyish girl; but then this impression vanished, only to re-emerge further on, except now it suggested rather an effeminate young man, sly and pensive; then this too disappeared, remained elusive. The quality of dreamy melancholy in the gaze, by its very contrast with the accessories belonging to the world of sensuality and the theatre, was not the least disturbing thing. One also felt it must be feigned, and that the young person who seemed to be inviting caresses in this provoking outfit had probably thought it arousing to add the romantic expression of a secret emotion, an unspoken sorrow. At the bottom of the portrait were the words *Miss Sacripant, October 1872*.* I couldn't contain my admiration. 'Oh, that's nothing! It's just a sketch I did when I was young. It was a costume for the Théâtre des Variétés.* That's all a long time ago now.' 'And what became of the model?' I asked. A look of surprise provoked by my question flashed on Elstir's face, followed quickly by casual nonchalance. 'Quick, hand me that canvas,' he said. 'I can hear Madame Elstir coming, and even though I can assure you that the young person in the bowler hat played no role in my life, there's no point in my wife seeing this watercolour. I only kept it as a sort of amusing footnote to the theatre of the time.' But before he hid the watercolour behind him, Elstir, who may not have seen it in a long time, gave it a careful look. 'The head's the only thing I should keep,' he murmured. 'Everything below it is really too poorly painted, the hands look as if they were done by a beginner.' I was exasperated by Madame Elstir's arrival, since she would delay us even more. The windowsill soon turned pink. Our outing would be quite pointless. There was no longer any chance of seeing the girls, and so it didn't really matter if Madame Elstir left sooner rather than later. As it happened, she didn't stay long. I found her very boring; she might have been beautiful, if she were twenty, leading a bull through the Roman countryside; but her dark hair was turning white, and she seemed common without being simple, because she thought a certain formality of manners and a regal bearing were required by her statuesque beauty, even though age had taken away all its charm. She was dressed with the utmost simplicity. It was touching, and surprising, to hear Elstir say, at every opportunity and with a tenderness full of respect, as if merely uttering the words moved him to affection and veneration: 'Ma belle Gabrielle!' Later, when I'd become familiar with Elstir's mythological paintings, I too saw Madame Elstir's beauty. I realized that to a certain ideal type summarized in certain lines and arabesques that continually reappeared in his work, and to a certain model of beauty, he had in fact ascribed a character that was almost divine, since all his time, all the mental effort of which he was capable—in a word, all his life—he had dedicated to the task of seeing these contours more clearly, and reproducing them more faithfully. What such an ideal inspired in Elstir was truly a form of worship so solemn, so demanding, that it never allowed him to be content; it was the most intimate part of himself: and so he had never been able to consider it with detachment, or to elicit emotion from it, until the day when he encountered it as an external manifestation, in the body of a woman, the body of the woman who was later to become Madame Elstir, and in whom he had been able—as we can't do unless it's something outside ourselves—to see it as praiseworthy, moving, and divine. What peace there was in pressing his lips on Beauty, which until then he'd had to extract from himself with so much difficulty, and which now, mysteriously incarnate, offered itself to him for a series of true communions! By that time, Elstir had left behind that first bloom of youth when we expect our thoughts to have the power to realize our ideals. He was nearing the age when we depend on the satisfactions of the body to stimulate the vitality of the mind, a time when the mind's fatigue inclines us to be more materialistic, when the diminution of its activity inclines us to be more passively influenced by things, and we begin to admit that there might well be certain bodies, certain vocations, certain privileged rhythms which might allow us to achieve our ideals quite naturally; that even without genius, but merely by copying the movement of a shoulder, or the tension of a neck, we could produce a masterpiece; it's the age when we like to caress Beauty with our eyes, outside us, near us, in a tapestry, in a beautiful sketch by Titian* we've discovered in an antique shop, in a mistress as beautiful as the Titian sketch. Once I had realized that, I could never see Madame Elstir without pleasure, and her body lost its substance, for I filled it with an idea: that she was an immaterial being, a portrait by Elstir. She was so for me, and for him as well, no doubt. The everyday things of life don't matter to the artist; they're merely an opportunity to reveal his genius. If you set side by side ten portraits of different people painted by Elstir, the strongest impression you'll have is that they are all by Elstir. Only, after this rising tide of genius which submerges life, when the brain tires, little by little, the balance is upset and, like a river resuming its course after the pull of a strong tide, life regains the upper hand. So long as his first period lasts, the artist is able, gradually, to develop the law, the formula, of his unconscious gift. He knows which situations, if he's a novelist, or which landscapes, if he's a painter, can best provide him with the material which, though unimportant in itself, is as necessary to his research as a laboratory or a studio. He knows he has made his masterpieces out of effects of subdued light, or out of the way remorse changes the way a person thinks about a transgression, or out of women posed under trees or half immersed in water like statues. A day will come when, owing to mental exhaustion, he will no longer have the strength, when faced with those materials that had served his genius so well, to make the intellectual effort that alone can produce his work; but he will go on looking for these materials, happy to find himself near them because of the spiritual pleasure, stimulating his work, that they awaken in him; and, enveloping them in a kind of superstition, as if they were superior to everything else, or as if a large part of the work of art already resided in them, which they somehow bear within them ready-made, he will do no more than frequent and adore his subjects. He will have lengthy conversations with repentant criminals whose remorse and rehabilitation used to be the subjects of his novels; he will buy a house in the country in a region where mist softens the light; he will spend long hours watching women bathing; he will collect fine fabrics. Thus the period that encompasses 'the beauty of life', a phrase somehow stripped of meaning, when beauty falls short of art (and a stage at which I'd seen Swann come to a standstill), was the phase at which, by a slackening of the creative genius, an idolatry of the forms that had furthered it, and a desire to expend as little effort as possible, would one day, little by little, cause even an Elstir to regress.

He had just given a final brushstroke to his flowers; I wasted a moment looking at them; there was no merit in my doing this, since I knew the girls would no longer be at the beach; but even if I had thought they were still there, and that these wasted minutes were caus-ing me to miss them, I would have looked all the same, since I would have told myself that Elstir was more interested in his flowers than in my meeting the girls. My grandmother's nature, a nature that was the exact opposite of my total selfishness, was nevertheless reflected in my own. In a situation where someone to whom I was indifferent, but for whom I'd always feigned affection or respect, might merely be inconvenienced, whereas I ran the risk of real danger, I couldn't have done otherwise than commiserate with him on his annoyance as if it were of grave importance, and treat my own danger as nothing, because that's how I thought our respective positions appeared to him. To speak plainly, it was a little more than that: not only would I refrain from complaining about the danger I myself ran, but I would even expose myself to this danger, and when it came to any danger others might be in, I'd try, even if this would increase the likelihood of my being harmed, to save them from it. There are several reasons for this, none of which are to my credit. One is that, so long as my reason was involved, I believed I valued my life; but whenever, in the course of my existence, I've been obsessed by moral problems, or merely nervous anxieties—sometimes so childish I wouldn't dare describe them here—if an unforeseen circumstance then arose, bringing with

it the risk that I might be killed, this new concern was so slight compared to the others that I'd welcome it with a feeling of relief bordering
on light-heartedness. In this way, even though I'm the least courageous man there is, I've found myself experiencing the very thing that
seemed, in my reasoning state, so foreign to my nature, so inconceivable: the intoxication of danger. But even if a danger, and a deadly
one, were to present itself during a period when I was completely
calm and happy, if I was with another person, I wouldn't be able to do
anything but shield him from it and place myself in danger in his
place. When I had experienced enough of these situations to realize
I always acted in this way, and with pleasure, I discovered, to my great
shame, that unlike what I had always believed and asserted, I was very
sensitive to the opinions of others. This sort of unprofessed self-
esteem, however, had nothing to do with vanity or pride. For what
might satisfy one or the other of these would bring me no pleasure,
and I've always abstained from them. But with people from whom
I've managed most thoroughly to hide the slight advantages of my
own that might have increased my esteem a little in their eyes, I've
never been able to deny myself the pleasure of showing them that
I take more care in averting death from their path than from my own.
Since my motive at such times is self-esteem and not virtue, I find it
quite natural for them to act differently in every situation. I'm far
from blaming them for this, as I might do if I'd been motivated by the
idea of a duty, which would then appear to me as obligatory for them
as it was for myself. On the contrary, I think they're being perfectly
sensible in protecting themselves, even though I can't help but regard
my own safety as less important, which is particularly absurd and
blameworthy when I realize that the lives of many of the people
I shield from an exploding bomb are less valuable than my own. In
any case, on that day of my visit with Elstir, the time when I'd become
aware of this difference in value was still far off; and there was no
question of danger, but simply—a harbinger of that pernicious
self-esteem—of not appearing to attach more importance to the pleasure
I so ardently desired than to his task of finishing his watercolour.
Now, finally, it was finished. And, once we were outside, I realized it
was not as late as I'd thought; we walked to the esplanade. How many
stratagems I employed to make Elstir stay in the place where I thought
the girls might appear! Pointing to the cliffs rising up next to us,
I kept asking him to talk about them, so as to make him forget the

hour and linger there. It struck me that we'd be more likely to spot the little band if we walked to the far end of the beach. 'I'd very much like to see those cliffs with you from a little closer,' I said, having noticed that one of the girls often went to this spot. 'In the meantime, tell me about Carquethuit. How I'd love to go there!' I added, without thinking that the freshness that showed through so powerfully in his *Harbour at Carquethuit* probably stemmed from the painter's vision rather than from any special quality in the place itself. 'Ever since I saw your painting, that's the place I'd most like to see, along with the Pointe du Raz, which would be quite a journey from here.'* 'Even if it wasn't closer, I'd still be inclined to recommend Carquethuit,' Elstir replied. 'The Pointe du Raz is admirable, but when it comes down to it, it's still the typical tall cliffs of Normandy or Brittany, which you know already. Carquethuit is completely different, with its rocks over the low shore. I don't know anything like it in France; it reminds me more of certain parts of Florida. It's quite something, and very wild too. It's between Clitourps and Nehomme, and you know how deserted that whole region is; the coastline is enchanting. Here, the coastline is like any other; but over there, I can't tell you how graceful, how lovely it is.'

Night was falling; it was time to go home; I was accompanying Elstir back to his villa when all of a sudden, like Mephistopheles materializing before Faust,* there appeared at the end of the avenue— like a simple objectification, unreal and diabolical, of the temperament opposite my own, the semi-barbaric, cruel vitality which, in my weakness and excess of painful sensitivity and intellectuality, I lacked—a few specks of the essence impossible to confuse with anything else, a few spores in the zoophytic band of girls,* who looked as if they didn't see me, but who were still without a doubt passing judgement on me in their ironic way. Feeling it was inevitable that we'd run into them, and that Elstir would call me over, I turned my back, like a bather about to meet a wave; I stopped short and, letting my illustrious companion continue on his way, I stayed behind, leaning towards the window of the antique shop we were passing at the moment, as if all my attention was suddenly absorbed by it; I wasn't bothered by seeming to have my mind on something other than these girls, and I already had a dim awareness that when Elstir called me over to introduce me, I'd have the sort of questioning look that conceals not surprise, but the wish to look surprised—since we're such poor actors, and our interlocutor is so good at reading faces—and that I'd even go so far as to point to my own chest, as if asking: 'Do you mean me?' and then hurry over, my head bent in obedience and docility, and my expression coldly masking my annoyance at being torn from contemplation of old china merely to be introduced to individuals I had no desire to know. All this time I was looking at the shop window, waiting for the moment when my name, shouted by Elstir, would strike me like an expected, harmless bullet. The certainty of being introduced to the girls had the result that not only did I feign indifference to them, but I felt it as well. Having become inevitable, the pleasure of making their acquaintance was compressed and reduced; it seemed smaller to me than the pleasure of talking with Saint-Loup, or dining with my grandmother, or going on excursions in the surrounding countryside, which, because of my having to associate with people who would no doubt have little interest in historical architecture, I'd feel reluctantly obliged to forgo. Moreover, the joy I was about to feel was diminished not only by the imminence, but by the incongruity, of its actually happening. Laws as precise as those of hydrostatics maintain the superimposition of images we form in a fixed order, which the impending nature of an event upsets. Elstir was about to call to me. This was not at all the way in which, on the beach, or in my room, I had often imagined I'd meet these girls. What was about to take place was another event for which I was not prepared. I recognized neither my desire, nor its object; I was almost sorry I'd gone out with Elstir. Above all, though, the shrinking of the pleasure I thought I was about to feel was due to the certainty that nothing, now, could take it away from me. And it resumed all its loftiness, as if by virtue of an elastic force, when it stopped undergoing the constraint of this certainty, the instant when, having made up my mind to turn my head, I saw Elstir, who had paused a few feet away with the girls, bid them farewell. The face of the girl closest to him, plump and lit up by her eyes, looked like a cake in which some room had been reserved for a little bit of sky. Her eyes, even when motionless, gave the impression of mobility, as on those windy days when the air, although invisible, hints at the speed with which it passes over the azure background. For an instant her gaze met mine, like those shifting skies on stormy days when a cloud overtakes a slower one, flows alongside it, touches it, and then passes on. But they don't know one another, and they're driven far apart. In this way our gazes met for an instant, each of us ignorant of what the heavenly continent facing it contained in the way of promises and dangers for the future. Except, at the exact instant when her gaze met mine, without slowing its movement, it grew slightly veiled, just as, on a clear, windy night, the moon passes behind a cloud, hiding its brilliance for an instant, and then quickly reappears. But already Elstir had taken his leave of the girls without calling me. They turned up a side street and he came towards me. All was lost.

I have said that Albertine didn't look the same to me on that day as on previous days, and that each time I saw her, she would seem different. But I felt at that moment that certain changes in the appearance, importance, or stature of a person can also stem from the variability of certain states that may come between ourselves and the other. One of the most important in that regard is belief: on that evening, my belief that I was going to meet Albertine, followed by the annihilation of that belief, within a matter of seconds, had made her seem almost insignificant to me, then infinitely precious; a few years later, my belief that Albertine was faithful to me, then the disappearance of that belief, would bring about similar results.

Indeed, long ago in Combray, depending on the time of day, and on whether I was entering one or the other of the two dominant modes of my sensibility, I had already experienced a diminution or expansion of my sorrow, which was as imperceptible all afternoon as moonlight is when the sun is still shining, but, as night fell, reigned alone in my anxious soul, replacing my recent, vanished memories. But that day, when I saw Elstir leaving the girls without calling me, I realized that the varying degrees of importance that pleasure or sorrow can take in our eyes can stem not just from the alternation of those two states, but from the shift in our invisible beliefs, which, for example, may make death seem unimportant to us because they bathe it in a glow of unreality, and thus allow us to attach importance to attending a musical evening, which would lose its charm if the belief colouring that evening were suddenly to dissolve because we learned we were about to be guillotined; it's true that something in me—my will—knew about the role belief plays; but this knowledge is pointless if our intellect and sensibility remain unaware of it; they act in good faith when they believe we want to leave a mistress to whom only our will knows we are attached. This is because they are clouded by the belief that we'll see her again in a moment. But let that belief vanish, in the sudden realization that she has gone forever, and the intellect and sensibility, having lost their bearings, become afflicted with a kind of madness, as the infinitesimal pleasure we had when we were with her grows infinitely great.

A variation in belief can also be a cause for the annihilation of love, which, pre-existent and mobile, settles on the image of a woman simply because that woman will be almost impossible to attain. From then on, we think less of the woman herself (whom we can barely even picture) than of the means by which we can get to know her. A whole sequence of anxieties then develops, causing our love to fixate on her as its scarcely known object. Our love becomes immense; we never reflect on how small a part the actual woman plays in it. And if it happens—as it did at the moment when I saw Elstir stop to talk with the girls—that we suddenly stop being anxious and fearful, since our love was based entirely on that anxiety, it seems abruptly to have vanished the instant we're finally able to grasp our prey, whose actual value we haven't sufficiently considered. What did I know of Albertine? One or two silhouettes in front of the sea, most certainly less striking than images of women by Veronese,* which, if I'd followed a purely aesthetic line of reasoning, I ought to have preferred to her. Could I have had other reasons to love her, since, once my anxiety had fallen away, I was left with nothing but these mute silhouettes? Ever since I'd seen Albertine, I'd entertained thousands of thoughts about her; I'd held, with what I called 'her', a whole interior conversation, in which I made her question me, reply, think, act; in the infinite series of imagined Albertines that followed each other hour after hour, the actual Albertine, glimpsed on the esplanade, was merely the forerunner, just as an actress, a star, having created a role, appears only in the first few of a long run of performances. This Albertine was little more than a silhouette; everything that was superimposed upon her was of my own making, for our own contribution to our love—even if considered from the perspective of quality alone—outweighs that of the person we love. This is true even for the most effective kinds of love. There are some kinds of love that can not only form but subsist on very little—even among those who have been granted fulfilment in the flesh. An old drawing master of my grandmother's had had a daughter by an obscure mistress. The mother died soon after the child was born, and the drawing master was so heartbroken that he did not long survive her. During the final months of his life, my grandmother and a few ladies from Combray, who hadn't even wanted to allude in his presence to the woman, with whom he hadn't officially lived or spent any significant amount of time, decided to ensure the girl's future by contributing to a life annuity for her. It was my grand-mother who suggested this; but some of her friends needed some persuading—was this girl truly so worthwhile, was she merely the daughter of someone who believed he was the father? With women like her mother, you could never be sure. Finally, it was decided. The little girl came to thank them. She was ugly and bore a marked resem-blance to the old drawing master, which removed any doubt; since her hair was her only redeeming feature, one lady said to the father, who had brought her: 'What lovely hair she has.' And, thinking that now that the guilty woman was dead and the drawing master half dead, an allusion to the past of which they had always feigned ignorance could do no harm now, my grandmother added: 'It must run in the family. Did her mother have such lovely hair?' To which the father gave the guileless reply: 'I don't know. I only ever saw her wearing a hat.'

I had to rejoin Elstir. I caught sight of myself in a mirror. In add-ition to the disaster of not having been introduced, I noticed that my tie was all askew, and that long strands of hair were showing from under my hat, which made me look unbecoming; still, it was a good piece of luck that they'd seen me with Elstir, even in such a state, and wouldn't be able to forget me; another piece of luck was that, on that day, at my grandmother's suggestion, I'd put on my handsome waist-coat, which I'd come close to replacing with a hideous one, and I'd carried my best walking stick; for even though an event we desire never occurs as we'd imagined, since it lacks the advantages we thought we could count on, others which we hadn't hoped for present themselves, making up for our disappointment; and we had been fearing the worst so intensely that we're finally inclined to feel that, taking one thing with another, chance has, on the whole, been on our side. 'I'd have been so happy to meet them,' I said to Elstir as I caught up with him. 'Then why did you stay miles away?'—He used this idiom not because it expressed what he was thinking, since if he had wanted to grant my wish, it would have been easy to call me over, but perhaps because he'd heard these sorts of phrases used by vulgar people when they've been caught in the act, and because even great men are similar in some respects to common folk and take their every-day excuses from the same repertoire, just as they buy their daily bread from the same baker; or because such words, which must in a way be read backwards, since their literal meaning is the opposite of the truth, are the inevitable effect, the photographic negative, of a reaction. 'In any case, they were in a hurry,' he added. I was convinced that they must have stopped him from introducing them to someone they didn't find very appealing; otherwise he wouldn't have failed to do so, after all the questions I'd asked him about them, and the interest he could clearly see I took in them. 'I was talking to you about Carquethuit,' he said, before I left him at his door. 'I did a little sketch where you can see the curve of the beach more clearly. The painting's not too bad, but it's not the same. If you like, as a token of our friendship, I could give you my sketch,' he added, for the people who deny you the things you desire do give you others.

'If you have one, I'd so like a photograph of your little portrait of Miss Sacripant! What sort of name is that, by the way?'

'It's the name of a character the model played in a stupid little operetta.'

'You seem to think I know who she is, but I assure you, Monsieur, I have no idea.'

Elstir said nothing. 'Oh! It isn't Madame Swann before her marriage, is it?' I said, in one of those sudden fortuitous ways whereby we stumble upon the truth, which are, when it comes down to it, quite rare, but which, later, are enough to give a certain basis to the theory of presentiments, if one takes care to forget all the wrong guesses that would invalidate it.

Elstir didn't reply. It was indeed a portrait of Odette de Crécy. She hadn't wanted to keep it for many reasons, a few of which are only too obvious. There were others as well. The portrait predated the time when Odette, disciplining her features, had made her face and figure into that creation whose broad outlines her hairdressers, her dressmakers, she herself—in her way of holding herself, talking, smiling, arranging her hands, directing her glances, thinking—would respect throughout the years to come. It required the depravity of a sated lover for Swann to prefer, over the numerous photographs of his beautiful wife as the Changeless Odette, the little photograph he had in his room, in which, beneath a straw hat trimmed with pansies, one saw a thin, rather plain young woman with full, frizzy hair and drawn features.

Even if, like Swann's favourite photograph, the portrait hadn't come before the systematic transformation of Odette's features into a new type, majestic and charming, but had come later, Elstir's vision would have been enough to disrupt this type. Artistic genius acts like those extremely high temperatures that have the power to break apart combinations of atoms and group them into a completely opposite order, which corresponds to a different type. All the artificial harmony a woman has imposed on her features, which she makes sure remains intact as she checks herself every day in the mirror, changing the tilt of the hat, the sleekness of the hair, the winsomeness of the gaze, so as to ensure this harmony's continuity, can be destroyed in a second by the eye of a great painter, and in its place he rearranges the woman's features, in such a way as to satisfy a certain feminine, pictorial ideal he carries within him. Similarly, it often happens that, after a certain age, the eye of a great researcher finds, wherever it looks, the elements he needs to establish the only connections that interest him. Such men, like those craftsmen or card players who, instead of making a fuss, are content with whatever falls to hand, could say of any material: this will do. In a similar vein, one of the Princesse de Luxembourg's cousins, a haughty woman of great beauty, having conceived a liking for an art that was new at the time, had asked the greatest of the naturalist painters to paint her portrait. Immediately the artist's eye had found what he always looked for. And so, on the canvas, instead of the great lady, there was an errand girl, with, behind her, a vast, sloping, purple background that called to mind the Place Pigalle.* But even without going to those lengths, not only will the portrait of a woman by a great artist make no attempt to satisfy any of the woman's requirements—such as those, for example, that make a woman beginning to age want to be photographed in outfits that are almost those of a young girl, which emphasize her still-youthful waist, and make her look like the sister or even the daughter of her daughter, who if necessary is made to stand next to her dressed unbecomingly for the occasion—but will, on the contrary, bring out the very disadvantages which she was trying to hide, and which (such as, for instance, a feverish, or even greenish, complexion) tempt the artist all the more since they have 'character'; but they're enough to destroy the illusions of the common viewer, and to reduce to dust the ideal he had, which the woman herself had so proudly upheld and which to her mind had placed her, in her unique, irreducible form, so far above and beyond the rest of humanity. Now deposed, driven outside her own type, where she had reigned supreme, she is nothing more than an ordinary woman in whose superiority we have lost all faith. We have so long regarded this type as constituting not only the beauty of an Odette, but her personality, her identity, that, faced with the portrait that has stripped her of it, we are tempted to exclaim not only: 'How ugly he's made her!' but: 'It looks nothing like her!' We can scarcely believe it is she. We don't recognize her. And yet there is a person in that portrait whom we sense we've seen before. But this being is not Odette; the face of this person, her body, her whole appearance, are familiar to us. They remind us, not of the woman, who never presented herself in that way, whose usual pose doesn't describe such a strange or provocative arabesque, but of other women, all the women Elstir has painted, those who, regardless of how different they might be from one another, he has always liked to portray full-face, with a high-arched foot showing under the skirt, and a large round in one hand, corresponding symmetrically, at the level of the knee which it covers, to that other round disc of the face. Not only does a brilliant portrait pick apart a woman's type, as defined by her coquetry and her egotistical conception of beauty, but, if it is an old portrait, it isn't content with ageing the original in the same way a photograph does, by showing it in outmoded attire. In the portrait, it's not only the way in which the woman is dressed that's dated; it's also the way in which the artist chose to paint her. This way—Elstir's earliest style—was the most devastating birth certificate for Odette, not just because, like her photographs of the time, it made her the youngest of the well-known courtesans, but because it made her portrait contemporary with one of the numerous portraits that Manet or Whistler painted* of so many models who have disappeared, consigned already to oblivion, or to history.

These thoughts, ruminated over in silence as I walked back with Elstir, and inspired by the discovery I'd just made about his model's identity, led me to a second discovery, which I found even more disturbing, concerning the identity of the artist. He had painted the portrait of Odette de Crécy. Could it be that this man of genius, this wise man, this solitary being, this philosopher with his brilliant conversation and looming presence, could be the ridiculous, wayward painter who had been taken up long ago by the Verdurins? I asked him if he'd known them, and if by chance they'd called him by the nickname of 'Monsieur Biche'. He replied, without any embarrassment, that this was the case, as if it had to do with a part of his life that was already

rather remote; and if he didn't suspect the extraordinary disappointment this aroused in me, he read it on my face when he raised his
eyes. His own assumed an expression of unhappiness. We had almost
reached his door; a more narrow-minded man, less knowledgeable in
matters of the heart, might simply have said a curt goodbye and
avoided me after that. But that was not how Elstir acted; as a true
master—and perhaps, from the point of view of pure creativity, to be
a master, at least in this sense of the word, may have been his only
defect, for an artist, in order to be entirely immersed in the truth of
the life of the mind, must be alone, and must not be lavish with his
inner self, even to his disciples—he sought to extract from every circumstance, whether it involved himself or others, whatever element
of truth it contained, in order to instruct those younger than himself
as best he could. And so, rather than saying something to avenge his
hurt pride, he chose to speak in a way that might be instructive for
me. 'There is no man, however wise,' he said, 'who hasn't, at some
time in his youth, uttered words, or even led a life, that he wished he
could wipe from his memory later on, and which he would gladly
undo. But he shouldn't regret it completely, because he can't be sure
he'd have become as wise as he is, insofar as that's possible, unless
he'd gone through all the ridiculous or odious incarnations that must
precede that final one. I know there are young people, sons and grand-
sons of distinguished men, whose tutors have instilled nobility of
mind and moral refinement in them since they were boys. They may
have nothing they wish to retract from their lives; they could publish
and sign everything they've said; but they are poor in spirit, feeble
descendants of doctrinaires, and their wisdom is negative and sterile.
We don't receive wisdom; we must discover it for ourselves after
a journey that no one can spare us or travel for us, for it is a way of
looking at things. The lives you admire, the attitudes you find noble,
have not been laid down by father or family or tutor; they have all
started out in very different ways, having been influenced by the evil
and the banality that were around them. Their lives represent a struggle and a victory. I understand how the image of what we've been in
our younger days might be unrecognizable, and certainly unpleasant.
It should not, however, be denied, for it is a testimony to the fact that
we have truly lived, that, in accordance with the laws of life and mind,
we have, from the common elements of life, from the life of studios
and artistic coteries (if one is a painter), gleaned something that

surpasses them.' We had arrived at his door. I was disappointed not to have met the girls. At least now, though, there was a possibility I might see them again in real life; they were no longer merely beings passing across a horizon where I thought they might never reappear. There no longer floated around them that sort of swirling eddy that kept us apart and that was only the translation of perpetually active desire, mobile, urgent, fed by anxiety, aroused by their inaccessibility, their possibly permanent flight from me. I could now, finally, set my desire for them to rest, keep it in reserve, along with all those other desires whose fulfilment, once I knew it was possible, I kept postponing. I left Elstir, and was once again alone. Then all of a sudden, despite my disappointment, I saw in my mind's eye the whole unlikely series of happenstances that I'd never have suspected could occur: that Elstir actually had a connection with these girls; and that these girls, who that very morning had been for me figures in a painting with the sea as background, had seen me, and had seen me accompanied by a great painter who now knew of my desire to know them and would no doubt do what he could do to further it. All this had brought me pleasure, but this pleasure had remained hidden from me; it was like one of those visitors who wait to let us know they're there until the others have left us alone together. Then we become aware of them, can say to them: 'I'm all yours', and can listen to them. Sometimes, between the moment when these pleasures have entered us and the moment when we can delve into them ourselves, so many hours have gone by, and we've seen so many people in the meantime, that we're afraid they haven't waited for us. But they are patient; they do not grow weary; and as soon as everyone has left, we find ourselves face to face with them. Sometimes we ourselves are so tired that it seems as though our weary mind won't have enough strength to retain these memories, these impressions, for which our fragile self is the only habitable place, the sole means of realization. And we would regret this, for existence has scarcely any interest except on those days when the dust of everyday things is mingled with magic sand, when some trivial incident in life becomes a source of romance. Then a whole promontory of the inaccessible world rises up from the illumination of dream and enters our life, our life in which, like the sleeper awakened, we see the people whom we've so ardently envisaged, whom we thought we'd never see again except in dreams.

The relief I felt at the likelihood that I could now meet these girls whenever I chose was all the more precious to me since I wouldn't have been able to look for them over the next few days, which were taken up with preparations for Saint-Loup's departure. My grandmother was anxious to show my friend how grateful she was for all his acts of kindness towards us both. I told her he was a great admirer of Proudhon,* and suggested she send for the many handwritten letters by the thinker, which she had bought; Saint-Loup came to look at them at the hotel when they arrived the day before his departure. He read them eagerly, handling each with respect, trying to memorize phrases from them; then, when he stood up to go, excusing himself for having stayed so long, he heard my grandmother reply:

'No, no; you must take them with you, they're yours. I sent for them so that you could have them.'

Saint-Loup was overcome with a joy that he could control no more than if it had been a physical state produced without the intervention of the will; he blushed as scarlet as a child who has just been punished, and my grandmother was far more moved by all the efforts he made (without success) to contain the joy surging through him than by all the thanks he could have expressed. The following day, fearing he hadn't sufficiently expressed his gratitude, he asked me to apologize to her again as he leaned out of the window of the little local train he was taking to return to his garrison, which was actually not far away. He had thought to go there, as he often did when he didn't have to stay long, but could return to Balbec in the evening, by carriage. But this time, he had a great deal of luggage to load into the train; and he found it simpler to take the train himself as well, following the advice of the hotel manager, who, when consulted, had replied that, whether he went by carriage or train, 'it would be more or less equivocal'. By that he meant 'equivalent' (roughly what Françoise would have expressed as 'it all comes down from similar to same'). 'So be it,' Saint-Loup had concluded: 'I'll take the little "twister".'* I would have taken it as well and accompanied my friend to Doncières if I hadn't been tired; I promised him, though, during the whole time we lingered in the Balbec station—that is, the time the engineer of the little train spent having a drink and waiting for friends who were late, without whom he didn't want to start—that I'd visit him several times a week. Since Bloch had also come to the station—to Saint-Loup's great annoyance—and since he saw that Bloch had overheard him inviting me to lunch, or dinner, or to stay at Doncières, Saint-Loup finally said, in an extremely cold tone of voice, intended to counter the forced friendliness of the invitation and to prevent Bloch from taking it seriously: 'If you're ever passing through Doncières on an afternoon when I'm free, you can ask for me at the barracks; but I'm hardly ever off duty.' Perhaps too Robert feared that I might not come on my own, and, thinking I was closer to Bloch than I claimed, was providing me with a travelling companion, someone to encourage me to make the trip.

I was afraid that this tone, this way of inviting someone while warning him not to come, might have hurt Bloch, and I thought it would have been better if Saint-Loup had said nothing. But I was wrong, for after the train left, as we were walking together as far as the intersection of two avenues, one going to the hotel, the other to Bloch's villa, Bloch never stopped asking me what day we'd go to Doncières, for after 'all the kindnesses Saint-Loup had shown me', it would have been 'too rude' of him not to accept the invitation. I was glad he hadn't noticed, or was not so unhappy that he couldn't pretend not to have noticed, the reluctant, scarcely polite tone in which the invitation had been given. I'd have liked, for his own sake, for Bloch not to make a fool of himself by going to Doncières right away. But I didn't dare offer him advice that could only have displeased him, by pointing out that Saint-Loup had been less insistent than Bloch thought. Bloch was all too eager, and even though all the faults he had in this respect were compensated for by remarkable qualities that other, more reserved, people might not have had, he became so importunate that it was alarming. From what he said, we couldn't let the week go by without visiting Doncières (he said 'we', for I think he counted a little on my presence to excuse his own). All along the way, in front of the tree-enclosed gymnasium, in front of the tennis court, in front of the town hall, in front of the shellfish stall, he kept stopping me, begging me to set a date, and since I didn't do so, he strode away in a huff, saying: 'As you like, Your Lordship. I at least am obliged to go, since he invited me.'

Saint-Loup was so afraid of not having thanked my grandmother enough that he asked me once again to convey his gratitude to her two days later, in a letter I received from him from the town where he was garrisoned, and which, with its name postmarked on the envelope, seemed to be rushing towards me, to be telling me that inside its walls, in the Louis XVI cavalry barracks,* he was thinking of me. The note-paper bore the arms of Marsantes, in which I could make out a lion surmounted by a crown capped with the bonnet of a peer of France.

'After a journey', he wrote, 'which went well, during which I read a book I bought at the station, by Arvède Barine* (a Russian writer, I believe; it seemed remarkably well written for a foreigner, but you can tell me what you think of it, for you must know it, as you've read everything and are a wellspring of knowledge), here I am again in the thick of this coarse life, where I feel very much like an exile, bereft as I am of everything I had to leave in Balbec; it's a life which holds no loving memories, no intellectual attraction, an environment on which you would certainly look with scorn—and yet it's not devoid of charm. Everything seems to have changed here since I left, for in the meantime, one of the most important periods of my life began: the one from which our friendship dates. I hope it will never end. I have spoken of it, of you, to one person only: my mistress, who has surprised me by coming to spend a little time with me here. She'd very much like to meet you, and I think you'd get along well with each other, for she too is extremely well read. In order to think back on our conversations and relive those hours that I will never forget, I've isolated myself from my comrades—excellent fellows, but they'd be completely incapable of understanding any of it. On my first day here, I'd almost have preferred to keep this memory of the times I spent with you all to myself, and not write to you. But I was afraid that you, with your subtle mind and ultra-sensitive heart, might begin to fret if you didn't receive a letter from me, if, that is, you have deigned to lower your thoughts to the coarse soldier you'll be hard put to refine, and make a little more subtle and worthy of you.'

This letter, with its affectionate tone, was very like those which, when I hadn't yet made the acquaintance of Saint-Loup, I'd imagined he'd write to me, in those daydreams which had been shattered by the coldness of his first greeting, when I was confronted with an icy reality that would, however, turn out not to be definitive. After I'd received that letter, every time the post was delivered, at lunchtime, I would immediately recognize a letter from him, for it always bore that second face a person shows when he is absent, in the features of which (the letters of his script) there is no reason not to believe we can perceive an individual's soul as clearly as we can see it in the shape of his nose or the inflections of his voice.

I would now happily remain seated as the tables were being cleared, and, if it wasn't a time when the girls of the little band might go by, I wouldn't look solely in the direction of the sea. Ever since I'd seen it in Elstir's watercolours, I cherished the poetic quality in things, and sought to find it in reality: the interrupted gestures of knives lying askew; the bulging folds of a used napkin, into which the sun had slipped a slice of yellow velvet; the glass now half empty, the better to show the noble flare of its curved lines, with, in the depths of its translucent glaze seemingly made from condensed daylight, a few dregs of wine, which, though dark, sparkled with lights; objects displaced, liquids transmuted by shifting perspectives; the deterioration of the plums, from green to blue, and blue to gold, in the fruit bowl already half despoiled; the peregrination of the old-fashioned chairs, which twice daily take their places around the cloth laid over the table as though over an altar on which the rites of gastronomy are celebrated, with a few drops of lustral water lingering in oyster shells as if in little stone fonts; I would try to find beauty where I had never imagined it could be, in the most ordinary things, in the profound life of 'still life'.

When, a few days after the departure of Saint-Loup, I had persuaded Elstir to hold a little gathering at which I might meet Albertine, I was sorry that the charm and elegance, temporary though they were, which people noticed as I was leaving the Grand-Hôtel—the result of a long rest and some extra expense lavished on my toilette—couldn't be reserved (along with the prestige of knowing Elstir) for the conquest of some other, more interesting person; I was sorry I was using it all up for the simple pleasure of meeting Albertine. My mind saw this pleasure, now that it was assured, as being of little worth. But the will in me did not share that illusion for an instant, for the will is the servant, ever-persevering and unwavering, of our successive personalities; it lies hidden in the shadows, scorned, tirelessly faithful, working ceaselessly, without any concern for the self's changefulness, making sure it will never lack what it needs. When a journey we've longed to make is beginning to become a reality, and our mind and sensibility are starting to wonder if it's really worth all the effort, the will, which knows that these lazy masters would immediately realize how wonderful this journey would have been, if it turned out it couldn't be made, leaves them to argue with each other in front of the station as they enumerate all their hesitations, while the will takes charge of buying the tickets and bustling us into the compartment before departure time. The will is as unchanging as the mind and sensibility are changeable; but since it is silent, and doesn't come forth with its reasons, it seems almost non-existent; its firm determination is what other parts of our self follow, but without realizing it so long as they can't clearly perceive their own uncertainties. So my sensibility and my mind started an argument about the value of the pleasure there might be in meeting Albertine as I was observing in the mirror the vain and fragile charms they would have preferred to keep intact for another occasion. But my will didn't forget the time at which I had to leave, and it was Elstir's address it gave to the coachman. My mind and sensibility were now at leisure, since the die was cast, to ruminate over what a pity it all was. If my will had given a different address, they would have been utterly confused.

When I arrived at Elstir's a little later, I thought at first that Mademoiselle Simonet wasn't in the studio. There was indeed a girl sitting there in a silk dress, her head bare; but this girl's magnificent hair was unknown to me, as well as her nose and complexion; I didn't recognize in these the entity I had created from a young cyclist in a toque strolling by the sea. But it was indeed Albertine. Even when I realized this, however, I paid no attention to her. Whenever we enter any fashionable gathering when we're young, we are no longer ourselves; we become a different person, since every salon is a new universe where, under the sway of the law of a different moral perspective, we direct our attention to individuals, dances, card parties, as if they will be forever important to us, even though we'll have forgotten them the next day. Having to follow, in order finally to end up in a conversation with Albertine, a path not of my own design, which stopped in front of Elstir, passed by other groups of guests to whom I was introduced, then went along the buffet, where I was handed, and where I consumed, some strawberry tarts, while I listened, motionless, to music that had just started up, I found myself giving to these various episodes the same importance as to my introduction to Mademoiselle Simonet, an introduction that was now only one among many, and which I'd completely forgotten had been, just a few minutes before, my only purpose in coming there. Isn't this always the case, in our busy daily lives, for our truest joys and our greatest sorrows? In the midst of other people, we receive, from the woman we love, the favourable or fatal answer we'd been awaiting for a year. But we must go on chatting; ideas come one after the other, developing a surface which may, at most, be silently pierced, from time to time, by the memory, profound but acute, that calamity has befallen us. If it's happiness instead of misfortune, it might not be until many years later that we remember that the most important event in our emotional life occurred, without our having the time to grant it much attention, but rather while almost overlooking it, during a fashionable gathering, say, which we had attended solely in anticipation of that event.

At the moment when Elstir called me over so he could introduce me to Albertine, who was sitting a little way off, I first finished eating a coffee eclair, then enquired eagerly of an old gentleman I'd just met, and to whom I was thinking of offering the rose he'd admired in my buttonhole, about certain agricultural fairs in Normandy. This isn't to say that the introduction that followed gave me no pleasure, or that it wasn't momentous to me. As to the pleasure, I would only experience it, naturally, a little while later, when, having returned to the hotel, and having been alone for a while, I had become myself again. Pleasure in this respect is like photography. What we take in the presence of the person we love is only a negative; we develop it later on, once we're home, when we have at our disposal that inner darkroom, the entrance to which is sealed off so long as we are with other people.

Though consciousness of my pleasure was thus postponed by a few hours, the gravity of this introduction, on the other hand, I felt immediately. During a moment of introduction, despite our sense of being instantly gratified and of becoming the owner of a 'voucher' good for future pleasures which we've been pursuing for weeks, we realize that its possession puts an end, not only to all our arduous searching—which of course fills us with joy—but also to the existence of a certain individual, the one our imagination had distorted, the one our anxious fear that we'd never be known by her had enlarged. The instant our name resonates in the mouth of the person making the introduction, especially if that person embellishes it, as Elstir did, with flattering commentary, this moment, as sacramental as the one in the fairy tale when the magician commands a person to turn suddenly into someone else, the woman we had been so longing to approach, vanishes; for one thing, how could she remain the same, since—by the attention the unknown woman is obliged to pay to our name and our person—the conscious gaze and unknowable thoughts that we had been seeking in her eyes, which only yesterday were infinitely remote from us, and which we thought our own eyes, wandering, unfocused, desperate, divergent, would never meet, have just been miraculously and quite simply replaced by our own image, depicted as though in a smiling mirror? If our reincarnation as an entity that had previously seemed utterly different from us is what most modifies the person to whom we've just been introduced, the form of this person still remains quite vague; and we might wonder if she'll turn out to be god, table, or bowl. But, as agile as those wax-modellers who can make a bust before our eyes in five minutes, the few words the stranger will say to us will give definition to this form, something final, which will exclude all the hypotheses conjured up in advance by our desire and imagination. Of course, even before coming to this gathering, Albertine was no longer entirely the sole phantom worthy of haunting our life that a passer-by about whom we know nothing and have scarcely glimpsed can become. Her connection with Madame Bontemps had already limited those fantastic hypotheses, by blocking off one of the paths on which they might have proliferated. The closer I came to the girl and the more I knew of her, this knowledge underwent a kind of subtraction, each part of the imagination and desire being replaced by a perception worth infinitely less, even though these perceptions were augmented by a sort of life equivalent of those 'continuing dividends' paid out by finance companies after the original investment has been reimbursed. Her name and her family connections had been the first restriction set on my suppositions. Her friendliness, as I was standing next to her and noticing again the little beauty mark on her cheek just beneath the eye, set another boundary; finally, I was surprised to hear her use the adverb 'perfectly' instead of 'completely' when talking of two people, saying about one of them: 'she's perfectly mad, but very nice all the same', and about the other: 'he's a perfectly common man, perfectly boring'. However inelegant this use of the word 'perfectly' may be, it indicated a degree of civilization and culture which I'd never have imagined this bacchante on a bicycle, this orgiastic muse of the golf course, had attained. Nevertheless, after this initial metamorphosis, Albertine would change many more times for me. The qualities and flaws that a person presents, as they appear on the surface of the face, take on a completely different aspect when seen from a different angle— just as the landmarks of a city, which seem to be scattered randomly along a single line, from another viewpoint take on a well-ordered depth, and their heights in relation to each other seem to change. At first Albertine struck me as being somewhat intimidated rather than unyielding; she seemed more well-bred than ill-mannered, judging by the epithets she used to describe all the girls I mentioned to her, such as 'she's a bit vulgar' or 'she's an odd sort'; and the focal point of her face was one of her temples, rather flushed and not very pleasant to look at, rather than the singular expression in her eyes, which until then had always lingered in my thoughts. But this was only my second view of her, and there would undoubtedly be other perspectives which I would successively experience. It's only after we've recognized, albeit with a great deal of fumbling in the dark, the optical illusions of our initial impression, that we can arrive at a precise knowledge of a person, if indeed this knowledge were possible. But it is not; for, during the time it takes for the vision we have of others to be rectified, they, who are not inert objects, change; when we think we can recapture them, they move; and, when we believe we can finally see them more clearly, we're seeing only old images that we've taken of them, which we've managed to make sharper, but which don't represent them.

Yet, whatever disappointments it is bound to bring, this approach to what we've only glimpsed, to what we've had the leisure to imagine, is the only one that is wholesome for the senses, the only one that whets the appetite. What dire boredom must fill the lives of people who, out of laziness or timidity, drive directly to the house of friends they've come to know without first having dreamed of them, without ever daring, on the way, to ponder what they desire!

I thought about this gathering as I walked home, seeing again in my mind's eye the coffee eclair I'd finished eating before allowing myself to be led by Elstir to Albertine, the rose I'd given the old gentleman—all those details chosen by circumstance without our realizing it and which compose for us, in a special and fortuitous arrangement, the tableau of our first meeting. But I'd feel I was seeing this picture from another perspective, at a great remove from myself, aware that it hadn't existed for myself alone, when, some months later, to my astonishment, when I was talking to Albertine about the first day I met her, she reminded me of the eclair, the flower I'd given away, everything I'd believed to have been, I can't say important only to myself, but noticed only by myself, which I rediscovered thus, transcribed in a version whose existence I hadn't suspected, in the mind of Albertine. After returning to my hotel on that first day, when I could examine the memory I'd brought back, I realized what a perfect conjuring trick had been executed, and how I had spent some time chatting with a person who, thanks to a magician's sleight of hand, had been substituted for the girl I'd followed for so long by the seaside, and who had nothing in common with her. I should in any case have suspected this beforehand, since the girl by the sea had been made up by me. Despite that, since I had identified her with Albertine in my conversations with Elstir, I felt, towards the real Albertine, the moral obligation to keep the promises of love made to the imaginary Albertine. We betroth ourselves by proxy, and we feel obliged afterwards to marry the one interposed. Besides, even though my life was at least temporarily free of an anxiety that could easily be appeased by remembering her proper manners, her use of the expression 'perfectly common', and her flushed temple, this memory awakened in me another kind of desire which, although sweet and not painful in the least, like a brotherly feeling, might in time become just as dangerous by giving me a constant urge to kiss this new person, whose good manners and shyness, and unexpected availability, stopped the useless course of my imagination, but at the same time gave birth to a tender gratitude. And, since memory immediately begins to take snapshots that are independent of one another, and suppresses any link, any progression, between the scenes it witnesses in the collection of those it displays, the latest memory doesn't necessarily obliterate all the previous ones. Faced with the ordinary, touching Albertine to whom I'd spoken, I could see the mysterious Albertine against the backdrop of the sea. Both of them were now memories, that is, pictures, neither truer than the other. Finally, concerning that afternoon of my first introduction to her, when I tried to visualize the little beauty spot on her cheek beneath the eye, I remembered that, the first time I was with Elstir in his studio, as she was leaving, I'd seen it on her chin. Whenever I saw Albertine, I noticed she had a beauty mark, but my wandering memory then moved it about on her face, placing it sometimes in one place, sometimes in another.

Even though I was disappointed at finding Mademoiselle Simonet not very different from all the other girls I knew, just as my disillusionment with the church at Balbec hadn't prevented me from wanting to go to Quimperlé, Pont-Aven, or Venice, I consoled myself with the thought that at least through Albertine I might come to know the other girls in the little band.

I thought at first that I'd fail in this endeavour. Since she was going to be staying on for quite some time in Balbec, as I was myself,

I thought it would be best not to try to seek her out, but to wait for some circumstance that would bring us together. But even if that were to happen every day, it was highly probable that she'd merely acknowledge my greeting from afar, which, if this was repeated daily for the rest of the season, would do nothing to further my cause.

Not long afterwards, one morning when it had rained and was almost cold, I was approached on the esplanade by a girl wearing a little toque and a muff; she was so different from the girl I'd seen at Elstir's gathering that recognizing her as the same person seemed an operation beyond the power of the human mind; my own, however, managed it, but only after a second's surprise, which I think didn't escape Albertine's notice. What's more, remembering her good manners, which had so impressed me, I was surprised in quite a different way by her rude tone and rough manners typical of the 'little band'. Moreover, her temple had stopped being the reassuring optical centre of her face, because I was standing on her other side, or because her toque concealed it, or because its flush wasn't always there. 'What weather we're having!' she said. 'But endless summers in Balbec are a huge joke, of course. Don't you do anything here? We never see you on the links, or at the Casino dances; and you don't go riding. How deadly bored you must be! Don't you find that sitting on the beach all day dulls your mind? Or do you like sunbathing? You must have lots of time on your hands. I see you're not like me, I adore every kind of sport! You didn't go to the races at La Sogne?* We went on the crawler, and I can see how riding on a rickety thing like that wouldn't be your cup of tea. It took us two whole hours! I could have gone there and back three times on my bike!' I'd admired Saint-Loup when he'd quite naturally called this little local train the 'twister', because of the countless meanderings it made, but I was intimidated by the ease with which Albertine said 'crawler' and 'rickety thing'. I sensed her mastery of a way of naming things, and I was afraid she'd notice my inferiority in this skill, and would scorn me for it; and this was even before the wealth of synonyms the little band used to designate the little train was revealed to me. When she spoke, Albertine kept her head still and her nostrils pinched, barely moving her lips. There resulted a kind of drawling, nasal sound which might have stemmed from a combination of provincial forebears, a youthful affectation of British phlegm, the lessons from a foreign governess, and a congestive hypertrophy of mucus in the nose. This enunciation, which soon disappeared and became more naturally girlish when she'd got to know people better, might have seemed unpleasant. But it was peculiar, and delighted me. Whenever I hadn't seen her for a few days, I'd cheer myself up by repeating 'We never see you on the links' with the same nasal tone she used while looking directly at me, without moving her head. And then I'd think there could be no one in the world more desirable. That morning, we were one of the couples who dotted the esplanade here and there as they came together, pausing just long enough to exchange a few words before parting to go their separate ways. I took advantage of this immobility to take a careful look and find out once and for all where her beauty mark was. Just like the phrase of Vinteuil that had delighted me in his sonata, and which my memory kept shifting from the Andante to the Finale until the day when I held the score in my hand and was able to locate and fix its place in my mind, in the Scherzo, so the beauty mark, which I recalled as being sometimes on her cheek, sometimes on her chin, came to rest finally on her upper lip beneath her nose. In the same way, we're amazed to come upon lines we know by heart, but in a poem in which we'd never have dreamed they belonged.

At that moment, as if in order for the whole decorative ensemble made by the beautiful procession of girls, rosy and golden, tanned by the sun and wind, to unfurl in all the variety of its forms against the background of the sea, Albertine's friends, with their shapely legs and slim waists, but all so different from one another, came into view in a cluster that grew larger as it came towards us, closer to the sea than we were, along a line parallel to ours. I asked Albertine if I could walk with her for a moment. Unfortunately, all she did was wave to them. 'Your friends will be upset if you don't join them!' I said, hoping we could all walk together. A young man with regular features, carrying some tennis racquets, sauntered up to us. It was the baccarat player whose fast ways so scandalized the first president's wife. With a cold, expressionless manner which he obviously regarded as the epitome of refinement, he greeted Albertine. 'Have you been playing golf, Octave?' she asked him. 'Did it go well? Were you in good form?' 'Oh, I'm disgusted with myself, I'm just a washout,' he replied. 'Was Andrée there?' 'Yes, she went round in seventy-seven.' 'Oh my! That's a record!' Albertine exclaimed. 'I went round in eighty-two yesterday,' he said. He was the son of an extremely wealthy industrialist who would one day play a rather important role in organizing the next World's Fair.*

I was struck by how knowledgeable this young man, and the other very few male friends of these girls, were in everything related to clothes, how to wear them, cigars, English drinks, horses—a knowledge which he wielded, down to its minutest details, with a proud infallibility verging on the silent modesty of the scholar, and one which he'd developed independently, without the aid of the slightest intellectual cultivation. He had no hesitation about the correct occasion on which to wear tails or pyjamas, but he had no inkling of when a certain word should or shouldn't be used, and was ignorant of even the simplest rules of grammar. This disparity between two cultures must have been shared by his father, the president of the Association of Property Owners of Balbec, for, in an open letter to his constituents, which he'd just posted on all the walls, he said: 'I desired to see the Mayor to discuss it with him; he did not, however, desire to listen to my just demands.' At the Casino, Octave won prizes in all the dance competitions, for the boston, the tango, etc., which, if he so wished, could serve as a qualification for him to make a good marriage in this 'seaside resort' setting, in which it's not in the figurative, but the literal, sense that young women end up marrying their 'partners'. Lighting a cigar, he said to Albertine: 'If you don't mind', as one would ask permission to finish an urgent task while talking. For he could never 'not do anything', despite the fact that he never did anything. And since complete inactivity ends up having the same effects as overwork, in the moral as well as the physical, muscular domain, the constant intellectual vacuum that lived behind Octave's pensive brow had the result, despite his calm manner, of giving him ineffectual urges to think, which kept him awake at night, as might happen to a metaphysician suffering from nervous exhaustion.

Thinking that if I knew the male friends of the little band I'd have more opportunities to see the girls, I'd been on the point of asking Albertine to introduce me to him. I said as much to Albertine as soon he walked away, still muttering: 'I'm just a washout.' I thought I might ask her to introduce us the next time.

'Look,' she exclaimed, 'I can't introduce you to a gigolo! This place is crawling with them. But they couldn't hold a conversation with you. This one is very good at golf, but that's it. I know what I'm talking about when I say he's not your type at all.'

'Your friends will be upset if you stay away from them,' I said, hoping she'd suggest we'd both go and join them.

'No, no, they don't need me at all.'

We ran into Bloch, who gave me a knowing, insinuating smile; and, embarrassed about Albertine, whom he didn't know, or rather knew 'without being acquainted with her', bobbed his head in a stiff, surly nod. 'Who is that brute?' she asked. 'I have no idea why he's greeting me—he doesn't know me. So I didn't acknowledge him.'

I had no time to reply, since Bloch walked straight over to us and said: 'Excuse me for interrupting, but I wanted to let you know I'm going to Doncières tomorrow. I can't wait any longer without seeming impolite; I wonder what Saint-Loup-en-Bray must think of me. So I'm letting you know I'm taking the train in two hours. It's up to you.'

But I was thinking only of seeing Albertine again and of trying to get to know her friends, and a visit to Doncières, since they never went there, and since I wouldn't get back until after the time they went to the beach, seemed like a trip to the ends of the earth. I told Bloch it would be impossible.

'Oh well, I'll go on my own. In the ridiculous alexandrines of old Arouet, I'll say to Saint-Loup, to appeal to his clericalism:

> Knowst thou that my duty on his does not depend;
> He may neglect his; but my own I must attend.'*

'I'll admit he's rather good-looking,' said Albertine, 'but I can't stand him!'

It had never occurred to me that Bloch might be good-looking; but he was. With his rather prominent forehead, his pronounced Roman nose, his air of extreme cleverness (and of being convinced of his own cleverness), he had a pleasant face. But there was no way Albertine could like him. This may have been because of Albertine's own short-comings, the coarseness and insensitivity of the little band, its rude-ness towards anything that was not part of its circle. Later, when I introduced them to each other, Albertine's antipathy did not dimin-ish. Bloch belonged to a milieu which, between the irony they directed at society, and society's regard for good manners which any 'decent' man must have, has reached a sort of special compromise which dif-fers from the manners of fashionable society yet is, despite everything, a particularly odious sort of urbanity. When you introduced him to someone, he'd bow his head with both a sceptical smile and an exag-gerated respect, and, if it was a man, he'd say: 'Delighted, Monsieur', in a tone that mocked the words it uttered, but made it clear that it belonged to someone who was not uncultivated. Having devoted that first instant to a custom he at once followed and scorned (just as he'd say, on New Year's Day, 'I wish you a Happy New One'), he'd then assume a shrewd, clever expression, and would 'let fall pearls of wisdom' which often had a good deal of truth in them but which, to Albertine, 'got on her nerves'. When, on that first day, I told her his name was Bloch, she exclaimed: 'I'd have bet anything he was a Yid! It's just like them to make your skin crawl!' Later on, Bloch would irritate Albertine in another way. Like many intellectuals, he was incapable of giving simple expression to simple things. He'd find some precious epithet for each of them, and would then make generalizations. Albertine, who didn't much like people paying attention to what she did, was annoyed that, when she'd sprained her ankle and was resting, Bloch said: 'She's lying on her chaise longue, but, being continuous, she continues simultaneously to haunt ghostly golf courses and dismal tennis courts.' This was only his way of using 'fine words'; but, because of the difficulties Albertine felt they might create with people whose invitations she'd refused with the excuse that she couldn't walk, was enough to make her develop a loathing for the sight and sound of the boy who said such things. Albertine and I parted company, promising to go out together soon. When I talked with her, I'd been as unaware of where my words went and what their fate would be as if I'd been throwing pebbles into a bottomless well. That in general our words are filled by the person to whom they are addressed with a meaning our interlocutor draws from their own inner resources, and that this meaning is very different from the one we'd placed in these same words, is a fact that everyday life constantly reveals to us. But if in addition the person to whom we're speaking is, as Albertine was for me, someone whose education I couldn't fathom, whose inclinations, choice of books, and principles are unknown to us, we have no idea if our words have any more semblance of meaning for her than they might for an animal, even a well-trained one. Trying to strike up a relationship with Albertine seemed like coming up against the unknown, or even the impossible, an exercise as difficult as training a horse, as restful as keeping bees or cultivating roses.

Only a few hours before, I'd thought that Albertine would do no more than give me a distant nod. Now we'd just parted with a plan for an outing together. I promised myself that, when I met Albertine next, I'd be bolder with her, and I sketched a plan for everything

I'd say to her, even (now that I had the strong impression that she wasn't at all prudish) all the favours I'd ask of her. But the mind, like plants or cells or chemical elements, is easily swayed, and the medium that effects the change is the circumstances in which the mind is immersed, a new setting. Made different by the mere fact of her presence, the things I said to her when I was with her again were not at all the things I'd planned to say. Then, remembering her flushed temple, I wondered if Albertine might be more appreciative of a kindness on my part that she knew was not motivated by self-interest. I was also flustered by some of the looks she gave me, and her smiles. They could signify either loose ways, or the slightly silly exuberance of a high-spirited girl who was actually quite respectable. Since the same expression, whether on her face or in her speech, could be interpreted in various ways, I was as hesitant as a pupil faced with the difficulties of translating Greek.

This time, almost at once, we met the tall Andrée, the one who had jumped over the first president, and Albertine had to introduce me. Her friend had extraordinarily limpid eyes, as bright as the entrance in a shadowy apartment, through an open door, into a room full of sunshine and the greenish reflection of the shining sea.

Five gentlemen walked past, men I knew very well by sight since I'd first come to Balbec. I'd often wondered who they were. 'They're not very classy,' Albertine said with a scornful snigger. 'The little old bloke, the one with the dyed hair and the yellow gloves—doesn't he look funny! He's the Balbec dentist, not a bad bloke really. The fat one's the mayor—not the little fat one, you must have seen him before, the dancing teacher; he's pretty ugly too, he can't stand us because we make too much noise in the Casino, we smash his chairs and want to dance without the carpet, so he's never given us the prize even though we're the only ones who can dance! The dentist's a nice fellow, I'd have said hello to him just to annoy the dancing teacher, but I couldn't because Monsieur de Sainte-Croix is with them; he's a leader of the Conseil général;* he comes from a good family but he's gone over to the republicans, for the money; all respectable people ignore him. He knows my uncle, because of the government, but the rest of my family have turned their back on him. The thin one in the raincoat is the orchestra conductor. Really, you don't know him? He plays divinely. You haven't gone to hear *Cavalleria Rusticana*?* Oh, I think it's just super! He's giving a concert tonight, but we can't go because it's in the Town Hall. The Casino's fine, but the Town Hall! Now that they've taken away the crucifix, Andrée's mother would have a fit if we went there. You'll say my aunt's husband is in government, but that's not what I mind—even though my aunt is my aunt, it doesn't make me like her any more. She's only ever wanted one thing in life: to get rid of me. The person who's really been a mother to me, and deserves twice the credit because she's not even related to me, is a friend I love like a mother. I'll show you her photo.' We were briefly joined by the golf champion and baccarat-player, Octave. I thought I might have discovered a link between us, for I'd learned in conversation that he was distantly related to the Verdurins, who were also quite fond of him. But he spoke scornfully of the famous Wednesdays, and added that Monsieur Verdurin had no idea how to wear a dinner jacket properly, which made it rather embarrassing to come upon him in certain music halls, where one would prefer not to hear 'Hello there, you little devil!' shouted at you by a gentleman wearing the suit and black tie of a small-town notary. Then Octave left us, and soon after it was Andrée's turn to go, as we had arrived at her villa, which she entered without having said a single word to me throughout the entire walk. I was sorry to see her go, especially because, as I was remarking to Albertine how cold her friend had been to me, and was comparing in my mind the difficulty Albertine seemed to have in introducing me to her friends with the hostility Elstir seemed to encounter on that first day when he tried to grant my wish for an introduction, two girls passed by, the d'Ambresac sisters, whom I greeted, and to whom Albertine also said hello.

I thought this greeting might improve my situation with Albertine. The two girls were the daughters of a relative of Madame de Villeparisis who also knew the Princesse de Luxembourg. Monsieur and Madame d'Ambresac, who had a little villa in Balbec, and were immensely wealthy, led a very simple life, the husband always wearing the same jacket, the wife a dark dress. Both would make deep bows to my grandmother, but would go no further than that. The daughters, both very pretty, dressed more elegantly, but with an elegance that was of the city and not the seaside. In their long dresses and wide hats, they looked as if they belonged to a different race from Albertine. She knew quite well who they were. 'Oh, you know the little d'Ambresac girls? You know some stylish people then. They're actually very simple,' she added, as if that were a contradiction in terms. 'They're very nice but so strictly brought up that they're not allowed to go to the Casino, mostly because of us, because we're such a bad lot. You like them? Not everyone does! They're such goody-two-shoes. Some people like that sort of thing, of course. If goody-two-shoes is what you like, look no further. They must have some sort of appeal, since one of them's already engaged to the Marquis de Saint-Loup. And that makes the younger one suffer no end, because she was in love with him. As for me, just their high-and-mighty way of talking down to you gets on my nerves. Plus they wear such ridiculous clothes. They go off to play golf in silk gowns! At their age they wear more pretentious outfits than older women who know how to dress. Just look at Madame Elstir, there's an elegant woman for you.' I replied that she'd seemed to me to be wearing very simple clothes. Albertine burst out laughing. 'She does dress very simply, that's true, but she has excellent taste, and to achieve what you call simplicity, she spends an enormous amount of money.' Madame Elstir's dresses passed unnoticed by anyone whose taste in clothing wasn't expert or refined. This was a taste I lacked. Elstir, however, possessed it in spades, or so Albertine said. I hadn't realized this in the least; nor did I suspect that the elegant but simple things that filled his studio were treasures he'd yearned for, which he'd pursued from auction to auction, knowing their whole history, until he'd earned enough money to be able to possess them. On that subject, however, Albertine, as ignorant as I was, could tell me nothing. When it came to clothing, though, prompted by her coquettish instinct and also perhaps by the sort of regretful longing of a poor girl who can appreciate, with greater objectivity and more delicacy of feeling, the things she'll never be able to afford when they're worn by the wealthy, she could speak very knowledgeably about Elstir's refined taste, which was so exacting that he thought every woman was poorly dressed, and that, investing every proportion, every nuance with paramount importance, he would spend exorbitant amounts to have his wife's parasols, hats, and cloaks made, whose charm he'd taught Albertine to appreciate, and which a person devoid of taste wouldn't have noticed any more than I did. Besides, Albertine, who had done a little painting, though without having, as she said, a 'knack' for it, had great admiration for Elstir, and, because of what he'd told her and shown her, had acquired a knowledge of painting that contrasted sharply with her enthusiasm for *Cavalleria Rusticana*. The truth is that, even though it wasn't yet apparent, she was highly intelligent; in the things she said, the stupidity was not her own, but that of her environment and her age. Elstir's influence had been good, but incomplete. Not all forms of intelligence were equally developed in her. Her taste in painting had almost caught up with her taste in clothing and other matters of elegance, but hadn't been followed by her taste in music, which lagged far behind.

Despite the fact that Albertine knew how important the d'Ambresacs were, just as one who is capable of the greatest things might not be capable of the smallest, she didn't seem any more inclined, after I'd greeted the girls, to introduce me to her friends. 'It's very sweet of you to attach so much importance to them. Don't pay any attention to them, they don't matter at all. What could a bunch of little kids like that mean to a man as smart as you? Andrée at least is rather intelligent. She's a nice girl, even though she's perfectly overstrung—the others, though, are incredibly stupid.' As soon as I bade farewell to Albertine, I was filled with sadness that Saint-Loup had hidden his engagement from me, and that he was so immoral as to contemplate marriage before he'd even broken up with his mistress. Just a few days later, I was introduced to Andrée, and since she spoke with me for quite some time, I seized the opportunity to tell her I'd like to see her the following day; but she replied that it wouldn't be possible, as she thought her mother was unwell, and didn't want to leave her alone. Two days later, when I went to see Elstir, he told me how much Andrée had liked me; I replied: 'But I'm the one who liked *her* so much, on the very first day! I asked to see her again the next day, but she refused.' 'Yes, I know, she told me,' Elstir said. 'She was rather sorry, but she'd agreed to go to a picnic over ten miles away, in a break,* and she couldn't get out of it.' Even though this lie was quite insignificant, since Andrée hardly knew me, I shouldn't have continued to see someone who was capable of it. For what people have done once, they will go on doing forever. If every year we go to see a friend who has broken our engagements the first few times, or has come down with a cold, we'll find he'll have caught another cold, or will fail to come to another engagement, always for the same reason, even though he thinks he has come up with many different circumstantial reasons.

One morning, soon after the day Andrée had told me she had to stay with her mother, I was taking a stroll with Albertine, whom I'd happened upon, and who was tossing up a peculiar device attached to the end of a string, which made her look rather like Giotto's

Infidelitas;* it was in fact called a 'diabolo',* and has fallen into such disuse that, faced with a portrait of a girl holding one, future critics, as if before one of the allegorical figures in the Arena Chapel, might debate what precisely it is that she's holding in her hand. A moment later, one of the little band, the one who looked tough and rather impoverished, who had sniggered so meanly on the first day I saw them and said: 'I almost feel sorry for him, the poor old bloke', referring to the old gentleman whose head had been brushed by Andrée's light feet, walked over and said to Albertine: 'Hello! Am I in the way?' She'd removed her hat, which was irritating her, and her hair, like some unknown, gorgeous variety of plant, lay on her forehead in all the detail and delicacy of its foliation. Albertine, possibly annoyed at seeing her bareheaded, keeping an icy silence, gave no reply; despite this, the other girl stayed, though she was kept at a distance from me by Albertine, who so arranged things as to be alone with her at some times, and to walk with me at others, leaving her behind. In order to be introduced, I was obliged to ask Albertine if she would do so, as the other looked on. As Albertine was saying my name, on the face and in the bright blue eyes of this girl, whom I'd thought so cruel when she'd said 'I almost feel sorry for him, the poor old bloke', I saw the flash of a brilliant, friendly, warm smile as she held her hand out to me. Her hair was not the only golden thing about her: although her cheeks were pink and her eyes blue, they looked like the rosy sky of morning, glinting and sparkling everywhere with gold.

Instantly aroused by her presence, I told myself she was a girl who turned shy when in love, and it was for me, out of love for me, that she'd remained with us, despite Albertine's rebuffs, and that she must have been happy finally to be able to confess, through this smiling, friendly gaze, that she'd be as gentle with me as she was cruel to others. She must have noticed me on the beach, even before I'd noticed her, and must have thought of me ever since; perhaps it was to impress me that she'd made fun of the old gentleman, and because she'd been unable to meet me that she'd looked so glum on the days that followed. From the hotel, I had often seen her in the evening, strolling along the beach. No doubt she was doing so in the hope of meeting me. And now, hindered by Albertine's presence as much as she'd have been by that of the whole little band, the only reason why she was keeping pace with us, despite her friend's increasingly frosty attitude, was obviously her hope that she'd manage to outstay

Albertine and arrange to meet me at a time when she'd find some way
to slip away without her family or friends noticing, and to come and
meet me at some safe place before Mass or after golf. It was all the
more difficult for me to see her since she was on bad terms with
Andrée, who detested her. 'I've put up too long', Andrée said, 'with
her awful duplicity, her low-down ways, the endless dirty tricks she's
played on me. I put up with all of it because of the other girls. But the
latest thing she did was the last straw.' And she told me about a rumour
this girl had spread which could, in fact, have serious consequences
for Andrée.

But the words Gisèle's eyes had promised me as soon as Albertine
left us alone had to remain unsaid, because Albertine went on stubbornly keeping us apart, giving her increasingly curt replies, and then
ceasing altogether to acknowledge her friend's remarks, so that at
length she gave up and walked away. I reproached Albertine for having been so unpleasant. 'That'll teach her to watch her tongue! She's
not a bad girl but she's so annoying. She doesn't have to keep sticking
her nose in everywhere. Why did she keep hanging on to us when no
one asked her to? I was just about to send her packing! Plus I hate her
hair like that, it looks so common.'

While Albertine was talking, I was looking at her cheeks, and wondering what perfume, what taste they might have: that day they didn't
look cool, but smooth, uniformly pink, with a mauve tinge, creamy,
like certain roses with a waxy sheen. I had the same sort of passion for
her cheeks as one might have for a particular kind of flower.

'I hadn't noticed,' I replied.

'Well you were certainly looking at her long enough, as if you
wanted to paint her portrait!' she said, not in the least mollified by the
fact that at that moment it was herself I was staring at with such
intensity. 'I don't think you'd like her, though. She's not at all a flirt.
You must like girls that flirt. Anyway, there won't be any more chances
for her to cling to us or keep popping up everywhere, because she's
going back to Paris today.'

'Are your other friends going with her?'

'No, just her, her and her governess, because she has to take her
exams over again—she has to cram for them, poor kid. It's no fun, let
me tell you. It's always possible you could get assigned an easy subject, though—you never can tell, luck being the way it is. One of our
friends got: "Describe an accident you have witnessed." How lucky is

that? But I know another girl who had to discuss (in writing, too!): "Who would you rather have as a friend, Alceste or Philinte?"* I'd have been completely stumped! For one thing, apart from everything else, it's not a question to ask young ladies! Girls are friends with other girls, they're not supposed to have gentlemen friends.' (This statement, with its implication that I'd have little chance of being admitted into the little band, made me tremble.) 'But in any case, even if the question was put to boys, what on earth are you supposed to say to such a thing? Lots of families have written to *Le Gaulois** to complain about the difficulty of questions like that. The worst thing is that in a collection of the best essays by prize-winning students, the same subject was given twice, but in completely opposite ways! It all depends on which examiner you get. One wanted them to say that Philinte was a deceitful flatterer, the other that you couldn't help admiring Alceste, but that he was too bad-tempered, and so as a friend you'd have to prefer Philinte. How are the poor students supposed to know what to say when the teachers can't even agree with each other? But that's not even the worst of it, it gets more difficult every year. There's no way on earth Gisèle can pass unless someone pulls a few strings for her.'

When I got back to the hotel, my grandmother wasn't there; I waited a long time for her; finally, when she arrived, I begged her to let me seize an unhoped-for opportunity to take an excursion that might last up to forty-eight hours; I lunched with her, ordered a carriage, and was driven to the station. Gisèle wouldn't be surprised to see me; once we'd changed trains in Doncières, in the train to Paris there would be a corridor carriage from which, while the English governess dozed, I could lead Gisèle into dark corners and arrange times for us to meet after my own return to Paris, which I'd try to make as soon as I could. Depending on how willing she seemed, I'd accompany her all the way to Caen or Évreux, and then would take the next train back. What might she have thought, though, if she'd known how I'd hesitated between her and her friends, how I'd have liked to fall in love with Albertine, or the girl with the bright eyes, or Rosemonde, just as much as with her! Now that a requited love was about to unite me with Gisèle, I felt remorse. I could assure her, however, quite truthfully, that Albertine didn't appeal to me. I'd seen her that morning walking away with her back almost turned to me, to talk to Gisèle. The hair behind her head, which was bent down sullenly, was different from the hair in front and even darker, and glistened as if she'd just come out of the water. It made me think of a wet hen, and it had made me see in Albertine another person, quite different from the one with the glowing complexion and mysterious gaze. For a moment, that glistening hair on the back of her head was all I could see of her, and it's all I continued to see. Our memory is like those shops that display in their windows, at different times, sometimes one photograph of a person, sometimes another. And it's usually the most recent that remains on view longest. As the coachman was urging on his horse, I could hear Gisèle's words of gratitude and tenderness, all of them springing from her warm smile and outstretched hand: the fact is that during the periods of my life when I was not in love but wanted to be, I carried within myself not only a physical ideal of beauty I'd seen, which I recognized from afar in each passer-by who was distant enough for her vague features not to contradict this identification, but also the mental phantom—always ready to be incarnated—of the woman who would fall in love with me, would act as my counterpart in the drama of love which I'd written out in my head ever since childhood and in which every friendly girl I met seemed to have the same desire to play, provided she had some of the physical attributes required for the role. In this play, no matter who I cast as the new 'star' to create or revive the role, the plot, all the main events, and even the text itself, remained ever the same.

Within a matter of days, despite Albertine's reluctance to introduce me to them, I'd met the entire little band I'd seen on the first day, all of them having stayed on in Balbec (except Gisèle, whom, because of a long delay at the level crossing in front of the station, and a change in the timetable, I'd been unable to join on the train, which had left five minutes before I arrived, and who was no longer in my thoughts in any case), along with two or three of their other friends whom I'd asked to meet. In this way, with my hope for the pleasure I'd find with a new girl springing from a previous girl who had introduced us, the most recent was then like one of those new varieties of rose developed from a rose of a different species. And as I passed from corolla to corolla in this chain of flowers, the pleasure of meeting a new girl would make me revert to the girl responsible for it, with a gratitude which was just as mingled with desire as my hope for the new one was. Soon I was spending all my time with these girls.

Alas, in the freshest flower one can discern the imperceptible signs which, to the skilled eye, indicate already what will be, by the desiccation or fructification of the flesh in blossom today, the immutable and already predestined form of the seed. Our eyes delight in studying a nose like a wavelet that deliciously swells the surface of an early morning sea and seems motionless enough to be sketched, because the sea is so calm that one can't perceive the tide. Human faces seem not to change at the moment we're looking at them, because the revolution they perform is too slow for us to perceive it. But one only had to see these girls standing next to their mother or aunt to measure the distances that, under a generally awful kind of internal attraction, these features will have travelled in less than thirty years, until the time when their eyes grow dim and their faces, having vanished altogether below the horizon, no longer receive light. I knew that, as deep, as ineluctable as Jewish patriotism or Christian atavism is in people who believe they've completely freed themselves from their race, there lurked, beneath the rosy inflorescence of Albertine, or Rosemonde, or Andrée, unbeknownst to themselves, held in reserve until circumstances align, a big nose, a prominent mouth, a bulging waist, which might seem surprising but which were waiting in the wings, ready to make their entrance, just as Dreyfusism or clericalism, or some nationalist, feudal heroism—sudden, unforeseen, and deadly—comes abruptly to the surface at the summons of circumstance from a nature that predates the individual himself, by which he thinks, lives, evolves, draws strength, or dies, without ever being able to distinguish it from the various motives he mistakes for it. Even mentally, we depend on natural laws much more than we may think, and our mind possesses already, like primitive cryptogams or grasses,* the particularities we think we've chosen ourselves. But we only grasp the secondary ideas, without perceiving the original cause (Jewish blood, French birth, etc.) which necessarily produced them and which we manifest at a time of its choosing. And perhaps, though we think our ideas are the result of our own deliberation, and our ills the consequence of an improvident and unhealthy way of life, we inherit from our family, just as papilionaceous flowers* pass down the shape of their seeds, both the ideas by which we live and the illness from which we'll die.

As if on a plant whose flowers ripen at different times, I'd seen them in old ladies, on the beach in Balbec, those hard seeds, those soft tubers, that my friends would one day become. But what did that matter? For now it was their season to blossom. And so, whenever Madame de Villeparisis invited me for a drive, I'd make up some excuse for not going. I'd visit Elstir only when my new friends could come with me. I couldn't even find an afternoon free to go to Doncières to see Saint-Loup, as I'd promised. Social engagements, serious conversations, even just a chat with a friend, if they'd taken the place of my outings with these girls, would have had the same effect for me as if at lunchtime I'd been taken out not to eat, but to look at a picture album. The men and youths, the old or middle-aged women, whose company we think we enjoy, exist for us only on a flat, shallow surface, because we're aware of them through visual perception alone; but when our eyes stray over to young women, it's as if they were delegates of the other senses, which follow close behind, seeking out one after the other the various qualities—of fragrance, touch, or taste—that they enjoy even without the help of hands or lips; and capable, thanks to the arts of transposition, and to the genius for synthesis in which desire excels, of reconstructing, beneath the colour of the cheeks or the bosom, the sensations of touching, or tasting, or forbidden contact, they give these girls the same honey-like consistency as they do when they inhale the fragrance of a rose garden, or feast their eyes on the grapes of a vine.

If it was raining, even though bad weather didn't bother Albertine in the least, since she could be seen in her raincoat speeding on her bicycle through downpours, we'd spend the day in the Casino, from which on such days I would have thought it unimaginable to stay away. I had the greatest contempt for the d'Ambresac girls, who had never set foot in it. And I was only too happy to help my friends play tricks on the dancing teacher. We'd usually suffer rebuke from the manager, or from employees standing in for him, because my friends (even Andrée, whose high spirits had led me to think of her as Dionysian,* but who on the contrary was fragile and intellectual and, that year, not at all well, but who, despite that, obeyed less the state of her health than the spirit of her age, which leaves everything behind in its wake, and, in its joy, confounds the sick with the sturdy) were incapable of entering the lobby, or the ballroom, without taking a running start, leaping over all the chairs, sliding across the floor while keeping their balance with a graceful wave of their arms, singing all the while, mingling all the arts, in this first bloom of youth, like those poets of antiquity for whom the different literary genres hadn't yet been separated, and who in the same epic poem mingle agricultural precepts with theological teachings.

The Andrée who had seemed the coldest of them all on that first day was infinitely more sensitive, affectionate, and astute than Albertine, to whom she showed the caressing, sweet tenderness of an older sister. She would come to the Casino and sit by my side, and she knew—unlike Albertine—when to refuse an invitation to waltz, or, if I was tired, she'd even give up an opportunity to go to the Casino and would visit me at the hotel instead. She would express her friendship for me, and for Albertine, in subtle terms that proved her exquisite understanding of matters of the heart, which might have stemmed from her fragile state. She always gave a cheerful smile to excuse the childishness of Albertine, who with childish impetuosity gave in to the irresistible temptation offered by outings and parties, which, unlike Andrée, she could not forgo in order to talk with me. When the time to go to a tea party at the golf club was approaching, if we were all together, Albertine would get ready to go, and then say to Andrée: 'Come on, Andrée, what's keeping you? You know we're having tea at the golf club.' 'No, I'll stay and talk with him,' Andrée replied, gesturing to me. 'But you know very well that Madame Durieux invited you,' Albertine exclaimed, as if Andrée's resolve to stay with me could only be explained by the fact that Andrée didn't know she'd been invited. 'Don't be silly, Albertine!' Andrée replied. Albertine didn't insist, afraid she'd be asked to stay as well. She shook her head and said: 'Fine, do as you like,' as you'd say to a sick person who takes pleasure in committing suicide little by little. 'I'm off, since I think my watch is running late,' and she fled. 'She's lovely, but totally impossible,' Andrée said, enveloping her friend in a smile that was both caressing and judgemental at the same time. If, in this taste for entertainment, there seemed to be something of the early Gilberte in Albertine, that's because a certain resemblance exists, though it evolves, between all the women we love; their resemblance stems from the unchanging nature of our own temperament, which is what selects them, eliminating all those who aren't both opposite and complementary to us, that is, capable of satisfying our senses and causing our heart to suffer. They are, these women, an inverted image or projection, a 'negative' of our own sensibility. So that a novelist, over the course of his hero's life, might portray his successive love affairs as being almost exactly the same, and thereby give the impression not of imitating himself but of creating, since there is less power in an artificial innovation than in a repetition intended to suggest a new truth. However, in the character of the lover, he should indicate a sign of variability, which becomes more pronounced as the lover moves into new regions and reaches other latitudes of life. And perhaps the novelist might express yet another truth if, endowing his other characters with particular qualities, he refrained from giving any to the woman his hero loves. We know the characters of people who mean nothing to us; how could we possibly grasp that of a person who is intertwined with our life, who soon becomes impossible for us to separate from ourselves, about whose motives we're constantly making anxious, perpetually revised hypotheses? Soaring past our reasoning mind, our curiosity about the woman we love goes beyond her character; we could linger over it, but we probably would rather not. The object of our anxious investigations is more essential than individual details of character, which are like the tiny lozenge-shapes on the skin, patterns whose varied combinations form the florid originality of the flesh. Our intuitive X-ray vision sees through them, and the images it sends back to us are not those of any particular face, but rather the bleak, distressing universality of a skeleton.

As Andrée was extremely wealthy, and Albertine poor and an orphan, she very generously shared her riches with her. As to Andrée's feelings towards Gisèle, however, they were not at all what I'd thought. News of the departed student soon came, and when Albertine showed everyone the letter she'd received, which Gisèle had written to describe to the little band her journey and arrival in Paris, apologizing for being too lazy to write to the others, I was surprised to hear Andrée, who I thought was at daggers drawn with Gisèle, say: 'I'll write to her tomorrow—if I waited for her to write first, I'd be waiting forever, she's such a scatterbrain.' And, turning to me, she added: 'You might not think much of her, but she's really a sweet girl, and I care about her a lot.' I concluded that for Andrée, quarrels were short-lived.

Except on those rainy days, since we usually went cycling along the cliffs or into the countryside, I'd spend an hour beforehand fussing over my appearance, and I'd complain if Françoise hadn't laid my things out properly.

Even in Paris, Françoise, who was charmingly humble and modest when her self-esteem was flattered, would proudly and indignantly stiffen her back, which was beginning to stoop with age, at the slightest hint of blame. Since pride in her work was the mainspring of her life, her satisfaction and good humour were in direct proportion to the difficulty of the things demanded of her. The tasks she had to perform in Balbec were so simple that she would almost always display a discontent that was suddenly magnified a hundredfold and accompanied by an ironic expression of pride if, as I was about to set off to meet my friends, I complained that my hat wasn't brushed or my ties were in disarray. Even though she was capable of going to any amount of trouble without a second thought, if I simply remarked that a jacket was out of place, she would not only boast about the care with which she had 'put it away rather than not let it gather dust', but, vaunting her own labours, would lament the fact that our stay in Balbec was no vacation for her, and that you couldn't find anyone else who would put up with such a life. 'It's beyond me how anyone can leave their things lying about like that—and you just go and see if you can find someone else to sort it all out! The devil himself would give up!' Or else she would merely assume a queenly air, look daggers at me, and remain silent until she'd closed the door and started off down the corridor, which then resounded with remarks I could guess were insulting, but which remained as indistinct as those of characters delivering their first lines in the wings before coming onstage. Moreover, whenever I was getting ready to go out with my friends, even if nothing was amiss and Françoise was in a good mood, she would still try my patience. For, making jokes about the girls which I myself had made in my need to talk about them to her, she would act as if she were revealing truths I'd have known better than she—if they had been true, but they weren't, since Françoise hadn't properly understood them in the first place. Like everyone else, Françoise had her own character; no one ever resembles a straight path, but we're always astonished by every person's singular, inevitable twists and turns, which others may not even notice, but which we have to do our best to tolerate. Whenever I ended a sentence with 'Hat not in place' or with Andrée's or Albertine's name, Françoise would subject me to a meandering diatribe that only caused further delay. The same would happen when I asked her to make Cheshire cheese and lettuce sandwiches and buy tarts which I'd share on the cliff later that afternoon with the girls, and which 'they should have taken turns to buy, if they weren't always out for what they could get', declared Françoise (who at those times was aided by a whole heritage of atavistic avarice and provincial vulgarity), as if the divided soul of the late Eulalie had been reincarnated, more graciously than at Saint Éloi, in the charming bodies of my friends in the little band. I would listen to these accusations with the rage of feeling myself coming up against one of those places where the rustic, familiar country lane that was Françoise's character became impassable, though fortunately not for long. Then, jacket found and sandwiches ready, I'd sally forth to meet Albertine, Andrée, Rosemonde, and sometimes others from the little band, and, on foot or bicycle, we would set off.

There was a time when I would have preferred an outing to take place in bad weather. Then I would try to see Balbec as 'the land of the Cimmerians', where there could be no such thing as a sunny day, and no intrusion of the vulgar summer of sea-bathers into that ancient region veiled in mist. But now, everything that I'd disdained, everything my eyes had shunned—not just the play of light and shadow, but even regattas and horse races—I would have passionately sought out for the same reason I used to desire only stormy seas, namely that all these things, then as now, were linked to an aesthetic idea. I had gone several times with my friends to see Elstir, and on the days when the girls were there, the pictures he chose to show us were sketches of pretty yachtswomen, or perhaps a drawing done at a racecourse near Balbec. I'd timidly confessed to Elstir that I hadn't at first wanted to go to the events that took place there. 'You were wrong,' he replied. 'They're such a pretty sight, and so interesting too. For one thing, that special figure, the jockey, on whom so many eyes are trained, who looks so lonely down there in the paddock, so nondescript in his brightly coloured silks, so at one with the prancing horse he reins in—how fascinating it would be to bring out his expert movements, to show the brilliant splash of colour he presents, along with the horses' glossy coats, on the racecourse. How everything is transformed in this luminous immensity of a racecourse where you're constantly surprised by so many shadows and reflections you can see nowhere but there! How pretty the women can look there! The first race meeting was especially magnificent, with women of extraordinary elegance, in a liquid, Dutch light, and you could sense the penetrating chill of the water rising up in the sunlight itself. Never have I seen women arriving in their carriages, or with binoculars held to their eyes, in such a light, which must come from the moist sea air. How I'd have loved to capture it! I went home from that race mad with desire to get to work!' He then spoke even more lyrically about the yachting events than about the horse races, and I understood that regattas and sporting competitions where well-dressed women bathe in the blue-green light of a seaside racetrack could be as interesting a subject for a modern artist as the festive celebrations that Veronese and Carpaccio so liked to depict.* 'Your comparison is all the more apt', Elstir said, 'because in the city where they painted, those celebrations were often nautical. Except the beauty of the vessels in those days lay chiefly in their ponderous heft and complexity. They did water jousting then, as we do here, usually in honour of a visiting embassy, like the one Carpaccio shows in *The Legend of Saint Ursula*.* The ships were massive, constructed like architecture, and seemed almost amphibious, like smaller Venices within the greater one, when they were moored with their broad, lowered gangways covered in crimson satin and Persian carpets, and they carried women in cherry-red brocades or green damask, close to balconies encrusted with multicoloured marble, on which other women leaned to get a good view, in gowns with black sleeves and white slashes that teemed with pearls or were decorated with lace. You couldn't tell where the land ended and the water began, which was palace or ship, caravel, galleass, or Bucentaur.'* Albertine listened with passionate attention to these details of dress, these images of luxury that Elstir was describing to us. 'Oh! I'd like so much to see that lace you speak of; Venetian point-lace is so lovely!' she exclaimed. 'How I'd love to go to Venice!' 'You may, before long,' Elstir replied, 'be able to gaze at the wonderful fabrics they used to wear. Until now, you could only see them in canvases by Venetian painters, or, very rarely, in church relics—sometimes a garment might even come up for auction. But they say that an artist from Venice, Fortuny,* has discovered the secret of how they were made, and that in a few years women will be able to stroll about and better still stay at home, in brocades as magnificent as those that Venice decorated, for its great ladies, with designs from the Orient. But I'm not sure I'd like that much; it might be a little too like a period costume for today's women, even if they were showing off at regattas, for, to come back to our modern pleasure boats, they're the complete opposite of those from the time when Venice was "Queen of the Adriatic". The most charming thing about a yacht—the fittings of a yacht, the clothes one wears on a yacht—is its seaside simplicity, and I so love the sea! I must confess I prefer today's fashions to the fashions of

Veronese's and even Carpaccio's time. The lovely thing about our yachts—the medium-sized ones especially, I don't like the really big ones, they're too much like ships (as with women's hats, there *is* a limit)—is how plain they are—simple, sparse, grey—which, on hazy, bluish days, takes on a creamy fluidity. The cabin where you sit should feel like a little café. It's the same with women's clothes on a yacht; the graceful ones are those light, white, plain dresses, in canvas, linen, lawn, duck, twill, which in the sunlight and on the blue of the sea are as white as a white sail. Not many women, for that matter, dress well; but there are a glorious few. At the races, Mademoiselle Léa had a little white hat and a little white parasol—it was enchanting. I'd have given a lot to have that little parasol.' I would have liked very much to know in what way exactly this little parasol was different from others, and, for other reasons having to do with feminine interest in fashion, Albertine must have been even more curious. But, just as Françoise used to say about her soufflés: 'It's all in the hands', the difference lay in the cut. 'It was quite small,' said Elstir, 'quite round, like a Chinese umbrella.' I mentioned the parasols of various other women, but they weren't at all the same. Elstir thought they were all hideous. A man of exacting and superlative taste, he would regard some tiny nothing as everything, since it made all the difference between what three-quarters of the women wore, which he found dreadful, and a pretty thing that delighted him, and which stimulated his desire (not like me, for whom all luxury was sterile), to paint 'in order to try to create things that were just as beautiful'.

'Now there's a young lady who's already understood what the hat and parasol were like,' Elstir said, pointing to Albertine, whose eyes were shining with envy.

'How I'd love to be rich so I could have a yacht,' she said to the painter. 'I'd ask you for advice on how to fit it out. What lovely excursions I'd go on. And how nice it would be to go to the regattas in Cowes!* I could get a motor car too! Do you think women's fashions for motoring are nice?'

'No,' Elstir replied, 'but that will come in time. There are hardly any dress designers, you see—one or two, like Callot, though they go in a little too much for lace, Doucet, Cheruit, sometimes Paquin.* The rest are all dreadful.'

'Is it true, then,' I asked Albertine, 'that there's such a huge difference between a dress by Callot and one by some other designer?'

'It's enormous, you silly boy!' she replied. 'I'm sorry! The only problem is that what costs three hundred francs from anyone else is two thousand francs from them. But they look completely different— except for people who don't know anything about such things, that is.'

'That's perfectly true,' replied Elstir, 'though I wouldn't go so far as to say that the difference is as profound as between a statue in Rheims Cathedral and one in the Saint-Augustin church.* Listen, speaking of cathedrals,' he said, addressing me in particular, since he was referring to a conversation in which the girls hadn't taken part, and which wouldn't have interested them in any case, 'I was talking to you the other day about how the Balbec church looks like a high cliff, a huge breakwater of stones from around here; well,' he said, showing me a watercolour, 'look at these cliffs (it's a sketch I made near here, in Les Creuniers*), look at these rocks, so powerfully but so delicately hewn; don't they remind you of a cathedral?'

They did in fact resemble immense pink vaulted arches. Painted on a scorching day, however, they looked as if they were reduced to dust, pulverized by the heat, which had drunk up half the sea, and had almost reduced it, throughout the entire extent of the canvas, to a gaseous state. On this day when the light had, so to speak, destroyed reality, reality itself was concentrated into dark, transparent figures which, by contrast, gave a more striking, more immediate impression of life: the shadows. Most of them, thirsty for coolness, and deserting the blaze of the open sea, had taken refuge at the foot of the rocks, sheltered from the sun; others swam slowly on the water's surface the way dolphins fasten on to the sides of moving boats, widening their hulls on the pale water with their smooth, blue bodies. It was perhaps the thirst for coolness communicated by them that did most to convey the sensation of that day's heat, and which made me exclaim how sorry I was not to know Les Creuniers. Albertine and Andrée assured me that I must have been there a hundred times. In that case, I must have gone without realizing it, or even suspecting that, one day, seeing them could inspire in me such a thirst for beauty, one that was not exactly natural, like what I'd sought until now in the cliffs of Balbec, but rather architectural. I, who had come here to see the realm of tempests, and who had never, in my excursions with Madame de Villeparisis, found the ocean, painted in the interstices between the trees, real enough, liquid enough, alive enough, or giving a sufficient impression that it was heaving masses of water into the air, who had never wanted to see the sea motionless except beneath a wintry shroud of mist, would never have thought that one day I'd dream of a sea that was nothing but a whitish vapour that had lost its consistency and colour. But Elstir, like the people dreaming in those boats made lethargic by the heat, had tasted its enchantment so deeply that he'd been able to convey, to fix on his canvas, the imperceptible ebbing of the tide, the throbbing beat of a moment of happiness; and to see it in this magic picture was to fall instantly so in love with it that one's only thought was to travel the world over to find that vanished day, in all its immediate, slumbering beauty.

Whereas before these visits to Elstir's studio, before I'd seen one of his seascapes in which a young woman, in a dress of barège or cotton lawn, on a yacht flying the American flag, planted in my imagination the spiritual double of a white lawn dress and a flag, which immediately ignited an insatiable, burning desire to see dresses of white lawn and flags by the sea, as if something like that had never happened to me before until then, I'd always tried, when looking at the sea, to banish from my field of vision not just the bathers in the foreground and the yachts, with their sails as glaringly white as beach outfits, but also anything that kept me from convincing myself that I was contemplating the age-old waves of the deep sea, which was already unfurling its same mysterious life before the appearance of humankind—I'd even try to block out the radiant days that seemed to me to be masking this coast of mists and storms with the banal look of a universal summer, and to be bringing everything simply to a pause, the equivalent of what in music would be called a rest; now, however, I was filled with a keen desire to go out and find in reality what thrilled me so greatly, and I hoped the weather would be favourable enough to see from the top of the cliffs the same blue shadows as in Elstir's painting.

Nor, as we walked along, did I continue to shield my eyes with my hands, as I did in those days when, conceiving of nature as being animated by a life dating from before the appearance of human beings, and in opposition to all those tedious improvements of industry which until then had made me yawn with boredom at world's fairs or milliners' windows, I tried to see of the sea only that section where there were no steamships, so that I could see it as timeless, as being contemporaneous with the ages in which it had been set apart from land, or at the very least contemporaneous with the first centuries of

Greece, which enabled me to keep reciting to myself the lines of 'old Leconte' so dear to Bloch:

> Gone are the kings far off now on their speeding ships,
> Bearing away, on the tempestuous ocean waves, alas,
> All the long-haired fighters from heroic Hellas*

I could no longer hold dressmakers in contempt, since Elstir had told me that he was just as interested in rendering the delicate gesture with which they give a final pleat, a supreme caress, to the bows and feathers on a completed hat, as he was in portraying the movements of jockeys (a statement which had delighted Albertine). But seeing the dressmakers again would have to wait until I returned to Paris, and as to the horse races and regattas, they would have to wait until my return to Balbec, since no more would be held until the following year. Even a yacht carrying women in white lawn was nowhere to be found.

We'd often meet Bloch's sisters, whom I'd been obliged to greet ever since I'd dined with their father. My friends didn't know them. 'I'm not allowed to play with Israelites,' Albertine said. The way she pronounced 'Issraelite' instead of 'Izraelite' would have sufficed to show, even if one hadn't heard the beginning of her sentence, that there was no love lost between the chosen people and these young bourgeois ladies from devout families, who must have found it easy to believe that Jews slit the throats of Christian children. 'Anyway, they have a dirty look about them, those friends of yours,' Andrée said to me with a smile that signified she knew very well they were not my friends. 'Like everything that touches that tribe,' replied Albertine in the sententious tone of a person of experience. And indeed, Bloch's sisters, at once overdressed and half naked, listless and bold, sumptuous and slovenly, didn't make the best of impressions. What's more, one of their cousins, who was only fifteen, was the scandal of the Casino for the admiration she displayed for Mademoiselle Léa, whose talent as an actress Monsieur Bloch senior valued highly, although her own tastes were thought not to extend to gentlemen.

On some days, we'd take tea in one of the neighbouring country inns. These are the farms known as Les Écorres, the Marie-Thérèse, the Croix-d'Heuland, the Bagatelle, the Californie, and the Marie-Antoinette. It was the last of these that the little band had adopted.

Sometimes, though, instead of going to an inn, we'd climb all the way to the top of the cliff and, once we got there and were sitting on the grass, we'd unwrap our packet of sandwiches and cakes. My friends preferred the sandwiches, and were surprised to see me eating only a chocolate cake with delicate Gothic icing, or an apricot tart. This was because the Cheshire cheese and lettuce sandwiches, a new and ignorant kind of food, had nothing to say for themselves. But the cakes were educated, the tarts talkative. The bland cream in the former and the fresh fruit in the latter knew a great deal about Combray and Gilberte, not only the Gilberte of Combray, but the Gilberte of Paris, whose tea parties had allowed me to become reacquainted with them. They reminded me of those cake plates decorated with images from the *Arabian Nights*,* their subjects providing my aunt Léonie with such entertainment when Françoise would bring her 'Aladdin and His Magic Lamp' on one day, or 'Ali Baba', 'The Sleeper Awakes', or 'Sinbad the Sailor Boarding Ship in Bassora with All His Riches' on another. I'd have liked very much to see them again, but my grandmother didn't know what had become of them, and in any case thought they were vulgar old plates bought in the country. No matter: in the greyness of Combray-en-Champagne,* they and their vignettes stood out in their many colours, like the stained-glass windows with their shifting jewel tones in a dark church, like the magic lantern projections in the twilight of my bedroom, like the buttercups from the Indies and the lilacs from Persia you see in front of the railway station and the little local line, like my great-aunt's collection of old china in her sombre dwelling, the home of an elderly lady in a little country town.

Stretched out on the cliff, I could see before me nothing but meadows, and, above them, not the seven heavens of Christian physics, but merely two superimposed: a darker one—the sea—and a paler one above. After our picnic, if I'd brought some little keepsake I thought one or another of my friends might like, joy would instantly turn their translucent faces red with such a vehement surge that their mouths were powerless to contain it, and they would burst out laughing. They were all gathered round me; and, between their faces, so close together, the air separating them traced azure paths, as if they'd been made by a gardener who had wanted to clear the way a little in order to be able to move more freely through a thicket of roses.

When we'd eaten all the food, we'd play games that earlier I would have found boring, sometimes ones as infantile as 'King of the Mountain' or 'Who Will Laugh First?', but which now I wouldn't have refused for all the world; the dawn of youth, with which the faces of these girls were still glowing, but which had already, at my age, faded from mine, illuminated everything before them, and, like the fluid painting of certain primitives, made the most insignificant details of their lives stand out against a background of gold. For most of them, the faces of these girls were confused with the hazy, reddish glow of dawn from which their actual features hadn't yet surfaced. Now all that could be seen was an enchanting colour; the profile that in a few years' time would emerge from beneath it was not yet discernible. There wasn't anything definitive about the present profile; it might have been nothing but a momentary resemblance to a long-lost family member to whom nature had granted this commemorative courtesy. It comes so quickly, the time when you have nothing left to look forward to, when your body is fixed in a state of immobility that promises no more surprises, when you lose all hope at the sight of faces that are still young framed by hair that's falling out or growing grey, like a tree in full summer with leaves that are already dead; it is so short, this radiant morning, that one comes to love only very young girls, the ones in whom the flesh, like a precious dough, is still rising. They are nothing but a pliable flow of matter, constantly moulded by whatever passing impression dominates them at the time. It's as if each of them is by turns a little statuette of cheerfulness, juvenile seriousness, tenderness, astonishment, each one shaped by an expression that is frank and open, but fleeting. This plasticity gives much variety and charm to the pretty little courtesies a girl shows us. Of course, these qualities are also indispensable in women, and in our eyes, any woman who does not like us, or who hides the fact that she does, takes on a tedious uniformity. But these same flirtatious ways, after a certain age, no longer bring any soft fluctuations to a face hardened by the struggles of existence, made forever combative or blissful. One face, through the constant pressure of obedience that subjects the wife to her husband, resembles a soldier's rather than a wife's; another face, sculpted by the sacrifices the mother has consented to make every day for her children, is the face of an apostle. Yet another, after years of obstacles and stormy setbacks, is the face of an old salt, of a woman whose clothes alone reveal her gender. It's true that the attentions a woman pays us can still, when we love her, fill with fresh delights the hours we spend beside her. But she is not a series of different women for us. Her cheerfulness remains external to her unchanging face. Adolescence, however, comes before complete solidification; and that's why, with teenage girls, we find so refreshing the spectacle of forms that are constantly changing, in a play of ever-shifting contrasts that is reminiscent of the perpetual recreation of the primordial elements of nature we contemplate when we look at the sea.

It wasn't only a society gathering, or an outing with Madame de Villeparisis, that I would have sacrificed for games of ring on a string* or charades with my friends. Several times, Robert de Saint-Loup had sent word to me that since I wasn't going to see him at Doncières, he had applied for twenty-four hours' leave and would spend it in Balbec. Every time he did so, I wrote to him to tell him to do no such thing, inventing the pretext that I was obliged to be away on precisely that day on a family visit it was my duty to make in the neighbourhood with my grandmother. No doubt he thought poorly of me when he learned from his aunt what exactly this 'family duty' consisted of, and which individuals were standing in for the role of grandmother. And yet I might not have been wrong to sacrifice the pleasures not only of society, but of friendship, to that of spending the day in this garden. The people who have the opportunity to live for themselves— it's true that they are artists, and I had long since been convinced I'd never be one—also have the duty to do so; friendship is a dereliction of this duty, an abdication of self. Even conversation, which is friendship's mode of expression, is a superficial digression that is ultimately unrewarding. We can spend all our lives conversing, without doing anything but repeating ad infinitum the emptiness of a minute, whereas the march of thought in the solitary work of artistic creation proceeds downwards, into profundity, in the only direction that is not closed to us, the only way in which we can progress (though, it's true, with more difficulty) towards an outcome of truth. Moreover, friendship is not just devoid of virtue, as conversation is; it is actually harmful. For the sense of boredom we can't help but feel in the presence of a friend—that is, the feeling of remaining on the surface of ourselves, instead of pursuing our voyage of discovery into the depths of ourselves—for those of us whose law of development is purely internal, friendship persuades us to correct this impression of boredom once we are alone, to look back with emotion on the words our friend has spoken to us, to regard them as a precious contribution, whereas we are not like buildings to which stones from outside can be added, but like trees, which draw from their own sap the burl that duly appears on their trunk, the upper layer of its foliage. I was lying to myself, I was stunting my growth in the very direction that could truly allow me to grow and be happy, when I congratulated myself on being loved and admired by a person as good, intelligent, and sought-after as Saint-Loup, when I applied my mind not to my own confused impressions, which should have been my duty to untangle, but to the words spoken by my friend, in which, when I repeated them to myself—when I forced them to be repeated by that being other than ourselves, who lives inside us, and on whom we are always so happy to shift our burden of thinking—I strove to find a beauty that was quite different from the beauty I silently pursued when I was truly alone, but one that would give more merit to Robert, to myself, to my life. In the life such a friend provided me, I appeared to myself as being safely preserved from solitude, with a noble desire to sacrifice myself for him—and thus, incapable of fully realizing myself. With these girls, however, even though the pleasure I enjoyed was selfish, at least it wasn't based on the lie that tries to make us believe we're not irremediably alone, and that, when we converse with someone else, prevents us from admitting that it's no longer we who are talking, but rather that we are modelling ourselves on the likeness of strangers and not on a self that differs from them. The words exchanged between the girls in the little band and myself were both uninteresting and rare, since they were broken up on my part by long silences. But that didn't prevent me from deriving, when I listened to them speaking to me, as much pleasure as I did when I looked at them, when I discovered in the voice of each of them a brightly coloured picture. I listened to their twittering with delight. Love helps us to discern, to differentiate. In the woods, a bird lover can immediately distinguish the warbling unique to each bird, which confuses the ordinary person. The lover of girls knows that human voices are even more varied. Each possesses more notes than the richest instrument. And the combinations in which she groups these tones are as inexhaustible as the infinite variety of personalities. Whenever I chatted with one of my friends, I'd notice that the original picture, unique in its individuality, was ingeniously drawn for me, tyrannically imposed as much by the inflections of her voice as by those of her face, and that these two displays were translating, each in its own way, the same singular reality. No doubt the lines of a voice, like those of a face, were not yet definitively fixed in place; the voice would break, just as the face would alter. Just as infants possess a gland whose secretion helps them digest milk, which adults have lost, there were, in the chirpings of these girls, notes that women don't have. And, on this more varied instrument, they played with their lips, with the application, the passion—qualities which are also the exclusive privilege of youth—of Bellini's little angel-musicians.* Later on, these girls would lose the accent of enthusiastic certainty that gave such charm to the simplest things, as when Albertine, in an authoritative tone, reeled off puns that the youngest listened to admiringly until an uncontrollable giggling fit seized them with the irresistible violence of a sneeze, or when Andrée began talking about their schoolwork, even more childish than their games, with an essentially juvenile seriousness; and their words changed notes, like those stanzas from ancient times when poetry, not yet very different from music, was chanted in varied tones. Despite all this, the voices of these girls already clearly indicated the attitude each of these young persons had towards life, a perspective that was so individual that it would be much too general to use phrases like 'She takes everything lightly' for one, or 'She's always laying down the law' for another, or, for a third, 'She lives in a constant state of cautious expectation'. The features of our face are little more than expressions that habit has fixed in place. Nature, like the catastrophe at Pompeii,* like the metamorphosis of a nymph, has frozen us in habitual gestures. Similarly, our intonations contain our philosophy of life, what we're always saying to ourselves about things. Of course, these traits did not belong just to the girls; they belonged to their parents as well. Individuals are steeped in something more general than themselves. By this token, parents hand down not just the habitual expressions of face and voice, but also certain ways of speaking, certain stock phrases, which are almost as unconscious and deeply rooted as intonation, and indicate an attitude towards life just as much as it does. It's true that for girls, some of these expressions are not given to them by their parents before a certain age, usually not before they've become women. They are kept in reserve. Thus, for example, if the conversation turned to some paintings by a friend of Elstir's, Andrée, whose waist-length hair was still worn loose, couldn't yet personally make use of the expression her mother and married sister favoured: 'Apparently the *man* is charming.' But that would come, along with permission to walk in the gardens of the Palais-Royal. And, ever since her First Communion, Albertine would say,

like a friend of her aunt's: 'I find that rather smashing.' Another gift
she'd received was the habit of having you repeat what you said, so
that she could appear to be interested and to be trying to form a personal opinion about the subject. If someone said a painter's work was
good, or his house nice, she'd say: 'Is that so, his work is good?' or 'Is
that so, he has a nice house?' Finally, even more general than family
legacy, there was the piquant addition imposed by the original province from which they drew their voices, and which even flavoured
their intonations. Whenever Andrée sharply plucked a low note, she
couldn't prevent the Périgourd string in her vocal instrument from
responding with a twanging sound, quite in harmony with the southern purity of her features; and to Rosemonde's constant childish
mannerisms, the matter of her northern face and voice replied, whatever her mood, with the accent of her province. In this play between
the province and temperament of whichever girl was dictating these
inflections, I perceived a charming dialogue. Dialogue, not discord.
Nothing could divide the girl from her native country. She is her
native land. This effect of local materials on the genius of the one who
uses them, and who is invigorated by them, does not make the result-
ing work any less individual; regardless of whether it's that of an
architect, a cabinetmaker, or a musician, it reflects no less minutely
the subtlest features of the artist's personality, because he has had to
work in the limestone of Senlis or the red sandstone of Strasbourg, or
has respected the knots inherent in the wood of ash, or in his score has
taken into account the resources and limitations, the potentialities
and sonorities, of the flute or the viola.

I was aware of all this, and yet we talked so little. Whereas with
Madame de Villeparisis or Saint-Loup I would have shown by my
words more pleasure than I felt since I was so weary from talking to
them, when I lay among the girls, the utter contentment I felt was
infinitely more powerful than the poverty and rarity of our remarks,
and flowed over my stillness and silence with waves of happiness that
lapped and subsided at the feet of these young roses.

For a convalescent who rests all day in a flower garden or orchard,
the fragrance of flowers and fruit impregnates the thousand trifles
that fill his idleness no more than the colour and aroma my eyes would
seek out in these girls, the sweetness of which would end up becoming
part of me, just as grapes are sweetened by the sun. And by their slow
continuity, these simple games had also wrought in me, as in those

who do nothing but repose as they lie by the sea breathing in the salt air and basking in the sun, a deep relaxation, a blissful smile, a vague dazzlement that overcame even my eyes.

From time to time, some attentive gesture from one or another of the girls would awaken in me profound vibrations that for a time lessened my desire for the others. Thus one day Albertine had said: 'Who has a pencil?' Andrée provided it while Rosemonde offered some paper. Albertine had said: 'Now then, little ones, I forbid you from looking at what I'm writing.' After carefully tracing each letter with the paper held firmly against her knees, she had handed it to me, saying: 'Be careful no one sees it.' I unfolded it and read: 'I like you.'

'But instead of writing all these silly things,' she exclaimed as she turned impetuously, with a serious look, towards Andrée and Rosemonde, 'I should show you the letter Gisèle wrote me this morning. How stupid of me, I've had it in my pocket all this while, and it could be so helpful to us!' Gisèle had thought of sending Albertine the essay she'd written for her final certificate examination,* so that she could share it with the others. Albertine's fears about the difficulty of the subjects that were assigned had been made even worse by the two topics from which Gisèle had to choose. One was: 'Sophocles* writes to Racine from the underworld to console him for the failure of *Athalie*'; the other, 'Imagine that after the first performance of Racine's *Esther*, Madame de Sévigné writes to Madame de La Fayette* to tell her how sorry she was that she couldn't have been with her'. Gisèle, out of an excess of zeal which must have touched the examiners, had chosen the first question, the more difficult of the two, and had discussed it in such a remarkable way that she'd been marked fourteen out of twenty and had been congratulated by the jury. She would have scored top marks if she hadn't 'made a mess of' her Spanish test. Albertine had immediately read the essay Gisèle had sent, since she had to pass the same exam herself, and so she was eager to have the advice of Andrée, who was by far the cleverest of them all and who could give her some good tips. 'How lucky she was!' Albertine said. 'This was just the thing her French teacher made her cram for while she was here!' Sophocles' letter to Racine, as written by Gisèle, began thus: 'My dear friend, forgive me for writing to you without having had the honour of meeting you personally, but doesn't your new tragedy, *Athalie*, show how thoroughly you've studied my modest works? You have put verses not only in the mouths of the protagonists, or the main characters in the play, but you have written some—delightful ones, even, if I may be allowed to say so without flattery—for the choruses, which didn't fare too badly, so they say, in Greek tragedy, but which in France are an absolute novelty. Moreover, your talent, so graceful, so polished, so charming, so fine, so discerning, has here acquired an energy for which I congratulate you. Athalie, Joad—those are characters whom your rival, Corneille, could not have delineated more perfectly. The personalities are forceful, the plot is simple and strong. Here is a tragedy in which love is not the driving force, and for this you have my sincerest compliments. The most famous precepts are not always the truest. As an example, let me quote these lines of Boileau:

> To portray passion with sensitive art
> Is the most certain way to reach the heart.*

You have shown that the religious sentiment that overflows from your choruses is no less capable of touching the heart. The masses may have been perplexed, but true connoisseurs recognize your real worth. I have felt compelled to send you my warmest congratulations, my dear colleague, as well as my heartfelt admiration.'

Albertine's eyes, as she read this to us, hadn't stopped sparkling. 'It's almost as if she'd copied it,' she exclaimed when she'd finished. 'I'd never have thought Gisèle was capable of coming up with an essay like that. And those lines she quotes—where on earth did she swipe those from?'

Albertine's admiration, despite having changed its centre of focus from Gisèle to Andrée, only grew, and, along with her ardent attention, kept making her eyes 'start out of her head' the whole time that Andrée, consulted as the oldest and most brilliant of them all, spoke about Gisèle's composition with a certain amount of irony at first, but then, with an offhand air that failed to conceal a genuine seriousness, revised the letter in her own way. 'It's not bad,' she said to Albertine, 'but if I were you and I'd been given the same subject, which could happen, since it's one they assign a lot, I wouldn't have done it like that. Here's how I'd go about it. First, if I'd been Gisèle, I wouldn't have let myself get carried away—I'd have started out by writing up an outline on a separate piece of paper. On the first line, I'd state the question and lay out the subject; then I'd list the general ideas to be worked into the discussion. Finally, assessment, style, conclusion.

That way, when you have a synopsis to help you along, you know where you're headed. You see, Titine, right from the setting out of the subject—or rather, since it's a letter, right from the introductory words—Gisèle botched it. Really, if he's writing to a man in the seventeenth century, Sophocles shouldn't write "My dear friend".'

'She should have had him say "My dear Racine" instead!' Albertine impetuously broke in. 'That would have been much better.'

'No, no,' Andrée replied in a slightly supercilious tone, 'she should have said just "Dear Sir". And at the end, she should have come up with something like: "Allow me, Sir" (or, at the very most, "dear Sir") "to assure you that I hold you in the highest esteem, and I have the honour to remain your humble servant" and so on. Also, Gisèle says that choruses are a new thing in *Athalie*. She's forgetting *Esther*, and two other tragedies that aren't very well known, but which the examiner himself has just written an analysis of this very year, so that all she had to do was mention them, since they're a hobby horse of his, and she'd pass with flying colours. They're called *Les Juives*, by Robert Garnier, and *Aman* by Antoine de Montchrestien.'* Andrée reeled off these two titles without managing to hide a sense of benevolent superiority, which showed through in her otherwise charming smile. Albertine couldn't contain herself any longer.

'You're *amazing*, Andrée!' she exclaimed. 'Be sure to write those two titles down for me. Just think how lucky I'd be if I got that subject, even just in the oral exam—I'd quote them right away and make such a splash!'

After that, however, whenever Albertine asked Andrée to repeat the titles of the two plays so she could note them down, her scholarly friend claimed to have forgotten them, and never in fact reminded her of them.

'And then,' Andrée went on in a tone of almost imperceptible disdain for her more childish schoolfellows, though obviously happy to be admired, and attaching more importance to the way in which she would have written her composition than she wanted to show, 'Sophocles in the underworld must be well informed. So he must know that it wasn't for the general public, but for the Sun King and a few of his privileged courtiers that *Athalie* was performed. What Gisèle says about the esteem of connoisseurs isn't bad at all, but it should be taken further. Since he's now immortal, Sophocles could very easily have the gift of prophecy, and could predict that Voltaire will say *Athalie* is "not just the masterpiece of Racine, but of the human mind".'*

Albertine was drinking in every word. Her eyes blazed. When Rosemonde suggested they play a game, she indignantly rejected her proposition.

'Finally,' Andrée said in the same detached, nonchalant, slightly mocking and quite passionately self-confident tone, 'if Gisèle had started out by calmly writing down the general ideas she was going to develop, she might have thought of what I myself would have done: show the difference there is between the religious inspiration of Sophocles' choruses and Racine's. I'd have made Sophocles say that even though Racine's choruses are just as full of religious feeling as the choruses in Greek tragedy, it's not for the same gods. The god of Joad has nothing to do with Sophocles' god. And that very naturally leads, after the end of the development, to the conclusion: "What does it matter that the beliefs are different?" Sophocles would make a point of insisting on that. He wouldn't want to offend Racine's convictions; and then he'd slip in a few words about Racine's masters at Port-Royal, so as to congratulate his disciple on the loftiness of his poetic spirit.'

Albertine had become so heated with admiration and attention that she was sweating profusely. Andrée, however, maintained the smiling composure of a female dandy.

'It wouldn't be a bad thing to quote the views of a few well-known critics,' she said, before we started playing again.

'Yes,' replied Albertine, 'that's what I've been told. Aren't the most respected ones Sainte-Beuve and Merlet?'*

'That wouldn't be entirely wrong,' replied Andrée (who still refused to write down the other two names, despite Albertine's pleas), 'Merlet and Sainte-Beuve aren't bad. But you should be sure to quote Deltour and Gasc-Desfossés especially.'*

In the meantime I'd been thinking of the little slip of paper torn from a notepad that Albertine had passed me: 'I like you', and an hour later, as we were walking down the paths that led, a little too steeply for my liking, back to Balbec, I was telling myself that it was with her that my great romance would be written.

The state characterized by all the signs by which we usually recognize the fact that we're in love, like the orders I gave at the hotel not to wake me for any visitor, unless it was one or another of these girls;

the palpitations I felt as I waited for them (regardless of which one was supposed to come); and my rage on those days if I hadn't been able to find a barber to shave me, and had to appear before Albertine, Rosemonde, or Andrée in an ugly form, no doubt this state, which arose anew every time I saw one of them, was as different from what we call 'love' as human life differs from the life of zoophytes, in which existence, or individuality (if it can be called that), is divided among different organisms. But natural history teaches us that such an organization of animal life can be observed, and that our own lives, provided we've lived a little while, prove just as much the reality of states which had hitherto been unsuspected by us, and which we must go through, even though it means growing out of them at a later stage: for me this was the loving state, simultaneously divided among several girls. Divided, or rather undivided: for most often what was delightful, different from the rest of the world, what began to become precious to me, to the point that the hope of finding it again the next day was the greatest joy of my life, was rather the entire group of these girls, taken in all those afternoons on the cliff, during those idle hours, on that strip of grass where these figures, so exciting to my imagination, of Albertine, Rosemonde, or Andrée, lay stretched out; and all this happened without my being able to say which girl made these sites so precious to me, which one I wanted most to love. In the beginning of a love affair, as at its end, we are not attached to the object of this love exclusively, but rather to the desire to love, which continues (leaving memories in its wake), and wanders voluptuously in a zone of interchangeable charms—charms that are sometimes simply of nature, or the table, or the places where we live—which harmonize with one another so well that it does not feel out of place in the presence of any one of them. Moreover, since, when I was with them, I was not dulled by habit, I was able to see them, that is to say, to feel profoundly surprised each time I found myself once again in their presence. No doubt some of this feeling of surprise stems from the fact that a person is constantly presenting us with a new side; but so great is the multiplicity of each individual, the richness of the lines of face and body, that they can rarely be retained once we are no longer with that person, and are left alone with the arbitrary simplicity of our memory. Since memory has chosen some particularity which has struck us, has isolated it and exaggerated it, making a woman who had appeared tall to us a sketch in which the length of her waist is enormous, or a woman who had seemed pink and blonde a pure *Harmony in Pink and Gold*, the moment this woman is with us again, all the other forgotten qualities which balanced that one assail us in their confused complexity, diminishing her height, drowning the pink, and substituting, for what we had come to look for exclusively, other particularities which we recall we'd noticed the first time, but which we can't understand how little we expected to see again. Our memory, our expectation, is of a peacock, but we find a peony. And this inevitable surprise is not the only one; for besides that, there is another, born out of difference, not between the stylized representations of memory and reality, but between the person we saw the last time, and the one that appears to us today from another angle, showing us a different aspect. The human face is truly like that of some god in Oriental theogony—a whole cluster of faces juxtaposed on different planes, which we can't see all at the same time.

For the most part, however, our surprise stems above all from the fact that the face a person presents to us is the same one. It would require such a great effort on our part to recreate everything that has been provided to us by what is not us—even if it's just the taste of a fruit—that no sooner have we received the impression than we begin imperceptibly to descend the slope of memory and, without realizing it, in a very short time, we are quite far from what we actually felt. So that each new glimpse is a kind of adjustment that brings us back to what we had truly seen. We've lost our recollection of this, since what we call 'remembering' a person is actually a process of forgetting him. But as long as we still know how to see, the instant the forgotten feature appears to us once again, we recognize it, we are obliged to rectify the line that had deviated; and in this way, the perpetual, fruitful surprise that made these daily meetings with the beautiful girls by the sea so salutary and relaxing for me was made up of reminiscence just as much as of discovery. If one adds to that the agitation aroused by what these girls were to me, which was never entirely what I had thought, and which made my expectation of the next meeting never align with my expectation, but rather with the memory, still vibrating, of the last conversation, one will understand how violently each outing wrenched my thoughts, and not at all in the direction that, in the solitude of my bedroom, I'd been able to outline for them. That direction was forgotten, wiped clean away, when I returned home, vibrating like a beehive with the remarks that had stirred me, and that continued to echo within me for a long time afterwards. Every person is destroyed when we stop seeing them; the person's next appearance is a new creation, different from the one that had immediately preceded it, if not from all previous appearances. For the minimum number of variations that can exist in these creations is two. When we remember a vivid gaze, a bold manner, it will inevitably be by an almost languid profile, a sort of dreamy tranquillity—things we had overlooked in our previous recollection—that we'll be surprised at our next encounter; or rather, they will be almost the only things we'll notice. In the clash between our memory and this new reality, it is this that will colour our disappointment or surprise, and will seem like a readjustment of reality by alerting us to the fact that we hadn't remembered it correctly. In its turn, the aspect of the face, overlooked the last time, and for that very reason the most striking one this time, the most real, the most correct, will become subject matter for reverie and memory. So it is a soft, languorous profile, a gentle, dreamy expression that we will long to see again. And then, the next time, the determined quality in that person's piercing eyes, in his sharp nose, in his tense lips, will correct the discrepancy between our desire and the object to which it had thought it corresponded. Of course, this fidelity to initial, purely physical impressions, rediscovered each time I was with the girls, didn't revolve around their facial features alone, since we've seen that I was also sensitive to their voices, which were perhaps even more disquieting (for not only does a voice offer the same singular and sensuous surfaces as a face, but it is also part of the inaccessible abyss that makes one reel with the thought of unattainable kisses)—voices that were like the unique sound of a little instrument, to which each girl gave herself wholly, and which belonged to her alone. A profound line in one of these voices, traced by a particular inflection, would surprise me when I recognized it again after having forgotten it. So much so that the amendments that at each fresh encounter I was obliged to make so as to ensure perfect accuracy were as much those of an instrument tuner or singing master as of a draughtsman.

The waves of feeling that these girls sent through me, neutralized for a time by the resistance each of them set against the expansion of the others, were held in a cohesive harmony which would be broken in Albertine's favour one afternoon when we were playing ring-on-a-string. This was in a little wood on the cliff. Positioned between two girls who were not part of the little band, whom Albertine had brought along because we wanted there to be more of us that day, I was looking enviously at Albertine's neighbour, a young man, and telling myself that if I'd been in his place I could have touched my friend's hands during those unhoped-for minutes that might never come again, and that such an opportunity could have taken me quite far. Just by itself, and even without the consequences it would probably have led to, the mere touch of Albertine's hands would have been a delight to me. Not that I'd never seen hands more beautiful than hers. Even just within her group of friends, Andrée's hands, slender and much more delicate, had a kind of special life of their own, obedient to the girl's command, but independent, and often they lay stretched out before her like noble greyhounds, indolent, dreamy, or with one finger suddenly flexed; Elstir had made several studies of them for this reason. In one of them, which depicted Andrée warming them before the hearth, they had, in the firelight, the golden translucency of two autumn leaves. But, though plumper, Albertine's hands, when grasped, yielded one instant, then resisted the pressure the next, producing a sensation that was quite unique. The pressure of Albertine's hand had a sensual softness that seemed in harmony with the pink, slightly mauve colouring of her skin. This pressure seemed to make you penetrate the girl's being and plumb the depths of her senses, like the resonance of her voice, indecent as the cooing of a dove or certain cries can be. She was one of those women with whom shaking hands was such a great pleasure that one was grateful to civilization for having made a handshake a permissible act between boys and girls meeting for the first time. If the arbitrary customs of politeness had replaced the handshake with some other gesture, I would have looked every day at Albertine's intangible hands, as curious to experience their touch as I would have been eager to get to know the savour of her cheeks. If I'd been next to her in the game of ring-on-a-string, my delight at holding her hands in mine for a long time wouldn't be the only pleasure I'd contemplate; what avowals, what declarations, silenced until now by shyness, I could have made by pressing her hands in certain ways; for her part, how easy it would have been, by responding with other pressings, to show me she welcomed them; what complicity, what a gateway to voluptuous delights! My love could make more progress in a few minutes spent thus next to her than it had since I'd met her. Sensing that these minutes were short-lived and would soon come to an end, since we couldn't go on playing this little game indefinitely, and since, once it was over, it would be too late, I didn't stay in my place. I contrived to let myself be handed the ring, and, once I was in the middle of the circle, as it was passed from hand to hand, I pretended not to see where it was going but followed it with my eyes, waiting for the moment when it reached the hands of the young man next to Albertine, who was laughing with all her might and, in the joy and excitement of the game, had turned quite pink. 'We really are in the pretty wood!' Andrée said to me, indicating the trees surrounding us with a smile in her gaze that was for me alone and seemed to pass over the other players, as if we two were the only ones intelligent enough to step outside ourselves and make a poetic remark about the game. She even had the wit to sing, as if as an after-thought: 'It passed by here, the ferret of the Wood, my ladies, it passed by here, the ferret of the pretty Wood',* like those people who can't go to Trianon without throwing a Louis XVI fancy-dress ball there, or who find it exciting to have an aria sung in the context for which it was composed. I would have been saddened that I didn't find this realization of Andrée's charming, if I'd had the time to think about it. But my mind was elsewhere. All the players were beginning to be surprised by my stupidity at not finding the ring. I was looking at Albertine, so beautiful, so carefree, so happy, who, without realizing it, would soon become my neighbour, when I finally managed to catch the ring when it was in the right hands, thanks to a ploy she didn't suspect, and which would have irritated her had she known. In the feverish heat of the game, Albertine's long hair had become partly undone, and, in curly ringlets, fell on to her cheeks, whose carnation pink they brought out even more with their plain brownness. 'Your hair is like Laura Dianti's or Eleanor of Aquitaine's, or her descend-ant, whom Chateaubriand loved so.* You should always wear your hair down a little,' I whispered in her ear, so as to get closer to her. All of a sudden the ring was passed to Albertine's neighbour. I pounced immediately, wrenched open his hands, and seized the ring, and he was obliged to take my place in the middle of the circle while I took his next to Albertine. Just a few minutes before, I'd been envying this young man when I saw that his hands, gliding over the string, might at any moment meet Albertine's. Now that my turn had come, too shy to seek out this touch and too excited to enjoy it, I could feel nothing but the quick and painful beating of my heart. At one point, Albertine bent her full, rosy face towards me with a conspiratorial look, pretending to have the ring in order to trick the ferret and keep him from looking over to where the ring was actually being passed. I understood immediately that this ruse was the purpose of Albertine's suggestive glances, but I was thrilled to see in her eyes, even though simulated for the purpose of the game, the image of a secret understanding, which hadn't existed between us before, but which from that moment seemed possible to me, and would have been heavenly. Just as I was feeling overjoyed by this thought, I felt a light pressure of Albertine's hand against mine, and her caressing finger slipped under mine; at the same time, I saw her give me a wink, which she tried to make imperceptible. Suddenly a mass of hopes, invisible to myself until then, crystallized: 'She's taking advantage of the game to let me know she likes me,' I thought; but I immediately fell from this pinnacle of joy when I heard Albertine say to me furiously: 'Come on, *take* it! I've been trying to pass it to you for an hour now.' Mortified, I let go of the string, the ferret saw the ring and swooped down on it; I had to go back to the middle of the circle, despairing, watching the frenzied game continuing around me, taunted by the jeers of all the players, forced, in reply, to laugh when I was so little inclined to do so, while Albertine kept saying: 'You shouldn't play if you can't pay attention and if you want to spoil everything for the rest of us. We won't invite him anymore on the days when we play, Andrée, or else I won't come.' Andrée, not caring about the game, chanting her 'pretty wood' song which Rosemonde had half-heartedly taken up in imitation, tried to make up for Albertine's reproaches by saying: 'We're very close to Les Creuniers, which you've wanted to see so much. Come with me, I'll take you there, along a pretty little lane, while these silly girls carry on acting like eight-year-olds.' Since Andrée was always so nice to me, on the way I said everything I could think of about Albertine that might make her love me. Andrée replied that she too liked her very much, and found her charming, but all the complimentary things I said about her friend didn't seem to please her very much. All of a sudden, in the little lane, I stopped short, my heart stirred deeply by a sweet childhood memory: I had just recognized, from the serrated, shiny leaves jutting out over the edge, a hawthorn bush that had, alas, been bare of flowers since the end of spring. Around me there floated an atmosphere of old months of Mary,* of Sunday afternoons, of beliefs and mistakes long forgotten. I wished

I could seize this moment. I paused for a second and Andrée, with her wonderful gift of intuition, let me converse for a moment with the leaves of the bush. I asked them for news of their flowers, those hawthorn flowers so like carefree, playful, pious girls. 'Those young ladies are long gone,' the leaves said to me. Perhaps they thought that for someone who claimed to be a close friend of theirs, I was singularly ill-informed about their habits. I *was* a close friend, but one who hadn't seen them again in many years, despite his promises. And yet, just as Gilberte had been my first love among girls, they had been my first love among flowers. 'Yes, I know, they go away about the middle of June,' I replied, 'but it makes me happy to see this place where they lived. They came to see me in my bedroom in Combray, brought by my mother when I was ill. And we'd meet again in church on Saturday evenings during the month of Mary. Are they allowed to come here too?' 'Of course! What's more, those ladies are very much in demand at the church of Saint-Denis-du-Désert, in the nearest parish.' 'Now, do you mean? I could see them there?' 'Oh no, not before next May.' 'But can I be sure they'll be there?' 'Regularly, every year.' 'I'm just not sure I'll be able to find this spot again, though.' 'Of course you will! My ladies are so cheerful, they only stop laughing to sing hymns—you can't possibly lose your way, you'll recognize their perfume from the top of the lane.'

I rejoined Andrée and carried on singing Albertine's praises. It seemed to me impossible that she wouldn't repeat what I said to her friend, given the insistence with which I spoke. And yet I never learned whether Albertine had been told. Andrée, however, was far more intuitive about things of the heart, more refined in her kindness; to find the look, or word, or action, that was most apt to please, to keep to herself a thought that might be hurtful, to sacrifice (while pretending it was not a sacrifice) an hour of playtime, or even an outing to a matinee or a garden party, in order to stay with a friend who was sad, and thus to show him or her that she preferred their simple company to frivolous pleasures: these kind attentions were habitual with her. But when you came to know her a little better, she reminded you of those heroic cowards who, because they don't want to be afraid, show exceptional bravery; it was as if deep within her, there was none of that kindness she showed at all times out of moral refinement, sensitivity, and a noble desire to seem to be a good friend. To hear her say to me all the charming things about the possibility of a growing affection between Albertine and myself, it seemed that she must have been doing everything in her power to bring it about. But, perhaps by chance, she never made use of any of the tiny things she had at her disposal to bring us together, and I couldn't swear that my effort to make Albertine love me, though it might not have spurred Andrée on to secret schemes to thwart it, at least provoked in her feelings of anger which she was careful to conceal, and which, out of certain moral scruples, she might have resisted. Of the thousand subtle touches of kindness Andrée showed, Albertine would have been incapable; and yet I was not as certain of the profound kindness of Andrée as I was later on of Albertine's. Always gently indulgent towards Albertine's exuberant frivolity, Andrée had words and smiles for her that were those of a friend; even more importantly, she behaved like one. I saw her, day after day, in order to share her wealth and make her poor friend happy, without any concern for herself, go to more trouble than a courtier seeking to win the favour of a king. She would be full of charming and sympathetic words of commiseration whenever anyone deplored Albertine's poverty, and would put herself out much more for her than she would have done for a wealthy friend. If anyone ventured to say that Albertine might not have been as poor as she was made out to be, a faint cloud would veil Andrée's eyes and brow and she would appear upset. And if anyone went so far as to say that, after all, Albertine's marriage prospects might not be quite as bad as was imagined, Andrée would vehemently contradict them and would repeat, almost angrily: 'I hate to say it, but that's not true! I know all about it, and it makes me so sad!' Even in matters concerning myself, she was the only one of the little band who would never have repeated some unpleasant remark that might have been made about me; even more importantly, if I myself was the one repeating it to her, she'd pretend not to believe it, or would give some explanation that made the remark inoffensive; all these qualities, taken together, are what we call tact. It is this sort of tact that causes someone, if we fight a duel, to congratulate us and to add that there was no need for us to accept the challenge, in order to make us feel even braver for having fought without being compelled to do so. This sort of person is the opposite of those people who say, in the same circumstance: 'It must have been so annoying for you to fight the duel, but you couldn't do otherwise; you couldn't just swallow an insult like that.' But since there are always two sides to everything, if our friends' pleasure, or at least indifference, in telling us something offensive that has been said about us, proves that they have no concern at all for our own feelings as they're talking, and that they're sticking pins and knives into us as if we were a stuffed doll, the art of always hiding from us the unpleasant things they've heard about our actions, or about the opinion they themselves may have formed about those actions, might be proof in that other category of friends, in those friends full of tact, of a strong dose of dissimulation. There is nothing harmful in that if, in fact, such people are incapable of evil thoughts, or if the evil they say makes them suffer just as much as it might make us suffer. I thought that such was the case for Andrée, but couldn't be absolutely sure.

By now we had emerged from the little wood and had followed a maze of little-used paths through which Andrée found her way quite easily. 'Look,' she said all of a sudden, 'here are your famous Les Creuniers!—and you're in luck, it's just the right time of day for the light to be the same as when Elstir painted them.' But I was still too sad at having fallen from such an acme of hope during the game of ring-on-a-string. And so it wasn't with the pleasure that I would otherwise have felt that I saw, suddenly laid out at my feet, crouching among the rocks where they were protecting themselves from the heat of the sun, those sea goddesses that Elstir had searched for and surprised, under a dark glaze as beautiful as one Leonardo might have used,* those wonderful Shadows, sheltered and furtive, agile and silent, ready at the first glimmer of light to slip under the rock and hide themselves in a hollow, and prompt, once the threat of sunlight had passed, to return to rock or seaweed, beneath the cliff-crumbling sun, by the bleached Ocean over whose drowsy slumber they seemed to be keeping watch, motionless, insubstantial guardians, showing just above its surface their clinging bodies and the watchful gaze of their dark eyes.

We went back to rejoin the other girls so we could make our way home together. I knew now that I loved Albertine; but, alas, I didn't think to let her know it. The fact is that, ever since the time when I played at the Champs-Élysées, my notion of love had become different, even though the people to whom my love was successively linked remained almost the same. On one hand, the avowal, the declaration of my affection to the one I loved no longer seemed one of the crucial, necessary scenes of love; and on the other, love itself no longer seemed to be an external reality, but only a subjective pleasure. And I thought that Albertine would do even more to keep this pleasure alive if she didn't know I thought it.

All the way home, the image of Albertine, bathed in the light that emanated from the other girls, was not the only one that existed for me. But, like the moon, which is nothing but a little white cloud more well-defined and fixed in place than the others during the day, takes on all its power as soon as the light has faded, so it was that when I was back at the hotel, it was the image of Albertine alone that rose from my heart and began shining. My room seemed suddenly new. Of course, it had long ago ceased to be the hostile room of my first night. We are constantly changing the space in which we live; and, as habit exempts us from feeling, we stop noticing the noxious elements of colour, dimension, and odour that had objectified our discomfort. By now, it was no longer even the room that had power over my sensibility, whether to make me suffer or give me joy, a reservoir of sunny days, like a swimming pool dappled halfway up with light-drenched azure, darkened for a moment by the fleeting reflection of a sail, impalpable and white as a shimmer of heat; nor was it the purely aesthetic bedroom of the evening vistas; it was merely the room where I had lived for so many days that I had stopped seeing it. But now I was starting to open my eyes to it again, this time from the selfish point of view of love. I mused that the beautiful slanting mirror and the elegant glass-fronted bookcases would give Albertine a high opinion of me if she came to visit. Instead of a place of transition where I spent a moment before hurrying to the beach or to Rivebelle, my room was once again becoming real and dear to me, was renewed, for I was looking at and appreciating each piece of furniture in it with the eyes of Albertine.

A few days after the game of ring-on-a-string, we'd let ourselves wander so far that we were very glad to find in Maineville a pair of little 'governess carts' with two seats each, which would enable us to get back in time for dinner; the intensity of my love for Albertine, which was already great, had the result that it was first Rosemonde and then Andrée that I asked to sit with me, never Albertine; and then, despite my seeming preference for Andrée or Rosemonde, I persuaded everyone, by means of secondary considerations such as the time, the path, and the cloaks they wore, to decide, as if against my will, that the most practical thing would be for Albertine to ride with me, while I pretended to resign myself half-heartedly to her company.

Unfortunately, as love aims at the complete assimilation of the other, since no one is actually edible through conversation alone, despite Albertine's being as friendly as possible on our way back, after I'd dropped her off at her door, I was left happy, but even more famished for her than I'd been at the start, counting the moments we'd just spent together as merely a prelude, without any great importance in itself, to those that would follow. It did have, however, that initial charm, which can never be regained. I had as yet asked nothing of Albertine. She might have imagined what I desired, but, not knowing for certain, she might suppose that I preferred having relationships with no specific goal in mind, in which my friend was bound to find that delicious vagueness, rich in expected surprises, which is what constitutes romance.

During the week that followed, I didn't try to see Albertine at all. I pretended to prefer Andrée. When love begins, we'd like to go on being, for our beloved, the stranger she can love, but we need her; we need to touch not so much her body as her attention, her heart. We slip a nasty remark into a letter which will force the apathetic recipient to ask for some kind gesture, and love, following an infallible procedure, engages the gears which set in motion the alternating movement in which we can neither love nor be loved. To Andrée I gave the hours when the others would be going to some matinee or other which I knew Andrée would gladly sacrifice for me, and which she would have sacrificed even with annoyance, out of a sense of moral superiority, so as not to give either the others or herself the idea that she attached any importance to even relatively fashionable things. In this way I arranged to have every evening wholly to myself, with the idea not of making Albertine jealous, but of increasing my prestige in her eyes, or at least not losing it by letting Albertine know it was her I loved and not Andrée. I didn't mention my love for Albertine to Andrée either, lest she repeat it to her friend. When I spoke about Albertine with Andrée, I affected a reserve which perhaps deceived her less than her apparent credulity deceived me. She pretended to believe in my indifference towards Albertine, and also to desire the most complete union possible between Albertine and myself. It is likely, however, that she believed in the former no more than she desired the latter. As I was telling her about how little I cared for her friend, I was thinking of one thing only: to try to meet Madame Bontemps, who was staying near Balbec for a few days, and in whose house Albertine was about to spend three days. Naturally, I didn't give Andrée any hint of this desire, and when I spoke to her about Albertine's family, it was in the most casual way. Andrée's straightforward replies seemed not to question my sincerity. Why, then, did she let slip on one of those days: 'I've *actually* just come from seeing Albertine's aunt'? Of course, she hadn't said: 'I could see through your words, which seemed so offhand, but implied that all you can think about is how you can get introduced to Albertine's aunt.' Yet it was the presence, in Andrée's mind, of such an idea, which she deemed more polite to hide from me, which the word 'actually' seemed to imply. The word was of a kind with certain glances, certain gestures, which, although they don't have any logical, rational form spelled out plainly for the mind of the one listening, still reach him with their actual meaning, just as human speech, changed into electricity on the telephone, turns back into speech that can be heard. In order to erase from Andrée's mind the idea that I was interested in Madame Bontemps, I spoke about the lady not merely absent-mindedly, but spitefully; I said I'd met that idiotic woman before, and that I very much hoped the event wouldn't be repeated. Whereas I was seeking any way possible to meet her.

I tried to persuade Elstir (without telling anyone I was doing so) to mention me to Madame Bontemps so we could meet. He promised an introduction, surprised though he was that I wished it, for he thought her a contemptible, scheming woman, as uninteresting as she was self-interested. Reflecting that if I saw Madame Bontemps, Andrée would hear about it sooner or later, I thought it best to tell her in advance. 'The things we try most to avoid are the very ones we can't manage to escape,' I said to her. 'Nothing in the world could bore me as much as meeting Madame Bontemps, and yet I can't get out of it, Elstir has organized a gathering.'

'I never doubted it for a second,' Andrée exclaimed in a bitter tone, as her eyes, enlarged and altered by annoyance, focused on some invisible object. Her words weren't the most accurately conveyed expression of what she thought, which can be summarized thus: 'I know very well that you love Albertine, and that you're moving heaven and earth to get closer to her family.' But these words were the shapeless but reconstructable debris of this thought that I had caused to explode, despite Andrée's best efforts to appear indifferent. Like her 'actually', these words had no literal meaning; that is, it's these sorts of expressions (not direct assertions) that inspire our respect for or mistrust of someone, or cause us to quarrel.

Since Andrée hadn't believed me when I told her I didn't care about Albertine's family, it meant that she thought I loved Albertine. And she probably wasn't happy about it.

She was usually the third party when Albertine and I were together. There were days, however, when I would see Albertine alone, days I awaited feverishly, but which passed without bringing me any decisive result, without having been that supreme day I expected; and so I would assign its role to the day that followed, which didn't live up to it either; and in this way the days went on collapsing, one after the other, like waves whose crests fall and are immediately replaced with others.

About a month after the day when we played ring-on-a-string, I heard that Albertine was about to leave the next morning to spend a few days with Madame Bontemps, and that, having to take an early train, she'd spend the night at the Grand-Hôtel, from which she would be able to take the bus to the station and catch the first train without disturbing the friends with whom she was staying. I mentioned this to Andrée. 'I don't think so at all,' she replied with an air of discontent. 'In any case it wouldn't be of any use to you, since I'm quite sure that Albertine won't want to see you, if she's coming to the hotel alone. It wouldn't be proper protocol,' she added, using an epithet she had recently come to like, in the sense of 'it's not the done thing'. 'I'm telling you this because I know how Albertine thinks. As for myself, I couldn't care less if you saw her or not. It's all the same to me.'

We were joined by Octave, who wasn't the least bit reluctant to tell Andrée how many strokes he'd gone round in at golf the day before, and later by Albertine, who, as she walked, was handling her diabolo like a nun with her rosary. Thanks to this game, she could be by herself for hours without ever getting bored. As soon as she joined us, the impish tip of her nose was apparent to me; I had omitted it whenever I thought of her during the last few days; beneath her dark hair, the verticality of her forehead contrasted—not for the first time—with the vague image of it that lingered in my mind, while my eyes were struck by its pallor; emerging from the dust of memory, Albertine was taking shape again in front of me. Golf makes one develop a taste for solitary pleasures. The pleasure provided by the diabolo is undoubtedly one of those. Yet after she had joined us, Albertine continued to play with it, chatting with us all the while, the way a lady being paid a visit by some friends doesn't stop crocheting. 'I hear', she said to Octave, 'that Madame de Villeparisis has lodged a complaint with your father.' Behind the word 'complaint' I heard one of those tones that were unique to Albertine; whenever I noticed that I'd forgotten them, I would simultaneously remember having already perceived behind them the determined French face of Albertine. Even if I'd been blind, I would have recognized some of her lively, slightly provincial qualities in those notes as clearly as I did from the tip of her nose. The two—her nose and the tone of her voice—were equivalent and interchangeable, and her voice was like the one we are told will be produced by the photo-telephone of the future: the sound of it gave a vivid image of her. 'And she hasn't written just to your father—she's written to the mayor of Balbec to get diabolos banned from the esplanade, since she got hit in the face by a ball.'

'Yes, I heard about that complaint. It's ridiculous. It's not as if there's much to do here for entertainment.'

Andrée didn't get involved in the conversation, since she didn't know Madame de Villeparisis (any more than Albertine or Octave did, for that matter). She did, however, say: 'I don't know why the lady made such a song and dance about it. Madame de Cambremer got hit too and she didn't complain.'

'I will explain the difference,' Octave replied in a serious tone as he lit a match. 'In my opinion, Madame de Cambremer is a real society lady, and Madame de Villeparisis is just an upstart. Are you coming to play golf this afternoon?' And he went off, accompanied by Andrée. I remained alone with Albertine. 'Look,' she said, 'I'm doing my hair the way you like it now—see my ringlet? Everyone's making fun of it, and no one knows who I'm doing it for. My aunt's going to laugh at me too. I won't tell her either.' I saw Albertine's cheeks from the side; though they often looked pale, seen this way, they were flushed with bright blood, which lit them from within, giving them the brilliance that certain winter mornings have when the rocks, partially illumined by the sun, look like pink granite, and fill us with joy. The joy I felt at this moment as I looked at Albertine's cheeks was just as keen, but led to another desire, not for a walk, but for a kiss. I asked her if what everyone was saying about her plans were true. 'Yes,' she said. 'I'm spending tonight at your hotel, and since I have a little bit of a cold,

I'm even going to go to bed before dinner. So you can come and sit by my bed while I'm having my dinner, and afterwards we can play at whatever you like. I'd have liked for you to come to the station tomorrow morning, but I'm afraid it might seem odd, not to Andrée, who's intelligent, but to the other girls who will be there; that could cause trouble if it got back to my aunt; but we can spend this evening together. My aunt won't know anything about *that*. I'm just going to say goodbye to Andrée, so I'll see you soon. Come early, so we can spend a nice long time together,' she added, smiling. At these words, I went further back in my mind than to the time when I loved Gilberte, to the days when my love seemed like an entity in itself, not just external to myself, but something that could become real. While the Gilberte I saw at the Champs-Élysées was a different Gilberte from the one I found in myself as soon as I was alone, suddenly in this real Albertine, the one I saw every day, whom I had thought full of bourgeois prejudices and so frank with her aunt, the imaginary Albertine had just become incarnate, the one who, when I didn't yet know her, I had thought was furtively watching me on the esplanade, the one who had seemed to be so reluctant to go home as she saw me walking away.

When I went in to dinner with my grandmother, I felt within me a secret she didn't know. Similarly, for Albertine, tomorrow her friends would be with her, but they wouldn't know this new thing there was between us; and when Madame Bontemps kissed her niece on the esplanade, she wouldn't know that I was between them, in this arrangement of hair which had the goal, hidden from everyone, of pleasing me, *me*, the person who, until then, had so envied Madame Bontemps because she was related to the same people as her niece, had to wear mourning at the same time she did, and had the same family visits to make; now I found I meant to Albertine more than her aunt herself. While she was with her aunt, it was about me that she'd be thinking. I didn't have a clear idea of what would presently happen between us. In any case, the Grand-Hôtel and the evening to come no longer seemed empty to me; they contained my happiness. I rang for the lift to go up to the room Albertine had taken, on the valley side. The least important movements, like sitting down on the bench in the lift, were full of sweetness, because they were in direct relation to my heart; I saw in the ropes that lifted the machine upward, in the few steps still to be climbed, only the materialized workings and stages of my joy. I just had two or three more steps to take in the corridor before

I reached the room in which the precious substance of that pink body was enclosed—that room which, even if delightful actions would soon take place there, would keep that permanence, that air, to an uninformed passer-by, of being just like all the other rooms, which make things into the stubbornly silent witnesses, the scrupulous confidants, the inviolable depositaries of our pleasure. These few steps from the landing to Albertine's room, these few steps that no one could now stop, I made with delight and care, as if I were immersed in some new element, as if, as I advanced, it was happiness itself that was slowly being stirred, and at the same time I had an unfamiliar feeling of omnipotence, of finally coming into an inheritance that had always belonged to me. Then I suddenly thought that I'd been wrong to harbour any doubts; she had told me to come when she was in bed. It was perfectly clear; I could barely contain my joy; I almost knocked over Françoise, who was in my way; I ran, eyes sparkling, to my friend's room. I found Albertine in bed. Leaving her throat bare, her white nightgown changed the proportions of her face, which, flushed from the bed, or her cold, or the dinner, seemed even pinker; I thought of the colours that had been near me just a few hours before, on the esplanade, which were now going to reveal their taste; her cheek was crossed from top to bottom by one of her long, curly, dark tresses, which, to please me, she had completely undone. She smiled at me. Alongside her, through the window, the valley was illumined by moonlight. The sight of Albertine's bare throat, of those excessively pink cheeks, threw me into such a state of intoxication—that is, shifted the reality of the world from nature to the torrent of sensations that I could scarcely contain—that this sight upset the balance between the immense, indestructible life that was roiling within me and the life of the universe, so meagre in comparison. The sea, which through the window I could see next to the valley, the swelling breasts of the first cliffs of Maineville, the sky where the moon hadn't yet reached its zenith—all of this seemed lighter to bear than feathers for the pupils in my eyes, which I could feel were dilating between my lids, strong, ready to hold many other burdens, all the mountains in the world, on their delicate surface. The whole horizon could no longer completely fill their orbits. And any life that nature could bring me would have seemed very meagre, the gusts from the sea very slight, compared to the immense yearning heaving in my chest. I leaned over to kiss Albertine. Even if death were to strike me down at that instant, it would have seemed a matter of no importance, or rather an impossibility, for life was not outside myself, it was inside me; I'd have smiled with pity if a philosopher had expressed the idea that one day, even far in the future, I would have to die, that the eternal forces of nature would survive me, those forces of nature beneath whose divine footsteps I was nothing but a grain of dust; that after me there would still be those round, swelling cliffs, this sea, this moonlight, this sky! How could that have been possible, how could the world last longer than me, since I was not lost in it, since it was the world itself that was enclosed in me, in *me* whom it was very far from filling, in me, where, feeling I had room to heap up so many other treasures there, I scornfully threw into a corner sky, sea, and cliffs. 'Stop it or I'll ring the bell!' Albertine cried, seeing me flinging myself on to her to kiss her. But I told myself that it wasn't for nothing that a girl sends for a young man secretly, making sure her aunt doesn't know, and that fortune favours the bold souls who know how to take advantage of such opportunities; in my state of exaltation, Albertine's round face, lit from a fire within as if by a lantern, appeared in such stark relief, imitating the rotation of a fiery sphere, that it seemed to me to be spinning, like those figures by Michelangelo being carried away by a motionless, vertiginous whirlwind.* I would soon know the fragrance, the taste, that this unknown pink fruit contained. I heard a sudden noise, shrill and prolonged. Albertine had pulled the bell with all her might.

I had thought that the love I had for Albertine was not based on any hope of physical possession. However, when it seemed obvious after that evening's experience that such possession was impossible; and when, after having never doubted for an instant, on that very first day on the beach, that Albertine was of easy virtue, and after going through various other later assumptions about her, it now seemed well established that she was thoroughly chaste; and when, upon returning from her aunt's a week later, she said to me coldly: 'I forgive you—I'm even sorry I hurt you—but make sure you never do that again', unlike what occurred after Bloch told me that one could have all the women one liked, and as if, instead of a real girl, it was a wax doll I'd known all this time, gradually, my desire to penetrate her life, to follow her into the places where she'd spent her childhood, to be initiated by her into the athletic life, became detached from her; my intellectual curiosity about what she thought about some subject or other didn't survive my conviction that I could kiss her. My dreams abandoned her as soon as they stopped being nourished by the hope of possessing her, of which I'd supposed them to be independent. From then on they were once again free to be transferred to one or another of Albertine's friends, depending on how alluring I found her on a particular day, but mostly on the likelihood of being loved by her; and it was Andrée I turned to first. If Albertine hadn't existed, though, I might not have felt the pleasure I began to find more and more in the kindness Andrée showed me over the days that followed. Albertine told no one about my failed attempt to kiss her. Albertine was one of those pretty girls who, from their earliest childhood, for their beauty, but above all for some sort of appeal, some charm, which remain wreathed in mystery, and which might spring from reserves of vitality to which those less favoured by nature come to quench their thirst, always, in their family, among their friends, in the world, have been better liked than girls who were more beautiful or more wealthy; she was one of those from whom, before the age of love is reached and even more so after its arrival, more is asked than they ask of themselves, and even more than they can give. Ever since her childhood, Albertine had had a circle of four or five admiring little playmates, among them Andrée, who was so superior to her, and who knew it (and perhaps this attraction that Albertine exercised, quite unwittingly, had been the origin of the little band, and its founding principle). This attraction reached a long way, even into circles that were, relatively speaking, more distinguished, where, if a pavane was to be danced, it was Albertine, rather than a girl of higher birth, who was asked. The consequence of this was that, having not a penny in her dowry, living, quite meagrely, in the care of Monsieur Bontemps, who was said to be corrupt, and who would rather have been rid of her, Albertine was nevertheless invited not only to dine, but to stay, with people who, in the eyes of Saint-Loup, might have been completely without distinction, but who, for the mothers of Rosemonde or Andrée—women who were quite wealthy but who didn't know such people—represented something immense. And so Albertine would spend a few weeks every year staying with the family of a governor of the Bank of France, who was also chairman of the board of directors of one of the principal railway companies. This financier's wife entertained important people but had never mentioned her 'day' to Andrée's mother, who thought this lady impolite, but was nevertheless extremely interested in everything that went on at her house. And so every year, she would urge Andrée to invite Albertine to their villa, because, she said, it was a good deed to offer a seaside stay to a girl who didn't herself have the means to travel, and whose aunt scarcely cared about her; Andrée's mother probably wasn't motivated by a hope that the governor of the Bank of France and his wife, upon learning that Albertine had been treated so kindly by her and her daughter, might form a high opinion of them both; still less did she hope that Albertine, although so good and clever, would be able to get an invitation for them both, or at least for Andrée, to the financier's garden parties. But every evening at dinner, while she assumed a look of cool indifference, she was delighted to hear Albertine tell her all about what had happened at the château during her stay and about the people who had been invited, most of whom she knew by sight or by name. The thought that she knew them only in this way, that is to say didn't know them at all (she called this knowing them 'forever'), gave Andrée's mother a tinge of melancholy as she asked Albertine questions about them with a haughty, casual air, as if she couldn't care less, and it could have planted a seed of uncertainty and anxiety in her mind about the importance of her own position in society if she didn't reassure herself and resume her place in 'real life' by saying to the butler: 'Tell the chef his peas aren't soft enough.' In this way she would recover her serenity. And she had made up her mind that Andrée would marry only a man from an excellent family, naturally, but also wealthy enough for her to have a chef and two coachmen. This was just an obvious fact, it was the simple truth that went with having a position. But the fact that Albertine had dined at the bank governor's château with some lady or other, and that one of these ladies had even invited her over for the following winter, made Andrée's mother view her with a special regard which went very well with the pity and even contempt aroused by her lack of wealth, a contempt increased by the fact that Monsieur Bontemps had proved to be a traitor to his cause and had gone over to the side of the government—there had even been talk of his being somehow involved in the Panama Affair.* This did not, however, prevent Andrée's mother, out of her love of truth, from directing her withering scorn at anyone who seemed to believe that Albertine was of low birth. 'Really, they're one of the best families there are—they're Simonets—with one *n*!' It is true that, given the fashionable circles in which all this was taking place, in which money plays such a large role and social standing wins invitations but not marriage proposals, it seemed there could be no useful outcome in the form of an 'acceptable' marriage, since the high regard she enjoyed did not compensate for her poverty. But even taken by themselves, bringing as they did no hope of a matrimonial consequence, these 'conquests' aroused the envy of certain spiteful mothers, furious at seeing Albertine being received like a member of the family by the bank governor's wife, even by Andrée's mother, whom they scarcely knew. Thus they said to friends shared by them and by those two ladies that the latter would be outraged if they knew the truth, namely that Albertine revealed to each of them everything she was imprudently allowed to learn by being admitted to their inner circle, a thousand little secrets which, if revealed, would have proved infinitely unpleasant to the interested party. These envious women spread these rumours so they would be repeated, and would cause Albertine to fall out of favour with her patronesses. But, as often happens, these machinations came to nought. The malice behind them was too apparent, and it only caused those who had plotted them to be held in a little more contempt. Andrée's mother was too fixed in her positive opinion of Albertine to change her mind about her. She thought of her as an 'unfortunate girl', but one who had an excellent nature, and who only made up stories to entertain people.

Even though the sort of popularity Albertine had won seemed not to carry with it any practical result, it had imparted to Andrée's friend the distinctive characteristic of people who, because they are always sought out, never need to make overtures (a trait that can also be found, for similar reasons, at the other end of the social scale, in ladies of great distinction), which consists in not flaunting their successes, but rather hiding them. She would never say to someone: 'He's eager to see me,' and spoke of everyone with great kindness, as if she were the one who ran after and sought out others. If someone mentioned a young man who a few minutes before had been showering her with bitter reproaches because she had refused to see him again, far from boasting publicly about her conquest of him, or being angry with him, she'd sing his praises and say: 'He's such a nice boy.' She was actually annoyed at being so admired, because it forced her to cause pain to others, whereas, by nature, she liked to please them. She was even so eager to please that she would sometimes make use of a kind of lie peculiar to people who want to be useful, or to social climbers.

Existing in embryo in a large number of people, this kind of insincerity consists of being unable to be content with pleasing a single person with a single act. For example, if Albertine's aunt wanted her niece to accompany her to a boring reception, Albertine, by going to it, could have found the moral satisfaction of having pleased her aunt sufficient. But, having been warmly welcomed by the hosts, she preferred to tell them that she'd wished to see them for so long that she'd seized this opportunity and had begged her aunt's permission to come. Even that wasn't enough: if one of Albertine's friends, who was suffering from heartbreak, was at this reception, Albertine would say to her: 'I didn't want to leave you on your own; I thought it would do you good if I kept you company. If you'd like us to leave the reception and go somewhere else, I'll do whatever you like—all I want is for you not to be so sad' (which was also quite true). Sometimes, though, the fictional goal destroyed the real goal. For instance, Albertine, having a favour to ask for one of her friends, went to see a certain lady who could help. But, having arrived at the home of this kind, sympathetic lady, Albertine, unwittingly obeying the principle of multiple uses for a single action, thought the more affectionate thing to do would be to pretend to have come solely for the pleasure she'd feel in seeing this lady again. The lady was extremely touched that Albertine had come such a long way out of pure friendship. Seeing how moved the lady was, Albertine liked her even more. But the result was this: Albertine felt so keenly the pleasure of friendship for which she had untruthfully claimed to have come that she feared making the lady doubt feelings that were actually sincere if she asked for the favour for her friend. The lady would think that Albertine had come for that reason alone, which was true, but she would conclude that Albertine derived no unselfish pleasure in seeing her, which was false. So that Albertine left without having asked for the favour, like a man who has treated a woman with such kindness in the hope of obtaining her favours that he doesn't declare his passion in order to make this kindness continue to seem noble. In other instances, it wasn't that the real goal was sacrificed to some secondary goal thought up later, but the former was so contrary to the latter that if the person whose heart Albertine softened by stating the apparent goal had learned of the real one, his or her pleasure would immediately have changed into the most profound distress. Much later on in this story, such contradictions will become clearer. For now we'll take an example from a very different realm of experience to prove that they occur quite frequently in the most diverse situations that life presents. A husband has set his mistress up in the town where he is garrisoned. His wife, still in Paris, and half aware of the truth, becomes increasingly distressed, and writes jealous letters to her husband. A time comes when the mistress has to spend the day in Paris. The husband can't resist her entreaties to come with her, and obtains twenty-four hours' leave. But since he is kind, and feels sorry for causing pain to his wife, he goes to see her, and tells her, shedding a few sincere tears, that, alarmed by her letters, he managed to get away so he could come console her and hold her in his arms. In this way he has found a way, by a single journey, to prove his love both to his mistress and his wife. But if the latter were to learn why he actually came to Paris, her joy would doubtless change into grief, unless her happiness at seeing the ungrateful wretch should outweigh, despite everything, the sorrow caused by his lies. One of the men who seemed most consistently to practise this system of multiple goals was Monsieur de Norpois. He would sometimes agree to act as an intermediary between two friends who had quarrelled, with the result that he was called the most obliging of men. But it wasn't enough for him to seem to be helping the one who had come to ask for his aid; he would present to the other the steps he was taking to influence him as undertaken not at the request of the former, but in the interests of the latter, something of which he could easily convince an interlocutor who had already heard that he was dealing with 'the most helpful of men'. In this way, playing two games at once, doing what brokers call operating 'against' his client, he never let his influence be jeopardized, and the services he rendered never took away from, but always added to, some aspect of his credit. What's more, each service, seeming to be twice rendered, increased all the more his reputation as a helpful friend, and an effectively helpful friend at that, one who doesn't waste your time and whose every action meets with success, as was demonstrated by the gratitude of both interested parties. This duplicity in helpfulness (with some contradictions, as in any human being) was an important part of Monsieur de Norpois' character. Often at the ministry, Norpois made use of my father, who was rather naïve, while leading him to believe he was being of use to him.

Pleasing others more than she'd like, and having no need to trumpet her conquests, Albertine said nothing about the scene she'd had with me by her bed, which a plainer girl might have wanted to proclaim to the world. And yet I couldn't for the life of me figure out her behaviour during that scene. My hypothesis of perfect virtue (a hypothesis which I had at first used to explain the vehemence with which Albertine had refused to let herself be kissed and possessed by me, which was, however, not at all incompatible with my conception of my friend's goodness and fundamental honesty) was one that I kept revising over and over. This hypothesis was diametrically opposed to the one I'd built up on the first day I'd seen Albertine. What's more, there were so many different actions, all acts of kindness towards myself (a soothing, sometimes worried or alarmed kindness, jealous of my predilection for Andrée) that completely enveloped the rude gesture she'd made to escape me by pulling the bell. Why, then, had she asked me to spend the evening by her bed? Why was she always speaking the language of love? What is the reason for wanting to see a friend—fear that he might prefer your friend to you, or an attempt to please him, to tell him romantically that the other girls won't know he's spent the evening with you—if you refuse him such a simple pleasure, and if it's not a pleasure for you? I couldn't bring myself to believe that Albertine's virtue was so all-encompassing, and I even began to wonder if in her violence there might not have been some coquettish reason (an unpleasant odour, for example, that she might have thought she had, which she feared might offend me), or a kind of squeamishness (if for instance she thought, in her ignorance of the realities of lovemaking, that she might somehow contract my frailty and nervous debility from a kiss).

Whatever the case, she was genuinely sorry that she hadn't been able to please me, and she gave me a little golden pencil, out of that virtuous perversity of people who, moved by your affection for them but unwilling to grant you what it clamours for, nevertheless want to do you some other favour: the critic whose article would flatter the novelist invites him out to dinner instead; the duchess doesn't bring a social climber with her to the theatre, but lends him her box one evening when she isn't using it. Thus a sense of conscientiousness, in those who do little and who could do nothing, compels them to do something. I told Albertine that I was pleased with the pencil she gave me, though not as pleased as I might have been if on the evening she had come to the hotel to spend the night she had allowed me to kiss her. 'That would have made me so happy!' I said. 'What harm could it have done? I'm surprised you refused.'

'What surprises me', she replied, 'is that you find it surprising. I wonder what sorts of girls you've known for you to be surprised by my behaviour!'

'I'm sorry I upset you,' I said. 'But even now, I can't say I think I was wrong. In my opinion, these sorts of things aren't the least bit important, and I don't understand why a girl who can so easily give pleasure doesn't agree to do so. Let me be clear,' I added, to lend some support to her sense of morality when I remembered how she and her friends had ostracized the girlfriend of the actress Léa, 'I don't mean a girl can do anything she likes, or that there's no such thing as immorality. For instance, what you were saying the other day about the Balbec girl and how she was carrying on with an actress—I think that's disgusting, so disgusting that I think it's not true, and that it's the girl's enemies who made it all up. It seems unlikely, impossible even. But to let yourself be kissed—by a friend at that, since you do *say* I'm your friend . . .'

'You are, but I've had other friends before you—I've known some boys who admired me just as much as you do, believe me. But not a single one of them would have dared to do such a thing! They knew how hard they'd get slapped. But it didn't even occur to them—we'd just shake hands nicely, the way friends do. There would never have been any talk of kissing! But that wouldn't prevent us from being friends. So, if you still want so much to be my friend, you can rest easy, because I must like you a lot to forgive you. But I'm sure you couldn't care less about me! Come on, admit it, it's Andrée you really like! You have every reason to, really—she's much nicer than me, and she's absolutely gorgeous! You men, you're all the same!'

Despite my recent disappointment, these honest words made me think very highly of Albertine, and filled me with affection. And perhaps this feeling of tenderness would have serious and unfortunate consequences for me later on, for it was this that caused an almost familial feeling to be born, the moral core that was always to remain at the heart of my love for Albertine. Such a feeling can be the cause of the greatest suffering. For to suffer truly for a woman, one must once have believed in her completely. For the time being, this embryo of moral esteem and friendship remained in my soul like a toothing-stone. It might have done nothing, by itself, to affect my happiness if it had stayed just as it was, without growing, unchanging as it was to remain during the following year, especially during the last week of my first stay in Balbec. It lived within me like one of those organisms it would really be wiser to get rid of, but which one leaves in place without disturbing them, so harmless for the time being do they seem, weak and lost in the depths of a foreign being.

My dreams were now free to fall back on one or another of Albertine's friends, Andrée first of all, whose kind gestures might have moved me less if I hadn't been sure they'd come to the attention of Albertine. Indeed, the preference I had long feigned for Andrée had provided me—by my habit of conversing with her, or declaring my affection— with material for a love that was ready-made for her, from which all that was lacking until now was the addition of a sincere feeling, which my heart, free once again, could have provided. But Andrée was too intellectual, too nervous, too frail, too like me for that to happen. If Albertine now seemed empty to me, Andrée was full of something I recognized only too well. On that first day I'd thought I'd seen on the beach the mistress of a racing cyclist, intoxicated with a love of sport; but Andrée told me that, by taking up some athletic activities, she was following her doctor's orders, in order to treat her neurasthenia* and nutritional disorders, but that she was never happier than when she was translating a novel by George Eliot into French.* My disappointment, because of an initial misconception about Andrée, was, in fact, of no consequence for me. But the error was like those that, if they allow love to be born, and are recognized as mistakes only when that love can no longer be changed, become a cause of suffering. Such errors—which can be different from mine about Andrée, and which can even be its exact opposite—often stem, and in Andrée's case especially, from our paying too much attention not to what people are, but to what they would like to appear to be, to create a false first impression. To that outward appearance, affectation, imitation, and the desire to be admired, whether by the good or the wicked, add the deceptions of word and gesture. There are many kinds of cynicism and cruelty which, when tested, prove no more genuine than some acts of kindness or generosity. Just as we often finally discover a vain miser beneath a man known for his charity, we can be led to mistake for a Messalina* a respectable girl full of middle-class prejudices who boasts about her sinful actions. I thought I'd found in Andrée a healthy, unsophisticated girl, but really she was only a person seeking health, just as many of those she'd thought healthy may have been no more so than an obese arthritic with a red face and a white flannel blazer is like a Hercules.* Similarly, there are circumstances in which our happiness can be affected when the person we've loved for seeming to be healthy was actually one of those invalids who only receive their health from others, the way planets borrow their light, or the way certain inert bodies only conduct electricity.

No matter: Andrée, like Rosemonde and Gisèle, and even more than they, was still a friend of Albertine's, sharing her life, imitating her manners to such an extent that on that first day I couldn't initially distinguish one from the other. Over these girls, these long-stemmed roses whose main charm was to stand out from the sea, there reigned the same inseparability as in the days when I didn't know them, and when the appearance of any one of them threw me into such turmoil by signalling that the little band wasn't far away. Even now, the sight of one of them gave me a pleasure into which there entered, to an extent I couldn't have defined, the thought of seeing the others following not far behind, and, even if they didn't come that day, I'd have the joy of talking with her about them, and of knowing they'd be told I'd been down to the beach.

It wasn't just the attraction of those first days, it was a vague desire to be in love that wavered between them all, so naturally did each girl answer for the other. My greatest sadness would not have been to be abandoned by whichever of the girls I preferred, since I'd only chosen the one who had abandoned me because I'd fixed on her the sum of sadness and fantasy that hovered indistinctly over them all. And when I was abandoned, it was all her friends, in whose eyes I'd quickly have lost all prestige, that I would have unconsciously missed, having declared for them the sort of collective love a politician or actor has for the public, whose desertion of them, after they have enjoyed all its favours, they can never get over. Even the favours I'd been unable to obtain from Albertine I would suddenly hope for from a girl who had parted from me that evening with an ambiguous word or glance, so that it was to her that, for a day, my desire would turn.

It wandered from one to the other all the more voluptuously in that over these changing faces a relative fixation of features had begun, just enough for the eye to distinguish—even if more changes occurred— a malleable, fluctuating likeness. The differences between these faces were far from corresponding to similar differences in the length or breadth of their features, which, from one girl to the next, however dissimilar they appeared, could have been almost superimposed, one over the other. But our knowledge of faces is not mathematical. It doesn't start out by measuring the different parts; it begins with an expression, an impression of the whole. In Andrée, for example, the subtlety of her gentle eyes seemed to go with her slender nose, as thin as a simple curve traced in order to continue on a single line the intention of delicacy divided previously in the twin smiles of her two eyes. An equally fine line was drawn in her hair, as supple and deep as a line furrowed in the sand by the wind. And this must have been hereditary, since the very white hair of Andrée's mother flowed in the same way, rising here, dipping there, like a snowdrift with hills or hollows, responding to the shifting terrain. Indeed, compared to the fine delineation of Andrée's nose, Rosemonde's seemed to offer wide surfaces, like a tall tower set on a strong base. While the expression of a face can be enough to convince us of enormous differences between things separated by infinitely little—and an infinitely small distinction can by itself create an absolutely unique expression, an individuality—in the case of the little band of girls, it was not just the minuteness of a line, or the originality of an expression, that made these faces seem irreducible to one another. It was their colouring that established an even more profound separation between my friends' faces, not so much by the varied beauty of tones it provided, so unlike one another that, with Rosemonde—whose face was suffused with a sulphurous pink over which the greenish light of her eyes reacted—and with Andrée—whose white cheeks were given such austere distinction by her dark hair—I felt the same sort of pleasure as if I'd looked at a geranium by the sunlit sea first and then at a camellia at night; but especially because the infinitely small differences of lines were enlarged out of all proportion, the relationships of surfaces wholly changed, by that new element of colour, which, as much as it is a dispenser of tints, is a great regenerator—or at least modifier—of dimensions. So that faces that may have been built along similar lines, if they were illumined by the colouring of reddish hair, a pink complexion, or the white light of matte pallor, were made to look longer or wider, turned into something entirely different, like the props of the Russian ballet, which sometimes consist, if seen in broad daylight, of a simple round paper cut-out, but which the genius of Bakst,* depending on the warm red or lunar grey in which he plunges the set, makes look as if deeply encrusted, like a turquoise in the façade of a palace, or softly blossom, like a Bengal rose in the middle of a garden. Thus, when we first become acquainted with faces, we take their measure carefully, but we do so as painters, not surveyors.

Albertine's face was like her friends' in this regard. On some days her face would look thin, with a grey complexion and a glum look, and a violet shade, oblique and transparent, somewhere deep in her eyes, as sometimes occurs in the sea, and she would seem to be feeling the sorrow of an exile. On other days, her face, smoother, fixed her desires to its polished surface, and kept them from going beyond it—unless I saw her suddenly from the side, so that her cheeks, matte as wax on the surface, looked transparently pink, which gave me such a desire to kiss them and reach that different tint hiding underneath. At other times, happiness bathed those cheeks in such a mobile clarity that her skin, having become fluid and vague, allowed a sort of underlying gaze to peer through, which made it seem to be a different colour, but not a different substance, from her eyes; sometimes, when you looked unthinkingly at her face punctuated by little brown dots, in which there floated two more spots, only bluer, it was as if you were looking at a goldfinch egg, or often like an opalescent agate cut and polished in only two places, where, in the middle of the brown stone, there gleamed, like the transparent wings of an azure butterfly, her eyes, in which flesh becomes mirror and gives us the illusion, more than other parts of the body, of letting us get closer to the soul. Most often, though, her face was more highly coloured, hence more animated; sometimes the only pink in her white face was the tip of her nose, as delicate as that of a sly little pussycat you'd like to play with; sometimes her cheeks were so smooth that one's gaze slid, as over the surface of a miniature, over their pink enamel, made to look even more delicate and inward by the half-open, superimposed lid of her dark hair; at times the tint of her cheeks attained the purplish red of a cyclamen, and sometimes even, when she was congested or feverish, making me think of a sickly complexion which reduced my desire to something more sensual and brought out a more perverse and unwholesome quality in her eyes, her cheeks took on the dark purple of certain roses, a red that was almost black; and each of these Albertines was as different as each appearance of a ballerina whose colours, shape, character, are transmuted according to the endlessly varied effects of a spotlight. Perhaps it was because the beings I contemplated within her were so diverse at the time that later on I developed the habit of becoming myself a different person, depending on which of the Albertines I was thinking of: and so I became a jealous man, an indifferent man, a voluptuary, a melancholic, a madman, depending not merely on which memory chanced to surface, but on the power of what I had come to believe in the meantime about that same memory based on the varying perspectives from which I viewed it. For it always comes down to this, to those beliefs which most of the time fill our minds without our realizing it, but which nevertheless are much more important for our happiness than the person we see in front of us, for it's through them that we see that person, it's they that endow the person seen with fleeting importance. To be entirely accurate, I should give a different name to each of the selves in me that would later think about Albertine; even more importantly, I should give a different name to each of those Albertines who appeared before me, never the same, like all those versions of the sea—called simply by me for the sake of convenience 'the sea'—that succeeded one another and in front of which, another nymph, she stood out. Above all, though, just as (except to far greater purpose here) a storyteller specifies what the weather was like on a certain day, I should always give her name to whichever belief was reigning over my soul when I saw Albertine on a particular day, defining its atmosphere, determining the way people look, just as the sea changes its appearance according to those barely visible clouds that change the colour of each thing, by their concentration, their mobility, their dissemination, their flight—like the cloud that Elstir had rent asunder that evening when he hadn't introduced me to the girls with whom he'd paused to talk and whose images had suddenly seemed more beautiful as they moved away—a cloud that had re-formed a few days later when I met them, veiling their brilliance, often coming between my eyes and them, opaque and soft, reminiscent of Virgil's Leucothea.*

No doubt each of their faces had taken on for me a meaning quite different from before ever since the way to read them had been to a certain extent indicated to me by their talk; and I could attribute an even greater value to their speech since I could provoke it as I liked with my questions, and make them vary their remarks, like an experimenter who cross-checks his results to verify his hypothesis. And that's as good a way as any, when it comes down to it, to solve the problem of existence, to come close enough to things and people that have seemed beautiful and mysterious to us from afar so that we can realize that they're devoid of mystery and beauty; it's one of the forms of mental hygiene we can choose, one which might not be advisable, but which can give us a certain sense of calm as we go through life, and also, since it allows us not to regret anything by convincing us that we've got the best out of life, and that the best isn't much, it helps us accept death.

From the minds of these girls, I had removed all contempt for chastity, any memory of daily assignations, and had replaced them with upright principles, which might be capable of wavering, but which had safeguarded from any misconduct those girls who had been taught them in their bourgeois milieu. When we've been mistaken at the start, however, even about small things, when a fake assumption, say, or a mistaken memory leads us in the wrong direction when we try to seek out the author of a piece of malicious gossip or the place where we've lost an object, it is possible, once we've discovered our mistake, for us to replace it not with the truth, but with another mistake. When it came to their way of life and my behaviour towards them, I drew all the conclusions possible from the word 'innocence', which, as I casually chatted with them, I had read on their faces. But perhaps I had been too hasty in my sight-reading and had misread it, and it was no more to be seen there than the name of Jules Ferry on the programme of the matinee at which I'd seen La Berma for the first time—although this hadn't prevented me from assuring Monsieur de Norpois that Jules Ferry, without the slightest doubt, was a writer of curtain-raisers.*

For any of my friends in the little band, how could the last face I'd seen not be the only one I remembered, since, from our memories of a person, our mind eliminates anything that doesn't contribute in an immediately useful way to our daily relations (even, and especially, if those relations are permeated by love, which, perpetually unsatisfied, lives in the moment still to come)? Our mind lets the chain of past days slip by, and holds fast only to the nearest end, which is often made of an entirely different metal from the links that have vanished in the dark; and in the journey we make through life, the only country the mind sees as real is the one in which we are at the present moment. All of my first impressions, already so remote, were powerless against their daily reshaping in my memory; during the long hours I spent talking, eating, playing with these girls, I didn't even remember that they were the same ruthless, sensual virgins whom I had seen as in a fresco, walking by against the background of the sea.

Geographers or archaeologists may well take us to Calypso's island or unearth the true palace of Minos.* But then Calypso becomes a mere woman, Minos just a king with nothing divine about him. Even the qualities and defects that history tells us belonged to those very real people often differ greatly from the ones we'd attributed to the mythical creatures who bore the same names. So it was that all the charming oceanic mythologies that I'd composed in those first days vanished into nothing. But it's not entirely unimportant that we come to spend some time, at least once in a while, in the company of those we'd so desired and thought inaccessible. Even in the midst of the factitious pleasure we might eventually feel when we're with people we've at first found unpleasant, there always persists the lingering aftertaste of the defects they've managed to hide. Even in relationships like those I had with Albertine and her friends, the real pleasure which was there at the start leaves a fragrance that no amount of artifice can give to hothouse fruit, to grapes that have not ripened in the sun. The supernatural beings they had once been for me could still, even without my realizing it, inject something marvellous into the most commonplace dealings I had with them, or rather keep those dealings from ever having anything ordinary about them. My desire had sought so eagerly the significance of the eyes which now knew me and smiled at me, but which, on that first day, had met my own like rays of light from another universe; it had so generously and meticulously distributed colour and perfume over the flesh-toned surfaces of these girls who, stretched out on the cliff, simply handed me sandwiches or played guessing games, that often as I sprawled there in the afternoon, I was like a painter who, seeking the grandeur of antiquity in modern life, gives a woman cutting her toenail the nobility of the *Spinario*, or who, like Rubens, has female acquaintances pose as goddesses to compose a mythological scene;* I would look at these beautiful fair and dark bodies, of such varied types, as they lay around me in the grass, without perhaps emptying them of all the mediocre contents with which everyday existence had filled them, but also without reminding myself explicitly of their celestial origin, as if, like Hercules or Telemachus, I were playing in the midst of nymphs.

Then the concerts came to an end, the bad weather arrived, and my friends left Balbec—not all together, like swallows, but within the same week. Albertine left first, abruptly, without any of her friends understanding, either then, or later, why she'd suddenly returned to

Paris, where neither work nor pleasure summoned her. 'Without any whys or wherefores she just up and left,' grumbled Françoise, who would have liked us to do the same. She thought we were being inconsiderate towards the staff, already greatly reduced in number but kept there by the few guests remaining, and towards the manager, who was 'eating up money'. It's true that the hotel, which would soon close, had for some time now been watching its guests depart; never had it seemed so pleasant. This was not the opinion of the manager; for the entire length of the lounges in which we were freezing, the doors of which had ceased to be guarded by any page, he would pace the corridors, dressed in a new frock coat, so attentively groomed by the barber that his drab face looked as if it were made of a composite mixture in which for each part of flesh there were three of make-up, and he was constantly changing his ties (such refinements cost less than the heating and the staff, just as a man who can no longer donate ten thousand francs to a charity still tries to appear generous by tipping with five the boy who brings him a telegram). He looked as if he were inspecting the empty space, as if, with his handsome sartorial appearance, he wanted to give a temporary look to the desolation that could be felt in this hotel that had had a poor season; he looked like the ghost of a king who returns to haunt the ruins of what had once been his palace. He was especially unhappy when the local railway, which no longer had enough passengers, suspended service until the following spring. 'What is lacking here', said the manager, 'are means of commotion.' Despite the deficit recorded, he was making grandiose plans for the years to come. And since he was still capable of accurately remembering fine expressions when they applied to the hotel industry and had the effect of glorifying it, he would say: 'I didn't have sufficient backup, though I did have a good team in the dining room; but the pages left a little to be desired. You'll see next year what a phalanx I'll muster!' Meanwhile, the suspension of services on the Balbec–Caen–Balbec line forced him to send a servant out to collect the post, and sometimes to see guests off in a wagonette. I would often ask to ride next to the coachman so that I could go on outings whatever the weather, as I'd done during the winter I'd spent in Combray.

Sometimes, however, the heavy rain would keep us, my grandmother and me, since the Casino was closed, in spaces that were almost completely empty, as in the lowest hold of a ship during a gale, and where every day, as during a journey, a different person from among the number of people in whose proximity we'd spent the last three months without making their acquaintance—the first president from Rennes, the *bâtonnier* from Caen,* an American lady and her daughters—came over to us, started a conversation, invented some way to make the hours seem less long, revealed a talent, taught us a game, invited us to take tea or listen to music or get together at a certain time, so that we could pool our resources to plan those amusements that possess the real secret of giving pleasure, which is not to strive for it, but merely to help us while away the time; in short, they formed friendships with us at the end of our stay that would be broken off the next day, one after another, by their departures. I even made the acquaintance of the rich young man, one of his aristocratic friends, and the actress who had come back for a few days; but their little group was composed of only three people now, the other friend having returned to Paris. They asked me to come and dine with them in their restaurant. I think they were rather relieved that I didn't accept. But they had extended the invitation in the friendliest way possible, and although it actually came from the rich young man, since the others, like the friend who was with him, the Marquis Maurice de Vaudémont,* who was of extremely noble descent, were only his guests, the actress who asked me to come said instinctively, in order to flatter me: 'Maurice would be so pleased.'

And when I met all three of them in the lobby, it was Monsieur de Vaudémont, not the self-effacing rich young man, who said: 'You won't give us the pleasure of dining with us, then?'

In the end I had derived little benefit from my stay in Balbec, but this only made me want to come back all the more. I felt my stay there had been too brief. This was not the opinion of my friends, who wrote to me to ask if I was planning to live there permanently. Seeing the name 'Balbec' that they were obliged to write on the envelope, since my window looked out not on a landscape or a street but on the plains of the sea, whose murmuring I could hear all night long, and to which, before falling asleep, I had entrusted my rest, as if to a ship, I had the illusion that this closeness to the waves must physically, without my realizing it, inculcate in me the sense of their charm, like those lessons you learn while asleep.

The manager offered me the best rooms for the following year, but I'd grown attached to mine, which I could now enter without ever smelling the odour of vetiver; and my mind, which had once found such difficulty in rising to the ceiling's height, had finally been able to take the room's dimensions so exactly that I was forced to submit it to a reverse process when I had to sleep in my old room in Paris, with its low ceiling.

For we did have to leave Balbec, since the cold and damp had become too penetrating for us to stay long in a hotel without fire-places or a heating system. In any case, I almost immediately forgot those final weeks. What I almost invariably saw in my mind's eye when I thought about Balbec were those times when, every morning, at the height of summer, because I was going out with Albertine and her friends in the afternoon, my grandmother, under the doctor's orders, forced me to remain in bed, in darkness. The manager gave orders that no noise be made on my floor, and took it upon himself to ensure they were obeyed. Because of the glaring light, I would keep the tall violet curtains, which had seemed so hostile to me on that first night, drawn for as long as possible. But since, despite the pins with which Françoise attached them every night so that the daylight wouldn't seep through, and which she alone knew how to undo, despite the blankets, the red cretonne tablecloth, the bits and pieces of fabric she tacked on, she never managed to join them completely together, the darkness was not complete, and they allowed something like a scarlet shower of anemone petals to dapple the carpet, in which I couldn't keep myself from immersing my feet for a moment. And opposite the window, on the partially illumined wall, a cylinder of gold, supported by nothing, stood upright, and moved slowly, like the pillar of fire which went before the Hebrews in the desert.* Then I would go back to bed; obliged to savour, without moving, in my imagination alone, and all at once, the pleasures of playing, swim-ming, and walking, whatever the morning prompted, joy would make my heart pound, like a machine working at top speed, but fixed to the ground, able to discharge its energy only by spinning on the spot.

I knew that my friends were on the esplanade, but I couldn't see them as they passed in front of the unevenly ranged peaks of the sea, far beyond which, nestled in the middle of its bluish crests like an Italian hamlet, there could sometimes be glimpsed in a shaft of sun-light the little town of Rivebelle, revealed in minute detail by the sun. I couldn't see my friends, but (as the shouts of the newsboys—'the journalists' as Françoise called them—wafted into my belvedere, along with the shouts of the swimmers and children playing, punctuating

like the cries of sea-birds the sound of the waves gently breaking)
I imagined their presence, I heard their laughter, enveloped like the
Nereids' in the gentle lapping sound that rose to my ears. 'We looked
up', Albertine would tell me in the evening, 'to see if you were coming
down. But your shutters were closed, even after the concert started.'
At ten o'clock, in fact, the concert would ring out beneath my windows. Slipping in among the instruments, if the tide was high, the
refrain of the susurrous lapping of a wave, smooth and continuous,
could be heard, seeming to envelop the notes of the violin in its crystal spirals and to spray its foam over the intermittent echoes of an
undersea music. I would grow impatient that no one had yet come to
give me the things I needed to get dressed. Twelve o'clock struck, and
at last Françoise would arrive. And for months on end, in that Balbec
I had so desired because I had imagined it only as beaten by storms
and lost in mist, the fine weather had been so bright and so unwavering that, when she came to open the window, I could expect, without
fail, to find the same strip of sunlight folded in the angle of the outside
wall, of a colour so unchanging that it was not so much an exciting
sign of summer as it was depressing, like the dull hue of lifeless, imitation enamel. And as Françoise removed the pins from the window
frame, took down the various fabrics, and drew back the curtains, the
summer day she revealed seemed dead, as immemorial as a splendid,
ancient mummy from which our old servant had done nothing but
carefully strip away all its linen wrappings, before allowing it to
appear, embalmed in its robe of gold.

EXPLANATORY NOTES

MADAME SWANN'S CIRCLE

5 *the Swann of the Jockey Club*: Charles Swann is a member of one of the most exclusive, elite gentlemen's clubs in Paris, founded in 1833–4. Swann's membership is indicative of his exalted social position.

an invitation to Twickenham or Buckingham Palace: a roundabout way of indicating Swann's exalted friends and acquaintances. Prince Philippe d'Orléans, Comte de Paris (1838–94), grandson of Louis-Philippe, King of the French, lived in exile at Twickenham, to the south-west of London, from 1848 to 1871. An invitation from Buckingham Palace implies Swann is acquainted with the British royal family.

6 *forty sous*: a very small sum of money. One sou was one-twentieth of a livre; in the nineteenth century, there were approximately 20–5 livres to one pound sterling.

the Patronne's home: for the Patronne, see note to p. 75.

the Champs-Élysées: the gardens of the Avenue des Champs-Élysées in central Paris, a popular location for leisurely strolling, were a place to see and be seen around the turn of the century.

Combray: the (fictional) provincial town where the narrator spends much of his childhood vacations and the principal site of *The Swann Way*, the first volume of *In Search of Lost Time*.

7 *talk about Nietzsche or Wagner*: Friedrich Nietzsche (1844–1900) was a German philosopher and one of the most influential thinkers of the twentieth century. He was an acquaintance of Richard Wagner (1813–83), the equally influential composer, conductor, and director. Nietzsche and Wagner were the epitome of the European highbrow at the time Proust was writing.

the war . . . the Sixteenth of May: the war is the Franco-Prussian War, waged between July 1870 and January 1871, and ending in the emphatic defeat of France at the hands of the German forces of the Kingdom of Prussia. The 'Sixteenth of May' refers to a turning point in the history of the French Third Republic: on that date in 1877, the President, Maréchal Mac-Mahon sought to oust the president of the Council of State and replace him with a monarchist successor. A fierce campaign followed in which, ultimately, republican values prevailed, prompting a significant shift of political and diplomatic personnel. That M. de Norpois should have held senior positions across this considerable period of turmoil indicates his high standing in political circles.

8 *Journal des débats*: a weekly newspaper (1789–1944) originally established to cover the debates of the French National Assembly. It identified as 'conservative republican' in 1890 and 'liberal republican' in 1895.

9 *An academician like Legouvé . . . by Claudel*: Ernest Legouvé (1807–1903) was a writer and critic, elected to the Académie française in 1856. Victor Hugo (1802–85), poet, playwright, and novelist, author of *Notre-Dame de Paris* (1831) and *Les Misérables* (1862), is one of the nineteenth century's most prolific and celebrated literary figures. Maxime Du Camp (1822–94) was a writer and close friend of the novelist Gustave Flaubert (1821–80) who, when elected to the Académie française in 1880, gave a speech celebrating Hugo. Alfred Mézières (1826–1915) was a politician and writer, also elected to the Académie in 1874. Paul Claudel (1868–1955) was a Catholic poet and dramatist who authored an essay in praise of the early modern poet Boileau (1636–1711), in which he argued Hugo's verses fell short of Boileau's accomplishments.

The same nationalism . . . the return of the King: these lines highlight the overlaps and complexities of French *fin-de-siècle* intellectual and political life. Maurice Barrès (1862–1923) was a novelist who was elected to the Chamber of Deputies in 1889 as a nationalist who, though republican, shared common ground with some right-wing monarchists. He finished his term in 1893, the year Georges Berry (1852–1915), initially a monarchist, was elected. Alexandre Ribot (1842–1923) and Paul Deschanel (1855–1922) were both republican progressives. The latter, like Barrès, was elected to the Académie française in 1906. Charles Maurras (1868–1952) and Léon Daudet (1867–1942) were both writers and right-wing monarchist politicians, founders of the nationalist periodical *Action française*.

the Commission: probably the 'Commission des Affaires étrangères' (Foreign Affairs Committee). 'Probably' since Proust never explicitly specifies the narrator's father's occupation. His various international 'missions' and close ties with the ex-ambassador Norpois suggest the likelihood of this role.

the war of '70: see note to p. 7.

10 *Monsieur de Norpois*: a characteristic Proustian blending of fictional and historical. Napoleon III and Bismarck are of course leading historical figures on their respective sides of the Franco-Prussian War, while Norpois and King Theodosius exist only in Proust's fiction. The state visit of the fictional king has much in common with that of Tsar Nicholas II to France in 1896.

Palais-Royal: originally built as a royal palace in the early seventeenth century, this group of buildings on the Rue Saint-Honoré in the centre of Paris long housed celebrated theatre spaces. It is now home to the Council of State and the Ministry of Culture.

11 *La Berma, in a matinee performance of Phèdre*: La Berma is a fictional creation of Proust's, though her accomplishments map quite closely on to those of the celebrated actress Sarah Bernhardt (1844–1923). *Phèdre* (1677) is a tragedy, the best-known play by Jean Racine (1639–99), in which Sarah Bernhardt made her name in the title role.

12 *the Guermantes way*: in Combray, as described in the first volume of Proust's novel, there are two walks around the town: one can go via Méséglise and the Swann residence ('the Swann way') or via the property owned by the aristocratic Guermantes family ('the Guermantes Way'), which is taken up as the title of the third volume of *In Search of Lost Time*.

La Revue des Deux Mondes: a journal covering literary and cultural affairs that first appeared in August 1829. It continues to be published monthly.

13 *Andromaque . . . Les Caprices de Marianne*: *Andromaque* (1667), like *Phèdre* (see note to p. 11), is a tragedy by Racine. *Les Caprices de Marianne* (1833) is a two-act Romantic comedy by Alfred de Musset (1810–57).

the Titian . . . San Giorgio dei Schiavoni: the Italian Renaissance artist Titian (~1488–1576) painted an *Assumption of the Virgin*, known as the 'Frari Assumption' or the *Assunta*, for the high altar of the Basilica di Santa Maria Gloriosa dei Frari (the Frari church) in Venice in 1515–18. It is the largest extant oil on wood panel painting in the world. The Scuola di San Giorgio degli (Proust writes 'dei') Schiavoni in Venice (one of the confraternities of the city) contains a series of panels painted between 1501 and 1507 by the celebrated artist Vittore Carpaccio (~1460/5–1525?). Proust most likely encountered these works via *The Stones of Venice* (see note to p. 278) by the English art historian John Ruskin (1819–1900).

They say . . . My Lord . . .: 'On dit qu'un prompt départ vous éloigne de nous, | Seigneur. . .'. From *Phèdre*, Act II, scene v: the start of Phèdre's declaration of incestuous love to her stepson, Hippolyte.

the golden voice: this was how Victor Hugo described Sarah Bernhardt after her performance in his play *Ruy Blas* (1872).

14 *Le Demi-monde*: a celebrated comedy of 1855 by Alexandre Dumas *fils* (1824–95) about a woman who marries into money to escape her questionable past.

Les Caprices de Marianne: see note to p. 13.

'Monsieur Anatole France': a writer and journalist, France (1844–1924) was best known for his novels, including *The Crime of Sylvestre Bonnard* (1881) and *Penguin Island* (1908). He was elected to the Académie française in 1896 and awarded the Nobel Prize in Literature in 1921. He provided a brief preface to Proust's first book, *Pleasures and Days* (1896).

15 *Balbec*: fictional seaside town based on Cabourg on the Normandy coast, where Proust spent every summer between 1907 and 1914.

They say . . . from us . . .: see note to p. 13.

Holy of Holies: the most sacred and innermost part of the Jewish Temple in Jerusalem, said to be where the Ark of the Covenant was kept.

'plastic mobility' . . . 'solar myth': the phrases 'quoted' here from the fictional writer Bergotte's booklet on *Phèdre* are in fact borrowed from Jules Lemaître's review of Sarah Bernhardt's performance as Phèdre on 27 November 1893, subsequently published in his *Impressions de théâtre* (1895).

16 *my daily posture as a stylite . . . theatre columns*: from the ancient Greek for 'pillar-dweller', 'stylites' were early Christian anchorites who lived on top of columns or porticos, demonstrating their faith through an isolated, ascetic existence. The narrator's metaphor is prompted by the fact that his devotion to La Berma is associated with the 'theatre columns', where bills of forthcoming productions are posted. These columns, cylindrical structures topped with an ornamental dome, are still visible in French cities today, known as 'Morris Columns', after the printer who held the original concession in the 1860s.

17 *boeuf à la gelée*: a traditional dish of braised beef and carrots, set in aspic (*à la gelée*) and eaten cold.

Les Halles: the central marketplace for fresh food and produce in Paris, next to the Saint-Eustache church on the right bank of the Seine. Émile Zola focused the action of his novel *Le Ventre de Paris* (*The Belly of Paris*, 1873) on life in and around Les Halles.

Julius II's monument: Michelangelo (1475–1564), Renaissance sculptor, painter, and poet, was commissioned to create the tomb of Pope Julius II in 1505, a monumental project that was eventually completed at the church of San Pietro in Vincoli, Rome in 1545. It includes his statue of Moses, much discussed by many, including Freud in his 1914 essay 'The Moses of Michelangelo'.

the creator of the Medici tombs in the Pietrasanta quarries: Michelangelo created the 'New Sacristy', one of the chapels celebrating the Medici family that were added to the Basilica of San Lorenzo, in the first decades of the sixteenth century. He spent long periods of time closely engaged in identifying and selecting the stone for his works in both Carrara and in Pietrasanta.

18 *the Nev'York*: Olida's, also known as the Maison du Jambon or 'House of Ham', was established in 1885 and located on the Rue Drouot in the 9th *arrondissement*.

the claque: individuals paid to attend theatre or opera performances and applaud.

19 *the imperious form of three knocks . . . a message from Mars*: in French theatres, three blows are struck on the floor with the butt of a stout stick just before a play begins, to quieten the audience and announce the imminent raising of the curtain.

21 *Phèdre's declaration to Hippolyte*: see note to p. 13.

22 *the Mona Lisa or Benvenuto's Perseus*: two of the most celebrated artworks of all time. Leonardo da Vinci (1452–1519) painted the portrait *La Gioconda* (known as the *Mona Lisa*) in 1503–6 and it has been displayed in the Louvre museum in Paris since 1797. *Perseus with the Head of Medusa* (1545–54) is the most famous work by Renaissance sculptor Benvenuto Cellini (1500–71) and stands in the Loggia dei Lanzi on the Piazza della Signoria in Florence.

23 *the wise Mentor . . . the young Anacharsis*: in Homer's *Odyssey*, Ulysses
entrusts his household to Mentor, a noble inhabitant of Ithaca. The goddess Athena on several occasions takes Mentor's form in order to protect
Ulysses or his son Telemachus. This is the derivation of the modern term
'mentor', meaning guide or wise protector. Anacharsis here most likely
refers to the eponymous hero of *The Travels of Anacharsis the Younger in
Greece* (1788), by Jean-Jacques Barthélemy, an early historical novel presented as the travel journal of a young man encountering the marvels of
the world for the first time.

24 *the Delphic oracle*: in ancient Greece the High Priestess at the Temple of
Apollo at Delphi, known as the Oracle, was the highest religious authority
and her ('oracular') pronouncements were taken to be prophecies.

   the Quai d'Orsay: location of the French Ministry of Foreign Affairs, built
between 1844 and 1855.

   Academy of Moral Sciences: the Académie des Sciences Morales et
Politiques is one of the five academies or learned societies of the Institut
de France (the best known of which is the Académie française), established
to support, perpetuate, and illuminate knowledge and understanding.

25 *English consols and Russian four-per-cents*: government-issue investment
bonds.

26 *Notre-Dame de Paris*: see note to p. 9.

   Gérard de Nerval: (1808–55), an influential Romantic poet and author,
much admired by Proust.

27 *the piano . . . in a concerto by Mozart*: the Austrian composer Wolfgang
Amadeus Mozart (1756–91) wrote twenty-seven piano concertos.

28 *John Bull . . . Uncle Sam*: John Bull emerged in the early eighteenth century as a satirical embodiment of British character; similarly, Uncle Sam
is an imaginary embodiment of the United States government in particular, physically taking the shape of an older man, usually dressed in clothes
bearing the colours or emblems of the US flag.

29 *your Vatel . . . a beef Stroganoff, for instance*: Norpois is here likening
Françoise to the famed majordomo in the court of Louis XIV, François
Vatel (1631–71), who was in charge of the feasting at a vast banquet held
for the King at the Château de Chantilly in 1671. Beef Stroganoff is
a Russian dish of beef prepared with mustard and sour cream.

   Attic wit: literally 'Athenian-style wit', characterized by simple and refined
elegance of expression.

30 *ukase*: in Russian, an edict or decree from the Tsar, with the force of law.

   the Élysée: the Élysée Palace in Paris is the official residence of the
President of the Republic.

31 *the Consulta . . . the Farnese Palace . . . the Carracci Gallery*: the Palazzo
della Consulta in Rome is the seat of the Ministry of Foreign Affairs and
the Constitutional Court of Italy. The French Embassy in Rome is housed

in the Palazzo Farnese, which is home to a gallery of frescoes executed in 1597–1606 by the Baroque painters, brothers Annibale and Agostino Carracci.

31 *the Wilhelmstrasse*: the site, in Berlin, of the German Ministry of Foreign Affairs.

32 *Court of Saint James's . . . Choristers' Bridge . . . Double-Headed Eagle . . . Montecitorio . . . Ballplatz*: Norpois' string of allusions here covers a considerable geographical terrain. The Court of St James is the official royal court of the United Kingdom, which receives all foreign ambassadors; the Choristers' Bridge is the seat of the Ministry of Foreign Affairs in St Petersburg, Russia; the Montecitorio Palace in Rome is where the Italian Chamber of Deputies sits; the 'Double-Headed Eagle' is the heraldic symbol of the Austro-Hungarian Empire, whose Ministry of Foreign Affairs is found at the Ballplatz in Vienna.

as Baron Louis used to say: Joseph Dominique, Baron Louis (1755–1837) was finance minister under Napoleon I and again, for three separate stints, under Louis XVIII.

33 *pass through Saint Petersburg*: a Franco-Russian alliance was signed in 1891.

the Oettingens: Oettingen in Bayern is a small town in Bavaria. Given that a few pages earlier we have been told of King Theodosius' presence at the Bavarian court, this seems to be an allusion to that time.

34 *the cathedrals of Rheims and Chartres . . . the Sainte-Chapelle here in Paris*: the former are two of France's most ancient and celebrated Gothic cathedrals, standing on the site of ancient churches dating back to the Merovingian period. Rheims Cathedral was constructed between 1211 and 75; that of Chartres between 1194 and 1230. The Sainte-Chapelle, on the Île de la Cité in Paris, was built between 1242 and 1248 as the private chapel of the French royal family.

Romanesque: as an architectural style, Romanesque predates the Gothic and is characterized by semicircular, rather than pointed, arches.

the Gothic architects, who could carve stone like lace: in architecture, the Gothic period spans from the mid-twelfth to the mid-fifteenth century. Proust's interest in cathedral design and construction stems from his study of, amongst others, the art historians John Ruskin and Émile Mâle (1862–1954).

35 *the tomb of Admiral de Tourville*: this is creative licence on Proust's part—the tomb of the admiral (1642–1701), a naval officer who served under Louis XIV, is found in the church of Saint-Eustache in Paris.

more than one of Panurge's sheep would have followed her lead: in *The Fourth Book* by François Rabelais (?1483–1553), a character called Panurge buys a sheep from a merchant and, incensed at having been overcharged, casts it into the sea, whereupon the rest of the flock follow, meeting a watery death. To be 'like Panurge's sheep' is an idiom that has entered the language, indicating mindless following and lack of autonomy.

36 *a Nesselrode pudding . . . a Lucullan feast!*: a Nesselrode pudding is a set custard made with cooked chestnuts and dried fruit soaked in Marsala wine, named after Karl Robert Reichsgraf von Nesselrode-Ehreshoven, a Russian diplomat of German birth. Lucullus (118–57/56 BC), was a Roman general and statesman, famed for his extravagant banqueting.

(you know Molière's word): a delicate way of indicating that Swann is a cuckold. Molière (Jean-Baptiste Poquelin, 1622–73) one of France's most famed playwrights, addressed the theme of cuckoldry and infidelity in a number of his plays, including *Sganarelle, ou le cocu imaginaire* (*Sganarelle, or the Imaginary Cuckold*, 1660).

urbi et orbi: (Latin) 'to the city and to the world'; taken to refer to certain papal addresses or blessings but more generally having the sense of 'something widely proclaimed'.

38 *Vermeer*: Johannes (or Jan) Vermeer (1632–75) is recognized as one of the finest painters of the Dutch Golden Age. Little known in his lifetime and with only thirty-four works attributed to his name, Vermeer was rediscovered by scholars in the nineteenth century. In the first volume of Proust's novel we learn that Swann is preparing a study of Vermeer, an artist quite unknown to Odette at the time of their meeting.

39 *cross-breeding of species as practised by the Mendelians*: Gregor Johann Mendel (1822–84) was a biologist who is acknowledged as the father of modern genetic science. His experiments with pea plants set out the rules of heredity, now known as Mendelian inheritance.

cocotte: a courtesan or prostitute serving an elite clientele.

40 *the Comte de Paris*: one of the titles of Prince Philippe d'Orléans (see note to p. 5).

41 *Bergotte*: Proust's invention—a fictional writer, first encountered by the narrator in the first volume of the novel.

42 *Art for Art's Sake*: English rendering of 'l'art pour l'art', an aesthetic slogan of the nineteenth century, associated in France in particular with the poets Théophile Gautier (1811–72) and Charles Baudelaire (1821–67), who argued that art should be freed of any political or utilitarian purpose.

43 *Loménie . . . Sainte-Beuve . . . Alfred de Vigny*: Louis-Léonard de Loménie (1815–78) was a critic and author of a ten-volume study of the 'great men' of his day, though his entry on Vigny doesn't include the critique mentioned here. Charles Augustin Sainte-Beuve (1804–69) was one of the most prominent critics and literary opinion-formers of his day. Vigny (1797–1863) was a Romantic poet, novelist, and dramatist.

Cinq-Mars . . . Le Cachet rouge: *Cinq-Mars* is a historical novel (1826) and *Laurette ou le cachet rouge* (*Laurette or the Red Seal*) a historical novella (1833), both by Vigny.

44 *Princesse de Metternich*: Pauline von Metternich (1836–1921) was a well-known Austrian socialite whom Proust met in a Parisian salon in 1898.

45 *a deity from Olympus . . . Minerva assumes*: in Greek mythology, Mount Olympus (found on the border of Thessaly and Macedonia) was the home of the gods. Minerva (for the Romans; Athena for the Greeks) is the goddess of poetry, crafts, and wisdom (as embodied in the sacred owl with which she is associated). In the *Odyssey* she takes male form as Mentor, prince of Taphos, to encourage Ulysses' son Telemachus to set off to find his father.

47 *Maspero . . . Ashurbanipal . . . ten centuries before Christ*: Gaston Maspero (1846–1916) was a distinguished Egyptologist and author of over twenty books on ancient Egypt and related subjects. Proust borrowed a volume by Maspero concerning 'The time of Ramses and Ashurbanipal' from a friend in 1906. Ashurbanipal (669–631 BC—Proust's 'ten centuries' is a slip) was an Assyrian king who ruled for thirty-eight years. Details of his hunts are preserved in cuneiform texts surviving on clay tablets from the Royal Library of Ashurbanipal at the ancient city of Nineveh, modern-day Mosul in Iraq; the British Museum conserves reliefs from Nineveh of the king's famed lion hunts.

49 *Chateaubriand's genius*: François-René de Chateaubriand (1768–1848) was a writer and politician who had a significant influence on Romantic literature. His best-known works include the novels *Atala* (1801) and *René* (1802) and the posthumously published *Memoirs from Beyond the Grave* (1849–50).

Beethoven: Ludwig van Beethoven (1770–1827), celebrated and prolific German composer much admired by Proust.

51 *Bressant's or Thiron's voice in L'Aventurière or in Le Gendre de Monsieur Poirier*: Prosper Bressant (1815–86) and Joseph Thiron (1830–91) were celebrated actors of their day. In *The Swann Way* we learn that Swann wears his hair like Bressant. Bressant performed in *L'Aventurière* (1848), a verse comedy by Émile Augier, when it played at the Comédie-Française in 1860; Thiron performed in *Le Gendre de Monsieur Poirier* (1854), a comedy in prose, co-written by Augier and Jules Sandeau.

53 *monde meant demi-monde*: the 'demi-monde' refers to the hedonistic fringes of respectable society ('le monde' or 'le beau monde') where elite men would indulge their desires with women of lower social standing ('demi-mondaines' or courtesans) whom they supported materially and financially. This world was at its peak during the period known as the Belle Époque, from around 1871 to 1914.

golden louis: golden coins introduced in France in 1640; on lower denominations, see note to p. 6.

the Henry . . . Weber's . . . Cirro's . . . the Café Anglais: popular, well-to-do Parisian restaurants around the turn of the century (Proust himself frequented Weber's). Proust adds an extra *r* to Ciro's.

54 *Pope Pius IX and Raspail*: Françoise's choices here seem somewhat at odds with each other. Pius IX was pope from 1846 to 1878, unpopular among liberals and promoter of the dogma of papal infallibility. François-Vincent Raspail (1794–1878) was a man of science and a revolutionary, active in the uprisings of 1830 and 1848.

55 *a Morris column*: see note to p. 16.

56 *'at evening, from deep within the woods'*: a quotation from Alfred de Vigny's poem 'Le Cor' ('The Horn', 1826), which opens and closes with a line alluding to the sound of the horn heard 'from deep within the woods' ('au fond des bois').

Gabriel's palaces: Jacques-Ange Gabriel (1698–1782) was an architect who designed and built the École Militaire in Paris, as well as the two Louis XVI-style palaces that are found at the north end of the Place de la Concorde, today the Hôtel Crillon and the Hôtel de la Marine.

Palais de l'Industrie . . . Trocadéro: the Palace of Industry was built for the Universal Exhibition of 1855 and modelled on London's Crystal Palace. It was dismantled and replaced by the Grand and Petit Palais between 1897 and 1900. The original Trocadéro Palace, facing on to the Champ-de-Mars, was built for the Universal Exhibition of 1878. It was destroyed in 1937 to make way for the Palais de Chaillot, which stands at the Trocadéro site today.

57 *these sordid arrondissements*: the two 'Portes' mentioned here are triumphal arches built in the early 1670s in homage to the achievements of Louis XIV.

Orphée aux Enfers: a popular operetta (1858) by Jacques Offenbach (1819–80) which sends up the classical myth of Orpheus and Eurydice.

59 *the disused tollbooths of old Paris*: over fifty tollbooths to manage (and tax) goods coming in and out of the city were established around Paris in the late eighteenth century.

water-closets: this appears in English in Proust's text.

Saint-Simon . . . 'belonging to the dregs of the people': the Duc de Saint-Simon (Louis de Rouvroy, 1675–1755) was a diplomat and writer whose voluminous *Mémoires* provide an extraordinary account of Louis XIV's court at Versailles and the Regency period of Louis d'Orléans, between 1694 and 1723. He uses this derogatory phrase on a number of occasions in his memoirs.

60 *Gouache's*: a high-end confectioners which, at the end of the nineteenth century, was situated on the Boulevard des Italiens.

64 *dyspnoea*: shortness of breath. Proust's father was a revered doctor and the author developed a detailed familiarity with the medical world and its vocabulary from an early age (Proust's younger brother would become a doctor too).

olé! au lait!: Cottard is punning on the homophony between the Spanish exclamation and the French phrase 'with milk'.

65 *Per viam rectam*: (Latin) by the straight line or direct route.

66 *cosa mentale*: (Italian) a thing of the mind. Leonardo da Vinci (see note to p. 22) uses this phrase to describe the painter's art in his *Treatise on Painting*, which first appeared in print in 1651.

68 *a kindly Eumenid*: Eumenids, in Greek mythology, sometimes called Erinyes and known as the Furies in English, were deities of vengeance in the underworld.

69 *one of the florets drawn by Leonardo*: da Vinci's technical and scientific drawings include studies of flowers.

the Candlestick in Scripture: the seven-branched golden candlestick or menorah placed by Moses in the Tabernacle (Exodus 25:31–7); a reminder of Swann's Jewish identity.

71 *it's Berlier who built them all*: Jean-Baptiste Berlier (1843–1911) was an engineer who created the pneumatic message delivery system used in Paris from the 1860s to the 1980s, and is credited with the thinking behind what became the Paris metro network.

Renan's Life of Jesus: Ernest Renan (1823–92) was a scholar and critic who published the controversial *Life of Jesus* in 1863, which focused on what was scientifically credible in the life of Christ, and was the first of eight volumes in his *History of the Origins of Christianity* (1863–81).

Kant's necessary universe: the German philosopher Immanuel Kant (1724–1804) is a key figure of the European Enlightenment and his writings cover a vast range of topics, including, above all, freedom, knowledge, and our relation to the world around us. Proust studied his work at the Lycée Condorcet.

an Asian temple as painted by Rembrandt: Rembrandt van Rijn (1606–69) was one of the most accomplished artists of all time, a Dutch painter, printmaker, and draughtsman. He painted *The Presentation in the Temple* (1631), though the reference may more widely seek to evoke the gloomy, atmospheric interiors of many of Rembrandt's paintings rather than a specific work.

the bastions of Darius' palace: the Palace of Darius was constructed between 550 and 330 BC at Persepolis, Iran and decorated with friezes, some of which Proust may have seen in the Louvre.

72 *that Ninevite pastry*: Nineveh was one of the largest and most powerful cities of the ancient world, the capital of Assyria, and was sacked in 612 BC, leaving widespread devastation.

73 *Gérôme's new painting*: the socialites talk about an academic, conservative painter Jean-Léon Gérôme (1824–1904), a declared enemy of the more radical Impressionist painters of the time.

Colombin's: a fashionable *salon de thé*, or teashop, in the exclusive 1st *arrondissement*.

toast: Proust's French text uses the English *toast(s)* throughout this passage.

74 *Wolf's theory*: the German scholar Friedrich August Wolf (1759–1824), a key figure in modern philology, gained fame through his *Prologomena ad Homerum* (1795) in which he argued that the *Iliad* and the *Odyssey* were not the work of a single author, but a patchwork of fragments by diverse hands, from different chronological moments.

75 *Saint Anthony of Padua*: a Portuguese priest (1195–1231) canonized a year after his death in Padua, and venerated as the patron saint for the recovery of things and people that have been lost.

as she'd heard the 'Patronne' do so often in the 'little clan': in the first volume of Proust's novel we learn that the bourgeois socialite Madame Verdurin is known as the 'Patronne' (colloquially the 'Boss') of her social circle, which she affectionately refers to as her 'little clan'.

76 *Officer of the Legion of Honour*: established by Napoleon Bonaparte in 1802, the National Order of the Legion of Honour is France's highest order of merit, 'Officer' being the second of five increasing degrees of eminence.

77 *the Union Générale crash*: the Société de l'union générale was a bank founded in 1876 that went bankrupt in 1882, prompting the crash of the Paris stock exchange.

"fast": this word appears in English in Proust's text.

78 *the Critique of Pure Reason*: the best known of Kant's philosophical works, published in 1781.

79 *the Massachutoes*: a name invented by Proust to evoke a foreign tribe, reminiscent of the name of the US state Massachusetts, which derives from a Wôpanâak word meaning 'by the blue hills'.

80 *'Stranger, go tell the Spartans!'*: this phrase is attributed to Leonidas, King of Sparta, who died alongside his three hundred troops at the Battle of Thermopylae in 480 BC. The warriors' tomb was inscribed with the words 'Stranger, go tell Sparta that we lie here in obedience to her laws', to commemorate their bravery. See Herodotus, *Histories*, Book 7.

President of the Horse Show: the *Concours central hippique de Paris* was established in 1865. The character mentioned here is Proust's invention.

81 *the Dreyfus Affair*: the case of a Jewish captain in the French army, Alfred Dreyfus (1859–1935), who was accused in 1894 of disclosing secrets to the Germans. He was tried, found guilty of treason, and condemned to solitary confinement on the Île du Diable, off French Guyana. Often fuelled by stark and growing anti-Semitism, public debates were fierce and the whole country was quickly divided over the question of whether or not Dreyfus was guilty. Ultimately the evidence against him was found to be falsified and he was finally exonerated in 1906.

82 *terra incognita*: (Latin) unknown land.

'Le Cousin Bête': literally 'the stupid cousin', punning on the homophony of the female name 'Bette' in the title of Balzac's 1846–7 novel, *La Cousine Bette* (*Cousin Bette*) and the French word for stupid (*bête*). Honoré de Balzac (1799–1850) is one of the most influential French novelists of the nineteenth century and author of the hugely ambitious series of interlinked novels *La Comédie humaine* (*The Human Comedy*, 1829–48).

the Rothschilds: while the Israels are a fictional family, the Rothschilds are not: they were a Jewish family of German origins, establishing a banking business in 1760s Frankfurt that grew to become first a European, then a global, financial empire. They held the greatest private fortune in the world during the nineteenth century.

82 *the Faubourg Saint-Germain*: the exclusive district on the left bank of the Seine, around the church of Saint-Germain-des-Prés, site of many of the capital's finest *hôtels particuliers* (private mansions) and historically home to the high nobility.

83 *he's the Duc de Chartres, not a prince*: Odette does not appreciate that the duke is referred to as a prince because he is a member of the royal family.

département: created in 1790 as an administrative division of France, the *département* serves a local function below that of the region.

84 *Liszt*: Franz Liszt (1811–86), Hungarian-born Romantic composer who lived and worked for much of his life in Paris.

85 *'Don Juan' attitude*: Don Juan is the embodiment of the male libertine, a figure who dedicates himself to the seduction of women. The name comes from the Spanish literary tradition, but the figure is memorably rendered in Molière's *Dom Juan* (1665) and Mozart's opera *Don Giovanni* (1787).

87 *Rue La Pérouse . . . jealousy in him*: in the novel's first volume we learn that Rue La Pérouse was Odette's address in the early days of her relationship with Swann.

whether . . . Odette had been in bed with Forcheville: during Swann's courtship of Odette, she favoured, for a time, another suitor, namely the Comte de Forcheville, a liaison encouraged by the Verdurins.

89 *landau*: a four-wheeled, horse-drawn, convertible carriage.

meeting: this word appears in English in Proust's text.

the tombs at Saint-Denis: the Abbey of Saint-Denis, to the north of Paris, was the burial site of the kings of France from the thirteenth century until the time of the Revolution of 1789.

a magnificent tie from Charvet's: Charvet's is a high-end shirt-maker and tailor, established on the Place Vendôme in 1838 and still trading today.

90 *as in Klingsor's laboratory*: in Wagner's music drama *Parsifal* (1882), Klingsor is an evil sorcerer.

92 *Vinteuil's sonata . . . the little phrase*: in *The Swann Way*, this work by Proust's fictional composer is introduced as the 'national anthem' of Charles Swann's love for Odette de Crécy. The 'little phrase' is a motif that recurs in the sonata and that Vinteuil reprises in another work the narrator encounters later in *In Search of Lost Time*.

93 *Saint Mark's in Venice . . . its domes in photographs*: the structure of the Basilica of St Mark in Venice, first consecrated in the eleventh century, incorporates five imposing domes.

94 *Beethoven's quartets (numbers 12, 13, 14, and 15)*: Proust mentions four of Beethoven's late string quartets, composed in 1825–6 towards the end of

his life. They were among Proust's favourite pieces of music. The narrator's point here is that great art is seldom understood as such by its first audiences, underlining the importance of time in the process of aesthetic appreciation.

Impressionism, the pursuit of dissonance, the exclusive use of the Chinese scale, Cubism, Futurism: with this list the narrator proffers a broad spread of examples of avant-garde artistic practice from the *fin-de-siècle* period. Impressionism, Cubism, and Futurism are currents in visual art, each concerned with providing alternative perspectives on the world as we find it. The pursuit of dissonance and the use of 'the Chinese scale' were experiments in early twentieth-century music (though not unprecedented in music history). The Chinese scale is a pentatonic (five-note) scale, by contrast to the more common seven-note scale of Western music, which repeats at the octave.

95 *gruppetto*: (Italian) 'little group'—refers to a turn, or four-note ornamentation, in music.

96 *"The Will-in-Itself" or "The Synthesis of the Infinite"*: probable allusion to Arthur Schopenhauer (1788–1860), whose *The World as Will and Representation* (1818) proposes music as a means of reproducing the structure of will.

the Palm Court at the Jardin d'Acclimatation: situated in the Bois de Boulogne and inaugurated in 1860, the Jardin d'Acclimatation is a zoo and amusement park. The Palm Court opened in 1893.

Armenonville: the Pavillon d'Armenonville was an elegant restaurant located in the Bois de Boulogne.

pushing: this word appears in English in Proust's text.

97 *the portrait of Savonarola by Fra Bartolomeo*: Girolamo Savonarola (1452–98) was a hardline Dominican friar and preacher in Renaissance Florence. Fra Bartolomeo (1472–1517), a fellow Dominican, painted his portrait which now hangs in the San Marco Museum in Florence.

Procession of the Magi . . . Gozzoli inserted the Medicis into their midst . . . after the time of the painter himself: Benozzo Gozzoli (1420–97) painted a fresco in the Palazzo Medici-Riccardi in Florence, *The Procession of the Magi*, between 1459 and 1462 and inserted into it, anachronistically, likenesses of two members of the Medici family, Pietro and Lorenzo. Swann continues this practice by 'identifying' his own contemporaries in the artworks he contemplates.

that scene in the Sardou play . . . all the noteworthy men of Paris . . . amused themselves . . . by appearing onstage: Victorien Sardou (1831–1909) wrote *Fédora*, which premiered in 1882 with Sarah Bernhardt in the leading role as a princess whose husband is assassinated. On successive nights, prominent Parisians and even the Prince of Wales, future Edward VII, played the role of the dead husband, over whom Bernhardt wept at the end of the first act.

98 *much more "in the know" about ethnography than I am*: between 1883 and 89 Paris hosted a number of 'exhibitions' of different ethnic groups from across the globe. This vignette reflects both the French colonial mindset and prevailing attitudes to racial and ethnic diversity of the time.

Coquelin's mulatto friend: Benoît-Constant Coquelin (1841–1909) was one of the Comédie-Française's most celebrated actors of the latter part of the nineteenth century. The identity of his mixed-race friend is unknown ('mulatto' was commonly used at the time).

99 *the Méséglise way*: see note to p. 12.

the crack, as the English say: thought to be a borrowing from English horse-racing jargon, referring to the favourite horse in a race.

100 *lobster à l'américaine*: lobster prepared with a sauce whose key ingredients are butter, white wine, tomatoes, and cognac.

101 *Louis XVI silks*: the last pre-Revolutionary king of France from 1774 until 1792, Louis XVI was guillotined in 1793. Silks, mostly manufactured in Lyons, were used for wall coverings in the royal residences at Versailles, Fontainebleau, and the Tuileries.

102 *the painting by Rubens*: Peter-Paul Rubens (1577–1640) was a Flemish Baroque artist, renowned in particular for his history paintings and altarpieces.

Tiepolo pink: Giambattista Tiepolo (1696–1770) was a Venetian Rococo painter and a major figure of eighteenth-century European art, noted for his colour work, especially his use of blues and pinks.

103 *a portrait by Winterhalter*: Franz Xaver Winterhalter (1805–73) was a pro-lific German painter, principally of court portraits and commissions.

the Princesse Mathilde . . . the niece of Napoleon I: Princess Mathilde Bonaparte (1820–1904) held a salon in Paris throughout the latter part of the nineteenth century, before and after the fall of the Second Empire, that connected her with the brightest and the best of society, including the three writers mentioned here (Flaubert, Sainte-Beuve, Dumas).

Taine: Hippolyte Taine (1828–93), a historian and philosopher, was one of the most influential thinkers of nineteenth-century France.

cochon . . . Bishop Cauchon: Pierre Cauchon (1371–1442), Bishop of Beauvais, was the judge in the trial of Joan of Arc. His surname is similar to the French word for pig, *cochon*.

I left him my card with p.p.c. written on it: *p.p.c.* stands for 'pour prendre congé', to take leave—an indication, on a visiting card, that the sender will not be back. The anecdote is true: Taine's article appeared in February 1887 and Princess Mathilde left him such a card, which the press, when news of her anger got out, suggested might also be read as 'Princesse pas contente' (Princess not happy).

104 *the Duchesse d'Orléans, née Princesse Palatine*: born into the German nobil-ity as Elisabeth Charlotte (1652–1722), of the House of Wittelsbach,

the 'Princess Palatine' was daughter of Karl Ludwig, Elector Palatinate (ruler of the Palatinate, part of the Holy Roman Empire).

Second Empire in style: the rule of Napoleon III, from 1852 to 1870, is known as the Second Empire.

the visit that Tsar Nicholas was to make two days later at the Invalides: a historical event—the Tsar visited Napoleon's tomb at Les Invalides during a state visit in October 1896.

105 *Prince Louis has joined the Russian army*: Louis-Napoléon (1864–1932), the nephew of Princess Mathilde, known as 'Prince Louis', did indeed join the Russian army, eventually becoming a general.

Compiègne: a town in the Oise department, where, in the Château de Compiègne, Napoleon III held court in the autumn.

107 *hansom cab*: a light, two-wheeled, horse-drawn carriage named after its designer, the English architect Joseph Hansom (1803–82); the name appears in English in Proust's text.

to meet: this appears in English in Proust's text.

112 *in the style of Saint-Simon . . . his portrait of Villars . . . a trifle mad*: Hector, Duc de Villars (1653–1734) was a soldier and diplomat under Louis XV, eventually rising to the position of Marshal of France. The memoirist Saint-Simon (see note to p. 59) writes somewhat disparagingly of him, perhaps through jealousy at his social ascension. The narrator's 'quotation' is approximate.

'a Cartesian diver trying to find his balance': named after the French philosopher and scientist René Descartes (1596–1650), 'Cartesian diver' (*ludion* in French) refers to a tube submerged in water that demonstrates the principle of buoyancy.

114 *difficult ever to understand, even in the Meistersinger . . . listening to birdsong*: Wagner's music drama, *Die Meistersinger von Nürnberg* (*The Mastersingers of Nuremberg*, 1868), includes a character who claims to have learned to sing by listening to birdsong.

116 *he detested Tolstoy, George Eliot, Ibsen, and Dostoevsky*: Bergotte here is said to detest some of the most important figures of nineteenth-century European literature, the Russians Leo Tolstoy (1828–1910) and Fyodor Dostoevsky (1821–81), Englishwoman Eliot pseudonym of Mary Ann Evans, (1819–80) and Norwegian Henrik Ibsen (1828–1906), all of whom were greatly admired by Proust.

I like the Chateaubriand of Atala . . . better than Rancé . . . he seems smoother: the works by Chateaubriand (see note to p. 49) mentioned here were written over forty years apart. *Atala* appeared in 1801 and *La Vie de Rancé*, his biography of the Abbé Armand Jean Le Bouthillier de Rancé (1626–1700), founder of the Trappist order, appeared in 1844.

119 *a Hesperid . . . the same gesture on a metope at Olympia . . . the ancient Erechtheion*: the Hesperides, in Greek myth, were the daughters of Atlas.

They are depicted in a metope (a decorative panel) of the temple of Zeus at Olympia and on the Erechtheion, the temple dedicated to Athena and Poseidon-Erechtheus at the Acropolis in Athens, where they make a gesture echoed by La Berma in her performance as Phèdre. Contemporary critics of Sarah Bernhardt commented on the statuesque quality of the positions she held during her performances.

119 *the Caryatids*: the Erechtheion's southern façade includes a renowned portico supported by six Caryatids (female figures also known as 'Korai' or maidens, which is the term Bergotte uses in what follows).

just like Hegeso on the stele in the Kerameikos: the grave stele of an Athenian woman, Hegeso, was discovered in 1870 in the Kerameikos or potters' district in Athens. The stele, a sort of standing slab or commemorative pillar, dates from the fourth century BC and depicts the woman, Hegeso, in the company of a servant, gazing at a piece of jewellery she holds before her.

120 *her Phèdre straight out of the sixth century*: this is something of an approximation (the statuary just mentioned is from the fourth century BC and the only surviving ancient version of the story of Phaedra is by Euripides and dates from the fifth century BC).

121 *I'm not saying that people should think solely of Port-Royal*: the Abbey of Port-Royal was the heart of the Jansenist movement in France and Racine received a Jansenist education. It has been suggested that his representation of fatalism and predestination in *Phèdre* is influenced by his Port-Royal education.

122 *an allusion to Scarron in the presence of Louis XIV*: Paul Scarron (1610–60) was a novelist and dramatist, married from 1652 until his death to Françoise d'Aubigné. The latter would later become Madame de Maintenon, Louis XIV's morganatic wife, so for Racine to mention her late husband's name in the king's presence was ill-advised. The anecdote is recounted in Saint-Simon's *Mémoires*.

124 *Mélusine*: a female figure from folklore, often depicted as having the body of a fish or serpent from the waist down. The different traits inherited from her parents make Gilberte, to the narrator's creative mind, like this alluring hybrid creature.

125 *the plot of the Menaechmi*: a five-act Roman comedy by Plautus (?254–184 BC), based upon the physical similarities of two twins (Shakespeare drew on the play for his *Comedy of Errors*).

the actress had said to Œnone: 'You knew it!': from *Phèdre*, Act IV, scene vi.

129 *the little Cartesian devil . . . up it bobs again*: see note to p. 112.

130 *in Luini's fresco*: Bernardino Luini (1480–1532) was a Renaissance painter who produced a fresco depicting the Adoration of the Magi (1520–5). It was acquired by the Louvre museum in 1867 and remains on show to this day.

132 *the use of 'Monseigneur' at the court of Louis XIV*: the title was an honorific typically used for men of high rank. Under Louis XIV it became formalized as the title of the dauphin (the heir to the throne).

133 *Mantegna*: Andrea Mantegna (1431–1506) was a Paduan painter much admired by Proust.

studies on the 'Cities of Art': the 'Villes d'art célèbres' was a series of illustrated art books published around the turn of the century, upon which Proust drew extensively.

134 *'Rachel, when of the Lord'*: a borrowing from the opera *La Juive* (*The Jewess*, 1835) by Fromenthal Halévy (1799–1862) and Eugène Scribe (1791–1861). The air from which the words are taken runs: 'Rachel! Quand du Seigneur la grâce tutélaire | À mes tremblantes mains confia ton berceau, | J'avais à ton bonheur voué ma vie entière' ('Rachel! When of the Lord his tutelary grace | gave unto my trembling hands your cradle, | I vowed my entire life to your happiness').

138 *leader article . . . the right man in the right place*: these words appear in English in Proust's text.

139 *the pas-de-quatre*: a dance for four participants.

140 *the Boston waltz*: as the name suggests, an American version of the traditional waltz, typically slower-paced.

146 *the Avenue des Acacias*: a promenade in the Bois de Boulogne, evoked at the close of *The Swann Way*, where elegant Parisians went to stroll and be seen.

147 *my Choufleury*: M. *Choufleury restera chez lui le 24 janvier* was an operetta by Offenbach, first performed in 1861. The eponymous character is an extreme snob always seeking out the company of high society. The remark is a knowing nod to Madame Swann's social circle.

P.-J. Stahl's New Year giftbooks: under this pseudonym, Pierre-Jules Hertzel (1814–86) published a great many novels and books for children, including the series of illustrated stories about Mademoiselle Lili mentioned later in the paragraph.

148 *the hôtels of those days*: *hôtels particuliers*, i.e. grand private houses, rather than hotels in the modern sense.

149 *the five o'clock tea*: this phrase appears in English in Proust's text.

senza rigore: (Italian) without rigour or strictness; musical terminology.

Julie de Lespinasse . . . stealing away . . . from the Madame du Deffand . . . its most attractive men: Julie de Lespinasse (1732–76) was a young woman invited in 1754 to the salon of the Marquise du Deffand (1696–1780), then 57 years old and almost completely blind. Lespinasse's role was to read to the marquise and keep her company. Eventually she grew more popular than the marquise, established a salon of her own, and entertained many of the most prominent writers and thinkers of the day, much to Madame du Deffand's displeasure.

150 *Henry Gréville*: pseudonym of Alice Durand (1842–1902). She authored more than twenty works of fiction, many of them set in Russia, where she lived some of her life.

151 *my Vatel*: see note to p. 29.

152 *babys*: this word appears in English in Proust's text with this spelling.

home: this word appears in English in Proust's text.

153 *Redfern fecit?*: Odette uses a Latin term here, in connection with the name of an English fashion designer with a boutique in Paris; a somewhat pretentious way of asking, 'Did Redfern make it?'

Raudnitz: another couturier with a boutique in Paris.

157 *Lemaître?*: florist established on the Boulevard Haussmann in 1885.

Debac . . . Lachaume: two more Parisian florists, found on the Boulevard Malesherbes and the Rue Royale respectively.

158 *Rebattet's*: a confectioner, established around 1820 on the Rue du Faubourg-Saint-Honoré.

Bourbonneux: another confectioner, established in 1846 on the Place du Havre.

nec plus ultra: (Latin) nothing more beyond, indicating something or someone who is unsurpassed.

159 *Lohengrin . . . I heard it's a riot!*: *Lohengrin*, Wagner's opera (see note to p. 7), written between 1845 and 1848, was first performed in Paris in 1891. It is not quite the sort of cabaret entertainment one would encounter at the Folies-Bergère music hall, which was opened in Paris in 1869.

161 *the electrician himself, Mildé!*: Charles Mildé (1851–1931) was an inventor and pioneer in creating and distributing electrical equipment, though around the turn of the century domestic electricity was enjoyed by only a tiny fraction of the population of Paris.

163 *Neurasthenics*: neurasthenia was the name given to a condition diagnosed frequently among the upper classes in the late nineteenth and early twentieth century in the US and in Europe, characterized by weakness, nervous tension, lethargy and fatigue, dyspepsia and neuralgia often experienced in combination. Proust's father co-authored a book on the subject, *L'Hygiène du neurasthénique* (*Treatment for Neurasthenia*), in 1897. Proust himself suffered from many if not all of these symptoms, as well as from severe asthma, with which neurasthenia was often associated.

the love potion . . . long after they drink it: the story of Tristan and Iseult (or Isolde) is an Arthurian romance in which the central couple fall passionately in love as a result of drinking, unawares, a love potion. Wagner's *Tristan und Isolde* (1865) was based on the tale and first performed in Paris in 1900.

168 *bonbonnières from Giroux's*: Alphonse Giroux (1776–1848) was a painter and cabinetmaker who established a high-end store selling furniture and small household items. These included *bonbonnières*, carefully crafted boxes or jars originally intended for holding sweets.

169 *Watteau dressing gowns*: Jean-Antoine Watteau (1684–1721) was a major figure of French eighteenth-century painting, his work characterized by

scenes of play and courtship among aristocratic figures in idyllic settings, known as 'fêtes galantes'. 'Watteau gowns' or 'Watteau-style' was used to refer to garments resembling those depicted in his paintings.

170 *Botticelli-like charm*: in *The Swann Way* we learn that Swann is captivated by a resemblance he perceives between Odette and Botticelli's depiction of Jethro's daughter, Zipporah, in his frescoes depicting *Scenes from the Life of Moses* in the Sistine Chapel.

the Virgin in the Magnificat: the *Madonna of the Magnificat* (1481) is a tondo (circular) painting by Botticelli that features a shawl round the neck of the Virgin, as described. The painting is held in the Uffizi in Florence.

La Primavera: Botticelli's work of this name, also known as the *Allegory of Spring*, dating from the 1470s or 1480s, is a large panel painting depicting seven principal figures in a garden setting, one of whom, Flora, the embodiment of spring, wears a dress decorated with a multitude of flowers. It can be seen at the Uffizi gallery.

171 *percaline*: a lightweight cotton fabric.

'monkey jacket': the French here is a *saute-en-barque* (literally 'jump on the boat'), which was a short-sleeved women's jacket or cape.

173 *wearing sweaters as they do*: the discussion of Madame Swann's wardrobe here spans influences from the sixteenth to the twentieth centuries, from Henri II of France to the most recent trends of the early 1900s. *Sweaters* appears in English in Proust's text.

175 *Good evening!*: this greeting appears in English in Proust's text at this point, though not throughout.

176 *La Bruyère says: 'It is sad to be a lover without wealth'*: Jean de La Bruyère (1645–96) was a philosopher and early member of the Académie française, best known for his book *Caractères* (*Characters*, 1688), a translation of Theophrastus' Greek text of the same title and an appended set of parallel reflections on the 'character(s)' of his own age. It is from this text that the given quotation is taken (from chapter 4 'Du cœur'—'Of the heart').

180 *Playing both Joseph and the Pharaoh, I set out to interpret my dream*: in the Old Testament, Joseph, son of Jacob, has dreams that are described in Genesis 37; he also interprets those of the Pharaoh: see Genesis 41.

184 *the Ice Saints*: in the Christian calendar, St Mamertus, St Pancras, and St Servatius are known as the 'Ice Saints', since their respective feast days (11, 12, 13 May) very often mark a late cold spell, sometimes known as 'the blackthorn winter'.

185 *the upright trees of the Pre-Raphaelites*: Proust's familiarity with these mid-nineteenth-century English artists derives principally from his reading of the art historian and critic John Ruskin. It is not clear if he has a particular painting in mind here.

Tansonville: as we learn in the novel's first volume, Tansonville is the site of Swann's country residence near the town of Combray.

185 *'Symphony in White Major'*: James Abbott McNeill Whistler (1834–1903), a painter much admired by Proust and one of the models for his fictional painter Elstir (see note to p. 203), created three paintings titled *Symphony in White*, each representing young women clad in white dresses. Théophile Gautier, an author well known to Proust, gave the title 'Symphonie en blanc majeur' to one of the poems in his 1849 collection *Émaux et camées*.

the Good Friday Spell in Parsifal: name given to the closing section of the first part of Act III of Wagner's music drama *Parsifal* (1882) and which celebrates the notions of rebirth and salvation that are associated with the Easter story.

187 *Good morning*: this greeting appears in English in Proust's text at this point, though not throughout.

188 *eight-spring victoria*: an open-topped, four-wheeled, horse-drawn carriage.

189 *Hypatia*: a fourth-century philosopher and mathematician; Leconte de Lisle (1818–94), the leading poet of the Parnassian School, included a poem to Hypatia in his *Poèmes antiques* (1852), which ends with a line echoed by Proust here: 'Et les mondes encor roulent sous ses pieds blancs!' (And worlds still turn beneath her feet!).

190 *drop*: Proust invents the word *dropiez* here.

Sagan: Charles Boson de Talleyrand-Perigord (1832–1910) was Prince de Sagan from 1859 and Duc de Talleyrand and Duc de Sagan upon the death of his father in 1898. His nephew, Boni de Castellane (1867–1932) was a friend of Proust.

Antoine de Castellane, Adalbert de Montmorency: two well-known aristocrats of the period. The former (1844–1917) was father of Boni de Castellane, just mentioned, and belonged to a noble lineage dating back to the eleventh century; the latter (1837–1915) was a relative of the Prince of Sagan, mentioned above.

PLACE NAMES: THE PLACE

193 *my departure for Balbec*: see note to p. 15.

195 *a departure by train or the Elevation of the Cross*: the narrator here picks out the (perhaps unanticipated) aesthetic qualities of the railway station, a site symbolic of modernity and progress, and connects them not to contemporary artists such as Claude Monet (1840–1926) and Whistler who both depicted stations, but to an artistic heritage reaching back to the Renaissance. Both Mantegna (see note to p. 133) and Paolo Veronese (1528–88) produced works related to the Crucifixion with dramatic skies: Mantegna's *Crucifixion* dates from 1457–9 and Veronese's *Calvary* from ?1580. Both works are held in the Louvre.

196 *'panorama'*: a visual device that first came to Paris in 1799. A precursor to moving pictures, the panorama presented a large-format circular image in a closed rotunda, viewed from a raised platform within the enclosure,

creating a powerful illusion of depth and an experience of vision without a limiting frame around the image.

Madame de Sévigné . . . from Paris to 'L'Orient': Madame de Sévigné (Marie de Rabutin-Chantal, 1626–96) was a prolific and celebrated writer of letters, particularly to her daughter, Madame de Grignan (1646–1705) and much admired by Proust. She is the narrator's grandmother's favourite author. 'L'Orient', as it was spelled in Sévigné's day (now Lorient) is a port town in Britanny. Her journey there from Paris is described in letters of April and May 1689.

197 *my aunts Céline and Victoire*: this is an authorial slip—the narrator's aunts are introduced as Céline and Flora in *The Swann Way*.

Cathedral of Saint-Lô: construction of the church of Notre-Dame de Saint-Lô in Normandy began in the late twelfth century. It is an example of the Flamboyant Gothic style of architecture.

198 *Saint-Cloud*: a prosperous commune to the west of Paris, near Versailles.

the joyful traveller Ruskin writes about: Ruskin writes in various places, including his autobiographical writings *Praeterita* (1885–9), about the joys of travel and encountering new places or re-encountering those previously known. He did not, however, appreciate train travel nor its impacts upon travellers and landscapes.

199 *following our every move with your eyes glued to a map*: in a letter of February 1671, Sévigné wrote to her daughter, 'I have a map before me; I know all the places where you will spend the night.'

in a portrait by Chardin or Whistler: Jean-Baptiste Siméon Chardin (1699–1779) and James Abbott McNeill Whistler, mentioned above, are two of the painters Proust admired the most in his artistic pantheon. Both men produced profound and affecting portraits marked by the sort of attention to detail alluded to here.

pictures of Anne de Bretagne painted by . . . in a book of hours: Anne of Brittany (1477–1514) was Duchess of Brittany, then Queen of France. She commissioned a prayer book or 'book of hours', *Les Grandes Heures d'Anne de Bretagne*, which was sumptuously illustrated by Jean Bourdichon between 1503 and 1508 and is held at the Bibliothèque nationale de France in Paris.

200 *"Regulus was accustomed, upon momentous occasions . . . ."*: Regulus was a roman general, renowned for his heroism in the wars against Carthage and celebrated by Cicero and Horace among others. By association the narrator's mother is encouraging him to be brave.

all the courage you lack: another borrowing from Madame de Sévigné's letters to her daughter, again from February 1671.

Montretout: part of the commune of Saint-Cloud, where the narrator's mother is staying.

201 *the Mémoires of Madame de Beausergent*: a fictional work and author, invented by Proust.

202 *Madame de Simiane . . . being so for your pleasure*: Pauline de Simiane (1674–1737) was Madame de Sévigné's granddaughter. The quotations from Simiane's letters included here are approximate and draw on missives sent in 1734–5.

203 *Elstir, who was to have such a profound influence on my way of seeing things*: the first mention, by name, of the fictional painter Elstir, whose name carries an echo of Whistler as well as of contemporary artist Paul Helleu (1859–1927), whose subjects and themes align closely to what we learn of Elstir's work. The latter figures in the novel's first volume but is referred to in the Verdurin circle only by his nickname 'Biche' or 'Tiche'.

'I couldn't resist . . . shrouded men upright against trees': an approximate quotation from Sévigné, letter to her daughter, June 1680.

the Dostoevsky side . . . of Madame de Sévigné's Letters: the narrator's suggestion here is that the seventeenth-century letter-writer and the nineteenth-century novelist (see note to p. 116) share an approach to depicting their world and the people in it.

207 *those towns' principal churches*: the cathedrals of Chartres, Bourges, and Beauvais, and the abbey at Vézelay, are indeed renowned in France and internationally for the beauty and detail of their architecture. Proust was fascinated by the symbolism, ambition, and multiple scales of church architecture and was an enthusiastic visitor of cathedrals, as well as the Abbey of Vézelay near Dijon, which he saw whilst en route to Evian in 1903.

the miraculous Christ statue: in AD 1001, crews fishing off the coast at Dives-sur-Mer, a village adjacent to Cabourg on the Normandy coast, discovered a statue of Christ and, separately, the cross to which the statue had once been attached. Dives subsequently became a site of pilgrimage.

the Trocadéro Museum: an ethnographical museum established in Paris in 1878. See note to p. 56.

209 *as beautiful as Siena*: the Tuscan hill town of Siena was an important medieval centre of finance and commerce, growing into a picturesque city that took shape round a spectacular piazza which hosts a twice-yearly horse race known as the 'Palio'.

Quimperlé . . . Pont-Aven: locales in western Britanny.

210 *Incarville . . . Maineville*: some of these place names, or names similar to those listed, can be found in various *départements* of the North of France, but not such that they would form stops on a single train-line. They are borrowings that lend a familiar colouring to Proust's fictional Norman topography.

211 *the glare of Minos, Aeacus and Rhadamanthus*: in Greek myth, the judges of the dead in the underworld, determining whether souls would be granted eternal life in Paradise (the 'Elysian Fields') or eternal suffering in Tartarus, the pit of hell.

212 *the colours Dante uses to depict Paradise and Hell*: the *Divine Comedy* (1321), by Dante Aligheri (*c.*1265–1321), tells of the journey of the soul after

death, in three parts: *Inferno* (*Hell*), *Purgatorio* (*Purgatory*), and *Paradiso* (*Heaven*). The landscape of *Inferno* is dark, gruesome, and foreboding; *Paradiso* is characterized by brightness, light, and clarity.

the statue of Duguay-Trouin: a statue of René Duguay-Trouin (1673–1736), a privateer who became an admiral, is to be found in his birthplace of Saint-Malo; another statue stood for a time on the Pont de la Concorde in Paris and was subsequently moved to Versailles. Placing such a statue in Balbec once more shows Proust interweaving reality and fiction.

'lift': this word appears in English in Proust's text.

where the lantern would be in a Norman church: a 'lantern' or 'lantern tower' in church architecture is a tower above the transept (the joining point of the four arms of a cruciform church) that lets in light.

214 *Cardinal La Balue in the cage in which he could neither stand nor sit*: Jean Balue or La Balue (*c.*1421–91) was a bishop under Louis XI's reign and a cardinal of the Catholic Church from 1467. He was imprisoned by the King at the Château de Loches from 1469 to 1480 as punishment for colluding with Charles 'the Bold' (1433–77). Historians doubt that he was in fact kept in such a cage, as the anecdote has it.

the assassination of the Duc de Guise: an allusion to Paul Delaroche's 1835 painting of the same name, in which the arrangement of the figures, and isolation of the murdered duke, enhances the viewer's perception of the vastness of the room in which the attack has taken place.

led by a guide from Cook's: Thomas Cook & Son was a travel agency established in England in 1841, which by the 1860s was offering tours across Europe and North America, and by the 1870s round-the-world trips.

cheval-glass: a long mirror mounted on a swivel that allows it to be tilted.

the aroma of vetiver: vetiver is a fragrant grass; essential oils extracted from the root have a range of medicinal properties and are commonly used in perfumes.

216 *that trifling introit of the day*: an *introit* (Latin: *introitus* = entrance) is a psalm that is sung to mark the opening of the celebration of the Eucharist.

219 *paintings by Tuscan primitives*: artists working between the 1200s and 1400s were often called 'primitives'. Proust visited an exhibition of 'Flemish Primitives' in Bruges in 1902.

220 *'sitting on the jetty' or 'in the boudoir' as in Baudelaire*: Charles Baudelaire (see note to p. 42) is one of the poets most admired by Proust. 'Sitting on the jetty' is a probable allusion to a prose poem, 'Le Port'; the mention of 'the boudoir' and the following reference to 'sun shining on the sea' are allusions to 'Chant d'automne' ('Autumn Song') from Baudelaire's best-known collection, *Les Fleurs du Mal* (*The Flowers of Evil*, first version 1857).

221 *smiling like Saint Blandina*: Christian saint and martyr (*c.* AD 162–177), who withstood horrific torture by Roman officials.

221 *eminent personalities . . . Le Mans*: Caen, near Cabourg, is a city in Normandy; Cherbourg is a city on the coast of Brittany; and Le Mans is a city in the Sarthe *département*, south of Caen and west of Chartres. The 'eminent personalities' are members of the legal profession: a first president is a senior magistrate and a *bâtonnier* is the name given to the president of the Bar.

222 *the Cour de Cassation*: France's supreme court for civil and criminal cases.

Rivebelle or Costedor: both are inventions of Proust's.

223 *the royal bathing machine at Ostend*: 'bathing machines' were wheeled contraptions, essentially small huts on wheels that were rolled or pulled into the sea to protect the modesty of those not wishing to be seen publicly in a bathing suit. Ostend is a city on the coast of Belgium, popular in the late nineteenth century in particular as a summer resort, and favoured by the wealthy, including the Belgian royal family.

226 *the Odéon*: a significant venue in Parisian theatre culture; it is an imposing building, established in 1782 in the 6th *arrondissement*.

227 *La Rochefoucauld*: the name of a celebrated and well-known aristocratic family, the most famous member of which is François, Duc de la Rochefoucauld (1613–80), a moralist and author of the widely read *Maximes* (1665).

the Café Anglais . . . the Tour d'Argent: for the Café Anglais, see note to p. 53. The Tour d'Argent (literally, The Silver Tower) is one of the most renowned restaurants in Paris, overlooking the Île Saint-Louis from the Quai de la Tournelle, tracing its origins back to 1582.

229 *the Shah of Persia or Queen Ranavalo*: a slip or misconstrual by the author, since the last queen of Madagascar was Ranavalona III ('Ranavalo' is Proust's approximation).

230 *The Life of Moses . . . in the guise of Jethro's daughter*: see note to p. 170.

231 *Rue Lord-Byron . . . Rue Hippolyte-Lebas*: the first three street names mentioned here derive from noble and distinguished families or individuals, yet these are not characteristics uniformly reflected in the streets themselves. The final two streets mentioned are named after an engineer and an architect respectively.

her cousin Mac-Mahon: Patrice MacMahon (1808–93), who led the French army in the Franco-Prussian War, was president of the Third Republic of France from 1873 to 1879. His relation to the fictional Madame de Villeparisis is Proust's invention.

Carnot, also a president of the Republic: Marie François Sadi Carnot (1837–94) was president from 1887 until his assassination in 1894.

Raspail . . . Pius IX: see note to p. 54.

232 *They were the de Cambremers, weren't they?*: the 'de' indicates nobility, but it is not typically included when a surname is used in isolation. This highlights the speaker's lack of familiarity with such social niceties.

distaff side: the female side.

'Of my Estate, must I give you half?': Racine, *Esther* (1689), Act II, Scene vii. Racine's three-act tragedy builds on the Old Testament story of Esther, a Jewish woman taken by Ahasuerus, King of Persia, as his queen.

bezique: a nineteenth-century card game requiring two packs of cards.

238 *those scenes in Molière . . . falling into each other's arms*: probable reference to Molière's *L'École des femmes* (*The School for Wives*, first performed 1662), Act I, scene iv.

'sumptuous enough to make you die of hunger': quotation from a letter from Madame de Sévigné to her daughter of July 1689.

to seek in it the effects described by Baudelaire: see note to p. 220.

239 *the mythical Cimmerians*: an ancient people that thrived to the north and south of the Black Sea (modern-day Russia and Turkey) in the eighth to the sixth century BC. The narrator seems to think of them as an example of a mysterious, ancient civilization, closely associated with maritime life.

rince-bouches: a small bowl of warm, scented water that was offered to guests at the end of a meal, so that they could rinse their mouth.

the Archduke Rudolf: Rudolf, Crown Prince of Austria (1858–89), found dead in his hunting lodge with his mistress, also dead. The circumstances of the case attracted considerable attention across Europe.

240 *'As soon as I've received one letter . . . what I feel' . . . 'I seek out those few . . . I avoid the others'*: the first quotation comes from a letter from Madame de Sévigné to her daughter in February 1671, the second is Proust's elaboration.

241 *no less than Plato distorted the words of Socrates, or Saint John those of Jesus*: Plato (429–347 BC) was an ancient Greek philosopher and a pupil/follower of Socrates (*c.*470–399 BC); it is via Plato's writings that Socrates' thought and method are conserved. Similarly, the Gospel of John the Evangelist is a major source for the 'words' of Christ, whom John often quotes in his text.

barouche: a large, four-wheeled carriage drawn by two horses.

242 *a few words were written in pencil*: the Princesse de Luxembourg is a fictional character, though one sharing a range of traits with Jeanne Seillière, Princesse de Sagan (1839–1905), a significant *fin-de-siècle* society figure known personally to Proust.

the Prelude to Lohengrin, the Overture to Tannhäuser: the two pieces mentioned are from major operas by Richard Wagner. *Lohengrin* is a Romantic opera first performed in 1850; *Tannhäuser* a slightly earlier composition, first performed in 1845. The Prelude and Overture mentioned here are often performed as stand-alone concert pieces.

243 *baby*: this word appears in English in Proust's text.

244 *Algeciras*: the Spanish town was the site of an important diplomatic conference in 1906, which sought to resolve the First Moroccan Crisis (the Franco-German dispute over the state of Morocco).

one of Titian's pupils: the name she cannot remember is provided by the narrator in the following paragraph: 'El Greco', the accepted moniker of Domenikos Theotokopoulos (1541–1614). He had worked with Titian earlier in his life, in Venice, but moved to Toledo in 1576–7 where he lived and worked until his death.

the Jupiter to whom Gustave Moreau . . . gave a superhuman stature: Gustave Moreau (1826–98) was best known as a Symbolist painter whose canvases lavishly depict mythological and biblical themes and motifs such as *Oedipus and the Sphinx* (1864) or *Salomé* (1876). His *Jupiter and Semele* dates from 1896 and depicts the mortal female Semele as a small, feeble figure lying across the lap of a vast, imposing, enthroned Jupiter.

246 *a Baronne d'Ange*: the faux-noble title adopted by Suzanne, a courtesan in Dumas *fils*' comedy *Le Demi-monde* (1855).

Mathurin Régnier and Macette: *Macette* is the title given to Satire XIII (1612) by Régnier (1573–1613); the work is a portrait of a procuress by that name who embodies both manipulation and hypocrisy.

247 *Nereid*: in Greek myth, the Nereids are sea nymphs, the fifty daughters of Nereus and Doris.

248 *the nymph Glauconome*: one of the Nereids, said to be especially given to laughter.

249 *the narthex or antechamber for catechumens in Romanesque churches*: the narthex is a lobby that permits entrance to those who are yet to be baptized; catechumen is the name given to those undertaking instruction in Scripture, who will seek baptism in due course (and then be permitted entrance to the nave—the main body of the church).

like Madame de Maintenon's charges . . . whenever Esther or Joad left the stage: an allusion to Racine's tragedies *Esther* (1689) and *Athalie* (1691), written at the request of Madame de Maintenon who had established the Maison royale de Saint-Louis as a school and whose pupils performed as the chorus in these plays.

250 *Baudelaire's 'radiant sunbeams'*: a further recollection of the poem 'Chant d'automne'; see note to p. 220.

Leconte de Lisle describes in his Oresteia . . . the waves of the bay: Leconte de Lisle (see note to p. 189) wrote a play entitled *Les Erinnyes* (1873), based on Aeschylus' *Oresteia*—the lines quoted are approximate.

251 *Chopin and Liszt had played there, Lamartine recited poetry*: Fryderyk Franciszek (or Frédéric François) Chopin (1810–49) was a musical prodigy born to a French émigré father and a Polish mother. He was a composer and pianist of genius, known above all for his preludes, waltzes, and nocturnes. Franz Liszt (1811–86) was a Hungarian composer and

performer and renowned as one of the most accomplished pianists of all
time. Alphonse de Lamartine (1790–1869) was a statesman and poet of the
Romantic era.

Croesus: king of Lydia (modern-day Turkey) from 560 to 546 BC and
famed for his vast wealth.

252 *the expulsions of the Jesuits*: the suppression and expulsion of the Jesuits
took place across Europe in the second half of the eighteenth century; the
order was abolished by the Holy See in 1773; Jesuits were expelled from
Spain and the Spanish Empire in 1767.

Louis-Philippe's wit and conversational skill: Louis-Philippe (1773–1850)
was king of the French (and known as 'the citizen king') from 1830 to
1848, a period known as the July Monarchy.

men like Molé . . . Daru: these eight men were all prominent figures in
nineteenth-century French politics but also made significant contribu-
tions to literary life and culture. Louis-Mathieu Molé was prime minister
from 1836 to 1839 and elected to the Académie française in 1840; Louis de
Fontanes was a poet and statesman who held a range of roles including as
a government minister during the Restoration; Eugène d'Arnauld, Baron
de Vitrolles, was a government minister during the Restoration; Pierre-
Ernest Bersot was a member of the Académie des sciences morales and
director of the École normale supérieure from 1871 to 1880; Étienne-
Denis, Baron then Duc de Pasquier was, among other roles, Prefect of
Police and a government minister, and elected to the Académie française in
1842; Pierre-Antoine Lebrun was a poet and playwright who was also
a peer during the July Monarchy and a Senator during the Second Empire;
Narcisse-Achille, Comte de Salvandy was a minister, ambassador, and
academician; finally, Pierre Bruno, Comte Daru was intendant-general of
Napoléon's armies, author of a history of Venice, and translator of Horace.

253 *Stendhal*: under this pseudonym, Henri Beyle (1783–1842) wrote two of
the most highly regarded novels of the nineteenth century: *The Red and
the Black* (1830) and *The Charterhouse of Parma* (1839).

Monsieur Mérimée's: Prosper Merimée (1803–70) was a dramatist and
writer of short fiction, notably the novella *Carmen* (1845) which was the
basis for Bizet's opera (1875).

Monsieur Sainte-Beuve: see note to p. 43. The attitude of the critic
articulated here is precisely the position that Proust took umbrage at: he,
Proust, was of the view that art should be evaluated and enjoyed on its own
terms, and in 1908–9 he drafted a critical essay 'Against Sainte-Beuve',
out of which the first drafts of what became *The Swann Way* would emerge.

255 *a fragmentary, fleeting passer-by . . . an imagination overwrought with regret*:
the image of the female passer-by here ('une passante fragmentaire et
fugitive' in the original) carries a marked echo of Baudelaire's poem
about beauty, chance, and the fleetingness of experience, 'A une passante'
('To a woman passing by'), from *Les Fleurs du mal*.

257 *an ogival window . . . the bulge of a capital*: an ogival window is one shaped like an arch that comes to a point; the 'capital' or head (Latin, *caput*—head) is the topmost part of a column.

258 *the steeples of Martinville*: in *The Swann Way*, the young narrator experiences a sense of awe and exhilaration on a carriage ride during which he witnesses shifting perspectives on a set of steeples that seem to come in and out of focus as his carriage makes its way along a winding road. It prompts him to write down an account of his experience: his first act of creative writing.

260 *a ring of witches or Norns offering to tell me their oracles*: in Scandinavian mythology Norns are female deities who tend Yggdrasil, the tree of life, and shape each individual's destiny, much like the Fates or Parcae of Roman myth.

261 *Chained to my back seat like Prometheus . . . Oceanids*: in Roman myth, Prometheus stole fire from the gods and was punished by being chained to a rock to have his (self-renewing) liver eternally pecked out by an eagle. In Aeschylus' *Prometheus Bound* (?479–424 BC) the Oceanids, daughters of Oceanus and Thetys, form a chorus that offers sympathy to Prometheus during his suffering.

262 *'She spread . . . melancholy' or 'weeping . . . fountains' or 'The shadows . . . august and solemn'*: the first quotation comes from Chateaubriand's *Atala*; the second from Vigny's long poem 'La Maison du Berger'; the third from Hugo's poem 'Booz endormi'.

predictions about the papal election: in March 1829 a Conclave was held and Cardinal Castiglioni was elected pope and took the name Pius VIII. Chateaubriand was French ambassador to Rome at the time and claimed to have anticipated this outcome.

Monsieur de Blacas: Casimir, Duc de Blacas d'Aulps (1771–1839) was French ambassador in Naples at the time of the election and took over from Chateaubriand in Rome when the latter resigned in August 1829.

263 *Cinq-Mars*: see note to p. 43.

the premiere of Hernani: the opening of Victor Hugo's *Hernani* (1830), a five-act play set in early sixteenth-century Spain about three men in love with the same woman, caused a very considerable stir, pitting the Romantics (embodied by Hugo and his supporters) against those supportive of the classical tradition in French theatre.

265 *godlike Alexanders of Macedonia*: Alexander of Macedonia (356–323 BC) is better known as Alexander the Great, ruler of one of the most vast empires ever known, stretching south from the Mediterranean into Egypt, and east as far as the Himalayas.

the Duc de Nemours: Louis-Charles-Philippe d'Orléans (1814–96), second son of King Louis-Philippe (see note to p. 252).

lovely woodwork—I think it was by Bagard: César Bagard (1639–1709) was a sculptor whose work in wood decorated a number of *hôtels particuliers* in Paris; much of his work was destroyed in the Revolution of 1789.

the unfortunate Duchesse de Praslin: the duchess (1807–47) was so called because she bore ten children by her husband, Charles de Choiseul, Duc de Praslin, who then left her for the children's governess; she was subsequently murdered (by the duke, her former husband, it is thought); he committed suicide before he could be tried. This extraordinary story is compressed into that brief adjective 'unfortunate'.

Madame de Praslin, who at the time was only Mademoiselle Sebastiani: the Duchesse de Praslin was born Françoise Sebastiani, daughter of a French army general.

266 *Madame de Choiseul*: the Choiseul family, from which Madame de Praslin's husband descends, is an important aristocratic family tracing its origins back many centuries (as Madame de Villeparisis goes on to say).

Louis 'the Fat': Louis VI was King of the Franks from 1081 to 1137.

Madame la Duchesse de la Rochefoucauld, Madame la Comtesse: on the Rochefoucauld family, see note to p. 227.

267 *ordinary men like Molé or Loménie*: on Molé, see note to p. 252; and on Loménie, see note to p. 43.

a Doudan . . . a Joubert: Ximinès Doudan (1800–72) was personal secretary to the Duc de Broglie (1785–1870), a diplomat and prime minister (1835–6); Charles, Comte de Rémusat (1797–1875) was a writer, government minister, and member of the Académie française; Joseph Joubert (1754–1824) was an essayist and thinker. It is characteristic of Proust's writing that Madame de Beausergent, Proust's fictional creation, mingles here with these celebrated figures.

the Baudelaires, the Poes, the Verlaines, the Rimbauds: Baudelaire is mentioned above; all these figures are major nineteenth-century poets. Edgar Allan Poe (1809–49) was an American writer whose work fascinated Baudelaire, who translated some of it into French; Paul Verlaine (1844–96) and Arthur Rimbaud (1854–91) were poets and lovers, as well as poetic successors to Baudelaire.

268 *preparing for Saumur . . . stationed in nearby Doncières*: the French École de cavalerie (Cavalry Academy) is located in the town of Saumur. Doncières is Proust's invention as the location of a military barracks.

269 *Marquis de Saint-Loup-en-Bray*: a fictional creation; numerous localities in France bear the name 'Saint-Loup', though none 'en-Bray'.

the young Duc d'Uzès: there have been seventeen Ducs d'Uzès to date. Proust may be referring to Emmanuel de Crussol, Duc d'Uzès from 1872 to 1878 or Jacques de Crussol, Duc d'Uzès from 1878 to 1893.

272 *Nietzsche and Proudhon*: on the former, see note to p. 7. Pierre-Joseph Proudhon (1809–65) was a thinker and politician. A committed socialist, he is thought of as the 'father of anarchism'.

'intellectuals': at the time this was a new coinage, first appearing in the 1898 'Manifesto of the Intellectuals', a protest against the injustice of the

handling of the Dreyfus case (see note to p. 81) and signed by many of the
most prominent writers and thinkers of the day, including Proust.

273 *yawned at Wagner and been passionate about Offenbach*: Saint-Loup's
father's tastes differ from his son's. The works of Wagner (see notes to
pp. 7 and 242) are often considered the pinnacle of highbrow artistic ambition. Offenbach (see notes to pp. 57 and 147) was a direct contemporary
of Wagner's and is remembered for his extensive work as the composer of
operettas, often light-hearted, comic, or satirical.

   a son of Boieldieu or Labiche: François-Adrien Boieldieu (1775–1834) was
   a prolific French composer in the opéra comique genre; Eugène Labiche
   (1815–88) for his part was a prolific writer of plays, especially vaudeville
   (light theatre incorporating song).

   La Belle Hélène: a popular and successful operetta by Offenbach, with
   a libretto by Henri Meilhac and Ludovic Halévy, based on the classical
   tale of the elopement of Helen of Troy with Paris, which triggered the
   Trojan War.

   the Ring: Wagner's tetralogy of music dramas (*Das Rheingold, Die Walküre,
   Siegfried, Götterdämmerung*) is known as the 'Ring Cycle' or simply the
   'Ring'.

274 *Rubinstein*: Anton Grigorievitch Rubinstein (1825–94) was one of the
finest pianists of the nineteenth century and founded the conservatories of
St Petersburg and Moscow.

277 *the Rue d'Aboukir*: the street is named after a Napoleonic victory in 1799
and historically was the site of many Jewish businesses.

   the Concours général . . . an université populaire: established in 1747, the
   Concours général is an annual competition to identify the most able students in the final two years of schooling in France. To win the top prize is
   a major achievement. *Universités populaires* were established in France in
   the second half of the nineteenth century with a view to ensuring adults
   from the working classes could attain the skills and technical know-how
   needed for their careers. That Saint-Loup should have met Bloch at such
   an institution is indicative of his radical views on social class.

278 *having to illustrate the Evangelists or the Arabian Nights*: in *The Swann Way*
we learn that *The Thousand and One Nights* are treasured by the young
protagonist, figuring on plates used in the family home at Combray and
becoming a frequent point of reference for the narrator.

   The Stones of Venaïce by Lord John Ruskin: Ruskin's study of the architecture of Venice (mispronounced by Bloch, who also misattributes a title of
   nobility to Ruskin) was published in three volumes in 1851–3. Proust consulted it when he visited Venice in 1900.

279 *'the commonest thing in the world'*: the philosopher René Descartes (see
note to p. 112) famously argued in *Le Discours de la méthode* (*Discourse
on Method*, 1637) that common sense is 'the commonest thing in the
world'.

283 *in the pages of Barbey d'Aurevilly*: Jules Barbey d'Aurevilly (1808–89) was a novelist, poet, and critic admired by Proust (and many others in the nineteenth and early twentieth century). He wrote a study of dandyism published in 1845, focused on the English Regency figure Beau Brummell (1778–1840).

284 *'by the Kroniôn Zeus, keeper of oaths'*: Bloch is pedantically pointing out that Kronos, in Greek myth, is father of Zeus. He often alludes to and speaks in the style of Leconte de Lisle's *Poèmes antiques* (1852) (see note to p. 189).

    the black Ker: also in Greek myth, a Ker is a winged spirit associated with death; Keres have an important role in Homer's *Iliad*, which was translated by Leconte de Lisle in 1866.

285 *Samuel Bernard*: (1651–1739) a famous banker who supported Louis XIV financially. The narrator seems to suggest Bernard was Jewish, though it is more likely he was of Protestant origin.

    cherished by Ares . . . Menier of the swift ships: in Bloch's mannered idiom, Saint-Loup is 'cherished by Ares', who is the Greek god of war, renowned as a 'tamer of horses'; Amphitrite is the goddess of the sea; 'Menier of the swift ships' probably refers to Gaston Menier, a wealthy owner of cacao plantations and a chocolate business, who had a luxurious (and much-talked-about) yacht named the Ariane.

286 *Heredia*: José-Maria de Heredia (1842–1905) was a Cuban-born poet established in Paris and associated with the Parnassian movement.

    the Suez Canal Company: the *Compagnie universelle du canal maritime de Suez* was established in 1858 by Ferdinand de Lesseps, a diplomat turned businessman, with the goal of connecting the Mediterranean to the Red Sea. Monsieur de Marsantes's presidency of the company is of course fictitious.

    they'd left the stereoscope in Paris: a stereoscope is an optical device, popular in the nineteenth century, that gives the illusion of depth in three dimensions via two identical images presented to the viewer at the same time, in binocular vision ('in stereo'). Such devices could be handheld, but given the Blochs are concerned about damaging their device in transit, and the details that follow, it seems likely theirs is of larger, cabinet-style design.

287 *some podestà or prince of the Church*: a *podestà* or *potestate* was the name of the senior magistrate or civic officer in Italian cities in the late medieval period; 'prince of the Church' is a term typically used to describe cardinals of the Catholic Church.

    a custumal: (or 'customary') a record of customs and laws relevant to a given locale or organization.

    a viola da gamba or a viola d'amore: the former is an instrument played upright like the cello, originating in the mid-fifteenth century; the latter dates from the sixteenth century and is played under the chin like a violin.

288 *'the Three Graces'*: in Greek myth, three female embodiments of beauty, grace, and harmony, known as the Charites or, individually, as Euphrosyne, Aglaea, and Thalia. They appear in Botticelli's *Primavera*; see note to p. 170.

289 *he invited some musicians to play them . . . for himself and a few friends*: in April 1916, Proust himself did just this, though he did not invite 'a few friends'—he listened to the performance in his apartment alone.

291 *claim descent from Geneviève de Brabant*: this (fictional) lineage is discussed in 'Combray', the first part of *The Swann Way*. Geneviève de Brabant is the heroine of a medieval legend.

our war cry, which later became "Passavant", started out as "Combraysis": *Passavant* suggests the forthrightness of the Guermantes (literally '[we] go before'); *Combraysis* indicates their roots in the town of Combray.

292 *Ovid's metamorphoses*: the Latin poet Ovid (43 BC–AD ?18) was author of a remarkable series of poems, grouped into fifteen books, titled *Metamorphoses*, each one narrating tales of transformation; they are one of the founding works of Western literature.

Carrière: Eugène Carrière (1849–1906), Symbolist artist and portrait painter.

a Whistler or a Velázquez: on Whistler, see note to p. 199; Diego Velázquez (1599–1660) is the most celebrated painter of the Spanish Golden Age.

Gustave Moreau: see note to p. 244.

293 *they were merely Barons of Île-de-France*: that is to say, the province of that name, and not the whole of France.

the Ducs de Nemours and the Princes de Lamballe: on the Duc de Nemours, see note to p. 265; Louis Alexandre de Bourbon (1747–68), Prince de Lamballe and great-grandson of Louis XIV, lived a short and indulgent life, dying of venereal disease aged just 20.

294 *Raphael . . . Boucher*: Raphael (1483–1520) was a Renaissance painter and architect; François Boucher (1703–70) was one of the finest painters of the eighteenth century. The span of great artists said to have portrayed Charlus' relatives is indicative of the grandeur of his heritage.

Lebourg . . . Guillaumin: Albert Lebourg (1849–1928) was a landscape painter, while his contemporary Armand Guillaumin (1841–1927) was an associate of the Impressionist Camille Pissarro and post-Impressionist Paul Cézanne.

an ode by Horace: Quintus Horatius Flaccus, known as Horace (65–8 BC) was a Roman poet and is best known for his *Odes* (Latin: *Carmina*).

295 *heraldic quarterings*: in heraldry, the division of a shield into four equal parts, each of which can display a different element or coat of arms; these quarters themselves may in turn be quartered.

a La Bruyère or a Fénelon as their tutor: Jean de la Bruyère (see note to p. 176) was tutor to the Duc de Bourbon (1668–1710); François de Salignac de la Mothe-Fénelon (1651–1715), known as Fénelon, was an archbishop and author, as well as tutor to the Duc de Bourgogne (1682–1712), Louis XIV's eldest son.

298 *La Fontaine's Monomotapa . . . the absence of the other pigeon*: in Book 8 of the *Fables* (1668–94) of Jean de La Fontaine (1621–95), we find reference to a fictional kingdom of this name in 'The Two Friends'; and in Book 9 we encounter the fable of 'The Two Pigeons'.

299 *"This separation . . . for which we yearn"*: approximate quotation/ paraphrase from two letters from Madame de Sévigné to her daughter, from February 1671 and January 1689.

"things so slight that only you and I would notice them": approximate borrowing from a letter of May 1675.

"To be close to those . . . is all the same": approximate quotation from La Bruyère's *Characters*, 'Du cœur' ('Of the Heart').

the young Sévigné: the reference here is to Madame de Sévigné's son Charles (1648–1713).

300 *a park designed by Le Nôtre*: André Le Nôtre (1613–1700) was Louis XIV's gardener from 1645 to 1700 and a master of garden design, conceptualizing and overseeing the works for the gardens and grounds of the Château de Versailles (amongst others).

Château de Blois: a château in the Loire Valley, developed over several centuries and occasional residence of various royals, including, as noted here, Mary Stuart (1542–87) who was married to François II from 1558 until his death in 1560.

Clara de Chimay: Proust makes a real figure of *fin-de-siècle* Parisian society into a relative of the fictional Charlus. Clara de Chimay, born in the United States as Clara Ward (1873–1916), married the Belgian Prince Joseph de Caraman-Chimay in Paris in 1890 but left him in 1896 to elope with a Hungarian violinist.

a photograph of the house when it was still pure: the Hôtel de Chimay in Paris, on the Quai Malaquais, had a garden designed by Le Nôtre.

301 *Poussin*: Nicolas Poussin (1594–1655) is the best-known painter of the classical baroque style.

the Petit Trianon: the smaller of two châteaux in the grounds of the Palace of Versailles.

Gabriel's façade . . . destroy the Hameau: on the architect Ange-Jacques Gabriel, see note to p. 56. He designed the Petit Trianon; the 'hameau' (hamlet) is the name given to the English garden and buildings that feature in it, described here.

303 *the Musset of 'L'Espoir en Dieu'*: Musset (see note to p. 13), was a Romantic novelist, dramatist, and poet. 'L'Espoir en Dieu' ('Hope in God', 1838) is a poem that enumerates a range of philosophical systems.

303 *Claudel*: Paul Claudel (1868–1955) was an important contributor to twentieth-century literary culture as part of the founding editorial board of *La Nouvelle Revue française* and as the author of poetry and plays underpinned by his Catholic faith.

304 *At Saint-Blaise . . . at ease . . .*: 'A Saint-Blaise, à la Zuecca, | Vous étiez, vous étiez bien aise. . .'; lines from Musset's 'Chanson' (1834).

Padua . . . Black Domino: 'Padoue est un fort bel endroit | Où de très grands docteurs en droit. . . | Mais j'aime mieux la polenta. . . | . . .Passe dans son domino noir | La Toppatelle'; lines from 'To my brother returning from Italy' (1844).

In Le Havre . . . to die: 'Au Havre, devant l'Atlantique, | À Venise, à l'affreux Lido, | Où vient sur l'herbe d'un tombeau, | Mourir la pâle Adriatique'; lines from Musset's 'La Nuit de décembre' (1835) from *Les Nuits*, four dialogues published between 1835 and 1837.

Madame Cornuel: Anne-Marie Cornuel (1605–94) held an important salon and was renowned for her wit and intelligence.

305 *the Russians would be victorious*: the Russo-Japanese War took place in 1904–5 and ended in a Japanese victory.

306 *your pepla with the lovely clasps*: a *peplos* was a garment worn by women in ancient Greece, formed of a single piece of fabric folded, draped, and pinned like a shawl.

He's not my father!: a line repeated on several occasions by the protagonist of Georges Feydeau's bawdy comedy *La Dame de chez Maxim's* (1899). 'Allez donc, c'est pas mon père!' came to have the sense of 'there's no harm in it!'

307 *the Duc d'Aumale*: Henri d'Orléans, Duc d'Aumale (1822–97), was the youngest son of Louis-Philippe, the last king of the French.

The Queen of Naples: Caroline-Berthier de Wagram (1832–84), Princesse Murat, adopted the title of Queen of Naples by her marriage to the grandson of the King of Naples in 1851.

Gramont-Caderousse himself: Charles-Robert de Gramont-Caderousse (1808–?65) was a relative of the revered Gramont family and was notorious for his dissolute lifestyle.

Le Radical: a left-wing daily newspaper with a circulation of around forty thousand in 1885 and over thirty thousand by 1912.

308 *the Cercle de la Rue Royale*: after the Jockey Club, the Cercle de la Rue Royale was the most prestigious, exclusive members' club in Paris, its members were memorialized in a famous 1868 painting by James Tissot (1836–1902) of the same name, which can be viewed in the Musée d'Orsay in Paris.

Old Codgers' Club: this club, the Cercle des Ganaches in French, was established in 1876 and its members consisted largely of retired military men. The name was a borrowing from a play by Victorien Sardou

(1831–1908) titled *Les Ganaches* (1862), a slang term for those whose views were outdated.

Villiers or Catulle: Auguste Villiers de Lisle Adam (1838–89) was a novelist, playwright, and short-story writer, playing an important role in the development of Symbolism in France; Catulle Mendès (1841–1909) was a poet and playwright who also wrote widely on the theatre and opera.

Schlemihl: (Yiddish) an unfortunate person, someone with bad luck. It is the name of the protagonist of a novella, *The Marvellous Story of Peter Schlemihl* (1814) by Count Adelbert Von Chamisso, about a man who sells his shadow to the Devil.

309 *Darius' palace*: see note to p. 71.

Madame Dieulafoy: Jeanne Dieulafoy (1851–1916) was an archaeologist and writer who, along with her husband, worked on a number of important digs in Persia.

made the wings of some androcephalous bull from Khorsabad float above it: Khorsabad is an ancient city with its origins in the seventh century BC. Androcephalous describes an animal (here a bull) with a human head; in the 1840s such sculptures were discovered in the Khorsabad palace of Sargon II, King of Assyria, which have been preserved in the Louvre.

310 *the greatest liar among mortals*: Homer, *Odyssey*, Book 13.

311 *Sardou, Labiche . . . Menander, Kalidasa*: the verbal jousting here sees Bloch and his father indicate their doubt at the veracity of Nissim Bernard's story by adding to the list of contemporary authors he claims to have dined with (Sardou, Labiche, and Augier) the names of not just three long-dead seventeenth-century dramatists (Molière, Racine, Corneille), but also three ancient authors (Plautus, Menander, and Kalidasa).

the agrégation: a highly competitive public examination required by those wishing to teach in secondary schools in France.

Monsieur Coquelin: see note to p. 98.

Rubens: see note to p. 102.

312 *Journal officiel*: the official journal of the French Republic, a government gazette publishing laws and decrees as well as parliamentary affairs.

Zephyros and Boreas . . . rose-fingered Eos: in Greek myth Zephyros is the god of the West wind and Boreas the god of the North wind; Eos is the name for Aurora, goddess of the dawn.

blessed denizen of Olympus: see note to p. 45.

313 *between Paris and the Point-du-Jour*: the Paris 'belt line' railway ('Chemin de fer de Ceinture') is no longer in use, but when it was operational, the 'Point-du-Jour' was the last station on the Rive Gauche section.

'those Monsieurs': Françoise often makes slips of expression in French; she should say 'Messieurs', which is the correct form.

314 *Amélie, that sister of Philippe's*: Marie-Amélie, Princesse d'Orléans (1865–1951) became queen consort of Portugal through marriage; she was sister of Philippe, Duc d'Orléans (1869–1926).

316 *valerian drops*: a perennial flowering plant, valerian is used as a light sedative or to relieve anxiety.

317 *some snapshots I took with my Kodak*: the Kodak handheld camera was released in 1888; Saint-Loup is therefore an early adopter of this modern technology.

318 *Ancilla Domini*: in Luke 1:38, to the angel that tells her she will bear a child, Mary is said to respond 'Ecce ancilla Domini' (Latin: 'Behold the servant or handmaiden of the Lord'). In depictions of this scene, Mary typically holds a lily in her hand.

322 *pushing her bicycle with one hand*: bicycles were popular by the end of the nineteenth century in France, but largely available only with a crossbar and its attendant challenges for anyone wearing a skirt. That young women should start riding bicycles and wearing clothing that allowed them to do so was a form of liberation (of movement and of the body) and a significant mark of changing social mores.

325 *as Chopin does with even his most melancholy phrase*: on Chopin, see note to p. 251.

327 *this little peri*: in Persian folklore, a *peri* is a beautiful winged spirit. The Ballets Russes (see note to p. 458) performed a piece titled 'La Péri' in Paris in 1912.

332 *the same singular form as Racine does when he says 'the poor man'*: in *Athalie*, Act II, scene ix and Act IV, scene iii.

Rembrandt shapes a windowsill or the handle of a well: considered as one of the most accomplished artists of all time, Rembrandt van Rijn (see note to p. 71) painted *The Good Samaritan* (1630) which features a well.

335 *from Pisanello's pencil . . . glassware by Gallé*: Antonio Pisano, known as Pisanello (1395–1455) was a painter and portrait medallist, his approach characterized by extraordinarily fine detail, even in larger works. Émile Gallé (1846–1904) was an innovative artist who worked in glass and ceramics, a vital figure in the Art Nouveau movement who produced vases and vessels of extraordinary beauty and finesse.

the predella of the altar: the base of an altarpiece, typically consisting of decorative panels above the altar itself.

337 *the signature emblem of the Chelsea master*: Whistler (see note to p. 199) formed his initials, J.M.W., into an ideograph of a butterfly that appears at the foot of some of his paintings. He lived and worked at 96 Cheyne Walk (formerly Lindsey Row) in Chelsea, London from 1866 to 1878.

338 *Dreyfus was guilty a thousand times over*: see note to p. 81.

Giotto: Giotto di Bondone (*c.*1266–1337) is one of the most celebrated painters of the thirteenth and fourteenth centuries, whose work, especially his frescoes in the Arena Chapel in Padua, was greatly admired by Proust.

341 *potatoes à l'anglaise . . . Pauillac lamb*: *pommes à l'anglaise* are simply boiled potatoes dressed with parsley; Pauillac lamb is a speciality from that particular area of the Bordeaux region, also famed for its fine red wines.

345 *ataxia*: a medical term describing the loss of an individual's ability to coordinate their movements.

351 *like the builder in the fable*: a vignette recorded in Book 11 of *The Odyssey* and in Horace's *Ars Poetica*, Amphion, son of Zeus and Antiope, is charged with building a wall around Thebes with his brother Zethos. The latter laboriously moves stones by hand; Amphion charms the stones into place by playing sweetly on his lyre.

353 *spores of the pale madrepore*: madrepore is another name for coral; spores may be a reference to the spawning of the coral.

355 *Sunrise over the Sea*: a common theme among the Impressionists. Turner painted at least two works with this title and Claude Monet famously painted *Impression, soleil levant* (*Impression, sunrise*, 1872), whose title gave rise to the label 'Impressionism'.

357 *like John Jeffreys in the portrait by Hogarth*: Jeffreys (1689–1741) was a London barrister; the portrait by William Hogarth (1697–1764) was painted in 1730; Jeffreys's wife (rather than a governess) is a straight-backed figure in the composition though not quite authoritarian in appearance.

361 *the land of King Mark, or on the site of the Forest of Broceliande*: Mark, King of Cornwall, features in the legend of Tristan and Iseult: Iseult is betrothed to Mark when she drinks the love potion. In Arthurian legend and tales of the Round Table, the forest of Broceliande is an important locus of the action and is thought to be based on what is today the Paimpont forest in Britanny.

363 *the harbour of Carquethuit*: a fictional port town.

365 *the Lilliputian grace of white sails*: in *Gulliver's Travels* (1726), Swift's hero encounters an island, Lilliput, whose inhabitants are only one twelfth of size of regular human beings.

366 *the finest illustrated Bible the people have ever read*: church statuary tells a story that can be read like a book. Indeed, John Ruskin's study of Amiens Cathedral is titled *The Bible of Amiens* (1885), Proust's French translation of which was published in 1904. Much of the detail of what follows draws on Proust's reading of *L'Art religieux du XIIIᵉ siècle en France* (*Religious Art in 13th-century France*, 1898) by the art historian Émile Mâle, with whom Proust corresponded and who had an important influence on his thinking.

368 *a subtlety unmatched by your Redon*: Odilon Redon (1840–1916) was a Symbolist artist. The mention of him here may relate to his *Apocalypse of Saint John* (1899).

the devil advising Potiphar's wife: in Genesis 39, Potiphar's wife is portrayed as a seductress; her advances to Joseph rejected, she succeeds in having him falsely imprisoned.

370 *these Dianas and nymphs*: in ancient mythology Diana is the goddess of nature, hunting, and the moon.

374 *Miss Sacripant, October 1872*: a few pages later, Elstir indicates this title is taken from a 'stupid little operetta'. *Sacripant* was indeed the title of a comic opera performed in Paris in 1866, whose male lead was played by a female actor; the character himself appears disguised as a woman in the work's final scenes. As a noun, *sacripant* means rascal, deriving from a character, Sacripante, in *Orlando innamorato* (1483–95) by the Italian poet Matteo Boiardo (1440–94).

Théâtre des Variétés: inaugurated in Montmartre in Paris in 1807, this popular theatre staged many successful runs of vaudeville and the works of Offenbach, mentioned above.

376 *Titian*: see notes to pp. 13 and 244.

379 *the Pointe du Raz, which would be quite a journey from here*: a rocky promontory that reaches out into the Atlantic from the western coast of Brittany.

like Mephistopheles materializing before Faust: in his tragic drama *Faust* (1808), the great German writer Goethe (1749–1832) casts the devil as the folkloric Mephistopheles, who appears to Faust who, in turn, eventually signs a pact with him.

zoophytic band of girls: 'zoophyte' (now obsolete) is a term designating an entity thought to be midway between plant and animal.

382 *Veronese*: see note to p. 195.

385 *the Place Pigalle*: in the 9th *arrondissement of Paris*, an area attracting artists in the nineteenth century, as well as sex workers and somewhat wild nightlife.

386 *the numerous portraits that Manet or Whistler painted*: on Whistler, see note to p. 199; Édouard Manet (1832–83), like Whistler, painted many portraits of female subjects. His notorious *Déjeuner sur l'herbe* was displayed alongside Whistler's *Symphony in White, no. 1* in 1863 in the 'Salon des refusés'.

389 *a great admirer of Proudhon*: see note to p. 272.

'I'll take the little "twister"': the word used for the local railway line in the French is 'tortillard', a familiar term for a slow train taking a route with multiple twists and turns.

390 *Louis XVI cavalry barracks*: Doncières, as noted above, is a fictional location, but Proust furnishes it with an eighteenth-century barracks (such as is found at the cavalry academy in Saumur).

391 *Arvède Barine*: in fact a pseudonym of Madame Charles Vincens (1840–1908), author of critical studies of Bernardin de Saint-Pierre (1891) and Musset (1893).

398 *La Sogne*: this town is just south of Évreux and about 70 miles from the Normandy coast.

399 *the next World's Fair*: given the events mentioned in the volume to this point, it seems likely this refers to the Exposition universelle held in Paris in 1900.

401 *Know thou . . . attend*: 'Apprends que mon devoir ne dépend pas du sien: | Qu'il y manque, s'il veut: je dois faire le mien.' '[T]he old Arouet' is Bloch's pretentious way of referring to the writer and thinker Voltaire (François-Marie Arouet, known as Voltaire, 1694–1778). Bloch, however, misattributes the lines: they come not from Voltaire but from Pierre Corneille's *Polyeucte* (Act III, scene ii).

403 *the Conseil général*: the department (or county) council.

Cavalleria Rusticana: a one-act opera (1890) by Pietro Mascagni (1863–1945), from which the symphonic Intermezzo has become a much-loved stand-alone piece. Proust found the work vulgar; Albertine's liking for it (which echoes Odette's in *The Swann Way*) is indicative, to the narrator, of her unsophisticated taste.

406 *a break*: an open, four-wheeled horse-drawn carriage.

407 *Giotto's Infidelitas*: one of Giotto's allegorical depictions of the Virtues and Vices in the Arena Chapel at Padua, mentioned above.

a 'diabolo': a toy formed of an hour-glass-shaped bobbin that can be spun or tossed on a string attached to two sticks.

409 *Alceste or Philinte*: the two male leads in Molière's *Le Misanthrope* (1666).

Le Gaulois: a Right-leaning daily newspaper, founded in 1868; Proust published some society journalism in its pages. It ceased circulation, merging with *Le Figaro*, in 1929.

411 *primitive cryptogams or grasses*: crytogamous plants are those that reproduce via spores rather than flowers or seeds.

papilionaceous flowers: those flowers (mostly legumes) with petals or corolla shaped like a butterfly.

412 *Dionysian*: given to passion, instinct, and emotion, characteristics of the Greek god of wine and pleasure, Dionysus. (Often contrasted with the rational, ordered qualities associated with Apollo, god of light, art, and reason.)

417 *the festive celebrations that Veronese and Carpaccio so liked to depict*: both painters, mentioned above, depicted richly detailed set-piece scenes of feasts or events, such as Veronese's *The Wedding at Cana* (1562–3) or Carpaccio's *The Sermon of St Stephen* (1514), both of which Proust could have seen at the Louvre.

The Legend of Saint Ursula: a cycle of paintings by Carpaccio, completed in the 1490s, and preserved in the Gallerie dell'Accademia in Venice. They depict the story of St Ursula from Jacobus de Voragine's *Golden Legend* (?1265); Proust most likely encountered Carpaccio and these works via his reading of Ruskin.

caravel, galleass, or Bucentaur: a caravel is a small sailing ship used by the Portuguese in the fifteenth and sixteenth centuries; a galleass was a large warship that combined sails and oars, used in the sixteenth and seventeenth centuries; Bucentaur was the name given to the state barge of

Venice which, between the fourteenth and eighteenth centuries, was used ceremonially every Ascension Day to 'wed Venice to the sea'.

Fortuny: Mariano Fortuny y Madrazo (1871–1949) was a Spanish-born artist and designer of textiles, fabrics, and garments as well as of stage lighting. Fortuny was eclectic in his sources of inspiration: he made dresses that drew on fabrics depicted in Carpaccio's paintings, by which Proust was quite enchanted. Fortuny was brought up in Paris and lived and worked in Venice from 1902 until his death.

418 *regattas in Cowes*: an English port town on the Isle of Wight, Cowes is famous for its regattas.

Callot . . . Doucet, Cheruit . . . Paquin: each of the four names mentioned here designates a celebrated fashion house or designer of women's clothes active in Paris at the *fin de siècle*.

419 *a statue in Rheims cathedral and one in the Saint-Augustin church*: Elstir here is comparing one of the most celebrated Gothic cathedrals in Europe, built in the thirteenth and fourteenth centuries with a (fairly unremarkable) city church built in the 1860s in the 8th *arrondissement* of Paris.

Les Creuniers: a range of cliffs found on the Normandy coast between Trouville and Villerville.

421 *Gone . . . heroic Hellas*: 'Ils sont partis, les rois des nefs éperonnées, | Emmenant sur la mer tempétueuse, hélas! | Les hommes chevelus de l'héroïque Hellas'; lines from Leconte de Lisle's tragedy *Érinnyes* (1873).

422 *those cake-plates decorated with images from the Arabian Nights*: see note to p. 278.

Combray-en-Champagne: in *The Swann Way*, published in 1913, Proust had located Combray near Chartres. In the 1919 re-edition, as reinforced here, he changes the location to the region of Champagne, near Rheims, so that later in the narrative he could incorporate reference to the advance of the German forces into this locale in the course of the First World War, which had not begun when he first planned his novel.

424 *games of ring on a string*: the *jeu de furet* is a game where a ring on a long loop of string is held by one individual and the others pretend to pass it from hand to hand along the string, while one player—the ferret—stands in the middle and tries to determine who in fact has the ring.

426 *Bellini's little angel-musicians*: Giovanni Bellini (1430–1516) was a Venetian painter who included two child-angels, playing a lute and a whistle respectively, at the foot of the central panel of his triptych altarpiece in the Frari church in Venice (see note to p. 13 on the Titian *Assumption* in the same church).

the catastrophe at Pompeii: in AD 79 the volcano Mount Vesuvius erupted, burying the city of Pompeii and its inhabitants in ash and lava.

428 *final certificate examination*: the *certificat d'études primaires supérieures* was a diploma awarded at the end of pupils' primary education in France

between the 1860s and its discontinuation in 1989. Assessment took the form of written and oral exams.

Sophocles: ancient Greek playwright (*c.*496–406/405 BC), believed to have written some 120 plays, only seven of which have survived in their entirety, including most famously *Oedipus Rex*.

Racine's Esther . . . Madame de La Fayette: on *Esther*, see note to p. 249. Madame de La Fayette (1634–93) was a writer and author of *La Princesse de Clèves* (1678), a tale of the frustrated love of a married woman for another man, once of France's best-known novels.

429 *To portray . . . the heart*: 'De cette passion la sensible peinture | Est pour aller au Cœur la route la plus sûre'; lines from *L'Art poétique* (1674) by Boileau (see note to p. 9).

430 *Les Juives, by Robert Garnier, and Aman by Antoine de Montechrestien*: Garnier (1544–90) and Montechrestien (?1575–1621) were part of a trend in the first half of the sixteenth century in reprising ancient tragedies with choruses. *Les Juives* (1583) and *Aman* (1601) are both based on Old Testament stories.

431 *"not just the masterpiece of Racine, but of the human mind"*: this claim is made a number of times in Voltaire's writing and in his correspondence, including in his *Le Siècle de Louis XIV* (1751).

Sainte-Beuve and Merlet: on Sainte-Beuve, see note to p. 43; for his part, Gustave Merlet (1828–91) taught rhetoric at the prestigious Lycée Louis-le-Grand in Paris and was the author of numerous critical and literary-historical works.

Deltour and Gasc-Desfossés especially: Nicolas-Félix Deltour (1822–1902) was another teacher and author of critical works, particularly of Racine, while Alfred and Léon Gasc-Defossés were scholars who gathered together all the essay titles students faced between 1881–5 into a popular reference work.

436 *'It passed . . . the ferret of the pretty wood!'*: Andrée is quoting from a traditional song, 'Le Furet du bois', which was sung like a nursery rhyme during the game of 'furet' (ring-on-a-string).

like Laura Dianti's or Eleanor of Aquitaine's, or her descendant, whom Chateaubriand loved so: Laura Dianti (1480–1573) was the model for Titian's *Flora*, the beautiful goddess of spring (*c.*1515), as well as his *Woman with a Mirror* (*c.*1515), which Proust could have seen in the Louvre. She is shown with deep blonde, almost auburn hair. Eleanor of Aquitaine (1122–1204) was famed for her long hair, but she was not related to Delphine de Sabran (1770–1826), who was Chateaubriand's beloved *c.*1802–5.

437 *months of Mary*: in the Catholic faith, traditionally the month of May is dedicated to acts of devotion and celebrations honouring Mary, mother of Jesus.

440 *as beautiful as one Leonardo might have used*: see note to p. 22.

448 *those figures by Michelangelo being carried away by a motionless, vertiginous whirlwind*: probable reference to the figures depicted on the ceiling of the Sistine Chapel, painted by Michelangelo.

450 *the Panama Affair*: the name given to a corruption scandal that came to a head between 1889 and 1892. A French company, headed up by Ferdinand de Lesseps (see note to p. 286), tried and failed to construct a canal across Panama, joining the Atlantic and Pacific Oceans. Many investors lost vast amounts of money through the company's bankruptcy and government ministers (among others) were believed to have accepted bribes to keep the company's troubles quiet.

456 *her neurasthenia*: see note to p. 163.

translating a novel by George Eliot into French: Eliot, mentioned above in relation to Bergotte (see note to p. 116), was author of seven novels, the best known of which is *Middlemarch* (1871–2).

Messalina: third wife of the Roman emperor Claudius, and relative of three previous emperors, Messalina (*c.* AD 22–48) was a powerful woman notorious for using her position to get what she wanted and to make others suffer. She was eventually executed for a plot against her own husband.

457 *Hercules*: in ancient myth, Hercules was the embodiment of strength and tenacity. He was a demigod—son of Zeus and a mortal mother, Alcmena.

458 *the props of the Russian ballet . . . the genius of Bakst*: Léon Bakst (1866–1924) was a painter and designer who produced many breathtaking sets and costume designs for the Ballets Russes, the Russian ballet company that toured Europe in the early twentieth century, led by the impresario Sergei Diaghilev (1872–1929).

460 *Virgil's Leucothea*: in Greek myth, Ino, daughter of Cadmus, was turned mad as a punishment; she leapt into the sea and was transformed into a sea-goddess, by the name of Leucothea. She is said to look out for sailors on the seas and in the *Odyssey* saves Ulysses from drowning. In Virgil's *Aeneid* she is mentioned in Book 5.

461 *Jules Ferry . . . a writer of curtain-raisers*: Jules Ferry (1832–93) was not a playwright, but a statesman, who served two stints as prime minister of France and is remembered in particular for the 'Jules Ferry laws' implemented in the early 1880s, which made education free, mandatory, and secular.

462 *Calypso's island . . . palace of Minos*: in the *Odyssey*, the nymph Calypso lives on an island called 'Ogygia'. Victor Bérard (1864–1931) was a French diplomat and classicist who published a two-volume work on the geography of Homer's *Odyssey*, identifying Ogygia with the real island of Perejil off the coast of Morocco. Minos was a king of Crete in Greek myth, associated with the palace at Knossos unearthed by the British archaeologist Sir Arthur Evans (1851–1941) in 1900.

the Spinario . . . a mythological scene: Boy with Thorn or *Spinario* in Italian, is a bronze sculpture of a boy, seated, trying to extract a thorn from the sole of his foot which is crossed over his knee; the original is thought to date from the first century BC and is held in the Palazzo dei Conservatori in Rome; Proust saw a copy in the Louvre. In Rubens's canvases depicting the life of Marie de' Medici, as well as his *The Feast of Venus*, it has been discerned that the painter's wife served as a model for the goddesses depicted.

464 *the first president from Rennes, the bâtonnier from Caen*: earlier we were told the first president was from Caen and the *bâtonnier* from Cherbourg. See note to p. 221.

the Marquis Maurice de Vaudémont: a fictional creation. Vaudémont is a commune in north-eastern France.

465 *before the Hebrews in the desert*: Exodus 13:21.

American Literature

British and Irish Literature

Children's Literature

Classics and Ancient Literature

Colonial Literature

Eastern Literature

European Literature

Gothic Literature

History

Medieval Literature

Oxford English Drama

Philosophy

Poetry

Politics

Religion

The Oxford Shakespeare

A complete list of Oxford World's Classics, including Authors in Context, Oxford English Drama, and the Oxford Shakespeare, is available in the UK from the Marketing Services Department, Oxford University Press, Great Clarendon Street, Oxford OX2 6DP, or visit the website at www.oup.com/uk/worldsclassics.

In the USA, visit www.oup.com/us/owc for a complete title list.

Oxford World's Classics are available from all good bookshops.

ANTHONY TROLLOPE

The American Senator
An Autobiography
Barchester Towers
Can You Forgive Her?
Cousin Henry
Doctor Thorne
The Duke's Children
The Eustace Diamonds
Framley Parsonage
He Knew He Was Right
Lady Anna
The Last Chronicle of Barset
Orley Farm
Phineas Finn
Phineas Redux
The Prime Minister
Rachel Ray
The Small House at Allington
The Warden
The Way We Live Now